D1499747

14 STORIES BY LUCIUS SHEPARD

ARTWORK BY JEFFREY K. POTTER

ARKHAM HOUSE PUBLISHERS, INC.

Library of Congress Cataloging-in-Publication Data
Shepard, Lucius.
  The ends of the earth : 14 stories / by Lucius Shepard ; artwork by Jeffrey K. Potter.—1st ed.
    p.   cm.
  ISBN 0-87054-161-7 (alk. paper)
  1. Fantastic fiction, American. I. Title.
PS3569.H3939E5 1991   90-933
813'.54—dc20

Printed in the United States of America
Title page by Dan X. Solo
First Edition

FOR PHIL AND M. K.

ACKNOWLEDGMENTS

I'd like to thank the following for their thoroughly generous—albeit often unwitting—assistance during the writing of these stories: my editor, James Turner, Robert Frazier, Karol Lindquist, James Patrick Kelly, Stan Robinson, John Kessel, Gardner Dozois, Sheila Williams, Ellen Datlow, Alice K. Turner, Edward L. Ferman, Ralph Vicinanza, Patrick Delahunt, Lisa Goldstein, Michaela Roessner, Mark Ziesing, Jack and Jeanne Dann, Roy Flanders, Charlie Walters, Nancy Thayer, Ford Seeley, Jeffrey K. Potter, Richard Burns, Patti Claflin, James Goff, John and Kate O'Connor, Courtney Shick, Sarah Conforti, Lauren Mascola, Lenny, Ernie, Corky, Carl, Jeff, Evans, and all the rest of the good people at the Atlantic Café.

CONTENTS

THE ENDS OF
THE EARTH

JK

T
hose whose office it is to debunk the supernatural are fond of
pointing out that incidences of paranormal activity most often
take place in backwaters and rarely in the presence of credible
witnesses, claiming that this in itself is evidence of the
fraudulent character of the phenomena involved; yet it has occurred to me that the agents of the supernatural, especially
those elements whose activities are directed toward evil ends, might
well exhibit reticence in appearing before persons capable of verifying
their existence and thus their threat to humankind. It seems surprising that such shadowy forces—if, indeed, they do exist—choose to appear before any witnesses at all, and equally surprising—if their powers
are as vast as described in popular fiction—that they do not simply
have done with us. Perhaps they are prevented from doing so by some
restraint, a limit, say, on how many souls they are allowed to bag,
and perhaps the fact that they manifest as they do is attributable to
a binding regulation similar to the one dictating that corporations (shadowy forces in themselves) must make a public notice of the date and
location of their stockholders' meetings. In order to avoid scrutiny
of their business practices, a number of corporations publish these
notices in shoppers' guides and rural weeklies, organs unlikely to pass
before the eyes of government agencies and reporters, and it makes
sense that the supernatural might emulate this tactic as a means of
compliance with some cosmic rule. That supposition may seem face-
tious, but my intent is quite serious, for while I cannot say with absolute certainty whether the circumstances that provoked my interest
in these matters were in essence supernatural or merely an extraordinary

combination of ordinary people and events, I believe that six months
ago in Guatemala, a place notable for its inaccessibility and unreliable
witnesses, I witnessed something rare and secret, something that may
have reflected the exercise of a regulatory truth pertaining to both the
visible and invisible worlds.

Prior to leaving for Guatemala I had been romantically involved
for the preceding three years with Karen Maniaci, a married woman
who managed a Manhattan art gallery, and it was our breakup, which
was marked by bitterness on my part and betrayal on hers, that persuaded me I needed a drastic change in order to get on with living.
This process of persuasion lasted several months, months during which
I wandered gloomily about New York, stopping in my tracks to stare
at dark-haired women of approximately five feet nine in height and
120 pounds; and at length I concluded that I had better get out of
town . . . either that or begin to play footsie with mental illness. I
was thirty-seven and had grown too cautious to want to risk myself
in a dangerous enterprise; yet there is a theatricality inherent in being
jilted, a dramatic potential that demands resolution, and to satisfy it,
I chose that other option of the heartbroken: a trip to some foreign
shore, one isolate from the rest of the world, where there were no
newspapers and no reminders of one's affair. Livingston, Guatemala,
seemed to qualify as such. It was described in a guidebook that I happened upon in The Strand bookstore as ". . . a quiet village at the
egress of the Río Dulce into the Caribbean, hemmed in against the
sea by the Petén rain forest. Settled by black Caribes and the descendants of East Indian slaves brought by the British to work the sugar
plantations upriver. There are no roads into Livingston. One reaches
it either by ferry from Puerto Morales or by powerboat from Reunión
at the junction of the Río Dulce and the Petén highway. The majority of the houses are neat white stucco affairs with red tile roofs. The
natives are unspoiled by tourism. In the hills above the village is a
lovely tiered waterfall called Siete Altares (Seven Altars), so named
because of the seven pools into which the stream whose terminus it
forms plunges on its way to the sea. Local delicacies include turtle
stew. . . ."

It sounded perfect, a paradise cut off from the grim political realities
of the mother country, a place where a man could go to seed in the
classic style, by day wandering the beach in a Bogart suit, waking each
morning slumped over a table, an empty rum bottle beside his elbow,
a stained deck of cards scattered around him with only the queen of
hearts showing its face. A few days after reading the guidebook entry,

following journeys by plane, train, and an overcrowded ferry, I arrived in Livingston. A few days after that, thanks to a meeting in one of the bars, I took possession of a five-room house of yellow stucco walls and concrete floors belonging to a young Spanish couple, doctors who had been studying with local *curanderos* and wanted someone to look after their pets—a marmalade cat and a caged toucan—while they toured for a year in the United States.

I have traveled widely all my life, and it has been my experience that guidebook descriptions bear little relation to actual places; however, though changes had occurred—most notably the discovery of the village by the singer Jimmy Buffett, whose frequent visits had given a boost to the tourist industry, attracting a smattering of young travelers, mainly French and Scandinavians who lived in huts along the beach—I discovered that the guidebook had not grossly exaggerated Livingston's charms. True, a number of shanty bars had sprung up on the beach, and there was a roach-infested hotel not mentioned in the book: three stories of peeling paint and cell-sized rooms furnished with torn mattresses and broken chairs. But the Caribe houses were in evidence, and the turtle stew was tasty, and the fishing was good, and Siete Altares was something out of a South Seas movie, each pool shaded by cciba trees, their branches dripping with orchids, hummingbirds flitting everywhere in the thickets. And the natives *were* relatively unspoiled, perhaps because the tourists kept to the beach, which was separated from the village by a steep drop-off and which—thanks to the bars and a couple of one-room stores—provided them with all the necessities of life.

Early on I suffered a domestic tragedy. The cat ate the toucan, leaving its beak and feet for me to find on the kitchen floor. But in general, things went well. I began to work, my mind was clearing, and the edge had been taken off my gloom by the growing awareness that other possibilities for happiness existed apart from a neurotic career woman who was afraid to trust her feelings, was prone to anxiety attacks and given to buying bracelets with the pathological avidity that Imelda Marcos once displayed toward the purchase of shoes. I soon fell into a pleasant routine, writing in the mornings, working on a cycle of short stories that—despite my intention of avoiding this pitfall—dealt with an unhappily married woman. Afternoons, I would lie in a hammock strung between two palms that sprouted from the patio of the house, and read. Evenings, I would stroll down to the beach with the idea of connecting with one of the tourist girls. I usually wound up drinking alone and brooding, but I did initiate a flirtation with an Odille LeCleuse, a Frenchwoman in her late twenties, with high cheekbones and milky skin, dark violet eyes and a sexy mouth that always looked as if she were about to purse her lips. She was in thrall— or so I'd heard—to Carl Konwicki, an Englishman of about my own age, who had lived on the beach for two years and supported himself by selling marijuana.

By all reports, Konwicki was a manipulator who traded on his experience to dominate less-seasoned travelers in order to obtain sex and other forms of devotion, and I couldn't understand how Odille, an intelligent woman with a degree in linguistics from the Sorbonne, could have fallen prey to the likes of him. I spotted him every day on the streets of the village: an asthenic olive-skinned man, with a scraggly fringe of brown beard and a hawkish Semitic face. He commonly wore loose black trousers, an embroidered vest, and a Moroccan skullcap, and there was a deliberate languor to his walk, as if he were conscious of being watched; whenever he would pass by, he would favor me with a bemused smile. I felt challenged by him, both because of Odille and because my morality had been enlisted by what I'd heard of his smarmy brand of gamesmanship, and I had the urge to let him know I saw through his pose. But realizing that—if Odille was involved with him—this kind of tactic would only damage my chances with her, I restrained myself and ignored him.

One night about two months after my arrival, I was going through old notebooks, searching for a passage that I wanted to include in a story, when a sheet of paper with handwriting on it slipped from between the pages and fell to the floor. The handwriting was that of my ex-lover, Karen. I let it lie for a moment, but finally, unable to resist, I picked it up and discovered it to be a letter written early in the relationship. A portion read as follows:

> . . . *When I went to the therapist today (I know . . . I'll probably tell you all this on the phone later, but what the hell!), I told her about what happened, how I almost lost my job by making love to you those days in the office, and she didn't seem terribly surprised. When I asked her how a responsible adult who cares about her job could possibly jeopardize it in such a way, she simply said that there must have been a great deal of gain in it for me. It seems she's trying to lead me toward you— she's quite negative about Barry. But that's probably just wishful thinking—what she's doing is trying to lead me toward what I want. Of course what I want is you, so it amounts to the same thing.*

It was curious, I thought, scanning the letter, how words that had once seemed precious could now seem so vapid. I noted the overusage of the words *terribly* and *terrible,* particularly in conjunction with the words *surprising* and *surprised.* That had been her basic reaction to falling in love, I realized. She had been terribly surprised. *My God,* she'd said to herself. *An emotion! Quick, I'll hie me to the head doctor and have it excised.* I read on.

> . . . *I can't imagine living without you, Ray. When you said something the other day about the possibility of getting hit by a bus, I suddenly got this awful chill. I had a terrible sense of loss just hearing you say that. This is interesting in that I used to try to figure out if I loved Barry by imagining something awful happening to him and seeing how I felt. I usually felt bad, but that's about it. . . .*

I laughed out loud. The last I'd heard on the subject was that Barry, who bored Karen, whom she did not respect, who had recently gotten into rubber goods, was back in favor. Barry had one virtue that I did not: he was controllable, and in control there was security. She could go on lying to him, having affairs with no fear of being caught—Barry was big into denial. And now she was planning a child in an attempt to pave over the potholes of the relationship, convincing herself that this secure fake was the best she could expect of life. She was due fairly soon, I realized. But it didn't matter. No act of hers could bring conscience and clarity into what had always been a charade. Her lies had condemned the three of us, and most of all she had condemned herself by engaging in a kind of method living, chirping a litany of affirmation. "I think I can, I think I can," playing The Little Adultress That Could, and thus losing the hope of her heart, the strength of her soul. I imagined her at sixty-five, her beauty hardened to a grotesque brittleness, wandering through a mall, shopping for drapes thick enough to blot out the twenty-first century, while Barry shuffled along in her wake, trying to pin down the feeling that something had not been quite right all these years, both of them smiling and nodding, looking forward to a friendly gray fate.

The letter brought back the self-absorbed anguish that I'd been working to put behind me, and I felt—as I had for months prior to leaving New York—on the verge of exploding, as if a pressure were building to a hot critical mass inside me, making my thoughts flurry like excited atoms. My face burned; there were numbing weights in my arms and legs. I paced the room, unable to regain my composure, and after ten minutes or so, I flung open the door, frightening the marmalade cat, and stormed out into the dark.

I did not choose a direction, but soon I found myself on the beach, heading toward one of the shanty bars. The night was perfect for my mood. Winded: a constant crunch of surf and palm fronds tearing; combers rolling in, their plumed sprays as white as flame. A brilliant moon flashed between the fronds, creating shadows from even the smallest of projections, and set back from the shore, half-hidden in deep shadow among palms and sea grape and cashew trees, were huts with glinting windows and tin roofs. The beach was a ragged, narrow strip of tawny sand strewn with coconut litter and overturned cayucos. As I stepped over a cayuco, something croaked and leaped off into the rank weeds bordering the beach. My heart stuttered, and I fell back against the cayuco. It had only been a frog, but its appearance made me aware of my vulnerability. Even a place like Livingston had its dangers. Street criminals from Belize had been known to ride motor-boats down from Belize City or Belmopan to rob and beat the tourists, and in my agitated state of mind I would have made the perfect target.

The bar—Café Pluto—was set in the lee of a rocky point: a thatched hut with a sand floor and picnic-style tables, lit with black lights that emitted an evil purple radiance and made all the gringos glow like sun-burned corpses. Reggae from a jukebox at the rear was barely audible above the racket of the generator. I had several drinks in rapid succes-sion and ended up out front of the bar beside a toppled palm trunk, drinking rum straight from the bottle and sharing a joint with Odille and a young blond Australian named Ryan, who was writing a novel and whose mode of dress—slacks, shirt, and loosened tie—struck an oddly formal note. I was giddy with the dope, with the wildness of the night, the vast blue-dark sky and its trillion watts of stars, silver glitters that appeared to be slipping around like sequins on a dancer's gown. Behind us the Café Pluto had the look of an eerie cave lit by seams of gleaming purple ore.

I asked Ryan what his novel was about, and with affected diffidence he said, "Nothing much. Saturday night in a working-class bar in Sydney." He took a hit of the joint, passed it to Odille. "It wasn't going too well, so I thought I'd set it aside and do something poetic. Run away to the ends of the earth." He had a look around, a look that in its casual sweep included the sea and sky and shore. "This *is* the ends of the earth, isn't it?"

I was caught by the poignancy of the image, thinking that he had inadvertently captured the essence of place and moment. I pictured the globe spinning and spinning, trailing dark frays of its own essen-tial stuff, upon one of which was situated this slice of night and stars and expatriate woe, tatters with no real place in human affairs. . . . Wind veiled Odille's face with a drift of hair. I pushed it back, and she smiled, letting her eyelids droop. I wanted to take her back to the house and fuck her until I forgot all the maudlin bullshit that had been fucking me over the past three years.

"I hear you're doing some writing, too," said Ryan in a tone that managed to be both defiant and disinterested.

"Just some stories," I said, surprised that he would know this.

" 'Just some stories.' " He gave a morose laugh and said to the sky, "He's modest . . . I love it." Then, turning a blank gaze on me: "No need to hide your light, man. We all know you're famous."

"Famous? Not hardly."

"Sure you are!" In a stentorian voice he quoted a blurb on my last book. " 'Raymond Kingsley, a mainstay of American fiction.' "

"Uh-huh, right."

"Even the Master of Time and Space thinks you're great," said Ryan. "And believe me, he's sparing with his praise."

"Who're you talking about?"

Ryan pointed behind me. "Him."

Carl Konwicki was coming down the beach. He ambled up, dropped onto the fallen palm trunk, and looked out to sea. Odille and Ryan seemed to be waiting for him to speak. Irritated by this obeisance, I belched. Konwicki let his eyes swing toward me, and I winked.

"How's she going?" I took a man-sized slug of rum, wiped my mouth with the back of my hand, and fixed him with a mean stare. He clucked his tongue against his teeth and said, "I'm fine, thank you."

"Glad to hear it." Drunk, I hated him, my hate fueled by the frustration that had driven me out of the house. Hate was chemical between us, the confrontational lines as sharply etched as the shadows on the sand. I gestured at his skullcap. "You lived in Morocco?"

"Some."

"What part?"

"You know . . . around." The wind bent a palm frond low, and for an instant, Konwicki's swarthy face was edged by a saw-toothed shadow.

"That's not very forthcoming," I said. "Do questions bother you?"

"Not ones that have a purpose."

"How about light conversation . . . that a worthwhile purpose?"

"Is that *your* purpose?"

"What else would it be?"

"Wow!" said Ryan. "This is like intense . . . like a big moment."
Odille giggled.

"I got it," I said. "What would *you* like to talk about? How about the translation you're doing . . . what is it?"

"The *Popol Vuh*," said Konwicki distractedly.

"Gee," I said. "That's already been translated, hasn't it?"

"Not correctly."

"Oh, I see. And you're going to do it right." I had another pull on the rum bottle. "Hope you're not wasting your time."

"Time." Konwicki smiled, apparently amused by the concept; he refitted his gaze to the toiling sea.

"Yeah," I said, injecting a wealth of sarcasm into my voice. "It's pretty damn mind-bending, isn't it?"

The surf thundered; Konwicki met my eyes, imperturbable. "I've been looking forward to meeting you."

"Me, too," I said. "I hear you sell great dope." I clapped a hand to my brow as if recognizing that I had made a social blunder. "Pardon me . . . I didn't intend that to sound disparaging."

Konwicki gave me one of his distant smiles. "You're obviously upset about something," he said. "You should try to calm down."

I sat close beside him on the palm trunk, close enough to cause him to shift away, and was about to bait him further, but he stood, said, "Ta ra," and walked into the bar.

"I'd score that round even," said Ryan. "Mr. Kingsley dominating the first half, the Master coming on late."

Odille was gazing after Konwicki, wrapping a curl of hair around one forefinger. She gave me a wave, said, "I'll be back, okay?" and headed for the bar. I watched her out of sight, tracking the oiled roll of her hips beneath her cutoffs, and when I turned back to Ryan, he was smiling at me.

"What is it with them?" I asked.

"With Odille and the Master? Just a little now-and-then thing." He gave me a sly look. "Why? You interested?"

I snorted, had a hit of rum.

"You can win the lady," said Ryan. "If you've a stout heart."

I looked at him over the top of the bottle, but offered no encouragement.

"You see, Ray," said Ryan, affecting the manner of a lecturer, "Odille's a wounded bird. The poor thing had a disappointment in love back in Paris. She sought solace in distant lands and had the misfortune of meeting the Master. It's not much of a misfortune, you understand. The Master's not much of a Master, so he can't offer a great deal in the way of good or ill. But he confused Odille, made her believe he could show her how to escape pain through his brand of enlightenment. And that involved a bit of sack time.''

Given this similarity in history between Odille and myself, I imagined fate had taken a hand by bringing us together. ''So what can I do?''

''Things a bit hazy, are they, Ray?'' Ryan chuckled. ''Odille's grown disillusioned with the Master. She's looking for someone to burst his bubble, to free her.'' He reached for the bottle, had a swig and gagged. ''God, that's awful!'' He slumped against the toppled palm trunk, screwed the bottle into the sand so that it stood upright. The surf boomed; the wildfire whiteness of the combers imprinted afterimages on my eyes.

''Anyway,'' Ryan went on, ''she's definitely looking for emotional rescue. But you can't go about it with *déclassé* confrontation. You'll have to beat the Master on his own terms, his own ground.''

Perhaps it was the rum that let me believe that Ryan had a clear view of our situation. ''What *are* his terms?'' I asked.

''Games,'' he said. ''Whatever game he chooses.'' He had another pull off the bottle. ''He's afraid of you, you know. He's worried that you're into disciples, and all his children will abandon him for the famous writer. He realizes he can't befuddle you with his usual quasi-erudite crap. So he'll come up with something new for you. I have no idea what. But he'll play some game with you. He's got to . . . it's his nature.''

''How's he befuddled you? You seem to have a handle on him.''

''He's got no need,'' said Ryan. ''I'm his fool, and a fool can know the king's secrets and make fun of them with impunity.''

I started to ask another question, but let it rest. The wind pulled the soft crush of the surf into a breathy vowel; the moon had lowered behind the hills above the village, its afterglow fanning up into the heavens; the top of the sky had deepened to indigo, and the stars blazed, so dense and intricate in their array that I thought I might—if I were to try—be able to read there all scripture and truth in sparkling sentences. And it was not only in the sky that clarity ruled. What Ryan had said made sense. Odille was testing me . . . perhaps unconsciously, but testing me nonetheless, unwilling to abandon Konwicki until she was sure of me. I didn't resent this—it was a tactic often used in establishing relationships. But I was struck by how clear its uses seemed on the beach at Livingston. Not merely the social implications, but its elemental ones: the wounded lovers, the shabby Mephistophelian figure of Konwicki with his sacred books and petty need to exercise power. Man, woman, and Devil entangled in a sexual knot.

"Did I ever tell you my theory of the Visible?" I asked Ryan.

"We only just met," he reminded me.

"God, you're right. And here I've been under the illusion we're old pals."

"It's the sea air. Affects everyone dele. . . ." Ryan hiccuped. "Deleteriously."

"Well, anyway." I plucked the rum bottle from the sand and drank. "In places like this, I've always thought it was possible to see how things really are between people. To discern relationships that are obscured by the clutter of urban life. The old relationships, the archetypes."

He stared blearily up at me. "Sounds bloody profound, Ray."

"Yeah, I suppose it is," I said, and then added: "Profundity's my business. Or maybe it's bullshit . . . one or the other."

"So," he said, "are you going to play?"

"I think so . . . yeah."

"Beautiful," said Ryan. "That's really beautiful."

A few moments later Konwicki and Odille came out of the bar and walked toward us, deep in conversation.

Ryan laughed and laughed. "Let the games begin," he said.

We talked on the beach for another hour, smoking Konwicki's dope, which smoothed out the rough edges of my drunk, seeming to isolate me behind a thick transparency. I withdrew from the conversation, watching Konwicki. I wasn't gauging his strengths and weaknesses; despite my exchange with Ryan, I had not formalized the idea that there was to be a contest between us. I was merely observing, intrigued by his conversational strategy. By sidestepping questions, claiming to know nothing about a subject, he managed to intimate that the subject was not worth knowing and that he possessed knowledge in a sphere of far greater relevance to the scheme of things. Odille hung on his every word for a while, but soon began to lose interest, casting glances and smiles at me; it appeared she was trying to maintain a connection with Konwicki, but was losing energy in that regard.

For the most part, Konwicki avoided looking at me; but at one point, he cut his eyes toward me and locked on. We stared at each other for a long moment, then he turned away with acknowledgment. During that moment, however, the skin on my face went cold, my muscles tensed, and a smile stretched my lips. A feral smile funded by a remorseless hatred quite different from the impassioned, drunken loathing I originally had felt. This emotion, like the smile, seemed something visited upon me and not an intensification of my emotions, and along with it came a sudden increase in my body temperature. A sweat broke on my forehead, on my chest and arms; my vision reddened, and I had a peculiar sense of doubled perceptions, as if I were looking through two different pairs of eyes, one of which was capable of seeing a wider spectrum. I decided to slack off on the rum.

At length Konwicki suggested we get out of the wind, which was blowing stronger, and go over to his place to listen to music. I was of two minds about the proposal; while I wasn't ready to give up on Odille, neither was I eager to mix it with Konwicki, and I was certain that if I went with them there would be some bad result. The dope had taken the edge off my enthusiasm. But Odille took my hand, nudged the softness of her breast into my arm.

"You *are* coming, aren't you?" she said.

"Sure," I said, as if a thought to the contrary had never occurred.

We walked together along the beach, trailing Konwicki and Ryan, and Odille talked about taking a trip to Esquipulas someday soon to see the Black Christ in the cathedral there.

"Women come from all over Central America to be blessed," she said. "They stand in line for days. Huge fat women in white turbans from Belize. Crippled old island ladies from Roatán. Beautiful slim girls from Panama. All waiting to spend a few seconds kneeling in the shadow of a black statue. When I first heard about it, I thought it sounded primitive. Now it seems strangely modern. The New Primitivism. I keep imagining all those female shadows in the bright sun, radios playing, vendors selling cold drinks." She gave her hair a toss. "I could use that sort of blessing."

"Is it only for women?"

She held my eyes for a second, then turned away. "Sometimes men wait with them."

I asked if what Ryan had told me about her love affair in Paris was the truth. I had no hesitancy in asking this—intimacies were the flavor of the night. A flicker of displeasure crossed her face. "Ryan's an idiot."

"I doubt he'd argue the point."

Odille went a few steps in silence. "It was nothing. A fling, that's all."

Her glum tone seemed to belie this.

"Yeah, I had a fling myself right before I came down here. Like to have killed me, that fling."

She glanced up at me, still registering displeasure, but then she smiled. "Perhaps with us it's a matter of. . . ." She made a frustrated gesture, unable to find the right words.

"Victims recognizing the symptoms?" I suggested.

"I suppose." She threw back her head and looked up into the sky as if seeking guidance there. "Yes, I had a bad experience, but I'm over it."

"Completely?"

She shook her head. "No . . . never completely. And you?"

"Hey, I'm fine," I said. "It's like it never happened."

She laughed, cast an appraising look my way. "Who was she?"

"This married woman back in New York."

"Oh!" Odille put a hand on my arm in sympathy. "That's the worst, isn't it? Married, I mean."

"The worst? I don't know. It was pretty goddamn bad."

"What was she like?"

"Frightened. She got married because she had a run of bad luck . . . at least, that's what she told me. Things started going bad around her. Her parents got divorced, her dog ran away, and that seemed a sign something worse might happen. I guess she thought marriage would protect her." I walked faster. "She's a fucking mess."

"How so?"

"She doesn't know what the hell she wants. Whenever she doubts something, she'll broadcast an opinion pro or con until the contrary opinion has been shouted down in her own mind." I kicked at the sand. "The last time we talked, she explained how she was happy in her marriage for the same reasons that she'd once claimed to be miserable. The vices of this guy whom she'd ridiculed . . . she told everyone how much he bored her, how childish he was. All those vices had been transformed into solid virtues. She told me she knew that she couldn't have the kind of relationship with Barry—that's her husband—that we'd had, but you had to make trade-offs. Barry at least always wore a neatly pressed suit and could be counted on not to embarrass—though never to scintillate—at business functions." I sniffed. "As a husband he made the perfect accessory for evening wear."

"You sound bitter."

"I can't deny it. She put me through hell. Of course I bought into it, so I've got no one to blame but myself."

"She was beautiful, of course?"

"She didn't think so." I changed the subject. "Was yours married?"

"No, just a shit." Her expression became distant, and I knew that for a moment she was back in Paris with the Shit. "For a long time afterward I threw myself into other relationships. I thought that would help, but it was a mistake . . . I can see that now."

"Everything seems like a mistake afterward," I said.

"Not everything," she said coyly.

I wasn't sure how to take that, and it wasn't just that her meaning was vague; it was also that I was put off by her coyness. Before I could frame a response, she said, "Talking to Carl has helped me a great deal."

"Oh, I see." I tried to disguise my disappointment, believing this to be a sign that her connection with Konwicki was still vital.

"No, you don't. Just having someone to talk to was helpful. Carl's a fraud, of course. Nothing he says is without guile. But he does listen, and it's hard to find a good listener. That's basically all there was between us. I helped him with his work, and . . . there was more. But it wasn't important."

I wondered if she was playing with me, making me guess at her availability, and was briefly angered by the possibility; but then, recalling how uncertain my own motivations and responses had been, I decided that if I couldn't forgive her, I couldn't forgive myself.

"What are you thinking about?" Odille asked.

Her features, refined by the moonlight, looked delicate, etched, as if a kind of lucidity had been revealed in them, and I believed that I could see down beneath the games and the layers of false construction, beneath all those defenses, to who she most was, to the woman, no longer an innocent in the accepted sense of the word, but innocent all the same, still hopeful in spite of pain and disillusionment.

"Konwicki," I lied. "You helped him translate the *Popol Vuh?*"

"He was being discreet. He's acquired an old Mayan game and some papers that go with it. That's what he's translating."

"What sort of game?"

"From what I've been able to gather, it's a role-playing game. The papers seem to imply that it has to do with spirit travel. The gods. All the old cultures have myths that deal with that. It might be something that the priests used to evoke trances . . . something like that."

For no reason I could determine, this news made me edgy.

"Is that really what you were thinking about?" Odille asked.

"I was being discreet," I said, and she laughed.

Konwicki's place was a thatched hut with one large room and a sand floor over which a carpet of dried palm fronds had been laid, and was a scrupulously neat advertisement for his travels. Wall hangings from Peru, a brass hookah, a Japanese scroll, a bowl holding some Nepalese jewelry—rings of coral and worked silver, pillows embroidered in a pattern of turquoise thread that I recognized as being from Isfahan. Gourd bowls and various cooking implements hung from pegs, and a hurricane lantern provided a flickering orange light. An old Roxy Music album was playing on a cassette recorder, Bryan Ferry's nostalgia seeming more effete than usual in those surroundings. In one corner was an orange crate containing a stack of papers covered with Mayan hieroglyphs. I started to pick up the top paper, and Konwicki, who was sitting against the rear wall, rolling a joint, said, "Don't touch that . . . please!"

"What's the problem? My vibes might unsettle the spiritual fabric?"

"Something like that." He licked the edge of the rolling paper.

Ryan had stretched out on his back between Konwicki and a cardboard box that held some clay figurines, a comic book spread over his eyes; Odille was on her knees facing Konwicki, watching him roll.

"Why don't you tell me what else is off-limits?" I said.

He lit the joint, let smoke trickle from his nostrils. "Did you come here just to be contentious?" he asked.

"I'm not sure why I came," I said. "I figured you'd tell me."

He gave a shrug, blew more smoke. "Why are you so hostile?"

I dropped down cross-legged next to Odille. "You know what's going on here, man. But for one thing, I don't like guys like you . . . guys who want to grow up to be Charles Manson, but don't have the balls, so they hang out and maneuver weaker people into fucking them."

I said this mildly, and that was not a pose; I felt calm, without malice, merely making an observation. My dislike of Konwicki—it appeared—had shifted into a philosophical mode.

"And what sort of person are you?" he asked with equal mildness.

"Why don't you tell me?"

He made a show of sizing me up. "How about this? A horny, lonely man who's having trouble adjusting to the onset of middle age."

"Gee, Carl," I said. "I like my kind of guy a lot better than I do yours."

He sniffed, amused. "There's no accounting for taste." He passed me the joint, and in the spirit of the moment, I took a hit, let it circulate, then took another, deeper one. Seconds later I realized that Konwicki had exercised the home-field advantage in our little war and pulled out his killer weed. Even though I was already ripped, I could feel its effects moving through me like a cool, soft wind; it was the kind of weed that immobilizes, the kind with which you need to plan where you want your body to fall. My thoughts became muddled, my extremities felt cold. Yet when the joint was passed to me again, I had still another hit, not wanting to seem a wimp.

"Good shit, huh?" said Konwicki, watching Ryan suck on the joint.

"Gawd!" said Ryan, leaking smoke. "What clarity!"

I'm not sure why I reached for the clay figurines in the box next to Ryan—the need to hold on to something, probably. The wind tattering the thatch made a sound like something huge being torn apart. The inconstant wash of orange light along the walls mesmerized me, and the lantern flame itself was too bright to look at directly. In every minute event I perceived myriad subtleties, and I could have sworn I was floating a couple of inches above the ground. Perhaps I thought the figurine would give me ballast, bring me back down, because I was blitzed, wrecked, fucked-up. My hand moved in slow motion, effecting a lovely arc toward the box that contained the figurines. But the second I picked one up, I was cured of my sensory overload and felt stone-cold sober, in absolute control.

"Christ!" said Konwicki with annoyance. "Put that down!"

The figurine was a pre-Columbian dwarf of yellowish brown clay with stumpy legs, a potbelly, a hooked nose, and thick brutish lips. The eyes were slitted folds. About the size of a Barbie doll. Ugly as a wart. Holding it gave me focus and made me feel not merely whole, but powerful. The only remnant of my buzz was a sense that the figurine was full of something heavy and shifting, like a dollop of mercury. It seemed to throb in my hand.

"Put it down!" Konwicki's tone had become anxious.

"Why? Is it valuable?" I turned the figure, examining it from every angle. "Don't worry, man. I won't drop it."

"Just put it down, all right?"

Holding the figurine in my left hand, away from Konwicki, I leaned forward and saw that the cardboard box contained five more figurines, all standing. "What are they? They look like a set."

Konwicki held out his hand for the figurine, but I was feeling more and more in control. As if the figurine were a strengthening magic. I wasn't about to let it go. Odille, I saw, was regarding Konwicki with distaste.

"I'm not going to drop it, man. You think I'm too stoned or something? Hey"—I flashed him a cheery grin—"I feel great. Tell me what they are."

Ryan, too, was staring at Konwicki; he laughed soddenly and said in an Actors' Equity German accent, "Tell him, Master."

Konwicki grimaced like a man much put upon. "They're part of a game. An old Mayan game. I bought it off a *chiclero* in Flores."

"Really?" I said. "How do you play?"

"I can set the figures up, but I don't know what happens after that."

"If you know how to set them up, you must know something about it."

An exasperated sigh. "All right . . . I'll set them up, but be careful."

A long piece of plyboard was leaning against the wall to his left; it was stained a rusty orange and marked with a mosaic of triangular zones. He laid the board flat and arranged the five figures, three at the corners, the other two at the center edge opposite one another. The corner nearest me was vacant, and after a brief hesitation I set the dwarf down upon it.

"What next?" I said.

"I told you. I don't know. Whoever's playing picks one of the figures to be his corner. But after that . . ." He shrugged.

"How many can play?"

"From two to six people."

"Why don't you and I give it a shot?" I said.

It was curious how I felt as I said that. I was giving him an order, one I knew he'd obey. And I was eager for him to obey. I wanted him on the board, vulnerable to my moves, even though I didn't know what moves existed. That animal grin that had first manifested itself in front of the Café Pluto once again spread across my face.

"Come on, Carl," I said mockingly. "Don't you want to play?"

He pretended to be complying for the sake of harmony, giving Odille a glance that said, *What can I do?* and stretched out his hand, letting it hover above the figurines as if testing a discharge that issued from the head of each. At last he touched a clay warrior with a feathered headdress and a long spear. I felt less competent, and my thoughts frayed once again; it appeared that my relapse had boosted Konwicki's spirits. His bland smile switched on, and he leaned back against the wall. The noise of wind and sea smoothed out into a slow oscillating roar, as if something big and winged were making leisurely flights around the outside of the hut.

On impulse, I picked up the dwarf, and, suddenly brimming with gleeful hostility, I set it down beside a figurine at the center of the board, a lumpy female gnome with a prognathous jaw and slack breasts. Konwicki countered by moving a figurine resembling a squat infant to the side of his warrior. Thereafter we made a number of moves in rapid succession using the same four figurines. Complex moves, each consisting of more than one figurine, sometimes in tandem, utilizing every portion of the board. The entire process could not have taken more than a few minutes, but I could have sworn the game lasted for an hour at least. The room had been transformed into a roaring cell that channeled the powers of wind and sea, drew them into a complex circuit. A weight was shifting inside me, shifting just as the interior weights of the figurines seemed to shift, as if some liquid were being tipped this way and that, guiding my hand. Along with the apprehension of strength was the feeling of a separate entity at work, a quick, nasty brute of a being with a potbelly and arms like tree trunks, grunting and scuttling here and there, stinking of clay and blood. And yet I maintained enough sense of myself to be afraid. Things were getting out of hand, I realized, but I had no means of controlling them. As I stared at the board it began to appear immense, to exhibit an undulating topography, and I could feel myself dwindling, becoming lost among those rust-colored swells and declivities, coming closer to some terrible danger.

And then it was over . . . the game, the feelings of power and possession. Konwicki tried a smile, but it wouldn't stick. He looked wasted, worn-out. Exactly how I felt. Despite the intensity and strangeness of what I had experienced, I blamed it all on substance abuse. And I was sick of games, of repartee. I struggled to my feet, held out a hand to Odille. "Want to take a walk?" I asked.

I'd expected that she would look to Konwicki for approval or for some sort of validation; but without hesitation she let me help her to stand.

"Carl," I said with my best anchorman sincerity. "It's been fun."

He kept his face deadpan, but in his eyes was a shine that struck me as virulent, venomous. "That's how it is, huh?" he said, directing his words, I thought, to neither me nor Odille, but to the space between us.

"Night, all," I said, and steered Odille toward the door. I kept waiting for Konwicki to make some hostile remark; but he remained silent, and we got through the door without incident. We went along the edge of the shore, and after we had gone about thirty yards, Odille said, "You don't want to walk, do you, Raymond? Tell me what you really want."

"This how it is in Paris?" I said. "Everything made clear beforehand?"

"This isn't Paris."

"How are you with honesty?" I asked.

"Sometimes not so good." She shrugged as if to say that was the best she could offer.

"You're a beautiful woman," I said. "Intelligent, appealing. I'm tired of being in pain. Whatever possibilities exist for us . . . that's what I want."

She made a noncommittal noise.

"What?" I said.

"I thought you'd say you loved me."

"I want to love you, and that's the same thing," I said. "What the depth of my feelings are at this moment doesn't matter. One thing I've learned about love . . . you're a fool if you judge it by how dizzy it makes you feel." To an extent this was a lie I was telling myself, but it was such a clever lie that it came cloaked in the illuminative suddenness of a truth recognized, allowing me to adopt the role of a sincere man struggling to be honest . . . which was the case. Perhaps we are all such fraudulent creatures at heart that we must find a good script before we can successfully play at being honest.

"But the dizziness," said Odille. "That's important, too."

"I'm starting to get dizzy now. How about you?"

"You're a clever man, Raymond," she said after a pause. "I don't know if I'm a match for you."

"If I'm so damned clever, don't try and baffle me with humility."

She said nothing, but the wind and surf and the thudding of coconuts falling onto the sand seemed an affirmation. At last she stood on tiptoe, and her lips grazed my cheek. "Let's go home," she whispered.

Late that night Odille came astride me. Her skin gleamed palely in the moonlight shining through the window, her black hair stuck to the sweat on her shoulders in eloquent curls, and each of her rapid exhalations was cored with a frail note as if she were singing under her breath. Her breasts were small and long and slightly pendulous, with puffy dark areolae, reminding me of *National Geographic* breasts, shaped something like the slippers Aladdin wears in illustrations from *The Arabian Nights;* and her features looked so cleanly drawn as to appear stylized. Her delicacy, its exotic particularity, inspired desire, affection, passion. And one thing more, an emotion that underlay the rest: the need to degrade her. Part of my mind rebelled against this urge, but it was huge in me, a brutish drive, and I dug my fingertips into her thighs, gripping hard enough to leave bruises, and began to use her roughly. To my surprise she responded in kind; her fingernails raked my chest, and soon our lovemaking evolved into a savage contest that lasted nearly until dawn.

I slept no more than a few hours, and even that was troubled by a dream in which I found myself in a dwarfish, heavily muscled body with ocher skin, crouching on the crest of a dune of rust-colored sand, one that overlooked a complex of black pyramids. A hot wind blew fans of grit into the air, stinging my face and chest. The complex appeared to be a mile or so away, but I knew this was an illusion created by the clarity of the air, and that it would take me hours to reach the buildings. I knew many things about the place. I knew, for instance, that the expanse of sand between the dune and the complex was rife with dangers, and I also knew that there was life within the complex . . . a form of life dangerous to me. I understood this was a dream, albeit of an unusual sort, and that awareness was, I thought, a kind of wakefulness, leading me to believe that the dangers involved were threats not only to my dream self but to my physical self as well. Yet despite this knowledge, I was moved to start walking toward the complex.

I walked for about an hour, growing dehydrated and faint from the heat. The buildings seemed no nearer to hand, and the sun was a violet-white monster seething with prominences that looked much closer than the sun with which I was familiar, and although great banks of silvery-edged gray clouds were crossing the sky with the slowness of cruising galleons, they never once obscured the sun, breaking apart as they drew near to permit its continued radiance, re-forming once they had passed. It was as if the light were a solid barrier, an invisible cylindrical artifact around which they were forced to detour. Crabs with large pincers, their shells almost the same color as the sand, burrowed in the dunes; they were quite aggressive, occasionally chasing me away from their homes . . . or hunting me.

After another hour I came to an exceptionally smooth stretch of sand, lying flat as a pond, in this wholly unlike the rest of the desert, which wind had sculpted into an infinite sequence of undulations and rises, and in color a shade more coppery. The world was so quiet that I could hear the whine of my circulatory system, and I was afraid to step forward, certain that the sand hid some peril; I supposed it to be something on the order of quicksand. At last, deciding to give it a test, I unbuckled the belt that held my sheathed knife (I was not in the least surprised to discover that I had a knife), and removing the weapon, I tossed the belt out onto the sand. For a moment it lay undisturbed. But then the sand beneath it began to circulate in the manner of a slow whirlpool. I sprang back from the edge of the sand, retreating into the lee of a dune, just as the whirlpool erupted, spraying coppery orange filaments high into the air, filaments that were—I realized as they fell back to earth around me—serpents with flat, questing heads, the largest of them seven or eight feet in length. The pit from which they had been spewed was expanding. I scrambled higher on the dune, clawing at the sand, and gazed down into a vast maw, where thousands of white sticks—human bones, I saw— were being pushed up and then scattered downward as if falling off the shoulders of a huge dark presence that was forcing its way up through them from some unimaginable depth. . . .

At that moment I waked, blinking against the sunlight, still snared by the tag ends of the dream, still trying to climb out of danger to the top of the dune, and discovered Odille propped on an elbow, looking down at me with a concerned expression. The sight of her seemed to nullify all the fearful logic of the dream, and I felt foolish for having been so caught up in it. The corners of Odille's lips hitched up in a faint smile. "You were tossing about," she said. "So I woke you. I'm sorry if. . . ."

"No," I said, "I'm glad you did. I was having a bad dream." I boosted myself to a sitting position. My muscles ached, and dried blood striped my chest. "Jesus Christ!" I said, staring at the scratches; I remembered how it had been the previous night and was embarrassed.

"Are you all right?" Odille asked.

"I don't know," I said. "You . . . did I . . .?"

"Hurt me? I have some bruises. But it looks to me"—she pointed at my abrasions—"that you lost the battle."

"I'm sorry," I said, still flustered. "I don't know what got into me. I've never . . . I mean, last night. I've never been like that . . . not so. . . ."

She put a forefinger to my lips. "Apparently it's what we both wanted. Maybe we needed it, maybe. . . ." She made an angry noise.

"What's wrong?"

"I'm sick of explaining myself in terms of the past."

I thought I knew her meaning, and I wondered if that was what it had been for both us—a usage of each other's bodies in order to inflict pain on phantom lovers. I pulled her down, let her rest on my shoulder; her hair fanned across my chest, cool and heavy and silky. I wanted to say something, but nothing came to mind. The pressure of her body aroused me, but I felt tender now, empty of that perverse lust that had enlivened me hours before. She shifted her head so she could see my eyes.

"I won't ask what you're thinking," she said.

"Nothing bad."

"Then I will ask."

"I was thinking about making love with you again."

She made a pleased noise. "Why don't you?"

I turned to face her, drawing her against me, but as we began to kiss, to touch, I realized I was afraid of making love, of reinstituting that fierce animalism. That puzzled me. In retrospect, I had been somewhat repelled by my behavior, but in no way frightened. Yet now I had a sense that I might be opening myself to some danger, and I recalled how I'd felt while playing the game with Konwicki—there had been a feeling identical to that I'd had during our lovemaking. One of helplessness, of possession. I forced myself to dismiss all that, and soon my uneasiness passed. The sun melted like butter across the bed, and the sounds of morning, of birds and the sea and a woman vendor crying, *"Coco de aguas,"* came through the window like music to flesh out the rhythm that we made.

For a month or thereabouts, I believe that I was happy. Odille and I began to make a life, an easy and indulgent life that seemed in its potentials for pleasure and consolation proof against any outside influence. It was not only our sexuality that was a joy; we were becoming good friends. I came to see that like many attractive women she had a poor self-image, that she had been socialized to believe that beauty was a kind of cheapness, a reason for shame, and that her disastrous affair might have been a self-destructive act performed to compensate for a sense of worthlessness. Saying it like that is an over-simplification, but it was in essence true and I thought that she had known her affair would be ill-fated; I wondered if my own affair had been similar, a means of punishment for a shameful quality I perceived in myself, and I wondered further if our budding relationship might not have the same impetus. But I should have had no worries in that regard. Everything—sex, conversation, domestic interaction—was too easy for us; there was no great tension involved, no apprehension of loss. We were healing each other, and although this was a good thing, a healthy thing, I missed that tension and realized that its absence was evidence of our impermanence. I tried to deny this, to convince myself that I was in love with her as deeply as I had been in love with Karen, and to an extent my self-deception was a success. Atop the happiness we brought to one another, I installed a level of passionate intensity that served to confound my understanding of the relation-ship, to counterfeit the type of happiness that I believed necessary to maintain closeness. Yet even at my happiest I had the intimation of trouble hovering near, of a menace not yet strong enough to effect its will. And as time wore on, I began to have recurring dreams that centered upon those black pyramids in the rust-colored desert.

At the outset all the dreams were redolent of the first, dealing with dangers overcome in the desert. But eventually I made my way into the complex. The pyramids were enormous, towering several hun-dred feet high, and as I've said were reminiscent of old Mayan struc-tures, with fancifully carved roof combs and steep stairways leading up the faces to temples set atop them, all of black stones polished to a mirror brilliance that threw back reflections of my body—no longer that of a dwarf, but my own, as if the dwarf were merely a transi-tional necessity—and were joined with incredible precision, the seams almost microscopic. The sand had drifted in over the ebony flagstones, lying in thin curves, and torpid serpents were coiled everywhere, some slithering along leisurely, making sinuous tracks in the sand. Here and there I saw human bones half-buried in the sand, most so badly splin-tered that it was impossible to tell from which part of the body they had come. Many of the buildings had been left unfinished or else had been designed missing one or more outer walls, so that passing beside them, I had views of their labyrinthine interiors: mazes of stairways that led nowhere, ending in midair, and oddly shaped cubicles.

Before entering the complex I had been visited with certain knowledge that the buildings were not Mayan in origin, that the Mayan
pyramids were imperfect copies of them; but had I not intuitively
known this, I might have deduced it from the nature of the carvings.
They were realistic in style and depicted nightmare creatures—demons
with spindly legs, grotesque barbed phalluses, and flat snakelike heads
with gaping mouths and needle teeth and fringed with lank hair—
who were engaged in dismembering and otherwise violating human
victims. In a plaza between two pyramids I came upon a statue of
one of these creatures, wrought of the same black stone, giving its
skin a chitinous appearance. It stood thirty feet in height, casting an
obscenely distorted shadow; the sun hung behind its head at an
oblique angle, creating a blinding corona of violet-white glare that
masked its features and appeared to warp the elongated skull. But the
remainder of its anatomy was in plain view. I ran my eyes along the
statue, taking in clawed feet; knees that looked to be double-jointed;
the distended sac of the scrotum and the tumescent organ; jutting
hipbones; the dangling hooked hands, each finger wickedly curved
and tipped with a talon the length of a sword; the belly swollen like
that of a wasp. I was mesmerized by the sight, ensnared by a palpable
vibration that seemed to emanate from the figure, by an alluring
resonance that made me feel sick and dizzy and full of buzzing, incoherent thoughts. From beneath heavy orbital ridges, the eyes glinted
as if cored with miniature suns, and my shock at this semblance of
life broke the statue's hold on me. I backed away, then turned and
sprinted for my life. . . .

I came back to consciousness thrashing around in the dark, hot
bedroom. Odille was still asleep, and I slid out from beneath the sheet,
being careful not to wake her. I crossed to the door that led to the
living room, my heart pounding, skin covered with a sheen of sweat.
The room beyond was slashed by a diagonal of moonlight spilling
through the window, and the furniture cast knife-edged shadows on
the floor. I wiped my forehead with the back of my arm and was startled by the coldness and smoothness of my skin. I looked at my arm,
and the feeling of cold ran all through me—the skin on my wrist and
hand was black and shining like polished stone, channeling streams
of moonlight along it. I let out a gasp, and holding the arm away from
me, I staggered into the living room and onward into the kitchen,
the arm banging against the door, making a heavy metallic sound.
I tripped, spun around, trying to keep my balance, and fetched up
against the sink. I didn't want to look at the arm again, but when

I did I was giddy with relief. Nothing was wrong with it; it was pale and articulated with muscle. A normal human arm. I touched it to make sure. Normal. I leaned against the sink, taking deep breaths. I stayed there for another fifteen minutes, trying to counter the dream and its attendant hallucination with rationalizations. I was smoking too much dope, I told myself; I'd lived for too long under emotional pressure. Or else something was terribly wrong.

Houses and intricate buildings in dreams, says Freud, signify women, and for this reason I supposed that the pyramids might be related to my experiences with Karen—a notion assisted by the patent sexuality of the serpent imagery. There was no doubt that I had been damaged by the affair. For a year and a half prior to falling in love with her I had been forced to watch my father die of cancer, and had spent all my time in taking care of him. My resources had been at a low ebb when Karen had come along, and I'd seen her as a salvation. I'd been obsessed with her, and the slow process of rejection—itself as lingering as a cancer—had turned the power of my obsession against me, throwing me into a terrible depression that I had tried to remedy with cocaine, a drug that breeds its own obsessions and eventually twists one's concept of sexuality. I wondered if I was still obsessed, if I was sublimating the associated drives into my dream life. But I rejected that possibility. All that was left of my feelings for Karen was a vengeful reflex that could be triggered against my will, and it occurred to me that this was a matter of injured pride, of anger at myself for having allowed that sad woman to control and torment me. The dreams, I thought, might well be providing a ground for my anger, draining off its vital charge. And yet I couldn't rid myself of the suspicion that the dreams and the game I had played with Konwicki were at the heart of some arcane process, and one morning as I walked along the beach, I turned my steps in the direction of Konwicki's hut, hoping that he might be able to shed some light on the matter.

I hadn't spoken to him since the night of the game, and I had seen him only twice, then at a distance; in the light of that, it was logical to assume that he had come to terms with what had happened. But the instant his hut came into view I tensed and began to anticipate a confrontation. Ryan was sitting outside, dressed with uncharacteristic informality in cutoffs and a short-sleeved shirt; his head was down, knees drawn up. When he heard my footsteps, he jumped to his feet and stood in front of the door.

"You can't go in," he said as I came up.

I was taken aback by that, and also by his pathetic manner. His eyes darted side to side as if expecting a new threat to materialize; nerves twitched in his jaw, and his hands were in constant motion, plucking at his cutoffs, fingers rubbing together. He looked paler, thinner.

"What's the problem, man?" I asked.

"You can't go in," he said stubbornly.

"I just want to talk to him."

He shook his head.

"What's the hell wrong with you?"

Konwicki's voice floated out from the hut. "It's all right, Ryan."

I brushed past Ryan, saying, "You better get yourself together," and went on in. The light was bad, a brownish gloom, and Konwicki was sitting cross-legged against the rear wall; beside him was something bumpy covered by a white cloth, and noticing a corner of orange wood protruding from the cloth, I realized that he had been fooling around with the game.

"What can I do for you?" he said in a dry tone. "Sell you some drugs?"

I sat down close to him, off to the side, so I could watch the door; the dried palm fronds crunched beneath my weight. "How you been?"

He made a noise of amusement. "I've been fine, Ray. And you?"

I gestured at the covered board. "Playing with yourself?"

A chuckle. "Just studying a bit. Working on my project, you know."

I didn't believe him. There was a new solidity to his assurance, and I suspected it had something to do with the figures and the board. "Are you learning how to play it?" I asked.

After a silence, framing his words with—it seemed—a degree of caution, he said, "It's not something you can learn . . . not like chess, anyway. It's more of a role-playing game. It's essential to develop an affinity with one's counter. Then the rules—or rather, the potentials—become evident."

The light was so dim that the details of his swarthy features were indistinct, making it difficult to detect nuances of expression. But I had the feeling he was laughing at me. I didn't want to let him know that I was leery about the game, and I changed the subject. "Sounds interesting. But that's not why I came here. I wanted to"—I pretended to be searching for the right words—"clear the air. I thought we could. . . ."

"Be friends?" said Konwicki.

"I was hoping we could at least put an end to any lingering animosity. We're all going to be living here for a while, and it's pointless to be carrying on petty warfare . . . even if it's only giving each other the cold shoulder."

"That's very reasonable of you, Ray."

"Are *you* going to be reasonable? You and Odille were done before I came along. You must be aware of that."

"If you knew me, you wouldn't approach me this way."

"That's why I'm here . . . to get to know you."

"Just like a Yank, to think he can know something through talking." Konwicki's hand strayed toward the board as if by reflex, but he did not complete the movement. "I don't let go of things easily. I hang on to them, even things I don't really want. Unless I'm made to let go."

I ignored the implicit challenge. "Why's that?"

Konwicki leaned back and folded his arms, a shift in posture that conveyed expansiveness. "I've traveled in America," he said. "I've seen slums in Detroit, New York, Los Angeles. Ghastly ruins. Much more terrible in their physical entity than anything in England. But there's still vitality in America, even in the slums. Some of the slums in London, they're absolutely without vitality. Gray places with here and there a petunia in a flowerpot brightening a cracked window, and old toothless women, and children with stick arms and legs, and women whose bodies are too sallow and sickly to sell, and men whose brains have shrunk to the size of their balls. All of them moving about like people in a dream. Bending over to sniff at corpses, poking their fingers in a fire to see how hot it is. So much trash and foulness lying about that the streets stink even when they're frozen. To be born there is like being born on a planet where the gravity is so strong you can't escape it. It's not something you can resist with anger or violence. It's like treacle has been poured over you, and you crawl around in it like a fly with your wings stuck together. I've never escaped it. I've run around the world; I've cultivated myself and given myself an education. I've developed refined sensibilities. But everywhere I've gone I've carried that gravity with me, and I'm the same ignorant bloody-minded sod I always was. So don't you tell me something's not good for me. I'll want it more than ever. Things that aren't good for me make me happy. And don't say that something's done. I'm too damn stupid to accept it. And too damn greedy."

Despite its passion, there was a hollowness to this statement, and after he had done I said, "I don't believe you."

He gave a caustic laugh. "That's good, Ray. That's very perceptive. I've other imperatives now. But it used to be true."

I let his words hang in the air for a bit, then said, "Have you been having odd dreams lately?"

"I dream all the time. What sort of dreams are you talking about?"

"About the game we played."

"The game? This game?" He touched the cloth covering the board. I nodded.

"No . . . why? Are you?"

His mocking voice told me that he was not being direct, and I realized there was no use in continuing the conversation; either he was lying or else he was running yet another game on me, hoping to make me think he knew something by means of arch denial. I tried to dismiss the importance of what I'd said. "A couple . . . just weird shit. I haven't been sleeping well."

"I'm sorry to hear that."

If Konwicki was dreaming of that strange desert, if there was an occult reality to the game we'd played, I knew—because of my partial admission—I must look like a fool to him; to me, with his arms folded, half-buried in the dimness, he seemed as impenetrable as a Buddha. The thatched roof crackled like a small fire in a gust of wind, and behind Konwicki, mapping the darkness of the wall, were tiny points of lights, uncaulked places between the boards through which the day was showing; they lent the wall the illusion of depth, of being a vast sky mapped with stars, all arranged in a dwindling perspective so as to draw one's eyes toward a greater darkness beyond them. I began to feel daunted, out of my element, and I told myself again that this was the result of manipulation on Konwicki's part, that by intimating through denial some vague expertise he was playing upon my fears; but this was no comfort. I tried to think of something to say that would pose a counterspell to the silent pall that was settling over me. I had a great faith in words, believing that their formal noise elegantly utilized could have the weight of truth no matter how insincere had been the impulse to speak, and so when words failed me, I felt even more at sea. I looked away from Konwicki, gathering myself. The doorway framed a stretch of pale brown sand and sun-spattered water and curving palm trunks, and the brilliance of the scene was such a contrast to the gloom within, I imagined that these things comprised a

single presence that was peering in at us like an eye at a keyhole, and
that Konwicki and I were microscopic creatures dwelling inside the
mechanism of a lock that separated dark and light.

The weight of the silence forced me to stand and squeezed me
toward the door. "We haven't settled anything," I said, brushing
off my trousers, making a bustling, casual business of retreat. "But
I hope you understand that I don't need any aggravation. Neither
does Odille. If you want to make peace, we're open to it." I stepped
into the doorway. "See you around."

Once outside under the sun, breathing the salt air, I felt easier,
confident. I had, I thought, handled things fairly well. But as I turned
to head back to the house, I tripped over Ryan, who had reclaimed
his place beside the door, sitting with his knees drawn up. I went
sprawling, rolled over, intending to apologize. But Ryan didn't appear to have noticed me. He continued to sit there, staring at a patch
of sand, fingers plucking at a fray on his cutoffs, and after getting to
my feet, watching him for a second or two, I started walking, maintaining a brisk pace, feeling a cold spot between my shoulder blades
that I imagined registered the pressure of a pair of baleful eyes.

That same night, following a bout of paranoid introspection, I
dreamed that I went inside one of the pyramids, a structure not far
from the statue of the snake-headed creature that I had encountered
in earlier dreams. Leery about entering, watching for signs that would
warn me off, I passed through a missing wall and climbed a stair that
ended several hundred feet above in midair and was connected to a
number of windowless cubicles, all of the same black stone. I considered exploring the cubicles, but when I put my hand to the door
of one, I heard a woman's muffled voice alternately sobbing and spewing angry curses; I pictured a harpy within, some female monstrosity,
and I withdrew my hand. On every side a maze of other stairways
lifted around me, rising without apparent support like a monumen-
tal fantasy by Escher or Piranesi, reducing perspective to a shadowy
puzzle, and I felt diminished in spirit by the enormity of the place.
Snakes lay motionless on the stairs, looking at a distance like cracks
admitting to a bright coppery void; black spiders, invisible until they
moved, scuttled away from my feet, and their filmy webs spanned
between each step. From a point three-quarters of the way up, the
desert appeared the color of dried blood, and set at regular intervals
about the complex were five more colossal statues, each similar to the
first in its repulsive anatomy, but sculpted in different poses: one

crouching, one with its head thrown back, and so on. I couldn't help wondering if these six figures were related to the counters of Konwicki's game.

I had intended to go all the way to the top, but I grew uncomfortable with the isolation, the silence, and started back down. My progress was slowed by an attack of dizziness. I could still hear the woman crying, and the percussive effect of her sobs made me dizzier. The spaces beneath were swelling upward like black gas, and afraid that I would fall, overcoming my nervousness concerning the cubicles, I flung open the door to one, thinking I would sit inside until my vertigo had passed. A fecal stink poured from the cubicle, and something moved in the darkness at the rear, startling me.

"Who's there?" called a man's voice.

There was something familiar about the voice, and I peered into the cubicle. A pale shape was slumped against the far wall.

"Come on out," I said. .

The man shifted deeper into the corner. "Why are you here?"

"I'm dreaming all this," I said. "I don't have much choice."

A feeble, scratchy laugh. "That's what they all say."

I stepped inside, closing until I had clear sight of the man. For a moment I failed to recognize him, but then I realized it was Ryan— Ryan as he might have looked after a hard twenty years, his blond hair grayed and the youthful lines of his face dissolved into sagging flesh. The creases in his skin had filled in with grime and looked to be deep cuts. His clothes were in tatters. "Jesus, Ryan!" I said. "What happened?"

"I'm in jail." Another cracked laugh. "I have to stay put until. . . ."

"Till what?"

He shook his head.

I knelt beside him. "Where are we, Ryan?"

He giggled. "The endgame."

"What the hell's that mean?"

"The game," he said, "is not a game."

I waited for him to continue, but he lost his train of thought. I repeated the question.

"The game is just a way of getting here. You've already done playing, and now you have to wait till all the moves have been made."

I asked him to explain why—if I'd done playing—moves were still to be made, and he replied by saying that a move wasn't a move until it had been made everywhere. "It's like this place," he said. "A place isn't really a place. One place leads to another, and that place leads to another yet, and on and on. There's nothing that's only itself." That thought seemed to sadden him, and he said, "Nothing."

The woman let out a piercing scream, and her curses echoed through the pyramid.

I tried to pull Ryan to his feet, thinking that there might be some more pleasant place for him to wait; he struck at my hands, a flurry of weak blows that did no damage, but caused me to release him.

"Leave me alone," he said. "I'm safe here."

"Safe from what?"

"From you," he answered. "The Master thinks he's the dangerous one, but I know it's you. He's made the wrong move. Sooner or later he'll see I'm right, and he'll try and stop it. But you can't stop it. The travelers have to come and go; the transitions have to. . . ." His speech became incoherent for a few seconds; then he snapped out of it. "Of course there are no right moves. Even the winner pays a price once the game is done. But not to worry, Ray," he said with a flash of his old cockiness. "It'll hurt, but it'll be a much cheaper price than the one the Master has to pay. Or else you can always keep playing if you want to be noble and take the risk."

He lapsed into incoherence once again; I attempted to bring him to his senses, but all he would say was to repeat that "it" couldn't be stopped, "it" had to happen, and to ramble on about "exchanges, necessary transitions." Giving up on him, I left the cubicle and went out onto the sand. The sun was low, its violet-white disk partially down on the horizon, and the shadows had grown indistinct. I strolled about the complex, feeling for the first time at ease among the buildings; I was comfortable even in proximity to the snake-headed statue. I stepped back from it, admiring its needle teeth and flat skull, all its obscene proportions, and although I felt as before a sense of resonant identity with it, on this occasion I was not frightened by the feeling, but rather was pleased. Indeed, I found the entire landscape soothing. The snakes, the crabs scuttling down the sanguine faces of the dunes, the black silence of the complex . . . all this had a bleak majesty and seemed the product of a pure aesthetic.

On waking and remembering the dream, however, I was more disturbed by my acceptance of that bizarre landscape than I had been by my fear of it. It was still dark, and Odille was asleep beside me. I eased out of bed, pulled on jeans and a shirt, and went into the patio. The edges of the tile roof framed a rectangle of stars and dark blue sky, with the crowns of palms showing half in silhouette, the ragged fronds throwing back pale green shines from the lights of the house next door. I dropped onto a lawn chair and lay back, trying to settle my thoughts. After a few minutes I heard the whisper of Odille's sandals on the concrete; she had thrown on a bathrobe, and her hair was in disarray, loose about her shoulders. She sat opposite me, put a hand on my knee, and asked what was wrong.

I had previously told her that I'd been having bad dreams, but had not been specific; now, though, I told her the entire story—the game, the feelings I'd had, the dreams, and my meeting with Konwicki. Once I had done, she lowered her head, fingering the hem of her robe, and after a pause she asked, "What are you worried about? The game . . . that it's real?"

I was ashamed to admit it.

"That's ridiculous!" she said. "You can't believe that."

"It's just the dreams . . . and Ryan. I mean, what's the matter with him?"

She made a noise of disgust. "He's weak. Carl's found a way to undermine him with drugs or something. That's all."

We were silent for several seconds; a palm frond scraped the roof, and the surf was a distant hiss.

"I knew something was bothering you," she said. "But . . ." She got to her feet, walked a couple of paces off, and stood with her arms folded. "Carl's getting to you. I wouldn't have thought it possible." She sighed, jammed her hands in the pocket of the robe. "I'm going to see him."

"The hell you are!"

"I am! And if *he* believes there's anything to the game, I'll find out about it." I started to object, but she talked over me. "You aren't worried about me, are you? About my going back to him?"

"I guess not."

"That doesn't sound like a vote of confidence." She knelt beside my chair. "Don't you understand how much I hate him?"

"I never understood why you were with him in the first place."

"I was vulnerable. He took advantage of my confusion. He confused me even more. He violated my trust; he weakened me. If I could, I'd. . . ." She drew a deep breath, let it out slowly. "Don't tell me you haven't ever done anything that you knew was bad for you even when you were doing it."

"No," I said, surprised by her vehemence. "I can't tell you that." I stroked her hair. "What did he do to you?"

Her face worked, suppressing emotion. "The same sort of thing he's trying to do to you . . . except I didn't have anybody to tell me what was going on. Listen! Nothing's going to happen. I'm just going to talk to him. He'll lie, but I know when he's lying. I'll be able to tell whether he's concerned for himself or looking for a way to hurt you. And that'll put your mind at ease."

"It's not necessary."

"Yes, it is!" She put her arms around my neck. "I want you to get past this so I can have your undivided attention."

There was an edge to her intensity, a hectic brightness in her eyes, that quieted my objections, and later that night when she said she loved me, I believed her for the first time.

Two nights later as we sat at dinner in a small restaurant, a one-room place of stucco and thatch lit by candles, Odille told me that she had spoken with Konwicki. "You don't have to be concerned about the game," she said. "Carl's only trying to unnerve you." She had a forkful of rice, chewed. "I told him all about your dreams . . . everything. You should have seen him. He was like a starving man who'd been handed a steak. He said, Yes, yes, it was the same for him. Dreams, odd intuitions. Then I described your last dream, the one with Ryan, and what he'd said about Carl's making the wrong move. He loved that. He said, Yes, that was true. And he didn't know how to stop it from happening. After that, he offered an apology for everything that had happened between us. He said the game had changed him, that he could see now what a reprehensible sort he'd been."

"A reprehensible sort?" I said. "Were those his words?"

"I believe so."

"Reprehensible . . . shit!" I stared at her over the rim of my coffee cup. "It sounds to me like he's corroborating the dreams. Why else would he admit that he'd made a bad move?"

"Because," said Odille, "he knows if he were to deny it, he'd have no way of affecting you. But now, claiming that it's all true, especially the part about him possibly losing, he has an excuse to talk to you, to play with your mind. He can pretend to be your ally. You watch. He'll come to see you. He'll try to align himself with you. He'll have a plan that'll involve the two of you working together to save each other from the game . . . its perils. Then he'll start manipulating." She had another bite, swallowed. "He thought he was fooling me, but he was transparent."

"Are you sure about all this?"

"Of course. Carl's a greedy little man who thinks he's smarter than the rest of the world. He can't imagine that anyone could see through him. If there was anything to the game, he never would have told me." She took my hand. "Just wait. Watch what happens. You'll see I'm right."

Odille's reassurances had not convinced me of the fecklessness of my fears. Recalling Konwicki's statement that familiarity with one's counter was important, I set out to reinhabit the feelings I'd had while playing, to recall the moves that had been made. It was not hard to recapture those feelings; they returned to me every night in dreams. But the moves were a different matter. Other than the first, I could remember only the last two: one in which all four figurines had been placed in close proximity, and another in which the figure of the infant had been placed in a zone adjoining that of the dwarf. I asked Odille what she could recall about the counters from working on the translation, and she said that all she knew was what Konwicki had told her.

"He used to joke with me about them," she said. "He identified himself with the warrior, and he said my counter was the female . . . the one you moved during the game. He described her to me. A real maniac, a terrible creature. Sluttish, foul-mouthed, vile. She was always throwing tantrums. Physically abusive."

"Maybe he was trying to demean you by describing her that way."

"I'm sure he was. But once he did show me some of the translation he'd done about her, and it looked authentic."

"What were they . . . the counters? Did he ever tell you that?"

"Archetypes," she said. "Mayan archetypes. Spirit forms . . . that was the term he used. I'm not sure what that meant. Whoever made the figures, whoever assigned them their characters, had a warped idea of human potential. All the characters were repellent in some way. . . . I remember that much. But when he told me all that, I was trying to pull away from him, and I didn't pay much attention."

A week went by, and I made no further progress. I was spinning my wheels, wasting myself in futile effort. Then I took stock of the situation, and suddenly all my paranoia seemed ludicrous. That I could have even half-believed I had been possessed by a Mayan spirit in the shape of a dwarf was evidence of severe mental slippage, and it was time to get a grip. The dreams must have some connection to the abuses I had suffered during the past few years, I thought, and to be this much of a fool for love was debasing, particularly in the face of the abuses I met with every day in Livingston. Malnutrition, tyranny, ignorance. I determined that I was going to take a hard line with my psyche. If I had dreams, so what? Sooner or later they would run their course. And I also determined to grant Odille's wish, to give her my undivided attention; I realized that while I hadn't been neglecting her, neither had I been utilizing the resources of the relationship as a lover should. Things were changing between us in a direction that I would never have predicted, and I owed it to her, to myself, to see where that would lead.

Our lives were calm for the next couple of weeks. The dreams continued, but I refused to let them upset me. Odille and I fell into the habit of taking twilight walks along the beach, and one evening after a storm, with dark blue ridges of cloud pressing down upon a smear of buttermilk yellow on the horizon, we walked out to the point beyond the Café Pluto, a hook of land bearing a few palms whose crowns showed against the last of sunset like feathered headdresses. Nearby stretches of cobalt water merged with purplish slate farther out, and there were so many small waves, it looked as if the sea were moving in every direction at once. We sat on a boulder at the end of the point, watching the light fade in the west, and after a minute Odille asked if I had ever been to Paris.

"A long time ago," I said.

"What did you think?"

"It was the winter," I said. "I didn't see too much. I had no money, and I was staying in a house that belonged to this old lady named Bunny. She was straight out of a Tennessee Williams play. She'd been Lawrence Durrell's lover . . . or maybe it wasn't Durrell. Somebody famous, anyway. She was an invalid, and the house was a mess. Cat shit everywhere. There was a crazy Romanian who was printing an anarchist newsletter in the basement. And Bunny's kids, they were true degenerates. Her fifteen-year-old raped the maid. The twenty-year-old was dealing smack. Bunny just lay around, and I ended up having to take care of her."

"God, you've lived!" said Odille, and we both laughed.

I put an arm around her. "Are you homesick?"

"Not so much . . . a little." She leaned into me. "I was just wondering how you'd like Paris."

We had talked about the future in only the most general of terms, but I felt comfortable now considering a future with her, and that surprised me, because even though I was happier than I'd been in a very long time, I had also been nervous about formalizing the relationship.

"I suppose we're going to have to leave here eventually," I said. She looked up at me. "Yes."

"It doesn't matter to me where we go. I don't have to be any particular place to do my work."

"I know," she said. "That's your greatest virtue."

"Is that so?" I kissed her, the kiss grew long, and we lay back on the boulder. I touched her breasts. In the darkness the whites of her eyes were aglow; her breath was sweet and frail. Waves slapped at the rock. Finally I turned onto my back, pillowed my head on my hands. Icy stars made simple patterns in the sky, and it seemed to me at the moment that everything in the world had that same simplicity.

"Someday," Odille said after a long silence, "I'd like to go back to Paris . . . just to see my friends again."

"Want me to go with you?"

She was silent for a bit; then she sat up and stared out to sea. I had asked the question glibly, thinking I knew the answer, yet now I was afraid that I'd misread her. At last she said, "You wouldn't like it. Americans don't like Parisians."

"The way I hear it, it's mutual," I said, relieved. "But there are exceptions."

"I guess so." She glanced down at me and smiled. "Anyway, we don't have to stay in Paris. We could come to the States. I wouldn't mind that." She tipped her head to the side. "You look puzzled."

"I wasn't sure we'd get around to talking about this. And even if we did, I thought it would be awkward."

"So did I for a while. But then I realized we were past awkwardness." With both hands she lifted the heft of her hair and pushed it back behind her head. "Sometimes I've tried to imagine myself without you. I can do it. I can picture myself living a life, being with someone else. All that. But then I realized how artificial that was . . . that kind of self-examination. It was as if I were wishing for that prospect, because I was afraid of you. To end doubt, or to learn whether my doubts were real, all I had to do was stop thinking about them. Just give in to the moment. That was easier said than done, I thought. But then I tried it, and it *was* easy." She ran a hand along my arm. "You did it, too. I could tell when you stopped."

"Could you, now?"

"Don't you believe me?"

Before I could answer, there was a crunching in the brush behind us, and two figures emerged from shadows about thirty feet away. It took me a second to identify them against the dark backdrop—Konwicki, with Ryan hanging at his shoulder. I stood, wary, and Odille came to her knees. "What the fuck are you doing?" I asked them. "Tracking us?"

"I have to talk with you," said Konwicki. "About the game."

"Some other time, man." I took Odille's arm and began steering her back along the point, giving Konwicki and Ryan a wide berth, but keeping an eye on them.

"Listen," said Konwicki, coming after us. "I'm not after mucking you about. We're in serious trouble." I kept walking, and he grabbed my shoulder, spun me around. "I've been having dreams, too. They're different from yours. But they're indicators all the same."

His face betrayed anxiety, but I wasn't buying the act. I shoved him back. "Keep your hands off me!"

"The game's a conduit," he said as we walked away. "A means of transport to another world, another plane . . . something. And to another form as well." He caught up with me, blocked our path; Ryan scuttled behind him. "I don't know how the Mayans discovered it, but it was a major influence on their architecture, on every facet of their culture. The ritual cruelties of their religion, the—"

"Get out of my way." I was cold inside—a sign that I was preparing for violence. My senses had grown acute. The slop of the waves, Konwicki's breathing, the leaves rustling—all were sharp and distinct. Ryan's pale face, peering from behind Konwicki, seemed as bright as a star.

"You're a fool if you don't listen to me," Konwicki said. "The game we played was real. I admit I wouldn't be here if I didn't think I was in danger, but there's—"

"You made the wrong move, that it?" I said.

"Yes," said Konwicki. "I didn't know it at the time. I didn't know we were actually playing. And later, after I realized something strange was happening, I didn't see the mistake I'd made." He wagged both hands as if dismissing all that. "We've got an option, man . . . I think. The winner can keep the game going for one more move at least. It'll be a risk, but a relatively minor one." He looked as if he were about to grab me in frustration, doing a fine imitation of a desperate man. "That way we have a chance of figuring out what else we can do."

"I'm not one of your goddamn chumps!" I said. "I know Odille told you about my dream. You're trying to use it against me."

"Yes, yes, you're right," he said. "I *was* using it. I wanted to fuck with you. I admit it. But after Odille talked to me, I began thinking about some of the things she'd told me. And some of the things you'd said, too."

I made a derisive noise.

"I'm telling the truth. I promise you!" he said. "After I talked to her, I had another look at the game . . . at the papers. Some of the things she'd told me gave me new insights into the translation." His words came in a rush. "You see, I believed that the figures—the dwarf, the warrior—that they were the entities involved. I thought they were conveyances that carried you to the pyramids. And they are. One of us was going to be transported. That much was certain. I thought it would be me, but it's not . . . it's you. And I'd overlooked the obvious." A dismayed laugh. "It's a matter of elementary physics. For every action there's a reaction."

He paused for breath, and having heard enough, I said, "Odille told me you'd come up with something clever. Guess she was wrong about that."

I started to push past him, but he shoved me back. "For God's sake, will you listen?"

"I'm going to tell you once more," I said. "Keep your hands off me."

"That's right, you stupid clot!" he said. "Just go home and bugger your stupid whore and don't worry about a bloody thing!"

"Such talk," I said; my arms had begun to tremble.

"Let's just go!" Odille pulled at me, and I allowed myself to be hauled along; but Konwicki planted a hand on my chest, bringing me up short.

"I'm trying to save your sodding life, you ass!" he said. "Are you going to listen to me, or. . . ." He was, judging from his disdainful expression, about to deliver some further pomposity.

"No," I said, and nailed him in the stomach, not wanting to hurt my hand. He caved in, went to his knees, then rolled up into a fetal position, the wind knocked out of him. Ryan darted toward me, then retreated into the shadows; a second later I heard him running off through the bushes.

It had been years since I'd hit anyone, and I was ashamed of myself; Konwicki had been no threat. I dropped to my knees beside him, counseled him to take shallow breaths, and once he had recovered somewhat, I tried to help him up. He pushed my hands away and fixed me with a hateful stare.

"Right, you bastard!" he said. "I warned you, but that's all right. You'll have to take what comes now."

After that night on the point I concluded that Livingston had lost its charm; I wanted to avoid further conflicts, and I was certain more would arise. Odille was in accord with this, and we planned to leave as soon as I could find someone responsible to take over the Spanish doctors' house. We decided to settle in Panajachel near Lake Atitlán until I finished my current writing project, and then to visit New York City en route to Paris; almost without acknowledging it, we had made an oblique, understated commitment to each other, one that by contrast to our pasts and the instability around us was a model of rigor. Perhaps our relationship had begun as an accommodation, a shelter from the heavy weather of our lives, but against all odds something more had developed; although I wasn't ready to admit it to her, unwilling to risk a total involvement, I had fallen in love with Odille. It wasn't any one instance or event that had brought this home to me, but rather a slowly growing awareness of my reactions to her. I had begun to focus more and more upon her, to treasure images of her. To savor all the days. And yet I detected in myself a residue of tension, one I also detected in her, and this was evidence that we were afraid of the obsessive bonding that had occurred and were preparing for disappointment, obeying the conditioning of our pasts.

Ten days passed, and I hadn't found anyone to take the house. I wrote to the Spanish doctors, telling them that an emergency had come up, that I had to leave and wanted to delegate my responsibilities to the local priest, who had become something of a friend, and who—aside from his clerical duties—maintained a small museum that displayed some Mayan artifacts of indifferent value. I began to pack my papers in anticipation of their response. Early one evening I went to the telegraph office to call my agent in the States and tell her about the move, to see if she had money for me. The office was a low building of yellow stucco next to the generator that provided the village's power, and was manned by a harried-looking clerk who was arguing with an Indian family, and was guarded by a soldier wearing camouflage gear and carrying a machine gun. The phones lined the rear wall of the office, and choosing the one farthest from the argument, I put in the call. Five minutes later I heard my agent's voice through a hiss of static, and after we had taken care of business, I asked what was new in the big city.

"The usual," she said. "Boring parties and editors playing musical chairs. You're better off down there . . . as long as you're working. *Are* you working?"

"Don't worry," I said.

My agent let some dead time accumulate, then said, "I guess I should tell you this, Ray. You're going to find out sooner or later."

"What's that?"

"Karen had her baby."

For an instant I felt strangely light, free of some restraint. "I didn't think she was due this soon."

"There were complications. But she's all right. So's the baby. It's a boy. It's really cute, Ray. A little doll. It just lies there and squeaks."

I let out a nasty laugh. "Just like his mama."

"I thought you went down there to let go of her. You don't sound like you're letting go."

"Must be the connection." I stared at the pocked, grimy wall, seeing nothing.

Another pause. "What're you working on, Ray?"

"You'll see it soon," I said. "Look, I've got to go."

"I didn't mean to upset you."

"I'm not upset. I'll call you in a couple of weeks, okay?"

I walked outside, cut down onto the beach. Dusk had given way to darkness, and the jungled shore was picked out by shanty lights; there was also a scattering of lights on the hills lifting behind the village, showing the location of small farms and platanals. The moon, almost full, had risen to shine through a notch between the hills, paving the chop of the water close to shore with silvery glitter; but threatening clouds and dark brooms of rain were visible farther out—a storm would be hitting the coast within a matter of minutes. I was angry as I walked, but my anger was undirected. Karen was no longer an object of hatred, merely a catalyst that opened me to violent emotion, and I realized that part of the reason she had maintained a hold over me for so long was due, not to any real feeling, but to my romantic nature, my stubborn denial that the light in the heart could be snuffed out. I had hung on to the belief that—despite Karen's betrayal—the good, strong core of my feelings would last; now I was forced to face the fact that they were dead, and that made me angry and caused me to doubt everything I felt for Odille.

A voice called to me as I was passing a stand of palmettos. I ignored it, but the voice continued to call, and I whirled around to see Ryan running down the beach, his blond hair flying, dressed in the cutoffs and soiled shirt that had become his uniform. He staggered to a halt a few feet away, gasping.

"What do you want?" I asked.

He held up a hand, trying to catch his breath. "Gotta talk to you," he managed. He looked alien to me, a pale little twist of a creature, and I felt vastly superior. Stronger, more intelligent. The fierceness of the loathing that fueled these feelings didn't strike me as unusual.

"Talk about what?" I said.

"Odille . . . you have to break it off with her."

"You jealous, Ryan?"

"Konwicki . . ."

"Fuck Konwicki!" I gave Ryan a shove that sent him reeling backward, catching at the air with his hands. "If he's got a problem, tell him to come talk to me himself."

"You have to stop seeing her," said Ryan defiantly. He slipped a hand beneath his shirtfront as if soothing a stomachache and kept his eyes lowered. "I'm warning you . . . bad things are going to happen if you don't."

"Goodness me, Ryan," I said, taking a little walk around him, examining him contemptuously, as if he were an unsightly objet d'art. "I wonder what they could be."

Ryan's chin quivered. "He's . . . he's. . . ."

"C'mon, man! Spit it out!" I said. "Has he been doing bad things to *you?* He must have been doing something nasty, mighty bad to turn you into such a twitchy little toad. Is it drugs? Is he feeding you bad drugs, or. . . ."

Anger came boiling out of him. "Don't talk to me like that!"

I knew at that moment that Ryan had a weapon. The way he kept shifting his right hand under his shirt as if adjusting his grip, keeping his weight back on his heels, balanced, ready to strike. And I wanted him to strike.

"I got it," I said. "Konwicki's into boys now. That's it, right? And you're his boy! That explains why I've never seen you with a girl."

"Stop it!" He set himself, the muscles of his right forearm flexing.

"What's it like with him, man? He make your little doggy sit up and beg?"

"You better stop!"

"Does he make a lot of noise, Ryan?" I laughed, and the laugh startled me, sounding too guttural to be my own. "Or is he the strong, silent type?"

With a shout, he pulled a knife from beneath his shirt and slashed at me. I caught his wrist, gave it a sharp twist. He cried out, the knife fell to the sand, and he backed away, cradling his wrist, his expression shifting between panic and anguish. "I'm sorry," he said. "I'm sorry. He told me I had to. . . ." Then he broke into a stumbling run and went crashing through the palmettos. I scooped up the knife and began to hunt him. That was how it seemed. A hunt. One in which I was expert. I've never been much of an athlete, yet that night I ran easily, with short chopping strides that carried me in a zigzagging path among the palmettos. I kept pace with Ryan, running off to his left and a little behind, intending to harry him until he dropped. He glanced back over his shoulder, saw me, and ran faster, frantically calling out to Konwicki.

On hearing that, I slowed my pursuit. It was Konwicki I really wanted, and since Ryan had been his messenger, it was likely that he was now going to see him. And yet we were heading away from the beach, away from Konwicki's house. I decided to trust my instincts. If Konwicki had somehow convinced Ryan to kill me—and I thought that must be the case, that he'd hoped to evade the judgment of the game by eliminating me—after the deed he would have wanted Ryan to meet him somewhere out of the way. I dropped back a bit, letting Ryan think he had lost me, keeping track of him by ear, picking out the sound of his passage through the foliage from the noises of insects and frogs and wind. We were moving onto the slope of one of the hills behind the village, and despite the uphill path, I was still running easily, enjoying myself. The musky scents of the vegetation were as cloying as perfume; clouds flowing across the moon, driven by a gusting wind, made the world go alternately dark and bright with an erratic rhythm that added to my excitement. I exulted in the turbulent weather, in my strength, and I threw the knife into the brush, knowing that I wasn't going to need it.

As I passed through a banana grove, a flickering yellow light penetrated the bushes to my left from one of the farmhouses. The wind was rapidly gaining in force, tattering the banana leaves, lifting them high like the feathery legs of giant insects, and something about their articulated shapes fluttering in a sudden wash of moonlight made me uneasy. I began to have an inconstant feeling in my flesh, a dull vibration that nauseated me; I tried to push it aside, to concentrate on the running, but it persisted. I estimated that I must be a quarter of the way up the hill, and I could hear Ryan jogging along almost parallel to me. He had stopped calling out to Konwicki, but now and then he would cry out, perhaps because of the pain in his wrist. I was having some pain myself. Twinges in my joints, in my bones. Growing sharper by the moment. And there was something wrong with my eyes. Every object had a halo, the veins of leaves glowed an iridescent green, and overhead I could see dozens of filmy layers between the clouds and the earth, drifting, swirling, coalescing. I shook my head, trying to clear my vision, but if anything it grew worse. The halos had congealed into auras of a dozen different colors; hot spots of molten scarlet and luminous blue were insects crawling in the dirt. The pain kept growing worse, too. The twinges became jolts of agony shooting through my limbs, and with the onset of each I staggered, unable to stay on course. Then a tremendous pain in my chest sent me to all fours, my eyes squeezed shut. I tried to stand, and in doing so caught sight of my left hand—gnarled, lumpy fingers thick as sausages, clawing at rusty orange sand, lengthening and blackening. A fresh surge of pain knocked me down, and I twisted about and gouged at the earth for what seemed a very long time. Rain started to fall, and another burst of pain dredged up a bassy scream from my chest that merged with the wind, like the massive flat Om of a foghorn wedded to a howl. One instant I felt I was splitting in half, the next that I was growing huge and heavy. I receded from the storm and the world, dwindling to a point within myself, and from that moment on I was incapable of action, only of mute and horrified observation as another "I" took control of my thoughts, one whose judgments were funded by an anger far more potent and implacable than my own.

I lashed out with my left arm, clutched something thin and hard, tore at it; the next second a banana tree fell across my chest. But the pain was diminishing rapidly, and after it had passed, rather than feeling exhausted, I felt renewed. I climbed to my feet and looked out over the treetops. The storm that during transition had seemed so chaotic and powerful now seemed inconsequential, hardly worth my notice. Lightning scratched red forking lines down the sky; inky clouds rushed overhead. A flickering nimbus of bluish white overlaid the jungle, and beneath it, the lights of the houses ranging the hill were almost too dim to make out. I could find no sign of the defeated. Frustrated, I moved toward the nearest house—a structure with board walls and a roof of corrugated metal—knocking away branches, pushing masses of foliage aside, my hair whipped into my eyes by the wind. When I reached the house I stood gazing down at the roof, trying to sense the occupants. The energy flows binding the metal, stitchings of coruscant lines and dazzles, could not hide the puny lives within: shifting clots of heat and color. My quarry was not there, but in a fury I swung my arm and tore a long rip in the roof, delighted by the shriek of the tortured metal. Dark frightened faces stared at me through the rip, then vanished. A moment later I spotted them running out the door and into the jungle, becoming streaks of red beneath the ghostly luminescence of the leaves. I would have enjoyed pursuing them, but my time was limited, and I was concerned that the completion of my task would be hampered by the victor—I felt him lodged like a stone in my brain—whose pitiful morality was a nagging irritant. I wondered at his motives for entering the contest. Surely he must have known what was at stake. There is no morality in this darkness.

I comforted myself with the thought that before too long the victor would have his due, unless—and I thought this unlikely—he chose to renew the challenge; and I pressed on through the jungle. Something ran across my path—an animal of some sort. It swerved aside, but before it could escape I grazed it with a claw, tearing its belly and flipping it into the air. The kill improved my temper. I had never relished employing my license here. The weak strains of life are barely a music, and the walls that hold back death are tissue-thin. But I was pleased to see the blood jet forth. I watched the animal's essence disperse, misting upward in pale threads to rejoin the Great Cloud of Being, and then continued on my way.

At the crest of the hill I paused and gazed back down the slope. From this vantage the landscape of that soft female world seemed transformed, infused with new strength. Great smoking clouds streamed from the sea, and the jungle pitched and tossed as if troubled by my sight. The souls of the trees were thin gold wires stretched to breaking. The thunder was a power, the lightning a name. I stood attuning myself to the night, absorbing its black subtleties and cold meanings, and thus strengthened, restored to the fullness of purpose, I went along the crest, searching the darkness for the defeated, listening among the whispers of the dead for the sound of one soon to die, for that telltale dullness and sonority. At last I heard him venting his rage against one of the alternates in a house a third of the way down the hill. His obvious lack of preparation dismayed me, and once again I felt less than enthusiastic about my duty. It would be a mercy to end these intermittent rituals of violence and let the brood come as an army to urge on this feeble race to the next plane.

The house was a glowing patch in the midst of a toiling darkness and was made of sapling poles and thatch; orange light striped the gaps between the poles and leaked from beneath the door. I called

to the defeated. The angry conversation within was broken off, but
no one came out. Perhaps, I thought, he had mistaken my call for
an element of the storm. I called again, a demanding scream that out-
voiced the thunder. Still he remained within. This was intolerable!
Now I would be forced to instruct him. I ripped aside the poles at
the front of the house, creating a gaping hole through which I saw
two figures shrinking back against the rear wall. I held out my hand
in invitation, but as the alternate collapsed to the floor, the defeated
went scuttling about like a frightened crab, running into the table,
the chairs. Disgusted, I reached in and picked him up. I lifted him
high, looked into his terrified face. He struggled, prying at my claws,
kicking, squealing his fear.

"Why do you struggle?" I asked. "Your life is an exhausted breath,
the failure of an enervated creation. You are food with a flicker of
intelligence. True power is beyond you, and the knowledge of pain
is your most refined sensibility." Of course he did not understand:
my speech must have seemed to him like a tide roaring out from a
cave. But to illustrate the point I traced a line of blood across his ribs,
being careful not to cut too deeply. "Your ideas are all wrong," I
told him. "Your concept of beauty a gross mutation; your insipid
notions of good and evil an insult to their fathering principles." Once
again I made him bleed, tracing the second line of instruction, slit-
ting the skin of his stomach with such precision that it parted in neat
flaps, yet the sac within was left intact. "Evil is as impersonal as mathematics. That its agencies derive pleasure from carrying out its charge
is meaningless. Its trappings, its gaud and hellish forms, are nuance,
not essence. Evil is the pure function of the universe, the machine
of stars and darkness that carries us everywhere." At the third line
I saw in his face the first light of understanding, and in his shrieks
I detected a music that reflected the incisiveness of my as-yet-
incomplete design. His eyes were distended, bloody spittle clung to
his lips and beard, and there was a new eagerness in his expression;
he would—had he been able to muster coherent thought—have inter-
preted this eagerness as a lust for death, yet I doubted he would be
aware that to feel such a lust was the signature of a profound lesson
learned. I thought, however, that once we returned to the desert,
once I had time to complete the design, our lessons would go more
quickly. I traced a fourth line. His body spasmed, flopping bonelessly,
but he did not lose consciousness, and I admired his stamina, envied
him the small purity of his purpose. The bond that held me in that
place was weakening, and I grasped him more tightly, squeezing a

trickle of darkness from his mouth. "You and I," I said, slicing the skin over his breastbone, "are gears of the machine. Together we interlock and turn, causing an increment of movement, a miniscule resolution of potential." With the barest flick I laid open one of his cheeks, and he responded with a high quavering wail that went on and on as if I had opened a valve inside him, released some pressure that issued forth with a celebratory keening. Beneath the wash of blood I had a glimpse of white. "I can see to your bone," I said. "The stalk of your being. I am going to pare you down to your essential things, both of flesh and knowledge. And when we return to the temples, you will have clear sight of them, of their meaning. They, too, are part of the machine." His head lolled back; his mouth went slack, and his eyes—they appeared to have gone dark—rolled up to fix on mine. It was as if he had decided to take his ease and bleed and study his tormentor, insulated from pain and fear. Perhaps he thought the worst was over. I laughed at that, and the storm of my laughter merged with the wind and all the tearing night, making him stiffen. I bent my head close to him, breathed a black breath to keep him calm during the transition, and whispered, "Soon you will know everything."

That is a mere approximation of what I remember, an overformal and inadequate rendering of an experience that seems with the passage of time to grow ever more untranslatable. Trapped by the limitations of language, I can only hint at the sense of alienness that had pervaded me, at the compulsions of the thing I believed I had become. I woke on the beach before dawn not far from Konwicki's house, and I thought that after the possession—or the transformation, or whatever it had been—had ended, in the resultant delirium I must have wandered down from the hillside and passed out. No other possibility offered itself. My muscles still ached from the experience, and my memories were powerful and individual and sickening. I remembered how it felt to have the strength to tear iron like rotten cloth; I remembered a cold disdain for a world I now embraced in gratitude and relief; I remembered the sight of a black hand wicked with curved talons closing around Konwicki and lifting him high; I remembered intelligence without sentiment, hatred without passion; I remembered a thousand wars of the spirit that I had never fought; I remembered killing a hundred brothers for the right to survive; I remembered a silence that caused pain; I remembered thoughts like knives, a wind like religion, a brilliance like fear, I remembered things for which I had no words. Things that made me tremble.

But as the sun brought light into the world, light brought doubt into my mind and caused the memories to diminish in importance. Their very sharpness was a reason to doubt them; memories, I believed, should be fragmentary, chaotic, and these—despite their untranslatable essence—were a poignant, almost physical, weight inside my head. Their vividness seemed a stamp of fraudulence, of the manufactured, and thus my problems with interpreting what had happened became complex and confusing. How much, for instance, had Odille known? Had she, out of hatred for Konwicki, manipulated me? Had she known more than she had said, trying to encourage a deadly confrontation? And if so, what sort of confrontation was she trying to encourage? And what about coincidence? The coincidence of so many elements of those days and the dreams and the game. Was it really coincidence, or could what seemed coincidental have been a matter of selective memory? And Konwicki . . . had he been honest with me that night on the point, or had he, too, been engaged in manipulation? Could Odille's desertion have left him more bereft than he had allowed, and was that a significant motivation? I wished I had let him finish speaking, that I had learned what he meant by the phrase "for every action there's a reaction." Was that merely another coincidence, or did it refer to an exchange of travelers between this world and that desert hell? And most pertinently, had my deep-seated anger against an old lover been a sufficiently powerful poison to cause me to imagine an unimaginable horror, to erect an insane rationalization for a crime of passion? Or had anger been the key that opened both Konwicki and me to the forces of the game? Each potential answer to any of these questions cast a new light upon the rest, and therefore to determine an ultimate answer became a problem rather like trying to put together a jigsaw puzzle whose pieces were constantly changing shape.

The sun had cleared the horizon, shining palely through thin gray clouds; clumps of seaweed littered the beach, looking at a distance like bodies washed up by the surf, and heaps of foam like dirty soapsuds demarked the tidal margin. My head felt packed with cotton, and I couldn't think. Then I was struck by an illumination, a hope. Maybe none of it had happened. A psychotic episode of some kind. I went stumbling through the mucky sand toward Konwicki's place, growing more and more certain that I would find him there. And when I burst into the darkened shack, I saw someone asleep on an air mattress against the wall, a head with brown hair protruding from beneath a blanket.

"Konwicki!" I said, elated.

The head turned toward me. A tanned teenage girl propped herself on an elbow, the blanket slipping from her breasts; she rubbed her eyes, pouted, and said grouchily, "Who're you?"

The air in the room stank, heavy with the sourness of sexual activity and marijuana. I couldn't tell if the girl was pretty; her environment suppressed even the idea of prettiness. "Where's Konwicki?" I asked.

"You a friend of Carl's?"

"Yeah, we're soul mates." Being a wiseass helped stifle my anxiety.

The girl noticed her exposure, covered herself.

"Where is he?" I asked.

"I dunno." She slumped back down. "He went somewhere with Ryan last night. He'll probably be back soon." She shaded her eyes, peered into the thin light. "What's it like out there? Still drizzling?"

"No," I said dully.

The girl shook her hair back from her eyes. "I think I'll catch a swim."

I stood looking down at the cardboard box that contained the Mayan figurines.

"That means I'd like to put on my suit," said the girl.

"Oh . . . right. Sorry." I started out the door.

"After I'm dressed," said the girl, "you can wait here if you want. Carl's real free with his place."

I stood outside, uncertain what to do. While I was considering my options, the girl came out the door, wearing a red bikini; she waved and walked toward the water's edge. I stared in through the door at the cardboard box. Konwicki would not be returning, I realized, and the answer to all my questions might lie in that box. I checked to make sure that the girl wouldn't be a problem—she was splashing through the shallows—and darted inside. I picked up the box, then remembered the papers; I stuffed as many of them as possible in among the figurines, stuck some more under my arm, and went jogging along the shore toward home.

These were the facts, then. Konwicki was missing. The police were indifferent to the matter. Gringos were prone to make unannounced exits of this sort, they said. Likely he had gotten a girl in trouble. Ryan had been found on the hill, incapable of rational speech, his wrist broken; I saw him once before he was flown home under sedation, and he looked very like the Ryan of my dream. Drugs, said the local doctor. An Indian family with a small farm claimed that a demon had torn a hole in their roof and chased them through the jungle; but the sightings of demons were commonplace among the hill people, and their testimony was disregarded, the hole in the roof chalked up to storm damage—a ceiba tree had fallen onto it. A deer had been found disemboweled in the jungle, but the wound could have been made by a machete. A shack had been destroyed, apparently by the wind. As the days passed and the memories of that night grew faint, I came to see this combination of facts as an indictment against myself. It was conceivable that in chasing Ryan I had frightened an Indian family who had already been terrified by a tree crashing down upon their roof, and that in my rage, a rage funded by the bizarre materials of Konwicki's game, I had erected a delusionary system to deny my participation in a violent act. Having reached this conclusion, I became desperate to prove it wrong. I refused to accept that I was a murderer, and I pored over Konwicki's notes, trying to legitimize the game. I discovered what he had meant by saying that the game could be prolonged; according to his notes, the winner could choose to continue alone for one more move and thereby negate the penalties that accrued to both winner and loser . . . though why anyone would choose this option was beyond me. Perhaps the Mayans ranked their priorities differently from those of our culture, and personal survival was not high among them. The fact that Konwicki had not told me that I, the winner, could save him and risk myself by continuing seemed to testify that he had been trying to trick me into going on. However, that wasn't sufficient proof. Even if he had not given the game any credence, he might—as Odille had suggested—have said the exact same thing in order to gain a hold on me. The events of that night lay on an edge between the rational and the irrational, and the problem of which interpretation to place upon them was in the end a matter of personal choice.

Yet I was obsessed with finding a solution, and for the next month I pursued the question. I no longer had dreams of the pyramids and the desert, but I had other dreams in which I saw Konwicki's tormented face. From these dreams I would wake covered with sweat, and I would go into my study and spend the remaining hours of the night staring at the four counters that had been employed in the game: the dwarf, the warrior, the woman, the infant. I grew distracted. My thoughts would for a time be gleefully manic, sharp, and then would become muzzy and vague. I was afflicted by the smell of blood; I had fevers, aural hallucinations of roaring and screams. And I fell into a deep depression, as deep as the one that had owned me in New York, unable to disprove to my own satisfaction the notion that I had killed a man.

Throughout this period, Odille was loving and supportive, exhausting herself on my behalf, and during moments of clarity I realized how fortunate I was to have her, how much I had come to love her. It was this realization that began to pull me out of my depression . . . that, and the further realization that she was beginning to fray under the pressures of dealing with my breakdown. Over the span of a week she grew sullen and short-tempered. I would find her pacing, agitated, and when I would try to console her, she would often as not react with hostility. Usually I was able to break through to her, to bring her back to normalcy. Then one night, returning from the corner store, where I had gone to buy olive oil, matches, some other things for the kitchen, as I came into the living room I heard Odille out on the patio, sobbing, cursing, her voice thickened like a drunkard's. It was the voice I'd heard in my dream, coming from one of the cubicles in the pyramid. I stopped in my tracks, and as I listened, a dissolute feeling spread through my guts. There was no doubt about it. Not only were the timbre and rhythms identical, but also the words.

"Bastard," she was saying. "Oh, you bastard. God, I hate you, I hate you! You . . ." A wail. "Dead man, that's what I'll call you. I'll say, 'How are you, dead man?' And when you ask what I mean by that, I'll say that I'm just anticipating . . . you fucking bastard!"

I went out onto the patio, walking softly. It was hot, and a few drops of rain were falling, speckling the concrete. Sweat poured off my neck and chest and back; my shirt was plastered to my skin. The lights were off, the moon high, printing a filigree of leaf shadow on the concrete, and Odille was perched on the edge of a chair in the shadows, her head down and hands clasped together—a tense, prayerful attitude. It seemed hotter the nearer I came to her. "Odille," I said.

She threw back her head, her strained face visible through strands of hair; she looked like a madwoman caught at some secretive act.

I started toward her, but she jumped up and backed away. "Don't touch me, you bastard!"

"Jesus, Odille!"

I moved forward a step or two, and she screamed. "You lied to me! Always lies! Even in Irún . . . even then you were lying!"

She had told me enough about her affair in Paris to make me think it was her old lover—and not me—that she was addressing. "Odille,"

I said. "It's me . . . Ray!" She blinked, appeared to recognize me; but when I came forward again, she said, "I won't listen to you anymore, Carl. Everything you say is self-serving. It has nothing to do with what I'm feeling, what I'm thinking."

I took her by the shoulders. "Look at me, Odille. It's Ray."

"Oh, God . . . Ray!" The tension drained from her face. "I'm sorry, I'm so sorry!" Her mouth twisted into an expression of revulsion, and she pushed me back. "Sitting there mooning about that bitch in New York. You think I don't know? I do . . . I know! Every time you touch me, I know!"

"Odille!"

Again her face grew calm, or rather, registered an ordinary level of distress. "Oh, God!" she said. "I feel out of control, I feel . . .!"

I tried to embrace her, and she slapped me hard, knocking me off-balance. She came at me, shouting, slapping and clawing, and I went backward over the arm of a chair. My head struck the concrete, sending spears of white light shooting back into my eyes. I grabbed at her leg as she stepped over me, but I was stunned, my coordination impaired, and I only grazed her calf with my fingernails. By the time I managed to stand, Odille was long gone.

I went into the living room and stood by a table that I had marked into zones like the game board; the four counters were set upon it, and on the floor was the box containing the remaining two counters. In the pool of lamplight the rough brownish orange finish of the clay had the look of pocked skin; shadows had collected in their eye sockets, making them appear ghoulish. I would have liked to break them, to scatter them with a sweep of my hand and dash them to the floor; but I was frightened of them. I recalled now what Ryan had said in my dream about the victor paying a price, and I also recalled Konwicki's description of the female counter. A maniac, Odille had said. Foulmouthed and physically abusive. It was possible to dismiss the evidence of dreams, to blame Odille's emotional state on stress, on the turbulent emotional climate of her past, to dissect experience and devise a logical system that would explain away everything inexplicable. But there had been one too many coincidences, and I knew now that the game and all its hallucinatory consequences had been real, that the potency of the game was in part due to the fact that this world and the one from which the game derived were ultimately coincidental, lying side by side, matching one another event for event; the game was a bridge between those worlds, allowing the evil character of one to tap into and transform the weak principles of the other. Maybe the Mayans had played the game too often; maybe it had infected them and they had fled their cities, looking for someplace untainted by that other world. Maybe that ominous vibration of the old ruins, of Tikal and Palenque and Cobán, was a remnant of the power of evil, a lingering pulse of the ancient machinery. The theory was impossible to prove or disprove, but I had the feeling that I was not far from right. And what was to happen now? Was I to lose Odille, watch her decline into a madness that accorded with the character assigned her counter by some impersonal agency, some functionary of a universal plan?

So it appeared.

It was curious, my calmness at that moment. I had no idea whether or not there was a remedy to the situation. I thought about Konwicki's notes, his declaration that the game could be prolonged if the winner chose to put himself at risk for one more move, and I remembered, too, how Ryan had hinted at much the same thing in the dream; but there was nothing in Konwicki's notes that explained how one should initiate the tactic. Still, I acted as if there was remedy, as if I had a decision to make. I sat down in a straight-backed chair, staring at the counters, and thought about what we make when we make love, the weave of dependencies and pleasures and habituations that arise from the simple act of bestowing love, which is an act of utter honesty, of revelation and admission, of being innocent enough to open oneself completely to another human being and take a step forward into the dangerous precinct of their wills, hoping that they have taken the same immeasurable step, hoping they will not backtrack and second-guess what they know absolutely—that here is a rare chance to deny the conventional wisdom, to attempt an escape from the logics that supposedly define us. Karen Maniaci had taken that step and then had become afraid. It was not blameful, what she had done; it was only sad. And perhaps her rejection of love, her sublimation of desire, and her decision to view the life of her heart in terms of an emotional IRA, a long-term yuppie investment, choosing the security of what she could endure over the potentials of hope—maybe that was all of which she was capable. But that was the imperfect past. I thought of Odille then—her childhood of white lace and Catholic virtue, her intelligence and her ordinary passage through schools and men and days to this beach at the ends of the earth, this place where one thing more than the expected had happened—and I thought of the risk we had taken with one another without knowing it . . . to begin with, anyway. At some point we must have known, and still we had taken it. As it had been with Karen, it was now—I did not understand how to step back from that commitment, even though it was clear that the prospect of yet another risk lay before me.

Perhaps the game was—as Konwicki had suggested—merely a matter of attunement, not of rules; and perhaps once I'd entered the game's sphere of influence, I had only to acknowledge it, to make a choice, and then that choice would be actualized within its boundaries. Whatever the case, I must have reached a decision that bore upon the game, because I realized that the table and the counters had undergone a transformation. The surface of the table had become an undulating surface of rusty orange upon which the counters stood like colossi, and in the distance, apparently miles and miles away, was a complex of black pyramids. It was as if I were a giant peering in from the edge of the world, looking out over a miniature landscape . . . miniature, but nonetheless real. The wind was blowing the sand into tiny scarves, and hanging above the pyramids was a fuming violet-white sun. Acting without thought, feeling again that sense of power and possession, I removed three of the counters, leaving the dwarf to stand facing the black buildings alone. After a moment I took one of the two remaining two counters from the cardboard box and set it close to the gnome. The figure depicted a youth, its proportions less distorted than those of the dwarf, yet with muscles not so developed as those of the warrior. I leaned back in my chair, feeling drained, wasted. The table had returned to normal, a flat surface marked with lines of chalk.

I was more than a little afraid. I wasn't sure what exactly I had done, but now I wanted to retreat from it, deny it. I pushed back my chair, becoming panicked, darting glances to the side, expecting to see an immense black talon poking toward me from window or door. The house seemed a trap—I remembered Konwicki and Ryan in the hut on the hill—and I scurried out into the night. It was spitting rain, and the wind was driving in steadily off the sea, shredding the palms, breaking the music from a radio in the house next door into shards of bright noise. I felt disoriented, needing—as I had that first night at Konwicki's—something to hold, something that would give me weight and balance, and I sprinted down onto the beach, thinking that Odille would be there. At the Café Pluto or one of the other bars. Maybe now that the game had been joined once again, she would have grown calm, regained her center. The moon flashed between banks of running clouds, and chutes of flickering lantern light spilled from shanty windows, illuminating patches of weeds, strips of mucky sand littered with fish corpses and offal and coconut tops. In the darkness above the tossing palms I glimpsed a phantom shape, immense and snake-headed, visible for a fraction of a second, and I picked up my pace, running now out of fear, the salt air sharp in my lungs, expecting a great claw to lay open my backbone. Then I spotted Odille—a shadow at the margin of the sea, facing toward the reef. The tide was going out, leaving an expanse of dark sand studded with driftwood and shells. I ran faster yet, and as I came near, she turned to me, backed away, saying something lost in the noise of the wind and surf. I caught her by her shoulders, and she tried to twist free.

"Let me go!" she said, pushing at my chest.

I glanced behind me. "Come on! We've got to get out of here!"

"No!" She broke loose from my grasp. "I can't!"

Again I caught hold of her.

"Leave me alone!" she said. "I'm. . . ." She brushed strands of wet hair away from her face. "I don't know what's wrong with me. I must be crazy, acting like that."

"You'll be all right."

"You can't know that!"

I pulled her close, pressed her head onto my shoulder. She was shaking. "Calm down, just calm down. You're all right. Don't you feel all right? Don't you feel better?" I stroked her hair, my words coming in a torrent. "It's just the pressure, all the pressure. We've both been acting crazy. But it's over now. We have to leave; we have to find a new place." I searched the sky for signs of the monster I'd seen earlier, but there was only the darkness, the rushing moon, the lashing fronds. "Are you okay, are you feeling okay?"

"Yes, but—"

"Don't worry. It's just the pressure. I'm surprised we both haven't gone nuts."

"You're not going to leave me?" Her tone was similar to that of a child who'd been expecting a beating and had been granted a reprieve.

"Of course not. I love you. I'm not going to leave you . . . ever."

Her arms tightened around my neck, and she said that she couldn't stand the idea of losing me; that was why, she thought, she'd lost control. She just couldn't bear going through the same heartbreak again. I reassured her as best I could, my mouth dry with fear, continuing to look in every direction for signs of danger. The sea rolled in, smooth swells of ebony that detonated into white flashes on the reef.

"Come on," I said, taking her hand, pulling her along. "Let's go back to the house. We have to get out. This place, it's no good anyway. Too much bad shit has happened. Maybe we can find a boat to take us upriver tonight. Or tomorrow morning. Okay?"

"Okay." She forced a smile, squeezed my hand.

We went stumbling along the shore, beating our way against the wind. As we were passing close to a clump of palms, their trunks curved toward the sea, a figure stepped from behind them, blocking our path, and said, "Dat's far as you go, mon!"

He was standing barely a dozen feet away, yet I had to peer in order to make him out: a cocoa-skinned boy in his teens, about my height and weight, wearing jeans and a shirt with the silk-screened image of a blond woman on the front. In his hand was a snub-nosed pistol. His eyes looked sleepy, heavy-lidded—Chinese eyes—and he was swaying, unsteady on his feet. His expression changed moment to moment, smiling one second and the next growing tight, anxious, registering the chemical eddies of whatever drug he was behind.

"Gimme what you got, mon!" He waggled the pistol. "Quickly, now!"

I fumbled out my wallet, tossed it to him; he let it slip through his fingers and fall to the sand. Keeping his eyes on me, the gun trained, he knelt and groped for the wallet. Then he stood, pried it open with the fingers of his left hand, and removed the contents. My vision was acting up; superimposed on the boy's face was another face, one with coarse features and pocked ocher skin—the image of the counter depicting the youth.

"Shit . . . boog muthafucka! Dis all you got? Quetzales all you got? I want gold, mon. Ain't you got no gold?"

"Gold!" I said, easing Odille behind me. To the surprise of half my mind, I felt in control of the situation. The bastard planned to kill me, but he was in for a fight. I was in the game again, flooded with unnatural strength and cold determination, my fear dimmed by my partnered consciousness with a muscular little freak who thrived on bloodlust.

"Ras clot!" said the boy, his face hardening with rage, jabbing the gun toward me, coming a few steps closer. "Gold! American dollars! You t'ink I goin' to settle fah dis?" He waved the fistful of Guatemalan currency at me.

The rain had let up, but the wind was increasing steadily; all along the beach the bushes and palms were seething. The sky above the hills had cleared, and the moon was riding just high enough so that the tip of the highest hill put a black notch in its lowest quarter. With ragged blue clouds sailing close above, their edges catching silver fire as they passed, it was a wild and lovely sight, and my heart stalled on seeing it. I felt suddenly calm and alert, as if attentive to some call, and I watched the tops of some silhouetted acacias inland sway-ing and straightening with a slow ungainly rhythm, bending low all to one side and lurching heavily back to upright again, like the shadows of dancing bears. At the center of the wind, I heard a silence, a vast pool of dead air, and I knew that other world, that place half my home, was whirling close, ready to loose its monsters upon whoever failed this test. I was not unnerved; I was empowered by that silence, unafraid of losing.

"Didn't you hear me, mon?" said the boy. "T'ink I foolin' wit' you? I ast if you got gold."

"Yeah, I got gold," I said coolly. "I got more gold than you can handle. Look in the secret compartment."

"What you mean?"

"There's a seam inside the billfold," I said, gloating over what was to come. "An inner flap. You have to look real close. Slit it open with your fingernail."

The boy stared into the wallet, and I flew at him, driving my shoulder into his abdomen, my arms wrapping around his legs, bring-ing him down beneath me. I clawed for his gun hand, caught the wrist as we went rolling in the wet sand left by the receding tide. I butted him under the jaw and smashed his hand against the sand again and again, butting him once more, and at last he let the gun fall. I had a glimpse of a dagger falling onto the rust-colored sand, and as we grappled together, face-to-face, in his eyes I saw the shadowy, depthless eyes of the counter, the coarse slitted folds, the hollowed pupils. I smelled cheap cologne, sweat, but I also smelled a hot desert wind. The boy spat out words in a language that I didn't recognize, tearing at my hair, gouging at my eyes; he was stronger than he had appeared. He freed one hand, punched at the back of my neck, brought his knee up into my chest, sending me onto my back. Then he straddled me, twisting my head, forcing my face into the sand and flailing away with his fist, punching at my liver and kidneys. There was sand in my nose and mouth, and the pain in my side was enor-mous. I couldn't breathe. Black lights were dancing behind my eyes, swelling to blot out everything, and in desperation I heaved up, unseating the boy, grabbing at his legs; I saw leaden clouds, a boiling sun, and then darkness filmed across the sky once again. The boy broke free, coming to his knees. But in doing so he turned away from me, and that was his undoing. I knocked him flat on his stomach, crawled atop him, and barred my forearm under his neck, locking him in a choke hold by clutching my wrist. We went rolling across the sand and into the water. A wave lifted us, black water coursed over my face, the moon blurred into a silver stream like the flashing of a luminous eel. I surfaced, sputtering. I was on my back, the boy atop me, humping, straining, his fingers clawing. His Adam's apple worked against my arm, and I tightened the hold, digging into his flesh with a twisting motion. He made a cawing noise, half gurgle, half scream. I think I laughed. Another wave swept over us, but we were anchored, heels dug into the sand. I heard Odille crying out above the tumult of wind and waves, and suddenly my glee and delight in the contest, the sense of possession, of abnormal strength . . . all that was gone.

The boy spasmed; his back arched like a wrestler bridging, trying to prevent a pin, then he went stiff, his muscles cabled. But I could feel the life inside him flopping about like a fish out of water, feel the frail tremor of his held breath. I didn't know what to do. I could release him. . . . I doubted he would have any fight left, but what if he did? And if he lived, wouldn't he continue to be a menace, wouldn't the game be unresolved, and—if not the boy—would not some new menace arise to terrorize me? I didn't so much think these things as I experienced a black rush of thought of which they were a part, one that ripped through me with the force of the tide that was sucking us farther from the shore, and once this rush had passed, I knew that the choice had already been made, that I was riding out the final, feeble processes of a death. Even this realization came too late, for at the moment the boy went limp and his body floated up from mine in the drag of the tide.

Horrified, I pushed him away, scrambled to my feet, and stood in the knee-deep water, fighting for balance. For the briefest of instants I spotted something huge, something with needle teeth and a flat skull, bending to the boy. Then Odille was clinging to me, dragging me away from the shore, saying things I barely heard. I turned back to the boy, saw his body lifting, sliding down the face of a swell, almost lost in the darkness. I searched the sky and trees for signs of that other world. But there was nothing. The game was over. Whatever had come for the boy already had him, already was tormenting the last of him in that place of snakes and deserts and black silences. That place forever inside me now. I looked for the boy again. He had drifted out of sight, but I knew he was there, and I would always know how his body went sliding into the troughs, rising up, growing heavier and heavier, but not heavy enough to prevent him from nudging against the reef, his skin tearing on the sharp rocks, then lifting in the race of outgoing tide and passing over the barrier, dropping down and down through schools of mindless fish and fleshy flowers and basking sharks and things stranger and more terrifying yet into the cold and final depths that lay beyond.

When I returned to the house, I discovered that the figurines depicting the youth and the warrior had been shattered. The marmalade cat fled from our footsteps and peered out from beneath a chair with a guilty look. I didn't puzzle over this; I was for the moment unconcerned with validation and coincidence . . . except for my comprehension that the life of one world was the shade of another, that the best and brightest instances of our lives were merely functions of a dark design. That and the memory of the boy dying in the shallows colored everything I did, and for a very long time, although I went about the days and work with my accustomed verve, I perceived a hollowness in every incidence of fullness and was hesitant about expressing my emotions, having come to doubt their rationality. Odille, while she had not been aware of the undercurrents of the fight on the beach, seemed to have undergone a similar evolution. We began to drift apart, and neither of us had the energy or will to pull things back together.

On the day she left for Paris, I walked her to the dock and waited with her as the ferry from Puerto Morales unloaded its cargo of fat black women and scrawny black men and chickens and fruit and flour. She leaned against a piling, holding down the brim of a straw hat to shield her eyes from the sun, looking very French, very beautiful. However, I was no longer moved by beauty. Some small part of me regretted her leaving, but mostly I was eager to have her gone, to pare life down to its essentials once again in hopes that I might find some untainted possibility in which to place my faith.

"Are you all right?" she asked. "You look . . . peculiar."

"I'm fine," I said, and then, to be polite, I added, "I'm sorry to see you go."

She tipped back her head so as to better see my face. "I'm sorry, too. I'll never understand what went wrong, I thought. . . ."

"Yeah, so did I." I shrugged. *"C'est la vie."*

She laughed palely, turned to the ferry, obviously nervous, wanting to end an awkward moment. "Will you be all right?" she asked suddenly, as if for an instant she were reinhabiting the depth of her old concern and caring. "I'll worry about you here."

"I'm not going to stay much longer . . . a couple of weeks. The doctors will be back by then."

"I don't know how you can stand to stay a minute longer. Aren't you worried about the police?"

"They're tired of hassling me," I said. "Hell, one of the lieutenants . . . you remember the one with the waxed mustache? He actually told me the other day that I was a hero." I gave a sarcastic laugh. "Like Bernhard Goetz, I'm keeping the city clean."

Odille started to say something, but kept it to herself. Instead, she let her fingers trail across my hand.

At last the ferry was empty, ready for boarding. She stood on tiptoe, kissed me lightly, and then was gone, merging with the crowd of blacks that poured up the gangplank.

The ferry veered away from the dock, venting black smoke, and I watched until it had rounded a spit of land, thinking that the saddest thing about Odille and me was that we had parted without tears. After a minute or so I headed back to the house. I had planned to work, but I was unable to concentrate. The inside of my head felt like glass, too fragile to support the weighty process of thought. I fed the cat, paced awhile; eventually I went into the living room and gazed down at the cardboard box that contained the four remaining figurines. I had been intending to destroy them, but each time I had made to do so, I'd been restrained by a fear of some bad result. It occurred to me that I enjoyed this irresolute state of affairs, that I found it romantic to cling to the belief that—mad from unrequited love—I had done terrible violence, and that I'd been shying away from anything that might prove the contrary. I became enraged at my self-indulgence and lack of fortitude; without thinking, I picked up a figurine and hurled it at the wall. It shattered into a hundred pieces, and to my astonishment, a stain began to spread where it had struck. A spatter of thick crimson very like a smear of fresh blood. I tried to blink the sight away, but there it was, slowly washing down the wall. I was less afraid than numb. I looked into the box and saw that the figurine I'd broken was the infant. Ryan. I glanced again at the wall. The stain had vanished.

I started laughing, infinitely amused, wondering if I should call New Zealand and check on the particulars of Ryan's health; but then I realized that I would never pin down the truth, that his health or illness or death could be explained in a dozen ways, and I was afraid that I might not stop laughing, that I would continue until laughter blocked out everything else. Everything was true. Insanity and the supernatural were in league. Finally I managed to get myself under control. I packed my papers, a few clothes, and after wrapping the three remaining figurines in crumpled newspaper, I carried them to the house of a local priest and donated them to his museum. He was delighted by the gift, though puzzled at my insistence that he not allow them to be handled, that they be treated with the utmost care. Nor did he understand my hilarity on telling him that I was placing my fate in God's hands.

At the jetty, I found a swarthy white-haired East Indian man with a powerboat who said he would transport me up the Río Dulce to the town of Reunión for an exorbitant fee. I did not attempt to haggle. Minutes later we were speeding north through the jungle along the green river, and as the miles slipped past I began to relax, to hope that I was putting the past behind me once and for all. The wind streamed into my face, and I closed my eyes, smiling at the freshness of the air, the sweetness of escape.

"You look happy," the old man called out above the roar of the engine. "Are you going to meet your sweetheart?"

I told him, no, I was going home to New York.

"Why do you want to do that? All those gangsters and slums! Don't tell me New York is as beautiful as this!" He waved at the jungle. "The Río Dulce, Livingston . . . nowhere is there a more lovely place!"

With a sudden jerk of the wheel, he swerved the boat toward the middle of the river, sending me toppling sideways, balanced for an instant on the edge of the stern, my face a foot above the water. Something big and dark was passing just beneath the surface. The old man clutched at my arm, hauling me back as I was about to overbalance and go into the water. "Did you see?" he said excitedly. "A manatee! We nearly struck it!"

"Uh-huh," I said, shaken, my heart racing, wondering if the priest had mishandled one of the figurines back in Livingston.

"I would wager," said the old man, unmindful of my close call, "that there are no manatees in New York. None of the marvelous creatures we have here."

No manatees, I thought; but dark things passing beneath the surface—we had plenty of those. They came in every form. Male, female, shadows in doorways, rooms in abandoned buildings with occult designs chalked on the walls. Everywhere the interface with an uncharted reality, everywhere the familiar world fraying into the unknown.

Escape was impossible, I realized. I had always been in danger, and I always would be, and it occurred to me that the supernatural and the ordinary were likely a unified whole, elements of a spectrum of reality whose range outstripped the human senses. Perhaps strong emotion was the catalyst that opened one to the extremes of that spectrum; perhaps desire and rage and ritual in alignment allowed one to slide from light to light, barely noticing the dark interval that had been bridged. There was a comforting symmetry between these thoughts and what I had experienced, and that symmetry, along with my brush with drowning, seemed to have settled things in my mind, to have satisfied—if not resolved—my doubts. This was not so simple an accommodation as my statement implies. I am still prone to analyze these events, and often I am frustrated by my lack of comprehension. But in some small yet consequential way, I had made peace with myself. I had achieved some inner balance, and as a result I felt capable of accepting my share of guilt for what had happened. I had, after all, been playing head games with Konwicki before taking up the counters, and I had to shoulder responsibility for that . . . if for nothing else.

"Well, what do you say?" the old man asked. "Have you anything in New York to rival this?"

"I suppose not," I said, and he beamed, pleased by my admission of the essential superiority of the Guatemalan littoral.

We continued along the peaceful river, passing through forbidding gulfs bordered by cliffs of gray stone, passing villages and reed beds and oil barges, and came at last to Reunión, where I parted company with the old man and caught the bus north, sadder and wiser, free both of hate and love, though not of trouble, returning home to the ends of the earth.

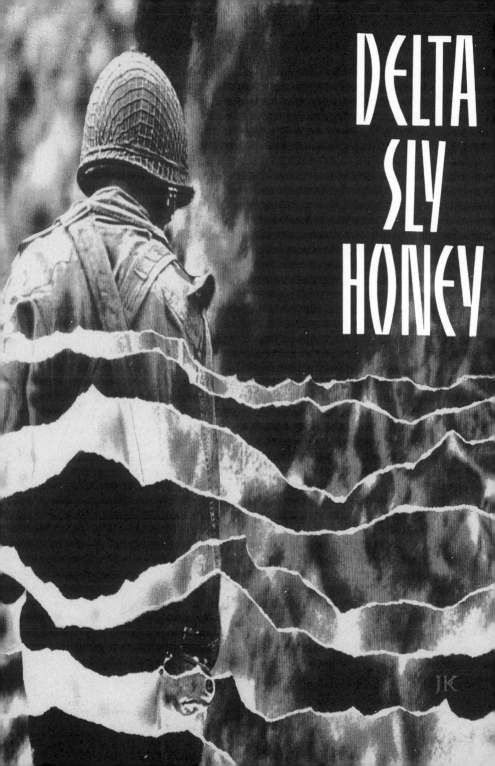

DELTA SLY HONEY

There was this guy I knew at Noc Linh, worked the corpse detail, guy name of Randall J. Willingham, a skinny red-haired Southern boy with a plague of freckles and eyes blue as poker chips, and sometimes when he got high, he'd wander up to the operations bunker and start spouting all kinds of shit over the radio, telling about his hometown and his dog, his opinion of the war (he was against it), and what it was like making love to his girlfriend, talking real pretty and wistful about her ways, the things she'd whisper and how she'd draw her knees up tight to her chest to let him go in deep. There was something pure and peaceful in his voice, his phrasing, and listening to him, you could feel the war draining out of you, and soon you'd be remembering your own girl, your own dog and hometown, not with heartsick longing but with joy in knowing you'd had at least that much sweetness of life. For many of us, his voice came to be the oracle of our luck, our survival, and even the brass who tried to stop his broadcasts finally realized he was doing a damn sight more good than any morale officer, and it got to where anytime the war was going slow and there was some free air, they'd call Randall up and ask if he felt in the mood to do a little talking.

The funny thing was that except for when he had a mike in his hand, you could hardly drag a word out of Randall. He had been a loner from day one of his tour, limiting his conversation to "Hey" and "How you?" and such, and his celebrity status caused him to become even less talkative. This was best explained by what he told us once over the air: "You meet ol' Randall J. on the street, and you gonna say, 'Why, that can't be Randall J.! That dumb-lookin' hillbilly couldn't recite the swearin'-in-oath, let alone be the hottest damn radio personality in South Vietnam!' And you'd be right on the money, 'cause Randall J. don't go more'n double figures for IQ, and he ain't got the imagination of a stump, and if you stopped him to say 'Howdy,' chances are he'd be stuck for a response. But lemme tell ya, when he puts his voice into a mike, ol' Randall J. becomes one with the airwaves, and the light that's been dark inside him goes bright, and his spirit streams out along Thunder Road and past the Napalm Coast, mixin' with the ozone and changin' into Randall J. Willingham, the High Priest of the Soulful Truth and the Holy Ghost of the Sixty-Cycle Hum.''

The base was situated on a gently inclined hill set among other hills, all of which had once been part of the Michelin rubber plantation, but now were almost completely defoliated, transformed into dusty brown lumps. Nearly seven thousand men were stationed there, living in bunkers and tents dotting the slopes, and the only building with any degree of permanence was an outsized Quonset hut that housed the PX; it stood just inside the wire at the base of the hill. I was part of the MP contingent, and I guess I was the closest thing Randall had to a friend. We weren't really tight, but being from a small Southern town myself, the son of gentry, I was familiar with his type—fey, quiet farmboys whose vulnerabilities run deep—and I felt both sympathy and responsibility for him. My sympathy wasn't misplaced: nobody could have had a worse job, especially when you took into account the fact that his top sergeant, a beady-eyed, brush-cut, tackle-sized Army lifer named Andrew Moon, had chosen him for his whipping boy. Every morning I'd pass the tin-roofed shed where the corpses were off-loaded (it, too, was just inside the wire, but on the opposite side of the hill from the PX), and there Randall would be, laboring among body bags that were piled around like huge black fruit, with Moon hovering in the background and scowling. I always made it a point to stop and talk to Randall in order to give him a break from Moon's tyranny, and though he never expressed his gratitude or said very much about anything, soon he began to call me by my Christian name, Curt, instead of by my rank. Each time I made to leave, I would see the strain come back into his face, and before I had gone beyond earshot, I would hear Moon reviling him. I believe it was those days of staring into stomach cavities, into charred hearts and brains, and Moon all the while screaming at him . . . I believe that was what had squeezed the poetry out of Randall and birthed his radio soul.

I tried to get Moon to lighten up. One afternoon I bearded him in his tent and asked why he was mistreating Randall. Of course I knew the answer. Men like Moon, men who have secured a little power and grown bloated from its use, they don't need an excuse for brutality; there's so much meanness inside them, it's bound to slop over onto somebody. But—thinking I could handle him better than Randall—I planned to divert his meanness, set myself up as his target, and this seemed a good way to open.

He didn't bite, however; he just lay on his cot, squinting up at me and nodding sagely, as if he saw through my charade. His jowls were speckled with a few days' growth of stubble, hairs sparse and black as pig bristles. "Y'know," he said, "I couldn't figure why you were buddyin' up to that fool, so I had a look at your records." He grunted laughter. "Now I got it."

"Oh?" I said, maintaining my cool.

"You got quite a heritage, son! All that noble Southern blood, all them dead generals and senators. When I seen that, I said to myself, 'Don't get on this boy's case too heavy, Andy. He's just tryin' to be like his great-grandaddy, doin' a kindness now and then for the darkies and the poor white trash.' Ain't that right?"

I couldn't deny that a shadow of the truth attached to what he had said, but I refused to let him rankle me. "My motives aren't in question here," I told him.

"Well, neither are mine . . . 'least not by anyone who counts." He swung his legs off the cot and sat up, glowering at me. "You got some nice duty here, son. But you go fuckin' with me, I'll have your ass walkin' point in Quanh Tri 'fore you can blink. Understand?"

I felt as if I had been dipped in ice water. I knew he could do as he threatened—any man who's made top sergeant has also made some powerful friends—and I wanted no part of Quanh Tri.

He saw my fear and laughed. "Go on, get out!" he said, and as I stepped through the door, he added, "Come 'round the shed anytime, son. I ain't got nothin' against *noblesse oblige*. Fact is, I love to watch."

And I walked away, knowing that Randall was lost.

In retrospect, it's clear that Randall had broken under Moon's whip early on, that his drifty radio spiels were symptomatic of his dissolution. In another time and place, someone might have noticed his condition; but in Vietnam everything he did seemed a normal reaction to the craziness of the war, perhaps even a bit more restrained than normal, and we would have thought him really nuts if he hadn't acted weird. As it was, we considered him a flake, but not wrapped so tight that you couldn't poke fun at him, and I believe it was this misconception that brought matters to a head. . . .

Yet I'm not absolutely certain of that.

Several nights after my talk with Moon, I was on duty in the operations bunker when Randall did his broadcast. He always signed off in the same distinctive fashion, trying to contact the patrols of ghosts he claimed were haunting the free-fire zones. Instead of using ordinary call signs like Charlie Baker Able, he would invent others that suited the country lyricism of his style, names such as Lobo Angel Silver and Prairie Dawn Omega.

"Delta Sly Honey," he said that night. "Do you read? Over."

He sat a moment, listening to static filling in from nowhere.

"I know you're out there, Delta Sly Honey," he went on. "I can see you clear, walkin' the high country near Black Virgin Mountain, movin' through twists of fog like battle smoke and feelin' a little afraid, 'cause though you gone from the world, there's a world of fear 'tween here and the hereafter. Come back at me, Delta Sly Honey, and tell me how it's goin'." He stopped sending for a bit, and when he received no reply, he spoke again. "Maybe you don't think I'd understand your troubles, brothers. But I truly do. I know your hopes and fears, and how the spell of too much poison and fire and flyin' steel warped the chemistry of fate and made you wander off into the wars of the spirit ' stead of findin' rest beyond the grave. My soul's trackin' you as you move higher and higher toward the peace at the end of everything, passin' through mortar bursts throwin' up thick gouts of silence, with angels like tracers leadin' you on, listenin' to the cold white song of incoming stars. . . . Come on back at me, Delta Sly Honey. This here's your good buddy Randall J., earthbound at Noc Linh. Do you read?"

There was a wild burst of static, and then a voice answered, saying, "Randall J., Randall J.! This is Delta Sly Honey. Readin' you loud and clear."

I let out a laugh, and the officers sitting at the far end of the bunker turned their heads, grinning. But Randall stared in horror at the radio, as if it were leaking blood, not static. He thumbed the switch and said shakily, "What's your position, Delta Sly Honey? I repeat. What's your position?"

"Guess you might say our position's kinda relative," came the reply. "But far as you concerned, man, we just down the road. There's a place for you with us, Randall J. We waitin' for you."

Randall's Adam's apple worked, and he wetted his lips. Under the hot bunker lights, his freckles stood out sharply.

"Y'know how it is when you're pinned down by fire?" the voice continued. "Lyin' flat with the flow of bullets passin' inches over your head? And you start thinkin' how easy it'd be just to raise up and get it over with. . . . You ever feel like that, Randall J.? Most times you keep flat, 'cause things ain't bad enough to make you go that route. But the way things been goin' for you, man, what with stickin' your hands into dead meat night and day—"

"Shut up," said Randall, his voice tight and small.

"—and that asshole Moon fuckin' with your mind, maybe it's time to consider your options."

"Shut up!" Randall screamed it, and I grabbed him by the shoulders. "Take it easy," I told him. "It's just some jerkoff puttin' you on." He shook me off; the vein in his temple was throbbing.

"I ain't tryin' to mess with you, man," said the voice. "I'm just layin' it out, showin' you there ain't no real options here. I know all them crazy thoughts that been flappin' 'round in your head, and I know how hard you been tryin' to control 'em. Ain't no point in controllin' 'em anymore, Randall J. You belong to us now. All you gotta do is to take a little walk down the road, and we be waitin'. We got some serious humpin' ahead of us, man. Out past the Napalm Coast, up beyond the high country . . ."

Randall bolted for the door, but I caught him and spun him around. He was breathing rapidly through his mouth, and his eyes seemed to be shining too brightly—like the way an old light bulb will flare up right before it goes dark for good. "Lemme go!" he said. "I gotta find 'em! I gotta tell 'em it ain't my time!"

"It's just someone playin' a goddamn joke," I said, and then it dawned on me. "It's Moon, Randall! You know it's him puttin' somebody up to this."

"I gotta find 'em!" he repeated, and with more strength than I would have given him credit for, he pushed me away and ran off into the dark.

He didn't return, not that night, not the next morning, and we reported him AWOL. We searched the base and the nearby villes to no avail, and since the countryside was rife with NLF patrols and VC, it was logical to assume he had been killed or captured. Over the next couple of days, Moon made frequent public denials of his complicity in the joke, but no one bought it. He took to walking around with his holster unlatched, a wary expression on his face. Though Randall hadn't had any real friends, many of us had been devoted to his broadcasts, and among those devotees were a number of men who . . . well, a civilian psychiatrist might have called them unstable, but in truth they were men who had chosen to exalt instability, to ritualize insanity as a means of maintaining their equilibrium in an unstable medium: it was likely some of them would attempt reprisals. Moon's best hope was that something would divert their attention, but three days after Randall's disappearance, a peculiar transmission came into operations; like all Randall's broadcasts, it was piped over the PA, and thus Moon's fate was sealed.

"Howdy, Noc Linh," said Randall or someone who sounded identical to him. "This here's Randall J. Willingham on patrol with Delta Sly Honey, speakin' to you from beyond the Napalm Coast. We been humpin' through rain and fog most of the day, with no sign of the enemy, just a few demons twistin' up from the gray and fadin' when we come near, and now we all hunkered down by the radio, restin' for tomorrow. Y'know, brothers, I used to be scared shitless of wakin' up here in the big nothin', but now it's gone and happened, I'm findin' it ain't so bad. 'Least I got the feelin' I'm headed someplace, whereas back at Noc Linh I was just spinnin' round and round, and close to losin' my mind. I hated ol' Sergeant Moon, and I hated him worse after he put someone up to hasslin' me on the radio. But now, though I reckon he's still pretty hateful, I can see he was actin' under the influence of a higher agency, one who was tryin' to help me get clear of Noc Linh . . . which was somethin' that had to be, no matter if I had to die to do it. Seems to me that's the nature of war, that all the violence has the effect of lettin' a little magic seep into the world by way of compensation. . . ."

To most of us, this broadcast signaled that Randall was alive, but we also knew what it portended for Moon. And therefore I wasn't terribly surprised when he summoned me to his tent the next morning. At first he tried to play sergeant, ordering me to ally myself with him; but seeing that this didn't work, he begged for my help. He was a mess: red-eyed, unshaven, an eyelid twitching.

"I can't do a thing," I told him.

"You're his friend!" he said. "If you tell 'em I didn't have nothin' to do with it, they'll believe you."

"The hell they will! They'll think I helped you." I studied him a second, enjoying his anxiety. "Who did help you?"

"I didn't do it, goddammit!" His voice had risen to a shout, and he had to struggle to keep calm. "I swear! It wasn't me!"

It was strange, my mental set at that moment. I found I believed him—I didn't think him capable of manufacturing sincerity—and yet I suddenly believed everything: that Randall was somehow both dead and alive, that Delta Sly Honey both did and did not exist, that whatever was happening was an event in which all possibility was manifest, in which truth and falsity had the same valence, in which the real and the illusory were undifferentiated. And at the center of this complex circumstance—a bulky, sweating monster—stood Moon. Innocent, perhaps. But guilty of a seminal crime.

"I can make it good for you," he said. "Hawaii . . . you want duty in Hawaii, I can arrange it. Hell, I can get you shipped Stateside."

He struck me then as a hideous genie offering three wishes, and the fact that he had the power to make this offer infuriated me. "If you can do all that," I said, "you ain't got a worry in the world." And I strode off, feeling righteous in my judgment.

Two nights later while returning to my hooch, I spotted a couple of men wearing tiger shorts dragging a large and apparently unconscious someone toward the barrier of concertina wire beside the PX—I knew it had to be Moon. I drew my pistol, sneaked along the back wall of the PX, and when they came abreast I stepped out and told them to put their burden down. They stopped but didn't turn loose of Moon. Both had blackened their faces with greasepaint, and to this had added fanciful designs in crimson, blue, and yellow that gave them the look of savages. They carried combat knives, and their eyes were pointed with the reflected brilliance of the perimeter lights. It was a hot night, but it seemed hotter there beside them, as if their craziness had a radiant value. "This ain't none of your affair, Curt," said the taller of the two; despite his bad grammar, he had a soft, well-modulated voice, and I thought I heard a trace of amusement in it.

I peered at him, but was unable to recognize him beneath the paint. Again I told them to put Moon down.

"Sorry," said the tall guy. "Man's gotta pay for his crimes."

"He didn't do anything," I said. "You know damn well Randall's just AWOL."

The tall guy chuckled, and the other guy said, "Naw, we don't know that a-tall."

Moon groaned, tried to lift his head, then slumped back.

"No matter what he did or didn't do," said the tall guy, "the man deserves what's comin'."

"Yeah," said his pal. "And if it ain't us what does it, it'll be somebody else."

I knew he was right, and the idea of killing two men to save a third who was doomed in any event just didn't stack up. But though my sense of duty was weak where Moon was concerned, it hadn't entirely dissipated. "Let him go," I said.

The tall guy grinned, and the other one shook his head as if dismayed by my stubbornness. They appeared wholly untroubled by the pistol, possessed of an irrational confidence. "Be reasonable, Curt," said the tall guy. "This ain't gettin' you nowhere."

I couldn't believe his foolhardiness. "You see this?" I said, flourishing the pistol. "Gun, y'know? I'm gonna fuckin' shoot you with it, you don't let him go."

Moon let out another groan, and the tall guy rapped him hard on the back of the head with the hilt of his knife.

"Hey!" I said, training the pistol on his chest.

"Look here, Curt . . ." he began.

"Who the hell are you?" I stepped closer, but was still unable to identify him. "I don't know you."

"Randall told us 'bout you, Curt. He's a buddy of ours, ol' Randall is. We're with Delta Sly Honey."

I believed him for that first split second. My mouth grew cottony, and my hand trembled. But then I essayed a laugh. "Sure you are! Now put his ass down!"

"That's what you really want, huh?"

"Damn right!" I said. "Now!"

"Okay," he said. "You got it." And with a fluid stroke, he cut Moon's throat.

Moon's eyes popped open as the knife sliced through his tissues, and that—not the blood spilling onto the dust—was the thing that froze me: those bugged eyes in which an awful realization dawned and faded. They let him fall facedownward. His legs spasmed, his right hand jittered. For a long moment, stunned, I stared at him, at the blood puddling beneath his head, and when I looked up I found that the two men were sprinting away, about to round the curve of the hill. I couldn't bring myself to fire. Mixed in my thoughts were the knowledge that killing them served no purpose and the fear that my bullets would have no effect. I glanced left and right, behind me, making sure that no one was watching, and then ran up the slope to my hooch.

Under my cot was a bottle of sour mash. I pulled it out and had a couple of drinks to steady myself; but steadiness was beyond me. I switched on a battery lamp and sat cross-legged, listening to the snores of my bunkmate. Lying on my duffel bag was an unfinished letter home, one I had begun nearly two weeks before; I doubted now I'd ever finish it. What would I tell my folks? That I had more or less sanctioned an execution? That I was losing my fucking mind? Usually I told them everything was fine, but after the scene I had just witnessed, I felt I was forever past that sort of blithe invention. I switched off the lamp and lay in the dark, the bottle resting on my chest. I had a third drink, a fourth, and gradually lost both count and consciousness.

I had a week's R & R coming and I took it, hoping debauch would shore me up. But I spent much of that week attempting to justify my inaction in terms of the inevitable and the supernatural, and failing in that attempt. You see, now as then, if pressed for an opinion, I would tell you that what happened at Noc Linh was the sad consequence of a joke gone sour, of a war twisted into a demonic exercise. Everything was explicable in that wise. And yet it's conceivable that the supernatural was involved, that—as Randall had suggested—a little magic had seeped into the world. In Vietnam, with all its horror and strangeness, it was difficult to distinguish between the magical and the mundane, and it's possible that thousands of supernatural events went unnoticed as such, obscured by the poignancies of death and fear, becoming quirky memories that years later might pass through your mind while you were washing the dishes or walking the dog, and give you a moment's pause, an eerie feeling that would almost instantly be ground away by the mills of the ordinary. But I'm certain that my qualification is due to the fact that I want there to have been some magic involved, anything to lessen my culpability, to shed a less damning light on the perversity and viciousness of my brothers-in-arms.

On returning to Noc Linh, I found that Randall had also returned. He claimed to be suffering from amnesia and would not admit to having made the broadcast that had triggered Moon's murder. The shrinks had decided that he was bucking for a Section Eight, had ordered him put back on the corpse detail, and as before, Randall could be seen laboring beneath the tin-roofed shed, transferring the contents of body bags into aluminum coffins. On the surface, little appeared to have changed. But Randall had become a pariah. He was insulted and whispered about and shunned. Whenever he came near, necks would stiffen and conversations die. If he had offed Moon himself, he would have been cheered; but the notion that he had used his influence to have his dirty work jobbed out didn't accord with the prevailing concept of honorable vengeance. Though I tried not to, I couldn't help feeling badly toward him myself. It was weird. I would approach with the best of intentions, but by the time I reached him, my hackles would have risen and I would walk on in hostile silence, as if he were exuding a chemical that had evoked my contempt. I did get close enough to him, however, to see that the mad brightness was missing from his eyes; I had the feeling that all his brightness was missing, that whatever quality had enabled him to do his broadcasts had been sucked dry.

One morning as I was passing the PX, whose shiny surfaces reflected a dynamited white glare of sun, I noticed a crowd of men pressing through the front door, apparently trying to catch sight of something inside. I pushed through them and found one of the canteen clerks—a lean kid with black hair and a wolfish face—engaged in beating Randall to a pulp. I pulled him off, threw him into a table, and kneeled beside Randall, who had collapsed to the floor. His cheekbones were lumped and discolored; blood poured from his nose, trickled from his mouth. His eyes met mine, and I felt nothing from him: he seemed muffled, vibeless, as if heavily sedated.

"They out to get me, Curt," he mumbled.

All my sympathy for him was suddenly resurrected. "It's okay, man," I said. "Sooner or later, it'll blow over." I handed him my bandanna, and he dabbed ineffectually at the flow from his nose. Watching him, I recalled Moon's categorization of my motives for befriending him, and I understood now that my true motives had less to do with our relative social status than with my belief that he could be saved, that—after months of standing by helplessly while the unsalvageable marched to their fates—I thought I might be able to effect some small good work. This may seem altruistic to the point of naïveté, and perhaps it was, perhaps the brimstone oppressiveness of the war had from the residue of old sermons heard and disregarded provoked some vain Christian reflex; but the need was strong in me, nonetheless, and I realized that I had fixed on it as a prerequisite to my own salvation.

Randall handed back the bandanna. "Ain't gonna blow over," he said. "Not with these guys."

I grabbed his elbow and hauled him to his feet. "What guys?"

He looked around as if afraid of eavesdroppers. "Delta Sly Honey!"

"Christ, Randall! Come on." I tried to guide him toward the door, but he wrenched free.

"They out to get me! They say I crossed over and they took care of Moon for me . . . and then I got away from 'em." He dug his fingers into my arm. "But I can't remember, Curt! I can't remember nothin'!"

My first impulse was to tell him to drop the amnesia act, but then I thought about the painted men who had scragged Moon: if they were after Randall, he was in big trouble. "Let's get you patched up," I said. "We'll talk about this later."

He gazed at me, dull and uncomprehending. "You gonna help me?" he asked in a tone of disbelief.

I doubted anyone could help him now, and maybe, I thought, that was also part of my motivation—the desire to know the good sin of honest failure. "Sure," I told him. "We'll figure out somethin'."

We started for the door, but on seeing the men gathered there, Randall balked. "What you want from me?" he shouted, giving a flailing, awkward wave with his left arm as if to make them vanish. "What the fuck you want?"

They stared coldly at him, and those stares were like bad answers. He hung his head and kept it hung all the way to the infirmary.

That night I set out to visit Randall, intending to advise him to confess, a tactic I perceived as his one hope of survival. I'd planned to see him early in the evening, but was called back on duty and didn't get clear until well after midnight. The base was quiet and deserted-feeling. Only a few lights picked out the darkened slopes, and had it not been for the heat and stench, it would have been easy to believe that the hill with its illuminated caves was a place of mild enchantment, inhabited by elves and not frightened men. The moon was almost full, and beneath it the PX shone like an immense silver lozenge. Though it had closed an hour before, its windows were lit, and—MP instincts engaged—I peered inside. Randall was backed against the bar, holding a knife to the neck of the wolfish clerk who had beaten him, and ranged in a loose circle around him, standing among the tables, were five men wearing tiger shorts, their faces painted with savage designs. I drew my pistol, eased around to the front, and—wanting my entrance to have shock value—kicked the door open.

The five men turned their heads to me, but appeared not at all disconcerted. "How's she goin', Curt?" said one, and by his soft voice I recognized the tall guy who had slit Moon's throat.

"Tell 'em to leave me be!" Randall shrilled.

I fixed my gaze on the tall guy and with gunslinger menace said, "I'm not messin' with you tonight. Get out now or I'll take you down."

"You can't hurt me, Curt," he said.

"Don't gimme that ghost shit! Fuck with me, and you'll be humpin' with Delta Sly Honey for real."

"Even if you were right 'bout me, Curt, I wouldn't be scared of dyin'. I was dead where it counts halfway through my tour."

A scuffling at the bar, and I saw that Randall had wrestled the clerk to the floor. He wrapped his legs around the clerk's waist in a scissors and yanked his head back by the hair to expose his throat. "Leave me be," he said. Every nerve in his face was jumping.

"Let him go, Randall," said the tall guy. "We ain't after no innocent blood. We just want you to take a little walk . . . to cross back over."

"Get out!" I told him.

"You're workin' yourself in real deep, man," he said.

"This ain't no bullshit!" I said. "I *will* shoot."

"Look here, Curt," he said. "S'pose we're just plain ol' ordinary grunts. You gonna shoot us all? And if you do, don't you think we'd have friends who'd take it hard? Any way you slice it, you bookin' yourself a silver box and air freight home."

He came a step toward me, and I said, "Watch it, man!" He came another step, his devil mask split by a fierce grin. My heart felt hot and solid in my chest, no beats, and I thought, He's a ghost, his flesh is smoke, the paint a color in my eye. "Keep back!" I warned.

"Gonna kill me?" Again he grinned. "Go ahead." He lunged, a feint only, and I squeezed the trigger.

The gun jammed.

When I think now how this astounded me, I wonder at my idiocy. The gun jammed frequently. It was an absolute piece of shit, that weapon. But at the time its failure seemed a magical coincidence, a denial of the laws of chance. And adding to my astonishment was the reaction of the other men: they made no move toward Randall, as if no opportunity had been provided, no danger passed. Yet the tall guy looked somewhat shaken to me.

Randall let out a mewling noise, and that sound enlisted my competence. I edged between the tables and took a stand next to him. "Let me get the knife from him," I said. "No point in both of 'em dyin'."

The tall guy drew a deep breath as if to settle himself. "You reckon you can do that, Curt?"

"Maybe. If you guys wait outside, he won't be as scared and maybe I can get it."

They stared at me, unreadable.

"Gimme a chance."

"We ain't after no innocent blood." The tall guy's tone was firm, as if this were policy. "But . . ."

"Just a coupla minutes," I said. "That's all I'm askin'."

I could almost hear the tick of the tall guy's judgment. "Okay," he said at last. "But don't you go tryin' nothin' hinkey, Curt." Then, to Randall. "We be waitin', Randall J."

As soon as they were out the door, I kneeled beside Randall. Spittle flecked the clerk's lips, and when Randall shifted the knife a tad, his eyes rolled up into heaven. "Leave me be," said Randall. He might have been talking to the air, the walls, the world.

"Give it up," I said.

He just blinked.

"Let him go and I'll help you," I said. "But if you cut him, you on your own. That how you want it?"

"Un-unh."

"Well, turn him loose."

"I can't," he said, a catch in his voice. "I'm all froze up. If I move, I'll cut him." Sweat dripped into his eyes, and he blinked some more.

"How 'bout I take it from you? If you keep real still, if you lemme ease it outta your hand, maybe we can work it that way."

"I don't know. . . . I might mess up."

The clerk gave a long shuddery sigh and squeezed his eyes shut.

"You gonna be fine," I said to Randall. "Just keep your eyes on me, and you gonna be fine."

I stretched out my hand. The clerk was trembling, Randall was trembling, and when I touched the blade it was so full of vibration, it felt alive, as if all the energy in the room had been concentrated there. I tried pulling it away from the clerk's neck, but it wouldn't budge.

"You gotta loosen up, Randall," I said.

I tried again and, gripping the blade between my forefinger and thumb, managed to pry it an inch or so away from the line of blood it had drawn. My fingers were sweaty, the metal slick, and the blade felt like it was connected to a spring, that any second it would snap back and bite deep.

"My fingers are slippin'," I said, and the clerk whimpered.

"Ain't my fault if they do." Randall said this pleadingly, as if testing the waters, the potentials of his guilt and innocence, and I realized he was setting me up the way he had Moon's killers. It was a childlike attempt compared to the other, but I knew to his mind it would work out the same.

"The hell it ain't!" I said. "Don't do it, man!"

"It ain't my fault!" he insisted.

"Randall!"

I could feel his intent in the quiver of the blade. With my free hand, I grabbed the clerk's upper arm, and as the knife slipped, I jerked him to the side. The blade sliced his jaw, and he screeched; but the wound wasn't mortal.

I plucked the knife from Randall's hand, wanting to kill him myself. But I had invested too much in his salvation. I hauled him erect and over to the window; I smashed out the glass with a chair and pushed him through. Then I jumped after him. As I came to my feet, I saw the painted men closing in from the front of the PX and—still towing Randall along—I sprinted around the corner of the building and up the slope, calling for help. Lights flicked on, and heads popped from tent flaps. But when they spotted Randall, they ducked back inside.

I was afraid, but Randall's abject helplessness—his eyes rolling like a freaked calf's, his hands clawing at me for support—helped to steady me. The painted men seemed to be everywhere. They would materialize from behind tents, out of bunker mouths, grinning madly and waving moonstruck knives, and send us veering off in another direction, back and forth across the hill. Time and again, I thought they had us, and on several occasions, it was only by a hairsbreadth that I eluded the slash of a blade that looked to be bearing a charge of winking silver energy on its tip. I was wearing down, stumbling, gasping, and I was certain we couldn't last much longer. But we continued to evade them, and I began to sense that they were in no hurry to conclude the hunt; their pursuit had less an air of frenzy than of a ritual harassment, and eventually, as we staggered up to the mouth of the operations bunker and—I believed—safety, I realized that they had been herding us. I pushed Randall inside and glanced back from the sandbagged entrance. The five men stood motionless a second, perhaps fifty feet away, then melted into the darkness.

I explained what had happened to the MP on duty in the bunker—a heavyset guy named Cousins—and though he had no love for Randall, he was a dutiful sort and gave us permission to wait out the night inside. Randall slumped down against the wall, resting his head on his knees, the picture of despair. But I believed that his survival was

assured. With the testimony of the clerk, I thought the shrinks would
have no choice but to send him elsewhere for examination and possible institutionalization. I felt good, accomplished, and passed the night
chain-smoking, bullshitting with Cousins.

Then, toward dawn, a voice issued from the radio. It was greatly
distorted, but it sounded very much like Randall's.

"Randall J.," it said. "This here's Delta Sly Honey. Do you read?
Over."

Randall looked up, hearkening to the spit and fizzle of the static.

"I know you out there, Randall J.," the voice went on. "I can
see you clear, sitting with the shadows of the bars upon your soul
and blood on your hands. Ain't no virtuous blood, that's true. But
it stains you alla same. Come back at me, Randall J. We gotta talk,
you and me."

Randall let his head fall; with a finger, he traced a line in the dust.

"What's the point in keepin' this up, Randall J.?" said the voice.
"You left the best part of you over here, the soulful part, and you
can't go on much longer without it. Time to take that little walk for
real, man. Time to get clear of what you done and pass on to what
must be. We waitin' for you just north of base, Randall J. Don't make
us come for you."

It was in my mind to say something to Randall, to break the disconsolate spell the voice appeared to be casting over him; but I found
I had nothing left to give him, that I had spent my fund of altruism
and was mostly weary of the whole business . . . as he must have been.

"Ain't nothin' to be 'fraid of out here," said the voice. "Only
the wind and the gray whispers of phantom Charlie and the trail leadin'
away from the world. There's good company for you, Randall J. Gotta
man here used to be a poet, and he'll tell you stories 'bout the Wild
North King and the Woman of Crystal. Got another fella, guy used
to live in Indonesia, and he's fulla tales 'bout watchin' tigers come
out on the highways to shit and cities of men dressed like women
and islands where dragons still live. Then there's this kid from Opelika,
claims to know some of your people down that way, and when he
talks, you can just see that ol' farmboy moon heavin' up big and yellow
over the barns, shinin' the blacktop so it looks like polished jet, and
you can hear crazy music leakin' from the Dixieland Café and smell
the perfumed heat steamin' off the young girls' breasts. Don't make
us wait no more, Randall J. We got work to do. Maybe it ain't much,
just breakin' trail and walkin' point and keepin' a sharp eye out for
demons . . . but it sure as hell beats shepherdin' the dead, now, don't

it?" A long pause. "You come on and take that walk, Randall J. We'll make you welcome, I promise. This here's Delta Sly Honey. Over and out."

Randall pulled himself to his feet and took a faltering few steps toward the mouth of the bunker. I blocked his path and he said, "Lemme go, Curt."

"Look here, Randall," I said. "I might can get you home if you just hang on."

"Home." The concept seemed to amuse him, as if it were something with the dubious reality of heaven or hell. "Lemme go."

In his eyes, then, I thought I could see all his broken parts, a disjointed shifting of lights and darks, and when I spoke I felt I was giving tongue to a vast consensus, one arrived at without either ballots or reasonable discourse. "If I let you go," I said, "be best you don't come back this time."

He stared at me, his face gone slack, and nodded.

Hardly anybody was outside, yet I had the idea everyone was watching us as we walked down the hill; under a leaden overcast, the base had a tense, muted atmosphere such as must have attended rainy dawns beneath the guillotine. The sentries at the main gate passed Randall through without question. He went a few paces along the road, then turned back, his face pale as a star in the half-light, and I wondered if he thought we were driving him off or if he believed he was being called to a better world. In my heart I knew which was the case. At last he set out again, quickly becoming a shadow, then the rumor of a shadow, then gone.

Walking back up the hill, I tried to sort out my thoughts, to determine what I was feeling, and it may be a testament to how crazy I was, how crazy we all were, that I felt less regret for a man lost than satisfaction in knowing that some perverted justice had been served, that the world of the war—tipped off-center by this unmilitary engagement and our focus upon it—could now go back to spinning true.

That night there was fried chicken in the mess, and vanilla ice cream, and afterward a movie about a more reasonable war, full of villainous Germans with Dracula accents and heroic grunts who took nothing but flesh wounds. When it was done, I walked back to my hooch and stood out front and had a smoke. In the northern sky was a flickering orange glow, one accompanied by the rumble of artillery. It was, I realized, just about this time of night that Randall had customarily begun his broadcasts. Somebody else must have realized this, because at that moment the PA was switched on. I half expected to hear Randall giving the news of Delta Sly Honey, but there was only static, sounding like the crackling of enormous flames. Listening to it, I felt disoriented, completely vulnerable, as if some huge black presence were on the verge of swallowing me up. And then a voice did speak. It wasn't Randall's, yet it had a similar countrified accent, and though the words weren't quite as fluent, they were redolent of his old raps, lending a folksy comprehensibility to the vastness of the cosmos, the strangeness of the war. I had no idea whether or not it was the voice that had summoned Randall to take his walk, no longer affecting an imitation, yet I thought I recognized its soft well-modulated tones. But none of that mattered. I was so grateful, so relieved by this end to silence, that I went into my hooch and—armed with lies—sat down to finish my interrupted letter home.

BOUND FOR GLORY

Tracy and I had boarded at White Eagle, which is the next-to-last stop before the train enters the Bad Patch, and we had bought tickets clear through to Glory, where I had some friends who still trusted me enough—or so I hoped—to front me a loan. I had screwed things up proper in White Eagle, running my business into the ground and skating a thin line between plain failure and out-and-out fraud. And I had known that Tracy was getting ready to make a move, that she was fed up with our life. I expect that was why I had risked the ride to Glory—the prospect of losing his only support has driven many a man to desperation. The wonder of it was, I realized, that Tracy must have felt equally as desperate about her own prospects, otherwise she wouldn't have joined me. And I could not decide if this was a good thing or bad, that we were each other's last, best hope.

Somehow we had managed to convince ourselves that the trip was a golden opportunity, but seeing the drawn faces of our fellow passengers brought home what a starve-out proposition it really was. Neither of us wanted to let on we felt this way, however, so we smiled and held hands and pretended to be full of spit and determination. That was easy to do at first. The sun hung high in a notch between two mountains, gilding the snow and throwing indigo shadows from the firs, making a rare beauty out of the decline of day, and since there was plenty of time before we would reach the Patch, before the changes would begin, we were able to relax somewhat and enjoy the scenery.

Following behind the conductor as he collected tickets was Roy Cole, who was an institution on the line. He was in his late forties,

rawboned, with salt-and-pepper hair and a seamed, tanned face whose
dour expression was accentuated by a ridged scar that ran from the
corner of his mouth along his jaw. He wore jeans and a loose black
shirt, and cradled in his arms was a shotgun with silver filigree embel-
lishing the stock. He stared at us hard as if searching for evidence of
guilt. Which was more or less the case. The train made the trip only
when Cole felt conditions were right, and since he knew better than
anyone the changes that could occur and the signs to look for, no
one objected to his scrutiny. If you were going to change, your best
chance for survival was that Cole could protect you. But when he fixed
those black eyes on mine, the pupils as oddly configured as chess pieces,
it felt like my skeleton was getting ready to jump out of my flesh and
run for the door at the end of the car. I wanted to ask whether or
not I was going to undergo a change; but before I could work up
the courage he had moved on and was examining yet another passenger.

For the first hour the ride was uneventful. Sunset was a sweep of
burnt orange above the western peaks, with lavender and a sprinkle
of stars higher up; the snow crystals in the air were fired and flurrying
like swarms of live jewels, and the glow shined up the tumble of Tracy's
black hair, put a gloss on the beauty of her face, which was something
special under even ordinary light—with its fine bones and sad eyes,
like the face of a troubled angel. And as we passed into the flat country I felt that we had left the bad times behind and were only alive
to the good parts of what had been. We talked some about our plans,
but mostly we reminisced about our days in White Eagle. From the
way we laughed and hugged each other, you might have thought we
were newlyweds and not two losers on the run from fate.

"'Member Gordon?" I asked Tracy at one point. "That ol' boy
rode a sorrel mare . . . you used to say he looked like he was always
poutin'? Well, back 'fore we got together, this tent show come to
town."

"Doctor Teague's Medicine Show," Tracy said, and I replied, Yes,
yes, now I thought of it, I believe that *had* been its name.

"Anyway," I went on, "they had these monkeys. Chimpanzees.
And the word was, the owner would pay fifty bucks to anyone who
could whup one of 'em. Wellsir, ol' Gordon considered himself a
helluva fighter. It wasn't just he thought he was good at it, he thought
it was a noble pursuit. Once I 'member we were drunk, and he got
this faraway look and says to me, "Ed," he says, "y'know, fightin'

ain't just rollin' 'round in the dirt and gettin' bloody. It's the purest form of physical 'spression there is."

Tracy giggled.

"So the thing was, when Gordon heard 'bout the monkeys, 'bout how they could whup any man, he was first in line to give 'er a try. He felt he was upholdin' the pride of all mankind against the animal kingdom." I chuckled. "Lemme tell ya, it was pitiful. There was this little pen with a dirt floor they fought in, and Gordon he's bouncin' up and down on the balls of his feet, throwin' left jabs at the air, and the monkey he's just squattin' in the dirt, starin' at Gordon like he never seen such a fool. Finally Gordon gets frustrated 'bout the monkey not doin' nothin', so he steps up and wings a roundhouse right"—I demonstrated—"aimin' for the monkey's head. That's all it took to get the monkey goin', 'cause the next thing y'know it's all over Gordon. I mean it happened so damn fast, it was a blur. One second the monkey's windmillin' its arms at Gordon's chest, and a second later Gordon's lyin' on his belly and the monkey's jumpin' up and down on his back and snatchin' out handfuls of his hair."

"Oh, my God!" said Tracy, laughing so hard that she started to cough.

"Gordon just wouldn't accept defeat," I went on. "After we'd got him patched up and he had a few drinks in him, he starts talkin' 'bout it ain't fair a man's gotta fight a beast without there bein' some kinda handicap imposed. A human bein's bone structure, he said, wasn't as strong as a monkey's, and if he'd had some protection, it wouldn'ta been no contest, he woulda kicked the monkey's butt 'cause his manner of fightin' was scientifically superior. So next day he goes to see Ben Krantz and gets him to carpenter up a helmet out of wood and leather that's got bars across the face and paddin' inside. Then he heads back down to the tent show and demands another crack at the monkey." I shook my head in dismay. "They started out the same, with Gordon bouncin' 'round and the monkey squattin' and givin' him this look that says, Fool. Then, 'fore Gordon can even think about throwin' a punch, the monkey jumps up and rips the helmet off Gordon's head and goes to poundin' him with it. He smashed the goddamn thing to pieces on Gordon's skull and laid him out worse'n before."

We collapsed against one another, laughing. I don't guess the story was all that amusing, but we needed laughter and so we milked the moment for every ounce. I was glad Tracy could manage it, because even under the best of circumstances she was not a happy woman. She had been raped by her daddy when she was just out of pigtails, and that had set her up for a string of disastrous relationships. She had told me more than once that I was the first man she'd been with who hadn't beat her, and I thought her feelings for me were less genuine attachment than relief. She had come to depend on men in an unhealthy way, to use their mastery as an excuse for not striving to better herself. I expect she figured it was easier to let a man keep her down than to face up to what she was becoming. Or maybe it was just that men had made her feel like that. Though I liked to see myself as being a step up in class for her, I knew that I was only the latest in a line of masters, that my uses for her—disguised as love—were crueler than bruises in their deceit, and would likely cause her more grief in the long run. Yet knowing this hadn't persuaded me to let her go; I kept telling myself that if I did, she would just find someone else to misuse her. And, too, I enjoyed dominating her. While I had my charitable moments, I was at heart a taker, a wielder of power—the problem was that I had no power to wield except where Tracy was concerned. I believe the most compelling reason that I clung to her, however, was fear. I was expert at denying that knowledge, but I had to work at it. And my most successful form of denial was holding out the hope that beneath the layers of our falsity there was something real, an ember of love, or at least honest emotion, that— given some kindling and a little wind to puff it alight—would warm us for the rest of our lives.

"Maybe," said Tracy, coming up for air, "maybe the monkey's how come Gordon was always poutin'."

"Could be," I said. "It's for sure he never did get over it. He'd talk 'bout that monkey like it was some sorta legendary hero . . . a great man whose like'd never come our way again. He was a funny ol' boy, that Gordon."

The train was pulling into Lorraine, a collection of shacks gathered around a couple of larger frame buildings, a hotel and one that housed an assay office and a general store. Beyond the town the terrain was rolling, snow-covered, with a few golden rectangles of winter wheat glowing in the decaying light, and beyond the wheat, beyond the Spring Hills, whose sheer granite faces showed slate-blue, lay a dark haze that signaled the beginning of the Patch. Seeing it sobered us, and we sat for a minute or two in silence.

"Maybe we should get off," Tracy said dully. "Lorraine seems 'bout far enough away from White Eagle."

"You know that ain't so," I told her. " 'Sides, won't nobody here lend me money."

"I can always go back to whorin'."

I was startled by the defeated tone in her voice. "The hell you say!"

"It ain't much different'n what I do with you."

That angered me, and I refused to respond.

"What's the point?" she said. "We go here, we go there . . . we still the same people."

I started to speak, but she cut me off.

"And don't go sayin' you gonna turn over a new leaf! I can't 'member how many times you promised. . . ."

"I ain't the only one who's got bad habits they can't cure."

That stopped her a moment. Like me, though she might not ad-mit it, she knew our union was a comfortable trap, that its comforts were a guarantee nothing better would come along for either of us.

"I still don't see the point," she said. "If we ain't gonna do nothin' different, what's it matter where we end up?"

"Well, go on then," I said. "Paint yourself up and be a whore if that's what you think's right. But I don't wanna watch ya at it."

She bowed her head, watched her hands clasping and unclasping in her lap. I could tell the crisis had passed.

"Why'd you'd come with me?" I asked. "You knew there'd be risk."

"I reckon I thought takin' a chance might be like magic or some-thin', and we might come through it better off than we was. I know that sounds stupid. . . ."

"Naw, it don't."

She looked up at me. "Why'd *you* wanna risk it?"

"Pretty much the same reason," I lied.

I pulled her into an embrace. Her hair smelled of lavender, and her breasts crushed against me. I touched them on the sly. They were firm and full, and just the thought of them could make me steamy. I felt the heat stirring in her by the way she arched against my hand. Then she drew back and pushed my hand away. Her eyes were filling.

"What's wrong?" I asked.

She shook her head, but I suspected she was thinking how pitiful it was that the good thing we made with our bodies had so little vital truth behind it, as if it were just a clever trick we could perform.

The whistle sounded high and forlorn, and as the train lurched forward, a fat woman in a black cloth coat with a fur collar half-staggered, half-dropped into the seat across the aisle.

"Goodness!" she said, and beamed at us. "That 'un almost threw me back into Culver County, it did." She flounced about, settling the folds of her coat; she was wearing white gloves that made her hands appear tiny by contrast to the voluminous sleeves from which they emerged. And her feet, too, appeared tiny, like a child's feet stuck onto swollen ankles and bloated black-stockinged calves. Her pasty chins trembled with the motion of the train. Eyes like currants stuck in the dough of her cheeks, and a Cupid's bow of a mouth painted cherry red. Looking at her, I imagined that she was an immense pastry come to life, her veins filled not with blood but with custard cream. She leaned toward us, bringing with her a wave of cloying perfume, and said, "This your first trip, ain't it? I always can tell. Now don't worry . . . it ain't so bad as you heered. I mean it's bad, I won't deny that. But it's tolerable." She heaved a sigh, causing the wrinkles in her coat to expand like a balloon plumping with gas. "Know how many times I crossed?"

"Naw, how many?" asked Tracy. By the edge in her voice I knew she was put off by the fat woman.

"Thirty-two," said the woman proudly. "This un'll make thirty-three. I 'spect you might find that curious, but when you get my age"—she tittered—"and you love good cookin' much as I do, and ain't no man in your life, you gotta find somethin' to take your mind off the lonelies. Guess you might say travelin' the Patch is my hobby. When I first started I was feelin' kinda low, and I didn't much care whether I made it to the far side or not. But it 'pears I'm immune to the changes like Roy Cole." She hauled a leather-bound diary out of her purse. "I keep a record of the trips. I figger someday it might be valuable to some explorer or somebody like that." She shook her head in wonderment. "The things I seen, you just wouldn't believe it."

I was a touch dismayed by the idea of someone traveling through the sickness and dark of the Patch for fun, but the look on Tracy's face was one of pure disgust. She turned to the window, wanting no part of the conversation. A fellow in striped overalls came along the aisle, lighting the gas lamps in the car, bathing us in a sickly yellow glow.

"It's a horrid place," the woman said. "I won't try and deny that. But it's a mystery, and things that's mysterious, they gotta beauty all their own. 'Course"—she adopted a haughty expression—"it ain't the mystery to me it once was. I 'spect I know more 'bout it than anybody 'cept Roy Cole."

I couldn't help being curious about her experiences; it would have been unnatural not to be after having lived near the Patch for all those years. Like everybody else, I'd heard stories about how it had come to be, how Indian wizards had been warring and stray magic had transformed a stretch of land that cut straight across the country. And how it had been fiery stuff falling from a comet that had done the trick, and how it was a section of hell surfaced from under the earth. But though the stories all differed as to its origins, they were unanimous concerning its nature: it was a place where everything changed, where things out of nightmares could appear, where time and possibility converged.

I asked the woman what she knew concerning the beginnings of the Patch, and she said, "This fella I know claims the Patch is like that place out East where you can see seven states from the top of a peak . . . 'cept it ain't states you see from the Patch, it's worlds. Hundreds of 'em, all packed in together. He claims that what with all the pressures on the Patch, y'know, from them hundreds of worlds crowdin' into each other, the place just plumb give way like a dam will in a flood, and the worlds got all mixed together."

I favored the story about Indian wizards, but I said, "Uh-huh."

"It don't really matter, though," said the woman. "Things is how they is, and knowin' why they got that way don't change diddley."

Tracy was looking strained, and I decided to change the subject. "You been livin' in Lorraine awhile, have you?" I asked the woman.

"I moved there once't I started ridin' the train. 'Fore that, I was over in Steadley for a number of years."

Steadley was a large silver-mining community on the other side of the Patch, and if I'd had a proper stake, that would have been my destination and not Glory. "S'posed to be a world of opportunity in Steadley," I said.

"Yes, indeed! A body can make hisself a fortune . . . if he's got the will and the wherewithal. That where you headin'?"

"I got plenty of will," I told her. "But I'm a bit shy of the wherewithal. We're bound for Glory. I'm hopin' I can get a stake there."

She clucked her tongue in sympathy. "Ain't that the way of it . . . when you get a bushel of 'taters, that's when you run outta stew meat." She shot me a coy look. "Y'know, I bet there's folks in Steadley who'd be willin' to help out a young fella like yourself. God knows, they do enough for the refugees."

"Refugees from the Patch, you talkin' 'bout?"

She nodded. "They pitiful devils, the ones that make it out."

"I hear there's a lotta trouble with refugees . . . on the train, I mean."

"Lord, yes! Ain't a trip when some don't try and board."

"I don't wanna hear 'bout none of it," said Tracy, but the woman made a gesture of dismissal.

"Your man'll protect you, hon," she said. "Don't you fret. But them refugees, Lord, they can be fearsome! More'n fearsome. They can purely freeze your heart."

"I told you I don't wanna hear about it," said Tracy, her voice tight.

"Yes, Jesus"—the woman's tone became exultant—"when they come aboilin' through the doors, bringin' all that foul air and magic with 'em, and it 'pears they grinnin', 'cause their lips is drawed back to show their teeth, they so desperate, and you can feel the power clawin' at 'em. . . ."

"Stop it!" Tracy shrilled. "You just stop, y'hear?"

She was gaping at the woman. Shivering, transfixed by some sight or feeling. Her cheeks were hollowed, and her eyes were aswarm with crazy lights; they looked like broken glass scattered on black velvet, like the eyes of a woman I'd known once who'd just gotten out of the looney bin. It was those eyes as much as anything that made me realize we had entered the Patch and that the changes had begun.

"Tracy?" I said, confused, reluctant to touch her for fear I'd disrupt the tension that seemed to be holding her together.

"You can't help but feel it," the woman went on, showing her teeth in a manner redolent of the poor souls she'd just finished describing. "It comes off 'em like the stink from an open grave. Sometimes their flesh just goes to saggin' off their bones."

"Hey," I said to her. "Leave it be, will ya?"

"Won't be long now 'fore we see 'em," she said, pointing out at the smoky blue twilight and the snow. "Sometimes their faces gets to glowin' like dead fish bellies, their teeth turn black and drop out, and they grow old right 'fore your eyes. They feel the strength ebbin' from 'em, and they go to their knees and pluck at ya with hands shrunk to skin and bones, and they beg for help in languages you can't understand. Devil languages. Their cheeks bulge, and the gut-strings come out of their mouths."

Tracy began shouting, and the woman's face reddened and looked to be crimping in on itself like a rotten apple; her white-gloved hands gripped the armrest, and she spat out the words as if they were poisoned daggers. I pushed Tracy back and told the woman to shut up, but she only got louder, her imagery more vile. The pictures she conjured made me shrivel inside, and I was tempted to hit her. I think I might have, but then the door of the car opened and Cole stepped in. He walked slowly down the aisle and stopped beside us, letting his shotgun angle down to cover the woman's breast. She stared wide-eyed at the double barrels and fell silent.

"'Pears you havin' some trouble, Marie," he said in a voice like iron.

"Naw," she said weakly, "naw, I just. . . ."

"Way you gettin' all puffed up and red-faced," he said, "looks to me like you 'bout to change. How you feel? Little shaky inside . . . like maybe somethin's shiftin' 'round in there?"

He cocked one barrel, burning her with those otherworldly black eyes, and she froze with her pouty red mouth open and one hand to her throat; a whistly guttering of breath came from her throat.

"Please, Cole," she said, putting real effort into sounding out the words. "I'm all right, I swear. You must can see that."

"You fuckin' sow," Cole said. "I'm 'bout sick to death of you scarin' my passengers. You don't shut your hole, I'm just gon' assume you changin' and blow your heart out through your damn spine. Ain't a soul here who'd blame me for it." He pushed the shotgun into the pillowy softness of her breast and worked it about as if fitting it to a socket. "How 'bout it, Marie? Don't you reckon I can get away with murder?"

"Naw, Cole," she whispered. "Please don't."

"You gon' leave these good people 'lone?"

Her eyelids fluttered down, and she nodded.

Cole made a disgusted noise, but he lowered the hammer. His eyes swung toward me; the scar along his jaw bunched like a sidewinder. "Keep your gun in reach, son," he said. "There's gon' be trouble in this car. Do the best you able, and if I can get back to you, I will."

He set out along the aisle, but I went after him and caught up as he was about to enter the next car.

"I think you just better lemme in on what's goin' on!" I said, grabbing his arm.

He nailed me with a fierce stare. "Take it easy, friend."

"You don't go tellin' a man to keep his gun handy and then walk away without sayin' why."

"I figgered it wasn't no mystery why," he said. "But awright. Let's you'n me have a talk."

He pulled me toward the door, away from the others. The window beside us was sectioned into four narrow panes, each enclosing a rectangle of blue darkness with a single star low in the right-hand corner, like a block of mystical postage stamps. It was such a symmetrical configuration, so subtly improbable, it made me realize how at sea I was.

"This here's gon' be a bad trip," Cole said. "I can't cover all the cars, so I'm leavin' you in charge of this 'un."

I was not eager for responsibility. "Why the hell you let 'em start out when you knew things was gonna be bad?"

"Son, I do the best I can makin' them judgments, but I ain't never claimed to be a hunnerd percent right. Now last time things was this bad, I lost me nine passengers. I'll leave it up to you. You wanna help out, or you just wanna stand around and watch it happen?"

"Tracy," I said, "the woman with me, is she gonna be . . . bad off?"

Cole kicked at the iron bar that attached one of the seats to the floorboards.

"Sometimes the changes ain't so bad, and you can get 'em through," he said. "Other times you gotta stop 'em. That's why I want you in charge here. Be better for everybody, you make that decision."

"You are talkin' 'bout Tracy, ain'tcha?"

" 'Fraid I am."

I touched my holstered pistol; it felt as snug and dry as a snake in a skull. "Naw," I said, "naw, I couldn't do nothin' to her. And I ain't no good with a gun, anyhow."

"I'm gon' be busy," Cole said. "Whatever happens here, it's gotta be your call."

I studied his weathered face, his strange eyes, wondering if he was telling me everything. He met my stare without any sign of dodginess. The rattle of the train seemed to be sounding out the tension between us, giving a voice to all the violent acceleration of our lives. I had a strong sense of his character then, and I understood that while the job had tied a few black twists in his soul, he was not especially good or evil, not wonderfully courageous, not mad with fear or a stone killer; he was just a man who had reached a difficult pass that was half his own making and half the sorry luck that comes with being born. He was simply doing what he could to get along. Knowing that he was like me, someone with no special magic or destiny, gave me confidence in him. And in myself. I'd never had to use my gun against another man. Now I believed I could.

"What I gotta do?" I asked him.

"There'll be refugees," he said. "Always is. They'll try and board a coupla hours from now, this place where the train slows on a steep grade. Don't ask no questions if they get inside. Just do for 'em quick. And don't waste no bullets." He inspected my gunbelt. "Y'see that squarehead back in the corner?"

He indicated a middle-aged blond man in a gray suit with a brooding Scandinavian face and told me to keep an eye on him. And on Tracy. The remaining seven were Marie, an elderly woman in a green print dress, and five dirt farmers—gloomy, roughly dressed men who had lost their holdings in a land grab and were, like me, aiming for a new start.

"Anything else happens," Cole said, "chances are you'll see it comin'. The Patch changes some for the worse and some hardly at all. Others like me and that fat bitch Marie—and you, maybe—it lets 'em see clear how bad things are for the rest. I don't know which way's more merciful. I come to see so damn much, I wish I was blind sometimes."

"You said 'maybe' I'd see things clear . . . I don't get it. Either I will or I won't, right?"

"That's the best I can do," he said. " 'Pears to me you 'bout a hair away from changin' yourself, so it's hard for me to read you. Tell ya one thing, though. If I was you I wouldn't be makin' this run too often. Sooner or later the Patch'll take you. I can see that much."

He squared his shoulders and settled his shotgun under his arm. He slapped my shoulder and flashed me a grin that didn't have much juice to it.

"Luck to you," he said.

I paced along the aisle, dismayed by Tracy, who was gone into some kind of fugue. And what I glimpsed out the train window dismayed me even more and made me fear for what I might see later inside the car. Once we passed a way station, an island of brilliance in the dark where sat a wooden building with a peaked roof and a peculiar bright white light stuck on a pole above a loading platform; ranked alongside the platform were rows of what appeared to be human figures wrapped in gray cloth, like rows of mummies. Then we hurtled past a snowy street lined with round stone buildings with glowing signs floating above them, spelling out words in a script I could not read. Then there came a time when all I could make out were thousands of lights ranging the darkness; we were traversing a smooth section of rail, and the noise of the wheels had diminished to a rushing sound, and it was as if I were traveling on a schooner under full canvas in a brisk wind, sailing just offshore from a jeweled coast.

More and more I came to regret my decision of risking the ride to Glory. All my life I had made the wrong or the too-hasty decision, and while I had always chalked this up to bad luck, now I understood it was a matter of weak character . . . or rather, of a strong character half-formed, one whose strength was sufficient to use the power it had, but not strong enough to seize power for itself. As a result I had constantly leaped from one fix to another, reacting to trouble like a scalded cat, and it struck me as odd that I hadn't seen this until now. Maybe, I thought, this was an instance of the clarity that Cole had said came to some who traveled through the Patch; but most likely it was just that I'd reached the bottom of my possibilities, and all that was left for me was to look back up and observe how I'd managed to fall so far.

At first I kept a close eye on Tracy and the Swede; soon, though, I began to relax, thinking that Cole must have overstated the danger just to make me stay alert. But as we passed into the Spring Hills, the Swede came to his feet, clasping his hands to his head and moaning, a hideous noise that issued from the black O of his mouth like a dozen voices all sounding the same tormented bass note. His fingers appeared unnaturally long, and to my astonishment, I realized they were growing longer yet, curving to encase the sides of his head like the bars of a birdcage. I could hear the skin and bone stretching, cartilage popping. His head, too, was elongating, becoming a caricature of Swedish despondency. Glints in his eyes flickered like lantern flames turned low, his fingernails were sprouting into talons, and his skin had pebbled like that of a lizard. Seeing this, I felt my guts clench, and for an instant I was too stunned to move.

Screams, and the passengers went crawling over the seats away from the Swede, scrambling along the aisle, blocking my line of fire. One farmer—a red-faced, round-bellied fool—made a grab for the Swede as he staggered past, and the Swede raked him with his hooked fingers, tearing away his cheek. I shoved somebody aside—the elderly lady in the bonnet, I think—and squeezed off a shot. The gun felt alive in my hand, its kick like a natural muscular reaction and not the uncontrollable spasm that usually resulted when I took target practice. The explosion cracked the inside of my skull, and the bullet painted the Swede's coat with blood. A twig of red sprouted from the corner of his mouth, and he stopped, but he didn't fall. He just came forward again, howling in that demon voice. My second bullet shattered his jaw. That dropped him to his knees, nuggets of scored bone showing through the gore. He stared daggers at me for a second, then his eyes rolled up and he keeled over onto his side. His chest lifted and fell. The blood was too dark for human blood, almost purplish in color, and was already congealing.

I spotted some coils of rope in the luggage, and I beckoned to a couple of farmers crowded behind me. "Tie him up," I told them, and gesturing at Tracy: "Her, too."

"I ain't gettin' near the son of a bitch," said one farmer, a skinny redhead peppered with freckles. "Seems to me, you oughta just finish him."

"Amen!" said Marie, pushing her way to the front of the bunched passengers. "Somebody's talkin' sense at last."

It wasn't so much compassion as curiosity as to how the Swede might continue to change that made me want to keep him alive. Curiosity wasn't that strong in me, but I would be judged, damned, and fried to a turn before I'd let this little redheaded puke tell me what to do. I aimed my gun at him and cocked it. "Tie 'em up," I said. "Then get rid of that." I gestured at the man the Swede had clawed; he was lying facedown, and it was obvious that his act of foolhardy courage had been the final signature of his life.

Gunfire sounded from the adjoining car, and the passengers surged forward, bumping and tussling, knocking one another off their feet. I forced them back and stood guard while two farmers tied up the Swede, dumping him into a seat, and then did the same for Tracy. She made no objection to being treated so roughly, just gazed out the window, refusing to answer when I asked how she felt—or maybe she didn't hear. Her eyes were black as bullet holes, muscles twitched in her jaw. It hit me hard to see her all trussed up, but I was terrified that she would end like the Swede, staggering along the aisle, spitting blood and fury. Marie caught my eye, triumph in her expression, and went to scribbling in her little book. In the panic she had popped most of the buttons from her blouse, and her breasts bulged from their lace armor, quivering like sick pudgy animals.

The train had slowed, chuffing up a steep grade. I peered out the window, searching for refugees, but all I could see were snow-laden pines and darkness and stars aligned into unfamiliar constellations. Most of the passengers sat staring at the seats in front of them, and a few were praying for some mercy of the world to rain down. Looking at Tracy, netted in rope, I couldn't tell if the pain I felt was for her or for myself at the prospect of losing her. The whole time we'd been together I'd been able to persuade myself that I must love her a little bit anyway. All my life, it seemed, I'd been trying to exert control, to do something for love, to create a miracle of being, one clean act, and yet all it had come to was a sense of spoilage and shame, a thickness clotting the flow of my thoughts. I was still certain that love was in me, buried beneath the topsoil of my character. Pools of it, dark reservoirs of crude compassion and caring. But now I knew that what I'd been calling "love" was merely the comforts of sex, the security of having a shoulder to cry on, childish dependencies, strident needs, and none of the generous emotions of a man. I could swear then I felt my life blow past me, like a train blowing past some-body standing on a weedy embankment, just that—life—just a fast freight with a roaring cargo, a streak of darkness with a hot wind behind; and you barely saw what it was before it was by, and only too late did you understand how you could have fleshed it out, all the things you could have noticed and savored. And at the end, if you were lucky, you might know the measure of your failure. I overheard one of the farmers mutter, "Oh, God, I'd do any-thing. . . ." So would I have given anything, but in exchange for what? A fiercer determination, or something to blot out my con-science, something that would weaken my desires? Those weren't the sort of things a good man is supposed to want, and even if I could escape the moral rule, the things I wanted were things weighed out from the dross of experience, not something you could pick up in a trade like you could with a gun or a pair of boots. I wondered if you decide to love, if love wasn't just an act of will, one I'd never chosen to make. Well, I chose to make it now, and although I was more wishing than choosing, crossing my fingers and whistling in the dark, I swore I would try to protect Tracy beyond the limits with which I'd fenced in my heart.

About halfway up the grade I forced myself to examine the Swede and Tracy once again. The Swede was still alive and had not undergone further changes. This gave me hope for Tracy, but when I checked on her, I found that she was smiling—a fixed, irrational smile—and as I watched, a black trickle leaked from the corner of her mouth. She flicked out a long slender tongue, crimson and rough, and licked it clean. Her skin had grown white, pulpy-looking, and was rippling under her dress. When she flexed her fingers, straining at her bonds, they appeared to be either boneless or many-jointed.

"Jesus!" I said, edging away, and Marie, who had come to peer over my shoulder, squealed, "You gotta kill 'er!"

I eased my gun out, half-convinced she was right, and held it with the muzzle up. The skin on my face thrummed as if covering hot wires instead of muscle and bone. But I had no heart for shooting Tracy.

"She's gon' be all right," I said.

A heavyset man with a thick shock of gray hair, wearing a threadbare corduroy jacket, shuffled forward and said, "I sympathize, friend. But this ain't no time to be takin' chances."

I kept my eyes on Tracy, recalling her fire and stubbornness, the wild look she got whenever she wanted me. I didn't care about any man.

"You can die for her, mister," I told the heavyset farmer. "It sure don't matter to me."

Another one came sneaking up on my left. I whirled and took aim at his face. "Take another step," I said. "Just one more'll do."

My frustration turned to anger, and I yelled at the rest. "C'mon and see what I got for ya! What you waitin' for?"

"Calm down, friend," said the heavyset farmer.

I laughed at that and gestured toward the rear of the car. "Get on back there, all of ya. And don't even think about tryin' me."

I herded them into the back, then sat down next to Tracy. Her eyes had gone a blazing yellow; membranes slid back and forth across them. The delicate lines bracketing her mouth had deepened, blackened. It looked as if her face were a white mask that was about to crack into pieces.

"Tracy?" I said. "Can y'hear me?"

She made a growly noise in her throat. Her torso rippled as if the muscles were sliding free beneath the skin, and as a result, the ropes were loosening. Her fingernails had turned dark blue. Like death, death's color, dark blue. I remembered the sight of her body naked in the light of a red dawn, rumpled sheets banked snowy around her, her breasts pinked with gleam, and the soft curve of her belly—as pure a shape as the sweep of a spring meadow—planing down to the dark swatch of her secret hair. I was dead inside, my thoughts like bitter smoke from a damped fire. I could feel the brimstone emptiness through which the train was tunneling, grinding along up the grade, and I wanted to throw back my head and howl.

"Tracy?" I had the urge to touch her, but couldn't bring myself to do it. Her skin would be moist, her flesh a cold tumescence like the flesh of a tomato worm. The ropes were getting slacker by the second, and though it was an agony to me, I knew it would be more merciful to shoot her now than to wait and watch her grow monstrous.

I caught movement out of the corner of my eye. Another goddamn farmer creeping up on me. The bastards were getting to be like mice. I half-turned to him, but said nothing, and after a moment's hesitation he scuttled back to the others. The elderly lady stretched out her hands to me.

"Don't let her hurt us . . . please!" she said.

"Y'gotta do it!" shrilled Marie. "Long as she's alive, she's a danger to us all."

The others murmured their assent.

With their skins all pasty and yellowed by the light, their gawping mouths and bugged eyes, they looked to have changed in some pitiful fashion. And maybe they had, I thought; maybe there's changes and then there's changes. There was a metallic taste in my mouth. I could feel a killing rage bubbling up inside me, and my head was full of terrible noises, a screech of metal being torn, of a hungry hawk screaming in frustration. I wanted the world to end, I hated these people so. I felt sick, dizzy, hot. The corners of the coach seemed to be pulling apart, as if the yellow ugly light had grown solid and was forcing back the walls. My eyes skidded across faces and shiny boards and gold lockets and glass—like everything had gone slippery and insubstantial. No place for my vision to catch on. It must be a change, I thought, a bad one. I fought against it, squinting, reducing the car to a fierce rippled brightness and a dark surround. That made things easier, and after a bit my vision steadied.

I got to my feet, rested a hand on the grip of my pistol, and told the passengers to stay back and stop their whimpering. "I don't give a frog's ass what you people want," I said. "You don't mean a thing to me, none of ya. So you might as well swallow that bullshit you're gettin' set to spout."

Saying this, I felt a swell of cold satisfaction, like a charge working inside me—it seemed not a change, but rather the expression of an attitude that I should have expressed long before, one that had been restrained in some way.

"Nobody's goin' to do nothin' to this woman here," I said, nodding at Tracy. "Not so long as I'm kickin'."

I was about to tell them what would happen if they challenged me when the rear door of the car blew open, a bitter wind gusted along the aisle, and the refugees came in. Three men—or almost-men

—wearing crudely sewn skins and furs. Everything was frozen. The refugees grouped by the door; the suddenly intensified noise of the wheels; the passengers standing in their seats, their eyes round with fright—all these things seemed elements of a vast tension that, I thought, must spread far beyond the car and the train, throughout the entire Patch. Apart from the raw cold, I felt a crawly sensation along my spine, and I recalled what Marie had said about how you could sense the magical power that enlivened the refugees.

The three of them eased forward, their shadows kinking over the warped floorboards, sliding flat as black silk over the smooth places. The passengers—ranged between me and the rear door—cowered in their seats. One of the refugees was a hunchback with a brutish heavy-jawed face, bulging prominences above his eyes, tufted eyebrows, and yellow teeth like an ape's. A second hid behind him. The third was a big man with grayish skin and a strangely unfinished face—a gash of a mouth and black eyes that were almost perfect circles, like holes cut in a dirty bed sheet. His domed skull was bald, ringed with maybe half a dozen bony knots, each the size of a baby's fist, as if he were growing a king's crown under his scalp. There was a hunting knife slung at his hip. I felt I knew something about his character—I couldn't define it, but if I could have made a stab at definition, I would have done so in terms of strength and intelligence and tenacity.

He spoke to me in a language whose words had the sound of a horse munching an apple. It might have been a question.

I wasn't sure why I didn't follow Cole's advice and shoot straight-away. Could be I had some hope for the big man, or at the bottom of my soul I felt he had the right to live, that I wasn't the one to be his executioner. And also I wondered if his question signaled a will-ingness to negotiate, if he wanted to bargain or trade. But I couldn't think how to communicate with him.

"Get on outta here!" I waved at the door. "Just go on, and there won't be no trouble."

He spoke again—the same words, I believe, but with a touch more intensity. He gave me a searching look . . . or so I took it. Meeting his eyes, I felt I had made a connection, that what lay behind those black surfaces was not inhuman.

The gray-haired heavyset farmer made a threatening move, and the big man held up a hand by way of warning. He spoke to me a third time. I eased my hand toward my gun and said, "Get on out! I ain't gon' be tellin' ya again."

I think the big man smiled, though he might just have been trying to frighten me by showing his filed teeth. But I do believe it was a smile, for when the hunchback scuttled toward me, moving with a peculiar crabwise gait, he made a grab for him, trying to haul him back. Then three of the idiot farmers went at him, and my options dwindled to one.

My heart was empty of caring, of fear, and the gun leaped easily in my hand. I punched out the hunchback's left eye with one round, opened up his belly with a second, and still he staggered toward me. My last shot, squeezed off at a range of no more than a couple of feet, cracked his chest. His shirt caught fire from the muzzle flash, and the flames danced merrily, so pale in the glare, they were almost invisible. I turned the gun on the big man, who was about to finish off the last of three farmers—half-conscious in his grasp—with a fist the size of a cannonball.

"Hold it!" I yelled, but he did not let the farmer fall. He stared at me, grave and unflustered, as if measuring the distance between himself and death. I was still reluctant to shoot him.

"Aim at his throat!" somebody shouted. "Or the eye! You shoot him anywhere's else, and y'can't kill him! There's too much bone."

I couldn't see the man who had shouted, but I didn't think it had been a passenger—they were crouched down behind the seats, those who were still capable of crouching, and not a one of them was displaying the poise of an expert. I lowered my aim to the throat as the voice had instructed, and the big man let go of the farmer and backed toward the door.

I put a bullet into the floorboards at his feet. "Go on!" I said. "You got the idea."

He kept on edging backward, but as he reached the door he stopped and roared at me. That was how it seemed—a roar, but one with words embedded in it—and I couldn't help but admire the purity of his rage. I had thought he was going to leave us to heaven and go back to his wilderness, but I had underestimated his desperation. He half-turned as if to jump from the car, but then plucked the hunting knife from its sheath and hurled it at me. It sang past my ear as I fired. The bullet took him in the Adam's apple and spun him down onto the floor. He flopped about, clutching at the wound, but still fixed me with his eyes, which remained bright with regard. He tried to talk, but blood was all that came from his mouth. Words of blood, trickles of lost meanings. Then he went all unstrung. Nothing violent or spasmodic. Just like he was laying down his head for a little nap. I holstered my gun. Outside, the snow and dark looked clean and inviting, and the idea of taking a long walk in it seemed for an instant to offer a more hopeful prospect than completing the ride to Glory.

Smoke hung on the air in the car, like misty trails winding through invisible mountains; the rattle of the wheels had acquired the rhythm of an enormous telegraph. I noticed that the Swede's head had slumped forward, and I could tell from the blood on his mouth and chest that something had busted inside him and he was dead. My head ached, and in my heart I felt the sick weight of killing. I searched around for the third refugee. Marie peeked over the top of a seat, staring dazedly at the blood rivering the floor. She had a lump coming beneath one eye. The others had started picking themselves up. Then a man called out, the same voice that had instructed me to aim for the throat.

"Don't shoot!" he said. "I won't hurt nobody, I swear!"

The voice was issuing from behind a rear seat. I aimed at it. "Stand up and lemme see ya," I said.

"I promise I won't hurt nobody! Didn't I help you? Don't that prove I'm on your side?"

"I hear ya," I told him. "Let's see your hands. Right now, or I'm gon' put a bullet right through that seat you're hidin' behind."

"For the love of God!" he said, his words rushing forth in a torrent. "Don't you unnerstand? The others, they were crazy. This is their home, this goddamn hole. They just wanted to kill you. But me, I'm hardly changed at all. I never wanted to kill nobody. I went along with the rest of 'em so's I could get on the train. I tried to help you, didn't I? I ain't after nothin', I just wanna live."

Though I had been listening to him, during his spiel I had become entranced by the bodies, the stink of gunpowder, the blood and the smoky yellow air. I was amazed to recollect my lack of fear, the ease with which I'd killed . . . all entirely out of character. I wondered if I looked in the mirror whether I'd see black eyes like Cole's, pupils in the shape of pentagrams or coiled serpents. And I wished I was my old, flawed, cowardly self once again.

"Last chance," I told the refugee. "Get your hands high, and then let's have a look at ya."

After a second he complied. He was a puny thing, several inches short of five feet, with a shaggy head of graying black hair. He had a pinched face the color of an old pumpkin, all seamed and wrinkled. I assumed him to be an old-timer, but then I noticed that his hands were those of a young man, that his neck wasn't crepey, but firmly fleshed. And I realized that what I had taken for wrinkles was actually ropy veins darker than the rest of his skin, and that his features were those of somebody my own age. What would he do out in the world, I wondered, looking like that?

"Don't trust him," said a farmer; and Marie chimed in, "That's right! Even the innocent-lookin' ones can be terrors."

What she had said had no influence upon me, but I wasn't about to trust the refugee; he had turned on his companions, and monstrous though they had been, it was nonetheless a betrayal. Besides, I wasn't certain that the big man had intended to hurt anybody.

"What's your name?" I asked.

"God, it's been so long since anybody asked me my name," he said. "I been livin' with them animals, pretendin' to be one of 'em. . . ." He gave himself a shake. "Name's Jimmy Crisp. I was a farmer over in Glory till this no-good son of bitchin' wife-stealer tied me up and put me on a handcar and set me rollin' into the Patch. It's been six years . . . six goddamn years."

A couple of the farmers urged me to shoot Crisp, and I told them to stuff their holes, that I was more likely to be shooting them if they gave me any more grief. Then I noticed Marie, her jaw dropped, staring at something behind me. I turned around just in time to see something whippet-thin and blue-black in color leaping across the aisle and down in back of a seat. In reflex, without thinking what it might be, I blew a hole in the seat and heard a pining cry, birdlike, yet more piercing than that of any bird I knew. And from that cry I realized that I had fired at Tracy—it was the perfect, pained expression of the trapped thing she had mostly been. I fired a second time at the seat, not wanting to know how she had changed. The next moment, as the cry sounded again, drilling through me, Jimmy Crisp grabbed my arm and prevented a third shot. The others yelled for me to shoot, but Crisp, his wizened face looking up close even more like a rotted vegetable, shouted them down.

"She ain't gon' hurt you!" he said. "She's changin' into this kinda animal what lives 'round here in the forests. They peaceful, they just wanna be left alone!"

I thought it strange that he would forget his own peril and go to the defense of a mere animal; I had the idea that he was trying to compensate for something.

The others kept on yammering, and Crisp screeched at them, waving his arms. "You stupid bastards! You wanna kill everything comin' outta the Patch, don'tcha? Y'wanna stomp 'em like bugs! But know who you killin'? Your friends, your sisters, your cousins. Folks who's either foolish or sinned against. It ain't no life out there, not for a man. But it's a life all the same, and you got no call to deny it to somethin's got only that much life left."

Some of the passengers appeared mortified, but then the thing behind the seat—I couldn't think of it as Tracy—set up a mewling, and they started in on me again.

"You don't finish 'er," Marie said, "then Cole will."

I made no response.

"Hell," she said, patting her dress into a semblance of order, "I think I'll go get him right now."

She came toward me, went sideways in order to scoot by, and when she did that, I caught her by the neck, forced her back over one of the seats, and shoved the barrel of the gun up under her chin. In the sickly light her doughy face with its bruises and dimples resembled something I might have dreamed after a heavy meal and too much brandy, even less human in its revolting stamp than Crisp's face. I cocked the gun, and her eyes swiveled down, trying to see my hand.

"Help me!" she said weakly; then she screamed it. "Help! Help me, Cole! He's killin' me!"

There was a scrabbling noise behind me, and I pushed Marie away. The animal was jumping about, moving with the sinuous speed of a ferret, clawing the windows, apparently terrified by Marie's screams. Through rips in Tracy's underclothes, which still clung to it, I saw that its body was all whipcord muscle. The skin had darkened to a midnight blue. The face, too, had darkened, though not so much as the rest, and it had simplified, the features acquiring a cast that was somehow both feline and reptilian, the mouth thinner, wider, and the nose a pair of curved slits. But the eyes, huge and yellow, with translucent membranes like crystal lenses—they carried the sadness I'd heard in that cry. And in the lineaments of the face, minimal though they were, I could still make out the remnant of Tracy's troubled beauty. It was awful to detect her essence in that creature. Weakness flooded me. I wanted to work some magic and call her back to the human. Yet at the same time I wanted to release her, and I had the thought that this might be the best she could hope for, not to have failed with me again, but to have changed utterly, to have gone beyond herself into a world where failure and success was a simple affair, something wholly of her own making.

Marie had stopped her squawling. She had slumped into one of the seats, holding her dumpling gut, and Crisp was standing over her, muttering curses. The farmers were keeping their distance. The animal was tearing away the remains of Tracy's clothing, letting out feral hisses, and I figured that if it couldn't escape soon, it might decide that attacking us was its only hope for survival. Having reached the steepest section of the grade, the train was barely moving, and I went to a window, intending to bust it out with my gun butt, thinking I might be able to persuade the animal to jump through. But as I took hold of the barrel, and prepared to swing, Cole came back into the car. I reversed my grip and threw down on him before he could bring his shotgun up to fire at the animal.

"Use that hogleg, and you're a dead man!" I told him.

He looked haggard, his black shirt was ripped. "Don't be foolin' with me, son," he said. "She ain't nothin' to you no more. Just you stand aside and lemme do my job."

"I mean it," I said, seeing that he was bracing himself in front of the open door.

"I should clean your plow for ya, boy," he said, his tone even and easy, "but I'm gon' give you a chance to reconsider 'cause you done me a service. Now you stop with this here bullshit. All you doin' is makin' things worse for ever'body . . . your woman included."

Cole was blind—I understood that now. He had been too long on the line, he was operating on the basis of judgments made years before and was incapable of weighing the case now before him. In the seams of his worn face was written a language of unyielding principle. He had, as he had said, seen too much, and so he came to disregard anything that demanded his attention. But my vision was new and clear. I could see his eerie pupils contracting, appearing to change like the spots on a magical deck of cards, going hearts to clubs to spades, each design more ominous than the last. I saw the muscles tense in his neck, his shoulders. I knew what he intended.

"I guess you're right," I said, letting my voice falter, my words thick with resignation. "I don't know what to do."

I dropped my eyes a mite, waited until I saw him relax, then I shot him in the hip, sending him spinning down against the wall. His shotgun discharged into the ceiling, and leaving a few last shreds of Tracy's petticoat on the floor, the animal bolted for the door, flowed through it and was gone. I jumped over Cole, who was twisting about, saying, "Shit! Oh, Jesus!" and went to stand between the cars. As I've mentioned, the train had slowed to a crawl, and so I had a good long look at what I'd learned to love too late running away from me.

The land sloped sharply down from the tracks, a decline of moonlit hummocky snow that gave out into evergreen forest, and beyond the base of the hill, beyond the edge of the trees, lay a plain that stretched to the horizon. It was the heart of the Patch. I'd never seen it before, but I could tell that's what it was. It was such a place, that plain, as you might envision after chewing some of those cactus buds that Indians sell in the Mexican marketplaces, and yet strangely enough, it was familiar too, comfortably familiar in the way of those cool rotten-leaf smells that drift up from shady rivers and the taste of larrup syrup and the sight of deer hiding in among some post oaks with their white flags raised. Wild stars and pale enormities of cloud overhead, a sky of such complex immensity that it seemed an entity unto itself, the embodiment of a profound emotion. Darkly iridescent points of land hooked out into water that had the gleam of tarnished silver, a great river feeding a country of virgin timber and solitary cabins—nodes of inconstant fire lodged in the vast gloomy sweep. There were fountains of light, gouts of indigo and crimson and viridian, spraying up from secret places like the souls of magicians taking flight, and areas where witchy glows flickered. Islands of phosphorescence effloresced and faded in the farthest reaches like universes being born, and shadows with no apparent source passed across the face of the water. Lightnings touched the earth and spread glittering tides. The place was lovely and evil, serene and fulminant, intimate and infinite. Impossible to characterize or judge. There was no end to its mysterious detail. And running over the snow toward all that majestic confusion and silent tumult was Tracy . . . I had accepted that weird lithe creature as being her, because I had finally given up on her, finally let her go, and because I knew just from seeing it that the Patch wasn't the hell I had imagined, that while it might seem inimical to me, for others it was the only home possible, and that it held out the opportunity for rewards that my world couldn't offer. Good and evil were more sharply defined within its perimeters, and there was a grandeur to its freedom and wildness, in the endless reach of the solitudes, in the feeling that whatever fate was to be yours, it was something worked out from your deeds and not a weakness bred into you and reinforced by lies. I had felt something of that freedom and wildness in the big gray-skinned man, though at the time I couldn't have put it into words. For certain I had known that he needed something other than our lives, something he had not been able to say and hadn't trusted me to understand. In truth, I could not have understood under the circumstances. But now, seeing more clearly than I had, I believed we might have made a compact, established a bond that would have prevented the deaths. And what about Crisp? What about all the pitiful refugees

who came wandering back to the world? Half-changed men, unsuited
for life in either place. That, I realized, had to be the case. Crisp had
hinted of it in his defense of Tracy, and I thought I must be like that
myself—born too much for one world, too little for the other. Wrong
by an inch for happiness. Or not happiness. I could no longer accept
that true happiness existed. For strength, for constancy.

As I contemplated this, I watched Tracy receding, growing smaller
and smaller, darkening against the snowfield. Sort of like watching
a hole being burned in white paper by a match held behind it, only
in reverse, the hole dwindling and ultimately vanishing. It was not
until after she had gone into the shadows of the trees that I felt her
loss, and it wasn't the tearing pain I might have expected; it was softer,
a sweet fall of darkness over the heart, a luminous ache that seemed
to light the gloom it created. I realized that I had lost Tracy long ago,
and that only this minute had I begun to miss her.

At last, shivering with cold, I went back into the car. My bullet
had ripped a furrow in Cole's hip, yet had done him no serious
damage. Someone had bandaged him, and he was sitting with his legs
straight out on the floor; his color was off, but otherwise he appeared
to be sound. He had a quart of Emerson's Bourbon in hand. He gazed
up at me sorrowfully.

"You a damn fool, y'know that?" he said without malice, just
making an observation.

I flopped down next to him. "You were wrong to wanna shoot
her, man. Dead wrong."

He was not interested in the topic. "I should lock you up," he
said. "Maybe that'd improve your judgment."

"I'll testify for ya, Cole," Marie said. "You can count on that."

She was back in her seat. They were all sitting, the battered and
bloodied farmers, the elderly lady, all displaying the same self-absorbed
attitudes that they had at the start of the trip. Only Crisp, who was
rocking back and forth, his face buried in his hands, showed any sign
of having endured a rough passage. He was talking to himself, agitated
words that I could not make out, and now and again slamming a fist
into his thigh. I had neither the energy nor the right pitch to console
him.

"You don't bring charges," Marie said to Cole, primping in a hand
mirror, dabbing powder onto her bruises, "then I will. I ain't about
to have my person assaulted way it's been this trip."

"Shut your hole, Marie," Cole said wearily; he shifted and winced.

"Sorry 'bout that." I nodded at his hip.

"I've had worse."

"Well, I'm amazed," I told him. "If I'd known people took get-tin' shot as good as you, I'd have shot a sight more of 'em in my time."

He grunted with amusement.

Marie stared at him, dumbfounded. "You ain't just gon' forget about this, are ya? He's committed a blood crime!"

"Puttin' this boy away ain't gon' cure nothin'," Cole said. "Hell, I could use him on the line if he. . . ."

"I doubt I'm up to it," I cut in. " 'Sides, that's your bad fortune, and not mine."

"You didn't let me finish," he said. "It's like I told you—you come into the Patch again, I doubt you'll be so lucky with the changes."

"I ain't been that damn lucky this time," I said.

We had reached the top of the grade and started down, picking up speed with every second. I gazed out the window at the sweep of the plain, the shining waters and dark curves of land—it seemed that the whole expanse formed a single fabulous image like a character in some ancient script or a symbol on a treasure map. And there must be treasure out there, I thought. There must be a million sights worth seeing, a million things worth having. I imagined Tracy somewhere, asleep in its shadows, her old life receded to a dream.

"I don't believe this!" Marie said. "Man puts a bullet in you, and you sayin' you'd offer him a job?"

"You can pick your nose," Cole said with a grin that spread a net of wrinkles across his face. "But you can't pick your friends."

"He almost got us killed!" Marie heaved up from her seat, hands on hips. "You do what you want, but I ain't gon' stand by and see him get off scot-free! I'm goin' straight to the sheriff in Steadley and have him swear out papers on this hellion! And if you think I'm . . ."

With an inarticulate yell, Crisp sprang to his feet. He turned this way and that as if unsure of whom he wanted to address. "There's this place in the Patch," he said, emoting like a preacher, "this place so bad can't nothin' but the worst of 'em stand to be there. The ones who's monsters, the ones who sleep on what they kill and shit their babies. It makes hell look like Sunday school. Fire don't warm you, it just hurts your eyes. The snow's white insects, the rain cuts like razors." He hustled over to Marie, whipped a knife out from his ragged sleeve; he put the edge to her throat. "I'm takin' you there, bitch! I'm takin' you right to there, 'cause that's where you fuckin' belong!" He hauled Marie into the aisle. "Don't nobody try and stop me! I'll bleed 'er here'n now!"

I regarded him wearily. Much as I would have liked to see Marie dragged out into the Patch, I couldn't let him do it. Maybe there was more of Cole in me than I'd figured. I came to my feet, and Crisp nicked her, bringing a rill of blood out from Marie's saggy jowl; she squeaked and went stiff.

"I ain't gon' interfere with ya, man," I said. "I just wanna ask you a coupla questions . . . all right?"

That didn't sit too well with him, but he said, "Yeah, I guess."

"Those men you come aboard with, you say they wanted to kill us, but that big fella was askin' me somethin'? What was he askin'?"

"I don't know."

"You said you was pretendin' to be one of 'em, you must know their language."

He opened his mouth slowly, reminding me of a fish trying to get its lips around a pebble it had mistaken for food; but he did not reply.

"I was thinkin' 'bout this woman y'got here," I said. " 'Bout why she's so damn nasty. Way I figger, she's just scared of who she is, hatin' herself 'cause she's so fat and useless and don't belong nowhere. She ain't got nothin' better to do than ride this stinkin' train back and forth. She can't hate herself enough to satisfy, so she takes it out on other people. She don't really wanna hurt 'em, she just ain't got the guts to hurt herself."

"What you talkin' about? You talkin' crazy!" Crisp looked to the others as if for confirmation.

"You come aboard with these other two, and you turn on 'em. Then you tell us you was always plannin' to turn on 'em, that you was just playin' along till you had a chance to switch sides. They was gonna hurt us, you say. But be that as it may, you wasn't square with 'em . . . and not 'cause you cared 'bout us, but 'cause you was afraid."

"What'd you want me to do? Let 'em kill you?"

"You would have done anything to get outta the Patch. You weren't like them others. Don't matter what they were, you just wasn't one of 'em. You didn't belong with 'em, and you was too scared to think about anything except that. But once you was shut of 'em, alone with us, it was the exact same situation. You was scared of us, you felt you didn't belong. You could feel that this wasn't your answer either, that you was as wrong here as you was in the Patch. Still, you had to make us believe you was one of us, so you went on 'bout how you betrayed your companions to save our lives. Like you said . . . just playin' along.''

"Naw," Crisp said, "naw, that ain't how it was."

" 'Course, then you started hatin' yourself 'cause you betrayed 'em, and 'cause you couldn't hate yourself enough to satisfy, you picked out ol' Marie here to hate. Now I admit she's easy to hate. But when you get right down to it, what she been doin' ain't no different than what you doin', now is it?"

The tension had drained from Crisp. He looked hopeless, beaten, and I knew I had him. I was full of truth and clear-seeing, as sure and righteous in my stance as a preacher with all the weight of scripture behind him. I had him given up and gone—all I had to do was to keep on talking, wearing him out with the dismal truth.

"Don't you see?" I asked him. "There ain't nowhere in this world you ever gon' feel at home. And stickin' some pathetic woman what's the same as you just gon' make things worse."

"Lemme be!" Crisp shouted. "Just lemme be!"

"What was the big man askin'?"

"Nothin'! I don't know!"

"What was he askin'?"

"I tell you, I don't know!"

"What'd he want? Food . . . is that it? Medicine? Fuel?"

It appeared that Crisp couldn't decide whether to smile at me, to try and win me over, or to snarl. That rotted jack-o'-lantern head wobbled like it was about to fall off his neck.

"You don't have to answer," I said. " 'Cause I don't know what exactly he wanted, but I do know it wasn't blood."

Crisp let out a terrible moan, a sound so full of pain it seemed the result of an actual blow.

"Our help's what he wanted," I said. "He wasn't hopin' for it too much, but he was willin' to chance askin' me a question just in case I was smart enough to understand."

The little man shoved Marie aside, facing me with the knife, swaying with the erratic motion of the train, his face working.

"That ain't gon' do nothin' for ya," I said calmly.

He jabbed with the knife, but in his face was the rumpled, unsteady look of death. As I'd been earlier, he was past caring, past even the limits of wanting to care.

"Whatever you done," I said, "it ain't no worse'n things we everyone of us done. Maybe you did wrong with your companions, but you saved a life once you got on board. Nobody here can fault ya. But y'can't go 'round hurtin' people to make yourself feel better. You think about that, now.''

He appeared to be obeying my instructions, to be thinking things over, but I guess there was just too much wrongness in his head, too much trouble in his past for thought to make any sense. I had relaxed a bit, expecting him to see reason, and when he came at me, quicker than I would have believed possible, I wasn't prepared and took a slice on my arm. I gritted my teeth against the pain and tried to grab him, but he ducked and darted past me and out the door. He stood between the cars, a shadowy figure hanging on to the safety railing. The train was rocketing along now, and I understood what he intended and that he had no chance. But he was no longer my responsibility, and so I only watched and waited. He glanced back into the car, and I could feel his yearning, the weight of his anguish, all the shattering displacement of what he'd hoped being overwhelmed by what he knew. Then he swung out over the rail and vanished into the black rush of night. If he gave a cry, it was lost in the thunder of our passage.

Dispirited, wondering why I had bothered to save Marie, wishing I could have done more for Crisp, I sat back down beside Cole, ignoring the gabble from the rear of the car. Marie was sobbing, the farmers all talking at once.

Cole passed me the bourbon. "You didn't handle that real good."

" 'Bout as good as you handled me." I had a slug of bourbon and began wrapping a bandanna about my arm.

We were moving down into the deep forest, and all I could make out of the great plain through the ragged silhouettes of the evergreens was intermittent glints of silvery water and unearthly fire. I finished wrapping my arm, had some more bourbon, and leaned back.

"Are we all right?" I asked Cole. "We past havin' more trouble?"

Cole said, "Most likely," and reclaimed his bourbon. After a while he asked what I planned to do now . . . now that everything had changed for me.

I gave a bitter laugh. "Guess I'm still bound for Glory."

He made a noncommittal noise and drank.

"That's sure one hell of a ride," I said.

I gazed off along the car, at the dried blood and the farmers, at Marie, huge and depressed, muffled in her coat. Despite everything, I couldn't work up hatred for her. All my emotions had been fired, leaving me with empty chambers and the stink of cordite. A shudder went through me, not of cold, but some last residue voiding itself, a dry heave of the spirit.

Tracy, I thought, and then even that was gone.

"What's there to do after you done this?" I asked, feeling hopeless and cold. "What's left?"

Cole had another swig of bourbon; he rinsed it around in his mouth before he swallowed, then looked out the window at the dark world rushing past. He was wearing a distant expression, and his pupils appeared to have shrunk into tiny black keyholes. Finally he shrugged and spread his hands in a gesture of helplessness.

"Turn around and go back the other way was all I could ever figger," he said.

I took a room in Glory. It was a tiny, crooked room with a slanted ceiling and leaning walls, dirty, cold as a penny. From the window I could see ramshackle buildings and rutted dirt streets marbled with crusts of snow. By day, buckboards slotted along the ruts while women in wool shawls and long skirts hustled past. Men loaded and unloaded kegs of nails and grain sacks and bales of straw, and stopped into the saloons for a drink or three. Their children chased one another, ducking under horses and wagons, pelting each other with snowballs. Nights, there was some wildness—tinny piano music, gunshots, shrieks—but not so much as there had been in White Eagle. As far as I could tell from living there a week, every town I'd ever known ought to have been called Glory, because they were all pretty damn much the same.

There were refugees, of course. They slept in alleys and doorways, wherever it was dark and there was a chance of making it through the night without being beaten. None of the citizens wanted them around, what with their peculiar habits and deformities, but they were tolerated due to some Christian twitch. I would sit by my window and watch them slink about and wonder if I wasn't one of them myself. I hadn't bothered looking up my friends to borrow money. That was a plan I'd concocted with Tracy, and even if she had been there, I doubt I could have stuck to it. I had changed, and few of my old obsessions had any meaning. Instead, I got a job swamping out a saloon, which paid enough for food and shelter and—on occasion— for a woman to share my crooked room. The women made me happy, but not for long. Once they were gone, I would go to stand in the dark and spy on life. I saw a thousand things I wanted, but none I wanted enough to seize, nothing that inspired me to grab and take a bite and laugh with the joy of fulfilled desire. I was as empty as I'd been at the beginning of the ride from White Eagle, and whenever I looked into mirrors I saw a man on the run from himself, a man who was growing sick and weak again.

Spring faded, summer died, fall ebbed. I won a horse in a poker game, a shit-brown, sore-kneed, mean-tempered animal that I kept only because I was in no position to throw anything away. I hated that horse, and I would have sooner gotten cozy with a skunk than put a saddle on him. But one morning I realized I had become so sick of myself that I couldn't stand the room any longer. It reeked of my hangovers, my sodden incapacities. I packed a bedroll, mounted up, and headed east for Steadley, again thinking that what I needed was a new place, a new start. But the ride came to be a remedy in itself. The air so crisp it flowed into my lungs like cool fire, and the sky that potent blue you only find on the backside of creation, with high scribbled lines of birds and snow peaks in the distance. I had intended to do some soul-searching, to try and gain a perspective on things. But it appeared that merely by leaving Glory I had gained sufficient perspective, and I experienced sweeps of emotion that in their purity seemed to embody the perfection of the sky, the shining mountains, and the momentum of the land, the great flow of it eastward, rising and declining with the smoothness of ocean swells. My body felt clean, my head free of worries. Even the horse's temper had improved.

A day and a half later when Steadley hove into view, a gaggle of weathered frame buildings that differed from Glory only by its greater size and the profusion of its squalor, I was not yet ready to end my ride, and I figured I would keep going awhile and pitch camp in the hills east of town. Weather closed in, the sky grayed, and fat white flakes started to fall. But when I reached the hills, I was still eager to continue, and as the light faded toward dusk, I told myself I'd ride a few miles more, close—yet not too close—to the edge of the Patch. I moved into evergreen forest, following the railroad tracks, which were banked high with snow that had fallen the previous week, finding peace among the dark trees. Tiny birds with white bellies and black caps were hopping thick as fleas beneath them; in their nervous agitation, they reminded me of how my thoughts had been working recently. Wind whirled up fresh powder from the snow crust, stretched it out into veils that went flowing across the banks and glittered for a moment before dissipating; the heavy snow-laden boughs of the firs barely trembled.

I was preparing to scout about for a campsite when I heard the train from Steadley coming and spotted its smoke unwinding above the treetops; a minute later I saw the locomotive round a bend, sparks fluming from its smokestack, a gigantic black beast out of hell, its brass cowcatcher looking like golden needle teeth in the decaying light. It was on an upgrade, moving at a relatively slow pace, and I urged the horse into a trot alongside, looking in the windows, studying the frightened faces of the passengers. As the end of a car passed, a man with a shotgun leaned out between cars and shouted for me to keep away. Cole. Even at that distance I had a strong impression of his eyes, a sense of their bizarre black configurations.

"Hey, Cole!" I called out. "Don't you recognize me?"

He peered at me, leaning farther out, hanging on to the safety rail. "Ain't you the ol' boy put a hole in my hip?"

I waved. "How you been?"

"Tolerable . . . and you?"

"Shit, I'm doin' fine as a man can do!" Strangely enough, I believed it.

"Where the hell you think you goin'?" Cole shouted as the train began to pick up speed. "We 'bout into the Patch!"

"Well, that's where I'm goin'!" His warning didn't affect me . . . or not the way I would have expected, anyway. I felt challenged, excited, alive. I urged the horse into a gallop, plunging through the snow, and was astounded by the ease with which he responded.

"You're crazy! Don't you 'member what I said? Ain't gon' be the same for ya this time! There's gon' be changes!"

I laughed. "Don't tell me you ain't never wanted to go out into it, to find what's there. You can't see it without feelin' that way."

He nodded. "Oh, yeah! I've had me that feelin' a time or two."

"Then c'mon with me!" I spurred the horse faster. "We'd make a pair, we would! We'd scare all the monsters into hidin'!"

He just grinned.

"C'mon!" I yelled. "What've you got to lose? We'll be the kings of the goddamn place! C'mon with me!"

And I believed that, too—that we could see all of the wonders and intricacies of the Patch, all its violent lights and darks, and come through victorious. I was heady with that knowledge.

A plume of smoke from the engine swirled between us, and after it had passed, he called, "Naw, that's *your* bad fortune, not mine!"

The train was pulling away from me, heading for another curve, and as it began to angle around it, Cole yelled, "Luck to you!"

"I don't need luck!" I told him. "I gotta special moon watches over me, I'm part of an infinite design. I got more fire in me than that ol' engine of yours. What do I need with luck?"

"Take it anyhow!" he cried, waving with his shotgun, and then the car jolted around the bend, and I saw him no more.

I had thought all my brave words were merely bluster, that once he had gone out of sight, I would rein in the horse and find myself a campsite, but I kept urging the horse to run faster. And it was not just my urging that commanded us, because I noticed then that the horse had changed, become a force of its own, a great dark engine with a steaming heart that pulled me along and helped me abide by a decision that I realized I had already made, that I'd made long before I left Glory. I recalled watching Tracy run for the cover of the woods, how I'd thought of her as running away from danger; but seeing her in my mind's eye, I knew that she had been running for joy, for life, fueled by all the brilliant thoughtlessness that was empowering me now. That was it, you see. There was no logic to my act, no sense, no plan. I was free of all that, free of fetters I'd never known existed, of impediments so subtle in their hold that I couldn't even name them, and I was running as I had not since I had been a boy, for the pure muscular exhilaration of the act, with the wind a fire at my back, and the snow blowing up into phantoms, and the dark trees like fortress towers, and the whole world ahead of me a richness of absolutes. The things I knew just from breathing in that snow-crystaled, stinging air! Philosophies were squeezed into shape by the clenching of my fist, principles bred like tears in the corners of my eyes. My mind was white with knowing.

To my amazement, we were beginning to catch up with the train. That horse of mine was a marvel, each of his strides carrying us an improbable distance. I could not see his face, but I knew the measure of his change, his eyes aglow like miners' lanterns, his teeth sharp and capable of tearing, his hooves driving sparks from the stones. And I felt as well the measure of my own change. It wasn't what I might have picked had I had a choice, but it was true to myself in a way that I would never have admitted before. My heart was a furious cell, my brain flocked with outlaw desires, my hands fit for loving and killing and little in between. For evil . . . though I didn't look at it that way, not anymore. Evil had ceased to be an abstraction to me. It was as plain and comprehensible as a lump of coal, a black fist that could burn and give off flame, a tool that enabled me to survive, and being no longer mysterious, it no longer deserved a fancy word like *evil* to describe it—it was merely a part of what I was, a talent, a quality as indistinguishable from my whole self as a single sparkle of a gemstone.

I spurred my horse and went coursing past the last car. I matched the train's pace and looked in through the window at a pretty woman in a blue dress. I stared at the plump swell of her breasts and wanted her with a blaze of dizzy passion that came near to unseating me. She drew back, pale and alarmed, a hand to her mouth. God only knew what face I presented to the world . . . or maybe I did have some idea, for when I swept off my hat, intending to salute her with a bow, I felt several bony projections rising from my cranium, like the knobs of a primitive crown, and I laughed at the thought that a gray demon king might be rising from the ashes of my faint heart. There was a vicious glee in my laughter that—had I heard it at any other time— would have made my spit dry and my balls shrivel into seeds. But now I loved to hear it, knowing it for the signal music of a new life. I considered swinging up onto the car and taking the woman, but she offered nothing I would not find in more vital form out upon the vast glowing plain that lay to the north. The other passengers pressed close to the window, peering out at me, and I wondered what they were thinking. Was I simply the personification of their fears, or did they see in me a man who had lost everything? Did they sense the sweetness of my release? Could they guess at the years of dismal self-deception that lay behind me? Did they realize that I was like themselves, someone who had come to the end of his dodges and been forced to travel a road that he had tried for years to avoid, only to discover that it was life itself he had been avoiding?

I rode alongside them awhile, engaging their eyes soberly, trying to convey the tragedy of my long decline and the good news of my escape. I would have shouted out to them, but I knew they would not understand me. We were separated not merely by a quarter-inch of glass and a few feet of snowy ground, but by the potent enchantment of the Patch and the lesser enchantment of my choice. Or perhaps the fact that they had yet to make their own choices was the greatest barrier between us. Then, giving up forever on the world, I reined my horse northward, swerving down through the evergreens, smashing aside the boughs with my strong right hand and sending up clouds of snow behind, bound at last for glory, the only kind accessible to those who have failed at ordinary grace, bound for heat and pleasure, for the end of limits and the final places of love and power, bound for death by dreaming, for the joys of hell and the pains of paradise and all the pretty mysteries beyond.

THE EXERCISE OF FAITH

JK

From my pulpit, carved of ebony into a long-snouted griffin's head, I can see the sins of my parishioners. It's as if a current is flowing from face to face, illuminating the secret meaning of every wrinkle and line and nuance of expression. They—like their sins—are an ordinary lot. Children as fidgety as gnats. Ruddy-cheeked men possessed by the demons of real estate, solid citizens with weak hearts and brutal arguments for wives. Women whose thoughts slide like swaths of gingham through their minds, married every one to lechers and layabouts. Yet for all their commonality, the congregation is remarkable in that their sins mesh, are wholly compatible with one another. For every potential pederast there is a young boy in the first flush of his deviancy, for every violent urge a seeker of pain, and for every bitter widow a lust of knitting-needle sharpness with which to mend the piecework of her days. This has always seemed to me a circumstance worth exploiting, though until recently I had no idea as to how that should be done.

Not only can I see my parishioners' sins, I am able to experience them, both talents visited upon me by, I believe, the church. It is an ancient house of worship, its white plaster walls and black beams emblematic of the Puritan rigor whose sanctity it was built to guarantee, and it is graced by twelve stained-glass windows, each depicting a beast framed by a border of grape leaves. Legend tells that its cool dry air seethes with the caliginous spirits of old killed witches, most of them dead at the hands of the first pastor here, one Jeremy Calder, a man gone bloody with the love of God. However, I doubt his astral presence or that of his victims is responsible for the inception of my psychic gifts. No, rather I feel these gifts are a product of the essence of the place and time, for that, it strikes me, is the nature of all extremes of reality, be they good or evil: that they are bred from the interaction of a thousand ephemera, the conjunction of congruent normalcies that together act to compound an anomaly. . . . But I was going to tell you how I experience my congregation's sins.

This morning as I stand on the steps in my surplice after the eleven o'clock service, with the red-and-yellow leaves of the sycamores and birches that line the street bristling and flashing like semaphores under the high sun, I greet each by name and shake their hands, and with every touch a vision opens in my brain. Take Emily Prideau, now. Child of Bess and Robert. Sixteen years old; nubile; sweet. Her breasts molded into prim curves by the pink starched decorum of her Sunday dress. Yet from her fingers courses the vision of a midnight wood, where cross-armed she lifts her sweater and those heavy breasts bound free, globed pale and perfect by the moonlight; and next, smiling, she looses her wraparound skirt, proving underwearless, erecting the dry-throated boy who gazes dumbstruck at her curly secret. "Do me first," she says, and as he kneels to her, I feel the jolt of pleasure triggered by his tongue.

"Wonderful sermon, Reverend," she says, parroting her dad, and I am forced to restrain a laugh, amused not by the incongruity of the compliment in relation to her thoughts, but by the fact of the compliment itself. My sermons are mild and cautionary nothings, annotated with announcements of bake sales and raffles, and do not attempt salvation. For what purpose should I save them? Heaven? That curdled fantasy has long since fled my brain, and God's absence is everywhere . . . although I have sensed a scrap of His divinity floating in the belfry, as flat and black as a shadow, and know that He only waits the proper summons to return transformed into a God suitable to the times. That, you see, is the core principle of the divine, that we must pour It full of sins—as, indeed, I have been filled during the six years of my ministry—and kill It, and then resurrect It in new form, a vessel suitable for the shapes of contemporary wrongdoing.

Purse clasped to her belly, Emily strolls off 'twixt Bess and Robert into the myth of her virginity, and I am confronted by the banker, Miles Elbee, a sapless twig of a sinner gone gray at forty, weathered and wrinkled as a man half-again his age. From his perfunctory shake I have a glistening of leather, a whipcrack, and an exultant scream. He always withdraws his hand so quickly. I wonder if he knows I see his passion for submissiveness and is ashamed. "Fine morning," he says, and with a tailored smile, he joins the menfolk on the walk to discuss the NFL. And here, Marge Trombley extends her white-gloved hand. Auburn hair and a pale face so delicately engraved with thirty years of suffering, it seems as exquisitely wrought as a cameo. Ah, Marge! Your sin is the sweetest fellow to my own. From the pressure of your fingertips I am blessed with the sight of you and me coupling in the choir stall. And something else beneath that sight, a dark knurl of more-than-secret sin (Have I mentioned that locked in every heart is the knotty shape of the last and greatest evil of which we are capable?). I return the pressure, letting it linger a moment too long for propriety, infusing those lovely features with a blush.

"I am hoping to see Jeffrey one Sunday," I say. This initiates a litany between us. Jeffrey is the ne'erest of ne'er-do-wells, given to weekend binges and wife-beating; he has never set foot in St. Mary's, and our exchanges concerning him rarely vary.

"He's been sick," she says. "And he's depressed about his job." A smile breaks the lock of suffering. "I'll try to bring him along next week." Then, leaning close, a whisper. "I must talk to you, Reverend."

I respond that unfortunately I'm off to a church conference for the week—a lie—but that the Saturday evening after my return will be free. If she would care to stop by around sevenish . . .? She would, indeed. Marge, Marge. Is this to be our flowering?

And so it goes, one Episcopal life after another: neatly decked-out shells enfolding a chaos of frustrations.

Once they have all made their way homeward or to lunch or tennis, I sit in the back pew, drinking the last of the Communion wine and staring at the animals in their light-stained, grape-bordered universe. They stare back from the windows, trembling with life. They are alive. I mean this not in the ordinary mystical sense, but in one common to a grander age, the age of Jeremy Calder and his witches, who knew the truth that life is an idea. Every bubbled imperfection in the glass holds a germ of principle, the lead mullions flow with the conception of rivers, and as I watch, the bear lifts his snout from a golden honeycomb and grumbles a prayer for my salvation; he is the holiest of the lot, a gentle monster whose last red meal was so long ago that he has forgotten the call of the blood and now passes the hours in monastic contemplation. The owl, a persnickety old darkness, nods judgmentally; the lamb gambols, beckoning me to sin with flirtatious wags of its bobbed tail. They each have some comment to make on my performance, my life . . . all, that is, except the lion. He has never moved or spoken in these six years, and because he is the most beautiful of them, the noblest, he withholds much commentary that I long to hear. I wonder for what stimulus he is waiting. I've heard that Jeremy Calder often carried out private interrogations of the witches beneath this particular window, and that at times the cries of pain issuing from the church were indistinguishable from cries of womanly pleasure. Could this have silenced my lion? And did Jeremy go probing after Satan, risking the very extent of his manhood in scouring those vessels clean, or like me, was he merely lustful? The intent once mattered, I suppose. But no more. This age suppresses the importance of intent, and what is valued is effect, result, profit.

I swallow the dregs of the wine, and pulp catches between my teeth. I'm pleased, seeing in this an omen, because it's the pulp of life I'm always seeking in the thin wine of existence. The palpable, the chewable. Difficult to minister without some knowledge of those wilds, for we live in a universe of black rules and rudderless stars, and how can one navigate without grounding oneself in the depths of that medium? Thus it is I must indulge my needs from time to time . . . though in truth I need no excuse for indulgence. I'm a hale man in my early forties, my wife is dead, and I have met no suitable replacement, unless good Marge Trombley were to unshackle from her Jeffrey. Sigh. Would that it were so! I gaze at my warped reflection in the bottle glass. Its emptiness is my own. But not for long. A sense of purpose has lately begun stealing over me, less an emotion than a physical condition, yet embodying qualities of both. Perhaps it will come clear at the "church conference."

Two hundred and eight miles from Fallon, where St. Mary's bides in whiteness, lies the town of Corn River, and on its southern outskirts stands an old brick house, home to the beautiful Serena de Miron (née Carla DiLuca), a purveyor of Greek, French, and various Third World nationalities so exotic in character that not even the Bible was sufficiently wise to warn against them. Other girls live in the house, but it is Serena I fancy . . . Serena who knows well the muscular analogues of my spiritual requirements. Black hair, pale unblemished skin, the face of an angel by Degas, and as fine a set of warheads as these eyes have ever seen. All coupled with a gum-chewing, airhead mentality. The perfect tour guide to the pulp of contemporary life. She is waiting for me in a room whose walls show as veins of a cream-colored mineral seaming a bedrock of posters, most depicting depraved-looking men with guitars. "Frankie!" she squeals, coming to her knees and bouncing on the bed. "Where you been?"

"Sales trip," I say, shrugging off my jacket. Franklyn is, indeed, my Christian name, but I have told Serena that I'm a traveler in costume jewelry, and on each visit I present her with some bit of gaud as proof. From my trouser pocket I remove a pair of long rhinestone earrings that twist and twinkle like gemmy worms. Serena snatches them, holds them to her ears, pulling back her hair to let me judge the effect . . . a witchily beautiful effect. Good thing for you, Serena, that old Jeremy has not come in my stead.

Some hours later, lying face to face, still joined, I mention my problematic attraction to Marge Trombley. "Ya like her, huh?" she says.

"Like?" I mull over the quality of my feelings. "Let's say I'm drawn to something in her, something I can't quite fathom."

Serena gives me a chummy internal squeeze. "You're so sensitive, Frankie. I wish you was a younger guy."

This inspires me to prove that age has not entirely drained my vitality, and we do not continue the conversation for another hour.

"I don't know what to tell ya," she says. "What's she alla 'bout?"

I have little more than intuition to draw on as regards Marge's character, but I make a stab at analysis. "Quiet, conservative," I say. "On the surface, at least. Repressed. And that's the thing I want to know in her. Whatever's buried under those years of repression."

"And her husband beats her?"

"Habitually."

"Y'know," Serena says, "sounds to me she ain't sure what she wants. I mean she *is* sure, but she might need convincin'. Like maybe gettin' beat up alla time . . . well, she probably don't enjoy it or nothin'. But she's probably used to bein' forced."

"I don't understand."

"Yeah, you do." Serena squirms, and I respond. She giggles. "Ooh, I like that!"

"What were you going to say?"

" 'Bout what?"

"Marge . . . convincing her."

"See"—a crease mars Serena's brow, and her tone grows earnest, knowing—"she's gonna go right to the edge with ya, and then she's gonna need a push, y'know. To make her fall."

"A push?"

Serena laughs. "Y'gotta be masterful, Frankie. Y'know how to be masterful, don'tcha?"

On cue, I become masterful.

Between bouts with Serena, I wander the brothel. It, too, is a place of worship, one with a more comprehensible god than that scrap of darkness who inhabits St. Mary's, and as such, I find its lessons apt. Standing in the gloomy corridor, listening to cries of pleasure both fraudulent and unfeigned, I remember my wife's cries of pain as the thing that ate her from within gnawed closer and closer to the quick. How I loved her, yet at the same time how I resented her unsightly dying. Sometimes I could scarcely determine whether my urge to put her out of her misery was funded by mercy or by an irrational murderous impulse. Those months of watching her die, of trying to soothe her agony, unhinged me, set me on a canted course from which I have not yet and perhaps never will recover. . . . Does it surprise you that I'm aware of my deviant sensibilities? Perhaps it is surprising; however, I've lived too long within my own cracked shell to be confounded by the eerie slants of light that penetrate and color thought. In any case, to be mad in this age is a form of wisdom, a lens through which one can view its oblique truths and gain knowledge by which to apply what is learned. So, though madder than most, I am also wiser, more capable of action, and the action, or rather the confluence of actions, that occurs to me while standing in the hallway strikes me as being the zenith of my mad wisdom. Why haven't I seen it before? It should have been obvious! Marge and our Saturday evening tryst, the compatible congregation of sin, Serena's advice, the traditions of the church, and on and on. Everything points to the fact that like any good shepherd I shall have to lead my flock by example, steer them onto the path of righteous wickedness, and bring forth the fire of a new god from the embers of the old. By example . . . and by the word that will spring from that example. Yes, yes! Finally a fit topic for a sermon, a fit occasion to commemorate. Smiling, my clouded sense of purpose in focus at last, I fling open the door to Serena's room, startling her. She rolls onto her back, her Naughty Girl nightie riding up over her thighs.

"Geez, Frankie," she says. "You look. . . ." She tips her head to the side, searching apparently for an appropriate term or word. "Different or something."

Could my illumination have worked a physical change? Anything is possible, I suppose. I study my reflection in the mirror backing the door, but see nothing out of the ordinary . . . except in the measure of my self-regard. I realize now that for months I have avoided mirrors, not wanting to view the hapless soul shriveling in my flesh. But that soul is not in evidence. In my mirror image I perceive confidence, a lion's-worth of confidence. And intent. Oh, I am ripe to bursting with intent.

"What you see before you," I say, turning to Serena, "is a man grown suddenly great with conviction."

Serena giggles and pats the mattress beside her. "Well, don't waste it, Frankie. Come on over 'fore it shrinks back to normal."

Saturday night, the last pallid light of an ashen day illuminating the stained-glass windows, and candles burning steadily on the altar, flanking a silver cross of a size suitable for the crucifixion of a small child. Separated from Serena and the Church of Fleshly Delights, my conviction—as Serena playfully intimated—has shrunk. I am nervous, full of doubt. Yet my intent remains firm. Doubt-ridden or not, I will do the deed. And as Marge enters through the front door, I slip the bolt into place, securing us within an unknown country, one whose boundaries we are soon to define. The snick of the bolt makes her jump, but I smile reassuringly. "Burglars," I say. "Or mischievous choirboys." She smiles in return, relaxing.

With a sly wink toward the lion, I lead her back into the rectory, which is attached by a corridor to the choir's dressing room, and I sit her down on the red velvet sofa. Her hair is sewn with glints by the dim track lighting, her lips are redder than the velvet gleaming curves, and in the cleavage of her frock I spot an inch of lace. One button more than usual undone. The final signal, Marge. I will not fail you.

I offer wine; she demurs; I insist. The wine is the same pale red of her hair, and as she sips, I enjoy the conceit that she is tasting her own substance. I sit beside her, not too close, not too far. A seductive distance, yet I disguise a tempter's propinquity with sincere concern, listening to complaints about her Jeffrey.

"He's been gone almost two weeks this time," she says. "And he swore he wouldn't be back."

Thank you, Jeffrey.

"He'll be back," I say, stroking her arm. "Don't worry." Not a flinch from Marge, only a shy glance.

"I know you're right," she says. "But . . ."

"Yes?"

"This will sound awful, Reverend, but. . . ."

"Franklyn," I say. "Please call me Franklyn."

"All right." Wan smile. "Franklyn." She sighs, and a curve of white flesh swells above the lace. "As I was saying, this will sound awful, but I'm not sure I want him back."

I pretend to be in a deep study. "It's not awful in the least," I say. "You've endured too much from him already."

She stares into her wine glass as if seeking an oracle. "I don't know."

"Marge," I begin.

She looks at me, startled.

"Forgive my familiarity," I say, drinking in those delicate features. "It's just I feel close to you, in your confidence."

"No, no. It's all right."

"Marge," I continue. "You've been married how long . . . almost ten years, isn't it?"

A nod.

"To stay and suffer more abuse would be foolhardy."

"I suppose, but it's not so simple a question. I'm afraid I might be leaving him for the wrong reason." This last accompanied by a flush.

"I see." And I do see: Marge is close to an admission. I pretend awkwardness. "I . . . uh." Clear my throat. "May I ask if there's someone else?"

She lowers her head, and this time the nod is almost imperceptible.

"You have strong feelings for this other man?"

"Yes."

"Love is nothing to be ashamed of, Marge. Not in your case, not given the loveless circumstance of your house. You have to seize what joy you can, you have to obey the imperatives of your heart."

I have planned a long drawn-out seduction, but fired by my own words I shift closer, our thighs nearly touching, and lean to her. "Marge," I say. "I know, I know."

She tries to harden her face, but melts. "I can't," she says. "I'm not sure." But her mouth opens to me. I undo a button, and she arches beneath my hands. Inch by inch the frock divides, and my palms glory in the weight of her breasts. I whisper, telling her of my long desire. I slide one strap of her slip off her shoulder, bury my face in softness. Feel her tense.

"No!" she says, pushing my head away. "No, please."

"Don't be afraid," I tell her, and burrow in again.

"No!" She yanks at my hair, beats a fist against my shoulder, and

I realize that we have reached the point that Serena in her wisdom predicted. Now is the proof of conviction, the honing of intent into action. I rip away the last buttons, and Marge screams, tries to claw me. But I beat her hands aside, and drag her from the sofa and into the bedroom.

"Go ahead," I say, panting. "Scream. No one will hear. You're going to get what you came for, witch!"

The venom in my voice astounds me, as does the epithet. It hardly seems that it was I who spoke. But I put it from mind and address her in a gentler fashion.

"It'll be sweet, Marge. You'll see. After tonight there'll be no regrets, no recriminations." All the while, I'm lashing her wrists and legs to the bedposts with four lengths of rope. Odd . . . I don't recall having cut them. Ah, well. In some fugue I must have foreseen the determination underlying her recalcitrance. "Witch," I realize, is a most fitting term. For though I have seen her form by day, humble and gentle, sightly to the moral eye, even then I glimpsed the hidden form that now confronts me: a voluptuous figure that might adorn a Tarot card, with hair and rags blown to cover her nakedness by a wind that none but she can feel. She looks at you—as Marge is looking at me this moment—with terror and anxiety, and you know her name is Woman, frail and sweet, demanding guidance. Yet penetrating that glaze of fear, you make out another eye, blue and calm, regarding you with measured appraisal, and you understand that the name of this interior self is Reason. Oh, she has many names, and none are wholesome, for all are funded by that last interior creature, that fuming golden thing with eyes as blank as suns, who stands in the scorched circle of the Devil's gaze, exposing to him the charms with which she seeks to govern all men, and it is she who is the Great Lie, the embodiment of intoxicating and corrupting principle, and her name, the men speak with awe and longing, unaware of its enervating effects, her name is Love. . . .

I feel a touch of dizziness and pinch the bridge of my nose in an attempt to stem it. The tenor of my thoughts disturbs me, yet I chalk them up to the extreme nature of my actions, the conflict between their necessity and the disciplines instilled in me at the seminary; it would be surprising if I were not somewhat disoriented. I stare down at Marge. Lashed tightly in the remnants of her clothing, heaving up from the bed, she is a pretty sight, and while I undress, I talk to her. . . . No, I make purring, rumbling comments that are less speech than animal promises. Then, kneeling between her legs, I find that despite

her protestations, reduced now to whimpers, the witch is ready for
our consummation.

After I'm done, I sit naked with pen and paper at my writing desk,
and, unmindful of Marge's pleading, begin the creation of my next
day's sermon. I have never felt so capable, so filled with thunderous
verbal potential.

"I won't tell," says Marge. "I won't tell anyone. Just let me go."
In the half-light her breasts gleam pale, inspiring me further. I choose
my text and scribble a brief introduction.

"I swear," says Marge, and breaks into sobs.

Exasperated, I let out a sigh and set down my pen. My duty as
lover must preempt my priestly duty for a while; I must finish Marge's
instruction, bring her wholly into the realm of the senses, unravel that
dark knot in her breast that I have only begun to loosen. "Darling,"
I say as I enter her again. "This, too, shall pass." Though she twists
her head aside, though she affects revulsion, her cry is of pleasure,
not of pain. She cannot fool me. I am expert in these matters.

I alternate bouts of lovemaking and sermon-writing. The two pursuits, I understand, are linked, and I come from each renewed and
eager for more of the other. Marge tries every ploy to deny her feelings, to cozen me into releasing her. For a time she pretends to pretend enjoyment, thinking to tempt me into untying her, not knowing I perceive her true ecstasy, her absolute involvement, her delight
in the bonds. I let her know that I am not persuaded by instructing
her in several of the exotic practices I have picked up at the brothel
in Corn River, disciplines foreign to Marge, yet ones to which she
swiftly adapts, growing ever more silent in contemplation of the new
sensations she experiences. And in that silence, the dark construct of
her secret sin starts to lose conformation, to send out threads through
her flesh and spirit. By first light she is all but its embodiment, and
had I another hour before the service, I would be able to complete
the work I have begun. But both it and she will wait. I check her
bonds, kiss her on the brow, look onto her staring eyes, wide-open
in the study of that internal unraveling. A bit vacant, I think. But
her color is good, she will mend. Yes, the witch will bless my name
for this night of liberation.

Eleven o'clock, and showered, serene in a freshly starched surplice,
I stand behind the griffin's ebony beak, gazing out over the congrega-

tion, listening to thunder, watching the rainy light penetrate the segments of stained glass, spreading a gray gloom over all. My flock seems edgy, no doubt the result of my minute-long consideration of the words I am about to speak. Soon, though, they will be relaxed as never before, freed from the bonds of propriety to enact their sly wishes. I smile, nod, and they glance nervously at one another. It may be that—as do I—they sense some vast imminence. At last, resting my hands on the griffin's head, I begin.

"The first part of my text for today," I say, "is taken from the French poet and playwright, Antonin Artaud."

This causes a general stirring . . . not that Artaud and his cabalistic creed are known in Fallon, but it unsettles them that I should stray from my usual course.

" 'Do evil,' Artaud says. 'Do evil and commit many sins. But do no evil to me.' " I allow no time for a reaction, but launch into the body of the sermon. "This direct instruction might be taken for a misstatement of the Golden Rule, but in truth it implies the essence of the rule, it gives a new reading of that truth appropriate to our time. For we are all evil, are we not? Whatever good resides in us, it is mediated by a quantity of evil, and locked together these two forces intertwine and darken in us, until in the end one and one alone establishes dominion. We may by force of habit effect good works, love a good life, sin only minimally, yet mostly we are not impelled to behave thus by the empowering radiance of good, but rather by the fear of admitting to evil, of facing it and giving it its due. We have been taught that to master evil we must suppress it. And this is wrong. The act of suppression twists us. We become vessels filled with repressed desires and needs that without light grow into gnarled and mutant shapes."

Rustling everywhere. Women whispering together; men sitting expressionless, refusing to confront their discomfort; a child giggling.

"This," I go on, "brings me to the second part of my text, a quote from the magus Aleister Crowley. 'Do what thou wilt be the whole of the law.' "

The rustling increases, but I pay it no heed.

"Crowley was not advising us to rape and murder, to do unnatural deeds. Rather, he was encouraging us to liberate our evil natures, to give vent to sin before it can grow great and malignant. And Artaud: '. . . do no evil to me.' This bespeaks a comprehension that evil thus vented rarely involves a crime with a victim, that it expresses itself in mild forms such as lust. Once expressed, then our good works—when we attempt them—become the products of a true saintly intent and not of fear.''

The word *lust* might have been a needle thrust into the bony rump of every old woman in the church, for they all sit up straight, fully attentive and unanimously grim. My fingers clench the griffin's skull, and I feel a force surging through the black wood. The stained-glass animals twitch in their rectangular confines. The moment is near. I lean forward, becoming folksy, gentling my tone.

"We of St. Mary's are much blessed," I nod, imbuing the gesture with a thespian measure of sagacity. "Much blessed. For our sins, though multiplicitous and diverse, have each a complement among our body. And so we need not venture out into the world and risk humiliation in order to express our desires. We need only do what we have always done, and that is, trust in the fellowship. Here amidst friends and neighbors, we can bare our secrets . . . and not merely bare them, but indulge them with those whose secrets are partner to our own. Here we can share joy and pleasure free from spying eyes and moral judgments, and in so doing find the new meaning of God."

Indignation and anger are creeping into their expressions, but I am not concerned. The truth will set them free.

"I know your sins," I say. "I know them as you believe only you know them. There is no reason for shame in this place. Here you may admit and openly engage those forbidden pastimes of which you have long dreamed. Join me now in an act of liberation, empty yourselves of the vile. Taste and touch and know the flavors and textures of freedom." I pause to let them absorb my meaning, to let them prepare for what will come. "I have chosen this day to introduce you one to the other, sin to compatible sin, desire to desire. This morning we will initiate our adventure in the prurient, and bring God's bud to bloom in an exaltation of joyous camaraderie."

I favor them all with a loving gaze; their agitation and discomfort compels me to cut short my preamble. I will not allow them to suffer more the imprisonment of joy. "Miles Elbee," I say, "meet Cory Eubanks. Submissive meet dominatrix." A gasp from the back row where pretty, plump Cory sits with her husband. "No need for alarm, Cory," I cry. "No need to hide those black leathers and spike heels in the closet any longer, for in Miles you have one who will bleed for you, who will crawl to kiss the braided tip of your whip."

Miles jumps to his feet, sputtering, and the stunned pale faces of the rest are fixed on me.

"Emily Prideau," I say. "Meet Billy Taggart, Joey Grimes, and Ted Dunning. Their dream, like yours, entails a three on one, the Holy Trinity made flesh."

Emily ducks her head into her mother's arm, but the boys smirk and nudge one another.

"Carlton Dedaux," I shout above the growing babble. "Meet little Jimmy Newly. Look into each other's eyes and see the wet imprint of your kindred lusts."

They are all standing, shaking fists, berating me as I continue to make my introductions. My voice falters. Could I have been wrong? It seems so. How can I have misjudged their temper, their readiness for the new?

Miles Elbee strides to the base of the pulpit. "You son of a bitch!" he screeches. "The bishop's going to hear about this! I'll. . . ."

Anger forks through me, and I lean down to him. "Go ahead," I say. "The bishop's underwear is the same style as yours, only his lace trim is a bit more provocative."

Miles glances at his waist to see if anything is showing, then backs away, cursing at me. Other men, Emily's father among them, are being restrained from attack by their fellows, and the women are streaming out the door. Children are laughing, playing tag around the baptismal font. The entire concept of spiritual advancement is in disarray, the revolution I have envisioned is overthrown before it is begun.

They bunch at the front door, looking back at me, and as the last of them exits, hopelessness takes the place of my anger. A rock splinters the window of the old bear, shattering for once and all his search for a honeyed philosophy. Someone calls to me, accusing me of evil as if evil were something I have avoided confronting. They did not hear a single word I spoke.

I step down from the pulpit, walk along the aisle, and slump into a pew beneath the lion, whose expression now seems one of disapproval or—at least—of stern judgment. He is right to think badly of me. Not only have I failed in my intent, I have lost my sinecure. What, I wonder, awaits me? Will I join the homeless, wandering the streets, my possessions in a Hefty bag? No, no, it will be worse than that. There's Marge to consider, after all. I doubt she will be forgiving in the face of my failure to enlist the congregation. An asylum, perhaps. Possibly jail. I think I would prefer the penitential solitude of jail to the gibbering complexities of straitjackets and Thorazine and electroshock.

Outside, the gray light darkens, and the eyes of the lion grow balled and leaden. Thunder, the scent of ozone as lightning cracks the sky with a ripping sound, starting me from my morose reverie, alerting me to a change in the atmosphere, in—it seems—the very fabric of reality. Steam is billowing from the griffin's snout, the walls are trembling, and except for the lion, all the stained-glass animals are pacing in their windows. I jump up, amazed. This is what I expected at the culmination of my sermon, at the conjoining of my flock. How can it be . . . I have failed, have I not? And then comprehension dawns. I see it clearly now. My sermon was not the event essential to provoke this change, or if it was, it was only the spark and not the true burning. And I see, too, that I have not failed. Oh, my flock will publicly disavow what I revealed, will disparage me. After the scandal dies down, however, they will look around at one another, recalling my litany of sins and compatibilities, and slyly at first, then more openly, they will seek each other out for the purposes in which I have instructed them. But what of the burning that must take place before this can come to pass? Suddenly dismayed, I sit back in the pew. Maybe I am seeing things, maybe nothing will happen, maybe the griffin is not writhing, tossing his ebony-feathered head, and maybe. . . . A noise behind the choir stall, a white shape moving in the shadows.

Marge!

Naked, with shreds of rope trailing from her wrists and something shiny in her hand.

On spotting me, she freezes, then starts forward, haltingly at first, but growing more assured with every step. Her eyes are black, no whites showing whatsoever, ovals of griffin-color, and as she descends from the altar to the aisle, she raises high a shining knife.

For an instant I am afraid, and I start to come to my feet, thinking to run to take the weapon from her. But a moment later understanding banishes fear. Of course, of course! Everything is plain to me. As with the birth of every new religion, a sacrifice is necessary. I've been a fool not to anticipate this, and now that my fate is at hand, I rejoice, because I also understand that for me death will be liberation. That it has ever been the one means by which I might elude the gravities of the ordinary. Marge is speaking to me in some pagan tongue, some evil parlance, drooling spittle, and from this evidence and that of her pupilless eyes, I reach a further understanding. I have been hasty in debunking the myth of Jeremy and his victims, shortsighted in assuming that the supernatural would play no part in the infinite congruency of events and moments essential to the creation of divinity.

It's an obvious truth that every fleck and fragment of the past must be represented in this seminal act. Marge's aspect is unshakable evidence of witchy possession, a spirit given purchase by the trauma of rape (perhaps this was the knot within her, no real thing itself, but rather a nest in which an incubus could lodge); and recalling my venomous abuse of her, seeing in new light the particular definition of my madness, it is apparent that Jeremy and I are more closely connected than by tradition alone.

Marge stops beside me, the knife trembling above, and with her sweaty breasts heaving, her deep sin unraveled and leaking forth, never has she seemed more beautiful; an object of pure license, pure chaotic principle.

"Ah . . . ah!" she says, seeking to translate the dictates of her Satanic duty into words I will understand, unaware that my understanding is at last complete.

"Do what you must," I say, fixing my gaze on the lion. Why does he refuse to bless me with his powerful knowledge? Soon it will be too late.

Another incoherent gasp from Marge, a spit-filled sound that seems to me redolent of frustration, of some internal struggle.

"No reason to feel remorse," I say.

Our eyes meet, our darknesses commingle, and I turn away, rapt in contemplation of my release, yet not wanting to witness the downward arc of the instrument of release. Several seconds slip by, and I begin to worry that some human weakness is restraining her.

"Hurry, Marge," I tell her.

"You . . . uh . . ." she says, her hand scrabbling at my shoulder. "You!"

She needs encouragement, needs to know that I welcome this ending, that I comprehend the requirements of divine resolution.

"Marge," I say, "you have never seemed so desirable as now. How much I truly love you."

A shriek breaks from her lips, and I feel the force of her firmed commitment in the instant before the knife sinks home. The pain is sharp, the shock all-absorbing. Yet there is sweetness in the pain, in the strength it dredges up, the profound confidence it rips loose from the recesses of my being. I refuse to fall, I want to savor every instant of my passage, to know everything left to know. The griffin howls, a long keening note, and I feel wetness on my chest. Truth is everywhere, the church is black with God. I am not dying, I realize. In some element of that dark force, I will continue. Like Jeremy, I will go on and on, the shadow of a shadow, the hint of a spectacular possibility. Marge shrieks again, weakness overwhelms me. My heart—though pierced—is glad, my soul at peace. And as I topple sideways on the pew, looking up to the window glowing with supernal light, the stained-glass lion—always my favorite—lifts its head and roars.

NOMANS LAND

JK

I

Four miles due south of the Gay Head Lighthouse on Martha's Vineyard lies Nomans Land, an island measuring one mile wide and a mile and a half in length, rising from sand dunes tufted with rank grasses and beach rose on its eastern shore to a cliff of clay and various other sedimentary materials some thirty feet high that faces west toward the Massachusetts coast. Prior to 1940 the island was the site of several small farms, but during World War II when German submarines began to be sighted along the coastline, the government confiscated the land, removed the inhabitants, and erected large concrete bunkers on the beaches from which military observers scanned the sea by day and night for enemy periscopes and conning towers. Following the war, the island was ruled off-limits to civilians and utilized as a target area for bombers and fighters stationed at Otis Air Force Base, a practice that continues, albeit sporadically, to this very day; on winter nights when the din of the tourist season has passed, it is possible to hear the rocket bursts as far away as the island of Nantucket some twenty-five miles to the east. Yet in spite of this, thousands upon thousands of gulls and terns and a lesser number of old squaw ducks—often seen flying in peppery strings against the sunsets—have chosen the island for their nesting place, and as a result it has been designated a National Wildlife Preserve. It may seem peculiar that a wildlife preserve should be subjected to bombing runs and rocket fire; however, the point has been made—and to many conservationists it is a point well taken—that these intermittent attacks do less harm to the avian populace than would the influx of human beings (no matter how high-minded their intentions) that would occur should the island's restricted military status be voided. And so Nomans Land remains isolate, its silence broken only by wind and surf, the mewing of gulls, the occasional barking of seals at sport on the beaches, and the inconsequential noises of the moles and other rodents that tunnel through its soil. All except the newest bomb craters have been filled in with grass and sand, but walking is a difficult chore because much of the land is dimpled rather like the surface of an enormous golf ball, and it is easy to make a misstep. Scrub pine covers most of the island, hiding all but the tallest ribs of the splintered farm buildings, and the sight of these ruins in conjunction with the lonely cries of the birds, the evidences of war and warlike activity, give the place an air of desolation wholly in concert with its name. And as to that name . . . could there be some profound significance to the running together of the words *no* and *man,* to the lack of an apostrophe implying possession? Or is this merely due to the carelessness of a clerk or a mapmaker? And even if it is such, does the inadvertency of the nomenclature reflect an unconscious knowledge of uncommon process or event? There are no evil rumors associated with the island, no legends, no sailors' lies about strange lights or wild musics issuing from that forlorn shore. But a lack of legend and rumor in these legended waters, where every minor shoal is the subject of a dozen supernatural tales, seems in itself reason for suspicion, for wonderment; and perhaps a more compelling reason yet for suspicion lies in the fact that despite the island's curious past, despite the penchant among New Englanders for collecting and transcribing local histories, not one has come forward to ask the many questions that might well be asked concerning Nomans Land, and no human voice exists to give the answers tongue.

II

On the night of October 16, 198-, during the worst storm of the season, the fishing trawler *Preciosilla,* with its engines dead and wheelhouse afire, was swept through the Muskeget Channel between Martha's Vineyard and Nantucket, then westward in heavy seas toward Nomans Land. Four of the ten-man crew had been lost in the explosion that had ripped apart the engines, and three more had been washed overboard. As the vessel drew near Nomans Land, the survivors caught sight of the island silhouetted in a lightning stroke against churning clouds, and knowing that the *Preciosilla* could not long stay afloat, they committed their souls to God and their bodies to the sea in an attempt to reach solid ground. One of the three, Pedro Arenal, a Portuguese man of New Bedford, was carried by the tidal rip past the island and never seen again. However, the remaining two, Odiberto "Bert" Cisneros, age forty-six, also Portuguese, and the ship's cook, Jack Tyrell, an Irishman just entering his thirtieth year, reached shore within fifty feet of one another and took shelter in the lee of a concrete bunker, where they sat shivering, too cold and shaken to think, stunned by the thunderous concussions, gazing out at the toiling darkness, at detonations of lightning that illuminated waves peaking higher than circus tents and plumed with phosphorescent sprays.

It was Tyrell, a thin black-haired man with a sly cast to his sharp features, who had the urge to move inside the bunker, feeling the cold more intensely than Cisneros, who was the better insulated of the pair, being muscular and bandy-legged, with the beginnings of a potbelly, a seamed, swarthy face, and—at the moment—a terrified grimace punctuated by two gold canines. He gave no sign of hearing Tyrell's shouts, and at last Tyrell came to his feet, staggering with the wind, his hair flying, and took hold of Cisneros under his arms. Cisneros let himself be hauled erect, but when he realized that Tyrell was trying to wrestle him inside the bunker, he tore loose from the Irishman's grasp and went stumbling farther down the slope of the dune. To his eyes the bunker, with its pale concrete bulk and black slit mouth, had the look of an immense jawbone from which the demented howling of the wind was issuing, and he wanted no part of it. A powerful gust buffeted him, driving him backward, his eyes rolling up toward the sky in time to spot a flash of amber radiance and the sweep of the beam from the Gay Head light across the bottoms of the racing clouds. Though he had sailed those waters for twenty years, in his panic he had no recollection of the lighthouse, and the blade of light seemed a portent from hell. He dropped to his knees in the mucky sand and crossed himself, deeper into fear than ever before, shreds of prayers running through his head like tattered distress flags.

Tyrell was tempted to leave him. He had no great love for the Portuguese, none whatsoever for Cisneros, who had twice menaced him with a knife aboard the *Preciosilla*. But their ordeal had welded something of a bond between them, and besides, Cisneros's fear acted to shore Tyrell up. "Damn your ass!" he shouted, fighting through the wind to Cisneros's side. "You stupid piece of shit! Do you want to freeze . . . is that it?" Once again he grappled with Cisneros, hauled him up, and began dragging him toward the bunker.

His brush with prayer had left Cisneros resigned to fate. What did it matter how he died, whether blown into the sea or crushed in the jaws of the bunker? At the last moment, as Tyrell pushed him in over the concrete lip and into the black maw, his fatalistic resolve eroded and he tried to break free; but strength had drained from his limbs and he toppled onto the floor. Tyrell crawled in after him, and they huddled together close to the wall. Lightning flashes strobed the interior of the bunker, revealing pocked walls streaked with whitish bird droppings, matted with cobwebs, and more cobwebs spanned the angles of the corners, billowing and tearing loose in the wind. Cisneros shut his eyes, preferring blindness to flickering glimpses of what seemed to him redolent of dungeons and torture chambers. He began to mutter the Stations of the Cross, repeating those consoling words until they had insulated him against the fierce battering of the storm, and before long, shrinking like a child from a confrontation with his fears, he sank into a deep sleep.

Tyrell, too, was afraid, but his fear derived not from the storm or the island, but from the past few hours aboard the *Preciosilla*. He stared into the darkness, seeing there the faces of the dead, the burning wheelhouse pitching like a great mad window inset into the darkness, with the blackened, shriveling figure of the captain erect amid the flames, still clutching the wheel, and the mate, his eyes slits of reflected fire, throwing up his arms like a benighted Christian to welcome the huge talon of ebony water that had plucked him up and borne him down to hell. . . . Tyrell shook his head, trying to clear it of those nightmarish images. He peeled away his slicker and rubbed at a cramp in his thigh. A shudder passed through his chest and limbs, seeming to liberate all the dammed-up weakness inside him, and he leaned back, resting his head against the wall, feeling distant from the storm, from all that had gone before.

What a bloody mess! he thought.

Still and all, he'd been in worse spots, he had. He was a survivor, and he had survivor's luck. Take the time he, Joe McIlrane, and Pepper Swayze had been trapped by the Brits at Pepper's house, with only one rifle and a hail of bullets shattering vases and pictures on the wall. And then prison. God, hadn't that been a stroke of fortune, to be stuck in the same cell as the best damn breakout artist in the IRA? And that same luck had been at work for him in fleeing Ireland, in making it to the States and the sweet life, with a nice girl and a clean bed and plenty of time for the muckle part and having a few beers in the evening. Of course, sooner or later he was bound to take up the struggle again. He couldn't be letting others have all the glory of driving the goddamn Brits back to their gloomy little bloat of a kingdom. . . . A violent burst of lightning split open the black moil of the storm, burning afterimages of the bunker walls on Tyrell's eyes, and he let out a squawk.

"Jesus!" he said to the sky. "Are you wanting to kill me?"

Thunder grumbled, the sea boomed.

"Well, fuck you, then."

He tried to force his thoughts back to Ireland, but found that his memories—that was how he related to the lies he'd told so often, as fond, brave memories, inhabiting them with more frequency than he did his actual past—he found that they had ceased to be a comfort. He wondered how much longer the storm would last. Probably no less than a day. Afterward he'd build a fire on the north shore, big enough so they'd notice the smoke at Gay Head. It was for certain *he'd* have to do whatever was necessary, because Cisneros wasn't going to be any help. The bastard had been all nails and sharp edges with a deck beneath him, but just tip him over, give him a shake, and he wasn't worth spit. Well, old Bert was a fortunate soul this night, for he had as companion the Scourge of Belfast, one Jack Tyrell, who never yet had been known to let a brother-in-arms fall untended by the way.

"Easy there, old son," he said, patting Cisneros's shoulder. "I'm ever with you, don't you know?"

Bert Cisneros moaned, the world cracked and dazzled, and Jack Tyrell, who once had laughed in the face of the firing squad of dreams, laughed now, believing there was no terror in the entire universe that could withstand the arsenal of his imagination.

III

Cisneros did not so much sleep as fall down the staircase of his forty-six years, tumbling slowly head over heels, bumping and rolling across the landings, taking long enough at each to register its consequential evils. The man he'd knifed when they'd put into Nantucket during a nor'easter; the friends he'd cheated; the women he'd beaten. He saw his wife, her face purpled and lumped with bruises, tearstained, clutching the little gold cross that hung from her neck, and for the first time he felt shame. His was a foul dark slant of a life, an inch of time fractioned by violent stupidities, energized by an ego convinced—despite all the evidence against—of its mental superiority, and looking at it in this wan light, he had a sense of relief on passing the final landing and plummeting back to where he had begun, lying curled

like a dark pearl in the mouth of a giant oyster, not asleep, but som-
nolent. He could see the whole island, see it from alternating perspectives and through a lens of perception that transformed each sight into
a strange jeweled design upon a black ground: birds with ruby eyes
tucked in among the dune grass, which showed as waving silvery cilia,
and ghostly pale clouds eddying above, and the shattered timbers of
an old ruin edged with an unholy shimmering of green fire amid the
winded pines, and jade blue waves marbled with an iridescent circuitry
of foam that broke over a cliff to the west, and the wind a whirling
gray-green fog. He wondered how he could be lying in the bunker
and yet appear to be hovering above different quarters of the island,
and then he noticed the thousands of golden wires extending from
his body, each connected to some point on the island. It was through
these wires, he realized, that his senses were being channeled, allowing him to overlook the place, to inspect every detail. He heard a voice
. . . no, two voices. One was muffled, agitated, calling him back to
the darkness of life, and he resisted it, listening instead to the second
voice, which was soft—more a musical sonority than actual speech—
and transmitted a feeling of tranquillity and power similar to that he'd
experienced as a child when kneeling in church: a feeling he associated
with God. He didn't believe that the god speaking to him was the
god of his childhood, but he was gratified that his prayers had reached
someone's ears, and since to his mind one god was much like another,
he had no moral problem with the transference of faith. And when
his thoughts began to change, becoming oddly angular and literate,
full of grim resolve, when he began to think of himself not as Bert
Cisneros but as Quentin Norcross, to see himself as a tall pale man
with hawkish features and deep-set eyes shaded by tufted eyebrows,
dressed in his Sunday suit of black broadcloth, he did not question
this, knowing that God's ways were not his to understand, and surrendered to those thoughts . . .
      . . . and found himself walking in a high blue day with mackerel
clouds far out to sea, planting each step firmly, squarely, as if intending to leave a clear track. When he reached the edge of the western
cliff, he took a stand in the knee-deep grass, leaned forward, and peered
down at the cliff face. With its fissured gray surface, it had the look
of an ancient decaying forehead rising from the sea, grooved by harrowing thoughts. The cauldron of waves at its base seemed to pull
at him, to lodge a knot of their chill tonnage in his stomach, and he
straightened, fixed his eyes on the sunstruck sea, on cobalt swells flowing away to the horizon. He thought it peculiar that he had no pain.

It had been the pain gnawing at his intestines that had brought him to this point, and now, as if his decision had proved a cure, he felt calm, translucent, free of affliction. If it had been only that, only pain, he would have seen it to the end; but he could no longer stomach the sight of his illness etching new lines on Martha's face, disfiguring her as hideously as the sea had disfigured the cliff. This was the best way, the moral way. She would never believe him a suicide; she would assume that he had been walking by the cliff, suffered a spasm, and lost his footing. She'd have the money from the land, and she was still pretty enough to find a new husband, a new father for the children. Blessedly they were too young to feel the true sting of grief. Oh, they would weep and think of him in heaven. But time would heal those wounds, and all that he could do for them now was to hasten their healing by dying swiftly. And that would not be as difficult as he'd thought. He was dead already, killed by the force of his commitment. Standing there, he felt walled off from the past, from life, and he thought he could feel the entire island at his back. The cove on the eastern shore where urchins clung to the rocks of a tide pool; the beachvine fettering the north slope, its complex shadows trembling in the breeze; a vole peeking from its tunnel, its black eyes starred like Indian sapphires; the white spiders—unique to the island—that annoyed him with their incessant biting, but wove webs of unsurpassed intricacy among the pines; the terns wheeling and wheeling above the deep. He felt them all summed up in a unity of tension, as if they were a power that stood beside him, joining him in what must be done. He was not a religious man. His pragmatic nature had not allowed him to accept the existence of a hereafter, and he could not accept that possibility now. However, he believed that if there was a god it would be—like the island—an isolate thing capable of absorbing the lesser quantities that came within its sphere, assimilating winds that had touched the tops of Balinese temples and tides that swept past the shores of Tenerife. In a sense the island *had* been his god, the object of his devotion, his labors and hopes, and he felt closer to it now than ever before. He loved the old place, and perhaps that, not some mystical abstraction, was the definition of a god: something labored over and nourished, a thing that through long process of devotion became indistinguishable from its devotee. It seemed his thoughts were being orchestrated by the crashing of the waves and the screams of the gulls into a kind of music, a flight of logic and poetry, and he realized then that he had stepped forward, that he was falling. He had an instant of fear, but the shock of impact, the stinging cold of the water, numbed his fear, and he went pinwheeling down in blue-green light, icy light, icy dark, slowly, slowly, into a dream of a storm, into a secret place where others shared the dream, and no man lived, and truth was form, and form was chaos, and chaos was ordered anew.

IV

Morning, and the storm held over Nomans Land. Slate-gray waves piled in onto the beach, eroding the shore; the clouds blackened and lowered, and the wind flattened the dune grass, keening across the island, driving slants of rain into the mouth of the bunker, stinging Tyrell awake. All his muscles ached, and there was grit in his mouth. He groaned, rubbed a cramp from his thigh, scratched an inflamed spot on his wrist, and noticed Cisneros still curled up asleep, his neck and head turtled beneath his slicker, several cobwebs spanning between his legs and the wall. Tyrell hawked, spat, and said, "Hey, Bert! Rise and shine, you filthy spic!"

Cisneros didn't move.

Tyrell reached out, gave his shoulder a nudge, and Cisneros mumbled, but remained asleep.

"Worthless bastard," said Tyrell. "I'm better off without you, anyway. Plucking at your damned rosary and complaining to the saints like an old woman! To hell with you!"

He sucked at the scummy coating on his teeth, glancing around at the bunker. Cobwebs everywhere fettering the pale yellow stone, with dozens of white spiders creeping along the skeins, some suspended like tiny stars on single threads. He felt itchy movement on his calf, let out a squawk, and crushed a spider that had climbed up under his jeans. He staggered to his feet, his flesh crawling, and began stamping on spiders that tried to scuttle away into the dark corners. When he was certain that the floor was clear, he stood shivering, hugging himself against the cold and keeping an eye cocked for any spider that might lower from the ceiling.

"Cisneros," he said shakily. "Wake up."

The sleeping man appeared to shudder.

"You want these dancey little fuckers traipsing all over you?" he said, cheered by the sound of his voice. "Fine then, Bert. That's just fine with me, old son. For myself, I've fucking had it. My stomach's empty as a country church on Tuesday midnight, and I'm going to find me an oyster or a dead bird or some damn thing to fill it." He climbed half-out of the bunker mouth, sat perched on the lip, turning up the collar of his slicker. "Can I bring back something for you, Bert? No? Well, maybe you'll feel differently after your nap. I'll be checking in on you. Sleep tight, now."

He swung his legs over the lip, sank to his ankles in the sand, then slogged up the face of the dune, stumbling, crawling on all fours to the crest. He got to his feet again, struck full by the wind and the slashing rain, and stared out across a broken ground: tufts of pale green grass sprouting from bowl-shaped depressions, some of them twenty feet wide, and beyond, where the land flattened out, stands of Japanese pine through which he could make out a fresh crater about a hundred feet off. Rising above the pines, near the center of the island, were spears of dark wood, obviously ruins. He started toward them, and something big and dirty white in color flew up from the grass, screeching, its wings flurrying at him, black beak punching the air in front of his face; he shrieked, threw up his arms, swung his fists, fell and went rolling down the dune.

He came to his knees at the bottom of the dune and looked around for the bird. A tern, it had been . . . he was pretty sure. It was nowhere in sight. He must, he realized, have come too near its nest, and he wondered if there were any eggs. Last resort, he thought. Last fucking resort. For one thing, raw eggs were low on his list, and for another, he wasn't eager to tangle with the tern again. He stood, brushed clots of wet sand from his jeans, and set off for the ruins, picking his way among the overgrown craters. The air in the pines was shaded to a greenish gloom, with raindrops beaded like translucent pearls on the tips of the needles; the ground was less broken here, but cobwebs were everywhere—the webs of white spiders like those that had infested the bunker. He tore them away, clearing a path, and after a few minutes' walk emerged from sparse cover into a large clearing centered by the ruins. From the spacing of the standing timbers, the shingles lying amid the other wreckage, he decided that they must have been part of a barn. And that mass of shattered boards to the right, smashed flat as if by a gigantic fist, that had likely been the main house. He walked over to the ruins, prodded the wreckage with his toe. Glistening dark planks with white brocades of mold, weeds poking up between their overlaps; shredded pieces of tin. He'd been hoping he might find an old store of canned food, but it was apparent there was nothing left that would do him any good.

The clouds frayed overhead, rips of ashen sky showing through for an instant, the rain diminishing; but then they closed in again, lowering thick slabs of blackish gray like fleshy dead leaves matted together, and the wind gusted in a mournful rush, bending the pines all to one side, then letting them snap back to upright, like a line of tattered green dancers. Tyrell turned, unsure of what course to follow, wondering if he could knock off one of the birds with a stone, and could have sworn he saw someone standing at the edge of the clearing. Someone slender, wearing a hooded black slicker. His heart stuttered, he took a backward step. Then he understood that what he must have seen had been no more than a roughly human shape formed by an artful combination of shadows and the actions of the wind and the textures of discolored needles in a niche between two of the pines. However, a moment later he heard movement, and this time he caught a glimpse of a figure slipping behind a pine trunk.

"Is that you, Bert!" he called anxiously, and when there was no response, he called again. "Who's there?"

The rain picked up, spattering off the splintered planks at his feet, blurring his view of the pines, seeming to measure the passage of seconds with the oscillating hiss of drops seething in the pine boughs.

"Hey!" Tyrell shouted. "Hey, who the hell are you?"

Again there was no response, and, unnerved, imagining the presence of a madman or worse, he was about to head back to the bunker when the figure moved out into the clearing and came toward him with a faltering step. A woman. Strands of whitish blond hair plastered to her forehead. In her late twenties, or maybe a bit younger. She had Nordic features, glacial blue eyes, a strong chin and mouth—a face that, while not beautiful, had a kind of imposing sensuality. She stopped a couple of feet away, fixing him with a look that seemed both hopeful and cautious, and made an incompleted gesture with her hand that caused him to think she had wanted to touch him. "You're from the boat," she said.

"How do you know that?" asked Tyrell, taken aback.

"I saw it burning last night." She pushed some stray blond hairs back beneath the hood of the slicker; a raindrop slid down her cheek to her chin. "I tried to get down to the beach, but the storm was too fierce. I lost my way. This morning I went to the bunker. I knew if anyone had survived, they'd take shelter there." She wiped rain from her face with the back of her hand. "Your friend's still asleep."

"Is he, now? Well, he had a hard night." Tyrell blinked at a drop that had trickled into the corner of his right eye. "My name's Jack Tyrell."

"Astrid." She pronounced the name tentatively, as if hesitant about identifying herself.

Entrusted with her name, he felt suddenly assured, masterful and in control, solicitous of the weaker sex.

"And just what are you doing here, Astrid?" he asked in an expansive tone.

"I was . . . studying. The spiders . . . the white ones. You must have seen them. I'm an entomologist."

"Bugs, is it?"

"Yes, I . . . I was supposed to be picked up, but the storm . . . the boat couldn't get out. My friends . . . they'll be here once it lets up."

Tyrell could understand her temerity—a woman alone in this god-forsaken place; but he sensed that her hesitancy was the product of something more than a simple fear of assault, that she was in the grip of some profound uncertainty.

"Maybe," he suggested, "we should go back to the bunker. Get out of the rain."

"No," she said, glancing behind her, to the side, then fixing Tyrell with a wide-eyed stare. "No, I've got a place. It's . . . closer. And there's food if you're hungry."

"God, yes! I'd be eternally grateful for anything you can spare." He flashed her his most winning smile, but it didn't brighten her; she kept darting glances in all directions as if to reassure herself that everything was as usual. He noticed the swell of her breasts beneath the slicker, the flare of her hips, and felt a pang of desire that—with a dose of Catholic guilt, chiding himself for such lustful thoughts—he put from mind. Besides, he told himself, her friends would be coming. Now if *she* wanted to get friendly . . . well, that was another story.

"There's no reason to be frightened," he said. "I won't harm you. Now Bert . . . that's my mate. He's a different matter. Beats his wife, he does. And carries a knife." He laughed. "And in spite of that, in spite of being ignorant as sin, the sod thinks he's a bloody genius. Yeah, you best watch yourself with him about. He's a menace even to himself. But I'll keep him in line, never you worry."

Her expression flowed between confusion and astonishment, and then those emotions resolved into a mournful laugh. "Oh, I'm not worried," she said. "I know there's nothing to fear."

V

Cisneros slept on, slipping from dream to dream, dreams that would have amazed him with their bizarre materials under any other circumstance, but which he had come to recognize as part of an intricate and consequential process that was most natural in its incidence, the underpinnings of creation itself. All life, he understood, was a dream. This was something his mother had told him when he was a child, and he had accepted it as a child's truth, the idea that one's days were but a fleeting image upon the mirrored pool of God's imagination; he doubted that his mother had seen it as other than a pleasant fairy tale. Now he realized that it was the ultimate truth. Life and dreams were, indeed, one and the same, and he had been fortunate enough by virtue of fatigue and terror to dive deeply enough beneath the surface of sleep so as to reach the source of dreams, the place from which life derived its impulse and meaning.

Millions upon millions of lives, of dreams, flowed to him along the golden skeins that held him fast, but with a connoisseur's selectivity he chose to inhabit only those who had been involved in some way with the island: Indians, farmers, soldiers, civilian observers, and those who, like him, had come there by chance. He dreamed that he was a boy playing atop the cliff, dropping stones into the boil of water at its base, lying on his back with the grasses tickling his nose, watching clouds so big and white and fat, they might have been famous souls. Then a young woman came with a man from Gay Head to take him as her first lover—he lingered in that dream, deriving prurient delight from her tremulousness, her pain and pleasure. Then a mad submarine commander who had been stranded by his crew and thought his craft was gilded with baroque ornamentation like something out of Jules Verne, that it was armed with crystalline torpedoes containing drugs and music, and believed that he had sailed in secret waters wherein he and his crew visited lost continents and sported with sea-green women and were borne to ecstasies of sensibility by the verses of rhapsodes with beards of kelp and black pearls beneath their tongues.

These dreams were more complicated than the others in aspect and particularly in their use in playing the game of the world. Compared to the rest, they were like rooks and bishops in relation to pawns . . . for an instant he didn't understand where he had gotten that image. He had never played chess, had no familiarity with the pieces or the moves. But then he realized that, informed by the dreams, he was becoming a new man. All the evil compulsions of his former life were falling away like an old skin; his petty lusts and avarice, all the intemperate qualities of his nature, were gradually being subsumed by a contemplative, sensitive character whose parameters were dic-

tated by the contagious sweetness of more civilized souls, and he began
to see that there was purpose to this change, that not by accident had
he been led to Nomans Land. He was to provide a new turn in the
affairs of God, to implement a new conceit. This knowledge dispelled
the remnants of his fear, and he gave himself over utterly to the usages
of the dreams, eager now to learn not only what deeds he must perform, but at whose agency he was to perform them. He felt that he
was dwindling, growing insubstantial, becoming merely another
dream, and rather than allowing this to unman him, he experienced
an intoxicating joy in the act of surrender, in the sense of unity that
pervaded him, in the understanding that despite all his human frailty
and faults, his sense of destiny and special purpose was soon to be
fulfilled, his sins had been forgiven, and he had been chosen to know
the lineaments of his God.

VI

Set back from the ruins of the old farm, half-hidden in the grayish
green shade of the pines, was a small shack with a tin roof . . . probably a toolshed that somehow had survived the years of rockets and
foul weather. Its weathered boards were black with dampness, and
the roof was half rust, but Astrid had done a good job in making a
home of the place. A hot plate—battery-operated, with two burners—
and a hurricane lamp were set on a rickety table, and beside them lay
a litter of scientific equipment: microscope, test tubes, and so forth.
The floor was covered with a carpet of dry grasses, and a supply of
canned food was stacked along one wall; the gaps in the boards had
been sealed with mud, and a sleeping bag was spread in the corner,
with a couple of blankets folded atop it. After a few minutes, with
the lamp giving off an unsteady orange glow and the hot plate heating
the little space, warming cans of stew, the shack took on a cheery air;
the sounds of the wind and rain seemed unimportant and faraway.
Only the cobwebs spanning the rafters struck a contrary note, and
when Tyrell, thinking they might be too high for Astrid to reach, asked
if she wanted him to beat them down, she said in a dispirited voice
that there wasn't any point.

"They'll just come back by morning." She handed him a scorched
can of stew, cautioning him to grip it with a rag because it was hot.
"They're all over . . . millions of them."

"Yeah, some of 'em were busy making a nest out of ol' Bert."
He sat down with his back to the wall, cradling the stew. Watched

her sit opposite him. She had taken off the slicker, and proved to be wearing jeans and a heavy white wool sweater. A bit on the skinny side, he thought; but not bad. She caught him staring at her, and he tapped his spoon on the can. "This is good."

She said nothing, continuing to stare, tension in her face.

"Is anything wrong?" he asked.

She gave a start as if her mind had been elsewhere, shrugged and said, "No."

"Must be something," he said. "You look like a little noise would put you through the roof."

She laughed nervously. "It must be the storm."

"Sure, now," he said in an arch tone. "That must be it."

She ducked her eyes, stirred her stew.

"Aren't you hungry?" he asked, and had another bite.

"Not very." She glanced up sharply, appeared about to say something else, but kept silent.

He spooned in more stew, chewed. "Tell me about yourself. Where are you from?"

"Woods Hole," she said listlessly.

"Never been there. I'm from New Bedford myself. And before that I was living in Belfast."

He had expected her to make some response, but she just kept on picking at the stew.

"I had to get out of there," he said. "Trouble with the Brits, y'know."

Silence.

"I was with the IRA," he added weakly, his mood hovering between anger at her disinterest and concern that she might not believe him. He decided on hostility. "Am I boring you?"

"In a way," she said. "In other ways . . . no."

"Oh, is that right?" He set down the can. "Then perhaps you should enlighten me as to how it is I'm boring you so I can avoid it in the future."

"It's not important," she said.

"Maybe not," he said. "But I've got a notion you're thinking badly of me."

"What if I am?"

"I'd prefer you didn't, that's all. Is it you're swallowing all the bloody Brit propaganda about the IRA? Because if that's it. . . ."

"Stop," she said. "Just stop."

"Because if that's it," he went on, "I'm here to tell you it's nothing but a heap of lies."

"I don't want to hear it!" Her voice shrilled. "Everything's enough of a lie as it is without you adding to it!"

"Listen to me, now!"

"No," she said. "You listen! You were born in Belfast, but you never had anything to do with the IRA. Three years ago you emigrated to work at your cousin's restaurant in New Bedford, and you've done nothing more notable since than get a local girl pregnant."

For a moment he sat stunned, unable to voice a denial. "How," he said finally, "how could you know that? I've never seen you before."

Her chin was trembling. "I've a gift," she said, and gave a despairing laugh.

"You mean you're psychic . . . something like that?"

She nodded.

He caught her wrist, angry, afraid that she knew all his secrets; but she wrenched free and stared at the place where he had held her as if expecting to see a bruise. She looked up at him, and he thought he detected a new fervor in her eyes; he took it for disgust with his lies, and wanted—for a reason he couldn't quite fathom—to repair the damage.

"I'm sorry," he said, deciding to confess everything, to explain that self-deception had sustained him against the guilt he felt on fleeing Belfast. "You see, I was. . . . My uncle was in the IRA. I never felt right that I didn't follow him. The family . . . he was all they ever talked about. My bloody Uncle Donald. Famous and in jail. But I couldn't take after Donald. I was afraid . . . that was part of it. But mostly I just never understood how it was you lifted a gun and killed a man. I mean, God, I hated the Brits. But I never could understand how it was you killed. You know what I'm telling you?"

She said nothing, but he could feel the pressure of her cold blue eyes.

"Are you listening to me?" he said. "Goddamn it, I'm talking to you. Are you listening?"

"I am."

"I'm a coward," he said. "I'm not ashamed of it, really. I was worried what other people might think of me. Donald was so goddamn famous! I didn't want to suffer by comparison, and that's why I've lied. But I'm quite satisfied being a coward. There's nothing wrong with it. If there were more of us cowards, maybe the world would be a better place." He held her eyes, trying to read her opinion.

"We're all of us frail." She said this with such wistfulness, he had the idea that she was not likely to judge him, that nothing he had done for bad or good was of any consequence to her. And that made him uncomfortable. Without the armor of lies, the motivation and structures of guilt to direct his conversation, he could think of nothing to say. He picked at a shred of beef with his fork.

"Do you want some more?" she asked.

"Not just yet."

Rain hissed against the shack, a gust of wind shuddered the boards, and thunder grumbled in the distance. "I should see about Bert," he said glumly. "He'll be hungry, too."

Astrid put a hand on his arm. "Stay awhile longer," she said. "Just a little while. I've been here alone for so long."

"How long have you been here?"

"Seems like years," she said distractedly.

Tyrell leaned back against the wall; despite his anxiety over having been caught in a lie, the warmth in his belly was making him feel relaxed and garrulous. "I suppose ol' Bert can wait for a bit." He gestured at the cobwebbed ceiling. "Why don't you tell me about our tiny friends here?"

Her face froze.

"You said you were studying them, didn't you?"

"That's right," she said, a catch in her voice.

"So . . . what's their story?"

She said something he couldn't hear.

"What's that?"

"They're poisonous," she said.

"Poisonous?" He sat up straight, feeling the inflamed spots on his arms and legs. "Shit, I must have half a dozen bites! What should I do?"

"Don't worry," she said. "The poison acts quickly. There'll be some hallucinations, probably. But if you've been bitten and you're still alive, then you're immune." She laughed palely. "Like me."

He remembered Cisneros. "I've got to get Bert! They were all over him. I . . ." Something in her face stopped him, and a chill point materialized between his shoulder blades, expanded and fanned out across his back. "You were down at the bunker. You said he was sleeping."

"You'd been through so much," she said. "I didn't want to

. . . I don't know. Maybe I should have told you. I was confused. I've been here so long with just the birds and spiders. . . ." Her chin trembled, and her eyes glistened.

"What happened to him?"

"Your friend wasn't immune."

"What are you saying . . . he's dead?"

"Yes."

"Jesus." Tyrell glanced up to the ceiling, to the star-shaped white spiders crawling along their webs. He remembered talking to Cisneros that morning, nudging him, and the man already half a corpse. Filled with loathing, he jumped to his feet, grabbed a stick from the tabletop, and began swatting at the webs.

"Don't . . . please!" Astrid caught him from behind, got a hand on the stick, and wrestled for control of it. She looked terrified, wide-eyed, a nerve twitching in her cheek, and more than her struggles, it was the sight of her face that made him quit.

"What's the matter?" He pushed her away, swung the stick at the webs. "You like the little bastards, is that it?"

"No, it's not that. It's. . . ."

He took her by the shoulders, gave her a shake. "Will you do me a favor? Tell me what it is with you? One second you act like I'm the last man in the world and you've a great inner need for my company. The next it's like you've heard the beating of leathery wings and the howling of wolves." He shook her again. "There's something not right here. I want you to tell me what's going on."

"Nothing," she said. "Nothing."

"Damn it!" He slapped her. "Tell me!"

"Nothing! Nothing!"

He slapped her a second time.

"It's the truth!" She began half to laugh, half to cry, building toward hysteria. "Absolutely nothing! I swear it!"

Ashamed of himself, he helped her to sit and put his arm around her, comforting her with muttered assurances. Maybe it was loneliness that had gotten to her . . . that and the morbid nature of her studies. She'd probably been stranded here a week or so, and knowing what he did now, he doubted he'd be able to take more than a week on Nomans Land without showing a few cracks. She sighed, collapsed against him, nestling beneath his arm, and he was astonished at how settled and solid that little show of trust made him feel. He couldn't recall having felt this way for a very long time—perhaps he never had—and he wondered if it was the fact that he'd been forced into honesty, into confession, that had cleared away the rubble and granted him such an unimpeded view of himself and the world. It seemed that in giving up his defenses, his lies, he had also given up guilt and fear; and now, sitting here with his arm around a strange woman in a strange place, as vulnerable as he had ever been to the assaults of chance, he felt capable of making real choices, ones determined by logic and the heart's desire, and not reactions to something dread, something he wished to forget. His fear, too, had fled, and he could see that fear for him had not been specific, not merely concern for his own life in the political moil of sad Belfast; he had been frightened of everything, of every choice and possibility. And he realized that not only had his fear been based upon falsity, but that everything he had loved as well—women, country, and all—had been emblems of that fear, objects upon which he could pin the flag of his lies and the affectation of morality. Staring at the grain of the weathered boards, as intricate and sharp as printed circuitry, he thought he could see the path ahead. How he would give up his illusory notions of heroism. Find a mild, strong life. Become an ordinary hero. Sacrificing for family, for friends. That was the best you could do. The world was too strong a spell for any single man or idea to break. No matter how passionate your outcry, how forceful your blood and intent, it went on and on in its wicked, convulsed web, spinning nightmares and tragedies. That was the lesson to be learned of Belfast, of all the wild boys and their warring heat. Surrender. Look within yourself for worlds to conquer and principles to overthrow.

He noticed that Astrid's breathing had grown deep and regular, and thinking she was asleep, he started to lower her to a prone position, intending to cover her with a blanket and then rub out the cramp that was developing in his arm. Her eyelids fluttered open, and she tightened her grip around his waist.

"Don't go," she whispered.

"You're asleep," he said.

"No, I'm not . . . I'm just resting."

"Well"—he chuckled—"maybe you better do your resting in the sleeping bag."

"All right."

She got to her feet sluggishly, went to the sleeping bag, and then, her eyes downcast, kicked off her shoes and skinned out of her jeans. That caught him by surprise. He watched her work the jeans past her hips, step out of them with the delicate awkward poise of a crane. Her legs were long and lovely, pale, pale white, and he could see the honey-colored thatch of her pubic hair through the opaque crotch of her panties. His mouth was dry. He looked away, looked back as, instead of getting inside the sleeping bag, she lay down atop it, covering herself with a blanket. Her hips bridged up beneath the blanket, her hands pushed at her thighs, and he knew she was removing her panties. She turned onto her side, facing him. In the shadowy corner her eyes were large and full of lights.

"Come be with me," she said.

The storm slammed a wall of wind against the shack, rain drummed on the roof, and although Tyrell felt in the grasp of a curious morality, put off by Astrid's invitation, because they were strangers and this should not be happening, the fury of the storm moved him to stand. He went over to the table, extinguished the hurricane lamp. The cherry red concentric circles of the hot plate's heating coils floated on the darkness like bizarre halos. He stripped off his clothing and, shivering, squirmed in beneath the blanket, turning to her as he did. She had pushed her sweater up around her neck, and her breasts rolled and flattened against his chest, warming him. In the dim effusion of light from the hot plate her features were rapt, her eyes half-lidded. He wanted to ask her a question, to understand why this was happening, to make certain that it was nothing low, nothing small, but rather something clean and strong, something to suit the tenor of his cleansed sensibilities; but as she pressed close to him, he knew that it was good. He thought he could feel the whiteness of her limbs staining him, and when he sank into her, he felt the movement as a sweet gravity in his belly, the kind of sensation that comes when you take a tight curve in a fast car and settle back into the straightaway with the whole world pushing you deep into the plush tension of the machine.

"It's been so long," she whispered, holding him immobile, her hands locked around his back. "So long."

He wasn't sure of exactly what she meant, but it seemed true for him as well, it seemed forever since he had felt this perfect immersion, and he hooked his fingers into the plump meat of her hips, grinding her against him, easing deeper, dredging up a soft cry from her throat, and, without understanding anything at all, said, "I know, I know."

Tyrell waked to find the storm unabated. Pine branches scraped the outside of the walls, and the wind was a constant mournful pour off the sea. Dim reddish light fanned up from the hot plate, seeming to diffuse into a granular dust near the ceiling, like powdered rust on black enamel. He was disoriented by the oscillating pitch of the wind, the incessant seething of the rain, and to ground himself in waking he turned to Astrid, letting his left arm fall across her waist. She didn't stir. He peered at her, his eyes adjusting to the darkness, and when he made out her face, his heart was stalled by what he saw. Empty sockets; desiccated strings of tendon cabled across the bare cheekbone; the teeth gapped and the jawbone visible between tatters of yellow skin; hanks of pale hair attached to a parchment scalp. The stink of the grave cloyed in his nostrils, and he could feel her clamminess beneath his arm. He let out a shriek, rolled off the sleeping bag and onto the dry grasses covering the floorboards, and crouched there, panting, resisting the impulse to give in to fear, trying to persuade himself that he hadn't really seen it.

"Astrid?" he said.

Not a sound.

He fumbled for his jeans, struggled into them. Called her name louder. Nothing. His skin pebbled with gooseflesh. He pulled on his sweater, slipped his feet into wet shoes.

"Astrid!" he said. "Wake up!"

He wanted to kneel beside her, to take a closer look and make sure of what he'd seen, but he couldn't work up the courage. He backed away. The corner of the table jabbed his thigh; the hurricane lamp swayed and nearly toppled. He caught it, fumbled on the table for a match. His hands were shaking so badly that he wasted three matches trying to light the lamp, and when the light grew steady, it took all his willpower to turn toward the sleeping bag. He shrieked again and staggered against the door, unable to catch his breath, transfixed by the sight of that horrid death's-head poking from beneath the blanket, sightless eyes focused on a white spider dangling on a single thread just above the face. Then the strand snapped. The spider dropped into one of the empty eye sockets, and for the briefest of instants the eye appeared to twinkle.

Tyrell's control broke. Screaming, he clawed the door open and ran full tilt through the pines, wet branches whipping his face and chest. He burst out into the clearing, stopped beside the wreckage of the main house. Rain slanted hard into his face, soaked the wool of his sweater. He wiped his eyes, started toward the beach, the bunkers, then pulled up, remembering that Cisneros was dead, not knowing in which direction safety lay. The winded pines bent their dark green tips, lightning made a vivid white crack in the massy leaden clouds of the eastern sky, and from the beach came the cannonading of the surf. Suddenly terrified that Astrid had followed him, he wheeled about. Someone was coming toward him from the pines. But it wasn't Astrid. It was Cisneros. Dressed in jeans and a wool hat and a slicker glistening with rain. Smiling.

Tyrell's thoughts were in chaos. He retreated from Cisneros, but as he did he realized that everything Astrid—ghost or whatever she was—had told him must have been a lie. Cisneros couldn't be dead. Obviously not. But he wasn't quite able to believe that, and he continued to retreat, calling out to Cisneros.

"Bert!" he shouted above the wind. "Where you been, Bert?"

"Hello, Jack! What's the problem, man?"

"Bert?" Tyrell was still uncertain who and what it was that confronted him. "I left you in the bunker. I was coming back, but I wanted to let you sleep."

"I had a real good sleep," said Cisneros, closing on him. "Nice dreams. What you been doing?"

"Trying to find some food."

"Find any?"

Tyrell's answer died stillborn. His stomach was full—no doubt about that. And if Astrid was a ghost, how could that be? He wiped his eyes clear of rain again, thoroughly befuddled. Cisneros had stopped a few feet away, his image blurred by the rain driving into Tyrell's face.

"You look fucked up, man," said Cisneros. "There's no reason to be fucked up. This is a good place."

Tyrell spat out a sardonic laugh. "Oh, right!"

"You having a bad time, man?" Cisneros chuckled. "Just take it easy. Relax. God is here."

"God?" A chill began to map Tyrell's spine; his scrotum tightened, and he blinked away the raindrops, trying to bring Cisneros into clearer focus. He felt at the center of a grayish green confusion, a medium without form, without border, the only real thing in a vast unreality. "What do you mean . . . 'God'?"

"I'm not talking 'bout Jesus," said Cisneros with another sly chuckle. "Oh, no! I'm not talking 'bout Jesus."

"Well, what *are* you talking about?"

"It's interesting," said Cisneros. "I wonder if the idea of God was based on a premonition of what exists here. It's possible, you know.

It's obvious there are some astounding similarities between the laws of karma, certain Christian tenets, and the true process of the"—he sniffed, amused—"the divine."

Cisneros's unnatural fluency and abstract self-absorption disconcerted Tyrell; he'd always been one to put on airs, but because he had nothing intelligent to say, the effect had been ludicrous. Now the effect was a little scary.

The rain intensified, and Cisneros wavered like a mirage. Something was dangling from his hand, swinging back and forth, and peering through the rain, Tyrell saw that it was an eight-pointed star that had been crudely carved from a piece of seashell, holed, and strung on a length of twine.

"What's that?" Tyrell asked.

"Just something I made while I was waiting for you." Cisneros flipped the star high, grabbed it in his fist. "Things have changed for me, Jack. I'm not the man I used to be."

"Well, none of us are, Bert old son," said Tyrell, trying to make light of it and taking a backward step. "It's been one hell of a night."

"That's true," said Cisneros. "But it's much more than that. It's the only truth there is."

Tyrell noticed for the first time that the rain didn't seem to be bothering Cisneros: it trickled into his eyes, yet he never even blinked. He wanted to run, but he didn't know if there was a secure place to hide, and neither did he know what exactly he would be hiding from.

"Tell me about God, Bert," he said, deciding against fear, hoping that this Cisneros's behavior was merely derangement resulting from exposure and fatigue.

"You really want that, Jack? You don't look like the kind of man cares too much 'bout God. But"—Cisneros twirled his little star on its string—"if you want to hear, you come to the right place. 'Cause I'm the man's going to tell everybody 'bout God. Soon as I get off this island, that's what I'm going to do. Preach the truth 'bout the God that is and the world that isn't." His smile seemed the product of absolute serenity. "You understand?"

"Not hardly," said Tyrell. "Why don't you explain it to me?"

"This world," said Cisneros, waving at the pines, "it's nothing but a dream." He giggled. "The thing is, nobody knows who's doing the dreaming. Nobody 'cept me."

"And who's that?"

"And when I tell everybody," Cisneros went on, ignoring the question, "when I tell 'em nothing's all there is, that anything they do is all right, 'cause there's nothing for anybody to hurt, it's all a dream . . . then there's going to be chaos. Maybe it'll be blood and sex and madness. A beautiful chaos of dreams. But maybe it'll be the beginning of a new and glorious potential. I believe that might just be the case, I really do. I believe that beauty and hope will be reborn. Why else would they bother?"

Tyrell kept up his bold front, but kept on sizing up the possibilities of flight and hiding. "Is that so, Bert?"

"You don't believe me, do you?"

"Nobody's going to believe you . . . an illiterate little Portugee. They'll laugh your ass back to New Bedford."

"Want me to prove it, Jack? They've taught me how to do quite a few tricks. I'm sure I can find one that'll impress you."

"I'd love it. Go ahead . . . show me your stuff."

"It'll be my pleasure." Cisneros's smile broadened, displaying his gold teeth; his dark seamed face looked to have an impish, stylized evil, its detail lost in the streaming rain. Then the face began to pale. "Dreams, Jack," he said. "That's all there is. Dreams like me, like you. Like your girlfriend back in the shack."

Tyrell started to ask how he had known about Astrid, but alarm stifled his curiosity, held him motionless and cold. Cisneros was fading, growing vague and indistinct, becoming a ghost in the rain. Yet his voice remained strong.

"You remember this, Jack, when you think you know something. You know nothing, man. Nothing. You're smoke, you're haze on the water, you're not even real as the dew. And what you feel and what you know is even less real than that. Just think of yourself as a spark flying up against the darkness, visible for a moment, then gone. But not gone forever, Jack. Gone forever, that's for real things, things that live and die. You're in the wind, a pattern, a shape that what's real calls back now and again to play with, to make new dreams, to amuse itself. You're part of a game, a dream actor in a play."

Cisneros had almost completely disappeared; all that remained was a roughly human shape hollowed from the rain, an indistinct opacity against the backdrop of the pines.

"Dreams," came Cisneros's voice, a sonorous whisper rising above the keening of the wind. "Sometimes they're beautiful, Jack. Beautiful and slow and serene."

More lightning in the east, accompanied by a savage crack of thunder.

"And sometimes they're nightmares."

VII

How, Cisneros thought, could he have sunk to the depths that he had in his former life? How could he have been such a posturing bully, a tormentor of women and the weak? He supposed that—like most of his friends—he had been enslaved by tradition, by the spiritual and physical meanness of life among the Portuguese of New Bedford. It was for certain that his father's constant abuse of his mother had informed his own behavior, and he had not been able to rise above those origins. Well, now he had been given a chance for redemption . . . more, his lifelong desire for knowledge and the skills with which to employ it had been satisfied, and he planned to take full advantage of the opportunity. And in the process of spreading the truth he would make up all the bad times to his wife and children, to everyone whom he had wronged. He, unlike Tyrell, had untapped potential; he was capable of change. He knew how foolish it was to take pride in himself considering his ephemeral nature; but although he was merely a creation, an illusion, that was no excuse to ignore the decencies or to deny his potential. Even if Tyrell was able to accept the way things were, which Cisneros doubted, he would never be able to maintain his humanity; he was not strong, not resilient. It was a pity, but Cisneros had no time to spare on pity. He had a world to teach, to enlighten, and Tyrell's fate was not his concern. Later he'd have another try at talking with him. But for now there was so much to learn, so much to understand. He let himself fade into the dream and the deep places beneath it, where he communed with the trillion forms of his Creator.

VIII

It was almost twilight, the storm still raging, before Tyrell screwed up the courage to approach the bunker. He was soaked to the skin, his sweater a foul-smelling matte of drenched wool, and he was shaking with cold; yet he stood at the side of the bunker for quite some time, leery of discovering what lay within. Huge slate-colored waves marbled with foam piled in from the sea, crashing explosively on the eroded beach, driving a thin tide to the bunker's lip, then retreating, leaving a slope of tawny sand cut by deep channels; the wind flattened the grass at the crest of the dunes. But despite the ferocity of the elements, Tyrell sensed that the worst of the weather was past, that by morning the sea would be calm and the sky clear and any fire set upon the beach would be noticed by the keeper of the Gay Head light. One more night, then, and he would be safe. But that one night loomed endlessly before him, and he realized that he was in great peril from the terrors of his mind . . . if from nothing else. That, he thought, must be the cause of everything he had seen and felt. The trauma of the fire aboard the *Preciosilla,* of the swim to shore . . . these things must have unhinged him in some way, because he was not about to believe in what he had seen. And if he was ever going to quell his fears, he had to take a look inside the bunker, to begin ordering his mind, firming it against the solitude of the night ahead.

Finally, steeling himself, he made his way down the slope, sinking to midcalf with every step in the wet sand. He paused at the corner of the bunker, drawing strength from the power of the sea, filling his chest with its power, its briny smell; then he slogged around the corner and peered in over the lip. He felt relief on seeing Cisneros lying curled up in the shadow of the lip, still wearing his black slicker and jeans, his face turned to the wall.

"Bert!" he shouted. "Wake up!"

Cisneros didn't move; cobwebs bridged between his shoulders and the bunker wall, and more cobwebs formed a linkage between his ankles, his knees. No spiders in sight . . . not on his body, anyway. And not as many as there had been on the fouled walls and ceiling.

"Come on, Bert," he said, a real wealth of anxiety and pleading in his voice. "Get the fuck up!"

Maybe he *was* dead, Tyrell thought. And what did that say about Astrid? He'd half-talked himself into believing that she hadn't been real, but if what she had told was true. . . . Christ, it was all craziness! He doubted he would ever be able to sort it out. He shouted again, and again Cisneros made no response. He drew a breath, held it, leaned in over the lip and poked the sleeping man with a forefinger.

The finger sank knuckle-deep into Cisneros's shoulder, and Tyrell felt ticklish movement along its length.

He cried out in shock, fell back. Cisneros's body rippled and shifted, and as Tyrell watched it began to break apart, the realistic-looking slicker, the jeans, the seam of swarthy skin visible between the ragged black hair and the slicker's collar, all dissolving into a myriad separate white shapes, thousands and thousands of spiders spilling, crawling over one another, proving that the body had been composed of nothing but tiny arachnid forms, a boiling nest of little horrors, a tide of them that scuttled across the floor and fumed toward him over the edge of the lip.

Tyrell screamed and screamed, scrambling away from the bunker, falling, wriggling on his back, then crawling toward the sea, right to the verge, into cold water. He sat up, staring at the bunker. The spiders had not followed him; they were poised on the lip, all in a row, riding one another, a fringe of them several inches thick, and he had the idea that they were watching him, amused by his panic. He got to his feet, gasping, choking on fear, and there was an explosion at his back. He turned just in time to be knocked flat by an enormous breaker that dragged him over the coarse sand of the slope. He scrambled up, coughing up saltwater. The mass of spiders was still perched on the lip, still watching. He started to his right. Stopped. Went to his left. Stopped. A sob loosened in his chest, and his eyes filled.

"Oh, Jesus God," he said, singing it out above the pitch of the wind. "Please don't do this!"

A lesser wave broke at his back, sending a flow of chill water rushing about his knees.

"Please," he said. "I don't want this anymore."

He wished there was someone who could answer, someone to whom he could appeal this thoroughly unfair circumstance. That, he thought, would be his best hope, because it was for certain there was nowhere to run, nowhere to hide. But at last, having no other option, he began to run, giving the bunker a wide berth, pumping his knees, mounting the dune and cresting it, picking his way nimbly among the overgrown craters and through the pines. He came to feel light in running, as if each step might lift him high above the island, even above the storm, and seizing upon this comforting irrationality among all the terrifying irrationalities that ruled over Nomans Land, he thought he might be able to run forever, or until he dropped, or until something even more irrational happened, something that through terror or pain would set him free once and for all from the fear that had ruled him for so long.

Night, a toiling darkness illuminated by strokes of red lightning that spread down the darkness like cracks in a black and fragile shell, and a flickering orange light was shining beneath the ill-fitting door of Astrid's shack. Tyrell stood in the pines, hugging himself for warmth, his teeth chattering, chilled to the bone. Hallucinations, she'd said. Maybe that had been responsible for all that had happened. Hallucinations brought on by the spiders' venom. If her version of things was accurate—hallucinations, Bert dead—then he had nothing to fear inside the shack. He wanted badly to believe her, because then he could get warm. Warmth seemed the most important quality in all the world, and he realized he was going to have to give it priority very soon or else he was not going to survive. He kept edging nearer to the shack, stopping, listening, hoping to pick up some sign of occupancy and from that sign to gauge the nature of the occupant. But the only sounds were the pissing of the rain in the pine boughs, the moaning of the wind, and the occasional concussion from the sky.

Tyrell crept to the side of the door, peered in through a gap in the boards, but could make out nothing apart from blurred orange light. He could feel the warmth inside, steaming out at him, and its allure drew him to pull the door open. The shack was empty. After a moment's hesitation he ducked inside and closed the door behind him. He stripped off his clothing, wrapped himself in one of the blankets, and stood by the hot plate, warming his hands over the coils, standing there until his shaking had stopped. Then he sat down on the sleeping bag, covered himself with a second blanket, and stared blankly at the ceiling, where dozens of white spiders patrolled the intricate strands of their webs. He felt weak in every joint, every extremity, too weak to consider doing anything about the spiders, and he became mesmerized by their delicate movements. There seemed to be patterns involved in their shifting, at the heart of which was the maintenance of a structure, a constant process of adjustment, of equalization. He laughed at himself. *Christ, you're really losing it, you are!* He settled back against the wall, let his eyes close; the light of the hurricane lamp acquired a dim yellowish orange value through his lids, like the color of a summer sunset, a clean, sweet color, and it seemed he was falling into it, drifting away on a calm breeze that carried him beyond this storm, beyond all storms.

He came awake to find Astrid looking down at him, shrugging out of her slicker. He sat up, tension cabling the muscles in his neck and shoulders, waiting for her to change back into a corpse. But no change occurred. She ran her hands along the sides of her head, pulling the damp heft of her hair into a sleek ponytail.

"I was worried about you," she said. "I didn't know where you'd gone."

He had trouble mustering speech. "I . . . uh . . ." He swallowed. "It was those hallucinations you talked about. I woke up and saw something that frightened me."

"What did you see?" She kneeled beside him, and he had to restrain himself from scrambling away.

He told her what he'd seen in the shack, in the bunker; once he had finished he laughed nervously and said, "When you said there might be hallucinations, I didn't think you had anything like that in mind."

She plucked at a wisp of grass, her features cast in a somber expression. "I have to tell you the truth," she said. "I don't suppose it's very important whether or not you believe me. Or maybe it is . . . maybe it's important in some way I don't understand. But I do have to tell you."

He felt something bad coming; a sour cold heaviness was collecting in his gut, and the weakness in his limbs grew more profound.

"I came here in the summer of 1964," she said. "I . . ." She broke off, reacting to his horrified stare. "I'm not a ghost . . . not in the way you think. Not any more than you are."

"What the hell's that mean?"

"Just listen," she said. "It's going to be very hard for you to believe this, and you won't have a chance of understanding unless you listen carefully and hear me out. All right?"

He nodded, too frightened to move, to do other than listen.

"I came here in '64," she continued. "To study the spiders. I'd heard about them from a botanist who'd spent time on the island, and I'd seen a specimen. That was enough to convince me that we were dealing with an entirely new subspecies and not just a variant. Their poison, in particular, fascinated me. It incorporated an incredibly complex DNA. Do you know what that is? DNA?"

"I've a fair idea," he said, thinking of '64, right, you crazy bitch!

"Okay." She put her hand to her brow, pinched the bridge of her nose, a gesture—it seemed to Tyrell—of weariness. "God, there's so much to tell!"

This sign of weakness on her part boosted his confidence. "Go ahead. We've got all night."

"At least that," she said; she drew a breath, let it sigh out. "Aside from the DNA, I found what appeared to be fragments of human RNA in the poison." She looked at him questioningly.

"Something to do with memory, storing memory or something . . . is that right?"

"Near enough."

Wind curled in beneath the door to rustle the dry grasses carpeting the floor; the flame of the hurricane lamp flickered, brightened, and a tide of orange light momentarily eroded the edge of the shadows on the walls. The rain had let up to a drizzle, and the thunder had quit altogether. The storm, Tyrell realized, was nearing its end. For some reason this made him anxious. He was not feeling very well. He kept wishing for something solid, some edifice of thought to hang on to; but there was nothing within reach, and this caused him even more anxiety. He tried to focus on Astrid's words.

"Anyway," she went on, "after a week or so I ran up against some pretty frightening questions. The poison, I'd discovered, was unbelievably potent. I figured that death would follow within seconds of a bite. Yet I'd been bitten many times and I was still alive. And I couldn't understand how the spiders had been isolated on the island. Surely, I thought, they must have been carried off on the boats that had landed here over the years ever since the Indians occupied the land. And if that had been the case, given their hardiness, their breeding capacity, there wouldn't be too many people left alive. Without a sophisticated technology, there was no way an antidote could have been produced. The poison was extremely complex." Another sigh. "Then I began having dreams."

Tyrell remembered Cisneros, his ravings. "What kind of dreams?"

"They weren't dreams, they were experiences of other lives. Men, women, children. All from different eras, some of them Indian lives from precolonial times. None earlier than that. It wasn't that I was watching them. I was inside their heads, living their days and nights. And it was from these dreams that I began to understand the truth, that the spiders had been transported off-island . . . a long, long time ago. They'd been carried to the mainland, back to Europe on the colonial vessels, and then gradually had spread to Asia, Africa. Everywhere. By my estimate their population had come to span the world by the mid–nineteenth century. I very much doubt that humanity survived into the twentieth. Of course what I know of human history belies that . . . that's part of their fabrication. But in reality the last hundred years or so of mankind must have been awful. People dying and dying. The population shrinking to a mere handful of souls who hadn't been bitten."

It took him a long moment to absorb what she had said. "Now wait a minute! We're living proof of. . . ."

"No, we're not," she said. "We're not alive. We never were." He tried to interrupt, but she talked over him. "I don't understand it completely. Or perhaps I do. I can't be sure. It's difficult to explain things in human terms, because though the spiders with their

poison have managed to ensure a kind of human survival, I have no
idea of their motivations . . . or if they even have motivations. This
may be all reflex on their part. Or maybe it's that they've become
a unity, intelligent in some way due to a symbiotic use of our genetic
material. A group mind or something of the sort. Maybe the best anal-
ogy would be to say. . . . Have you heard about the concept of
people's personalities being translated into computer software? That's
similar to what the spiders have done. Transformed our genetic material into a biological analogue of software." She blew out a sharp
breath between her pursed lips. "I think sometimes it's all a game
to them, a pageant, this continuation of the history of a dead race.
The way they appear to attach special significance to this island, for
instance. Once in a while they act out a scene or two on the island,
and the human creations involved. Like you and me. It's as if they
develop a fondness for them. They bring them back over and over,
and occasionally they'll let them live"—she laughed—"happily. As if
they were celebrating us, thanking us for what we've done for them
by dying, by affording them a new level of consciousness." She took
his hand. "Do you remember asking me why it was that one moment I'd be looking at you with longing, and the next I'd be frightened? It's because I think they mean for us to live happily for a while.
I want that so much! I don't want to lose the chance. Maybe it's
only a dream, an illusion. But it feels so good, so strong, to be even
this much alive compared to what I've been . . . almost nothing, a
flicker of consciousness subsumed into a hive of dreams."

He pulled his hand away from her. "You're fucking crazy!"

"I know that's how it sounds. . . ."

"No, it doesn't *sound* crazy. It *is* crazy!" He drew up his knees,
shifted deeper into the corner; the lamplight fell across his toes, and
when he pulled them back into shadow he felt much more secure.
"You sit here and tell me that we're the figments of the imagination of a bunch of goddamn spiders, and that they've been carrying
out the evolution of human history in this fantasy world they've
created. . . ."

"Yes, I . . ."

"And you expect me to swallow *that?* Jesus Christ, woman!"

"I'd think," she said stiffly, "that of all people you'd be able to
comprehend it . . . what with your living in a fantasy of your own
all these years."

"When it comes to fantasy, lady, I can't hold a candle to you."

"It's not so alien as it seems," she said. "Philosophers have
been . . ."

He snorted in contempt.

". . . saying more or less the same thing for centuries. Think about it. Didn't your friend say what I have? Didn't he?"

His shock at her knowing what Cisneros had said must have showed on his face, because she laughed.

"How could I have known that?" she said. "I couldn't have . . . not unless his truth had been communicated to me through dreams." Again she took his hand. "You'll understand sooner or later. It's always hard for those of us who're brought to the island to accept. It's like waking up to find you're dreaming. But eventually you become sensitized to what they intend, what their patterns are, their tendencies."

Tyrell shook free of her, his mind whirling. Had everything he'd seen and felt since his arrival been a hallucination? That couldn't be right. The hallucination theory, that was *hers,* and so it had to be wrong. No, wait. She'd denied that one when she'd tried to convince him about the spiders. So maybe it *was* right after all. Maybe this whole thing had been a fever dream, maybe he was lying passed out in the bunker, or maybe even back in his berth aboard the *Preciosilla.* His thoughts went skittering away into the corners of his brain, hiding like spiders in the convolutions, and he sat empty and unknowing, bewildered by the infinity of confusions accessible to him. Astrid said something, but he refused to listen, certain that whatever she would tell him would only offer more confusion. He could hear his thoughts ticking in secret, little bombs waiting to explode. His heart was ticking, too. The entire world was running on the same pulse, building and building to an explosive moment. He closed his eyes, and the light seemed to be growing brighter, more solid, to pry beneath his lids with thin glowing orange talons.

"Jack! Look at me!"

Oh, no! He remembered what had happened the last time he'd had a look at her after a long interval.

"Are you all right, Jack?"

Let me be, damn you!

She was very near, her breath warm on his cheek, and he couldn't resist taking a peek. That close to him, her face was a touch distorted; but it was her face. Strong Scandinavian features framed by hair like white gold. She looked beautiful in her concern, and he didn't trust that. Not one bit.

"Don't leave me, Jack," she said. "You have to understand . . . they've given us a chance to live, for more of a life than anyone else can have. But you have to accept things, you can't go against them. They'll simply . . . stop you. Do you understand?"

"Yes . . . yes, I understand."

He couldn't take his eyes off her, waiting for the smooth skin and icy eyes and white teeth to give way to corruption and pocked bone.

"Do you remember earlier?" she asked. "Making love?"

"Uh-huh."

"Make love to me now. I want to feel that way again."

Her face drew closer yet, and he knew what the plan was now. They would wait until he was kissing her to make the change, and he would find himself kissing death, his tongue probing into a joyless void of rotted gums and broken teeth. Revolted, he shoved her hard, sending her back against the table. Her head struck the corner, cutting short her scream, and she fell on her side. He sat there, breathing rapidly, expecting her to get up. Then he noticed the blood miring the back of her pale blond head.

"Astrid!"

He threw off the blanket, crawled over to her, searched for a pulse. She was dead.

Well, he thought, that proved she was wrong. You had to be alive in order to die.

Didn't you?

He was repelled by his insensitivity, by how casually he could accept the death of this woman with whom he had made love only hours before.

But maybe they *hadn't* made love, maybe. . . .

He scrambled to his feet. Time to stop this shit, stop this ridiculous metaphysical merry-go-round. He'd killed a woman. She'd been a lunatic, but he was liable for the act, and he'd damn well better cover his tracks. He struggled into his wet clothes, trying to think, but his thoughts were muddy, circulating with sluggish inefficiency. Then in pulling on his trousers, he lurched into the table and nearly overturned the lamp. He grabbed it by the handle, held it above the table a moment. A mad little idea crackled in his head. Kill two birds with one stone, he would. He wedged his feet into his shoes, avoiding looking at the body. But as he shrugged on his slicker, his eyes fell upon it and emotion tightened his chest. A tear leaked down onto his cheek.

"Aw, Jesus!" he said. "I didn't mean to."

As if Jesus were listening.

He made promises to God. *Lord,* he said to himself, *get me out of*

*this. I swear I'll live a clean life. I'll go back to Ireland, I'll take a stand
for God and country.*

And then he chastised himself for his weakness. He'd done the
deed, and he'd have to face up to the consequences.

*Damn! Did every fucking thing you decided about your life, your moral-
ity, sound as feckless and unattached to reality as the things he was trying
to decide?*

He backed to the door, pushed it open, and held the lamp high.
Astrid's body receded into shadow; only her feet were in the light.
He said a prayer for her, for himself. Then he dashed down the lamp,
and as the grass upon the floor burst into flames, he sprinted out into
the darkness.

Within seconds the entire shack was ablaze, flames snapping,
shooting into the starless sky, high and bright enough that they would
surely be seen by the keeper at Gay Head. Tyrell had become so accustomed to the violence of the storm that the relative calmness of
the night felt unnatural, inimical. He glanced behind him, expecting
some threat to show itself; but there were only the pines, the faintly
stirring dark. When he turned back to the shack, however, he saw
that the threat he most feared had materialized.

It was a spectacular sight, with the flames leaping, wisping into
thin smoke and sparks that shot out into eloquent curves over the
pine tops, and the shack itself a skeleton with molten knots of fire
peeping between the boards . . . so spectacular, in fact, that at first
Tyrell didn't notice movement inside the building. And when he did
notice it, something dark and spindly twisting and rippling behind
a wall of flame, he thought it merely some internal structure being
eaten by the fire. But then that something came toward the door,
paused in the doorway, a black streaming figure with fiery hair and
stick-thin limbs, reminding him of the captain in the burning wheelhouse of the *Preciosilla*. But he knew this was not the captain. The
figure stood for a few seconds without moving; then, with the slow
precision of a signalman, it began to wave its arm back and forth, back
and forth, each repetition of the gesture charging Tyrell with the
voltage of fear. He would have liked to bellow, to scream, to roar,
anything to release the tension inside him; but he was enervated, on
the verge of collapse, and he managed only a muted squawk. The muscles of his jaw trembled, and his heart seemed to have tripled its
rhythm, less beating than quivering in the hollow of his chest.

He was too frightened to turn his back on the burning figure, and he retreated slowly, carefully, feeling behind him, brushing aside clumps of wet needles, dragging his feet so he wouldn't stumble and pitch over into one of the craters. Only after he had put a hundred feet between himself and the shack, its fierce reddish orange glow like that of a miniature sun fallen from the heavens, casting the pine trunks in stark silhouette . . . only then did he run, breaking free of the pines, climbing to the crest of the dune overlooking the bunker, and there sinking to his knees. Neither exhausted nor out of breath, of strength, but rather totally confused, seeing no point in further flight. He sat cross-legged, watching the amber sweep of the Gay Head light across the bottom of pale scudding clouds, feeling empty, hollow, barely registering the gentle touch of the wind on his face, watching the pitch and roil of the sea, which was still heavy and running high.

"Hello, Jack," said a man's voice to his right.

Nothing could shock Tyrell anymore. He felt a prickle of cold traipse along his neck like the tiptoeing of a spider, but nothing more. He turned his head a quarter of an arc and saw a man standing some ten or twelve feet away. A most unusual man, a man who in outline displayed the short, bandy-legged form of Bert Cisneros, complete to the shape of the wool hat atop his head, but whose substance was the blue darkness of the night sky beset with a sprinkling of white many-pointed stars.

"That you, Bert?" asked Tyrell.

"More or less," said Cisneros. "You know how it is."

"No, I don't, Bert. Maybe that's my problem. I don't have a fucking clue about how it is."

"I tried to tell you." Cisneros flung out a starry arm, gesturing inland. "And so did she."

The stars in his body were moving, shifting into strange alignments, like living constellations. It was troubling to see, and Tyrell lowered his eyes to the sand.

"Was that the truth, then?" he asked.

"The truth." Cisneros laughed. "No matter how illusory a species we are, every man's still his own truth. I've heard you say much the same thing, Jack."

"Did I, now? I wonder what I meant by it."

"You'll understand soon enough."

An immense slow wave lifted from the dark, towering over the beach, and came crashing down, its vast tonnage exploding into splinters of white spray. The smell of brine was strong.

"So what's to happen now?" asked Tyrell.

"For you?"

"Yeah, for me."

"I'm afraid you're just not cut out for the next part, Jack," said Cisneros. "It sometimes happens that the created prove unsuitable. Not even the creators are infallible."

Tyrell sniffed. "I was ever a disappointment to my mother, too." He was silent a moment, tracing a line in the sand with his forefinger. "I'd like to believe that Astrid's alive somehow . . . that either what you're saying's true, or else that I'm round my fucking twist and none of this is happening."

"Don't worry about it," said Cisneros. "Nothing I tell you is going to be a solid assurance one way or the other. It's not in your nature to accept that from me. But you haven't done anything to be ashamed of . . . not really."

"From all you're telling me, Bert, can I assume that given your version of reality is accurate, we still have a bit of free will left to us?"

"If you want to call it that. Things are actually little different from how you always thought they were. The only salient difference is that instead of an unknown mystical creator, there's a knowable, explicable one. Of course in the beginning"—Cisneros shrugged—"who can say?"

Tyrell glanced at him, then away. "Even if you are a hallucination, you're still an asshole. I never could figure how an ignorant git like yourself could think he knew *any*thing. But maybe you do know something now. Whatever, you *are* a changed man, Bert. And I'm not talking about the suit of special effects. Quite erudite, you are. They must have something important in mind for you."

"It's as I told you," said Cisneros. "As I've shown you. I am to instruct with words and miracles. To invest the play with a new spirit. Who knows what the result may be?"

"You sound pretty much in control, Bert. You sure about that? You sure the fucking spiders haven't got something nasty in mind for you? I mean, how come an asshole like you, a real punk . . . how come you get to win the world?"

"God works in mysterious ways."

A broken laugh guttered out between Tyrell's teeth. "I wish I could buy all this crap."

"So do I, Jack. So do I." Cisneros sidled off a couple of feet. "I'm going to leave you now. Things are at an end here, and I can't help you. Perhaps someday we'll meet again. You never know."

"I suppose I should be hoping for that eventuality," said Tyrell without taking his eyes from the patch of sand before him. "But tell you the truth, I don't hope for it a hell of a lot."

When he looked up after a minute or so, Cisneros was gone. But he was not alone. Horribly burned, her face melted and blackened, her eyes like shattered opaque crystals, breasts smeared into shapeless masses, bone showing through the crispy meat of her right leg, Astrid was standing where Cisneros had been. Tyrell's gorge rose, his fear returned. But nonetheless he remained sitting on the dune top. "Go away, damn you," he said.

He heard a horrid wheezing and recognized it for the sound of air passing in and out of charred lungs; the breeze rustled frays of burned skin on her arms. He buried his face in his hands. "Oh, God!" he said. "Just let me be for a little while, all right? Just let me be."

A throaty husk of a noise, speech trying to issue from her throat. "Ahh!" He pushed himself erect, tripped, rolled down the face of the dune. He got to one knee, gazed back up to the crest. For a moment he thought she had vanished, but then the Gay Head light flashed across her, etching an image into Tyrell's mind: a female thing with black crusted thighs, her flesh displaying shiny fracture lines like overlapping slabs of anthracite. Blind eyes. Bits of papery skin fluttering like hanks of hair from her skull in the fitful wind. The image wouldn't fit inside his head. It kept expanding, forcing out thoughts, until there was no room for anything else, and still it continued to expand, driving a hoarse cry out of his chest, sending him staggering toward the edge of the shore.

He couldn't see Astrid, but he felt the push of her vision, and to escape that he waded out into the water, going waist-deep, breasting into a crawl that took him flush into a breaking wave. He dived underwater into the heart of the wave, felt it billow above him, and surfaced in a trough so deep that he could not locate the shore. The water was terribly cold, but after a few seconds his flesh grew numb, and this lack of sensation inspired him. He stroked away from the island, realizing that this way led to death, but no longer caring, no longer willing to suffer the obscenities that sprouted from the darkness of Nomans Land. Another wave lifted above him, and again he dived into its heart, surfacing far beyond it. All around, the sea was peaking into enormous waves whose flowing slopes carried him high, then sent him hurtling into pitch-black valleys. He tried to swim, but it was futile. The weight of his soaked clothing was dragging him under, and his feeble strokes were merely exertion, serving no purpose. Fear overwhelmed him. A cry formed in his throat. But as he went slipping into yet another valley, the momentum of that rushing decline dissipated the cry and he felt exhilarated, like a child on a carnival ride. He went under, came up choking, flailing, spitting saltwater. The tilting side of a swell bore him under a second time. He beat his way to the surface, thrusting his head into the air, knowing that he was drowning, that the cold had robbed him of strength, regretting now his decision to flee the island, regretting everything, his lost opportunities, his failures, the loss of fleeting moments of happiness, so few by comparison to the long periods of doldrums that had dominated his life. But as he sank for a last time, a white nail driving itself into the black flesh of the sea, at the core of his panic and regret was a profound satisfaction, the knowledge that he was dying, *really* dying, that madness had afflicted him and nothing of what he had undergone on the island had the least reality. That he was a man and not a pale imagined thing. He had a moment of bitterness amid his fear. What had he done to deserve this? He was no worse than most, no more a coward or charlatan. He didn't think these things as much as he experienced them in a bleak current of emotion, and once that current had exhausted itself, he accepted—along with the unfairness of life—the cold embrace of the sea and sank twisting into the depths, his arms floating up with the grace of a slow dancer, his lungs filling, his mind growing as black and serene as the water surrounding him, dwindling to a point of ebony stillness that seemed to hang in a suspension, a peaceful place between dread and the object of dread in which he perceived the pure thing of his soul, his essential things, touched them, found them strong and unafraid, and then, this necessary business done, he went without reservation about the small and final business of dying.

IX

Two nights after being rescued by the Coast Guard from Nomans Land, Bert Cisneros sat drinking beer at a table in the Atlantic Café on Nantucket, where just that afternoon he had been interviewed by members of a review board assembled by the Maritime Union and by the owners of the *Preciosilla*. Marvelous detail, he'd thought, and he had treated the board with the ironic respect that he considered it deserved. He was accompanied by two friends from New Bedford, Portuguese sailors who were in aspect and temperament much like his former self and hailed from the fishing vessel *Cariño*, which had put into port during the storm and was currently undergoing engine repairs. One of the men, José Nascimento, after listening to the relation of Cisneros's adventures with spiders and dreams, asked if this was the same story he had told the investigative board.

"No," said Cisneros. "The time wasn't right then to begin the process of illumination."

His companions exchanged looks of concern; they had never heard their friend speak in such a manner.

"But now," Cisneros went on, "now the time has come." His gaze swept over the dark monkeylike faces of his companions. "You don't believe anything I've said, do you?"

"Hey, Bert," said Nascimento. "You been through some rough shit, man. You a little fucked up right now. Don't worry 'bout it."

"That's right," said the second man, Arcoles Gil. "You be fine pretty soon. Just take it easy, have another beer."

"Don't you notice a difference in me?" Cisneros asked.

"Well," said Gil, "you talkin' funny, that's for sure."

"It's not only my way of speaking that's changed," said Cisneros. "I've changed utterly. When I think back to the man I was, the things I did, particularly the things I did to women. . . ."

"You gotta hit a woman sometimes, man," said Nascimento. "Shit, Bert. You know that. Sometimes they put you in a position where you ain't got no choice, where if you don't hit 'em, they cut off your balls."

Cisneros felt sad for Nascimento. Looking at his friend was like looking into a mirror that reflected his own past foulness and brutal stupidity. It would be easy now, given his new perspective, to try and put his old life behind him, to hide the past away and neglect his friends in the interest of complacency and contentment. But Bert Cisneros was a man of honor. It was his duty, his trust, to bring enlightenment to men like Nascimento. To all men.

"When I think back on what I've done," he said, "despite the fact I realize that my entire life is a beautifully articulated fantasy, I'm sick to my stomach." He paused, thoughtfully rubbing the little eight-pointed star he had brought from the island with the tips of his fingers. "I often wonder if this violent dream the spiders have made of the twentieth century is an accurate reflection of what would have occurred had humanity survived . . . if through some biochemical genius they've managed to predict the exact twists and turns that would have resulted from human greed and lust. I don't suppose the answer's important any longer. Now that I've been called to inform the world of its insubstantial nature, perhaps things will be returned to a kind of normalcy. Perhaps we'll be able to regain control of our destiny . . . no matter how illusory it is. After all, who can judge the potentials of an illusion? But I really believe they want something good for us."

The men's faces displayed both pity and alarm, and Cisneros laughed. "Come, my friends," he said, getting to his feet. "I'll prove it to you." They remained seated. "Come on! I'll prove it in a way you won't be able to deny. I'll show you what the world really looks like. Come on!"

Grudgingly, they followed him through the crowd at the bar to the door of the café, and then along the sidewalk until they came to the main street of the town. Buildings of brick and wood frame, cobblestones, a few cars moving, pedestrians looking into hotly lit shop windows. Graceful old trees leaning in over the rooftops.

"What do you see?" Cisneros asked.

Gil and Nascimento once again exchanged concerned glances.

"The street," said Gil with a puzzled expression.

"No," said Cisneros. "You only see a dream. I'll show you the *street.*"

He concentrated his will, and within seconds the scene before him rippled, wavered, like something melting in the rain, and in its place, lit by a bone-white full moon, was a ruin. Sad fragments of another time, another dream. The broken shells of weathered gray houses fettered in ivy, their windows shattered, half-hidden by brush and oak and hawthorn. The cobblestones were thick with moss. Mice scampered in the complex skeins of shadow beneath the boughs. Something long and yellowish brown protruded from a pile of leaves—a human bone. They were probably all around, he realized, the bones of the spiders' last victims. And spanning between limbs of trees, the cross-pieces of windows, everywhere, were veils of cobwebs tenanted by white spiders. After the bustle of the street of dreams, the emptiness of reality was harrowing. The emptiness and solitude of the place made Cisneros feel old, as if the weight of the years was a kind of contagion.

"There . . . you see," said Cisneros, turning to his friends.

But they, along with the shops and the cars and the pedestrians, had vanished.

Cisneros was startled but not afraid. Perhaps, he thought, he had misunderstood the discretion of his control, perhaps it was impossible to reveal the totality of the actual without eliminating all observers.

Of course, he told himself. That must be it. He tried to reinhabit the world of the dream, but—and this did frighten him—he could not remember how it was done. The knowledge of how to manipulate the materials of the unreal had seemed innate, as uncomplicated and natural a process as breathing, and yet now. . . . He ran a little ways forward into the center of the deserted street, panicked, slipping on the damp mossy stones. He tried again, focusing his will on the act of return, clenching his fists, squeezing his eyes shut. But when he opened them he discovered that nothing had changed. He could sense the forms and tensions of the dream just beyond his range, just out of reach, tantalizing, unattainable. Could the spiders have tricked him? Could all their promises merely have been a terrible deceit? Had they been playing with him, weaving another duplicitous web of his needs and desires? He whirled around, expecting to see some vast trap closing shut on him. But there were only the shattered buildings, the trees, the desolate moon, and he realized that the trap had already been sprung. They had raised him high and left him in a place where wit and knowledge had no audience, no use, no meaning, and thus were nothing but a torment.

The ruins appeared to have inched nearer, the network of shadows was shrinking to encage him. The bone-knob moon with its scatter of ashy markings looked to have lowered and been caught in the fork of two oak limbs, pinning him in place with its strong light. Rustles and skitterings from within the abandoned houses. Something tickled his cheek; he brushed at it, and a spider came away on his hand, perched like an ornate ring on the middle joint of his forefinger. With a shout, he knocked it off. The sound of his fear was swallowed by the silence.

"No, please, you can't do this, please," he said in a tone of hurried bargaining, like a drunk trying to reason with the police. "I'll do anything, I'll. . . ."

What, he thought, what could he do for those who could do anything, who could make a world and people it with the fictions of chemistry?

"I'm begging you," he said. "There must be something . . . something I can do. Please!" Tears were coming, and though he had the urge to stop them, to be a man, to live up to his old ideals of machismo, he let them come, having for the moment a childlike faith that they would move his tormentors to mercy. "Really," he said, "there must be something. I mean"—he spread his hands like a lawyer beseeching a jury—"you don't just create something complicated and fine, and then throw it away."

The wind kicked up a flurry of dead leaves, fluted through the gapped windows and doors, and Cisneros, once again driven to panic, began to run along the street, peering this way and that, hoping to find a sign that all this might be temporary, that they were only slapping his wrist for some inadvertent failure, some mistake of judgment or pride. That must be it, he thought, coming to a stop. His pride . . . they wanted to humble him, to make him aware of their supremacy.

"Believe me," he said to the sky, the ruins, "I know who you are. I'm not a fool, I have no intention of trying to usurp your place." He bowed his head, he choked back a sob. "Please believe me."

The only response was the banging of a loose shutter on the shop across the street.

"I love you," Cisneros said. "I swear . . . all I want to do is serve you."

He laughed at the fecklessness of the lie, at the pitiful blindness that had inspired it.

As if they would not be aware that he was lying.

After a few seconds he walked over to a shop, to a window in which hung an icicle of broken glass. He worked the piece of glass loose from the dried, crumbling putty and studied it, seeing his opaque reflection in its warped surface. He ran a finger along the edge. Sharp enough. It was hard to think about setting the point to his throat, but he did it anyway. They must want death of him, as they had wanted it of Tyrell, and he would give it to them. Sooner or later they would summon him for another act in the dream, and then perhaps they would confer upon him the power that they had promised. He closed his eyes, firmed his grip on the glass, and with all his strength, shoved the point into his jugular vein.

There was no pain, no weakness, no sensation of any sort, and when he opened his eyes, he saw that the glass knife had vanished.

This, then, was what they had in store for him. This was to be his prison for eternity, and he would not even be permitted the escape of death. He knew this with the clarity that had attended the knowledge visited upon him in dreams, and horrified, he spun about, his eyes locking onto wreckage and decay, the artifacts of his new home, the dissolution through which he would scurry like a rat in an abandoned museum. He started running again, trying to believe that they would relent, that he would turn a corner and find himself back in the dream. That would be like them, he told himself, that would be in character with their spidery ways—to allow him to lose faith and then restore it. At last despair heavied him, and he dropped to his knees, wanting to call upon God, the God who had lived in the minds of men centuries before, and who might yet live. Yet he understood the futility of prayer. He was full of useless comprehensions. Why . . . why had they done this? He had believed in them, he had believed in the possibility of redemption. He would have entertained them, injected a new subtlety into their ancient game, and they had betrayed him. Or perhaps it had not been a betrayal, perhaps fate was a matter of chemistry. What if all personality and fate, he wondered, were the resolution of biochemical laws that the spiders enacted within their dream of the human world? Perhaps they had merely allowed him to act out the essential directives of his personality? More useless insight. He leaked a fuming noise of frustration. Then he clasped his hands to his head, trying to stop thought, to contain fear, and yet thinking, thinking, always thinking, imagining that the last men living in these ruins, in other ruins all over the world, must have experienced this same harrowing loneliness and bewilderment, bereft of love and the possibility of salvation, of the least good thing. He tracked his gaze across the ruins of Nantucket Town, taking in the gaunt oaks and the skeletal shadows, the blind windows, the husks of old grogshops and apothecaries, and feeling in the depths of his soul the finality of his circumstance, he let out a terrified wail, a white plume of a cry that seemed to go up and up, arcing out over the emptiness, a hopeless, directionless signal that carried with it all the fears and cares and heart of the solitary, eternal inhabitant of that country of failed dreams and broken lives, that endless gray absence known as Nomans Land.

LIFE OF BUDDHA

Whenever the cops scheduled a raid on the shooting gallery to collect their protection money, old cotton-headed Pete Mason, who ran the place, would give Buddha the day off. Buddha rarely said a word to anyone, and Pete had learned that cops were offended by silence. If you didn't scream and run when they busted in, if like Buddha you just sat there and stared at them, they figured you were concealing a superior attitude, and they then tended to get inside your head.

They had beaten Buddha half to death a couple of times for this very reason, and while Buddha hadn't complained (he never complained about anything), Pete did not want to risk losing such a faithful employee. So on the night prior to the September raid, Pete went downstairs to where Buddha was nodding on a stained mattress by the front door and said, "Why don't you hang out over at Taboo's place tomorrow? Police is comin' 'round to do they thang."

Buddha shook himself out of his nod and said, "Talked to him already. Johnny Wardell's gon' be over sometime makin' a buy, but he say to come ahead anyway." He was a squat black man in his late thirties, his head stone bald, with sleepy heavy-lidded eyes and the beginning of jowls; he was wearing chinos stippled with blood from his last fix, and a too-small T-shirt that showed every tuck and billow of his round belly and womanly breasts. Sitting there, he looked like a Buddha carved from ebony that somebody had outfitted with Salvation Army clothes, and that was why Pete had given him the name. His real name was Richard Damon, but he wouldn't respond to it anymore. Buddha suited him just fine.

"Beats me why Taboo wanna do business with Johnny Wardell," Pete said, hitching his pants up over his ample stomach. "Sooner or later Wardell he be gettin' crazy all over a faggot like Taboo . . . y'know?"

Buddha grunted, scratched the tracks on his wrist, and gazed out the window beside the front door. He knew Pete was trying to draw him into a conversation, and he had no intention of letting himself be drawn. It wasn't that he disliked Pete; he liked him as much as anyone. He simply had no opinions he wanted to share; he had cultivated this lack of opinion, and he had found that the more he talked, the more opinions came to mind.

"You tell Taboo from me," Pete went on, "I been livin' in Detroit more'n sixty years, and I done business wit' a lotta bad dogs, but I ain't never met one meaner than Wardell. You tell him he better watch his behavior, y'understan'?"

"Awright."

"Well . . ." Pete turned and with a laborious gait, dragging his bad leg, mounted the stairs. "You come on up 'round two and get your goodnighter. I'll cut ya out a spoon of China White."

" 'Preciate it," said Buddha.

As soon as Pete was out of sight, Buddha lay down and stared at the flaking grayish-white paint of the ceiling. He picked a sliver of paint from the wall and crumbled it between his fingers. Then he ran the back of his hand along the worn nap of the runner that covered the hallway floor. All as if to reassure himself of the familiar surroundings. He had spent the best part of fifteen years as Pete's watchdog, lying on the same mattress, staring at that same dried-up paint, caressing that same runner. Before taking up residence on the mattress, he had been a young man with a future. Everybody had said, "That Richard Damon, he's gon' be headlines, he's gon' be *Live at Five,* he's gon' be *People* magazine." Not that he had started out different from his peers. He'd been into a little dealing, a little numbers, a little of whatever would pay him for doing nothing. But he'd been smarter than most and had kept his record clean, and when he told people he had his eye on the political arena, nobody laughed. They could see he had the stuff to make it. The trouble was, though, he had been so full of himself, so taken with his smarts and his fine clothes and his way with the ladies, he had destroyed the only two people who had cared about him. Destroyed them without noticing. Worried his mama into an early grave, driven his wife to suicide. For a while after they had died, he'd gone on as always, but then he'd come up against guilt.

He hadn't known then what that word *guilt* meant; but he had since learned its meaning to the bone. Guilt started out as a minor irritation no worse than a case of heartburn and grew into a pain with claws that tore out your guts and hollowed your heart. Guilt made you sweat for no reason, jump at the least noise, look behind you in every dark place. Guilt kept you from sleeping, and when you did manage to drop off, it sent you dreams about your dead, dreams so strong they began to invade your waking moments. Guilt was a monster against which the only defense was oblivion. . . . Once he had discovered that truth, he had sought oblivion with the fervor of a converted sinner.

He had tried to kill himself but had not been able to muster the necessary courage and instead had turned to drugs. To heroin and the mattress in the shooting gallery. And there he had discovered another truth: that this life was in itself a kind of oblivion, that it was carving him slow and simple, emptying him of dreams and memories. And of guilt.

The porch steps creaked under someone's weight. Buddha peered out the window just as a knock sounded at the door. It was Marlene, one of the hookers who worked out of Dally's Show Bar down the block: a pretty cocoa-skinned girl carrying an overnight bag, her breasts pushed up by a tight bra.

Her pimp—a long-haired white kid—was standing on a lower step. Buddha opened the door, and they brushed past him. "Pete 'round?" Marlene asked.

Buddha pointed up the stairs and shut the door. The white kid grinned, whispered to Marlene, and she laughed. "John think you look like you could use some lovin'," she said. "What say you come on up, and I'll give you a sweet ride for free?" She chucked him under the chin. "How that sound, Buddha?"

He remained silent, denying desire and humiliation, practicing being the nothing she perceived. He had become perfect at ignoring ridicule, but desire was still a problem: the plump upper slopes of her breasts gleamed with sweat and looked full of juice. She turned away, apparently ashamed of having teased him.

"Take it easy now, Buddha," she said with studied indifference, and hand-led the white kid up the stairs.

Buddha plucked at a frayed thread on the mattress. He knew the history of its every stain, its every rip. Knew them so thoroughly that the knowledge was no longer something he could say: it was part of him, and he was part of it. He and the mattress had become a unity of place and purpose. He wished he could risk going to sleep, but it was Friday night, and there would be too many customers, too many interruptions. He fixed his gaze on the tarnished brass doorknob, let it blur until it became a greenish-gold sun spinning within a misty corona. Watched it whirl around and around, growing brighter and brighter. Correspondingly his thoughts spun and brightened, becoming less thoughts than reflections of the inconstant light. And thus did Buddha pass the middle hours of the night.

At two o'clock Buddha double-bolted the door and went upstairs for his goodnighter. He walked slowly along the corridor, scuffing the threadbare carpet, its pattern eroded into grimy darkness and worm trails of murky gold. Laughter and tinny music came from behind closed doors, seeming to share the staleness of the cooking odors that pervaded the house. A group of customers had gathered by Pete's door, and Buddha stopped beside them. Somebody else wandered up, asked what was happening, and was told that Pete was having trouble getting a vein. Marlene was going to hit him up in the neck. Pete's raspy voice issued from the room, saying, "Damn it! Hurry up, woman!"

Getting a vein was a frequent problem for Pete; the big veins in his arms were burned-out, and the rest weren't much better. Buddha peered over shoulders into the room. Pete was lying in bed, on sheets so dirty they appeared to have a design of dark clouds. His freckly brown skin was suffused by a chalky pallor. Three young men—one of them Marlene's pimp—were gathered around him, murmuring comforts. On the night table a lamp with a ruffled shade cast a buttery yellow light, giving shadows to the strips of linoleum peeling up from the floor.

Marlene came out of the bathroom, wearing an emerald-green robe. When she leaned over Pete, the halves of the robe fell apart, and her breasts hung free, catching a shine from the lamp. The needle in her hand showed a sparkle on its tip. She swabbed Pete's neck with a clump of cotton and held the needle poised an inch or two away.

The heaviness of the light, the tableau of figures around the bed, Marlene's gleaming skin, the wrong-looking shadows on the floor, too sharp to be real: taken all together, these things had the same richness and artful composition, the same important stillness, as an old painting that Buddha had once seen in the Museum of Art. He liked the idea that such beauty could exist in this ruinous house, that the sad souls therein could become even this much of a unity. But he rejected his pleasure in the sight, as was his habit with almost every pleasure.

Pete groaned and twisted about. "Stop that shit!" Marlene snapped. "Want me to bleed you dry?"

Other people closed in around the bed, blocking Buddha's view. Pete's voice dropped to a whisper, instructing Marlene. Then people began moving away from the bed, revealing Pete lying on his back, holding a bloody Kleenex to the side of his neck. Buddha spotted his goodnighter on the dresser: a needle resting on a mirror beside a tiny heap of white powder.

"How you doin'?" Pete asked weakly as Buddha walked in.

He returned a diffident wave, went over to the dresser, and inspected the powder: it looked like a nice dose. He lifted the mirror and headed off downstairs to cook up.

"Goddamn!" said Pete. "Fifteen years I been takin' care of you. Feedin' your Jones, buyin' your supper. Think we'd have a relationship by now." His tone grew even more irascible. "I should never have give you that damn name! Got you thinkin' you inscrutable, when all you is is ignorant!"

Nodding on his mattress in the moonlit dark, feeling the rosy glow of the fix in his heart, the pure flotation of China White in his flesh, Buddha experienced little flash dreams: bizarre images that materialized and faded so quickly, he was unable to categorize them. After these had passed he lay down, covered himself with a blanket, and concentrated upon his dream of Africa, the one pleasure he allowed himself to nourish. His conception of Africa bore no relation to the ethnic revival of the sixties, to Afros and dashikis, except that otherwise he might have had no cognizance of the Dark Continent. Buddha's African kingdom was a fantasy derived from images in old movies, color layouts in *National Geographic,* from drugs and drugged visions of Nirvana as a theme park. He was not always able to summon the dream, but that night he felt disconnected from all his crimes and passionate failures, stainless and empty, and thus worthy of this guardian bliss. He closed his eyes, then squeezed his eyelids tight until golden pinpricks flowered in the blackness. Those pinpricks expanded and opened into Africa.

He was flowing like wind across a tawny plain, a plain familiar from many such crossings. Tall grasses swayed with his passage, antelope started up, and the gamy smell of lions was in the air. The grasslands evolved into a veld dotted with scum-coated ponds and crooked trees with scant pale foliage. Black stick figures leaped from cover and menaced him with spears, guarding a village peopled by storytellers and long-legged women who wore one-eyed white masks and whose shadows danced when they walked. Smoke plumed from wart-shaped thatched huts and turned into music; voices spoke from cooking fires. Beyond the village stood green mountains that rose into the clouds, and there among the orchids and ferns were the secret kingdoms of the gorillas. And beyond the mountains lay a vast blue lake, its far reaches fringed by shifting veils of mist in whose folds miragelike images materialized and faded.

Buddha had never penetrated the mists: there was something ominous about their unstable borders and the ghostly whiteness they enclosed. At the center of the lake a fish floated halfway between the surface and the bottom, like the single thought of a liquid brain. Knowing that he must soon face the stresses of the outside world, Buddha needed the solace offered by the fish; he sank beneath the waters until he came face-to-face with it, floating a few inches away.

The fish resembled a carp and measured three feet from its head to its tail; its overlapping scales were a muddy brown, and its face was the mask of a lugubrious god, with huge golden eyes and a fleshy downturned mouth. It seemed to be regarding Buddha sadly, registering him as another of life's disappointments, a subject with which it was quite familiar, for its swollen belly encaged all the evil and heartache in the world, both in principle and reality. Buddha gazed into its eyes, and the pupils expanded into black funnels that connected with his own pupils, opening channels along which torrents of grief and fear began to flow. The deaths of his wife and mother were nothing compared with the hallucinatory terrors that now confronted him: demons with mouths large enough to swallow planets; gales composed of a trillion dying breaths; armies of dead men and women and children. Their bodies maimed by an infinity of malefic usage. Had he witnessed these visions while awake, he would have been overwhelmed; but protected by the conditions of the dream, he withstood them and was made strong.

And before long he fell asleep in the midst of this infinite torment contained within the belly of the fish in his dream, contained in turn within his skull, within the ramshackle frame house, within the gunshot-riddled spiritual realm of the Detroit ghetto, whose agonies became a fleeting instance of distress—the fluttering of an eyelid, the twitching of a nerve—within the dreamed-of peace of Buddha's sleep.

The shooting gallery was located in the Jefferson-Chalmers district, the section of the ghetto most affected by the '67 riots. Hundreds of gutted houses still stood as memorials to that event, and between them—where once had stood other houses—lay vacant lots overgrown with weeds and stunted trees of heaven. The following afternoon, as he walked past the lot adjoining the shooting gallery, Buddha was struck by the sight of a charred sofa set among weeds at the center of the lot, and obeying an impulse, he walked over to it and sat down. It was the first day of fall weather. The air was crisp, the full moon pinned like a disfigured cameo of bone to a cloudless blue sky. In front of the sofa was a pile of ashes over which somebody had placed a grill; half a dozen scorched cans were scattered around it. Buddha studied the ashes, the grill, the cans, mesmerized by the pattern they formed. Sirens squealed in the distance, a metallic clanging seemed to be issuing from beyond the sky, and Buddha felt himself enthroned, the desireless king of a ruined world in which all desire had faltered.

He had been sitting for perhaps an hour when a teenage boy with a freckly complexion like Pete's came running along the sidewalk. Dressed in jeans and a sweatshirt and lugging an immense ghetto blaster. The boy looked behind him, then sprinted across the lot toward Buddha and flung himself down behind the sofa. "You tell 'em I'm here," he said breathlessly, "I'll cut ya!" He waggled a switchblade in front of Buddha's face. Buddha just kept staring at the toppled brick chimneys and vacated premises. A dragonfly wobbled up from the leaves and vanished into the sun dazzle of a piece of broken mirror canted against the ash heap.

Less than a minute later two black men ran past the lot. Spotting Buddha, one shouted, "See a kid come this way?" Buddha made no reply.

"Tell 'em I headed toward Cass," the kid whispered urgently, but Buddha maintained his silence, his lack of concern.

"Y'hear me?" the man shouted. "Did a kid come this way?"

"Tell 'em!" the boy whispered.

Buddha said nothing.

The two men conferred and after a second ran back in the direction from which they had come. "Damn, blood! You take some chances!" said the boy, and when Buddha gave no response, he added, "They come back, you just sit there like you done. Maybe they think you a dummy." He switched on the ghetto blaster, and rap music leaked out, the volume too low for the words to be audible.

Buddha looked at the boy, and the boy grinned, his nervousness evident despite the mask of confidence.

"Ain't this a fine box?" he said. "Fools leave it settin' on the stoop, they deserve to get it took." He squinted as if trying to scry out Buddha's hidden meaning. "Can't you talk, man?"

"Nothin' to say," Buddha answered.

"That's cool. . . . Too much bullshit in the air, anyhow."

The boy reminded Buddha of his younger self, and this disquieted him: he had the urge to offer advice, and he knew advice would be useless. The boy's fate was spelled out by the anger lying dormant in the set of his mouth. Buddha pitied him, but pity—like love, like hate—was a violation of his policy of noninvolvement, an impediment of the emptiness to which he aspired. He got to his feet and headed for the sidewalk.

"Hey!" yelled the boy. "You tell them mothafuckas where I'm at, I'll kill yo' ass!"

Buddha kept walking.

"I mean it, man!" And as if in defiance, as if he needed some help to verbalize it, the boy turned up the ghetto blaster, and a gassed voice blared, "Don't listen to the shuck and jive from Chairman Channel Twenty-Five. . . ."

Buddha picked up his pace, and soon the voice mixed in with the faint sounds of traffic, distant shouts, other musics, absorbed into the troubled sea from which it had surfaced.

From the shooting gallery to Taboo's apartment should have been about a twenty-minute walk, but that day—still troubled by his encounter with the boy—Buddha cut the time in half. He had learned that it was impossible to avoid involvement on his day off, impossible not to confront his past, and in Taboo he had found a means of making the experience tolerable, letting it be the exception that proved the rule. When he had first met Taboo seven years before, Taboo's name had been Yancey; he had been eighteen, married to a pretty girl, and holding down a steady job at Pontiac Motors.

Three years later, when he had next run into him, Taboo had come out of the closet, was working as a psychic healer, curing neighborhood ladies of various minor complaints, and through hormone treatments had developed a small yet shapely pair of breasts, whose existence he hid from the world beneath loose-fitting clothes.

Buddha had caught a glimpse of Taboo's breasts by accident, having once entered his bathroom while he was washing up, and after this chance revelation, Taboo had fixed upon him as a confidant, a circumstance that Buddha had welcomed—though he did not welcome Taboo's sexual advances. He derived several benefits from the relationship. For one thing, Taboo's specialty was curing warts, and Buddha had a problem with warts on his hands (one such had given him an excuse to visit that day); for another, Taboo—who dealt on the side—always had drugs on hand. But the most important benefit was that Taboo provided Buddha with an opportunity to show kindness to someone who brought to mind his dead wife. In their solitary moments together, Taboo would don a wig and a dress, transforming himself into the semblance of a beautiful young woman, and Buddha would try to persuade him to follow his inner directives and proceed with the final stage of his sex change. He would argue long and hard, claiming that Taboo's magical powers would mature once he completed the transformation, telling Taboo stories of how wonderful his new life would be. But Taboo was deathly afraid of the surgeon's knife, and no matter how forcefully Buddha argued, he refused to pay heed. Buddha knew there had to be an answer to Taboo's problem, and sometimes he felt that answer was staring him in the face. But it never would come clear. He had the notion, though, that sooner or later the time would be right for answers.

It was a beautiful spring day in Taboo's living room. The walls were painted to resemble a blue sky dappled with fluffy white clouds, and the floor was carpeted with artificial grass. In Taboo's bedroom where he did his healing, it was a mystical night. The walls were figured with cabalistic signs and stars and a crescent moon, and the corner table was ebony, and the chairs upholstered in black velour. Black drapes hid the windows; a black satin quilt covered the bed. Muted radiance shone from the ceiling onto the corner table, and after he had fixed, it was there that Buddha sat soaking his wart in a crystal bowl filled with herb-steeped water, while Taboo sat beside him and muttered charms.

Taboo was not in drag because he was waiting for Johnny Wardell to show; but even so he exhibited a feminine beauty. The soft lighting applied sensual gleams to his chocolate skin and enhanced the delicacy of his high cheekbones and generous mouth and almond-shaped eyes. When he leaned forward to inspect Buddha's wart, the tips of his breasts dimpled the fabric of his blousy shirt. Buddha could make out his magic: a disturbance like heat haze in the air around him.

"There, darlin'," said Taboo. "All gone. Your hand back the way it s'posed to be."

Buddha peered into the bowl. At the bottom rested a wrinkled black thing like a raisin. Taboo lifted his hand from the water and dried it with a towel. Where the wart had been was now only smooth skin. Buddha touched the place; it felt hot and smelled bitter from the herbs.

"Wish Johnny'd hurry up," said Taboo. "I bought a new dress I wanna try on for ya."

"Whyn't you try it on now? If the buzzer goes, you can pretend you ain't at home."

" 'Cause I just have to deal wit' him later, and no tellin' what kinda mood Johnny be in then."

Buddha had no need to ask Taboo why he had to deal with Johnny Wardell at all. Taboo's reason for risking himself among the bad dogs was similar to Buddha's reason for retreating from life: he felt guilty for the way he was, and this risk was his self-inflicted punishment.

Taboo pulled out a packet of white powder and a drinking straw and told Buddha to toot a few lines, to put a shine on his high. Buddha did as he suggested. A luxuriant warmth spread through his head and chest, and little sparkles danced in the air, vanishing like snowflakes. He started getting drowsy. Taboo steered him to the bed, then curled up beside him, his arm around Buddha's waist.

"I love you so much, Buddha," he said. "Don't know what I'd do without you to talk to . . . I swear I don't." His soft breasts nudged against Buddha's arm, his fingers toyed with Buddha's belt buckle, and despite himself, Buddha experienced the beginnings of arousal. But he felt no love coming from Taboo, only a flux of lust and anxiety. Love was unmistakable—a warm pressure as steady as a beam from a flashlight—and Taboo was too unformed, too confused, to be its source.

"Naw, man," Buddha said, pushing Taboo's hand away.

"I just wanna love you!"

In Taboo's eyes Buddha could read the sweet fucked-up sadness of a woman born wrong; but though he was sympathetic, he forced himself to be stern. "Don't mess wit' me!"

The buzzer sounded.

"Damn!" Taboo sat up, tucked in his shirt. He walked over to the table, picked up the white powder and the drinking straw, and brought them over to Buddha. "You do a little bit more of this here bad boy. But don't you be runnin' it. I don't want you fallin' out on me." He went out into the living room, closing the door behind him.

There seemed to be a curious weight inside Buddha's head, less an ache than a sense of something askew, and to rid himself of it he did most of the remaining heroin. It was enough to set him dreaming, though not of Africa. These dreams were ugly, featuring shrieks and thuds and nasty smears of laughter, and once somebody said, "The man got tits! Dig it! The man's a fuckin' woman!"

Gradually he arrived at the realization that the dreams were real, that something bad was happening, and he struggled back to full consciousness. He got to his feet, swayed, staggered forward, and threw open the door to the living room.

Taboo was naked and spread-eagled facedown over some pillow, his rump in the air, and Johnny Wardell—a young leather-clad blood with a hawkish face—was holding his arms. Another man, darker and heavier than Wardell, was kneeling between Taboo's legs and was just zipping up his trousers.

For a split second nobody moved. Framed by the vivid green grass and blue sky and innocent clouds, the scene had a surreal biblical quality, like a hideous act perpetrated in some unspoiled corner of the Garden of Eden, and Buddha was transfixed by it. What he saw was vile, but he saw, too, that it was an accurate statement of the world's worth, of its grotesque beauty, and he felt distanced, as if he were watching through a peephole whose far end was a thousand miles away.

"Lookit here," said Wardell, a mean grin slicing across his face. "The ho already done got herself a man. C'mon, bro'! We saved ya a piece."

Long-buried emotions were kindled in Buddha's heart. Rage, love, fear. Their onset too swift and powerful for him to reject. "Get your hand off him," he said, pitching his voice deep and full of menace.

Wardell's lean face went slack, and his grin seemed to deepen, as if the lustful expression engraved on his skull were showing through the skin, as if he perceived in Buddha an object of desire infinitely more gratifying than Taboo.

Wardell nodded at the man kneeling between Taboo's legs, and the man flung himself at Buddha, pulling a knife and swinging it in a vicious arc. Buddha caught the man's wrist, and the man's violence was transmitted through his flesh, seeding fury in his heart. He squeezed the man's wristbones until they ground together, and the knife fell to the floor. Then he pinned the man against the wall and began smashing his head against it, avoiding the fingers that clawed at his eyes. He heard himself yelling, heard bone splinter.

The man's eyes went unfocused, and he grew heavy in Buddha's grasp; he slumped down, the back of his head leaving a glistening red track across a puffy cloud. Buddha knew he was dead, but before he could absorb the fact, something struck him in the back, a liver punch that landed with the stunning impact of a bullet, and he dropped like a stone.

The pain was luminous. He imagined it lighting him up inside with the precise articulation of an X ray. Other blows rained in upon him, but he felt only the effects of that first one. He made out Wardell looming over him, a slim leathery giant delivering kick after kick. Blackness frittered at the edges of his vision. Then a scream—a sound like a silver splinter driven into Buddha's brain—and there was Taboo, something bright in his hand, something that flashed downward into Wardell's chest as he turned, lifted, flashed down again. Wardell stumbled back, looking puzzled, touching a red stain on the shirtfront, and then appeared to slide away into the blackness at the corner of Buddha's left eye. Buddha lay gasping for breath: the last kick had landed in the pit of his stomach. After a second his vision began to clear, and he saw Taboo standing above Wardell's body, the other man's knife in his hand.

With his sleek breasts and male genitalia and the bloody knife, he seemed a creature out of a myth. He kneeled beside Buddha. "You awright?" he asked. "Buddha? You awright?"

Buddha managed a nod. Taboo's eyes reminded him of the eyes of the fish in his dream—aswarm with terrors—and his magic was heavy wash in the air, stronger than Buddha had ever seen it.

"I never wanted to kill nobody," said Taboo tremulously. "That's the *last* thing I wanted to do." He glanced at the two corpses, and his lips quivered. Buddha looked at them, too.

Sprawled in oddly graceful attitudes on the green grass amid a calligraphy of blood, they appeared to be spelling out some kind of cryptic message. Buddha thought if he kept staring at them, their meaning would come clear.

"Oh, God!" said Taboo. "They gon' be comin' for me, they gon' put me in jail! I can't live in jail. What am I gon' do?"

And to his astonishment, looking back and forth between the corpses and Taboo's magical aura, Buddha found he could answer that question.

The answer was, he realized, also the solution to the problem of his life; it was a means of redemption, one he could have arrived at by no other process than that of his fifteen-year retreat.

Its conception had demanded an empty womb in which to breed and had demanded as well an apprehension of magical principle: that had been supplied by his dream of Africa. And having apprehended the full measure of this principle, he further realized he had misunderstood the nature of Taboo's powers. He had assumed that they had been weakened by the wrongness of his birth and would mature once he went under the knife; but he now saw that they were in themselves a way of effecting the transformation with a superior result, that they had needed this moment of violence and desperation to attain sufficient strength. Buddha felt himself filling with calm, as if the knowledge had breached an internal reservoir that had dammed calmness up.

"You need a disguise," he said. "And you got the perfect disguise right at your fingertips." He proceeded to explain.

"You crazy, Buddha!" said Taboo. "No way I can do that."

"You ain't got no choice."

"You crazy!" Taboo repeated, backing away. "Crazy!"

"C'mon back here!"

"Naw, man! I gotta get away, I gotta. . . ." Taboo backed into the door, felt for the knob, and—eyes wide, panic-stricken—wrenched it open. His mouth opened as if he were going to say something else, but instead he turned and bolted down the hall.

The pain in Buddha's back was throbbing, spreading a sick weakness all through his flesh, and he passed out for a few seconds.

When he regained consciousness, he saw Taboo standing in the doorway, looking insubstantial due to the heavy wash of magic around him; in fact, the whole room had an underwater lucidity, everything wavering, like a dream fading in from the immaterial. "See?" said Buddha. "Where you gon' go, man? You barely able to make it here!"

"I don't know, I'll . . . maybe I'll. . . ." Taboo's voice, too, had the qualities of something out of a dream; distant and having a faint echo.

"Sheeit!" Buddha reached out to Taboo. "Gimme a hand up."

Taboo helped him to his feet and into the bedroom and lowered him onto the bed. Buddha felt as if he might sink forever into the black satin coverlet.

"Show me that new dress you bought," he said. Taboo went to the closet, pulled out a hanger, and held the dress against his body to display its effect. It was white silk, low-cut, with a scattering of sequins all over.

"Aw, man," said Buddha. "Yeah, that's *your* dress. You be knockin' the boys' eyes out wearin' that . . . if they could ever see it. If you'd just do what's right. You'd be too beautiful for Detroit. You'd need to get someplace south, place where the moon shines bright as the sun. 'Cause that's what kinda beautiful you gon' be. Moon beautiful. Miami, maybe. That'd suit ya. Get you a big white car, drive down by them fancy hotels, and let all them fancy people have a look at ya. And they gon' lay down and beg to get next to you, man. . . ."

As Buddha talked, conjuring the feminine future with greater seductiveness and invention than ever before, the heat haze of Taboo's magic grew still more visible, taking on the eerie miragelike aspect of the mists beyond the lake in Buddha's Africa; and after Buddha had finished, Taboo sat on the edge of the bed, holding the dress across his lap. "I'm scared," he said. "What if it don't work?"

"You always been scared," said Buddha. "You bein' scared's what got them two men dead out there. Time for that to stop. You know you got the power. So go on!"

"I can't!"

"You ain't got no choice." Buddha pulled Taboo's head down gently and kissed him openmouthed, breathing into him a calming breath. "Do it," he said. "Do it now."

Hesitantly Taboo came to his feet. "Don't you go nowhere now. You wait for me."

"You know I will."

"Awright." Taboo took a few steps toward the bathroom, then stopped. "Buddha, I don't. . . ."

"Go on!"

Taboo lowered his head, walked slowly into the bathroom, and closed the door.

Buddha heard the tub filling, heard the splashing as Taboo climbed into it. Then heard him begin to mutter his charms. He needed to sleep, to fix, but he kept awake as long as he could, trying to help Taboo with the effort of his will. He could feel the vibrations of the magic working through the bathroom door. Finally he gave in to the pressures of exhaustion and the throbbing in his back and drifted off to sleep; the pain followed him into the blackness of sleep, glowing like the core of his being. He woke sometime later to hear Taboo calling his name and spotted him in the darkest corner of the room—a shadow outlined by painted stars.

"Taboo?"

"It don't feel right, Buddha." Taboo's voice had acquired a husky timbre.

"C'mere, man."

Taboo came a step closer, and though Buddha was still unable to see him, he could smell the heat and bitterness of the herbs.

"It worked, didn't it?" Buddha asked. "It musta worked."

"I think. . . . But I feel so peculiar."

"You just ain't used to it is all. . . . Now c'mere!"

Taboo moved still closer, and Buddha made out a naked young woman standing a few feet away. Slim and sexy, with shoulder-length black hair and high, small breasts and a pubic triangle that showed no sign of ever having been male.

The air around Taboo was still and dark. No ripples, no heat haze. The magic had all been used.

"I told ya," said Buddha. "You beautiful."

"I ain't. . . . I just ordinary." But Taboo sounded pleased.

"Ordinary as angels," Buddha said. "That's how ordinary you are."

Taboo smiled. It was faltering at first, that smile, but it grew wider when Buddha repeated the compliment: the smile of a woman gradually becoming confident of her feminine powers. She lay down beside Buddha and fingered his belt buckle. "I love you, Buddha," she said. "Make me feel right."

Love was a steady flow from her, as tangible as a perfume, and Buddha felt it seeping into him, coloring his calm emptiness. On instinct he started to reject the emotion, but then he realized he had one more duty to fulfill, the most taxing and compromising duty of all. He reached down and touched the place between Taboo's legs. Taboo stiffened and pushed her hips against his finger.

"Make me feel right," she said again.

Buddha tried to turn onto his side, but the pain in his back flared. He winced and lay motionless. "Don't know if I can. I'm hurtin' pretty bad."

"I'll help you," she said, her fingers working at his buckle, his zipper. "You won't have to do nothin', Buddha. You just let it happen now."

But Buddha knew he couldn't just let it happen, knew he had to return Taboo's love in order to persuade her of her rightness, her desirability. As she mounted him, a shadow woman lifting and writhing against the false night of the ceiling stars, strangely weightless, he pinned his dead wife's features to her darkened face, remembered *her* ways, *her* secrets. All the love and lust he had fought so long to deny came boiling up from nowhere, annihilating his calm. He dug his fingers into the plump flesh of her hips, wedging himself deep; he plunged and grunted, ignoring the pain in his back, immersed again in the suety richness of desire, in the animal turbulence of this most alluring of human involvements. And when she cried out, a mournful note that planed away to a whisper, like the sound a spirit makes falling through eternity, he felt the profound satisfaction of a musician who by his dominance and skill has brought forth a perfect tone from chaos. But afterward as she snuggled close to him, telling him of her pleasure, her excitement, he felt only despair, fearing that the empty product of his years of ascetic employment had been wasted in a single night.

"Come with me, Buddha," she said. "Come with me to Miami. We can get us a house on the beach and. . . ."

"Lemme be," he said, his despair increasing because he wanted to go with her, to live high in Miami and share her self-discovery, her elation. Only the pain in his back—intensifying with every passing minute—dissuaded him, and it took all his willpower to convince her of his resolve, to insist that she leave without him, for Taboo and his dead wife had fused into a single entity in his mind, and the thought of losing her again was a pain equal to the one inflicted by Johnny Wardell.

At last, suitcase in hand, she stood in the doorway, the temptation of the world in a white silk dress, and said, "Buddha, please won'tcha. . . ."

"Damn it!" he said. "You got what you want. Now get on outta here!"

"Don't be so harsh wit' me, Buddha. You know I love you."

Buddha let his labored breathing be the answer.

"I'll come see ya after a while," she said. "I'll bring you a piece of Miami."

"Don't bother."

"Buddha?"

"Yeah."

"In the bathtub, Buddha . . . I just couldn't touch it."

"I'll take care of it."

She half-turned, glanced back. "I'll always love you, Buddha." The door swung shut behind her, but the radiance of her love kept beaming through the wood, strong and contaminating.

"Go on," he murmured. "Get you a big white car."

He waited until he heard the front door close, then struggled up from the bed, clamping his hand over his liver to muffle the pain. He swayed, on the verge of passing out; but after a moment he felt steadier, although he remained disoriented by unaccustomed emotion. However, the sight of the pitiful human fragment lying in the herb-steeped water of the bathtub served to diminish even that. He scooped it up in a drinking glass and flushed it down the toilet. Then he lay back on the bed again. Closed his eyes for a minute . . . at least he thought it was just a minute. But he couldn't shake the notion that he'd been asleep for a long, long time.

Buddha had to stop and rest half a dozen times on the way back to the shooting gallery, overcome by pain, by emotions . . . mostly by emotions. They were all around him as well as inside.

The shadows of the ruined houses were the ghosts of his loves and hates; the rustlings in the weeds were long-dead memories with red eyes and claws just waiting for a chance to leap out and snatch him; the moon—lopsided and orange and bloated—was the emblem of his forsaken ambitions shining on him anew. By loving Taboo he had wasted fifteen years of effort and opened himself to all the indulgent errors of his past, and he wished to God now he'd never done it. Then, remembering how dreamlike everything had seemed, he had the thought that maybe it *hadn't* happened, that it had been a hallucination brought on by the liver punch. But recalling how it had felt to make love, the womanly fervor of Taboo's moves, he decided it had to have been real. And real or not, he had lived it, he was suffering for it.

When he reached the shooting gallery he sat cross-legged on his mattress, heavy with despair. His back ached something fierce. Pete was angry with him for being late, but on seeing his discomfort he limped upstairs and brought down a needle and helped him fix. "What happened to ya?" he asked, and Buddha said it wasn't nothin', just a muscle spasm.

"Don't gimme that shit," said Pete. "You get hit by a goddamn car, and you be tellin' me it ain't 'bout nothin'." He shook his head ruefully. "Well, to hell wit' ya! I'm sick of worryin' 'bout ya!"

Buddha began to feel drowsy and secure there on his mattress, and he thought if he could rid himself of the love that Taboo had imparted to him, things might be better than before. Clearer, emptier. But he couldn't think how to manage it. Then he saw the opportunity that the old man presented, the need for affection he embodied, his hollow heart.

Pete turned to go back up the stairs, and Buddha said, "Hey, Pete!"

"Yeah, what?"

"I love you, man," said Buddha, and sent his love in a focused beam of such strength that he shivered as it went out of him.

Pete looked at him, perplexed. His expression changed to one of pleasure, then to annoyance. "You *love* me? Huh? Man, you been hangin' out with that faggot too much, that's what you been doin'!" He clumped a couple of steps higher and stopped. "Don't bother comin' upstairs for your goodnighter," he said in gentler tones. "I'll send it down wit' somebody."

" 'Preciate it," said Buddha.

He watched Pete round the corner of the stairwell, then lay down on the mattress. He was so free of desire and human connections that the instant he closed his eyes, golden pinpricks bloomed behind his lids, opened into Africa, and he was flying across the grasslands faster than ever, flying on the wings of the pain that beat like a sick heart in his back. The antelope did not run away but stared at him with wet, dark eyes, and the stick figures of those who guarded the village saluted him with their spears. The shadows of the masked women danced with the abandon of black flames, and in one of the huts a bearded old man was relating the story of a beautiful young woman who had driven a white car south to Miami and had lived wild for a time, had inspired a thousand men to greater wildness, had married and. . . . Buddha flew onward, not wanting to hear the end of the story, knowing that the quality of the beginning was what counted, because all stories ended the same. He was satisfied that Taboo's beginning had been worthwhile. He soared low above the green mountains, low enough to hear the peaceful chants of the gorillas booming through the hidden valleys, and soon was speeding above the lake wherein the solitary fish swam a slow and celebratory circle, arrowing toward the mists on its far side, toward those hallucinatory borders that he previously had neither the necessary courage nor clarity to cross.

From behind him sounded a distant pounding that he recognized to be someone knocking on the door of the shooting gallery, summoning him to his duty. For an instant he had an urge to turn back, to reinhabit the world of the senses, of bluesy-souled hookers and wired white kids and punks who came around looking to trade a night's muscle work for a fix. And that urge intensified when he heard Pete shouting, "Hey, Buddha! Ain't you gon' answer the goddamn door?" But before he could act upon his impulse, he penetrated the mists and felt himself irresistibly drawn by their mysterious central whiteness, and he knew that when old Pete came downstairs, still shouting his angry question, the only answer he would receive would be an almost impalpable pulse in the air like the vibration of a gong whose clangor had just faded beneath the threshold of hearing, the pure signal struck from oblivion, the fanfare announcing Buddha's dominion over the final country of the mind.

This little gook cadre with a pitted complexion drove me through the heart of Saigon—I couldn't relate to it as Ho Chi Minh City—and checked me into the Hotel Heroes of Tet, a place that must have been quietly elegant and very French back in the days when philosophy was discussed over Cointreau rather than practiced in the streets, but now was filled with cheap production-line furniture and tinted photographs of Uncle Ho. Glaring at me, the cadre suggested I would be advised to keep to my room until I left for Cam Le; to annoy him I strolled into the bar, where a couple of Americans—reporters, their table laden with notebooks and tape cassettes—were drinking shots from a bottle of George Dickel. "How's it goin'?" I said, ambling over. "Name's Tom Puleo. I'm doin' a piece on Stoner for *Esquire*."

The bigger of them—chubby, red-faced guy about my age, maybe thirty-five, thirty-six—returned a fishy stare; but the younger one, who was thin and tanned and weaselly handsome, perked up and said, "Hey, you're the guy was in Stoner's outfit, right?" I admitted it, and the chubby guy changed his attitude. He put on a welcome-to-the-lodge smile, stuck out a hand, and introduced himself as Ed Fierman, *Chicago Sun-Times*. His pal, he said, was Ken Witcover, CNN.

They tried to draw me out about Stoner, but I told them maybe later, that I wanted to unwind from the airplane ride, and we proceeded to do damage to the whiskey. By the time we'd sucked down three drinks, Fierman and I were into some heavy reminiscence. Turned out he had covered the war during my tour and knew my old top. Witcover was cherry in Vietnam, so he just tried to look wise and to laugh in the right spots. It got pretty drunk at that table. A security cadre—fortyish, cadaverous gook in yellow fatigues—sat nearby, cocking an ear toward us, and we pretended to be engaged in subversive activity, whispering and drawing maps on napkins. But it was Stoner who was really on all our minds, and Fierman—the drunkest of us—finally broached the subject, saying, "A machine that traps ghosts! It's just like the gooks to come up with something that goddamn worthless!"

Witcover shushed him, glancing nervously at the security cadre, but Fierman was beyond caution. "They coulda done humanity a service," he said, chuckling. "Turned alla Russians into women or something. But, nah! The gooks get behind worthlessness. They may claim to be Marxists, but at heart they still wanna be inscrutable."

"So," said Witcover to me, ignoring Fierman, "when you gonna fill us in on Stoner?"

I didn't care much for Witcover. It wasn't anything personal; I simply wasn't fond of his breed: compulsively neat (pencils lined up, name inscribed on every possession), edgy, on the make. I disliked him the way some people dislike yappy little dogs. But I couldn't argue with his desire to change the subject. "He was a good soldier," I said.

Fierman let out a mulish guffaw. "Now that," he said, "that's what I call in-depth analysis."

Witcover snickered.

"Tell you the truth"—I scowled at him, freighting my words with malice—"I hated the son of a bitch. He had this young-professor air, this way of lookin' at you as if you were an interestin' specimen. And he came across pure phony. Y'know, the kind who's always talkin' like a black dude, sayin' 'right on' and shit, and sayin' it all wrong."

"Doesn't seem much reason for hating him," said Witcover, and by his injured tone, I judged I had touched a nerve. Most likely he had once entertained soul-brother pretensions.

"Maybe not. Maybe if I'd met him back home, I'd have passed him off as a creep and gone about my business. But in combat situations, you don't have the energy to maintain that sort of neutrality. It's easier to hate. And anyway, Stoner could be a genuine pain in the ass."

"How's that?" Fierman asked, getting interested.

"It was never anything unforgivable; he just never let up with it. Like one time a bunch of us were in this guy Gurney's hooch, and he was tellin' 'bout this badass he'd known in Detroit. The cops had been chasin' this guy across the rooftops, and he'd missed a jump.

Fell seven floors and emptied his gun at the cops on the way down. Reaction was typical. Guys sayin' 'Wow' and tryin' to think of a story to top it. But Stoner he nods sagely and says, 'Yeah, there's a lot of that goin' around.' As if this was a syndrome to which he's devoted years of study. But you knew he didn't have a clue, that he was too upscale to have met anybody like Gurney's badass." I had a slug of whiskey. " 'There's a lot of that goin' around' was a totally inept comment. All it did was to bring everyone down from a nice buzz and make us aware of the shithole where we lived."

Witcover looked puzzled, but Fierman made a noise that seemed to imply comprehension. "How'd he die?" he asked. "The handout says he was KIA, but it doesn't say what kind of action."

"The fuckup kind," I said. I didn't want to tell them. The closer I came to seeing Stoner, the leerier I got about the topic. Until this business had begun, I thought I'd buried all the death-tripping weirdness of Vietnam; now Stoner had unearthed it and I was having dreams again and I hated him for that worse than I ever had in life. What was I supposed to do? Feel sorry for him? Maybe ghosts didn't have bad dreams. Maybe it was terrific being a ghost, like with Casper. . . . Anyway, I did tell them. How we had entered Cam Le, what was left of the patrol. How we had lined up the villagers, interrogated them, hit them, and God knows we might have killed them—we were freaked, bone-weary, an atrocity waiting to happen—if Stoner hadn't distracted us. He'd been wandering around, poking at stuff with his rifle, and then, with this ferocious expression on his face, he'd fired into one of the huts. The hut had been empty, but there must have been explosives hidden inside, because after a few rounds the whole damn thing had blown and taken Stoner with it.

Talking about him soured me on company, and shortly afterward I broke it off with Fierman and Witcover, and walked out into the city. The security cadre tagged along, his hand resting on the butt of his sidearm. I had a real load on and barely noticed my surroundings. The only salient points of difference between Saigon today and fifteen years before were the ubiquitous representations of Uncle Ho that covered the facades of many of the buildings, and the absence of motor scooters: the traffic consisted mainly of bicycles. I went a dozen blocks or so and stopped at a sidewalk café beneath sun-browned tamarinds, where I paid two dong for food tickets, my first experience with what the Communists called "goods exchange"—a system they hoped would undermine the concept of monetary trade; I handed the tickets to the waitress, and she gave me a bottle of beer and a dish of fried peanuts. The security cadre, who had taken a table opposite mine, seemed no more impressed with the system than was I; he chided the waitress for her slowness and acted perturbed by the complexity accruing to his order of tea and cakes.

I sat and sipped and stared, thoughtless and unfocused. The bicyclists zipping past were bright blurs with jingling bells, and the light was that heavy leaded-gold light that occurs when a tropical sun has broken free of an overcast. Smells of charcoal, fish sauce, grease. The heat squeezed sweat from my every pore. I was brought back to alertness by angry voices. The security cadre was arguing with the waitress, insisting that the recorded music be turned on, and she was explaining that there weren't enough customers to warrant turning it on. He began to offer formal "constructive criticism," making clear that he considered her refusal both a breach of party ethics and the code of honorable service. About then, I realized I had begun to cry. Not sobs, just tears leaking. The tears had nothing to do with the argument or the depersonalized ugliness it signaled. I believe that the heat and the light and the smells had seeped into me, triggering a recognition of an awful familiarity that my mind had thus far rejected. I wiped my face and tried to suck it up before anyone could notice my emotionality; but a teenage boy on a bicycle slowed and gazed at me with an amused expression. To show my contempt, I spat on the sidewalk. Almost instantly, I felt much better.

Early the next day, thirty of us—all journalists—were bussed north to Cam Le. Mist still wreathed the paddies, the light had a yellowish green cast, and along the road women in black dresses were waiting for a southbound bus, with rumpled sacks of produce like sleepy brown animals at their feet. I sat beside Fierman, who, being as hung over as I was, made no effort at conversation; however, Witcover— sitting across the aisle—peppered me with inane questions until I told him to leave me alone. Just before we turned onto the dirt road that led to Cam Le, an information cadre boarded the bus and for the duration proceeded to fill us in on everything we already knew. Stuff about the machine, how its fields were generated, and so forth. Technical jargon gives me a pain, and I tried hard not to listen. But then he got off onto a tack that caught my interest. "Since the machine has been in operation," he said, "the apparition seems to have grown more vital."

"What's that mean?" I asked, waving my hand to attract his attention. "Is he coming back to life?"

My colleagues laughed.

The cadre pondered this. "It simply means that his effect has become more observable," he said at last. And beyond that he would not specify.

Cam Le had been evacuated, its population shifted to temporary housing three miles east. The village itself was nothing like the place I had entered fifteen years before. Gone were the thatched huts, and in their stead were about two dozen small houses of concrete block painted a quarantine yellow, with banana trees set between them. All this encircled by thick jungle. Standing on the far side of the road from the group of houses was the long tin-roofed building that contained the machine. Two soldiers were lounging in front of it, and as the bus pulled up, they snapped to attention; a clutch of officers came out the door, followed by a portly white-haired gook: Phan Thnah Tuu, the machine's inventor. I disembarked and studied him while he shook hands with the other journalists; it wasn't every day that I met someone who claimed to be both Marxist and mystic, and had gone more than the required mile in establishing the validity of each. His hair was as fine as corn silk, a fat black mole punctuated one cheek, and his benign smile was unflagging, seeming a fixture of some deeply held good opinion attaching to everything he saw. Maybe, I thought, Fierman was right. In-fucking-scrutable.

"Ah," he said, coming up, enveloping me in a cloud of perfumy cologne. "Mr. Puleo. I hope this won't be painful for you."

"Really," I said. "You hope that, do you?"

"I beg your pardon," he said, taken aback.

"It's okay." I grinned. "You're forgiven."

An unsmiling major led him away to press more flesh, and he glanced back at me, perplexed. I was mildly ashamed of having fucked with him, but unlike Cassius Clay, I had plenty against them Viet Congs. Besides, my wiseass front was helping to stave off the yips.

After a brief welcome-to-the-wonderful-wacky-world-of-the-Commie-techno-paradise speech given by the major, Tuu delivered an oration upon the nature of ghosts, worthy of mention only in that it rehashed every crackpot notion I'd ever heard: apparently Stoner hadn't yielded much in the way of hard data. He then warned us to keep our distance from the village. The fields would not harm us; they were currently in operation, undetectable to our senses and needing but a slight manipulation to "focus" Stoner. But if we were to pass inside the fields, it was possible that Stoner himself might be able to cause us injury. With that, Tuu bowed and reentered the building.

We stood facing the village, which—with its red dirt and yellow houses and green banana leaves—looked elementary and innocent under the leaden sky. Some of my colleagues whispered together, others checked their cameras. I felt numb and shaky, prepared to turn away quickly, much the way I once had felt when forced to identify the body of a chance acquaintance at a police morgue. Several minutes after Tuu had left us, there was a disturbance in the air at the center of the village. Similar to heat haze, but the ripples were slower. And then, with the suddenness of a slide shunted into a projector, Stoner appeared.

I think I had been expecting something bloody and ghoulish, or perhaps a gauzy insubstantial form; but he looked no different than he had on the day he died. Haggard; wearing sweat-stained fatigues; his face half-obscured by a week's growth of stubble. On his helmet were painted the words *Didi Mao* ("Fuck Off" in Vietnamese), and I could make out the yellowing photograph of his girl that he'd taped to his rifle stock. He didn't act startled by our presence; on the contrary, his attitude was nonchalant. He shouldered his rifle, tipped back his helmet, and sauntered toward us. He seemed to be recessed into the backdrop: it was as if reality were two-dimensional and he was a cutout held behind it to give the illusion of depth. At least that's how it was one moment. The next, he would appear to be set forward of the backdrop like a pop-up figure in a fancy greeting card. Watching him shift between these modes was unsettling . . . more than unsettling. My heart hammered, my mouth was cottony. I bumped into someone and realized that I had been backing away, that I was making a scratchy noise deep in my throat. Stoner's eyes, those eyes that had looked dead even in life, pupils about .45 caliber and hardly any iris showing, they were locked onto mine and the pressure of his stare was like two black bolts punching through into my skull.

"Puleo," he said.

I couldn't hear him, but I saw his lips shape the name. With a mixture of longing and hopelessness harrowing his features, he kept on repeating it. And then I noticed something else. The closer he drew to me, the more in focus he became. It wasn't just a matter of the shortening distance; his stubble and sweat stains, the frays in his fatigues, his worry lines—all these were sharpening the way details become fixed in a developing photograph. But none of that disturbed me half as much as did the fact of a dead man calling my name. I couldn't handle that. I began to hyperventilate, to get dizzy, and I believe I might have blacked out; but before that could happen, Stoner reached the edge of the fields, the barrier beyond which he could not pass.

Had I had more mental distance from the event, I might have enjoyed the sound-and-light that ensued: it was spectacular. The instant Stoner hit the end of his tether, there was an earsplitting shriek of the kind metal emits under immense stress; it seemed to issue from the air, the trees, the earth, as if some ironclad physical constant had been breached. Stoner was frozen midstep, his mouth open, and opaque lightnings were forking away from him, taking on a violet tinge as they vanished, their passage illuminating the curvature of the fields. I heard a scream and assumed it must be Stoner. But somebody grabbed me, shook me, and I understood that I was the one screaming, screaming with throat-tearing abandon because his eyes were boring into me and I could have sworn that his thoughts, his sensations, were flowing to me along the track of his vision. I knew what he was feeling: not pain, not desperation, but emptiness. An emptiness made unbearable by his proximity to life, to fullness. It was the worst thing I'd ever felt, worse than grief and bullet wounds, and it had to be worse than dying—dying, you see, had an end, whereas this went on and on, and every time you thought you had adapted to it, it grew worse yet. I wanted it to stop. That was all I wanted. Ever. Just for it to stop.

Then, with the same abruptness that he had appeared, Stoner winked out of existence and the feeling of emptiness faded.

People pressed in, asking questions. I shouldered them aside and walked off a few paces. My hands were shaking, my eyes weepy. I stared at the ground. It looked blurred, an undifferentiated smear of green with a brown clot in the middle: this gradually resolved into grass and my left shoe. Ants were crawling over the laces, poking their heads into the eyelets. The sight was strengthening, a reassurance of the ordinary.

"Hey, man." Witcover hove up beside me. "You okay?" He rested a hand on my shoulder. I kept my eyes on the ants, saying nothing. If it had been anyone else, I might have responded to his solicitude; but I knew he was only sucking up to me, hoping to score some human interest for his satellite report. I glanced at him. He was wearing a pair of mirrored sunglasses, and that consolidated my anger. Why is it, I ask you, that every measly little wimp in the universe

thinks he can put on a pair of mirrored sunglasses and instantly acquire magical hipness and cool, rather than—as is the case—looking
like an asshole with reflecting eyes?

"Fuck off," I told him in a tone that implied dire consequences
were I not humored. He started to talk back, but thought better of
it and stalked off. I returned to watching the ants; they were caravan-
ning up inside my trousers and onto my calf. I would become a legend
among them: The Human Who Stood Still for Biting.

From behind me came the sound of peremptory gook voices, angry
American voices. I paid them no heed, content with my insect pals
and the comforting state of thoughtlessness that watching them induced. A minute or so later, someone else moved up beside me and
stood without speaking. I recognized Tuu's cologne and looked up.
"Mr. Puleo," he said. "I'd like to offer you an exclusive on this
story." Over his shoulder, I saw my colleagues staring at us through
the windows of the bus, as wistful and forlorn as kids who have been
denied Disneyland: they, like me, knew that big bucks were to be
had from exploiting Stoner's plight.

"Why?" I asked.

"We want your help in conducting an experiment."

I waited for him to continue.

"Did you notice," he said, "that after Stoner identified you, his
image grew sharper?"

I nodded.

"We're interested in observing the two of you in close proximity.
His reaction to you was unique."

"You mean go in there?" I pointed to the village. "You said it
was dangerous."

"Other subjects have entered the fields and shown no ill effects.
But Stoner was not as intrigued by them as he was with you." Tuu
brushed a lock of hair back from his forehead. "We have no idea of
Stoner's capabilities, Mr. Puleo. It *is* a risk. But since you served in
the Army, I assume you are accustomed to risk."

I let him try to persuade me—the longer I held out, the stronger
my bargaining position—but I had already decided to accept the offer. Though I wasn't eager to feel that emptiness again, I had convinced myself that it had been a product of nerves and an overactive
imagination; now that I had confronted Stoner, I believed I would
be able to control my reactions. Tuu said that he would have the others
driven back to Saigon, but I balked at that. I was not sufficiently secure
to savor the prospect of being alone among the gooks, and I told Tuu

I wanted Fierman and Witcover to stay. Why Witcover? At the time I might have said it was because he and Fierman were the only two of my colleagues whom I knew; but in retrospect, I think I may have anticipated the need for a whipping boy.

We were quartered in a house at the eastern edge of the village, one that the fields did not enclose. Three cots were set up inside, along with a table and chairs; the yellow walls were brocaded with mildew, and weeds grew sideways from chinks in the concrete blocks. Light was provided by an oil lamp that—as darkness fell—sent an inconstant glow lapping over the walls, making it appear that the room was filled with dirty orange water.

After dinner Fierman produced a bottle of whiskey—his briefcase contained three more—and a deck of cards, and we sat down to while away the evening. The one game we all knew was Hearts, and we each played according to the dictates of our personalities. Fierman became quickly drunk and attempted to Shoot the Moon on every hand, no matter how bad his cards; he seemed to be asking fate to pity a fool. I paid little attention to the game, my ears tuned to the night sounds, half expecting to hear the sputter of small-arms fire, the rumor of some ghostly engagement; it was by dint of luck alone that I maintained second place. Witcover played conservatively, building his score through our mistakes, and though we were only betting a nickel a point, to watch him sweat out every trick you would have thought a fortune hung in the balance; he chortled over our pitiful fuckups, rolling his eyes and shaking his head in delight, and whistled as he totaled up his winnings. The self-importance he derived from winning fouled the atmosphere, and the room acquired the staleness of a cell where we had been incarcerated for years. Finally, after a particularly childish display of glee, I pushed back my chair and stood.

"Where you going?" asked Witcover. "Let's play."

"No, thanks," I said.

"Christ!" He picked up the discards and muttered something about sore losers.

"It's not that," I told him. "I'm worried if you win another hand, you're gonna come all over the fuckin' table. I don't wanna watch."

Fierman snorted laughter.

Witcover shot me an aggrieved look. "What's with you, man? You been on my case ever since the hotel."

I shrugged and headed for the door.

"Asshole," he said half under his breath.

"What?" An angry flush numbed my face as I turned back.

He tried to project an expression of manly belligerence, but his eyes darted from side to side.

"Asshole?" I said. "Is that right?" I took a step toward him.

Fierman scrambled up, knocking over his chair, and began pushing me away. "C'mon," he said. "It's not worth it. Chill out." His boozy sincerity acted to diminish my anger, and I let him urge me out the door.

The night was moonless, with a few stars showing low on the horizon; the spiky crowns of the palms ringing the village were silhouettes pinned onto a lesser blackness. It was so humid, it felt like you could spoon in the air. I crossed the dirt road, found a patch of grass near the tin-roofed building, and sat down. The door to the building was cracked, spilling a diagonal of white radiance onto the ground, and I had the notion that there was no machine inside, only a mystic boil of whiteness emanating from Tuu's silky hair. A couple of soldiers walked past and nodded to me; they paused a few feet farther along to light cigarettes, which proceeded to brighten and fade with the regularity of tiny beacons.

Crickets sawed, frogs chirred, and listening to them, smelling the odor of sweet rot from the jungle, I thought about a similar night when I'd been stationed at Phnoc Vinh, about a party we'd had with a company of artillery. There had been a barbecue pit and iced beer and our CO had given special permission for whores to come on the base. It had been a great party; in fact, those days at Phnoc Vinh had been the best time of the war for me. The artillery company had had this terrific cook, and on movie nights he'd make doughnuts. Jesus, I'd loved those doughnuts! They'd tasted like home, like peace. I'd kick back and munch a doughnut and watch the bullshit movie, and it was almost like being in my own living room, watching the tube. Trouble was, Phnoc Vinh had softened me up, and after three weeks, when we'd been airlifted to Quan Loi, which was constantly under mortar and rocket fire, I'd nearly gotten my ass blown off.

Footsteps behind me. Startled, I turned and saw what looked to be a disembodied white shirt floating toward me. I came to one knee, convinced for the moment that some other ghost had been lured to the machine; but a second later a complete figure emerged from the dark: Tuu. Without a word, he sat cross-legged beside me. He was smoking a cigarette . . . or so I thought until I caught a whiff of marijuana. He took a deep drag, the coal illuminating his placid features, and offered me the joint. I hesitated, not wanting to be pals; but tempted by the smell, I accepted it, biting back a smartass remark about Marxist permissiveness. It was good shit. I could feel the smoke twisting through me, finding out all my hollow places. I handed it back, but he made a gesture of warding it off, and after a brief silence he said, "What do you think about all this, Mr. Puleo?"

"About Stoner?"

"Yes."

"I think"—I jetted smoke from my nostrils—"it's crap that you've got him penned up in that astral tiger cage."

"Had this discovery been made in the United States," he said, "the circumstances would be no different. Humane considerations—if, indeed, they apply—would have low priority."

"Maybe," I said. "It's still crap."

"Why? Do you believe Stoner is unhappy?"

"Don't you?" I had another hit. It was *very* good shit. The ground seemed to have a pulse. "Ghosts are by nature unhappy."

"Then you know what a ghost is?"

"Not hardly. But I figure unhappy's part of it." The roach was getting too hot; I took a final hit and flipped it away. "How 'bout you? You believe that garbage you preached this mornin'?"

His laugh was soft and cultivated. "That was a press release. However, my actual opinion is neither less absurd-sounding nor more verifiable."

"And what's that?"

He plucked a blade of grass, twiddled it. "I believe a ghost is a quality that dies in a man long before he experiences physical death. Something that has grown acclimated to death and thus survives the body. It might be love or an ambition. An element of character . . . Anything." He regarded me with his lips pursed. "I have such a ghost within me. As do you, Mr. Puleo. My ghost senses yours."

The theory was as harebrained as his others, but I wasn't able to deny it. I knew he was partly right, that a moral filament had snapped inside me during the war and since that time I had lacked the ingredient necessary to the development of a generous soul. Now it seemed that I could feel that lack as a restless presence straining against my flesh. The sawing of the crickets intensified, and I had a rush of paranoia, wondering if Tuu was fucking with my head. Then, moods shifting at the chemical mercies of the dope, my paranoia eroded and Tuu snapped into focus for me . . . or at least his ghost did. He had,

I recalled, written poetry prior to the war, and I thought I saw the features of that lost poet melting up from his face: a dreamy fellow given to watching petals fall and contemplating the moon's reflection. I closed my eyes, trying to get a grip. This was the best dope I'd ever smoked. Commie Pink, pure buds of the revolution.

"Are you worried about tomorrow?" Tuu asked.

"Should I be?"

"I can only tell you what I did before—no one has been harmed."

"What happened during those other experiments?" I asked.

"Very little, really. Stoner approached each subject, spoke to them. Then he lost interest and wandered off."

"Spoke to them? Could they hear him?"

"Faintly. However, considering his reaction to you, I wouldn't be surprised if you could hear him quite well."

I wasn't thrilled by that prospect. Having to look at Stoner was bad enough. I thought about the eerie shit he might say: admonitory pronouncements, sad questions, windy vowels gusting from his strange depths. Tuu said something and had to repeat it to snap me out of my reverie. He asked how it felt to be back in Vietnam, and without forethought, I said it wasn't a problem.

"And the first time you were here," he said, an edge to his voice. "Was that a problem?"

"What are you gettin' at?"

"I noticed in your records that you were awarded a Silver Star."

"Yeah?"

"You must have been a good soldier. I wondered if you might not have found a calling in war."

"If you're askin' what I think about the war," I said, getting pissed, "I don't make judgments about it. It was a torment for me, nothing more. Its geopolitical consequences, cultural effects, they're irrelevant to me . . . maybe they're ultimately irrelevant. Though I doubt you'd agree."

"We may agree more than you suspect." He sighed pensively. "For both of us, apparently, the war was a passion. In your case, an agonizing one. In mine, while there was also agony, it was essentially a love affair with revolution, with the idea of revolution. And as with all great passions, what was most alluring was not the object of passion but the new depth of my own feelings. Thus I was blind to the realities underlying it. Now"—he waved at the sky, the trees—"now I inhabit those realities and I am not as much in love as once I was. Yet no matter how extreme my disillusionment, the passion continues. I want it to continue. I need the significance with which it imbues my past actions." He studied me. "Isn't that how it is for you? You say war was a torment, but don't you find those days empowering?"

Just as when he had offered me the joint, I realized that I didn't want this sort of peaceful intimacy with him; I preferred him to be my inscrutable enemy. Maybe he was right, maybe—like him—I needed this passion to continue in order to give significance to my past. Whatever, I felt vulnerable to him, to my perception of his humanity. "Good night," I said, getting to my feet. My ass was numb from sitting and soaked with dew.

He gazed up at me, unreadable, and fingered something from his shirt pocket. Another joint. He lit up, exhaling a billow of smoke. "Good night," he said coldly.

The next morning—sunny, cloudless—I staked myself out on the red dirt of Cam Le to wait for Stoner. Nervous, I paced back and forth until the air began to ripple and he materialized less than thirty feet away. He walked slowly toward me, his rifle dangling; a drop of sweat carved a cold groove across my rib cage. "Puleo," he said, and this time I heard him. His voice was faint, but it shook me.

Looking into his blown-out pupils, I was reminded of a day not long before he had died. We had been hunkered down together after a firefight, and our eyes had met, had locked as if sealed by a vacuum: like two senile old men, incapable of any communication aside from a recognition of the other's vacancy. As I remembered this, it hit home to me that though he hadn't been a friend, he *was* my brother-in-arms, and that as such, I owed him more than journalistic interest.

"Stoner!" I hadn't intended to shout, but in that outcry was a wealth of repressed emotion, of regret and guilt and anguish at not being able to help him elude the fate by which he had been overtaken.

He stopped short; for an instant the hopelessness drained from his face. His image was undergoing that uncanny sharpening of focus: sweat beads popping from his brow, a scab appearing on his chin. The lines of strain around his mouth and eyes were etched deep, filled in with grime, like cracks in his tan.

Tides of emotion were washing over me, and irrational though it seemed, I knew that some of these emotions—the fierce hunger for life in particular—were Stoner's. I believe we had made some sort of connection, and all our thoughts were in flux between us. He moved toward me again. My hands trembled, my knees buckled, and I had to sit down, overwhelmed not by fear but by the combination of his familiarity and utter strangeness. "Jesus, Stoner," I said. "Jesus."

He stood gazing dully down at me. "My sending," he said, his voice louder and with a pronounced resonance. "Did you get it?"

A chill articulated my spine, but I forced myself to ignore it. "Sending?" I said.

"Yesterday," he said, "I sent you what I was feeling. What it's like for me here."

"How?" I asked, recalling the feeling of emptiness. "How'd you do that?"

"It's easy, Puleo," he said. "All you have to do is die, and thoughts . . . dreams, they'll flake off you like old paint. But believe me, it's hardly adequate compensation." He sat beside me, resting the rifle across his knees. This was no ordinary sequence of movements. His outline wavered, and his limbs appeared to drift apart: I might have been watching the collapse of a lifelike statue through a volume of disturbed water. It took all my self-control to keep from flinging myself away. His image steadied, and he stared at me. "Last person I was this close to ran like hell," he said. "You always were a tough mother-fucker, Puleo. I used to envy you that."

If I hadn't believed before that he was Stoner, the way he spoke the word *motherfucker* would have cinched it for me: it had the stiffness of a practiced vernacular, a mode of expression that he hadn't mastered. This and his pathetic manner made him seem less menacing. "You were tough, too," I said glibly.

"I tried to be," he said. "I tried to copy you guys. But it was an act, a veneer. And when we hit Cam Le, the veneer cracked."

"You remember. . . ." I broke off because it didn't feel right, my asking him questions; the idea of translating his blood and bones into a best-seller was no longer acceptable.

"Dying?" His lips thinned. "Oh, yeah. Every detail. You guys were hassling the villagers, and I thought, Christ, they're going to kill them. I didn't want to be involved, and . . . I was so tired, you know, so tired in my head, and I figured if I walked off a little ways, I wouldn't be part of it. I'd be innocent. So I did. I moved a ways off, and the wails, the shouts, they weren't real anymore. Then I came to this hut. I'd lost track of what was happening by that time. In my mind I was sure you'd already started shooting, and I said to my-self, I'll show them I'm doing my bit, put a few rounds into this hut. Maybe"—his Adam's apple worked—"maybe they'll think I killed somebody. Maybe that'll satisfy them."

I looked down at the dirt, troubled by what I now understood to be my complicity in his death, and troubled also by a new understanding of the events surrounding the death. I realized that if anyone else had gotten himself blown up, the rest of us would have flipped out and likely have wasted the villagers. But since it had been Stoner, the explosion had had almost a calming effect: Cam Le had rid us of a nuisance.

Stoner reached out his hand to me. I was too mesmerized by the gesture, which left afterimages in the air, to recoil from it, and I watched horrified as his fingers gripped my upper arm, pressing wrinkles in my shirtsleeve. His touch was light and transmitted a dry coolness, and with it came a sensation of weakness. By all appearances, it was a normal hand, yet I kept expecting it to become translucent and merge with my flesh.

"It's going to be okay," said Stoner.

His tone, though bemused, was confident, and I thought I detected a change in his face, but I couldn't put my finger on what the change was. "Why's it gonna be okay?" I asked, my voice more frail and ghostly-sounding than his. "It doesn't seem okay to me."

"Because you're part of my process, my circuitry. Understand?"

"No," I said. I had identified what had changed about him. Whereas a few moments before he had looked real, now he looked more than real, ultrareal; his features had acquired the kind of gloss found in airbrushed photographs, and for a split second his eyes were cored with points of glitter as if reflecting a camera flash . . . except these points were bluish white, not red. There was a coarseness to his face that hadn't been previously evident, and in contrast to my earlier perception of him, he now struck me as dangerous, malevolent.

He squinted and cocked his head. "What's wrong, man? You scared of me?" He gave an amused sniff. "Hang in there, Puleo. Tough guy like you, you'll make an adjustment." My feeling of weakness had intensified: it was as if blood or some even more vital essence were trickling out of me. "Come on, Puleo," he said mockingly. "Ask me some questions? That's what you're here for, isn't it? I mean this must be the goddamn scoop of the century. Good News From Beyond the Grave! Of course"—he pitched his voice low and sepulchral—"the news isn't all that good."

Those glittering cores resurfaced in his pupils, and I wanted to wrench free; but I felt helpless, wholly in his thrall.

"You see," he went on, "when I appeared in the village, when I walked around and"—he chuckled—"haunted the place, those times were like sleepwalking. I barely knew what was happening. But the rest of the time, I was somewhere else. Somewhere really fucking weird."

My weakness was bordering on vertigo, but I mustered my strength and croaked, "Where?"

"The Land of Shades," he said. "That's what I call it, anyway. You wouldn't like it, Puleo. It wouldn't fit your idea of order."

The lights burned in his eyes, winking bright, and—as if in correspondence to their brightness—my dizziness increased. "Tell me about it," I said, trying to take my mind off the discomfort.

"I'd be delighted!" He grinned nastily. "But not now. It's too complicated. Tonight, man. I'll send you a dream tonight. A bad dream. That'll satisfy your curiosity."

My head was spinning, my stomach abubble with nausea. "Lemme go, Stoner," I said.

"Isn't this good for you, man? It's very good for me." With a flick of his hand, he released my wrist.

I braced myself to keep from falling over, drew a deep breath, and gradually my strength returned. Stoner's eyes continued to burn, and his features maintained their coarsened appearance. The difference between the way he looked now and the lost soul I had first seen was like that between night and day, and I began to wonder whether or not his touching me and my resultant weakness had anything to do with the transformation. "Part of your process," I said. "Does that. . . ."

He looked me straight in the eyes, and I had the impression he was cautioning me to silence. It was more than a caution: a wordless command, a sending. "Let me explain something," he said. "A ghost is merely a stage of growth. He walks because he grows strong by walking. The more he walks, the less he's bound to the world. When he's strong enough"—he made a planing gesture with his hand—"he goes away."

He seemed to be expecting a response. "Where's he go?" I asked.

"Where he belongs," he said. "And if he's prevented from walking, from growing strong, he's doomed."

"You mean he'll die?"

"Or worse."

"And there's no other way out for him?"

"No."

He was lying—I was sure of it. Somehow I posed for him a way out of Cam Le. "Well . . . so," I said, flustered, uncertain of what to do and at the same time pleased with the prospect of conspiring against Tuu.

"Just sit with me awhile," he said, easing his left foot forward to touch my right ankle.

Once again I experienced weakness, and over the next seven or eight hours, he would alternately move his foot away, allowing me to recover, and then bring it back into contact with me. I'm not certain what was happening. One logic dictates that since I had been peripherally involved in his death—"part of his process"—he was therefore able to draw strength from me. Likely as not, this was the case. Yet I've never been convinced that ordinary logic applied to our circumstance: it may be that we were governed by an arcane rationality to which we both were blind. Though his outward aspect did not appear to undergo further changes, his strength became tangible, a cold radiation that pulsed with the steadiness of an icy heart. I came to feel that the image I was seeing was the tip of an iceberg, the perceptible extremity of a huge power cell that existed mainly in dimensions beyond the range of mortal vision. I tried to give the impression of an interview to our observers by continuing to ask questions; but Stoner sat with his head down, his face hidden, and gave terse, disinterested replies.

The sun declined to the tops of the palms, the yellow paint of the houses took on a tawny hue, and—drained by the day-long alternation of weakness and recovery—I told Stoner I needed to rest. "Tomorrow," he said without looking up. "Come back tomorrow."

"All right." I had no doubt that Tuu would be eager to go on with the experiment. I stood and turned to leave; but then another question, a pertinent one, occurred to me. "If a ghost is a stage of growth," I said, "what's he grow into?"

He lifted his head, and I staggered back, terrified. His eyes were ablaze, even the whites winking with cold fire, as if nuggets of phosphorus were embedded in his skull.

"Tomorrow," he said again.

During the debriefing that followed, I developed a bad case of the shakes and experienced a number of other, equally unpleasant, reactions; the places where Stoner had touched me seemed to have retained a chill, and the thought of that dead hand leeching me of energy was in retrospect thoroughly repellent. A good many of Tuu's subordinates, alarmed by Stoner's transformation, lobbied to break off the experiment. I did my best to soothe them, but I wasn't at all sure I wanted to return to the village. I couldn't tell whether Tuu noticed either my trepidation or the fact that I was being less than candid; he was too busy bringing his subordinates in line to question me in depth.

That night, when Fierman broke out his whiskey, I swilled it down as if it were an antidote to poison. To put it bluntly, I got shit-faced. Both Fierman and Witcover seemed warm human beings, old buddies, and our filthy yellow room with its flickering lamp took on the coziness of a cottage and hearth. The first stage of my drunk was maudlin, filled with self-recriminations over my past treatment of Stoner: I vowed not to shrink from helping him. The second stage . . . Well, once I caught Fierman gazing at me askance and registered that my behavior was verging on the manic. Laughing hysterically, talking like a speed freak. We talked about everything except Stoner, and I suppose it was inevitable that the conversation work itself around to the war and its aftermath. Dimly, I heard myself pontificating on a variety of related subjects. At one point Fierman asked what I thought of the Vietnam Memorial, and I told him I had mixed emotions.

"Why?" he asked.

"I go to the Memorial, man," I said, standing up from the table where we had all been sitting. "And I cry. You can't help but cryin', 'cause that"—I hunted for an appropriate image—"that black dividin' line between nowheres, that says it just right 'bout the war. It feels good to cry, to go public with grief and take your place with all the vets of the truly outstandin' wars." I swayed, righted myself. "But the Memorial, the Unknown, the parades . . . basically they're bull-shit." I started to wander around the room, realized that I had forgotten why I had stood and leaned against the wall.

"How you mean?" asked Witcover, who was nearly as drunk as I was.

"Man," I said, "it's a shuck! I mean ten goddamn years go by, and alla sudden there's this blast of media warmth and government-sponsored emotion. 'Welcome home, guys,' ever'body's sayin'. 'We're sorry we treated you so bad. Next time it's gonna be different. You wait and see.' " I went back to the table and braced myself on it with both hands, staring blearily at Witcover: his tan looked blotchy. "Hear that, man? 'Next time.' That's all it is. Nobody really gives a shit 'bout the vets. They're just pavin' the way for the next time.' "

"I don't know," said Witcover. "Seems to—"

"Right!" I spanked the table with the flat of my hand. "You don't know. You don't know shit 'bout it, so shut the fuck up!"

"Be cool," advised Fierman. "Man's entitled to his 'pinion."

I looked at him, saw a flushed, fat face with bloodshot eyes and a stupid reproving frown. "Fuck you," I said. "And fuck his 'pinion." I turned back to Witcover. "Whaddya think, man? That there's this genuine breath of conscience sweepin' the land? Open your goddamn eyes! You been to the movies lately? Jesus Christ! Courageous grunts strikin' fear into the heart of the Red Menace! Miraculous one-man missions to save our honor. Huh! Honor!" I took a long pull from the bottle. "Those movies, they make war seem like a mystical opportunity. Well, man, when I was here it wasn't quite that way, y'know. It was leeches, fungus, the shits. It was searchin' in the weeds for your buddy's arm. It was lookin' into the snaky eyes of some whore you were bangin' and feelin' weird shit crawl along your spine and expectin' her head to do a Linda Blair three-sixty spin." I slumped into a chair and leaned close to Witcover. "It was Mordor, man. Stephen King–land. Horror. And now, now I look around at all these movies and monuments and crap, and it makes me wanna fuckin' puke to see what a noble hell it's turnin' out to be!"

I felt pleased with myself, having said this, and I leaned back, basking in a righteous glow. But Witcover was unimpressed. His face cinched into a scowl, and he said in a tight voice, "You're startin' to really piss me off, y'know."

"Yeah?" I said, and grinned. "How 'bout that?"

"Yeah, all you war-torn creeps, you think you got papers sayin' you can make an ass outta yourself and everybody else gotta say, 'Oh, you poor fucker! Give us more of your tortured wisdom!' "

Fierman muffled a laugh, and—rankled—I said, "That so?"

Witcover hunched his shoulders as if preparing for an off-tackle plunge. "I been listenin' to you guys for years, and you're alla goddamn same. You think you're owed something 'cause you got ground around in the political mill. Shit! I been in Salvador, Nicaragua, Afghanistan. Compared to those people, you didn't go through diddley. But you use what happened as an excuse for fuckin' up your lives . . . or for being assholes. Like you, man." He affected a macho-sounding bass voice. " 'I been in a war. I am an expert on reality.' You don't know how ridiculous you are."

"Am I?" I was shaking again, but with adrenaline not fear, and

I knew I was going to hit Witcover. He didn't know it—he was smirking, his eyes flicking toward Fierman, seeking approval—and that in itself was a sufficient reason to hit him, purely for educational purposes: I had, you see, reached the level of drunkenness at which an amoral man such as myself understands his whimsies to be moral imperatives. But the real reason, the one that had begun to rumble inside me, was Stoner. All my fear, all my reactions thus far, had merely been tremors signaling an imminent explosion, and now, thinking about him nearby, old horrors were stirred up, and I saw myself walking in a napalmed ville rife with dead VC, crispy critters, and beside me this weird little guy named Fellowes who claimed he could read the future from their scorched remains and would point at a hexagramlike structure of charred bone and gristle and say, "That there means a bad moon on Wednesday," and claimed, too, that he could read the past from the blood of head wounds, and then I was leaning over this Canadian nurse, beautiful blond girl, disemboweled by a mine and somehow still alive, her organs dark and wet and pulsing, and somebody giggling, whispering about what he'd like to do, and then another scene that was whirled away so quickly, I could only make out the color of blood, and Witcover said something else, and a dead man was stretching out his hand to me and. . . .

I nailed Witcover, and he flew sideways off the chair and rolled on the floor. I got to my feet, and Fierman grabbed me, trying to wrestle me away; but that was unnecessary, because all my craziness had been dissipated. "I'm okay now," I said, slurring the words, pushing him aside. He threw a looping punch that glanced off my neck, not even staggering me. Then Witcover yelled. He had pulled himself erect and was weaving toward me; an egg-shaped lump was swelling on his cheekbone. I laughed—he looked so puffed up with rage—and started for the door. As I went through it, he hit me on the back of the head. The blow stunned me a bit, but I was more amused than hurt; his fist had made a funny *bonk* sound on my skull, and that set me to laughing harder.

I stumbled between the houses, bouncing off walls, reeling out of control, and heard shouts . . . Vietnamese shouts. By the time I had regained my balance, I had reached the center of the village. The moon was almost full, pale yellow, its craters showing: a pitted eye in the black air. It kept shrinking and expanding, and—as it seemed to lurch farther off—I realized I had fallen and was lying flat on my back. More shouts. They sounded distant, a world away, and the moon had begun to spiral, to dwindle, like water being sucked down a drain. Jesus, I remember thinking just before I passed out, Jesus, how'd I get so drunk?

I'd forgotten Stoner's promise to tell me about the Land of Shades, but apparently he had not, for that night I had a dream in which I was Stoner. It was not that I thought I was him: I *was* him, prone to all his twitches, all his moods. I was walking in a pitch-dark void, possessed by a great hunger. Once this hunger might have been characterized as a yearning for the life I had lost, but it had been transformed into a lust for the life I might someday attain if I proved equal to the tests with which I was presented. That was all I knew of the Land of Shades—that it was a testing ground, less a place than a sequence of events. It was up to me to gain strength from the tests, to ease my hunger as best I could. I was ruled by this hunger, and it was my only wish to ease it.

Soon I spotted an island of brightness floating in the dark, and as I drew near, the brightness resolved into an old French plantation house fronted by tamarinds and rubber trees; sections of white stucco wall and a verandah and a red tile roof were visible between the trunks. Patterns of soft radiance overlaid the grounds, yet there were neither stars nor moon nor any source of light I could discern. I was not alarmed by this—such discrepancies were typical of the Land of Shades.

When I reached the trees I paused, steeling myself for whatever lay ahead. Breezes sprang up to stir the leaves, and a sizzling chorus of crickets faded in from nowhere as if a recording of sensory detail had been switched on. Alert to every shift of shadow, I moved cautiously through the trees and up the verandah steps. Broken roof tiles crunched beneath my feet. Beside the door stood a bottomed-out cane chair; the rooms, however, were devoid of furnishings, the floors dusty, the whitewash flaking from the walls. The house appeared to be deserted, but I knew I was not alone. There was a hush in the air, the sort that arises from a secretive presence. Even had I failed to notice this, I could scarcely have missed the scent of perfume. I had never tested against a woman before, and, excited by the prospect, I was tempted to run through the house and ferret her out. But this would have been foolhardy, and I continued at a measured pace.

At the center of the house lay a courtyard, a rectangular space choked with waist-high growths of jungle plants, dominated by a stone fountain in the shape of a stylized orchid. The woman was leaning against the fountain, and despite the grayish-green half-light—a light that seemed to arise from the plants—I could see she was beautiful. Slim and honey-colored, with falls of black hair spilling over the shoulders of her *ao dai*. She did not move or speak, but the casualness of her pose was an invitation. I felt drawn to her, and as I pushed through the foliage, the fleshy leaves clung to my thighs and groin, touches that seemed designed to provoke arousal. I stopped an arm's length away and studied her. Her features were of a feline delicacy, and in the fullness of her lower lip, the petulant set of her mouth, I detected a trace of French breeding. She stared at me with palpable sexual interest. It had not occurred to me that the confrontation might take place on a sexual level, yet now I was certain this would be the case. I had to restrain myself from initiating the contact: there are rigorous formalities that must be observed prior to each test. And besides, I wanted to savor the experience.

"I am Tuyet," she said in a voice that seemed to combine the qualities of smoke and music.

"Stoner," I said.

The names hung in the air like the echoes of two gongs.

She lifted her hand as if to touch me, but lowered it: she, too, was practicing restraint. "I was a prostitute," she said. "My home was Lai Khe, but I was an outcast. I worked the water points along Highway Thirteen."

It was conceivable, I thought, that I may have known her. While I had been laid up in An Loc, I'd frequented those water points: bomb craters that had been turned into miniature lakes by the rains and served as filling stations for the water trucks attached to the First Infantry. Every morning the whores and their mama sans would drive out to the water points in three-wheeled motorcycle trucks; with them would be vendors selling combs and pushbutton knives and rubbers that came wrapped in gold foil, making them look like those disks of chocolate you can buy in the States. Most of these girls were more friendly than the city girls, and knowing that Tuyet had been one of them caused me to feel an affinity with her.

She went on to tell me that she had gone into the jungle with an American soldier and had been killed by a sniper. I told her my story in brief and then asked what she had learned of the Land of Shades. This is the most rigorous formality: I had never met anyone with whom I had failed to exchange information.

"Once," Tuyet said, "I met an old man, a Cao Dai medium from Black Virgin Mountain, who told me he had been to a place where a pillar of whirling light and dust joined earth to sky. Voices spoke from the pillar, sometimes many at once, and from them he understood that all wars are merely reflections of a deeper struggle, of a demon breaking free. The demon freed by our war, he said, was very strong, very dangerous. We the dead had been recruited to wage war against him."

I had been told a similar story by an NLF captain, and once, while crawling through a tunnel system, I myself had heard voices speaking from a skull half buried in the earth. But I had been too frightened to stay and listen. I related all this to Tuyet, and her response was to trail her fingers across my arm. My restraint, too, had frayed. I dragged her down into the thick foliage. It was as if we had been submerged in a sea of green light and fleshy stalks, as if the plantation house had vanished and we were adrift in an infinite vegetable depth where gravity had been replaced by some buoyant principle. I tore at her clothes, she at mine. Her *ao dai* shredded like crepe, and my fatigues came away in ribbons that dangled from her hooked fingers. Greedy for her, I pressed my mouth to her breasts. Her nipples looked black in contrast to her skin, and it seemed I could taste their blackness, tart and sour. Our breathing was hoarse, urgent, and the only other sound was the soft mulching of the leaves. With surprising strength, she pushed me onto my back and straddled my hips, guiding me inside her, sinking down until her buttocks were grinding against my thighs.

Her head flung back, she lifted and lowered herself. The leaves and stalks churned and intertwined around us as if they, too, were copulating. For a few moments my hunger was assuaged, but soon I noticed that the harder I thrust, the more fiercely she plunged, the less intense the sensations became. Though she gripped me tightly, the friction seemed to have been reduced. Frustrated, I dug my fingers into her plump hips and battered at her, trying to drive myself deeper. Then I squeezed one of her breasts and felt a searing pain in my palm. I snatched back my hand and saw that her nipple, both nipples, were twisting, elongating; I realized that they had been transformed into the heads of two black centipedes, and the artful movements of her internal muscles . . . they were too artful, too disconnectedly in motion. An instant later I felt that same searing pain in my cock and knew I was screwing myself into a nest of creatures like those protruding from her breasts. All her skin was rippling, reflecting the humping of thousands of centipedes beneath.

The pain was enormous, so much so that I thought my entire body must be glowing with it. But I did not dare fail this test, and I continued pumping into her, thrusting harder than ever. The leaves thrashed, the stalks thrashed as in a gale, and the green light grew livid. Tuyet began to scream—God knows what manner of pain I was causing her—and her screams completed a perverse circuit within me. I found I could channel my own pain into those shrill sounds. Still joined to her, I rolled atop her, clamped her wrists together, and pinned them above her head. Her screams rang louder, inspiring me to greater efforts yet. Despite the centipedes tipping her breasts, or perhaps because of them, because of the grotesque juxtaposition of the sensual and the horrid, her beauty seemed to have been enhanced, and my mastery over her actually provided me a modicum of pleasure.

The light began to whiten, and looking off, I saw that we were being borne by an invisible current through—as I had imagined—an infinite depth of stalks and leaves. The stalks that lashed around us thickened far below into huge pale trunks with circular ribbing. I could not make out where they met the earth—if, indeed, they did—and they appeared to rise an equal height above. The light brightened further, casting the distant stalks in silhouette, and I realized we were drifting toward the source of the whiteness, beyond which would lie another test, another confrontation. I glanced at Tuyet. Her skin no longer displayed that obscene rippling, her nipples had reverted to normal. Pain was evolving into pleasure, but I knew it would be short-lived, and I tried to resist the current, to hold on to pain, because even pain was preferable to the hunger I would soon experience. Tuyet clawed my back, and I felt the first dissolute rush of my orgasm. The current was irresistible. It flowed through my blood, my cells. It was part of me, or rather I was part of it. I let it move me, bringing me to completion.

Gradually the whipping of the stalks subsided to a pliant swaying motion. They parted for us, and we drifted through their interstices as serenely as a barge carved to resemble a coupling of two naked figures. I found I could not disengage from Tuyet, that the current enforced our union, and resigned to this, I gazed around, marveling at the vastness of this vegetable labyrinth and the strangeness of our fates. Beams of white light shined through the stalks, the brightness growing so profound that I thought I heard in it a roaring; and as my consciousness frayed, I saw myself reflected in Tuyet's eyes—a ragged dark creature wholly unlike my own self-image—and wondered for the thousandth time who had placed us in this world, who had placed these worlds in us.

Other dreams followed, but they were ordinary, the dreams of an or-dinarily anxious, ordinarily drunken man, and it was the memory of this first dream that dominated my waking moments. I didn't want to wake because—along with a headache and other symptoms of hang-over—I felt incredibly weak, incapable of standing and facing the world. Muzzy-headed, I ignored the reddish light prying under my eyelids and tried to remember more of the dream. Despite Stoner's attempts to appear streetwise, despite the changes I had observed in him, he had been at heart an innocent and it was difficult to accept that the oddly formal, brutally sexual protagonist of the dream had been in any way akin to him. Maybe, I thought, recalling Tuu's theory of ghosts, maybe that was the quality that had died in Stoner: his inno-cence. I began once again to suffer guilt feelings over my hatred of him, and, preferring a hangover to that, I propped myself on one elbow and opened my eyes.

I doubt more than a second or two passed before I sprang to my feet, hangover forgotten, electrified with fear; but in that brief span the reason for my weakness was made plain. Stoner was sitting close to where I had been lying, his hand outstretched to touch me, head down . . . exactly as he had sat the previous day. Aside from his pose, however, very little about him was the same.

The scene was of such complexity that now, thinking back on it, it strikes me as implausible that I could have noticed its every detail; yet I suppose that its power was equal to its complexity and thus I did not so much see it as it was imprinted on my eyes. Dawn was a crimson smear fanning across the lower sky, and the palms stood out blackly against it, their fronds twitching in the breeze like spiders impaled on pins. The ruddy light gave the rutted dirt of the street the look of a trough full of congealed blood. Stoner was motionless—that is to say, he didn't move his limbs, his head, or shift his posi-tion; but his image was pulsing, swelling to half again its normal size and then deflating, all with the rhythm of steady breathing. As he expanded, the cold white fire blazing from his eyes would spread in cracks that veined his entire form; as he contracted, the cracks would disappear and for a moment he would be—except for his eyes—the familiar figure I had known. It seemed that his outward appearance—his fatigues and helmet, his skin—was a shell from which some glow-ing inner man was attempting to break free. Grains of dust were whirl-ing up from the ground beside him, more and more all the time: a miniature cyclone wherein he sat calm and ultimately distracted, the likeness of a warrior monk whose meditations had borne fruit.

Shouts behind me. I turned and saw Fierman, Tuu, Witcover, and various of the gooks standing at the edge of the village. Tuu beck-oned to me, and I wanted to comply, to run, but I wasn't sure I had the strength. And, too, I didn't think Stoner would let me. His power surged around me, a cold windy voltage that whipped my clothes and set static charges crackling in my hair. "Turn it off!" I shouted, pointing at the tin-roofed building. They shook their heads, shouting in return. ". . . can't," I heard, and something about ". . . feedback."

Then Stoner spoke. "Puleo," he said. His voice wasn't loud, but it was all-encompassing. I seemed to be inside it, balanced on a tongue of red dirt, within a throat of sky and jungle and yellow stone. I turned back to him. Looked into his eyes . . . fell into them, into a world of cold brilliance where a thousand fiery forms were materialized and dispersed every second, forms both of such beauty and hideousness that their effect on me, their beholder, was identical, a confusion of terror and exaltation. Whatever they were, the forms of Stoner's spirit, his potentials, or even of his thoughts, they were in their momentary life more vital and consequential than I could ever hope to be. Compelled by them, I walked over to him. I must have been afraid—I could feel wetness on my thighs and realized that my bladder had emptied—but he so dominated me that I knew only the need to obey. He did not stand, yet with each expansion his image would loom up before my eyes and I would stare into that dead face seamed by rivulets of molten diamond, its expression losing coherence, features splitting apart. Then he would shrink, leaving me gazing dumbly down at the top of his helmet. Dust stung my eyelids, my cheeks.

"What . . ." I began, intending to ask what he wanted; but before I could finish, he seized my wrist. Ice flowed up my arm, shocking my heart, and I heard myself . . . not screaming. No, this was the sound life makes leaving the body, like the squealing of gas released from a balloon that's half pinched shut.

Within seconds, drained of strength, I slumped to the ground, my vision reduced to a darkening fog. If he had maintained his hold much longer, I'm sure I would have died . . . and I was resigned to the idea. I had no weapon with which to fight him. But then I realized that the cold had receded from my limbs. Dazed, I looked around, and when I spotted him, I tried to stand, to run. Neither my arms nor legs would support me, and—desperate—I flopped on the red dirt, trying to crawl to safety; but after that initial burst of panic, the gland that governed my reactions must have overloaded, because I stopped crawling, rolled onto my back and stayed put, feeling stunned, weak, transfixed by what I saw. Yet not in the least afraid.

Stoner's inner man, now twice human-size, had broken free and was standing at the center of the village, some twenty feet off: a bipedal silhouette through which it seemed you could look forever into a dimension of fire and crystal, like a hole burned in the fabric of the world. His movements were slow, tentative, as if he hadn't quite adapted to his new form, and penetrating him, arcing through the air from the tin-roofed building, their substance flowing toward him, were what appeared to be thousands of translucent wires, the structures of the fields. As I watched, they began to glow with Stoner's blue-white-diamond color, their substance to reverse its flow and pour back toward the building, and to emit a bass hum. Dents popped in the tin roof, the walls bulged inward, and with a grinding noise, a narrow fissure forked open in the earth beside it. The glowing wires grew brighter and brighter, and the building started to crumple, never collapsing, but—as if giant hands were pushing at it from every direction—compacting with terrible slowness until it had been squashed to perhaps a quarter of its original height. The hum died away. A fire broke out in the wreckage, pale flames leaping high and winnowing into black smoke.

Somebody clutched my shoulder, hands hauled me to my feet. It was Tuu and one of his soldiers. Their faces were knitted by lines of concern, and that concern rekindled my fear. I clawed at them, full of gratitude, and let them hustle me away. We took our places among the other observers, the smoking building at our backs, all gazing at the yellow houses and the burning giant in their midst.

The air around Stoner had become murky, turbulent, and this turbulence spread to obscure the center of the village. He stood unmoving, while small dust devils kicked up at his heels and went zipping about like a god's zany pets. One of the houses caved in with a *whump,* and pieces of yellow concrete began to lift from the ruins, to float toward Stoner; drawing near him, they acquired some of his brightness, glowing in their own right, and then vanished into the turbulence. Another house imploded, and the same process was initiated. The fact that all this was happening in dead silence—except for the caving in of the houses—made it seem even more eerie and menacing than if there had been sound.

The turbulence eddied faster and faster, thickening, and at last a strange vista faded in from the dark air, taking its place the way the picture melts up from the screen of an old television set. Four or five minutes must have passed before it became completely clear, and then it seemed sharper and more in focus than did the jungle and the houses, more even than the blazing figure who had summoned it: an acre-sized patch of hell or heaven or something in between, shining through the dilapidated structures and shabby colors of the ordinary, paling them. Beyond Stoner lay a vast forested plain dotted with fires . . . or maybe they weren't fires but some less chaotic form of energy, for though they gave off smoke, the flames maintained rigorous stylized shapes, showing like red fountains and poinsettias and other shapes yet against the poisonous green of the trees. Smoke hung like a gray pall over the plain, and now and again beams of radiance—all so complexly figured, they appeared to be pillars of crystal—would shoot up from the forest into the grayness and resolve into a burst of light; and at the far limit of the plain, beyond a string of ragged hills, the dark sky would intermittently flash reddish orange as if great batteries of artillery were homing in upon some target there.

I had thought that Stoner would set forth at once into this other world, but instead he backed a step away and I felt despair for him, fear that he wouldn't seize his opportunity to escape. It may seem odd that I still thought of him as Stoner, and it may be that prior to that moment I had forgotten his human past; but now, sensing his trepidation, I understood that what enlivened this awesome figure was some scrap of soul belonging to the man-child I once had known. Silently, I urged him on. Yet he continued to hesitate.

It wasn't until someone tried to pull me back that I realized I was moving toward Stoner. I shook off whoever it was, walked to the edge of the village, and called Stoner's name. I didn't really expect him to acknowledge me, and I'm not clear as to what my motivations were: maybe it was just that since I had come this far with him, I didn't want my efforts wasted. But I think it was something more, some old loyalty resurrected, one I had denied while he was alive.

"Get outta here!" I shouted. "Go on! Get out!"

He turned that blind, fiery face toward me, and despite its featurelessness, I could read therein the record of his solitude, his fears concerning its resolution. It was, I knew, a final sending. I sensed again his emptiness, but it wasn't so harrowing and hopeless as before; in it there was a measure of determination, of purpose, and, too, a kind of . . . I'm tempted to say gratitude, but in truth it was more a simple acknowledgment, like the wave of a hand given by one workman to another after the completion of a difficult task.

"Go." I said it softly, the way you'd speak when urging a child to take his first step, and Stoner walked away.

For a few moments, though his legs moved, he didn't appear to be making any headway; his figure remained undiminished by distance. There was a tension in the air, an almost impalpable disturbance that quickly evolved into a heated pulse. One of the banana trees burst into flames, its leaves shriveling; a second tree ignited, a third, and soon all those trees close to the demarcation of that other world were burning like green ceremonial candles. The heat intensified, and the veils of dust that blew toward me carried a stinging residue of that heat; the sky for hundreds of feet above rippled as with the effects of an immense conflagration.

I stumbled back, tripped, and fell heavily. When I recovered I saw that Stoner was receding, that the world into which he was traveling was receding with him, or rather seeming to fold, to bisect and collapse around him: it looked as if that plain dotted with fires were painted on a curtain, and as he pushed forward, the fabric was drawn with him, its painted distances becoming foreshortened, its perspectives exaggerated and surreal, molding into a tunnel that conformed to his shape. His figure shrank to half its previous size, and then—some limit reached, some barrier penetrated—the heat died away, its dissipation accompanied by a seething hiss, and Stoner's white fire began to shine brighter and brighter, his form eroding in brightness. I had to shield my eyes, then shut them; but even so, I could see the soundless explosion that followed through my lids, and for several minutes I could make out its vague afterimage. A blast of wind pressed me flat, hot at first, but blowing colder and colder, setting my teeth to chattering. At last this subsided, and on opening my eyes I found that Stoner had vanished, and where the plain had been now lay a wreckage of yellow stone and seared banana trees, ringed by a few undamaged houses on the perimeter.

The only sound was the crackle of flames from the tin-roofed building. Moments later, however, I heard a patter of applause. I looked behind me: the gooks were all applauding Tuu, who was smiling and bowing like the author of a successful play. I was shocked at their reaction. How could they be concerned with accolades? Hadn't they been dazzled, as I had, their humanity diminished by the mystery and power of Stoner's metamorphosis? I went over to them, and drawing near, I overheard an officer congratulate Tuu on "another triumph." It took me a while to register the significance of those words, and when I did I pushed through the group and confronted Tuu.

" 'Another triumph'?" I said.

He met my eyes, imperturbable. "I wasn't aware you spoke our language, Mr. Puleo."

"You've done this before," I said, getting angry. "Haven't you?"

"Twice before." He tapped a cigarette from a pack of Marlboros; an officer rushed to light it. "But never with an American spirit."

"You coulda killed me!" I shouted, lunging for him. Two soldiers came between us, menacing me with their rifles.

Tuu blew out a plume of smoke that seemed to give visible evidence of his self-satisfaction. "I told you it was a risk," he said. "Does it matter that I knew the extent of the risk and you did not? You were in no greater danger because of that. We were prepared to take steps if the situation warranted."

"Don't bullshit me! You couldn't have done nothin' with Stoner!"

He let a smile nick the corners of his mouth.

"You had no right," I said. "You—"

Tuu's face hardened. "We had no right to mislead you? Please, Mr. Puleo. Between our peoples, deception is a tradition."

I fumed, wanting to get at him. Frustrated, I slugged my thigh with my fist, spun on my heel, and walked off. The two soldiers caught up with me and blocked my path. Furious, I swatted at their rifles; they disengaged their safeties and aimed at my stomach.

"If you wish to be alone," Tuu called, "I have no objection to you taking a walk. We have tests to complete. But please keep to the road. A car will come for you."

Before the soldiers could step aside, I pushed past them.

"Keep to the road, Mr. Puleo!" In Tuu's voice was more than a touch of amusement. "If you recall, we're quite adept at tracking."

Anger was good for me; it kept my mind off what I had seen. I wasn't ready to deal with Stoner's evolution. I wanted to consider things in simple terms: a man I had hated had died to the world a second time and I had played a part in his release, a part in which I had no reason to take pride or bear shame, because I had been manipulated every step of the way. I was so full of anger, I must have done the first mile in under fifteen minutes, the next in not much more. By then the sun had risen above the treeline and I had worked up a sweat. Insects buzzed; monkeys screamed. I slowed my pace and turned my head from side to side as I went, as if I were walking point again. I had the idea my own ghost was walking with me, shifting around inside and burning to get out on its own.

After an hour or so I came to the temporary housing that had been erected for the populace of Cam Le: thatched huts; scrawny dogs slinking and chickens pecking; orange peels, palm litter, and piles of shit in the streets. Some old men smoking pipes by a cookfire blinked at me. Three girls carrying plastic jugs giggled, ran off behind a hut, and peeked back around the corner.

Vietnam.

I thought about the way I'd used to sneer the word. 'Nam, I'd say. Viet-fucking-nam! Now it was spoken proudly, printed in Twentieth Century-Fox monolithic capitals, brazen with hype. Perhaps between those two extremes was a mode of expression that captured the ordinary reality of the place, the poverty and peacefulness of this village; but if so, it wasn't accessible to me.

Some of the villagers were coming out of their doors to have a look at the stranger. I wondered if any of them recognized me. Maybe, I thought, chuckling madly, maybe if I bashed a couple on the head and screamed "Number Ten VC!" maybe then they'd remember.

I suddenly felt tired and empty, and I sat down by the road to wait. I was so distracted, I didn't notice at first that a number of flies had mistaken me for a new and bigger piece of shit and were orbiting me, crawling over my knuckles. I flicked them away, watched them spiral off and land on other parts of my body. I got into controlling their patterns of flight, seeing if I could make them all congregate on my left hand, which I kept still. Weird shudders began passing through my chest, and the vacuum inside my head filled with memories of Stoner, his bizarre dream, his terrible Valhalla. I tried to banish them, but they stuck there, replaying themselves over and over. I couldn't order them, couldn't derive any satisfaction from them. Like the passage of a comet, Stoner's escape from Cam Le had been a trivial cosmic event, causing momentary awe and providing a few more worthless clues to the nature of the absolute, but offering no human solutions. Nothing consequential had changed for me: I was as fucked up as ever, as hard-core disoriented. The buzzing sunlight grew hotter and hotter; the flies' dance quickened in the rippling air.

At long last a dusty car with a gook corporal at the wheel pulled up beside me. Fierman and Witcover were in back, and Witcover's eye was discolored, swollen shut. I went around to the passenger side, opened the front door, and heard behind me a spit-filled explosive sound. Turning, I saw that a kid of about eight or nine had jumped out of hiding to ambush me. He had a dirt-smeared belly that popped from the waist of his ragged shorts, and he was aiming a toy rifle made of sticks. He shot me again, jiggling the gun to simulate automatic fire. Little monster with slit black eyes. Staring daggers at me, thinking I'd killed his daddy. He probably would have loved it if I had keeled over, clutching my chest; but I wasn't in the mood. I pointed my finger, cocked the thumb, and shot him down like a dog.

He stared meanly and fired a third time: this was serious business, and he wanted me to die. "Row-nal Ray-gun," he said, and pretended to spit.

I just laughed and climbed into the car. The gook corporal engaged the gears, and we sped off into a boil of dust and light, as if—like Stoner—we were passing through a metaphysical barrier between worlds. My head bounced against the back of the seat, and with each impact I felt that my thoughts were clearing, that a poisonous sediment was being jolted loose and flushed from my bloodstream. Thick silence welled from the rear of the car, and not wanting to ride with hostiles all the way to Saigon, I turned to Witcover and apologized for having hit him. Pressure had done it to me, I told him. That, and bad memories of a bad time. His features tightened into a sour knot and he looked out the window, wholly unforgiving. But I refused to allow his response to disturb me—let him have his petty hate, his grudge, for whatever good it would do him—and I turned away to face the violent green sweep of the jungle, the great troubled rush of the world ahead, with a heart that seemed lighter by an ounce of anger, by one bitterness removed. To the end of that passion, at least, I had become reconciled.

AYMARA

y name is William Page Corson, and I am the black sheep of the Buckingham County Corsons of Virginia. How I came to earn such disrepute relates to several months I spent in Honduras during the spring and summer of 1978, while doing research for a novel to be based on the exploits of an American mercenary who had played a major role in regional politics. That novel was never written, partly because I was of an age (twenty-one) at which one's concentration often proves unequal to lengthy projects, but mainly due to reasons that will be made clear—or if not made clear, then at least brought somewhat into focus—in the following pages.

One day while leafing through an old travel book, *A Honduran Adventure* by William Wells, I ran across the photograph of a blandly handsome young man with blond hair and mustache, carrying a saber and wearing an ostrich plume in his hat. The caption identified him as General Lee Christmas, and the text disclosed that he had been a railroad engineer in Louisiana until 1901, when—after three consecutive days on the job—he had fallen asleep at the wheel and wrecked his train. To avoid prosecution he had fled to Honduras, there securing employment on a fruit company railroad. One year later, soldiers of the revolution led by General Manuel Bonilla had seized his train, and rather than merely surrendering, he had showed his captors how to armor the flatcars with sheet iron; thus protected, the soldiers had gained control of the entire north coast, and for his part in the proceedings, Christmas had been awarded the rank of general.

From other sources I learned that Christmas had taken a fine house in Tegucigalpa after the successful conclusion of the revolution, and had spent most of his time hunting in Olancho, a wilderness region bordering Nicaragua. By all accounts, he had been the prototypical good ol' boy, content with the cushy lot that had befallen him; but in 1904 something must have happened to change his basic attitudes, for it had been then that he entered the employ of the United Fruit Company, becoming in effect the company enforcer. Whenever one country or another would balk at company policy, Christmas would foment a rebellion and set a more malleable government in office; through this process, United Fruit had come to dominate Central American politics, earning the sobriquet El Pulpo (The Octopus) by virtue of its grasping tactics.

These materials fired my imagination and inflamed my leftist sensibility, and I traveled to Honduras in hopes of fleshing out the story. I soon unearthed a wealth of anecdotal detail, much of it testifying to Christmas's irrational courage: he had, for instance, once blown up a building atop which he was standing to prevent the armory it contained from falling into counterrevolutionary hands. But nowhere could I discover what event had precipitated the transformation of an affable, easygoing man into a ruthless mercenary, and an understanding of Christmas's motivations was, I believed, of central importance to my book. Six weeks went by, no new knowledge came to light, and I had more or less decided to create a fictive cause for Christmas's transformation, when I heard that some of the men who had fought alongside him in 1902 might still be alive on the island of Guanoja Menor.

From the window of the ancient DC-3 that conveyed me to Guanoja, the island resembled the cover of a travel brochure, with green hills and white beaches fringed by graceful palms; but at ground level it was revealed to be the outpost of an unrelenting poverty. Derelict shacks were tucked into the folds of the hills, animal wastes fouled the beaches, and the harbors were choked with sewage. The capital, Meachem's Landing, consisted of a few dirt streets lined with weather-beaten shanties set on pilings, and beneath them lay a carpet of coconut litter and broken glass and crab shells. Black men wearing rags glared at me as I hiked in from the airport, and their hostility convinced me that even the act of walking was an insult to the lethargic temper of the place.

I checked into the Hotel Captain Henry—a ramshackle wooden building, painted pink, with a rust-scabbed roof and an electric pole lashed to its second-story balcony—and slept until nightfall. Then I set out to investigate a lead provided by the hotel's owner: he had told me of a man in his nineties, Fred Welcomes, who lived on the road to Flowers Bay and might have knowledge of Christmas. I had not gone more than a half-mile when I came upon a little graveyard confined by a fence of corroded ironwork and overgrown with weeds from which the tops of the tombstones bulged like toadstools. Many of the stones dated from the turn of the century, and realizing that the man I was soon to interview had been a contemporary of these long-dead people, I had a sense of foreboding, of standing on the verge of a supernatural threshold. Dozens of times in the years to follow, I was to have similar apprehensions, a notion that everything I did was governed by unfathomable forces; but never was it stronger than on that night. The wind was driving glowing clouds across the moon, intermittently allowing it to shine through, causing the landscape to pulse dark to bright with the rhythm of a failing circuit, and I could feel ghosts blowing about me, hear windy voices whispering words of warning.

Welcomes's shanty sat amid a banana grove, its orange-lit windows flickering like spirits in a dark water. As I drew near, its rickety shape appeared to assemble the way details are filled in during a dream, acquiring a roof and door and pilings whenever I noticed that it seemed to lack such, until at last it stood complete, looking every bit as dilapidated as I supposed its owner to be. I hesitated before approaching, startled by a banging shutter. Glints of moonlit silver coursed along the warp of the tin roof, and the plastic curtains twitched like the eyelids of a sleeping cat. At last I climbed the steps, knocked, and a decrepit voice responded, asking who was there. I introduced myself, explained that I was interested in Lee Christmas, and—after a considerable pause—was invited to enter.

The old man was sitting in a room lit by a kerosene lantern, and on first glance he seemed a giant; even after I had more realistically estimated his height to be about six-five, his massive hands and the great width of his shoulders supported the idea that he was larger than anyone had a right to be. It may be that this impression was due to the fact that I had expected him to be shriveled with age; but though his coal-black skin was seamed and wrinkled, he was still well-muscled: I would have guessed him to be a hale man in his early seventies. He wore a white cotton shirt, gray trousers, and a baseball cap from which the emblem had been ripped. His face was solemn and long-jawed, all its features so prominent that it looked to be a mask carved of black bone; his eyes were clouded over with milky smears, and from his lack of reaction to my movements, I came to realize he was blind.

"Well, boy," he said, apparently having gauged my youth from the timbre of my voice. "What fah you want to know 'bout Lee Christmas? You want to be a warrior?"

I switched on my pocket tape recorder and glanced around. The furniture—two chairs and a table—was rough-hewn; the bed was a pallet with some clothes folded atop it. An outdated calendar hung from the door, and mounted on the wall opposite Welcomes was a small cross of black coral: in the orange flux of the lantern light, it looked like a complex incision in the boards.

I told him about my book, and when I had done he said, "I 'spect I can help you some. I were wit' Lee from the Battle of La Ceiba till the peace at Comayagua, and fah a while after dat."

He began to ramble on in a direction that did not interest me, and I cut in, saying, "I've heard there was no love lost between the islanders and the Spanish. Why did they join Bonilla's revolution?"

"Dat were Lee's doin'," he said. "He promise dat dis Bonilla goin' to give us our freedom, and so he have no trouble raisin' a company. And he tell us that we ain't goin' to have no difficulty wit' de Sponnish, 'cause dey can't shoot straight." He gave an amused grunt. "Nowadays dey better at shootin', lemme tell you. But in de backtime de men of de island were by far de superior marksmen, and Lee figure if he have us wit' him, den he be able to defeat the garrison at La Ceiba. Dat were a tall order. De leader of de garrison, General Carrillo, were a man wit' magic powers. He ride a white mule and carry a golden sword, and it were said no bullet can bring him down. Many of de boys were leery, but Lee gather us on the dock and make us a speech. 'Boys,' he say, 'you done break your mothers' hearts, but you no be breakin' mine. We goin' to come down on de Sponnish like buzzards on a sick steer, and when we through, dey goin' to be showin' to de bone.' And by de time he finish, we everyone of us was spittin' fire."

As evidenced by this recall of a speech made seventy-five years before, Welcomes's memory was phenomenal, and the longer he spoke, the more fluent and vital his narrative became. Everything I had learned about Christmas—his age (twenty-seven in 1902), his short stature, his background—all that was knitted into a whole cloth, and I began to see him as he must have been: an ignorant, cocky man whose courage stemmed from a belief that his life had been ruined and so he might as well throw what remained of it away on this joke of a revolution. And yet he had not been without hope of redemption. Like many of his countrymen, he adhered to the notion that through the application of American know-how, the inferior peoples of Central America could be brought forward into a Star-Spangled future and civilized; I believe he nurtured the hope that he could play a part in this process.

When Welcomes reached a stopping point, I took the opportunity to ask if he knew what had motivated Christmas to enter the service of United Fruit. He mulled the question over a second or two and finally answered with a single word: "Aymara."

So, Aymara, it was then I first heard your name.

Perhaps it is passionate experience that colors my memory, but I recall now that the word had the sound of a charm the old man had pronounced, one that caused the wind to gust hard against the shanty, keening in the cracks, fluttering the pages of the calendar on the door as if it, too, were a creature playing with time. But it was only a name, that of a woman whom Christmas and Welcomes had met while on a hunting trip to Olancho in 1904; specifically, a trip to the site of the ruined city of Olancho Viejo, a place founded by the Spanish in 1589 and destroyed by a mysterious explosion not fifty years thereafter. Since that day, Welcomes said, the vegetation there had grown stunted and malformed, and all manner of evil legend had attached to the area, the most notable being that a beautiful woman had been seen walking in the flames that swept over the valley. Though the city had not been rebuilt, this apparition had continued to be sighted by travelers and Indians, always in the vicinity of a cave that had been blasted into the top of one of the surrounding hills by the explosion. Christmas and Welcomes had arrived at this very hilltop during a furious storm and. . . . Well, I will let the old man's words (edited for the sake of readability) describe what happened, for it is his story, not mine, that lies at the core of these complex events.

That wind can blow, Lord, that wind can blow! Howlin', rippin' branches off the trees, and drivin' slants of gray rain. Seem like it 'bout to blow everything back to the beginnin' and start all over with creation. Me and Lee was leadin' the horses along the rim of the valley, lookin' for shelter and fearin' for our lives, 'cause the footin' treacherous and the drop severe. And then I spot the cave. Not for a second did I think this the cave whereof the legend speak, but when I pass through the entrance, that legend come back to me. The walls, y'see, they smooth as glass, and there were atremble in the air like you'd get from a machine runnin' close by . . . 'cept there ain't no sound. The horses took to snortin' and balkin', and Lee pressed hisself flat against the wall and pointed his pistol at the dark. His hair were drippin' wet, plastered to his brow, and his eyes was big and starin'. "Fred," he says, "this here ain't no natural place."

"You no have to be tellin' me," I say, and I reckon the shiver in my voice were plain, 'cause he grins and say, "What's the matter, Fred? Ain't you got no sand?" That were Lee's way, you understand— another man's fear always be the tonic for his own.

Just then I spy a light growin' deeper in the cave. A white light, and brighter than any star. Before I could point it out to Lee, that light shooted from the dark and pass right through me with a flash of cold. Then come another light, and another yet. Each one colder and brighter than the one previous, and comin' faster and faster, till it 'pears the cave brightly lit and the lights they flickerin' a little. It were so damn cold that the rainwater have froze in my hair, and I were half-blinded on top of that, but I could have swore I seen somethin' inside the light. And when the cold begin to heaten up, the light to dwindle, I made out the shape of a woman . . . just her shape at first, then her particulars. Slim and black-haired, she were. More than pretty, with both Spanish and Indian breedin' showin' in her face. And she wearin' a garment such as I never seen before, but what in later years I come to recognize as a jumpsuit. There were blood on her mouth and a fearful expression on her face. The light gathered 'round her in a cloud and dwindle further, fadin' and shrinkin', and right when it 'bout to fade away complete, she take a step toward us and slump to the ground.

For a moment the cave were pitch-dark, with only the wind and the vexed sounds of the horses, but directly I hear a clatter and a spark flares and I see that Lee have got one of the lanterns goin'. He kneel beside the woman and make to touch her, and I tell him, "Man, I wouldn't be doin' that. She some kinda duppy."

"Horseshit!" he say. "Ain't no such thing."

"You just seen her come a-whirlin' outta nowhere," I say. "That's the duppy way."

'Bout then the woman give out with a moan, and her eyelids they flutter open. When she spot Lee bendin' to her, the muscles in her face start strainin' and she try to speak, but all that come out were this creaky noise. Finally she muster her strength and say, "Lee . . . Lee Christmas?" Like she ain't quite sure he's who she thinks.

Lee 'pears dumbstruck by the fact she know his name and he can't say nothin'. He glance up to me, bewildered.

"It *is* you," she say. "Thank God . . . thank God." And she reach out to him, clawin' at his hand. Lee flinched some, and I expected him to go a-whirlin' off with her into white light. But nothin' happen.

"Who are you?" Lee asks, and the question seem to amuse her, 'cause she laugh, and the laugh turn into a fit of coughin' that bring up more blood to her lips. "Aymara," she say after the fit pass. "My name is Aymara." Her eyes look to go blank for a second or two, and then she clutch at Lee's hand, desperate-like, and say, "You have to listen to me! You have to!"

Lee look a little desperate himself. I can tell he at sea with this whole business. But he say, "Go easy, now. I'll listen." And that calm her some. She lie back, breathin' deep, eyes closed, and Lee's starin' at her, fixated. Suddenly he give himself a shake and say, "We got to get you some doctorin'," and try to lift her. But she fend him off. "Naw," she say. "Can't no doctor help me. I'm dyin'." She open her eyes wide as if she just realize this fact. "Listen," she say. "You know where I come from?" And Lee say, No, but he's been a-wonderin'. "The future," she tell him. "Almost a hundred years from now. And I come all that way to see you, Lee Christmas."

Wellsir, me and Lee exchange looks, and it's clear to me that he thinks whatever happened to this here lady done 'fected her brain.

"You don't believe me!" she say in a panic. "You got to!" And she hold up her wrist and show Lee her watch. "See that? You ain't got watches like that in 1904!" I peer close and see that this watch ain't got no hands, just numbers made up of dots that flicker and change as they toll off the seconds. But it don't convince me of nothin'—I figure it's just some foreign thing. She must can tell we still don't believe her, 'cause she pull out a coupla other items to make her case. I know what them items was now—a ballpoint pen and a calculator—but at the time they was new to me. I still ain't convinced. Her bein' from the future were a hard truth to swallow, no matter the manner of her arrival in the cave. She start gettin' desperate again, beggin' Lee to believe her, and then her features they firm up and she say, "If I ain't from the future, then how come I know you been talkin' to United Fruit 'bout doin' some soldierin' for 'em."

This were the first I hear 'bout Lee and United Fruit, and I were surprised, 'cause Lee didn't have no use for them people. "How the hell you know that?" he asks, and she say, "I told you how. It's in the history books. And that ain't all I know." She take to reelin' off a list of names that weren't familiar to me, but—from the dumbstruck expression on Lee's face—must have meant plenty to him. I recall she mention Jacob Wettstein and Andrew Colby and Machine Gun Guy Maloney, who were to become Lee's second-in-command. And then she reel off another list, this one of battles and dates. When she finish, she clutch his hand again. "You gotta 'cept their offer, Lee. If you don't, the world gonna suffer for it."

I could tell Lee have found reason to believe from what she said, but that the idea of workin' with United Fruit didn't set well with him. "Couldn't nothin' good come of that," he say. "Them boys at the fruit company ain't got much in mind but fillin' their pockets."

"It's true," she say. "The company they villains, but sometimes you gotta do the wrong thing for to 'chieve the right result. And that's what *you* gotta do. 'Less you help 'em, 'less America takes charge down here, the world's gonna wind up in a war that might just be the end of it."

I know this strike a chord in Lee, what with him always carryin' on 'bout good ol' American ingenuity bein' the salvation of the world. But he don't say nothin'.

"You gotta trust me," she say. "Everything depends 'pon you trustin' me and doin' what I say. I come all this way, knowin' I were bound to die of it, just to tell you this, to make sure you'd do what's necessary. You think I'd do that to tell you a lie?"

"Naw," he says. "I s'pose not." But I can see he still havin' his doubts.

She sigh and look worried and then she start explainin' to us that the machine what brought her have gone haywire and set her swayin' back and forth through time like a pendulum. Back to the days of the Conquistador and into the future an equal ways. She tell us 'bout watchin' the valley explode and the old city crumblin' and finally she say, "I only have a glimpse of the future, of what's ahead of my time, and I won't lie, it were too quick for me to have much sense of it. But I have a feelin' from it, a feelin' of peace and beauty . . . like a perfume the world's givin' off. When I 'cepted this duty, I thought it were just to make sure things wouldn't work out worse than they has, but now I know somethin' glorious is goin' to come, somethin' you never would 'spect to come of all the bloodshed and terror of history."

It were the 'spression on her face at that moment—like she's still havin' that feelin' of peace—that's what put my doubts to rest. It weren't nothin' she coulda faked. Lee he seemed moved by it, but maybe he's stuck with thinkin' that she's addled, 'cause he say, "If you from the future, you tell me some more 'bout my life."

A shudder pass through her, and for a second I think we gonna lose her then and there. But she gather herself and say, "You gonna marry a woman named Anna and have two daughters, one by her and one by another woman."

Not many knew Lee were in love with Anna Towers, the daughter of an indigo grower in Trujillo, and even less knew 'bout his illegitimate daughter. Far as I concerned, this sealed the matter, but Aymara didn't understand the weight of what she'd said and kept goin'.

"You gonna die of a fever in Puerto Cortés," she says, "in the year. . . ."

"No!" Lee held up his hand. "I don't wanna hear that."

"Then you believe me."

"Yes," he say. "I do."

For a while there weren't no sound 'cept the keenin' of the wind from the cave mouth. Lee were downcast, studyin' the backs of his hands like he were readin' there some sorry truth, and Aymara were glum herself, like she were sad he did believe her. "Will you do it?" she asks.

Lee give a shrug. "Do I got a choice?"

"Maybe not," she tell him. "Maybe this how it have to be. One of the men who . . . who help send me here, he claim the course of time can't be changed. But I couldn't take the chance he were wrong." She wince and swallow hard. "Will you do it?"

"Hell," he say after mullin' it over. "Guess I ain't got no better thing to do. Might as well go soldierin' awhile."

She search his face to see if he lyin' . . . 'least that's how it look to me. "Swear to it," she say, takin' his hand. "Swear you'll do it."

"All right," he say. "I swear. Now you rest easy."

He try doctorin' her some, wettin' down her brow and such, but nothin' come of it. Somethin' 'bout the manner of travel, she say, have tore up her insides, and there's no fixin' 'em. It 'pear to me she just been hangin' on to drag that vow outta Lee, and now he done it, she let go and start slippin' away. Once she make a rally, and she tell us more 'bout her journey, sayin' the strange feelin's that sweep over her come close to drivin' her mad. I think Lee's doubtin' her again, 'cause he ask another question or two 'bout the future. But it seem she answer to his satisfaction. Toward the end she take to talkin' crazy to someone who ain't there, callin' him Darlin' and sayin' how she sorry. Then she grab hold of Lee and beg him not to go back on his word.

"I won't," he say. But I think she never hear him, 'cause as he speak, blood come gushin' from her mouth and she sag and look to be gazin' into nowhere.

Lee don't hardly say nothin' for a long time, and then it's only after the storm have passed and he concerned with makin' a grave. We put her down near the verge of the old city, and once she under the earth, Lee ask me to say a little somethin' over her. So I utter up a prayer. It were strange tryin' to talk to God with the ruined tower of the cathedral loomin' above, all ivied and crumblin', like a sign no prayers would be answered.

"What you gonna do?" I ask Lee as he saddlin' up.

He shake his head and tighten the cinch. "What would you do, Fred?"

"I guess I wouldn't want to be messin' with them fruit company boys," I say. "They takes things more serious than I likes."

"Ain't that the truth," he say. He look over to me, and it seem all the hollows in his face has deepened. "But maybe I ain't been takin' things serious enough." He worry his lip. "You really think she from the future?" He ask this like he wantin' to have me say No.

"I think she from somewhere damn strange," I say. "The future sound 'bout as good as anything."

He scuff the ground with his heel. "Pretty woman," he say. "I guess it ain't reasonable she just throw her life away for nothin'."

I reckoned he were right.

"Jesus Christ!" He smack his saddle. "I wish I could just forget alla 'bout her."

"Well, maybe you can," I tell him. "A man can forget 'bout most anything with enough time."

I never should have say that, 'cause it provide Lee with somethin' to act contrary to, with a reason to show off his pride, and it could be that little thing I say have tipped the scales of his judgment.

"Maybe *you* can forget it," he say testily. "But not me. I ain't 'bout to forget I give her my word." He swing hisself up into the saddle and set his horse prancin' with a jerk of the reins. Then he grin. "Goddamn it, Fred! Let's go! If we gotta win the world for ol' United Fruit, we better get us a move on!"

And with that, we ride up from the valley and into the wild and away from Aymara's grave, and far as I know, Lee never did take a backward glance from that day forth, so busy he were with his work of forgin' the future.

I asked questions, attempting to clarify certain points, the exact date of the encounter among other things, but of course I did not believe Welcomes. Despite his aura of folksy integrity, I knew that Guanoja was rife with storytellers, men who would stretch the truth to any dimension for a price, and I assumed Welcomes to be one of these. Yet I was intrigued by what I perceived as the pathos surrounding the story's invention. Here was the citizen of a country long oppressed by the economic policies of the United States, who—in order to earn a tip from an American tourist (I had given him twenty *lempira* upon the conclusion of his tale)—had created a fable that exonerated the United States from guilt and laid the blame for much of Central America's brutal history upon the shoulders of a mystical woman from the future. On returning to my hotel, I typed up sections of the story and seeded them throughout a longer piece that documented various of Christmas's crimes along with others committed by his successors. I entitled the piece "Aymara," and the following day I sent it off to *Mother Jones,* having no real expectations that it would see print.

But "Aymara" *was* published, as was my next piece, and the next. . . . And so began a journalistic career that has lasted these sixteen years.

During those years, my espousal of left-wing causes and the ensuing notoriety inspired my family to break off all connections with me. (They preferred not to acknowledge that I also lent my support to populist rebellions against Soviet-sponsored regimes.) I was not offended by their action; in fact, I took it for a confirmation of the rightness of my course, since—with their stock portfolios and mausoleumlike homes and born-again conservatism—they were as nasty a pack of capitalist rats as one could meet. I traveled to Argentina, South Africa, the Philippines, to any country that offered the scenario of a superpower-backed dictatorship and masses of the oppressed, and I wired back stories that sought to undermine the Commie-hating mentality engendered by the Reagan years. I admit that my zeal was occasionally misplaced, that I was used at times by corrupt men who passed themselves off as populist leaders. And I will further admit that in some cases I was motivated less by passionate concern than by a desire to increase my own legend. I had, you see, become a media figure. My photograph was featured on the covers of national magazines concomitant with such headings as "William Corson and the

New Journalism"; my books made the best-seller lists; talk shows pestered my agent. But despite the glitter, I truly cared about the causes I espoused. Perhaps I cared too much. Perhaps—like Lee Christmas—I made the mistaken assumption that my American citizenship was a guarantee of wisdom superior to that of the peoples whom I tried to help. In retrospect, I can see that the impulses that provoked my writing of "Aymara" were no less ingenuous, no more informed, than those that inspired his career; but this is an irony I do not choose to dwell upon.

In January of 1994, I returned to Guanoja. The purpose of the trip was partly for a vacation, my first in many years, and also to satisfy a nostalgic whim to visit the place where my career had begun. The years had brought little change to Meachem's Landing. True, there was now a jetport outside of town, and a few of the shanty bars had been replaced by more pricey watering holes of concrete block; but it remained essentially the same confluence of dirt streets lined with weathered shacks and populated by raggedly dressed blacks. The most salient differences were the gaggle of lower-echelon Honduran civil servants who spent each day hunched over their typewriters on the second-story verandah of the Hotel Captain Henry, churning out reams of officialese, and the alarming number of CIA agents: cold-eyed, patently anonymous men who could be seen sitting in the bars, gazing moodily toward Nicaragua and the Red Menace. Despite the Chamorro presidency, the Sandinistas had once again begun to make expansionist noises. War was in the offing, its onset as inevitable as the approach of a season, and this, too, was a factor in my choice of a vacation spot. I had received word of a mysterious military installation on the Honduran mainland, and—after having nosed around Washington for several weeks—I had been invited to inspect this installation. The Pentagon apparently wanted to assure me of its harmlessness and thus prevent their benign policies from being besmirched by more of my yellow journalism.

After checking into the hotel, I walked out past the town to the weedy little graveyard, where I expected I would find a stone marking the remains of Fred Welcomes. There was, indeed, such a stone, and I was startled to learn that he had survived until 1990, dying at the age of 106. I had assumed that he could not have lived much past the date of my interview with him, and the fact that he had roused my guilt. All my good fortune was founded upon his eloquent lie, and I could have done a great deal to ease his decline. I leaned against

AYMARA   **249**

the rusted fence, thinking that I was no better than the businessmen whose exploitative practices I had long decried, that I had mined gold from the old man's imagination and given him a pittance in return. I was made so morose that later the same night, unable to achieve peace of mind, I set out on a drunk . . . at least this was my intent.

Across the street from the hotel was a two-story building of white stucco with faded lettering above the door that read MAUD PRICE'S GOLDEN DREAM. I remembered Maud from my previous trip—a fat, black woman who had kept an enormous turtle in a tin washtub and would entertain herself by feeding it chicken necks and watching it eat—and I was saddened to discover that she, too, had passed away. Her daughter was now the proprietor, and I was pleased to find that she had maintained Maud's inimitable decor. Strung across the ceiling were dozens upon dozens of man-shaped paper dolls, colored red and black, and these cast magical-looking shadows on the walls by the light of two flickering lanterns. Six wooden tables, a bar atop which rested a venerable stereo that was grinding out listless reggae, and a number of framed photographs whose glass was too flyspecked to permit easy observation of the subject matter. I ordered a beer, a Salvavidas, and was preparing for a bout of drunken self-abnegation when I noticed a young woman staring at me from the rear table. On meeting my eyes, she showed no sign of embarrassment and held her gaze steady for a long moment before turning back to the magazine she had been reading. Even in that dim light, I could see she was beautiful. Slim, long-limbed, with a honeyed complexion. Curls of black hair hung over the front of her white blouse, their shapes as elegant as the tail feathers of exotic birds. Her face . . . I could tell you that she had large dark eyes and high cheekbones, that her features had an impassive Indian cast. But that does nothing more than to define her by type and illuminates her not at all. This was a woman with whom I was soon to be in love, if I was not somewhat in love with her already, and the most difficult thing in the world to describe is the face of your lover, because though it is familiar in every detail, it tends to become a mirror of your devotion, to reflect the ideals of passion, and thus is less a human face than the face of love itself.

I continued to watch her, and after a while she looked up again and smiled. There was no way I could ignore this contact. I walked over, introduced myself (in Spanish, which I assumed to be her native tongue), and asked if I could join her. "Why not?" she replied in English, and after I had taken a seat, she pushed her magazine toward me, pointing to an inset photograph of me, one snapped some years before when I had worn a mustache. "I thought it was you," she said. "You look much more handsome clean-shaven."

Her name, she told me, was Ivie Solis. She was employed by a travel agency in La Ceiba and was on a working vacation, having arrived the day before. We talked of this and that, nothing of consequence, but the air between us seemed to crackle. Everything about her, everything she did, struck a chord within me, and I was mesmerized by her movements, entranced, as if she were a magician who might at any moment loose a flight of birds from her fingertips.

Eventually the conversation turned to my work, of which she had read the lion's share, and she told me that her favorite piece was my first, "Aymara." I expressed surprise that she had seen it—it had never been reprinted—and she explained that her parents had run a small hotel catering to American tourists, and the magazine had been left in one of the rooms. "It had the feel of being part of a puzzle," she said. "Or the answer to a riddle."

"It seems fairly straightforward to me," I said.

She tucked a curl behind her ear, a gesture I was coming to recognize as characteristic. "That's because you didn't believe the old man's story."

"And you did?"

"I didn't leap to disbelief as you did." She settled back in her chair, picking at the label of her beer bottle. "I guess I just like thinking about what motivated the woman."

"Obviously," I said, "according to the logic of the story, she came from a world worse off than this one and was hoping to initiate a course of events that would improve it."

"I thought that myself at first," she said. "But it *doesn't* fit the logic of the story. Don't you remember? She knew what would happen to Christmas. His military career, his triumphs. If she'd come from a world in which those things hadn't occurred, she wouldn't have had knowledge of them."

"So . . ." I began.

"I think," she cut in, "that if she did exist, she came from this world. That she knew she would have to sacrifice herself in order to ensure that Christmas did as he did. It may be that your article was the agency that informed her of her duty."

"Even if that's the case," I said, "why would she have tried to inspire Christmas's crimes? Why wouldn't she have tried to make him effect good works? Perhaps she could have destroyed United Fruit."

"That would be the last thing she'd want. Don't you see? If her actions were politically motivated, she would understand that before real change could occur, the circumstances, the conditions of life under American rule, would have to be so oppressive that violent change would become a viable option. Revolution. She'd realize that Christmas's violences were necessary. They set the tone for American policies and licensed subsequent violence. She'd be afraid that if Christmas didn't work for United Fruit, the process of history that set the stage for revolution might be slowed down or negated. Perhaps the American stranglehold might be achieved with such subtlety that change would be forever impossible."

She spoke these words with marked intensity, and I believe I realized then that there was more to Ivie than met the eye. Her logic was the logic of terrorism, the justification of bloodshed in terms of its consciousness-raising effects. But I was so intent upon her as a woman, I scarcely noticed the implication of what she had said.

"Well," I said, "given that your scenario is accurate, it still doesn't make sense. The idea of time travel, of tinkering with the past . . . it's absurd. Too many paradoxes are involved. What you're supposing isn't a chain of events wherein one action predicates another. It's a loop, a metaphysical knot tied in reality, linking my article and some woman and a man years dead. There's no end, no beginning. Things don't work that way."

"They don't?" She lowered her eyes and traced a design in the moisture on the table. "It seems to me that life *is* paradox. Things occur without apparent reason between nations." She looked up at me. "Between people. Perhaps there are reasons, but they're impossible to unravel or define. And dealing with such an unreasonable quantity as time, I wouldn't expect it to be anything other than paradoxical."

We moved on to other topics, and shortly afterward we left the bar and walked along the road to Flowers Bay. A few hundred yards past the last shanty, at a point where the road meandered close to the shore and the sea lay calm beneath a sheen of starlight, visible through a labyrinthine fringe of mangrove, there I kissed her. It was the kind of kiss that holds a lifetime of promise, tentative, then growing more assured and involving as the contact surpasses all your expectations. I had thought kisses like that existed solely in the province of romance novels, and on discovering this was not so, all my cynicism was dissolved and I fell wholly in love with Ivie Solis.

I do not propose to detail our affair, the evolution of our feelings.

While these things seemed to me remarkable, I doubt they were more so than the interactions of any other pair of lovers, and they are pertinent to my story only in the volatility that attached to our moments together. Despite Ivie's thesis that love—like time—was an inexplicable mystery, I sought to explain it to myself and decided that because I had never had any slack in my life, because I had never allowed myself the luxury of deep emotional involvement, I had therefore been ripe for the picking. I might, I told myself, have fallen in love with anyone. Ivie had simply been the first acceptable candidate to happen along. All I knew of her aside from her work and place of birth was a few bits and pieces: that she was twenty-six; that she had attended the University of Miami; that—like most Hondurans—she resented the American presence in her country; that she had a passion for coconut candy and enjoyed the works of Manuel Puig. How, I wondered, could I be obsessed with someone about whose background I was almost completely ignorant. And yet perhaps my depth of feeling was enhanced by this lack of real knowledge. Things are often most alluring when they are not quite real, when your contact with them is brief and intense, and in the light of the mind they acquire the vivid artfulness of a dream.

We spent nearly every moment of every day in each other's company, and most of this in making love. My room, our clothing, smelled of sex, and we became such a joke to the old woman who cleaned the hotel that whenever she saw us she would let loose with gales of laughter. The only times we were apart were an hour or so each afternoon when Ivie would have to perform her function as a travel agent, securing—she said—cheap group rates from various resorts that would be offered by her firm to American skin divers. On most of these occasions I would pace back and forth, impatient for her return. But then, ten days after we had initiated the affair, thinking I might as well make some use of the interval, I rented a car and drove to Spanish Harbor, a small town up the coast where there had lately been several outbreaks of racial violence, highly untypical for Guanoja; I was interested in determining whether or not these incidents were related to the martial atmosphere that had been gathering about the island.

By the time I arrived in the town, which differed from Meachem's Landing hardly at all, having a larger harbor and perhaps a half a dozen more streets, I was thirsty, and I stopped in a tourist restaurant for a beer. This particular restaurant, The Treasure Chest, consisted of a small room done up in pirate decor that was fronted by a concrete deck where patrons sat beneath striped umbrellas. Standing at the bar,

I had a clear view of the deck, and as I sipped my beer, wondering how best to pursue my subject, I spotted Ivie sitting at a table near the railing. With her was a man wearing a gray business suit. I assumed him to be a resort owner, but when he turned to signal a waiter, I recognized him by his hawkish features and fringe of salt-and-pepper beard to be Abimael Sotomayor, the leader of *Sangre y Verdad* (Blood and Truth), one of the most extreme of Latin American terrorist groups. I had twice interviewed him and I knew him for a charismatic and scary man, a poet who excelled at torture, whose followers performed quasi-mystical blood rituals in his name prior to each engagement. The sight of him with Ivie numbed me, and I began to construct rationalizations that would explain her presence in innocent terms. But none of my rationalizations held water.

I left the restaurant and drove full-tilt back to Meachem's Landing, where I bribed the cleaning woman into admitting me to Ivie's room. It was identical to mine, with gray boards and a metal cot and a night table covered in plastic and a single window that opened onto the second-story verandah. I began by searching the closet, but found only shoes and clothing, apparel quite in keeping with her purported job. Her overnight case contained makeup, and the rest of her luggage was empty . . . or so it appeared. But as I hefted one of the suitcases, preparing to stow it beneath the cot, I realized it was heavier than it should have been. I laid it on the cot, and before long I located the catch that opened a false bottom; inside was a machine pistol.

I sat staring at the gun. It was an emblem of Ivie's complicity with an organization so violent that even I, who sympathized with their cause, was repelled by their actions. Yet despite this, I found I loved her no less; I only feared that she did not love me, that she was using me. And, too, I feared for her: the fact that she was at the least an associate of *Sangre y Verdad* offered little hope of a happy ending for the two of us. Finally I replaced the false bottom, restored the suitcase to its original spot beneath the cot, and went to my room to wait for Ivie.

That night I said nothing about the gun, rather I tested Ivie in a variety of ways, trying to learn whether or not her affections for me were fraudulent. Not only did she pass every test, but I came to understand much about her that had been puzzling me. I realized that her distracted silences, her deferential attitude concerning the future, her vague references to "responsibilities," all these were symptomatic of the difficulty our relationship was causing her, the contrary pulls exerted by her two passions. Throughout the night, I kept thinking of horror stories I had heard about *Sangre y Verdad*, but I loved Ivie too much to judge her. How could I—a citizen of the country which had created the conditions that bred organizations like Sotomayor's—ever hope to fathom the pressures that had brought her to this pass?

For the next three days, knowing that our time together was likely to be brief, I tried to put politics from mind. Those days were nearly perfect. We swam, we danced, we rented a dory and rowed out past the reef and threw out lines and caught silkfish, satinfish, fish that gleamed iridescent red and blue and yellow, like talismans of our own brilliance. Yet despite our playfulness, our happiness, I was constantly aware that the end could not be far off.

Four days after her meeting with Sotomayor, Ivie told me she had an appointment that evening, one that might last two or three hours; her nervous manner informed me that something important was in the works. At eight o'clock she drove off along the road to Flowers Bay, and I tailed her in my rented car, maintaining a discreet distance, my headlights dark. She parked by the side of the road about a mile past Welcomes's shanty, and seeing this, I pulled my car into a thicket and continued on foot.

It was a moonless night, but the stars were thick, their light revealing every shadowy rut, silhouetting the palms and mangrove. Mosquitoes whined in my ear; the sound of waves on the reef came as a faint hiss. A couple of hundred feet beyond Ivie's car stood a largish shanty set among a stand of coconut palms. Several cars were parked out front, and two men were lounging by the door, obviously on sentry duty. Orange light flickered in the window. I eased through the brush, making my way toward the rear of the shanty, and after ascertaining that no guards were posted there, I duckwalked across a patch of open ground and flattened against the wall. I could hear many voices speaking at once, none of them intelligible. I inched along the wall to the window whose shutter was cracked open. Through the gap I spotted Sotomayor sitting atop a table, and beside him, a thin, agitated-looking man of thirty-five or so, with prematurely gray hair. I could see none of the others, but judging by their voices, I guessed there to be at least a dozen men and women present.

With a peremptory gesture, Sotomayor signaled for quiet. "I would much have preferred to use my organization alone," he said. "But Dr. Dobler"—he acknowledged the gray-haired man with a nod—"insisted that the entire spectrum of the left be included, and I had no choice but to agree. However, in the interests of security, I wish to limit participation in this operation to those in this room. And, since some of you are unknown to the rest, I suggest that we not increase our intimacy by an exchange of names. Let us choose false names. Simple ones, if you please." He smoothed back his hair, glancing around at his audience. "As I am to lead, I will take a military rank for my name." He smiled. "And as I am not overly ambitious, you may refer to me as the Sergeant." Laughter. "Perhaps if we are successful, I will receive a promotion."

Each of the men and women—there were fourteen in all—selected a name, and I heard Ivie say, "Aymara."

The hairs on the back of my neck prickled to hear it, but knowing her fascination with my article, I did not think it an unexpected choice.

"Very well," said Sotomayor, all business now. "The matter under consideration is the American military project known as Longshot."

I was startled—Longshot was the code name of the installation I was soon to inspect.

"For some months," Sotomayor went on, "we have been hearing rumors concerning Longshot, none likely to inspire confidence in our neighbors to the north. We have been unable to substantiate the rumors, but this situation has changed. Dr. Dobler was until recently one of the coordinators of the project. He has come to us at great personal risk, because he believes there is terrible danger associated with Longshot, and because, with our lack of bureaucratic impediments, he believes we may be the only ones capable of acting swiftly enough to forestall disaster. I will let him explain the rest."

Sotomayor stepped out of view, leaving the floor to Dobler, who looked terrified. Thinking what it must have taken for him to venture forth from his ivory tower and out among the bad dogs, I awarded him high marks for guts. He cleared his throat. "Project Longshot is essentially an experiment in temporal displacement . . . that is to say, time travel."

This sparked a babble, and Sotomayor called for quiet. I wished I could have seen Ivie's face, wanting to know if she were as stunned and frightened as I was.

"The initial test is to be conducted twenty-three days from now," said Dobler. "We have every reason to believe it will succeed, because evidence exists in the past. . . ." He broke off, appearing confused. "There's so much to. . . ." His eyes darted left to right. "I'm sorry. I . . ."

"Please be calm," advised Sotomayor. "You're among friends."

Dobler squared his shoulders. "I'm all right," he said, and drew a deep breath. "The site of the project is a hill overlooking the ruins of Olancho Viejo, a colonial city destroyed in 1623 by an explosion. I say 'explosion,' but I believe I can safely state that it was not an explosion in the typical sense of the word. For one thing, eyewitness accounts testify that while, indeed, some of the buildings were blown apart, others appeared to crumble, to collapse into powder and chunks of rotten stone, the result of being washed over by a wave of blinding white radiance. Of course these accounts were written by superstitious men—mainly priests—and are thus suspect. Some tell of a beautiful woman walking in the midst of the light, but I think we can attribute that to the Catholic propensity for seeing the Virgin in moments of stress." This elicited a few chuckles, and Dobler was braced by the response. "However, allied with readings we have taken, with other anomalies we've discovered on and near the site, it's evident that the destruction of Olancho Viejo was a direct result of our experiment. Though our target date is in the 1920s, it seems that the displacement will create a kind of shock wave that will produce dire effects 360 years in the past."

"How does that affect us?" someone asked.

"I'll get to that in a minute," said Dobler. He was warming to his task, becoming the model of an enthused lecturer. "First it's important you understand that although the initial experiment will merely consist of the displacement of a few laboratory animals and some mineral specimens, plant life, and so forth, the target purpose of the project is the manipulation of the past through assassination and other means."

Expressions of outrage from the gathering.

"Wait!" said Dobler. "That's not what you should be worried about, because I don't think it's possible."

"Why not?" A woman's voice.

"I really don't think I could explain it to you," said Dobler. "The mathematics are too complex . . . and my conclusions, I admit, are arguable. Several of my colleagues are in complete disagreement; they believe the past *can* be altered. But I'm convinced otherwise. Time, according to my mathematical model, has a fixed shape. It is not simply a process that affects physical objects; it has its own physicality, or—better said—the process of time involves its own spectrum of physical events, all on the particulate level, and it is the isolation of this spectrum that will allow us to displace objects into the past." He must have been the focus of bewildered stares, for he threw up his hands in helplessness. "The language isn't capable of conveying an accurate explanation. Suffice it to say that, in my opinion, any attempt to alter the course of history will fail, because the physical potentials of time will compensate for that alteration."

"It sounds to me," said Sotomayor, "as if you're embracing the doctrine of predestination."

"That's a rather murky analogue," said Dobler. "But, yes, I suppose I am."

"Then why are you asking us to stop something which, according to you, cannot be stopped? If evidence exists that the experiment was carried out, we can do nothing . . . at least if we are to accept your logic."

"As I stated, I may be wrong in this," said Dobler. "In which case, an attack on the project might succeed. But even if time does prove to be unalterable, what is unalterable in this circumstance is the destruction of Olancho Viejo. It's possible that our experiment can be stopped, and the malleability of time will enlist some other causal agent."

"There's something I don't understand." Ivie's voice. "If you are correct about the unalterability of time, what do we have to fear?"

"For every action," said Dobler, "there must be a reaction. The action will be the experiment. One small part of the reaction can be observed in what happened three centuries ago. But my figures show that the greater part of the reaction will occur in the present. I've gone over and over the equations, and there's no error." Dobler paused, summoning thought. "I've no idea what form this end of the reaction will take. It may be similar to the explosion in 1623; it may be entirely different. We know nothing about the forces involved . . . except how to trigger them and how to perform a few simple tricks. But I'm sure of one thing. The reaction will affect matter on the subatomic levels, and it will be on the order of a billion times more extensive than what happened in 1623. I doubt anything will survive it."

A silence ensued, broken at last by Sotomayor. "Have you shown these equations to your colleagues?"

"Of course." Dobler gave a despairing laugh. "They believe they've solved the problem by constructing a containment chamber. It's a solution comparable to wrapping a blanket around a nuclear device."

"How can we discount their opinion?" someone asked.

"Look," said Dobler, peeved. "Unless you can understand the mathematics involved, there's no way I can prove my case. I believe my colleagues are too excited about the project to accept the fact that it's potentially disastrous. But what does it mean for me to tell you that? The best evidence I can give you is the fact that I am here, that I have in effect thrown away my career in order to warn you." He looked down at the floor. "Though perhaps I can offer one further proof."

They began to bombard him with questions, most of them challenging in tone, and—concerned that the meeting might suddenly break up and my car be discovered—I slipped away from the window and headed back toward town.

It is a measure, I believe, of the foolishness of love that I was less worried about the fate of the world than about Ivie's possible involvement in the events of Welcomes's story, a story I was now hard put to disbelieve; it seemed I was operating under the assumption that if Ivie and I could work things out, everything else would fall into place around us. I drove back to the hotel, waited awhile, and then, deciding that I wanted to talk to her somewhere more private, somewhere an argument—I thought one likely—would not be overheard, I left a note asking her to meet me on the far side of the island, at an abandoned construction site a short ways up the beach from St. Mark's Key—the skeleton of a large house belonging to the estate of an American who had died shortly after work had begun. This site was of special moment for Ivie and me. It was set back from the shore, hidden from prying eyes by dense growths of palms and sea grape and cashew trees, and we had made love there on several occasions. By the time I reached it, the moon had risen and the unfinished house—with its gapped walls and skewed beams and free-standing doorways—had the look of a surreal maze of silver light and shadow. Sitting inside it on the ground floor, I felt it posed an apt metaphor for the labyrinthine complexity of the situation.

Until that moment, I had not brought my concentration to bear on this complexity, and now, trying to unravel the problem, I found I could not do so. The circumstances of Welcomes's story, of Dobler's, Ivie's, and my own . . . all this smacked of magical serendipity and was proof against logic. Time, which had always been for me a commodity, something to be saved and expended, seemed to have been revealed as a vast fabulous presence cloaked in mystery and capable of miracles, and I had as little hope of comprehending its processes as I would those of a star winking overhead. Less, actually. I attempted to narrow my focus, to consider separate pieces of the puzzle, beginning with what Welcomes had told me. Assuming it was true, I saw how it explained much I had not previously given thought to.

Christmas's courage, for instance. Knowing that he would die of a fever would have made him immune to fear in battle. All the pieces fit together with the same irrational perfection. It was only the whole, the image they comprised, that was inexplicable.

At last I gave it up and sat staring at the white combers piling in over the reef, listening to the scattery hiss of lizards running in the beach grass, watching the colored lights of the resort on St. Mark's Key flicker as palm fronds were blown across them by the salt breeze. I must have sat this way an hour before I heard a car engine; a minute later, Aymara—so I had been thinking of her—walked through the frame of the front door and sat beside me. "Let's not stay here," she said, and kissed me on the cheek. "I'd like a drink." In the moonlight her face looked to have been carved more finely, and her eyes were aswim with silvery reflections.

I could not think how to begin. Finally, settling on directness, I said, "Did you know what Dobler was going to tell you? Is that why you chose the name Aymara?"

She pulled back from me, consternation written on her features. "How . . ." she said; and then: "You followed me. You shouldn't have done that."

"Why the hell not?" Anger over her betrayal, her subterfuge, suddenly took precedence over my concern for her. "How else am I going to keep track of who's who in the revolution these days?"

"You could have been killed," she said flatly.

"Right!" I said, refusing to let her lack of emotionality subdue me. "God knows, Sotomayor might have had you drink my blood for a nightcap! What the hell possessed you to get involved with him?"

"I'm not involved with him!" she said, her own temper surfacing.

"You're not with *Sangre y Verdad?*"

"No, the FDLM."

I was relieved—the FDLM was the most populist and thus the most legitimate element of the Honduran left. "You haven't answered my first question," I said. "Why did you choose that name?"

"I was thinking of you. That's all it was. But now . . . I don't know."

"You're going to do it, aren't you? Play out the story?" I slugged my thigh in frustration. "Jesus Christ! Sotomayor will kill you if he finds out! And Dobler, he might be a crazy! A CIA plant! Right now he's. . . ."

"You didn't stay until the end?" she cut in.

"No."

"He's dead," she said. "He told us that if we attacked, we should destroy all the computers and records, anyone who had knowledge of the process. He said that when he was younger, he would have supported any evil whose goal was the increase of knowledge, but now he had uncovered knowledge that he couldn't control and he couldn't live with that. He said he hoped what he intended to do would prove something to us. Then he went onto the porch and shot himself."

I sat stunned, picturing that nervous little man and his moment of truth.

"I believe him," she said. "Everyone did. I doubt we would have otherwise."

"Sotomayor would have believed him no matter what," I said. "He yearns for disaster. He'd find the end of the world an erotic experience."

"I shouldn't have to explain to you what produces men like Abimael," she said stiffly. She reached behind her to—I assumed—adjust the waistband of her skirt. "Are you going to inform on us?"

Her voice was tremulous, her expression strained, and she continued holding her hand behind her back; it was an awkward posture, and I began to suspect her reasons for maintaining it. "What have you got there?" I asked, knowing the answer.

A car passed on the beach, its headlights throwing tattered leaf shadows over the beams.

"What if I said I *was* going to inform on you?"

She lowered her eyes, sighed, and brought forth a small caliber automatic; after a second, she let it fall to the floor. She studied it despondently, as if it were a failed something for which she had entertained high hopes. "I'm sorry," she said. "I'm. . . ." She put her hand to her brow, covering her eyes.

The gun showed a negative black against the planking, an ugly brand marring the smooth grain. I picked it up. Its cold weight fueled my anger, and I heaved it into the shadows.

"I love you." She trailed her fingers across my arm, but I refused to speak or turn to her. "Please, believe me! It's just I don't know what to do anymore." Her voice broke, and it seemed I could smell her tears.

"It's all right." My voice was harsh, burred with anger.

We sat in silence. The crunch of waves on the reef built louder, the wind seethed in the palm crowns, and faint music from the resort added a fractured tinkling—I felt that the things of nature were losing definition, blending into a dissolute melodic rush. Finally I asked her what she intended to do, and she said, "I doubt my intentions matter. I don't think I can avoid going back."

"To 1902? Is that what you mean?" I said this helplessly, sensing the gravity of events sweeping toward us like a huge dark fist. "How can you even consider it? You heard Dobler, you know the dangers."

"I don't believe it's dangerous. Only inevitable."

I turned to her then, ready with protests, arguments. Christ, she was beautiful! It was as if tears had washed her clean of a film, exposed a new depth of beauty. The words caught in my throat.

"Just before Dobler killed himself," she said, "I asked him what he thought time was. He'd been talking about it as a mathematical entity, but I had the idea he wasn't saying what he really felt, and I wanted to know everything he did . . . because I was afraid. It seemed something magical was happening, that I was being drawn into some incomprehensible scheme." She brushed a strand of hair from her eyes. "Dobler said that when he had begun to develop his equations, he'd had a feeling like mine. 'An apprehension of the mystical,' he called it. There was something hypnotic about the equations . . . they reminded him of mantras the way they affected him. The further his work progressed, the more he came to think of time—its event spectrum—as evidence of divinity. Its basic operation, its mechanics. Abimael laughed at this and asked if he was talking about God. And Dobler said that if by God he meant a stable energy system governing the actions of all matter on a subatomic level, then yes, that's exactly what he was talking about."

I wanted to refute this, but it was so similar to my own thoughts concerning the nature of time, I could not muster a contrary word.

"You feel it, too," she said. "Don't you?"

I took her by the shoulders. "Let's leave here. Tonight. We can hire a boat to run us over to La Ceiba, and by tomorrow. . . ."

She put a finger to my lips, then kissed me. The kiss deepened, and from that point on I lost track of what happened. One moment we were sitting on the floor of that skeleton house, and the next— our clothes magicked away—we were lying in the grass behind the house, in a tiny clearing bordered by banana trees. The way Ivie's hair was fanned out around her head, its color merging with the dark grass, she looked to be a pale female bloom sprouting from the sandy soil, and her skin felt like the moonlight, smooth, coated with a cool emulsion. I thought I could taste the moonlight on the tips of her breasts. She guided me between her legs, her expression grave, focused on the act, and as I entered her she arched her neck, staring up into the banana leaves, and cried, "Oh, God!" as if she saw there some enrapturing presence. But I knew to whom she was really crying out. To that sensation of heat and weakness that enveloped us, sheltered us. To that sublimation of hope and fear into a pour of pure desiring. To that strange thoughtless and self-adoring creature we became, all hip and mouth and heart. *That* was God.

Afterward as we dressed, among the sibilant noises and wind and sea, I heard a sharper noise, a click. But before I could categorize it, I put it from my mind. My head was full of plans. I would knock Ivie out, drug her, carry her off to the States. I would allow the guerrillas to destroy the project, and at the last moment come swinging out of nowhere and snatch her to safety. I envisioned even more improbable heroics. Strong with love, all these plans seemed workable to me.

We walked around the side of the house, hand in hand, and I did not notice the figure standing in the shadow of a cashew tree until it spoke, saying, "Aymara!" Ivie gave a shriek of alarm, and I stepped in front of her, shielding her. The figure moved forward, and I saw it was Sotomayor, his sharp features set in a grim expression, his neatly trimmed beard looking fake in the moonlight. He stopped about six feet away, training a pistol on us, and fixed Ivie with a contemptuous stare. *"Puta!"* he said. He pulled something from his pocket and flung it at our feet. A folded piece of paper with writing on it. "You should be more discreet in your correspondence," he said to me.

"Listen . . ." I began.

He swung the pistol to cover my forehead. "You may have value as a hostage," he said. "But I wouldn't rely on that. I don't like being betrayed, and I'm not in the best of moods."

"I haven't betrayed you!" Ivie stepped from behind me. "You don't understand."

The muscles of Sotomayor's face worked, as if he were repressing a scream of rage.

"He's on our side," said Ivie. "You know that. He's always supported the cause."

Sotomayor smiled—a vicious predator's smile—and leveled the pistol at her. "Did you enjoy your last fuck, bitch? I could hear you squealing down on the beach."

The muscles on his forearms bunched, preparing for the kick, and I dove for him. Too late. The pistol went off an instant before I knocked him over, the report blending with Ivie's cry, and we rolled in the grass and sand, clawing, grappling. Sotomayor was strong, but

I was fighting out of sheer desperation, and he was no match for me. I tore the pistol from his grasp and brought the butt down on his temple. Brought it down a second time. He sagged, his head lolling. I crawled to where Ivie had fallen. Her legs were kicking in spasms, and when I touched her hair, I found it mired with blood. The bullet had entered through the side of her head and lodged in the brain. She must have been clinically dead already, but obeying some dumb reflex, she was trying to speak. Each time her mouth opened, blood jetted forth. She was bleeding from the eyes, the nostrils. Her entire face was slick with blood, and still her mouth kept opening and closing, making glutinous choking sounds. I wanted to touch her, to heal her with a touch, but there was so much broken, I could not decide where to lay my hands. They fluttered above her like stupid animals, and I heard myself screaming for it to stop, for her to stop. Her arms began to flop around, her hips to thrash, convulsing. A broken, bloody doll. I aimed the pistol at her chest, but could not bring myself to pull the trigger. Finally I covered her with my body, and, sobbing, held her until all movement ceased.

I came to my feet, staggered over to Sotomayor. He had not yet regained consciousness. Tears streaming down my cheeks, I pointed the pistol at him. But it did not seem sufficient that he merely die. I kneeled beside him, then straddled his chest.

A voice called out from behind me. "What goin' on dere, mon?" Visible as shadows, two men were standing at the water's edge.

"Man killed somebody!" I answered.

"You call de police?"

"No!"

"Den I'll be goin' to de Key, ax 'em to spark up dere radio!"

I waved acknowledgment, watched the men sprint away. Once they were out of sight, I pried Sotomayor's mouth open and inserted the pistol barrel. "Wake up!" I shouted. I spat in his face, slapped him. Repeated the process. His eyelids twitched, and he let out a muffled groan. "Wake up, you son of a bitch!" He gazed at me blearily, and I wiggled the pistol to make him aware of it. His eyes widened. He tried to speak, his eyebrows arching comically with the effort. I cocked the pistol, and he froze.

"I should turn you in," I said. "Let the police torture your ass. But I don't trust you to be a hero, man. Maybe you'd talk. Maybe you know something worth trading for your life."

He gurgled something unintelligible.

"Can't hear you," I said. "Sorry."

Using the pistol as a lever, I began turning his head from side to side. He tried to keep his eyes on mine. Sweat popped out on his brow, and he was having trouble swallowing.

"Here it comes," I said.

He tensed and shut his eyes.

"Just kidding," I told him. I waited a few seconds, then shouted, "Here it comes!"

He flinched.

I started sobbing again. "Did you see what you did to her, man? Did you see? You fucking son of a bitch! Did you see!" The pistol was shaking, and Sotomayor bit the barrel to keep it still.

For a minute or thereabouts I was crying so hard, I was blinded. At last I managed to gain control. I wiped away the tears. "Here it comes," I said.

He blinked.

"Here it comes!"

Another blink.

"Here it fucking comes!"

His stare was mad and full of hate. But his hatred was nothing compared to mine. I was dizzy with it. The stars seemed very near, wheeling about my head. I wanted to sit astride him forever and cause him pain.

I dug the fingers of my left hand in back of his Adam's apple, forcing his jaws apart, and I battered his teeth with the barrel, breaking a couple. Blood filmed over his lower lip, trickled down into his beard. He gagged, choking on the fragments.

"Like that?" I asked him. "How about this?"

I broke his nose with the heel of my hand. Tears squeezed from his eyes, bloody saliva and mucus came from his nose. His breath made a sucking noise.

Shouts from the direction of St. Mark's Key.

I leaned close to Sotomayor, my face inches away, the blood-slimed barrel sheathed in his mouth.

"Here it comes," I whispered. "Here. It. Comes."

I know he believed me, but he was mesmerized by my proximity, by whatever he saw in my eyes, and could not look away. I screamed at him and met his terrified gaze as I fired.

Perhaps I would have been charged with murder in the States, but in Honduras, where politics and passion license all manner of violence, I was a hero.

I was a hero, and insane . . . for grief possessed me as powerfully as had love.

Now that Ivie was dead, it seemed only just that the others join her on the pyre. I told the police everything I knew. The island was sealed off, the guerrillas rounded up. The press acclaimed me; the President of the United States called to commend my actions; my fellow journalists besieged the Hotel Captain Henry, seeking to interview me but usually settling for interviews with the cleaning woman and the owner. I was in no mood to play the hero. I drank, I wept, I wandered. I gazed into nowhere, seeing Ivie's face. Aymara's face. In memoriam, I accorded her that name. Brave-sounding and lyrical, it suited her. And I wished she could have died wearing that name in 1902—that, I realized, should have been her destiny. Whenever I saw a dark-haired young woman, I would have the urge to follow her, to spy on her, to discover who her friends were, what made her laugh, what movies she liked, how she made love, thinking that knowing these details would help me regain the definition that Aymara had brought to my life. Yet even had this not been a fantasy, I could not have acted upon it. Grief had immobilized me. Grief . . . and guilt. It had been my meddling that had precipitated her death, hadn't it? I was a dummy moving on a track between these two emotions, stopping now and again to stare at something that had caught my eye, some curiosity that would for a moment reduce my self-awareness.

Several days after her death, the regional director of the CIA paid me a call. My visit to Project Longshot had originally been scheduled for two weeks prior to the initial test, but he now told me that since I knew about "our little secret down here," the President had authorized my presence at the test. This exclusive was to be my reward for patriotism. I accepted his invitation and came close to telling him that I would be delighted to stand at ground zero during the end of the world.

I had been too self-absorbed to give much thought to Dobler's warnings, but now I decided I wanted the world to end. What was the point in trying to save it? We had been heading toward destruction for years, and as far as I was concerned the time was ripe. A few days before I might have raised a mighty protest against the project, but my political conscience—and perhaps my moral one—had died with Aymara, and I was angry at the world, at its hollow promise and mock virtues and fallacious judgments. Anger made my grief more endurable, and I nourished it, picturing it to be a tiny golden snake with ruby eyes. A familiar. It would feed on tears, transform them into venom.

It would be my secret, coiled and ready to strike. It would fit perfectly inside my heart.

On the day prior to the test, I was flown by small plane to a military base on the mainland, and from there by helicopter to the project site, passing over the valley in which lay the ruined city of Olancho Viejo, with its creeper-hung cathedral tower sticking up like an eroded green fang. Three buildings of white concrete crowned a massive jungled hill overlooking the valley, and on the hillside facing away from the valley were other buildings—living quarters and storage rooms and sentry posts. The administrator, a middle-aged balding man named Morrel, briefed me on the test; but I cut this short, informing him that I had heard most of what he was telling me from Dobler. His only reaction was to cluck his tongue and say, "Poor fellow."

Afterward, Morrel led me downhill to the commissary and introduced me to the rest of the personnel. Ostensibly this was a joint US-Honduran project, but there were only two Hondurans among the twenty-eight scientists—an elderly man clearly past his prime, and a dark-haired young woman who tried to duck out the door when I approached. Morrel urged her forward and said, "Mr. Corson, this is Señorita Aymara Luján."

I was nearly too stunned to accept her handshake. She refused to meet my eyes, and her hand was trembling. I could not believe that this was mere coincidence. Though to my mind she was not as lovely as my Aymara, she was undeniably beautiful and of a type with my dead love. Slim and large-eyed, her features displaying more than a trace of Indian blood. I had a mental image of a long line of beautiful dark-haired women stretching across the country, each prepared to step forward should an accident befall her sisters.

"I'm pleased to meet you," this one said. "I've always admired your work." She glanced around in apparent alarm as if she had said something indiscreet; then, recovering her poise, she added, "Perhaps we'll have a chance to talk at dinner."

She placed an unnatural stress on these last words, making it plain that this was a message sent. "I'd like that," I said.

For the remainder of the day I was shown a variety of equipment and instrumentation to which I paid little attention. The appearance of this new Aymara undermined my anger somewhat, and Dobler's thesis concerning the inalterability of time, its capacity to compensate for change, seemed to embody the menace of prophecy. But I made no move to reveal what I suspected. This development had brought my insanity to a peak, and I was gripped by a fatalistic malaise.

Who the hell was I to trifle with fate, I reasoned. And besides, it was unlikely that any action I took would have an effect. Maybe it *was* coincidence. I retreated from the problem into an almost puritanical stance, as if dealing with the matter was somehow vile, beneath me, and when the dinner hour arrived, deciding it would be best to avoid the woman, I pleaded weariness and retired to my quarters.

My room was a white cubicle furnished with a bed, a desk and chair, and a word processor. The window provided a view of the jungle that swept away toward Nicaragua, and I sat by it, watching sunset resolve into a slate-colored dusk, and then into a darkness figured by stars and a half-moon. With no one about to engage my interest, grief closed in around me.

A few minutes after eight o'clock, small-arms fire began to crackle on the hilltop. I went to the door and peered out. Muzzle flashes were probing the darkness higher up. I had an impulse to run, but my inertia prevailed and I went back to the chair. Soon thereafter, the door opened and the woman who called herself Aymara entered. She wore a white project jumpsuit that glowed in the moonlight, and she carried an automatic rifle, which she kept at the ready but aimed at a point to my right.

Neither of us spoke for several seconds, and then I said, "What's going on?" and laughed at the banal tone that comment struck.

Another burst of fire from above.

"It's almost over," she said.

I allowed several more seconds to elapse before saying, "How did you pull it off? Security looked pretty tight."

"Most of them died at dinner." She tossed her head, shaking hair from her eyes. "Poison."

"Oh." Again I laughed. "Sorry I couldn't make it."

"I didn't want to kill you," she said with urgency. "You've . . . been a friend to my country. But after what you did on Guanoja. . . ."

"What I did there was execute a murderer! An animal!"

She studied me a moment. "I believe you. Sotomayor was an evil man."

"Evil!" I made a disparaging noise. "And what force for good do you represent? The EDP? The FDLM?"

"We acted independently . . . I and a few friends."

Silence, then a single gunshot.

"Is that really your name?" I asked. "Aymara?"

She nodded. "I've often wondered how much influence your article has had on me. On everything. Because of it, I've always felt I was involved in. . . ."

"Something mystical, right? Magical. I know all about it."

"How could you?"

"How could I have written the article in the first place? I don't have any answers." I turned back to the window. "I suppose you're going to try to contact Christmas."

"I don't have a choice," she said defiantly. "I feel. . . ."

"Believe me," I cut in. "I understand why. When did you decide to do this?"

"I'd been considering it for some time, but I wasn't sure. Then the news came about Sotomayor. . . ."

"Jesus God!" I leaned forward, burying my face in my hands.

"What's wrong?"

"Get out!" I said. "Kill me, do whatever you have to . . . just get out of here."

"I'm not going to kill you."

I sensed her moving close, and through my fingers saw her lay some papers on the desk.

"I'm giving you a map," she said. "At the foot of the hill, next to the sentry post, there's a trail leading east. It's well-traveled, and even in the dark it won't be difficult to follow. Less than a day's walk from here, you'll come to a river. You'll find villages. Boats that'll take you to the coast."

I said nothing.

"We won't be able to go operational until dawn," she went on. "You have about ten hours. Things might not be so bad once you're out of the immediate area."

"Go away," I told her.

"I . . ." She faltered. "I think we. . . ."

"What the hell do you want from me?" Angry, I spun around. But on seeing her, my anger evaporated. The moonlight seemed to have erased all distinction between her and my Aymara—she might have been my lover reborn, her spirit returned. "What do you want?" I said weakly.

"I don't know. But I do want something from you. For so long I've felt we were linked. Involved." She reached out as if to touch me, then jerked back her hand. "I don't know. Maybe I just want your blessing."

I could smell her scent of soap and perfume, sharp and clean in that musty little room, and I felt a stirring of sexual attraction. In my mind's eye I saw again that endless line of dark-haired women, and I suddenly believed that love was the scheme that had enforced our intricate union, that—truly or potentially—we were all lovers, myself and a thousand Aymaras, all tuned to the same mystical pitch. I got to my feet, rested my hands on her hips. Pulled her close. Her lips grazed my cheek as she settled into the embrace. Her heart beat rapidly against my chest. Then she drew back, her face tilted up to receive a kiss. I tasted her mouth, and her warmth spread through me, melting the cold partition I had erected between myself and life. At last she pushed me away and—averting her eyes—walked to the door.

"Goodbye." She said it in Spanish—*"Adiós"*—a word that sounded too gentle and mellifluous to embody such a terminal meaning.

I heard her footsteps running up the hill.

I was tempted to go after her, and to resist this temptation, not to save myself, I took her map and set out walking the trail east. Yet as I went, my desire to survive grew stronger, and I increased my pace, beating my way through thickets and plaited vines, stumbling down rocky defiles. Had I been alone in the jungle at any other time, I would have been terrified, for the night sounds were ominous, the shadows eerie; but all my fear was focused upon those white buildings on the hilltop, and I paid no mind to the threat of jaguars and snakes. Toward dawn, I stopped in a weedy clearing bordered by ceibas and giant figs, their crowns towering high above the rest of the canopy. I was bruised, covered with scratches, exhausted, and I saw no reason to continue. I sat down, my back propped against a ceiba trunk, and watched the sky fading to gray.

I had thought brightness would fan across the heavens as with the detonation of a nuclear bomb, but this was not the case. I felt a disturbance in the air, a vibration, and then it was as if everything—trees, the earth, even my own flesh—were yielding up some brilliant white essence, blinding yet gradually growing less intense, until it seemed I was in the midst of a thick white fog through which I could just make out the phantom shapes of the jungle. Accompanying the whiteness was a bone-chilling cold; this, however, dissipated quickly, whereas it turned out that the fog lingered for hours, dwindling to a fine haze before at last becoming imperceptible. At first I was full of dread, anticipating death in one form or another; but soon I began to experience a perverse disappointment. The world had suffered a cold flash, a spot of vagueness, like the symptoms of a mild fever, and the idea that my lover had died for this made me more heartsick than ever.

I waited the better part of an hour for death to take me. Then, disconsolate, thinking I might as well push on, I glanced at my watch to estimate how much farther I had to travel, and found that not only had it stopped but that it could not be rewound. Curious, I thought. As I brushed against a bush at the edge of the clearing, its leaves crumbled to dust; its twigs remained intact, but when I snapped one off, a greenish fluid welled from the cortex. I tasted it, and within seconds I felt a burst of energy and well-being. Continuing on, I observed other changes. An intricate spiderweb whose strands I could not break, though I exerted all my strength; a whirling column of dust and light that looked to be emanating from the site of the project; and in the reflecting waters of a pond I discovered that my hair had gone pure white. Perhaps the most profound change was in the atmosphere of the jungle. Birds twittered, monkeys screeched. All as usual. Yet I sensed a vibrancy, a vitality, that had not been in evidence before.

By the time I reached the river, the fog had cleared. I walked along the bank for half an hour and came to a village of thatched huts, a miserable place littered with feces and mango rinds, hemmed in by brush and stands of bamboo. It appeared deserted, but moored to the bank, floating in the murky water, was a dilapidated boat that— except for the fact it was painted bright blue, decorated with crosses and bearded, haloed faces—might have been the twin of the scow in *The African Queen*. As I drew near, a man popped out of the cabin and waved. An old, old man wearing a gray robe. His hair was white and ragged, his face tanned and wrinkled, and his eyes showed as blue as the painted hull.

"Praise the Lord!" he yelled. "Where the hell you been?"

I glanced behind me to make sure he was not talking to someone else. "Hey," I said. "Where is everybody?"

"Gone. Fled. Scared to death, they were. But now they'll believe me, won't they?" He beckoned impatiently. "Hurry up! You think I got all day. Souls are wastin' for want of Jerome's good news." He tapped his chest. "That's me. Jerome."

I introduced myself.

Again he signaled his impatience. "Got all eternity to learn your name. Let's get a move on." He leaned on the railing, squinting at me. "You're the one sent, ain'tcha?"

"I don't think so."

" 'Course you are!" He clasped his hands prayerfully. "And, lo, I fell asleep in the white light of the Rapture and the Lord spake, sayin', 'Jerome, there will come a man of dour countenance bearin' My holy sign, and he will aid your toil and lend ballast to your joy.' Well, here you are, and here I am, and if that hair of your'n ain't a sign, I don't know what is. Come on!" He patted the railing. "Help me push 'er out into the current."

"Why don't you use the engine?"

"It don't work." He cackled, delighted. "Nothin' works. Not the radio, not the generator. None of the Devil's tools. Ain't it wonderful?" He scowled. "Now, come on! That's enough talk. You gonna aid my toil or not?"

"Where are you headed?"

"Down the Fundamental Stream to the Source and back again. Ain't no other place to go now the Lord is come."

"To the coast?" I insisted, not in the least taken with this looney.

"Yeah, yeah!" Jerome put his hands on his hips and regarded me with displeasure. "You gotta lighten up some, boy. Don't know as I'm gonna be needin' all this much ballast to my joy."

I have been a month on the river with Jerome, and I expect I will remain with him awhile longer, for I have no desire to return to civilization until its breakdown is complete—the world, it seems, has ended, though not in the manner I would have thought. I am convinced Jerome is crazy, the victim of long solitudes and an overdose of religious tracts; yet he has no doubt I am the crazy one, and who is to say which of us is right. At every village we stop to allow him to proclaim the Rapture, the advent of the Age of Miracles . . . and, indeed, miracles abound. I have seen a mestizo boy call fish into his net by playing a flute; I have witnessed healings performed by a matronly Indian woman; I have watched an old German expatriate set fires with his stare. As for myself, I have acquired the gift of clairvoyance, which has permitted me to see something of the world that is aborning. Jerome attributes all this to an increase in the wattage of the Holy Spirit; whereas I believe that Project Longshot caused a waning of certain principles—especially those pertaining to anything mechanical or electrical—and a waxing of certain others—in particular those applying to ESP and related phenomena. The two ideas are not opposed. I can easily imagine some long-dead psychic perceiving a whiteness at the end of time and assigning it Godlike significance. Yet I have no faith that a messiah will appear. It strikes me that this new world holds greater promise than the old (though perhaps the old world merely milked its promise dry), a stronger hope of survival, and a wider spectrum of possibility; but God, to my way of thinking, darts among the quarks and neutrinos, an eternal signal harrying them to order, a resource capable of being tapped by magic or by science, and it may be that love is both the seminal impulse of this signal and the ultimate distillation of this resource.

We argue these matters constantly, Jerome and I, to pass green nights along the river. But upon one point we agree. All arguments lapse before the mystery and coincidence of our lives. All systems fail, all logics prove to zero.

So, Aymara, we have worked our spell, you and I and time. Now I must seek my own salvation. Jerome tells me time heals all wounds, but can it—I wonder—heal a wound that it has caused? Though we had only a few weeks, they were the central moments of my life, and their tragic culmination, the sudden elimination of their virtues, has left me irresolute and weak. The freshness and optimism of the world has made your loss more poignant, and I am not ashamed to admit that—like the most clichéd of grievers—I see your face in clouds, hear your voice in the articulations of the wind, and feel your warmth in the shafts of light piercing the canopy. Often I feel that I am breaking inside, that my heart is turning in my chest like a haywire compass, trying to fix upon some familiar pole and detecting none, and I know I will never be done with weeping.

Buck up, Jerome tells me. You can't live in the past, you gotta look to the future and be strong.

I reply that I am far less at home in the fabulous present than I am in the past. As to the future, well . . . I have envisioned myself walking the high country, a place of mountains and rivers without end, of snowfields and temples with bronze doors, and I sense I am searching for something. Could it be you, Aymara? Could that white ray of science pouring from the magical green hill have somewhere resurrected you or your likeness? Perhaps I will someday find the strength to leave the river and find answers to these questions; perhaps finding that strength is an answer in itself. That hope alone sustains me. For without you, Aymara, even among miracles I am forlorn.

A WOODEN TIGER

There was a goddess in Katmandu named Kumari, a living, breathing incarnation chosen from among the daughters of wealthy Newar families—chosen by oracular sign, some said, and by political necessity, said others—and until she reached the age of puberty and a new incarnation was selected, she lived in a temple on Durbar Square, where she was worshiped and pampered and paraded before the faithful on festival days. It astonished Clement that no one apart from himself found this notable, that people dismissed Kumari's existence as an atavism left over from a simpler time, from an age when superstition had not yet been overthrown by logic. They seemed to neglect the fact that no matter how completely the phenomenon had been explained away, there *was* a goddess in Katmandu, an actual goddess whose followers numbered in the hundreds of thousands . . . and, even more remarkable in Clement's opinion, scattered throughout the country were thirteen women who had once been Kumari and were now shunned, deemed unlucky and thus unsuitable for marriage.

If there was one overwhelming reason that Clement was so taken with Kumari's divinity, so insistent upon its importance, it was that he needed something larger than himself on which to focus, something whose nature might afford relief from the grim realities of his profession. He was thirty-eight, a compact muscular man with sandy hair and what seemed a permanent case of sunburn, and blue-gray eyes that in certain lights appeared colorless. His face had a bland, boyish innocence, the face of an aging athlete or a young cleric, of someone to whom duplicity and violence were shameful but minor matters;

for the past three years, however, he had served as the CIA station chief in Calcutta, a position that required him to commit duplicity and violence on a grand scale. Many considered him a murderer, while others considered him a man who was doing a nasty but essential job. For his own part, Clement refused to characterize himself, because life had grown too complex for him to accept the emotionality attaching to either label. In his business such uncertainty led inevitably to mental sloppiness and fatal error, and Clement knew he was in danger; but he had a secret that allowed him to defer hopelessness, to believe in salvation of a kind. He wasn't sure it was a real secret, but it was at the least a mystery, and in order to determine its true nature, every now and then he would take a long weekend, and—accompanied by his wife, Lily—he would travel to small Asian hill towns and wander through the markets and inquire after an elderly foreigner who carved animals out of wood.

It was during one of these trips that Clement learned of Kumari, and he asked the station chief in Katmandu, Carl Rice, to assist him in tracking down the women who had once been incarnations. Within a matter of hours, Rice—a lanky olive-skinned Southerner, whom Clement had known for years—presented him with a list. "Most of 'em are locked away by their families," he said as they sat in the bar of the Soaltee Oteri, a simulation of a Hilton Lounge, with floors and walls of black marble, a teakwood bar, and a lethargic jazz trio presided over by a busty Japanese singer, whose accent and shrill upper register were turning "That Old Black Magic" into a cryptic lamentation. Rice gazed at her admiringly and waggled his fingers in a clandestine wave.

"Why they do that?" Clement asked.

Rice said, "Huh?"

"The families . . . how come they lock 'em up?"

"They're embarrassed 'bout 'em bein' unlucky. They're delighted to have a goddess in the family, but an ex-goddess . . . 'pears they just as soon be kin to a rat. This 'un"—Rice pointed to a name—"she went insane. Couple of others are prostitutes. They'd just bullshit you. But this un', now. Cheni Abdurachan. She ran away and got herself educated. Hung out with some Westernized Tibetans. She's pretty damn Westernized herself, speaks good English. I don't know if she'll talk to you, but I can get you to 'er. Fix you up with a plane tomorrow."

Clement inspected the list and saw that Cheni was thirty years old. "Where's Tasang-partsi?"

"Mustang. We'd fly you to Ra-lung. That's a four-hour walk away. I wouldn't advise takin' Lily. There's lotsa hill crime." Rice sipped his drink and studied the Japanese singer, who was striking center-fold poses. "So you want the tour?"

"Yeah, tomorrow'll be fine."

"This isn't business, is it?" asked Rice, and sipped his drink.

"Just curiosity."

"Curiosity." Rice pronounced it syllable by syllable, as if perplexed by the word. "You gettin' a weird reputation, man. People wonderin' 'bout you."

"People?" said Clement.

"You know . . . people." Rice wadded a strip of cocktail napkin between his thumb and forefinger. "Y'gotta watch your behavior. It ain't like you got a spotless record."

"You talking about D'allessandro?"

Rice shrugged and pegged the wad at the bartender.

"D'allessandro's dead," said Clement.

"Now there's two schools of thought 'bout that, ain't there?"

"I saw the fucking car blow up, man."

"Ri-ight," said Rice with a sardonic drawl.

"You got something on your mind," said Clement, annoyed, "why don't you spit it out?"

"Okay." Rice's long bony face was imperturbable. "Here we are, six years after D'allessandro pulls off the biggest scam anybody's ever pulled on our ass. I mean, we're talkin' a Barnum & Bailey produc-tion. Right before his plot thickens, the man's terminated. Terrorists, looks like. But a few days later when the shit hits the fan, people start sayin', 'All we got here's bits and pieces. Could be our boy's done a Houdini. No way to prove it, but we got his right-hand man.' " Rice poked Clement's shoulder. "Whyn't we keep him on a string and see which way he jumps?"

"Think I don't know all that?"

"You don't act like you do," said Rice. "You're becoming a god-damn eccentric. People watch you makin' these funny moves, and they start seein' hidden agendas. Anybody else was actin' like you, their butt would have been sanctioned. But what I'm leadin' up to is this. Time's a gonna come when they gonna say, 'D'allessandro's probably dead by now, anyway. So what're we gonna do with this chump we got runnin' Calcutta?' "

Clement forced a grin. "But that time hasn't come yet. And being watched but not leashed, that gives a man a certain freedom, doesn't it?"

Rice leaned back as if trying to see him in a better light. "What're you up to?"

"Good things." Clement sucked on a piece of ice to calm his nerves. "If I'm going to keep the assholes off my back, I need to count some coup. So"—he cracked the ice—"I'm going to count me some goddamn coup."

Rice stared at him deadpan. "Square business?"

"Scout's honor. I'm going to give 'em a prime-time spectacular." He fingered out another ice chip. "Since this is official. . . ."

"Wait a minute!" Rice was offended.

"C'mon, pal," said Clement. "We haven't had a heart-to-heart like this in years."

Rice looked down at his drink. "Y'unnerstand it ain't like I enjoyed this shit. I don't get off on hasslin' my friends."

"That Old Black Magic" ended in a tortured shriek and a drumroll that covered the lack of applause; the Japanese singer announced a break.

"No problema," said Clement. "But how 'bout doing me a favor? Tell 'em I'm going to do big things real soon. Sell it to 'em, okay?"

"You got it," said Rice, the soul of sincerity. "I'll sell it hard." He glanced at the stage. "I owe you, man." He stood, patted Clement on the arm. "Hang out. . . . I'll be back in a flash with the first installment."

Clement lowered his head, slowly letting out a breath. He was going to have to pull off a big-yardage play, he thought. Find somebody useful to hand over. Somebody with political sex appeal. It was too late in the game for anything else. And probably too late for that.

"Hey, when's Lily comin' back from the market?" asked Rice, sitting back down.

"She's going to meet us for dinner."

"How you two doin', anyway? You still in love?"

"Love." Clement made a derisive noise. "It's better than love."

Rice smiled. "Miko!" he called, and the Japanese singer came to stand between the two men. She gave Clement an arch look. "Miko here's been dyin' to meet you, Roy," said Rice. "She's a . . . how'd you put it, babe?"

"Pal-ty animal," said Miko, and inhaled for Clement.

Clement said, "Shit," laughed, and draped an arm around Miko. He lifted his glass to Rice, who joined him in the toast.

"To good company," said Rice, placing strong emphasis on the word *company*. Their eyes engaged over the rims of their glasses. It felt like a moment of bonding, a moment during which assurances were offered and confirmations exchanged. But Clement wasn't fool enough to trust it.

At twenty-nine, with light brown hair falling to the middle of her back, Lily still looked like a college girl. Willowy; long-limbed; the marks of age—faint lines bracketing her mouth, the hint of crow's-feet—barely sketched in. Her face was lean, finely boned, a bit horsey, and her features had an assertive refinement that Clement associated with East Hampton and West Palm Beach; she was beautiful, but one only noticed that after noticing her aura of health and style, as if beauty were merely an accessory that she displayed whenever she wished to show to advantage. Moving about the hotel room, preparing for bed, her gestures were eloquent and precise, and this, too, was a quality that Clement associated with the milieu of polo matches and expensive claret, with lives that had the clarity of sparkling water. In the beginning, her elegance had made him painfully aware of the commonality of his own roots, and this had caused him to view her as an acquisition, something he had obtained by nefarious means; sooner or later, he'd believed, she would see through to his essential crudity and leave him. But four years of marriage had erased most of those feelings, and despite his infidelity with Miko—a tactical infidelity to ratify the masculine contract he had made with Rice—he loved her. And more importantly, he trusted her.

Trust, to Clement's mind, was better than love, a thing of far greater rarity and consequence. He had only trusted one other person in his life—Robert D'allessandro—and he realized that the strain of emotion he'd felt for D'allessandro was akin to what he felt for Lily. In each instance he had surrendered himself not like a lover, but like a child, sensing that the object of his affections was more competent than he in a sphere of existence to which he could only aspire, an altitude of feeling denied him by the abuses of an orphaned childhood. He had permitted D'allessandro to steer him through this unfamiliar medium, and after the old man had died, he had been lost until Lily had come along and reoriented him. She had been doing graduate work in economics and had interviewed him in regard to the financial resurgence of Calcutta, a matter of sensitivity to Clement, since it had been instrumental in stalling his career. He'd had her investigated, and during the course of the investigation, he had become fascinated by her. With her Vassar education and aristocratic blood-lines, she had seemed alien, unfathomable, and it had taken him a long time to accept that she could sympathize with his work. But the upshot had been that she had renewed his enthusiasm for the Company by imbuing him with a sense of his own worth. And that had been the beginning of trust.

She dimmed the lights and slipped into bed, turning to face him, her breasts flattening against his chest. He grew hard against her belly, and he started to pull away, knowing that she was worn out from her day in the market; but she hooked her fingers into his back and kept him close.

"Thought you were too tired," he said.

She kissed his chest. "I just want you inside me a minute, okay?" She rested a knee on his hip, letting him slip between her legs.

"A minute, huh?"

"Maybe two."

Her breath quickened, warming his cheek, and when he entered her, she tensed until he had gone deep.

"God," she said. "God, you feel good."

He fucked her heavily, watching her face grow slack, slivers of white showing beneath her eyelids. After a few seconds he stopped, content to hold her and touch her breasts. The knowledge that he was possessing a rich man's woman, having her in a rich man's hotel, with its cool sheets and androgynous luxury . . . this never failed to give him a venal satisfaction.

"I want you to finish," she said, her eyes still closed.

"You're falling asleep."

"It's nice . . . falling asleep like that." She ran a hand along his arm. "Roy?"

"Yeah."

"Why do you want to see that woman?"

"The one in Mustang? I just want to find out what it was like to be a goddess."

"Oh." She sounded distressed.

"What's the matter?"

"I was hoping it was business. I wouldn't be jealous of business."

"You've got no reason to be jealous."

She opened her eyes; in the half-light they were small puzzles of gleam and shadow. "Maybe not."

"Definitely not."

"I don't know. You're always looking for something else . . . like with D'allessandro. You say he's dead, and still you keep looking for him."

"That's not real," he said. "I know he's dead, but I just keep hoping that somebody'll beat the game. It's got nothing to do with us."

"Yes, it does. It's like saying I'm not enough." She twisted her head away, stared at the ceiling. "Christ, that sounds stupid!"

Clement was losing his erection, and wanting to maintain intimacy, he pulled her hard against him. "Would you like me to cancel the trip?"

"Of course I would. You're going to see a goddess."

"An ex-goddess. She probably looks like a fucking yak."

"It isn't just that I'm jealous," she said after a bit. "All this with D'allessandro, and now Kumari, it's covering up something else. You've got a problem, and you're using this to avoid dealing with it. That's not like you."

He slipped out of her, and she gasped, tried to guide him back in.

"I've kinda lost the mood," he said.

"Are you angry with me?"

"Nah. I'm a little screwed up right now is all." He flopped onto his back. He wanted to be open with her, but openness seemed arduous, a chore demanding too much energy. "I need a couple of days to sort things out. When I get back, we'll talk about it . . . all right?"

"All right," she said, disappointment in her voice. She settled against him, her head tucked into the join of his neck and shoulder, an arm flung across his chest. Her breathing soon became deep and regular.

Clement felt he had passed some crisis and realized that although he had been giving evasive answers to Lily's questions, he had believed every word he'd said. That was SOP, lying to oneself. It had taken him a while to understand that the name The Company referred as much to an acting company as to a business concern. Agents were accomplished actors. They went from role to role, less interpreting than inhabiting them, and by doing so they often lost track of their identities. But that was a survival trait. If you had no solid identity, you could shrug off morality with the same ease that you removed a costume, and that immunized you to an extent against pain. Clement's problem was that he had begun to remember who he was, and he blamed Robert D'allessandro for this.

He recalled sitting with D'allessandro and watching the old man—as slow and ponderous as a gray bear—carve his toy animals, his form of stress therapy, and talking about how he wished he could get away and live up in the hills. Malaysia, maybe. Thailand. On one occasion he had laughed and said, "Y'know, Roy, I used to want to own a goddamn country, and now all I want is to sit somewhere peaceful and learn how to get these bastards right." He'd held up a half-finished tiger, regarding it sourly. "Fuckers always turn out looking like striped dogs."

It occurred to Clement that D'allessandro had carved him into shape just as he had his wooden animals, and that he had done as clumsy a job on him as he had with the tigers. He had taken a rough chunk of human material and created a new man, one with a conscience and the capacity for love, and so had rendered him totally unfit for his job. What Rice had said, that he was becoming an eccentric . . . no doubt about it. Lately he had been screwing up everything, and he didn't much care. It was as if he had admitted his sins, and by that admission had lost the ability to endure them. And maybe Lily had been right, too. Maybe in searching for D'allessandro, for Kumari, he was really searching for an alternative to supplant every facet of his life.

He tried to answer Lily's question about why he wanted to see Cheni Abdurachan; but instead he began to assemble a portrait of the Newar woman, giving her a slim body and large eyes and black hair braided into a pigtail, seeing her as neither beautiful nor ugly, but passable, with delicate features obscured beneath a mask of grime. Once he had finished, she hovered at the center of a diffuse golden light, an island of Buddhist glow, and appeared to be staring directly into his eyes. He had the impression that she was afraid, that although she possessed a core of strength, she was losing a battle against some menacing force. His sense of her grew more specific, so intense and individual that he became unnerved and the image flew apart. He lay blinking, confused. Everything, the shadowed drapes, the dim reflection in the mirror, even Lily, seemed ghostly by comparison to his apprehension of Cheni. This was more than eccentricity, he thought; he was slipping badly. He'd given lip service to the idea of sorting things out, but that might be exactly what he should do. Take the trip and try to get a grip on his life. He almost laughed out loud. *His* life. Christ! Life had never been his. From orphanage to Army to CIA, he'd always been part of a bureaucratic nightmare, always owned, controlled.

Lily stirred, her arm tightening about his chest. "You say something?"

He stroked her hair. "Go back to sleep."

She was silent a few seconds and then said, "I'm scared, Roy. I know something's going on with you, and it scares me."

He started to reassure her, but didn't think he could be convincing. He felt very fragile in his head, very shaky. If there were one problem, one wall against which to hurl himself, he might be able to pull it together. But everything was becoming a problem now, and he had no idea what to do.

An hour from Tasang-partsi. The air was bitter cold, unbelievably clear, the dark blue of the sky overhead shading down toward the horizon on every side to a band of pale turquoise. Miles to the east, the crevasses of glaciers on the slopes of a snowy peak looked as defined as the folds of the dun-colored rock above him. He was negotiating a trail along the flank of a hill; below, at the base of a cliff, a thin torrent of silvery water coursed down the center of a wide gravel bed and flowed off into a cut between the hills. Stunted thistles and gray brushes of wormwood sprouted alongside the trail; ahead lay pinnacles of reddish rock, their eastern faces shadowed to purple. D'allessandro would have loved this country, Clement thought. Clean and empty, yet with a feel of spiritual fecundity. Maybe he would have learned how to carve a tiger by now.

Clement had been twenty-eight when he had been assigned to D'allessandro, who was living then in Costa Rica, unable to leave for fear of being extradited on charges of fraud and extortion; however, D'allessandro had devised a plan that had engaged the favorable attention of the CIA. It was at heart altruistic, though he hid that fact from almost everyone; but eventually it became apparent that he wanted to leave a legacy, something to absolve his sins. The plan took seven years to implement and incorporated—among other elements—a bogus breakthrough in cinematic technology, an effective synthetic cocaine, a string of gambling resorts built in the Maldives and along the Malabar Coast, and, most importantly, a foundation whose purpose was to create low-cost housing outside Calcutta and stimulate the economy of the city. The foundation, fronted by respectable Hindu businessmen who had no idea of the skulduggery taking place around them, served as the holding company for the various properties; the foundation's accounts, seeded by a sizable investment of CIA funds, were swelled by investments in the billions solicited from every major criminal organization in the world. The CIA believed they were pulling off the greatest sting in history, an operation that would throw the criminal world into chaos and increase American influence on the subcontinent by a thousand percent. The criminal organizations had been led to believe that they would wind up in control of the world's entertainment industry, that their own political influence would increase. The plan was a masterpiece of misdirection, a work of genius depending upon dozens of lesser plans and ruthless covert maneuvers, most engineered by Clement, whom D'allessandro had at last taken into his confidence and revealed the ultimate misdirection—that at some point a series of traps would be sprung and the foundation's funds would be channeled into several UN agencies, who were ready with schemes for their charitable disposition.

D'allessandro's recruitment of Clement to be his accomplice had been a beautifully managed seduction. He'd played upon Clement's orphaned childhood in Wyoming and an attendant sympathy for the disenfranchised, and had made himself into a father figure. Clement had genuinely loved the old man, and D'allessandro, he believed, had loved him; he had certainly taken pains to make sure that Clement had not been implicated. As he scrambled up a rise, it seemed for the first time that he could feel how large a space the old man had filled in his life; he had been father, brother, friend . . . and creator. By contrast, the space filled by Lily, that of lover, was small indeed. Thinking this hurt Clement, and because he was no longer a competent actor, he was unable to disregard his feelings, but could only force himself to walk faster and faster, until the aching of his muscles overwhelmed thought.

It was late afternoon by the time he reached Tasang-partsi. Ridges of leaden cloud seamed with tin-colored glare draped the hills. The wind blew in fitful gusts, whirling up a pale grit that appeared to sparkle as it vanished. The village consisted of about thirty black sod houses with slate roofs that sheltered against a cliff, mired in its shadow; a hill rose from the summit of the cliff, resembling more a pile of granitic rubble than an actual geologic formation. The river had narrowed to a fouled trickle that meandered over a gravelly flat, and a couple of mangy yaks with paper flowers tied to their horns were drinking from it; they looked as unreal to Clement, cumbersome and stupid as dinosaurs. Comic-strip beasts. They twitched their tails and gazed mournfully at him as he passed. The row of houses paralleled the stream, and the path that ran alongside them was of deeply rutted frozen mud; protruding from a glaze of cracked yellowish ice at its center was the decaying body of a mastiff, and this added a hint of cloying mustiness to the fearsome stink of the place. Two ravens perched atop the carcass had the look of bizarre ornaments until they spread their wings and flapped away toward the clifftop. Garbage and offal had been banked against the walls of the houses to the level of the first-floor windows, which were framed with rickety match-boarding; holes had been chopped in the filth to permit access to the doors. The squalor was appalling, yet was so absolute, so in keeping with the gloomy sky and bleak surround, it lent a kind of morbid grandeur to the village, as if Tasang-partsi were an outpost on the border of some doomed mythical kingdom.

A young boy guided Clement to a house at the far end of the village, and after paying the boy, he stood staring at the door—three blackened planks and a huge brass padlock, a construction that seemed at once simple and complex, like a child's puzzle. He knocked, feeling foolish now at having come all this way on a whim. The instant before the door opened, he recalled the portrait he'd conjured of Cheni Abdurachan back in Katmandu—a slim woman with doe eyes and a pigtail—and when she appeared in the doorway, wearing jeans and a plaid shirt, she was so like that portrait, he was stunned and a little afraid of what this might mean. She was prettier than he had imagined, and less dirty, her skin bronzed by a fine layer of soot; but the resemblance was startling, nonetheless. Her hair was tied back with a piece of red velvet.

She met his eyes for a second or two, then, pinching the bridge of her nose with thumb and forefinger, lowering her head, gestures that spoke to him of impatience and weariness, she said, "You're from the university?"

He had the impression that unless he came up with a good excuse, he would be turned away. "My name's Roy Clement," he said. "And I'm not from the university. I had a dream about you . . . a hallucination or something. I saw your face, I pictured it just like you are now. I know it sounds crazy, but I thought it was important to come visit you."

"You think you're lying," she said after giving him a searching look. "That's interesting. You're telling the truth, and you think you're lying."

She stepped aside to let him enter and laughed—the laughter had a distressed, erratic quality.

The front room was choked with bluish haze that seeped from a stone oven, and was dimly lit by butter lamps—brass bowls with floating wicks—resting on a table at the back. A wooden trapdoor was inset into the ceiling. Every visible surface was coated with sooty residue, even the brass cooking utensils hung on pegs above the oven. Tips of yak bones and horns used to strengthen the construction stuck out from the walls like gray blunted teeth. Clement took a chair at the table, and Cheni removed a wheel of bread from the oven. She set it on the table, handed him a knife, and dropped into the chair opposite him. The bread was hot and crusty, but the stink of burning yak dung was so powerful, it ruined the taste. Clement chewed stoically, watching Cheni's face. Her features were, he decided, all too voluptuous for her delicate bone structure. Huge eyes, prominent nose, full mouth. They made it appear that something behind the face, some terrible pressure, was causing her skin to bulge. And yet viewed in another light, with an eye for the overall effect, that voluptuousness was her most attractive quality. It was hard to look at her, he thought; the dissonant values of her face forced you to choose a way of seeing, to decide whether or not she was pretty.

"You want to learn about Kumari," she said after a while.

"Everybody asks you about her, huh?"

Again, that disturbing laugh. It had the rhythm of a fading echo and conveyed no feeling of amusement.

"Not at all," she said. "The anthropologists come here and ask what I had to eat in the temple, who instructed me, who cared for me. They're not interested in Kumari."

"Then why assume that's what I want?"

"Because it's true," she said. "Would you like me to make up a lie and pretend that's true instead?"

"The plain truth'll do just fine."

She plucked at a splinter on the table's edge. She was, he realized, always fidgeting, picking at something.

"I know all about you," she said with a hint of defiance. "I know who you are."

"I don't see how that's possible," he said, but felt a trace of alarm.

"You're a violent man," she said. "You've never had any qualms about it until lately. Now you've developed qualms, and you're in a position where they're a liability. But that's not your biggest problem." She planted her hands palms-down on the table, glanced back and forth between them as if gauging their relative size. "The trouble is you haven't changed enough. It's as if you're half-formed. Violence is ingrained in you, and you haven't been able to exorcise it. And now you've been led here . . . but not to learn about Kumari. I can't help you with that, anyway."

The possibility of clairvoyance and all that she had said threatened him. He felt compelled to deny at least part of it.

"I wasn't led here," he said. "I'm just taking a few days off."

She shrugged; a silence lengthened between them.

"Why can't you tell me about Kumari?" he asked.

"Oh, I can tell you a little, but it won't be enough for you," she said. "It seems I woke up one day and discovered I was twelve years old, a little girl being led out of the temple. Before that, my memories are vague. Whispers, golden rooms . . . and fighting. I remember always fighting. Kumari was dark, though there was light at her heart. Not evil. Dark by necessity . . . because she dealt with darkness. The only thing I'm sure of is that she was with me for a while."

She pried at the splinter, peeling it back, working with what seemed fierce stubbornness; she cut her eyes toward him, then looked away.

"Am I making you uncomfortable?" he asked.

"No more than most people."

"I'm sorry," he said. "I don't mean to upset you."

She shook her head wildly as if trying to shake bees from her hair.

"You won't listen," she said. "I can't talk with you if you won't listen."

"I'm not sure what you're telling me."

She nodded, a twitch as much as an affirmation, and when she spoke again, she bit off each word as if restraining herself from a more forceful expression.

"I'm uncomfortable around people because I'm unlucky for them. I'm not talking about the kind of luck that brings a bad run at cards or a streak of household accidents. There's death in me." She glanced up at him. "You may not believe that, but you should heed it. There's virtually no difference between how the two of us think. I say you were led here, and you claim that you were curious. I tell you I'm unlucky, and you might say that what happens to those around me is merely fate. What you consider ordinary seems magical to me. Where I see the workings of gods or devils, you may see the actions of logical consequence. For me the world is a vast spell, for you an intricate coincidence. There's scarcely any distance between those poles. So when I tell you something, don't belittle it. If you have to justify it in logical terms, that's all right. But you have to accept what I say, or else we can't talk."

She leaned back, her hands at rest on the tabletop, and this sudden transition from tension to calm, more than any of the other signs, made it apparent to Clement that she was fighting for control, that she was traveling along the same path of madness down which he had been sliding. And he remembered that had been part of his original vision of her . . . though back in Katmandu he had assumed that she was struggling against an external adversary. Maybe he *had* been led here, he thought, maybe her knowledge of him was no more explicable than his knowledge of her, no less real.

She gave another of her unsettling laughs, and he had the idea that she knew what he had been thinking.

"It's a matter of seeing," she said. "You either see things or you don't. Perhaps that's why you're here—to learn to see."

He could not be sure if what she had said was responsive to what he had thought, or if he had worked himself up into such an excited and delusionary state that anything she said would seem responsive. He had, he realized, no clue as to what they had really been discussing, and he decided to change his tack, to force her to talk about herself, and not him.

"Why do you live here?" he asked. "There can't be very much to interest you."

"It's an unlucky place, it suits me. And I have a great deal to do. I read, I walk, I practice *chod*."

"Is that a religion?"

She hesitated. "It's a ritual of Tibetan Buddhism, a test of the soul against demons."

"You fight the demons?"

"I confront them. There's no point in fighting, they always win."

"Then why bother?"

"It's Kumari," she said. "Everything I do relates to her. To some part of her. *Chod* . . . I don't know. There's part of her I never understood. It seemed different, somehow. Not really her, but joined to her. Her ally, her shield against the darkness. The *chod*, I think, relates to that part."

"Why would a goddess need an ally?"

"Not even Kumari can stand alone against the demons." Cheni gave a wave of dismissal as if to erase what she had said. "It's as I told you, I don't remember much."

From the corner she took a pole with a rope loop at one end and pushed up the trapdoor in the ceiling. Where the door had been was now a square of rich deep blue and stars and a half-moon. Silence seemed to pour into the room along with the chill air. Laughter came from an adjoining house, sounding unnaturally bright. And then from somewhere high above, a man's voice chanting. Cheni scowled and appeared to be listening to the voice.

"What is it?" Clement asked.

"A crazy man," she said. "A hermit. He lives up there." She gestured toward the hilltop. "In the old monastery. The villagers think he's a shaman. And the children dote on him . . . they call him 'uncle.' But he's just crazy."

"Maybe he's a children's shaman."

Cheni sniffed. "He's afraid of everything. He won't say a word to anybody. Sometimes he helps me, but mostly he just hides in the ruin."

"He sounds harmless."

"Is that one of your American virtues?" she said with heavy sarcasm. "Harmlessness?"

Thin glowing clouds began to pass across the moon, and gazing at them, Clement recalled having had a similar feeling of isolation during his childhood, the nights after he had run away from the orphanage and hidden in culverts, in abandoned houses, in the woods. It suddenly seemed strange that he could have come so far from those empty nights, that he had lived and fought and killed and wound up in Mustang with a woman who had once been the goddess Kumari. Thinking this made him feel vulnerable, open to unseen influences, and for a moment he entertained the paranoid notion that the clouds overhead might be edging close to the light that shined him into being, threatening to blot him out. He turned to Cheni. She was staring at him, aghast; she pushed back her chair and came to her feet.

"What's wrong?" he asked.

She felt behind her, groping for the door to the back room. "Don't come near me!" she said. "Do you understand? I see you now! Keep away from me." She darted into the room and closed the door. Clement heard the latch click.

"Hey!" he shouted. "What's wrong? What'd I do?"

No response.

He got up and went to the door. "Hey, are you all right?" When she refused to answer, he said, "Is it okay if I sleep out here?"

Nothing.

"Fuck," he said mildly, less disappointed than confused. The chanting from the hilltop began to annoy him. He reached for the pole and pulled the trapdoor shut. He stood awhile, nourished by the silence, unsure whether to go or to stay. His eyes caught on the bones sticking from the walls, and he pictured himself a crazy little man in a barbarous black house with walls of teeth and dirt, a miniature resting on a dusty shelf behind toy mountains. It pleased him to think of himself as inconsequential, as lost and small, and he decided that he would stay. For a night, at least. Cheni might come around, he thought. He sensed an unalloyed place inside her that madness had not touched, a place where her being was intact, as if madness were not central to her, but rather a kind of corruption infecting her from without . . . like his own madness. Kumari, perhaps. This persuaded him to conclude what he had been tempted to conclude ever since meeting her, that there was a bond between them, a basic compatibility, and he imagined lying down beside her amid the stench of burning yak dung, becoming one with her unluckiness and engaging a cosmic doom.

At length he snuffed out the butter lamps and spread his sleeping bag on the floor; he took out his automatic, wormed into the bag, and zipped it shut. The darkness closed in around him. He lay there alert, unable to sleep. Every few minutes he checked his watch, worried about insomnia. After an hour he heard a keening sound, and because of its complex modulation, he thought it must be an animal voicing pain or loneliness; but when the cry came again, he realized it was only the voice of the land in its emptiness, the white violin whisper of the wind flowing through the passes. He listened to it sounding over and over, hypnotized by its eerie music, and soon began to feel that he too was being drawn thin and fine and pure, reduced to a melody winded from the cuts and notches of his life, from the wasted and cratered terrain of his endless war, becoming a cold song that drifted into silence.

He dreamed about murders, but the murders were not dreams, though they had the artful lucidity of the imagined. He dreamed of knives and the feeling of knives, the tremor that preceded the rush of the blood, and he dreamed of explosive truth, of tiny figures blowing up into heaven, and he dreamed of the incisive meaning of hollow-points, of breast pockets centered by cross hairs, and of an old Hindu man riddled with cancer, strapping a bomb to his waist, shaking Clement's hand, thanking him for the benefits paid to his family . . . and that waked him. At first he thought the sight of Cheni going through the front door was part of the dream, but once he realized it was not, he scrambled up, gun in hand, and pulled on his jacket and went out into the street, heavy with sleep yet curious about what she could be up to at such a late hour. He followed her along a trail that ascended the cliffside and then wound around the hill surmounting it, picking his way among loose rocks, slipping on gravel. The moon was still high, and he remembered other moonlit nights spent tracking a target; from those nights he appropriated a feeling of icy competence and calculation that dissipated the residue of dreams and transformed his pursuit into a logistical game. On several occasions he had the notion that he was being followed himself, but this he chalked up to a need to experience danger and an overactive imagination. At the summit of the hill, barely distinguishable from the pitch of stones beneath it, a jumbled patchwork of shadows and grays, stood a large ruin—the monastery—and it was toward this that Cheni was heading. The final ascent was rough going. Clement had to proceed along rocky defiles and up steep faces, and by the time he had reached the base of the walls, he was thoroughly winded.

The walls were about thirty feet high, crumbled away in sections, and the gate consisted of two massive wooden doors hanging askew, many of the planks shattered inward as if by an enormous fist. Flat *mani* stones with prayers graven in Tibetan script were propped beside the gate, and Clement sat down on one to catch his breath. He came to appreciate the hushed atmosphere, the imposing blankness of the walls, the resounding emptiness, the edged appliqués of shadow, and he began to feel akin to this irrational heap of stone, to the fundamental denials of hope and joy at its heart, with its echoes of animism and droning chants, old insect gods brought low to buzz among the haze of butter lamps and the fumes of ghastly revelation rising from the machineries of prayer. He laughed, alight with his own irrationality, his mind firing on all circuits as with the first rush of a cocaine high, and when he looked out over the village toward the snowy moonstruck peaks of the Himalayas, he felt the accomplished tranquillity of a conqueror, as if he had just completed an assault on some heretofore untraveled height. Everything he saw he claimed for his own; he named the foothills after old girlfriends and the highest mountain after Lily. He was Clement pukkah sahib, Clement of Nepal. At last, still chuckling, he dusted himself off and went inside the ruin.

He crossed a courtyard toward a windowless building of grayish white limestone that resembled an oversized bunker. Strung above the entrance were a number of tattered prayer flags: pale blue pennons inscribed with spidery characters, lashing and snapping in the wind. He climbed a flight of steps and entered a wide corridor lined with musty cells. The moonlight penetrated only a short way into the corridor, illuminating faded frescoes that depicted flayed bodies, skulls filled with blood, heaps of entrails, and demons standing among them—squat, muscular, with fanged mouths and glaring round eyes. Even the fiercest of them had a cartoonish aspect that reminded Clement of creatures created to represent tooth decay or bad breath. He was intrigued by them, and as he inspected the frescoes, he recognized that they were staring out over their terrestrial kingdom, and that he was at the forefront of a vast throng whose individual natures became evident to him, for he seemed to see them reflected in the demons' eyes, an intricate conceit of contorted limbs and twisted sinews and tears and droplets of blood glistening like gemmy fruit, the whole mass seething in ferment as with a constant pour of wind, and beetles were feasting in the eyes of these damned, and women mated with serpents, and men with cancers that had consumed half their faces were clawing at their bellies, trying to dig out some vital organ that would end their suffering, and here a fat man was feeding on gobbets of his own flesh, and here an addict was injecting fire into his genitals, and behind this host of humanity were the legions of the netherworld, hunchbacks whose humps had spindly arms and bony hands, and flies with female mouths, and creatures such as griffins and chimeras and basilisks in whose eyes were registered the enigmatic record of entropic decay, and they were crowding forward, forcing mankind toward its doom, toward the terrible negative fates rendered on the corridor wall, and Clement tried to claw his way back from the brink, drawing moans from those whom he shoved aside, and . . . . He pushed away from the wall, realizing that he had been in the process of losing it and that the moaning was real, coming from farther along the corridor. Still unsteady, he switched off the safety of his automatic, held it barrel-up beside his jaw, and eased along the wall, seeing tag ends of his hellish vision floating on the darkness. As he reached a corner of a cross-corridor the moan sounded again, and at the far end of it he spotted a vertical seam of moonlight. He moved quickly toward it. The way was blocked by a curtain of stringy dark hair that was coarse and dry and stiff to the touch. Yak hair, he realized. He twitched the curtain aside with the gun barrel. Directly opposite, some twenty yards away across an expanse of broken flagstones, was a doorway flanked by two stone columns. Cheni was spread-eagled between the columns, her arms and legs secured by ropes. She had sagged, her head hung down, face veiled by the black shawl of her hair. Clement assumed that she was unconscious, but then she lifted her head and stared through the strands of her hair at a point somewhere above him.

His instincts were to go to her, but it was such a strange and unexpected development that he held back. It was the perfect setup for an assassin. He recalled his feeling of being followed and wondered if Rice's warning had not been merely a general caution, if he'd been hinting that definite action was being contemplated. He opened the curtain a few inches wider to get a view of the rest of the interior courtyard. It was a long notch between buildings, closed in by the monastery's outer walls—a little stage of bone-white and ebony shadow. Apart from Cheni, it was deserted. Dark stems of dead nettles poked from the cracks. Clement glanced back along the corridor, but could detect no sign of movement. He turned again to the courtyard. Cheni had slumped, her head lolling drunkenly. He was, he decided, being overly paranoid. There had been a hundred opportunities for someone to take him since he'd left Katmandu, and he could see no reason why they would want to involve Cheni.

He stepped out into the courtyard, crossing toward her, wondering who could have done this, training his automatic on the darkness at her rear. Before he had gone halfway, she began to struggle against her ropes, and—her eyes rolling up to the strip of starry sky between the buildings—she let out a wild scream. In reflex, Clement looked up. Part of Orion was visible, and there was a feathery cloud passing off to the south. Then an almost imperceptible rippling like heat haze that disappeared within seconds. Some form of condensation, he thought.

"Take it easy," he said to Cheni, who was thrashing about, spitting out phrases in Newari. Yet he did not think that her struggles were fearful, but were bent at getting at something, and it seemed that her scream, too, had been enraged, not frightened. He reached for the knot that secured her right arm. The second his fingers touched it, he was overcome by dizziness. He shook his head, trying to clear it, and in doing so had a fleeting impression of something towering fifteen or twenty feet above him, something huge and indistinct that was gradually assuming a coherent shape, that of a demon similar to those on the walls of the corridor. Colorless, a mere outline, as if—like the frescoes—it had faded with time and hard weather. Thick-legged, barrel-chested. Talons tipped with moonlight. A fleshy tongue caged by fanged jaws. Its silence was terrifying, and Clement wanted to run, but weakness prevailed. He fell back, striking his head against the base of the column. His heart felt sluggish and hot, a flabby muscle whose weakness made a sick pressure in his chest. The demon's form began to solidify, to acquire traces of color and detail, and lifting his gun hand—a tremendous effort, because the pull of gravity seemed to have increased—Clement fired at the thing.

Firing had been an act of desperation, and he had not expected it to have the least effect, believing that the demon was a hallucination or else immune to earthly deterrents. But there was an effect . . . though it was not one he would have cared to elicit. The bullet traced a fiery line through the dusky light, impacting with a splash of vivid gold at the center of the demon's chest; then from the edges of the splash an inky darkness began to spread like oil throughout the demon's form, until it appeared that a hole had been punched through into interstellar space, a hole that had roughly a human shape and was figured by a single golden star. It looked to be inset into the air, to give out onto a great depth, and it had for Clement the chill allure of a gorge that had suddenly opened at his feet. He scrambled back from it, clawing at the flagstones, but the blackness bulged toward him like a membrane under pressure. Then the membrane burst, and the undammed blackness flowed forth and swept over him.

As he fell—and it was a fall, slow yet out of control, pinwheeling down and down—he understood that he was passing along the channel that the bullet was forging through the demon's flesh. He could see the bullet ahead of him—a golden dot maintaining its distance. He was terribly cold, and an aching emptiness was filling him the way that blackness had filled the outline of the demon. He cried out, but the cry offered no release. It seemed rather a spewing forth of the petty details of his life, as if life itself were no more than a cry. All his specifics, every violence, every affection, were—he realized—emblems of the horrid vacuum through which he had been falling for thirty-eight years. He touched and tasted each one, and was harrowed by their vacancy. He wanted to hide from the knowledge of what they were, what he was, but he could not. The golden light of the bullet was dwindling, and he saw that he would soon be trapped inside the demon, that his own hellish emptiness would become the bars of his prison. He twisted about, hoping to straighten out his fall, to move toward the light, but made no progress. Even if he managed to escape, he thought, what purpose would it serve? Emptiness and failure were everywhere, and the particulars of his life were demons in themselves. He had no choice but to confront them.

Reaching that accord, accepting it, acted to calm him, and when he tried once again to straighten out his fall, this time he succeeded.

The cold began to diminish, the darkness seemed to be thickening, to be providing a resistance that slowed him, and he discovered that he could use this resistance to guide himself, to shift direction. The golden light acquired a gravity that drew him faster and faster; it became a diffuse golden circle, a sun toward which the darkness was funneling him, and soon, with the barest sense of transition, he found himself at its center, lying on a pallet, staring at a butter lamp set into a niche in a black wall from which the tips of bones protruded.

Cheni was kneeling beside him. He struggled to sit up, bewildered, unable to accept that he was safe, back in her bedroom; but she forced him to lie down and adjusted the pillow beneath his head. Her face was like the face of a *gopi* girl, one of those women who danced and played the flute for Krishna. Almost a parody of femininity, too sensuous by a degree. Yet he was drawn to her, attracted in much the way that he had been attracted to the demon and then to the light, physically compelled, and he shifted his right hand so that it pressed against her leg. She tensed, but did not move away.

"What happened up there?" he asked. "You were tied up."

"*Chöd,*" she said. "The hermit helps me with the ropes. He helped carry you down, too." She glanced behind her. "He gave me something for you. I must have left it in the other room."

"I don't get why you have to tie yourself up," Clement said. "You saw the demon?"

"I saw *something*." He laughed. "Way it's been lately, I'm liable to see anything."

"Demons thrive on fear. To practice *chöd* you must put yourself in a position that forces you to confront them. If you have nowhere to run, you have to make a stand."

Nothing she said made any sense . . . or if it did, it was not the sort of sense that mattered to him. He ran his hand along her thigh, and the contact warmed him. He wanted her to take away all the cold inside him, to be a new meaning, a new level of pleasure. He sensed this was possible, that she would no longer reject him.

"Do you understand?" she asked.

"Uh-huh."

He turned on his side and put his other hand on her hip. He waited for her to resist, and when she did not, he pulled her down next to him. Her face was stoic, impossible to read. He touched her breasts, let the soft weight of one settle in his palm. Her eyelids drooped.

"Last night you locked yourself away from me," he said. "And now you're . . . you're letting me get close."

"I saw that we might be lovers. I needed a lover, but I was afraid for you. Then at the monastery you were courageous. It wasn't necessary, but you didn't know that."

"And this is my reward?"

"It's no reward," she said. "I know why you're here now. I saw it at the monastery."

The light from the butter lamps seemed to be melting over them, thickening into a languorous atmosphere. Clement tugged down the zipper of her jeans, worked his hand beneath the stiff denim, his fingers pushing into silky hair. She was already wet, open, and she arched against the pressure of his hand, making a scratchy noise in the back of her throat. Despite his arousal, he felt odd touching her so intimately. It was as if their sexuality was purely genital, as if their closeness was unemotional, a kind of intricate fitting together, satisfying in the sense that solving a puzzle is satisfying.

"Why *am* I here?" he asked, easing her jeans down past her hips.

"Kumari led you," she whispered.

"I don't understand."

"Kumari," she said, and repeated the name several times, her tone growing frantic, the rhythm of her speech effecting a counterpoint to the clumsy struggle they made of shedding their clothes. It seemed that her inability to explain things was unsettling her, and Clement told her that it was all right, that he had no need to understand.

"You're going to know Kumari . . . her light," she said. "Luck doesn't matter for you anymore."

He pushed her onto her back, propped himself above her, and thought how fine it was that a kid from a Wyoming orphanage was about to fuck a goddess.

"It never did," he said.

As he entered her, he imagined himself engaging bad luck, terrible luck, and something cold trickled along his spine; yet even the thought of death was arousing now, inspiring, enlisting his adventurousness, and for a few moments it was good with her. Her fingernails raked his sides, her ass churned beneath him. In the hazy, buttery light her face was a lover's face, softened and rapt, and her words were the breathy affirmatives of passion, the broken phrases and hissed endearments of a tender madness. It had been a long time for her between lovers—he knew that from the way her body responded—and this pleased him. But though clinically fulfilling, their lovemaking never matched his expectations. It remained clumsy, tentative, curiously uninvolving, never attaining the ease of a true compatibility, and afterward he felt that he had taken advantage of a sick woman and was ashamed. He left her sleeping, then dressed and went into the front room. It seemed that all his emotion and tumult had come to no result, and he had needed a result; he believed he had been promised a result by the place and the woman and his desire for resolution. Maybe, he thought, he should spare them both embarrassment and leave while she was still asleep.

He lit a butter lamp and sat down, resting an elbow on the table, cupping his chin. His elbow nudged against something, and he cocked an eye toward it. At first he could scarcely believe what he was seeing, and even after he had picked the thing up, he half-expected it to vanish, to prove to be another hallucination. But it was solid, real. A cunningly carved wooden tiger. Painted orange and black, with a red mouth and white fangs and eyes of vivid green. Flawless. A feral talisman. The hermit, he thought, recalling what Cheni had said about the man giving him a gift. D'allessandro was the hermit, he was up there right now . . . up in the monastery. Clement felt so much, he could not put a name to any of his emotions. He got to his feet, clutching the tiger, and paced back and forth, wondering if this could be a trap. If D'allessandro was there, why would he choose to make his presence known? He'd be afraid . . . even of Clement. And that, Clement realized, must be the answer. D'allessandro would figure that Clement would find him sooner or later, and he wanted to arrange a meeting on his own terms. He wouldn't have risked firing at Clement in front of Cheni, and he couldn't kill Cheni without arousing the suspicions of the villagers. This way, however, he could discover how many people knew of his whereabouts. And he'd give Clement a chance to prove himself—Clement was sure of that. Exhilarated, he looked about for his coat and spotted it crumpled in a corner. He grabbed it, and the automatic fell from the pocket. He scooped it up. The gun reminded him of what had happened the previous night, and he had second thoughts about returning. But no, he realized, it had been Cheni who had brought the demon—if the demon had really been there—and that if D'allessandro could live in the monastery, then he—Clement—would be all right. He shrugged into his coat, tucked the gun into his belt at the small of his back, and stepped out into the street. The sun was high, shining whitely through fraying storm clouds, and Clement set out walking briskly, enlivened by the cold thin air and the prospect of seeing D'allessandro.

Bad luck, my ass, he said to himself.

By day, the courtyard where Cheni had been tied up seemed more abandoned and ruinous than it had by night. Wind whirled up dust from the flagstones, and the outer wall showed itself to be deeply pocked, with fist-sized chunks of rock and mortar lying at its base. The clouds had moved on, and the strip of sky between the two buildings was a bright burning blue. Clement called out to D'allessandro, and the name seemed to stir a little something in the shadows. He shivered, took out the wooden tiger, and examined it again. Plush red jewel box of a mouth, and painted muscles flowing. The cunning white teeth were absolutes of biting. He closed his fist around it, feeling anger and love and frustration.

"It's me!" he shouted. "It's Roy!"

A snick, a small solidity among the whisperings of wind.

He squeezed the tiger more tightly; its pointed ears pricked his palm.

"D'allessandro!"

He had a sense of presence nearby, and he laughed, a cracked laughter that trailed away and left him empty. A bird, visible as a black incision in the blue void, soared overhead, and the sight caught at Clement, filling him with longing. He walked into the courtyard, out of the shadows and into the glittering silence.

"C'mon, man!" he said. "I don't want to hurt you!"

He listened, but heard only the wind. He stood straight, hands clasped at his back, and faced the curtain of yak hair covering the doorway from which he had come.

"Know what I can't figure, man? Why you didn't convince me you were dead. You could convince people of anything, you were a fucking genius at that. It's like you wanted me to know you were alive . . . isn't that right?"

The wind fluted through the ruins, cutting a thin breathy passage of melody.

"Well," Clement said, "if you're not going to come out, I'll just talk, okay?" He let out a sigh and that weakened him, opened him to greater emotion. "Remember what I did for you? All the killings, all the bloody detail work? I hated it, y'know. But I owed you, man. I really appreciated what you'd done for me. Really! I wouldn't know shit if it wasn't for you. And when all the shit I know is screwing me up, I'm still very appreciative." He scuffed his heel against the flagstones. "I guess this must sound a little . . . uh . . . a little confused. I realize that. But what can I tell you? I probably am a little confused. That's how you gotta be if you want to keep the assholes off-balance, right? You taught me that, too, remember? You said I had to learn to act irrationally for rational reasons." The silence was eroding his control; the sun seemed to be making a fuming noise. "What is this crap! If you're paranoid, man, do what you gotta do! Otherwise get your grimy ass out here!"

A faint scraping sound.

"For Christ's sake!" Clement was suddenly close to tears. "I'm not going to hurt you, okay? I've missed you!"

Another stretch of silence, and then a hoarse baritone said, "Put your hands on top of your head, Roy."

Clement did as ordered, his heart racing.

A massive figure in a maroon robe pushed through the curtain of yak hair to stand at the top of the stairs leading down into the courtyard. Wearing sandals and carrying an Uzi. Filthy gray hair twisted into strands that fell to his shoulders. Jowly, glum face dyed mahogany. Six years had worn new lines in the face, but Clement would have known it anywhere, no matter how effective its disguise. He felt eager and anxious like a child hoping for approval, and he couldn't think what to say. D'allessandro's dark eyes, set amid folds and pouches of skin, were narrowed, fixed on him, and he shifted uncomfortably.

"You look like a fucking gypsy," he said at last, and laughed.

His expression solemn, D'allessandro came down the stairs, keeping the Uzi trained on Clement. "What am I going to do with you, Roy?"

"Do with me? What the fuck you mean, do with me?" He held up the wooden tiger. "Finally got 'em right, huh?"

D'allessandro ignored this. "Are you alone?"

"Hell, yes! You know I wouldn't bring anybody else."

"Why did you come here?"

Nothing was going as Clement had anticipated. He had thought that the emotion of their reunion would overwhelm suspicion; he had expected that D'allessandro would have grown simple and beatific like Gepetto, reduced to his saintly essentials; he had pictured them embracing, weeping.

"You look terrific," he said. "Really terrific."

"Answer me." D'allessandro gestured with the Uzi. "Why did you come?"

"Kumari . . . I wanted to learn about Kumari. Jesus, I couldn't believe it when I saw the tiger. I couldn't fucking believe you were here."

He started forward, but D'allessandro waved him back.

"Are you certain you're alone? I thought I saw someone else."

"Fuck, yeah! I'm alone, all right?"

After a pause D'allessandro said, "It's good to see you." But his tone was neutral, and he did not lower the gun.

"I've been looking all over hell for you!" Clement said, his frustration boiling over. "Six goddamn years! And all you got to say is, 'It's good to see you?' Shit!"

"You should have left well enough alone."

"Damn it! You wanted me to find you!"

D'allessandro gave an exasperated sigh and glanced up to the sky as if seeking guidance. "Roy," he said sadly.

"How are you?" Clement asked. "Are you happy?"

D'allessandro appeared startled. "Yes, I suppose I am."

"That's good, that's good." Clement searched for something else to say, wanting to gain the old man's trust. "So what do you do here? Just hang out and carve the animals?"

"I have books, music . . . a cassette recorder." D'allessandro wore a bemused look. "It may sound austere to you, but it's a welcome simplicity."

"Great," said Clement, still at a loss for words, but beginning to think that they were going to get past this moment, that they would soon be sitting in the sun and talking about the future, being like father and son, clear of their bloody convoluted history, and they would make new plans, achieve tremendous successes, and D'allessandro would teach him the secrets of absolution and forgetfulness; and that was important, for without absolution and forgetfulness, he was not going to make it, but seeing how contented the old man was, he knew those secrets must exist, that there must be a way to lift memory from the brain as easily as those magical little screens that kids draw on; and when they peel back the plastic sheet, what they had drawn would be erased.

"Roy!"

Clement realized that D'allessandro had been speaking. "Yeah, what?"

"Put your hands back on your head!"

Clement was surprised to find his hands dangling at his sides. "Sorry," he said. "I was just. . . ."

A little sound like the whiff of a vacuum can being punctured, and D'allessandro's head exploded. Sprays of blood painted the wall behind him, bone fragments clittered on the flags. As the old man toppled, Clement threw himself into a shoulder roll toward the wall, digging for his automatic, and came up firing at the curtain of yak hair. Continuing to fire, he crawled over to the body, plucked up D'allessandro's Uzi; then he sent a burst of fire into the curtain, making it jerk and dance. He got to his feet, edged along the wall toward the curtain; he lifted the braided edge away with the barrel of the Uzi, and return fire tore through the hair. He glanced around, searching for an option to the corridor. The outer wall. By using the pitted sections for handholds, he should be able to scale it. Whoever had shot D'allessandro would pull back, knowing that Clement would have to make a break sooner or later. They would take cover in the boulders outside the gate. At least that was how Clement himself would handle the situation. They would not be looking for him atop the wall. And even if they did, he wouldn't present much of a target.

He sent another burst through the curtain, screaming his rage at the assassin; then he sprinted for the wall, hit it running, hooking his fingers into the rotten stone, digging in with his toes. Less than twenty seconds, and he had reached the top. It was barely a foot wide and planed away to a sheer drop, to the roofs of Tasang-partsi several hundred feet below. The wind tugged at him, his guts seemed to squirm, his balls shriveled. He looked down at the body. Blood had pooled beneath the head, its scarlet startling against the bleached flagstones; strands of gray hair lifted in the breeze with the dreamlike irresolution of kelp. Clement's eyes filled. They had been so close, so goddamn close. Everything would have been all right—he knew it. They would have come to an accord, they would have reminisced and made plans. His anger was consolidated by the sight of the blood. The bastards were going to pay. Not just the assassin, not just Rice. He knew it had to be Rice behind this particular move. But he wouldn't stop with Rice. All the major assholes. They were going to rue the fucking day.

He gripped the wall with his knees, and pushing the Uzi ahead of him, he started inching his way along. By the time he reached the corner where the wall angled toward the gate, the wind had nearly dislodged him twice. His hands were scraped raw, his shoulders ached. But he felt very clear, very controlled. Absorbed in the play, at one with his character, artless in the single-mindedness of his intent. He lay flat atop the wall, scanning the pitch of boulders. About seventy-five feet downslope from the gate—a slice of bright blue. Seconds later, the slice expanded to include a speck of white. A wool hat, he thought. And the blue must be a down parka. He aimed, but the target disappeared. The assassin kept shifting, exposing different sections of his body, never remaining still long enough for Clement to be sure of a hit. He edged forward again, trying for a better angle and closer range. After about thirty feet he stopped and assumed his firing position, waiting for the right moment. He relaxed and regulated his breathing. He drew a breath and held it. Sliver of white. Too little exposure. Sliver of blue. No, no, not yet. He released his held breath, took in another. Finally there it was—a perfect blue ace centering a gray blur. He squeezed the trigger and heard a shrill cry above the popping of the Uzi. He saw an upflung arm and more blue exposed. Gleeful, he poured round after round into the target. Painting it with speckles of red. And then he listened. Only the humming vibration of the ruins and the ghosting of the wind.

He was pretty sure the assassin was dead, but as he clambered down the broken slanting planks of the gate, he maintained his readiness. He went in a crouch among the boulders until he came to the body. There was too much blood, too many holes in the parka, for any life to remain. He nudged the body onto its back with his toe. Long chestnut hair spilled out as the wool hat slipped off. Lily's eyes stared at him jellied and unseeing above the wreckage of her jaw. Unable to move, to react, Clement stared back at her, revulsion growing in him, trying to probe with his mind inside the bullet holes and stroke something back to life. But the next moment, though he had begun to cry, he would have liked to smoke her again.

The goddamn Company!

Oh, man! What a great little actress, a fucking natural for the part!

You feel so good in me, you fit me so perfectly, I love your mouth on me.

Clement's fury erupted in a scream. He fired into the sky, picturing black holes stitched in blue flesh. The clip emptied, and he flung the Uzi aside. He felt huge with grief, towering over the events of the morning . . . events that had been contrived especially for him. They had really gotten his ass, they had. He had never seen it coming.

"But you fucked up, guys," he said. "You really should have left me something to care about . . . just in case."

He went for a little stroll through the boulders. He would have to deal with the bodies, he knew that. He didn't want anyone getting suspicious before he had his innings. But now . . . now he just wanted to pretend that he could walk away and feel nothing.

"Aw, Jesus," he said, remembering Lily on their last morning together, stepping from the shower. Something wrapped long curving talons around his heart and squeezed.

Nothing to do except face the demons.

Things were stirring behind him, the corpse was getting to its feet, combing its beautiful chestnut hair, tossing it back, smoothing down its lace peignoir, preparing for bed.

Baby, it said, darling, just come inside me for a minute, that'll be long enough for you to know all my moves, all my sweet tricks, all the honey in my groin, come on in, killer, we'll do it slow and forever, glistening and slick, a new kind of sex, writhing and choking, tongues slippery with cyanide and kisses that sting.

"Shut the hell up!" Clement said. "I don't care anymore."

Lily, Lily . . . damn!

She must have loved me, she really must have, she had been too good an actress not to buy her act.

So, she loved you, so what's that mean?

Nothing, I guess.

Right you are, chump. All that truefine feelgood, all that midnight clutch and tumble, it was just cheap sugar.

A tear trickled into the corner of his mouth. It had no taste.

He had an option, he realized. Tasang-partsi. Maybe something for him there, some new reason for caring.

Naw, un-uh, he didn't understand what that had been about, Cheni, their desultory sex, and maybe it had not been worthy of understanding, just a little wasted treat, a kind of mystical sloppy seconds.

He stared out over the boulders, over the flats and the foothills toward the Himalayas, deriving strength from their distant grandeur. No answers there, however. No alternatives. The assholes had started something that he would have to finish.

"Stupid fuckers," he said to the mountains. "You write yourself a great play, get yourself prime talent, then you blow the ending."

But that was cool.

He had an idea for a terrific third act.

A week after Clement's return from Tasang-partsi, a week during which fires bloomed in American embassies all over Asia, he broke into Rice's home in Katmandu and prowled about the place, digging into drawers, discovering little of interest apart from several handguns and a variety of sexual aids. He unloaded all of the guns except for a .44 Magnum, which he fitted with a silencer. Then he sat down to wait for Rice in the den. Rice had fixed the room up with walnut paneling, a green shag carpet, bookshelves, a wet bar, leather chairs and sofa, and Clement liked the American ambience, although the lighting was a touch too yellow for his tastes. He laid the gun on the arm of a chair, leafed through some old *Time* magazines, and having exhausted these, opened the latest Robert Ludlum thriller. Shouts and laughter and music came from the street—it was a festival night, and the city was thronged with celebrants. Listening to them, Clement felt lighthearted and clear in his mind; but this was mostly because he knew he was cutting his final ties with a world in which he had lived his entire life, that once the night was done he would be irrevocably disconnected. The thought sobered him, yet was not in the least displeasing. He went to the bar, poured himself a bourbon on the rocks, and toasted his freedom. Then he sat down again and reopened the Ludlum. He was three murders into the book when he heard Rice's car pulling up.

He killed the lights and went into the darkened living room; through the window he saw Rice and a heavyset balding man in a tweed overcoat, whom he recognized as Clark Settlemyre, an assistant to the Director. That Settlemyre was along both gladdened his heart and rekindled his anger. The more the fucking merrier, he thought. He went back into the den and stood behind the door, certain that they would be having a nightcap. A minute later the door opened, the lights were switched on, and the two men entered and walked over to the bar. Hidden by the door, watching through the crack below one hinge, Clement enjoyed the feeling of cold implacability that the sight of their backs gave him.

"Have a seat," said Rice, shrugging out of his overcoat.

"I've been sitting all day," said Settlemyre; he had a deep presidential voice that matched the blunt strength of his features. He ran his eye along the bookshelves.

Rice mixed, poured. "I think you're wrong about Clement."

Settlemyre shrugged as if Rice's opinion were unimportant.

"Clement's a doer," said Rice. "Not a schemer. I can see him gettin' in a snit and blowin' somebody's brains out. But whoever's been mailin' these bombs has. . . ."

"Whoever it is," said Settlemyre, "knows security procedures like the back of his hand. It has to be someone with Clement's level of clearance."

"True," said Rice. "But I'm gonna withhold judgment till I hear from Lily."

"*If* we hear from her."

"I think I can clear this up, fellas," said Clement, stepping from behind the door. "It was me what did for all yer buddies."

Rice's hand darted toward the inside of his coat. Clement blew a wine decanter at his elbow into a shower of icy splinters, and Rice ducked, then froze.

"A wise choice, pal," said Clement. "Because I'm crazy to kill. So why don't you take the gun out with your left hand and toss it over here?"

"What is this shit, man?" said Rice.

Clement aimed the Magnum at Rice's forehead, and Rice did as he'd been told.

"How 'bout you, Clark?" said Clement. "Are we packing tonight, or are we dressed for success?"

"I don't have a weapon," said Settlemyre.

"Let's be certain, now," said Clement brightly. "The punishment for wrong answers is lots and lots of pain." He injected menace into his tone. "I mean it."

"I have no weapon."

"Know what, Clark? I believe you. I bet you'd rather die than fib. But why don't we just open our coat . . . just to make me happy."

Settlemyre complied; his face was unreadable, but Rice looked anxious.

"You gonna tell us what this is alla 'bout?" he asked.

Clement arched an eyebrow. "You don't know? Golly, I would have bet you had to know." He ordered his face into a solemn mask and affected a Southern accent. "Miz Lily has met with a tragic fate." Saying that hurt him, and he covered his emotion with a laugh. "As has that dastard D'allessandro. In both instances, it was not a fate worse than death . . . get my meaning?"

Rice said, "Jesus," and Settlemyre said, "D'allessandro is in Mustang?"

"Was," said Clement, restraining his anger.

"I think . . ." Settlemyre began.

"You motherfucker," said Clement. "I'm going to go easy on Rice. But you, I'm going to do you slow. Know why? Because you're the one wanted D'allessandro. It was your pride on the line. You and all the major assholes in McLean. That's all it was . . . goddamn pride."

"You should take time to examine the situation, Clement," Settlemyre said. "Things may not be quite so cut-and-dried as they seem."

"Terrific idea! Clark, why don't you sit down over there." Clement gestured with the gun to one of the leather chairs. "And you"—he looked at Rice—"you come over here."

"C'mon, man," said Rice. "I . . ."

"Over here!" said Clement. "Now!"

He directed Rice to stand at the right of the leather chair opposite the one in which Settlemyre had taken a seat; then he sat down and jammed the silencer into Rice's groin. He could feel Rice quivering.

"Please," said Rice. "Please, don't."

"Everybody comfy?" asked Clement. "Good." He smiled at Settlemyre. "Okay . . . talk."

"You have to be a realist about all this," said Settlemyre. "I know you're upset, and I realize you don't particularly want to hear that. But you know that's how you should deal with it."

"Roy," said Rice plaintively.

"Shut the fuck up!" Clement glanced up at him. "This could be an important lesson for you . . . that is, if you believe in reincarnation. You believe in reincarnation, man?"

"Don't do this, Roy."

"All you're going to hear, pal, is a little whiff. Pffft! Then you're going to blow backwards into the wall and slide down like a dead snake. I don't know if you'll feel any pain. Gunshot wounds were never my best subject. But I bet your balls will be dead before you are."

Rice started to plead his case again, but Settlemyre told him to keep quiet.

"Do you want retribution?" he said to Clement. "Or would you prefer to live?"

"You mean I dare hope?"

"Your sarcasm is amusing," said Settlemyre. "But this situation surely merits more than sarcasm." He crossed his legs, pulling his features into a grave expression. "Now I realize, of course, that you can't trust me. But you're aware of my power, and you must know that with the use of a little acumen you can win guarantees from me that I won't be able to rescind until you've reached safety. You can survive this if you decide to be a realist. If, however, you insist on playing the role of grief-stricken avenger, then there's nothing I can do for you."

Rice was easing back from the gun, and Clement prodded him hard to keep him still.

"I can understand how you've become such a mover and shaker,

Clark," said Clement. "That was nicely spoken, nicely done . . . the way you tried to turn the tables on me. Under any other circumstance, it would have been incredibly effective. Really, I mean it. But the problem is, I just don't give a fuck about alternatives. I'm not playing anymore, and there's not a thing you can do for me except die. Besides, I might have a few moves that would surprise you."

"Oh?" said Settlemyre, maintaining his poise. "What might they be?"

"I *could* tell you, Clark. I know you'd keep it to yourself. But I don't care that much about satisfying your curiosity. I hate your guts. You're the kind of slug that makes nights like this an inevitability." He looked up at Rice, who was staring ahead, his chin trembling. "So how you doing there, pal?"

Rice's Adam's apple bobbed, and he let out a sobbing breath; his hands shook, his fingers curled.

"No shit . . . that bad, huh?"

With a marked effort, Rice steadied himself. "Lemme go, man. You know none of this was my decision."

"Lily," said Clement, his heart aching with hatred. "That one hurt."

"I'm just a fuckin' soldier, man . . . like you."

"How long?" asked Clement. "How long was she working for you?"

When Rice seemed reluctant to answer, Clement jabbed with the gun, doubling him over, and repeated the question. Rice sucked in air, tears spilled from his eyes. "Was it from the beginning?" asked Clement. "Just nod."

Rice nodded.

"From the beginning." Clement was having a problem holding on to his train of thought. "This was all about D'allessandro? That's all?"

Settlemyre said, "What would you expect?"

"I'll be right with you, Clark," said Clement; then, to Rice: "Remember what I said about learning a lesson?"

"What? No . . . yeah. I . . ."

"Don't strain yourself, pal. The lesson is, free will can be fun."

Rice blinked, swallowed. He kept his eyes on the wall, his mouth opening and closing.

"Remember that little sound I told you about? Pffft?"

"Roy . . . Christ!"

"Listen," said Clement, and fired.

As Rice flew backward, Clement caught movement out of the corner of his eye and threw himself sideways in the chair. He felt a tremendous jolt high in his chest that added to his momentum, heard an explosive report, and he went over onto the floor, firing in the general direction of Settlemyre. After a bit he sat up, his back to the wall. He blinked, trying to focus; but though his vision cleared, nothing in the room seemed to fit together—it was as if true clarity were a product of some indefinable strata underlying the visual, one whose dissolution preceded that of the six accredited senses. He blinked again. Better. Sofas on rugs, rugs on floors, walls containing light and bodies. The usual arrangement. One of the bodies, Settlemyre, was still sitting in his chair. The upper portion of his skull was missing . . . or not exactly missing. Most of it had gone to create a Jackson Pollock effect in reds and grays on the wall behind him. Despite this grotesque insult to his flesh, he had maintained something of his basic imperturbability; his mouth set in lines of stern disapproval, as if death had struck him as an example of unsatisfactory policy. Rice was curled beside the bookcase, his head wedged upright. He appeared to be gazing with intent interest at the lowest shelf, hunting for some pertinent reference work. Islands of his blood figured the tangles of a green shag sea. Clement closed his eyes. He probed his wound gingerly, feeling the ridged-up flesh of the bullet hole just under the collarbone.

You should have patted down the bastard, he told himself, you should have known he'd use Rice to make a move.

A fuckup to the last.

He probed his wound again.

Couldn't have been much of a gun. Fucking sissy gun. The shithead had probably carried it tucked in his garter belt.

But 'tis enough, t'will serve.

He had another look at the room. Hell, he thought, would open like this. Under the sickly yellow lights, a flat of carnage and gore, dapplings of red and gray, a still life with corpses painted upon a curtain that, once lifted, would allow the everlasting blackness to flow out over the audience.

Goddamn! Fuck, that hurts!

He gritted his teeth, pushed against the edges of the wound, trying to stifle the pain.

Fuck, fuck, fuck!

After a minute he hauled himself to his feet. He wavered, almost fell. Black nebular shapes floated before his eyes. Pain was beating in-

side him, the steady beat of oarsmen. Stroke, stroke. Once it had subsided a bit, he wobbled over to the bar and poured a double bourbon. He slugged it down. Poured another. He repeated the process
twice more and felt much better. Maybe, he thought, he could make
it back to Tasang-partsi.

Not hardly, bozo, not without you growing wings.

The funny thing, though, was why he should keep wanting to
return there. He wouldn't have minded seeing Cheni again. Birds of
a feather, that sort of thing. And they'd had something going, something that had seemed of importance. What it was, he had no way
of telling. Maybe it was merely a delusion.

Delusion was always a possibility.

But he could have sworn there had been something, some unity,
some tie. Nothing mystical . . . or if it was, then mystical in a nuts-
and-bolts sort of way, in a pragmatic sense.

What the hell was he doing, just standing here and thinking about
this dumb crap?

Time to flee, to hie thee hence, to make tracks.

The whiskey had steadied him, and he thought it would be good
to get away from the house. Take a walk somewhere.

Been a long time since you've had a chance just to walk around
and feel the breeze without having mean things on your mind.

Not since . . . shit! Not since Eddie Lavigne.

Eddie, Christ! How long's it been, man?

Twenty-three years, pal. What the fuck you been doing with
yourself?

Dying, Eddie. I've been dying all that time.

You always were a morbid asshole. Hey, remember when we busted
out of the orphanage?

Fucking A . . . it was great!

Great? You ran out on me!

What'd you expect, man? You freaked out!

The hell I did!

Hell you didn't, Eddie! We were crossing a field, remember, and
we saw this old horse grazing, and you said we should steal the fucker
. . . ride it. But we were too short to get up on it, so you started
jumping up and down, waving your arms, and the son of a bitch just
keels fucking over. Dead. You claimed you'd killed it, that you had
vast mental powers. You said if I didn't do what you told me, you'd
zap me with your mind rays.

Clement.

A cold, intimidating voice snapped him back to an awareness of Rice's den. He spun about, the Magnum at the ready.

I need you, Clement.

"Oh, man," he said, easing out of the room into the darkened corridor. "I don't need this shit!"

You have done evil, but your heart is pure.

"Who the fuck's there?" he shouted, dropping into a crouch.

Kumari.

Cold, black, deep as forever.

Clement laughed giddily, realizing that he was starting to lose it in a big way. Time to flee. Yes, indeed. He stepped back into the den. His shirtfront was soaked with blood. He grabbed Rice's overcoat, pulled it on, and buttoned it to cover the mess. He shoved the Magnum into his belt, then poured another bourbon. He glanced down at Settlemyre and Rice. Brothers in the bond, no matter how despicable. He toasted them and wondered how it would feel to be innocent and clean and full of hope.

This world is a shadow, Clement. What you have done is cause for neither contrition nor pride.

"No lie?" said Clement, and giggled; the bourbon was doing its job.

Purity is a condition of fate. It has been your fate to be a child at war and pure. Thus you can be useful to me.

"Sorry," he said. "Got a previous engagement."

He went staggering through the house, out onto the street. Swarthy wild-eyed men in loose white cotton shirts and trousers milled everywhere, going arm-in-arm, singing drunkenly. The night was music and incense and shrieks, the darkness slashed by channels of torchlight and glitter. As Clement moved with the crowd toward the heart of the city, he spotted three men in suits. They had the cut of Company men. They were craning their necks, peering in every direction, and Clement thought that they might have been watching Rice's house in hopes that he would show up; they probably had seen him leaving. He worked his way to the middle of the crowd in order to hide from the men, and then, feeling weaker, disoriented, he let the press carry him along, turning this way and that, and finally pouring into a wide street lined by wooden stalls with hotly lit interiors and necklaces of light bulbs that illuminated signs lettered in both English and Newari. Like little stages in which dozens of two- and three-character plays were being performed. Tinsmiths, basketsellers, men

hunched over sewing machines, cobbler's benches, men hammering
inlay into copper plates, offering scarves and rings and silver charms.
The jostling of the crowd had worn away Clement's reserves. He
pushed toward the nearest of the stalls, a place no larger than a toolshed
in which a pudgy man wearing an old tweed coat and a green turban
was embroidering a shirt; he slumped against the wall, slid down into
a sitting position, and stared at the forest of legs moving past, growing numb and thoughtless. Somebody tapped him on the shoulder.
The stallkeeper, his face crimped by a frown. He shook a finger under
Clement's nose.

"No stay here!" he said, shaking his head. "No!"

Clement fumbled in his pockets, hauled out a handful of bills and
thrust them at the man. "Just a few minutes, okay? I just want to
rest up for a few minutes."

The money vanished along with the frown.

"Okay!" said the stallkeeper, beaming. "No problem, no big
deal."

The music swirled around Clement, no longer seeming an assault
on his senses, but rather comforting him, supporting him on billows
of sound, and he began to feel at peace. This troubled him. By all
rights, he thought, he should not be granted peace, he should be
tormented for his crimes.

But peace was cool with him if it was cool with everyone else.

How 'bout it, guys? Little time-out? Little King's X?

Beyond the market stood a three-story building of crumbling friated
brick, with slices of light leaking through shuttered windows. Shadows
were hundreds of deaths passing behind them.

Can't scare me, man.

I live with those fucking shadows.

Hey, Cheni! There's worse than being unlucky.

"Right, D'allessandro?"

Absolutely, Roy.

You know how it goes. . . . Born under a bad sign, I been down
since I began to crawl, if it wasn't for bad luck, I wouldn't have no
luck at all.

No luck at all, Cheni, that's really the pits.

But no luck wasn't an excuse, he wasn't going to hide behind ex-
cuses, not at this point.

He fingered the wooden tiger from his pocket and looked it in
the eyes. "What do you think?"

You were hard wood to work, Roy, but I finally got you right.

I loved you, old man.

Please, Roy . . . love?

The stallkeeper tapped him on the shoulder again and handed him a cup. Tea. Clement thanked him and set the cup down.

Can't drink it, might spring a leak.

I'm a little teapot, short and stout, just tip me over and pour me. . . .

Fuck that shit!

He put the tiger down beside the cup.

You stay there, pal, and keep watch for demons.

His wound throbbed like a sick heart.

Clement.

That cold voice again.

"Go away," he said.

Look at me, Clement.

Wearily, he lifted his head. Torchbearers were approaching, and the crowd parted before them. Following the torchbearers came a platform borne on the shoulders of six men, and seated on it was a Newar girl of about twelve, clad in embroidered gilt cloth. Her black eyes opened like tunnels through golden flesh, and he flowed along them, passing through the bleak serenity of the girl's presence, a presence that struck him as being both masculine and feminine, until he touched a more erratic presence, touched it briefly, but for long enough to acknowledge an intimacy that was better than love, better than trust, one he had been too earthbound to accept and Cheni had been too distraught to convey, a unity that was too individual to have a name. Then the contact was broken and he found himself looking up at the Newar girl. She had descended from her platform. Her eyes were swelling, pushing toward him, threatening to burst and loose a flood of blackness.

"No," he said, "no, I don't want this."

Then, before he had time to doubt what was happening, the blackness of Kumari's eyes poured over him, and he saw, mounted upon a field of darkness, like a rip in the fabric of night, a Tibetan man, a soldier weary of war who joined company with an anguished, distraught woman, an unlucky woman, and shortly thereafter, wounded by his enemies, lay dying at the feet of a little girl dressed in gilt cloth.

Clement felt a searing pain that did not seem associated with his wound. He ignored the pain and watched the Tibetan tumbling through the darkness toward a golden light, and knew that the man was melding with the blackness of Kumari, becoming part of an ancient process, and when the blackness penetrated the light, it would be wedded to the soul of a newborn girl child, and soon priests would come for her and bear her away to the temple where she would be pampered and paraded before the faithful on festival days, and do battle with the fuming emptinesses who menaced all and everything, aided by that soldierly essence with whom she had allied herself, until the time arrived when a new incarnation would be chosen and the worn scrap of the Tibetan man's soul would be granted release, and the girl stood in the market of Katmandu above a dying American and instructed him on the nature of his fate.

I need you, Clement.

He recalled what Cheni had told him about Kumari's ally. More craziness, he thought. More delusion. Why, after all, would he be the one chosen?

It's no reward.

Oh, yeah . . . right.

He wanted to pull back from the vision, but discovered that he could not, that he was falling toward a distant golden light. Frightened, he twisted and turned, but had no option other than to confront the pain that assaulted him from every side, huge ebony shadows veering close to tear at him, and it wasn't fair, he thought, it just wasn't fair for him to have to keep on fighting, even though he recognized that there was a certain justice involved. He fixed on the golden light, hoping that concentrating would help ease his pain. It didn't look much like an opening, he thought. It was solid and serene, like a fat autumn moon floating over the emptiness of a Wyoming night, and he remembered having seen it before from this same angle, hiding in a barn on the night he split from Eddie Lavigne, wondering what monster might come out of the dark to rend him with its teeth, wondering if there would ever be an end to solitude, to grief.

Clement!

Another cold voice, or was it the same one?

Coincidence or magic?

And then his grief was subsumed into the light, and it felt strange to be free of grief, as if half his weight had been taken away, and he drifted toward the golden moon, drowsing, afraid that something would snatch him if he slept, but too sleepy to sustain fear.

Clement! Goddamn you!

His thoughts eddied, and he gazed at the wooden tiger that somebody had given him, liking the way it stood there, facing the battles ahead with a fierce frozen glare. Seeing it gave him courage.

C'mon, Clement! Talk to me!

Courage made anything bearable. Sorrow, pain, even being shaken . . . shaken hard. And he thought someday he would look back on this night, this one night that seemed emblematic of the entire character of his life, with the clean smell of hay and the sound of semis hitting the spacers on the highway down through the mountains, and loneliness fitting around him like a heavy coat, muffling emotion . . . yeah, someday he might think back on this night and realize that it had been a pretty good time.

Clement!

More shaking.

The pain had started again. His eyes blinked open, and he saw a man in a suit kneeling beside him, another man standing above him, holding a machine pistol.

Demons.

No doubt about it.

Their suits and pale skins were containers of emptiness and cold.

Behind them, the celebrants had cleared a space about the three men, formed a loose rank, and were looking on with sober expressions. Some were whispering one to another. Clement could no longer see Kumari. Her keepers must have hustled her away, but he could feel her off somewhere in the midst of the crowd.

Her Serene Darkness, waiting for him.

He focused on the man with the gun. Deep within the black tunnel of the barrel a golden full moon was shining.

"Oh," he said, and gave a feeble laugh.

The man with the gun laughed, too, and said, "Hey, dying must be fun, huh, Clement?"

"I don't think he's dying, I think we might be able to patch him up," said the man kneeling. He had a receding hairline and curly brown hair and the lined, rugged face of a sympathetic counselor, like a football coach or a juvenile probation officer; his tone, however, was anything but sympathetic. "Hear that, asshole? You might just live to do a little suffering."

"You're not such bad guys," Clement said. "You're just in a lousy play."

The two men exchanged glances, then the kneeling man asked Clement a question. Clement paid it no attention.

The pain was getting very bad. He stared at the shining moon within the gun barrel.

If you have nowhere to run, you have to make a stand.

Shut your ass, bitch!

Clement tried to collect himself, to gather his thoughts into a coherent pattern and make a judgment. This was all wrong, this shit about goddesses and soldiers, this crazy bullshit about demons. He was going to live. Okay. What then? Figure a way to buy some time. Tell them a tall tale, a Tru-Life Adventure.

There I was, guys, surrounded by an old man and my wife, with only my body for a weapon.

What for? Why make the effort?

The faces of the crowd glistened, flat and unreal, facades pressured by the blackness behind them. Screams of joy and deliverance, wild men drunk on holiness.

Swirling music and moonlit clouds on fire.

Aw, what the hell!

He wanted to remember something, something sustaining, enabling, something that would shore him up, but he realized that there had never been anything of the sort in his life. His world had consisted of the apparent, the illusory, of moments whose vividness and poignancy had been the product of a misapprehension or a sleight of hand. He could conjure sweet words, the softness of a woman's breast, the feeling of accomplishment, of conquest, but they were all funded by lies or a lying sensibility. He could see in his mind's eye Lily's lips curving up as he touched her, that sly, sexy way she'd had, he could see into the heart of a thousand such moments, and they were all wormwood, all betrayal and dust. What did it matter if his ending was colored by another lie, by a clever delusion, a delusion so clever that it didn't matter if it was real, because it offered nothing but pain?

You've always been a sucker for punishment, right, slugger?

Bet your ass!

Pretty goddamn remarkable, he said to himself, I mean this is very tricky how you've managed to work the whole deal in Tasang-partsi and everything since into a nifty little metaphysical gig, a nice job opportunity out on Fifth Dimension Avenue.

Well, ready or not, here I come.

The man kneeling beside Clement asked another question, but Clement only smiled. He squeezed the wooden tiger tightly in his fist, imagining that his soul was shrinking to fit within that lethal compact shape.

I love you, he said under his breath, talking to Lily, to D'allessandro, to Cheni, to anyone who might receive with understanding the minute spark of love that he had nourished, the spark that had weakened and killed him.

What's next? There must be something next, some final formality. Any last words, pal?

Forgot about that.

Clement searched out the eyes of the kneeling man. Watery blue eyes, little humid puddles empty of feeling.

"I give," he said to him.

He focused on the tiny golden moon within the barrel of the machine pistol. Then, summoning all his strength, he kicked the man, sending him onto his back, and made a quick, crafty move toward the Magnum tucked inside his overcoat. For an instant he was dismayed, thinking that he might have moved so quickly, he had caught the other man by surprise.

Then he fell through darkness into the light.

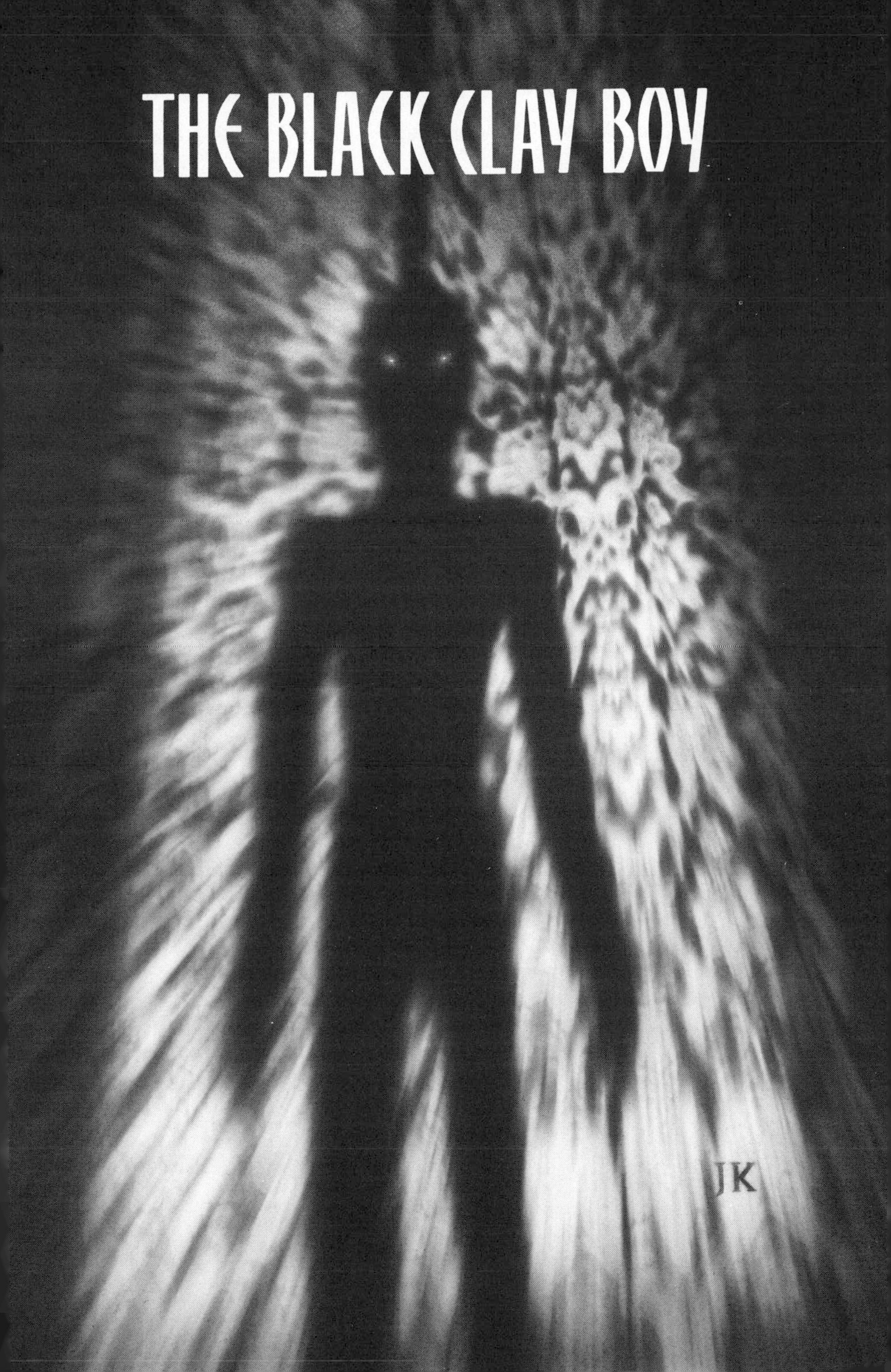
THE BLACK CLAY BOY
JK

They'd robbed her of her life, sucked out the middle of her joy like marrow-eating ghouls. Memories she had, but they'd drained them of juice and left the husks stuck in her head like dead flies in a web. Left her bitter and dotty, an old cracked hag fit for taunting by the neighborhood children.

Take those Kandell boys.

Always traipsing across her lawn and peeing their initials in the snow-crust, shaking their tiny pale things at her as if the sight would do an injury. There they were now, sneaking up to the house, clumping onto the porch. A piece of notebook paper scrawled with a kid's crooked letters was slipped under the door. Hanging on to the knob for balance, teetering, Willa picked it up and read: "Old lady Selkie is a fuking bitch!"

She snatched open the door and saw them humping toward the fence, two blue-coated wool-hatted dwarfs sinking to their knees in the snow. "You got that right," she squalled. "Fucking with a *C!*" Yelling took the wind out of her, and she stood trembling, her breath steaming in ragged white puffs, her eyes tearing.

The Kandells stopped at the fence-line, and one gave her the finger.

"I see you back there," she shrilled. "I'll go down in my cellar and make me a Black Clay Boy. Jab pins in its eyes, and prick you blind!"

Now where the hell had she gotten that idea? A Black Clay Boy? Some senile trick of broken thoughts happening right for once. Well, maybe she *could* hex 'em. Maybe she'd shriveled up that pure and mean.

She shut the door, leaned against it, her heart faltering. The next second, a snowball splintered one of the side windows, spraying sparkles of glass and ice over her new sofa. She was too weak to shout again.

Smelly little shits!

A Black Clay Boy might be just the ticket, she thought. Might scare 'em. They'd run to their mommy, their father would come over to have a serious talk. She'd pretend to be a tired and desperate old woman, scared to death of his vicious brood.

No need to pretend, Willa.

Muttering under her breath, she hobbled down to the cellar, and with popping joints and many a gasp, she troweled a bucketful of the rich black bottomland that did for a floor. Then she lugged the bucket upstairs to the kitchen and set it on the table. The kitchen whined, buzzed, and hummed with the workings of small appliances and the electric motor inside the cold box . . . or could be the hum was the sound of her mind winding tight, getting ready to spew out shattered gears and sprung coils.

The wall clock ticked loud and hollow like someone clicking her tongue over and over.

Willa made the Boy's torso first, patting a lump of clay into a fat black lozenge. She added tubular arms and legs, rolling them into shape between her palms the way she did with dough before flattening it into a crust. Finally she added a featureless oval head. The whole thing was about two and a half feet long, and it reminded her of those shapes left by frightened men crashing through doors in the Saturday morning cartoons. Black crumbs of it were scattered like dead bugs on the white Formica. She reached into her apron pocket for a pincushion and. . . . Steam vented from the teakettle with a shriek, stopping Willa's heart for a dizzy split second.

Oh, God! Now she'd have to get up again.

It took her three tries to heave out of the chair. Sweat broke on her forehead, and she stood panting for almost a minute. Once she'd regained her breath, she crossed to the stove and shut off the flame. She kept a hand on the stove, stretched out the other hand to catch the edge of the table for balance, and hauled herself back across. She dropped heavily into the chair and nearly slipped off the edge.

One day soon she'd do that and fracture her damn spine.

She plucked a pin from the pincushion, and, hoping to hear a distant scream, she shoved it into the Boy's face. Pressed it home until the pinhead was flush with the clay, a tiny silver eye. It shimmered and seemed to expand. She blinked, denying the sight. It expanded again. Somehow it didn't resemble an eye any longer. More of a silver droplet, a silver bead. Her memories would be that way, she thought. Hardened into pearls. The bead melted at the edges, puddling outward like mercury (*Don't tell me I need glasses!*), and a memory began to unfold.

It was rich, clear, and full of juice.

"Oh, God!" she said. "It's a miracle."

The recollection rolled out from fifty years ago, during her marriage to Eden McClaren, the wealthiest citizen of Lyman, Ohio. She hadn't wanted to marry him. He was old, fiftyish, and even older in spirit, a dried-up coupon-counter. But her father had persuaded her. *Man's so rich he builds his house on the finest piece of bottomland in the state,* he'd said. *You won't do any better than a man who can afford to waste land like that. Marry him, marry him, marry him.* And her mother, who'd had her doubts, what with Eden being an atheist, had eventually chimed in, *Marry him, marry him, marry him.*

What was an eighteen-year-old girl to do?

Eden courted her in a manner both civil and distant. He'd sit on the opposite end of the porch swing, as far from her as possible, gazing out at the hedge, and say, "I'm quite taken with you, girl."

She would stare at her clasped hands, watching her fingers strain and twist, wishing he'd blow away in a puff of smoke. "Thank you," she'd say.

After their wedding supper of overdone beef and potatoes and stale bread pudding, he sat her down and informed her that she would have to perform her wifely duty once a week. More would fray the moral fiber, and less would be unsalubrious. Then he took her upstairs and deflowered her in a perfunctory fashion, propping himself above her, thrusting in and out, maintaining a rhythm of one, two, one, two, regular as a metronome, until he sighed and gave a quiver and rolled off, leaving her with a fair degree of pain and no pleasure, wondering why people made such a fuss over sex.

But she knew why.

Knew it in her heart, her loins.

She wanted a lover like lightning who'd split her wide open and leave her smoldering. And if Eden couldn't give her that pleasure, she'd pleasure herself. She'd done it a few times before, despite her mother's depiction of the horrid consequences. She didn't care about the consequences. But she had been frightened by having so much pleasure without someone to hold on to afterward, and so she decided to do it in front of the full-length mirror in her bedroom. That way at least she'd have her reflection for company.

She stripped and posed before the mirror. She was a beauty, though she'd never understand how beautiful. Red hair, green eyes, milky skin. Pretty breasts tipped with pink candy, and long legs columning up to that curly red patch a shade lighter than the hair on her head. She cupped the undersides of her breasts, thumbed the nipples hard, and ran her palms down her hips, her flanks. Then she touched the place, already slippery and open to its hooded secret. Her knees buckled, weakness spread through her, and she hung on to the corner post of the mirror stand to keep her feet. Her eyelids fluttered down, her breath came harsh. She forced herself to hold her eyes wide, wanting to see what happened to her face when the pleasure started to take. Her cries fogged the mirror, and her mouth twisted, and her eyes tried to close, tried to squeeze in all that good feeling, and. . . .

"Slut!" Eden shouted from the door. "Bitch!"

Despite his rage, he seemed to have enjoyed the show. His face was flushed, his crotch tented.

"I'll not have it!" he said. "I'll not have you trailing your slime . . . your filth. Fouling my house!"

For the next three days he railed at her, and on the afternoon of the third day he suffered a coronary and was confined to bed by Dr. Malloy, who tsk-tsked, and warned her to prepare for the worst.

"Curse you!" Eden said when she went into his room. As weak as he was, he warped his mouth into a frown and spat out, "Curse you!"

She wondered then what sort of curse a godless man could lay, but later she concluded it must have been one of rules and joyless limits.

They buried Eden in a corner of the bottomland. In a dream she saw his bones floating in blackness like the strange money of a savage isle. And from that dream she knew him more than she ever had. She followed the track of his blue-faced primitive ancestors with their bone knives and their terrified little gods hiding in the treetops, and she trod the rain-slick stones of Glasgow town, where black-suited Calvinists screwed their souls into twists, and she crossed the great water with a prissy man of God and his widow-to-be, watched their children breed the bloodline thin and down to this miserable cramped sputter of a soul, this mysteryless little man, sad birthright of the clan.

Scratch one McClaren, sound the horn.

Willa wanted to sell the bottomland and move to the city. She wanted to live free, to kick up her heels, to have life take her in its arms and then to a nice restaurant and maybe afterward to a hotel. What harm could come of that? Twenty-two, and she'd never had any fun.

Sell the bottomland? her family said. *That'd be like selling Plymouth Rock! Bottomland's something you hang on to, something you cherish. We won't let you do it.*

And they didn't.

She did Eden widow's service for a year, and for a year after that she hardly set foot off the land. One day her high-school friend Ellie Shane came to visit and said, "Willa, there's gonna be a party Friday at the old Hoskins place." She glanced left and right as if to defeat the wiles of eavesdroppers. "Gonna be college men and coupla businessmen from Chicago . . . and every one's a looker. You gotta come."

Willa couldn't say no.

This was in October, the air crisp, the leaves full turned. Bright lights sprayed from the windows of the old house, outshining the moon, and inside couples danced and groped and sought out empty rooms. Willa's man was lean and dark. He had a sharp chin and the Devil's toothy white grin, and he carried a silver pint flask that he kept forcing on her. She saw his thoughts working. . . . He'd get this townie ripped, slip it to her quick, and leave her spinning. But Willa passed on the liquor. He'd read law at Michigan, he said, but had left school to run his father's *nationwide* trucking firm. He tried all night to impress her with his money, never knowing he didn't have to try, that it wasn't his money she wanted. He guided her out onto the porch. A blond man was sitting with a girl on a bottomed-out sofa there, his hand hunching up under her skirt, a rat-sized creature looking for its burrow. Willa stood by the porch rail, gazing at the moon-dappled woods. Her man hemmed her in against the rail, moved in for a kiss. Willa slipped away and went halfway down the steps.

"My kisses are for my husband," she said. "But all the rest is yours." And with that she skipped down from the steps and ran into the woods.

She found an old oak with gnarly bark and a lightning scar, and leaned against it. Moonlight streamed through the webbed branches, illuminating the red-and-yellow leaves. . . . Wind seethed through them, and they looked to be shaking in separate dances, red-and-yellow spearpoints of flame. She undid the top two buttons of her blouse and touched the slope of her right breast. God! The chill of that touch went through her like something sharp and silver. She undid a third button. The wind coiled inside the blouse, fondling her. She lifted her skirt, skinned down her panties, and flung them behind the oak. She could feel herself moist and open. The man's footsteps crunched in the dead leaves. He peered into the shadows, his mouth set grim. Probably angry at her, thinking her a tease. He spotted her and came forward at a slow pace. Dark head, gleaming eyes. When he saw that she had unbuttoned the blouse, he walked faster. Stopped and tipped back the flask. His Adam's apple bobbed twice. He tossed the flask away and reached inside her blouse. His hands moved over her breasts, squeezing, molding, knowing their white rounds from every angle. "Christ," he said. "Oh, Christ." She closed her eyes and arched to his pressure. Moonlight penetrated her lids. After a few seconds she pushed him off and hiked up her skirt.

The man swallowed hard at the sight, made a soft noise deep in his throat. He tore at his buckle, ripped down his zipper, sprung out at her, a needle seeking its pole. He lifted her the necessary inch, settled into place, and plunged into her. She threw her arms back around the oak trunk, dug in with her fingers. Rough bark scraped her buttocks, but even the pain was good. He battered at her. The leaves hissed, the limbs shook, and a vibration went through the oak, as if what was going on between Willa and the man were threatening to uproot it. "Go slow," she said, the words pushed out hoarse by a thrust. "Slow, slow." That made him treat her too gently, and she told him how she needed it to build, guiding his moves. "There," she said. "There . . . like that." And even before her pleasure came, she cried out just for the joy of finally having a man hot and urgent inside her.

Afterward she went back to the party and paid no attention to him. He couldn't understand her, and his lack of understanding anointed her a mystery. He trailed her around, saying he had to see her again, he'd fly her to Chicago. Willa could have owned him, married him, and secured her future. But she had lights dancing in the miles of her eyes, and she wasn't worried about the future.

More's the pity, Willa.

Ah, God, Willa thought. Why hadn't they let her live? That part of her, that need, it was nothing sinful. How could they have wanted to be with her and not accept her all in all? She shook her head, ruing the wasted years, then glanced at the Black Clay Boy.

Was it her imagination, or was he quivering a little, as if he'd been trying to roll himself off the table?

Calm yourself, Willa . . . that's just the trembling of your head on its feeble stalk of a neck.

The Boy's silver-dot eye stared up at her. Hmm, Willa said to herself. Wonder what'd happen if I give him another. She plucked out a second pin and rammed it home.

The pinhead shimmered, began to expand into a memory.

"Lord Almighty," said Willa. "I can do magic."

After that night at the Hoskins place, Willa cut a wild track through the tame fields of Ohio possibility. Roadhouses knew her, hotels took messages for her, and midnight dirt roads where nobody drove echoed to her backseat music. Rumors smoked up from her footprints, and the word went around that while she wouldn't kiss you, you just hadn't lived till Willa McClaren doctored your Charlie. The people of Lyman scandalized her name. That Willa, they said, she wasn't never nothin' more than hips and a hole, and I hear it was her evil needs what put ol' Eden in the ground. Willa didn't care what they said. She was having her life in sweet spasms, and for now that was enough. When the time was right, she'd settle down.

Tom Selkie, a supervisor at the seat-belt factory over in Danton, knew Willa's reputation and asked her out to get himself a sample of that real fine Charlie-doctoring. That was all Willa'd had in mind, but in the back of Tom's Packard they experienced one of those intoxicating mistakes that people often confuse for love, and Willa let him kiss her. His tongue darted into her mouth, and though she liked how that felt, it startled her more than some.

"What's the matter?" Tom asked, and Willa blushed and said, "Me and Eden never did it with tongues."

Well, knowing this innocence in her made Tom feel twice a man, and he asked her straight off to marry. "Yes," said Willa, confident that fate had finally done her a turn by giving her both a good man and the Power of True Romance. But True Romance lasted a matter of weeks. Tom kissed better than he tickled, so to speak, and was more interested in drinking with the boys after work than in getting prone and lowdown with Willa. When she tried to awaken his interest, he rejected her; his rejections grew more and more blunt, until at last he suggested that something must be wrong with her, that her needs were unnatural. Bored with marriage and having little else to engage her, she got pregnant with her firstborn, Annie. The year after Annie, she bore a son. Tom, Too, his proud dad called him. The kids grew, Tom's belly sagged, and life just dragged along.

It was at the age of thirty-six that Willa next had Big Fun. She left the kids with Tom and caught the train to Cleveland to talk with a broker about some stock Eden had hidden under the fireplace bricks. On the train she struck up a conversation with Alvah Medly, a pricey hooker with silkburns on her hips and fingers prone to breaking under the weight of her many diamonds. She was a big sleepy cat of a woman, her languid gestures leading Willa to believe she had syrup instead of marrow in her bones. Voluptuous to the point that it seemed an ounce more weight would cause everything to slump and decay. She had long black hair and big chest problems and a rear end just made for easy motion. But she was no finer a looker than Willa, who had held on to beauty and could still pass for her twenty-two-year-old self.

Willa was curious about Alvah's fancyhouse life and asked dozens of questions, and Alvah, perhaps sensing something more than mere curiosity, said, "Honey, if you wanna know all about it, whyn't you give it a whirl?"

Willa was flabbergasted. "Uh," she said, "well . . ." And then, finding refuge in the dull majority of her life, added, "I'm married."

"Married!" Alvah said the word like it was something you'd scrape off your shoe. "Everybody's been married." She inhaled from a slim black cigar and blew a smoke ring that floated up to the corner of the compartment and spelled out a lie. "The life ain't nothin' but one long lazy lack of limitations."

The train rattled as it went over a crossing, and everything inside Willa's head rattled. Could what Alvah was saying be true? The whole vital world was barreling east, shaking side to side, and blasting out its warning to the sexless villages of the heartland.

"You come on over to Mrs. Gacey's tonight," said Alvah, "and I bet she'll give you a try."

"I don't know," said Willa distractedly.

" 'Course you don't, honey," said Alvah. "How you gonna know 'less you explore the potentials?" She chuckled, "And believe you me, there's some mighty big potentials come through the door of Mrs. Gacey's."

Willa couldn't think of anything to say. Her mind was miles ahead in Cleveland, in a room with a dark and faceless stranger.

"You come on over," said Alvah. "Mrs. Gacey'll fix you up with a room and a trick or two."

"Well," said Willa hesitantly. "Maybe . . . maybe just one."

That night she lay amid perfume and shadow on a harem bed draped in filmy curtains, wearing a scrap of silk and a few of Alvah's spare jewels. The door opened, and a gray-haired monument of a man walked in. His face had a craggy nobility that looked as if it should be printed on money. Willa was tense, but when she saw how the man stared. . . . Oh, she could almost see how she appeared to him. A red-haired, green-eyed bewitchment with her silk pushed up to reveal a hint of that down-pointed curly patch of fire between her thighs. The man parted the curtain and sat on the edge of the bed, drinking her in.

"Good evenin'," he said.

"Evenin'," said Willa, a little confused. She hadn't thought she'd have to talk.

"Now where in the world did Mrs. Gacey find a girl like you?" asked the man.

"Lyman," said Willa.

"Lyman." The man loosened his tie and seemed to be trying to locate the place in some interior atlas.

"It's near Danton . . . that's the Winton County seat."

"Ah, yes. I carried Winton three to one."

"Whatcha mean you carried it?"

The man looked at her askance. "You don't recognize me?"

"No," said Willa. "You famous or somethin'?"

"I'm the governor," said the man, unbuttoning his shirt.

"You *are?* I voted for you!"

The man unbuckled his belt and smiled a warm professional smile. "I trust your enthusiasm for my candidacy has remained undimmed."

Willa enjoyed her evening with the governor. It gave her a chance to try some things that Eden and Tom had considered either unnatural or unmanning. But there was a distance to this kind of passion that didn't appeal to her, and when Alvah came in to find out how things had gone, she told her she didn't think she had the stuff it took for the life.

"Oh, you got what it takes, honey," said Alvah, sitting beside her. "You just don't know it."

Her robe had fallen partway open, and the globes of her breasts were visible, marble-white and moon-smooth. Looking at them, Willa suddenly perceived in Alvah a kind of sad blankness, as if a greater sadness had been erased or paved over, and she felt a wave of affection for this sculpture of a woman. And maybe her affection washed across the space between them, because Alvah put a hand on Willa's stomach and caressed its curve, resting it on her upper thigh. One of her fingertips brushed the margin of Willa's curly hair.

"You're so beautiful," said Alvah, her voice a tongue of shadow in that perfumed place.

There was a squirmy feeling in Willa's stomach, and she was a bit scared . . . but not scared enough to ask Alvah to take her hand away. "You're prettier than me," she said meekly, entranced by the desire in Alvah's face and by an anticipation of forbidden fruit.

Alvah eased her hand an inch south and down between. "No, honey," she said. "It's you, it's you."

Willa tried not to respond, but she could feel her pulse tapping out the message, "Yes, I will," against Alvah's fingertip.

"Please," whispered Alvah, and that word was a little wind that went everywhere through Willa, that told her a thousand things no one had ever troubled to tell her, that elevated her to something perfect and needed, that showed Alvah's need to be as strong and unalloyed as her own. *Please, please.* The word lowered over her like a veil, like the veil of Alvah's black hair fanning across her stomach, curtaining her off from the moral precincts of Lyman and her marriage. Willa wouldn't have believed a woman could make her burn, and true, it felt strange to be loved and not have a body covering her upper half, but Alvah's kisses and touches gave a tenderness to pleasure that she had never known from a man's rough bark. And though Willa had dreaded the idea of doing to Alvah what Alvah had done for her, though she set to it out of duty not desire, she came to desire. It seemed she had entered some Arab kingdom of musk and honey, some secret temple where a new god basked in its own heat, and when Alvah's white stomach quaked and her thighs clamped tight, Willa knew for the first time what it was to have the power and pleasure of a man.

For six years thereafter Willa guest-starred at Mrs. Gacey's and passed the idle hours in Alvah's arms. Eden's stocks had proved worthless, but Willa's one-trick stands gave her the profit required to justify her Cleveland weekends to Tom, and she let him think that the stocks were the source of this extra money. Her relationship to Alvah was the closest thing to love she had ever known, soft and slow and undemanding, and she would have told far greater lies to maintain it. But all good things must come to an end, or such was the regulation of Eden's curse. When Tom got fired from the seat-belt factory

(*Woman, don't you even think 'bout sellin' that bottomland!*), Willa was forced to take a job, and her weekends were no longer her own.

The memory evaporated, and Willa pinched up a nose from the Black Clay Boy's face. His chest rose and fell rapidly, and breath whined through his tiny nostrils. But no new memory breathed from him. She gouged out a mouth and listened hard. Heard a noise that brought to mind those lumps of sadness often disgorged from her own chest. But maybe that was his first word, because the noise opened just like the widening of a silver eye into a world as fresh as yesterday.

"What's happening?" Willa asked, becoming terrified now of magic and miracles.

The kitchen ticked and buzzed, and the Black Clay Boy lay silent. But Willa thought this absence was an answer all the same.

Willa waited tables at O. V. Lindley's Dirtline Café, its name deriving from the line of dirt that showed on the wrists of the farm boys who ate there when they took off their work gloves. They would come in drunk and sit swaying at the counter, pawing and teasing Willa, plugging the leaks in their souls with quarters'-worths of country and western philosophy from the glowing sage of the jukebox. She searched among them for a lover, but found no one of the proper measure. Sometimes she would go into the john on her break, skin down her panties, sit on the toilet, and remember Alvah, her hand moving between her legs. Sweat would pour off her, and she would bite back her cry. But even so, they caught her on occasion and would offer to help scratch her itch.

"What I got right here," she'd say, holding up her hand, "can do the job a damn sight better than any one of you."

And because she was still beautiful, they worried that she might be right.

Three years of this.

Time seemed to speed up, to turn a corner on an entire era and accelerate into an unfamiliar country, a place without hope or virtue. Before Willa knew it, she was wrapped in a web of trouble so intricate and thick that her own needs were suffocated. First, Annie—herself a redhead and possessing a streak of Willa's wildness—got pregnant by an unknown agency, her teenage stomach stretched by a baby boy who weighed fourteen pounds on delivery, and whom she was dissuaded from naming Nomad. Bruce, her second choice, was deemed acceptable. Willa went through Annie's high-school yearbook, looking for Bruces. Found two. One deceased, one long departed. After giving birth, Annie took to her room and would pass the days listening to vapid love songs on the radio and gazing out the window, leaving Willa to care for the infant. She spooned jar after jar of purée into its mouth, watching it pale and fatten under the harsh kitchen lights, wondering if this monster child might not be the ultimate credential of the efficacy of Eden's curse. She had begun to believe in the curse, that Eden had breathed some vileness out with the words that enveloped her like an aura and restricted her life—all her pleasures seemed to run a minimal course and span that accorded with Eden's notions of moderation.

Tom developed cancer (*Don't sell the bottomland*), and Tom, Too took something that caused him to vomit blood and avoid mirrors for almost a month. Not long thereafter he ran away from home. Willa found a note on his pillow confessing that he was Bruce's father. From his bed of pain, Tom shouted that all this was the fault of Willa's abnormal sexual urges, and while she did not accept his reasoning, she knew it was her fault in that she had not entered motherhood with love but out of boredom. Four years after his departure, Tom, Too returned, a convert to that mean, squinty-eyed form of Christianity that everywhere spies out its enemies. He begged forgiveness and received his father's blessing. The two of them would go bowling on Wednesday nights and walk home along the river, discussing philosophy (his brush with cancer had provided Tom with the insight that We Are Everyone of Us All Alone) and real estate (Tom, Too's chosen profession). Annie had moved with Bruce into a newly built garage apartment, and Tom, Too would visit them frequently, proclaiming that the boy needed a dad. One night Willa saw him coming down Annie's stairs long after the lights had been switched off. Two weeks later, following a whirlwind courtship, Annie married a fishing-tackle salesman and moved to Akron, vowing never to set foot in Lyman again.

Willa turned fifty-one.

Amazingly she looked to be in her early thirties, an age not without a hint of maturity yet nonetheless appealing. However, there was no one in sight who might respond to her appeal, and hoping to subsume her desires in spiritual pursuits, she began attending church with Tom and Tom, Too. And, lo, her faith was rewarded. The new pastor, the Reverend Robert Meister, was a ruggedly handsome man of thirty-five, with piercing blue eyes and a virile physique. A heavenly hunk. But his most attractive feature was his bachelorhood. Willa noticed the tension that flooded his face when he talked to the young girls after services, when they stuck out their gloved hands for him to shake. The poor man, she thought, imagining his solitary bouts of guilt-ridden self-abuse in a dark rectory bedroom. He didn't look at her the way he looked at the younger girls, but she determined that one day soon he would.

With a fervor that even drew grudging praise from Tom, Too, who had become the family's spiritual drill sergeant, Willa threw herself into church work. Nothing was too inconsequential for her attentions. She served on the Ladies' Auxiliary, she taught Sunday School, she organized fund-raisers and baked truckloads of cakes and cookies, all the while carrying on a flirtation with the Reverend, contriving to brush against him, touching his hand in conversation, gradually making him aware of her fundamental charms. And when the Reverend timorously suggested that she accompany him to a church conference on famine in New York, Willa knew that paydirt was near.

But two days passed at the conference, and the Reverend had yet to make his play. At last Willa contrived a trap. She ordered from room service, went to take a shower, and called out to the Reverend—who had at least been sufficiently bold to reserve adjoining rooms—asking him to answer her door when her order arrived. Then when she heard the waiter close the door behind him, heard the Reverend wrestling with the food cart, she walked buff naked into the room, affecting surprise that he was still there. The Reverend's jaw went slack, his eyes bugged, and turning back to the bathroom, Willa gave him a full view of her pert breasts, her long legs, and thighs undimpled by cellulite.

That evening over dinner, though nothing was said, Willa was, as ever, familiar with the Reverend, touching him often, letting him know that she was not displeased by the afternoon's event. But again he made no move to deepen their relationship. Desperate now, that night Willa disrobed and waited beside the connecting door until the Reverend's light was dimmed. She pressed her ear to the crack, and when she heard the beginning of heavy breathing, of creaking bedsprings, she threw open the door and walked in. The Reverend tried to conceal his actions, pretending to be wrestling with the bedclothes. But Willa was not to be denied. She flung back the covers, exposing the limp yet still tumescent evidence, and then with all the wiles she had learned while in Mrs. Gacey's employ, she proceeded to restore it to its former fisted grandeur.

The Reverend Meister proved Willa's equal in need, and together they explored the realm of Position, tying complex knots of heat and sinew that often took hours to unravel. Once Position had been exhausted, they began a study of Location. There was scarcely a place in Lyman that did not know their clandestine passion, and each grunting thrust, each stifled cry, was a godsend to Willa after those long and joyless years. She came half to believe that the Christian God had truly blessed her. "Hallelujah," she whispered as they lay in sweet congregation beneath the church's midnight altar. "Thank you, Jesus," she sighed as she stood pressed into a corner of the closet below the choir stalls, her skirts lifted high and the Reverend kneeling down to take communion. "Praise the Lord," she breathed, bending over a projector in the darkened Sunday School basement, while the Reverend mounted her from behind, and a dozen children sat in front, munching cookies and ice cream, their eyes fixed on a slide show of the Holy Land *sans* narration.

Willa lived in a green world again, in a world where hope and possibility conjoined. Her relationship with the Reverend was that rarest of commodities—they were friends who could make love and not allow their carnality to lead away from friendship. And in their lovemaking . . . well, let it suffice to say that the depth of Willa's devotion and the extent of the Reverend's commitment to excellence were compatible in every extreme.

But, lo, this too shall pass.

One night at the suggestion of Tom, Too, they had the Reverend over for dinner, and after the dessert dishes had been cleared away, Tom, Too displayed a packet of photographs he had taken, their subject being Willa and the Reverend. "Now this here," he said, handing one around, "it'll blow up real nice for the church newsletter. And this here"—he handed over another displaying a complex tangle of flesh, half of which comprised an illegality in the state of Ohio—"I was figurin' to do up some eight-by-ten glossies."

The Reverend lowered his eyes, and Willa shut hers.

"This has really got to stop," said Tom, Too. "Right, Dad?"

Tom was trembling, apoplectic, squeezing the arms of his chair.

Tom, Too held up yet another photograph that showed the lovers beneath the altar, the moonlit shadow of the cross thrown across them. "This one's got dandy symbolic value. Oughta raise a few eyebrows in the bishop's office." He searched among the remaining photographs. "Hey, Dad," he said breezily, picking one and sliding it over. "Check that out. . . . Never woulda thought Mom was so limber."

Despite his choler, Tom looked broken, frail, on the verge of passing out, and two weeks later, he suffered a stroke that left him paralyzed and requiring constant nursing.

"Wouldn't sell the bottomland if I were you," Tom, Too advised

Willa, reminding her of the leverage of his photographs. "I been considerin' puttin' up a shoppin' mall . . . after it's mine legal, of course. I 'spect the state'll take care of Dad if you can't."

That tore it for Willa. She crumbled all at once. It was as if her beauty had been its own self, had been hanging on for hope of some lasting appreciation, and now had just given up. By the time she reached the age of sixty, she looked it. At seventy, she looked a spry seventy-five, and at seventy-eight, morticians would perk up when she passed, clasp their hands and say, "How you feelin' today, Mrs. Selkie," in a tone that made clear they really wanted to know.

Tom died nine years after the disclosure of the photographs, having never spoken another word, and after the funeral, the Reverend Meister dropped over to see Willa. He had married a mousy little woman, and had written a book that everyone said was going to make him famous. Willa had never expected him to stay alone and didn't resent his marriage. In truth, she rarely thought about him anymore, being already a little distracted, halfway to dotty. But she was pleased about his book, and even more pleased when he told her that she was partly responsible for his writing it.

"Me?" she said. "What'd I do?"

"It was your intensity," he said. "When you made love, it was pure, an expression of something that had to come out. It was all of life you were taking in your arms. And if you'd been allowed to express it fully, it would have taken other forms as well. You made me want to find a way to express my own truth, to equal that intensity."

She often thought she might have done something with her life, but was glad to hear it from somebody else. "That's the second nicest thing anybody ever said to me," she told him.

"What was the nicest?"

" 'Please,' " she said, remembering.

He didn't press for clarification, and for a while they talked about trivial matters.

"How's it being married?" she asked.

"I don't love her," he said. "I just . . ."

"I know," she said. "What's it like?"

He thought a second or two. "It's like being sick . . . nothing serious. Like being in mild constant pain, and having a nurse and air conditioning."

For some reason that started her crying. Maybe it was because having him near made her notice her old-lady smell. Because he still looked young and she looked like death warmed over. He put an arm around her, but she shrugged it off. "Leave me be," she said.

"Willa . . ."

"You can't help me," she said. "I'm crazy."

"You're not crazy."

"Not now," she said. "But the minute you go, I'm gonna be wanderin' around the house, talking to myself, thinking all kinds of crazy thoughts. Now you get outta here and leave me to it."

He got to his feet, pulled on his coat, looking helpless and grim. "God bless you, Willa," he said.

"Ain't no such thing as God," she told him. "And don't argue with me 'bout it, 'cause I can feel the place where he ain't."

"Maybe you can at that," he said glumly.

When he closed the door, she had the idea that he stood outside for a long time . . . or could be he'd just left a thought leaning against the door, a wish for her, like an umbrella he had forgotten.

Night had fallen. Out the window, bare trees cast blue shadows on the rippled snow, and the air was so crystal clear it seemed you might be able to reach out and break off a chunk with a star inside it and put it in the fridge to save for Christmas. Oh, God . . . but it was a lonely clarity. And oh, God, there was life in the old girl yet, and wouldn't she love to move her hips again, and wouldn't it be more than love to know that sweet feeling of being filled, of being needed, instead of sitting here with liver spots a plague on her hands, with her son a Christian villain, and her daughter estranged, and her grandchild a hulking teenage monster who visited once a year and stole money from her purse. With no future and all her memories played, all her lovers dead . . .

Not all, whispered the Black Clay Boy.

Yes, all! Even the Reverend Meister gone, a victim of that new disease taking the gay boys. Who'd have thought it? If she'd have stayed with him, she'd bet he wouldn't have strayed that far from heaven.

The Black Clay Boy seemed to smile at that.

"Quit makin' fun of me!" she said. "You're worse than them Kandell brats."

Much worse, Willa.

Lewd little bastard! I hear that sly tone, I know what you want!

And what's wrong with that? It's what you want, too.

She made a disparaging noise. "A runt like you couldn't give me a tickle."

You might be surprised, Willa.

Willa studied him. With his silver eyes and gouged mouth, he looked like a surreal Little Black Sambo. And, she realized, he favored Eden some. Eden had had that same unfinished look. She could, she supposed, give him hands and feet. But then he'd be traipsing his footprints all over her nice carpet, strewing black crumbs everywhere.

Crazy old bat, she thought.

But he *did* look unfinished.

And of course she knew just what he needed.

What we both need, Willa.

"Do you really think. . . ."

I'm absolutely sure.

"I don't know, I. . . ."

How you gonna know 'less you explore the potentials?

"Well," she said hesitantly. "Maybe just once."

More would be unsalubrious, said the Black Clay Boy.

She came to her feet effortlessly, as if the idea was a power, and she went rummaging through the kitchen drawer until she found the perfect accessory, long and sharp and silver. She wedged the handle into the crotch of the Black Clay Boy, jammed it in, and tried to wiggle it. . . . It held firm. She'd always hated the bottomland for the hold it exerted, but now she was grateful for this quality.

God! She felt twenty-two again, all heart and hip, all nudge softness and clever muscle.

She picked up the Black Clay Boy, held him at arm's length, and went whirling into the living room, each whirl bringing her hot thoughts closer to a boil. Oh, she was mad, mad as the pattern on the wallpaper, mad as the wind shaping her name from the eaves, saying *Willa, Willa, Willa,* with each and every spin, mad and whirling among the dark armoires and the huge iron-colored sideboard and the Victorian mahoganies. The shadows watched her, and the furniture was leaning together, gossiping, and in the folds of the drapes were cores of indigo that she recognized to be the cores of ghosts waiting to live their wispy lives once she had done.

"Won't be a minute," she told them gaily, and went whirling into the bedroom where the Black Clay Boy would have her once and silent, where love would once more be red and biting. She lifted him high. His silvery member was God's measure of a man, flashing with moonlight, tipped with pure charge . . . and the measure, too, of Eden's curse. She knew that clear, now. Knew that Eden's bones and dry flesh and even drier spirit infused this little devil she held in her hands. She could smell his meager scent of talcum powder and stale sweat, could sense his spirit hovering inside this loamy shell, and she

knew she could expect only an Eden's worth of pleasure from his embrace, but that was so much more than she had for years, well.
. . . She not fell but floated down onto the bed, sinking into its bridal deep, and oh, she was eager, and oh, she could scarcely wait.

"Love," she said.

You never had it, Willa, whispered the Black Clay Boy.

"Love!" she cried. "Love, love, love."

Forever, said the Black Clay Boy, his voice acquiring a male sternness, a tone of command.

Forever, she thought she said, the word soft as a pillow. *Love forever, Love for now, pin me deep and darling into the bottomland. Split me wide, and take me where the pleasure lies.*

Lies, echoed the Black Clay Boy.

He quivered in her hands, wanting her, but she held him off, tasting the delicious anticipation of the pure silver moment of going inside.

Now, Willa, now!

"When I'm ready," she said, laughing, teasing. "When I'm ready and not a moment before."

Now!

"Yes!" she said, arching toward him, her eyelids fluttering down. "Yes, now!"

With the powerful thrust of a man, with all the violent sweet force of a man's need, she pulled him to her hard, and there was pain, yes, there was pain, but it was filling and deep and real, and if she'd had the strength, she would have plucked him out and pulled him in again and again and again.

Forever.

The perfect companion of that perfect gentleman, that perfect lover, the Black Clay Boy.

His strange blank face was inches away, his eyes appeared to widen. Maybe, she thought, this was the beginning of another memory.

Not hardly.

"Oh," she said sadly, and she could see the word come white from her lips like a spirit, like the white poor thing of her life, her need, her sorrowful ending. Like a blown kiss.

Better luck next time, he told her.

"Next time?" she said, hopeful. "You mean. . . ."

Just kidding, Willa, said the Black Clay Boy as he winked shut first one silver eye and then the other.

FIRE ZONE EMERALD

A in't it weird, soldier boy?" said the voice in Quinn's ear. "There you are, strollin' along in that little ol' green suit of armor, feelin' all cool and killproof . . . and wham! You're down and hurtin' bad. Gotta admit, though, them suits do a job. Can't recall nobody steppin' onna mine and comin' through it as good as you."

Quinn shook his head to clear the cobwebs. His helmet rattled, which was not good news. He doubted that any of the connections to the computer in his backpack were still intact. But at least he could move his legs, and that was very good news, indeed. The guy talking had a crazed lilt to his voice, and Quinn thought it would be best to take cover. He tried the computer; nothing worked except for map holography. The visor display showed him to be a blinking red dot in the midst of a contoured green glow: eleven miles inside Guatemala from its border with Belize, in the heart of the Petén rain forest, on the eastern edge of Fire Zone Emerald.

"Y'hear me, soldier boy?"

Quinn sat up, wincing as pain shot through his legs. He felt no fear, no panic. Although he had just turned twenty-one, this was his second tour in Guatemala, and he was accustomed to being in tight spots. Besides, there were a lot worse places he might have been stranded. Up until two years before, Emerald had been a staging area for Cuban and guerrilla troops; but following the construction of a string of Allied artillery bases to the west, the enemy had moved their encampments north and—except for recon patrols such as Quinn's— the fire zone had been abandoned.

"No point in playin' possum, man. Me and the boys'll be there in ten, fifteen minutes, and you gonna have to talk to us then."

Ten minutes. Shit! Maybe, Quinn thought, if he talked to the guy, that would slow him down. "Who are you people?" he asked.

"Name's Mathis. Special Forces, formerly attached to the First Infantry." A chuckle. "But you might say we seen the light and opted outta the Service. How 'bout you, man? You gotta name?"

"Quinn. Edward Quinn." He flipped up his visor; heat boiled into the combat suit, overwhelming the cooling system. The suit was scorched and shredded from the knees down; plastic armor glinted in the rips. He looked around for his gun. The cable that had connected it to the computer had been severed, probably by shrapnel from the mine, and the gun was not to be seen. "You run across the rest of my patrol?"

A static-filled silence. " 'Fraid I got bad tidin's, Quinn Edward. 'Pears like guerrillas took out your buddies."

Despite the interference, Quinn heard the lie in the voice. He scoped out the terrain, saw that he was sitting in a cathedrallike glade: vaults of leaves pillared by the tapering trunks of ceibas and giant figs. The ground was carpeted with ferns; a thick green shade seemed to well up from the tips of the fronds. Here and there, shafts of golden light penetrated the canopy, and these were so complexly figured with dust motes that they appeared to contain flaws and fracture planes, like artifacts of crystal snapped off in midair. On three sides the glade gave out into dense jungle; but to the east lay a body of murky green water, with a forested island standing about a hundred feet out. If he could find his gun, the island might be defensible. Then a few days' rest and he'd be ready for a hike.

"Them boys wasn't no friends of yours," said Mathis. "You hit that mine, and they let you lie like meat on the street."

That much Quinn believed. The others had been too wasted on the martial-arts ampules to be trustworthy. Chances were, they simply hadn't wanted the hassle of carrying him.

"They deserved what they got," Mathis went on. "But you, now . . . boy with your luck. Might just be a place for you in the light."

"What's that mean?" Quinn fumbled a dispenser from his hip pouch and ejected two ampules—a pair of silver bullets—into his palm. Two, he figured, should get him walking.

"The light's holy here, man. You sit under them beams shinin' through the canopy, let 'em soak into you, and they'll stir the truth from your mind." Mathis said all this in dead earnest, and Quinn, unable to mask his amusement, said, "Oh, yeah?"

"You remind me of my ol' lieutenant," said Mathis. "Man used to tell me I's crazy, and I'd say to him, 'I ain't ordinary crazy, sir. I'm crazy gone to Jesus.' And I'd 'splain to him what I knew from the light, that we's s'posed to build the kingdom here. Place where a man could live pure. No machines, no pollution." He grunted as if tickled by something. "That's how you be livin' if you can cut it. You gonna learn to hunt with knives, track tapirs by the smell. Hear what weather's comin' by listenin' to the cry of a bird."

"How 'bout the lieutenant?" Quinn asked. "He learn all that?"

"Y'know how it is with lieutenants, man. Sometimes they just don't work out."

Quinn popped an ampule under his nose and inhaled. Waited for the drugs to kick in. The ampules were the Army's way of ensuring that the high incidence of poor battlefield performance during the Vietnam War would not be repeated: each contained a mist of pseudoendorphins and RNA derivatives that elevated the user's determination and physical potentials to heroic levels for thirty minutes or thereabouts. But Quinn preferred not to rely on them, because of their destructive side effects. Printed on the dispenser was a warning against abuse, one that Mathis—judging by his rap—had ignored. Quinn had heard similar raps from guys whose personalities had been eroded, replaced in part by the generic mystic-warrior personality supplied by the drugs.

" 'Course," said Mathis, breaking the silence, "it ain't only the light. It's the queen. She's the one with the light."

"The queen?" Quinn's senses had sharpened. He could see the spidery shapes of monkeys high in the canopy and could hear a hundred new sounds. He spotted the green-plastic stock of his gun protruding from beneath a fern not twenty feet away; he came to his feet, refusing to admit his pain, and went over to it. Both upper and lower barrels were plugged with dirt.

" 'Member them Cuban 'speriments where they was linkin' up animals and psychics with computer implants? Usin' 'em for spies?"

"That was just bullshit!" Quinn set off toward the water. He felt disdain for Mathis and recognized that to be a sign of too many ampules.

"It ain't no bullshit. The queen was one of them psychics. She's linked up with this little ol' tiger cat—what the Indians call a *tigrillo*.

We ain't never seen her, but we seen the cat. And once we got tuned to her, we could feel her mind workin' on us. But at first, she can slip them thoughts inside your head without you ever knowin'. Twist you 'round her finger, she can."

"If she's that powerful," said Quinn, smug with the force of his superior logic, "then why's she hidin' from you?"

"She ain't hidin'. We gotta prove ourselves to her. Keep the jungle pure, free of evildoers. Then she'll come to us."

Quinn popped the second ampule. "Evildoers? Like my patrol, huh? That why you wasted my patrol?"

"Whoo-ee!" said Mathis after a pause. "I can't slide nothin' by you, can I, Quinn Edward?"

Quinn's laughter was rich and nutsy: a two-ampule laugh. "Naw," he said, mocking Mathis's corn-pone accent. "Don't reckon you can." He flipped down his visor and waded into the water, barely conscious of the pain in his legs.

"Your buddies wasn't shit for soldiers," said Mathis. "Good thing they come along, though. We was runnin' low on ampules." He made a frustrated noise. "Hey, man. This armor ain't nothin' like the old gear . . . all this computer bullshit. I can't get nothin' crankin' 'cept the radio. Tell me how you work these here guns."

"Just aim and pull." Quinn was waist-deep in water, perhaps a quarter of the way to the island, which from that perspective—with its three towering vine-enlaced trees—looked like the overgrown hulk of a sailing ship anchored in a placid stretch of jade.

"Don't kid a kidder," said Mathis. "I tried that."

"You'll figure it out," Quinn said. "Smart peckerwood like you."

"Man, you gotta attitude problem, don'tcha? But I 'spect the queen'll straighten you out."

"Right! The invisible woman!"

"You'll see her soon enough, man. Ain't gonna be too long 'fore she comes to me."

"To *you?*" Quinn snickered. "That mean you're the king?"

"Maybe." Mathis pitched his voice low and menacing. "Don't go thinkin' I'm just country pie, Quinn Edward. I been up here most of two years, and I got this place down. I can tell when a fly takes a shit! Far as you concerned, I'm lord of the fuckin' jungle."

Quinn bit back a sarcastic response. He should be suckering this guy, determining his strength. Given that Mathis had been on recon prior to deserting, he'd probably started with around fifteen men.

"You guys taken many casualties?" he asked after slogging another few steps.

"Why you wanna know that? You a man with a plan? Listen up, Quinn Edward. If you figgerin' on takin' us out, 'member them fancy · guns didn't help your buddies, and they ain't gonna help you. Even if you could take us out, you'd still have to deal with the queen. Just 'cause she lives out on the island don't mean she ain't keepin' her eye on the shore. You might not believe it, man, but right now, right this second, she's all 'round you."

"What island?" The trees ahead suddenly seemed haunted-looking.

"Little island out there on the lake. You can see it if you lift your head."

"Can't move my head," said Quinn. "My neck's fucked up."

"Well, you gonna see it soon enough. And once you healed, you take my advice and stay the hell off it. The queen don't look kindly on trespassers."

On reaching the island, Quinn located a firing position from which he could survey the shore: a weedy patch behind a fallen tree trunk hemmed in by bushes. If Mathis was as expert in jungle survival as he claimed, he'd have no trouble discovering where Quinn had gone; and there was no way to tell how strong an influence his imaginary queen exerted, no way to be sure whether the restriction against trespassing had the severity of a taboo or was merely something frowned on. Not wanting to take chances, Quinn spent a frantic few minutes cleaning the lower barrel of his gun, which fired miniature fragmentation grenades.

"Now where'd you get to, Quinn Edward?" said Mathis with mock concern. "Where *did* you get to?"

Quinn scanned the shore. Dark avenues led away among the trees, and as he stared along them, his nerves were keyed by every twitching leaf, every shift of light and shadow. Clouds slid across the sun, muting its glare to a shimmering platinum gray; a palpable vibration underscored the stillness. He tried to think of something pleasant to make the waiting easier, but nothing pleasant occurred to him. He wetted his lips and swallowed. His cooling system set up a whine.

Movement at the margin of the jungle, a shadow resolving into a man wearing olive-drab fatigues and carrying a rifle with a skeleton stock—likely an old M-18. He waded into the lake, and as he closed on the island, Quinn trained his scope on him and saw that he had black shoulder-length hair framing a haggard face; a ragged beard bibbed his chest, and dangling from a thong below the beard was a triangular piece of mirror. Quinn held his fire, waiting for the rest to emerge. But no one else broke cover, and he realized Mathis was testing him, was willing to sacrifice a pawn to check out his weaponry.

"Keep back!" he shouted. But the man kept plodding forward, heaving against the drag of the water. Quinn marveled at the hold Mathis must have over him: he *had* to know he was going to die. Maybe he was too whacked out on ampules to give a shit, or maybe Mathis's queen somehow embodied the promise of a swell afterlife for those who died in battle. Quinn didn't want to kill him, but there was no choice, no point in delaying the inevitable.

He aimed, froze a moment at the sight of the man's fear-widened eyes; then squeezed the trigger.

The hiss of the round blended into the explosion, and the man vanished inside a fireball and geysering water. Monkeys screamed; birds wheeled up from the shoreline trees. A veil of oily smoke drifted across the lake, and within seconds a pair of legs floated to the surface, leaking red. Quinn felt queasy and sick at heart.

"Man, they doin' wonders with ordnance nowadays," said Mathis.

Infuriated, Quinn fired a spread of three rounds into the jungle.

"Not even close, Quinn Edward."

"You're a real regular-Army asshole, aren't you?" said Quinn. "Lettin' some poor fucker draw fire."

"You got me wrong, man! I sent that ol' boy out 'cause I loved him. He been with me almost four years, but his mind was goin', reflexes goin'. You done him a favor, Quinn Edward. Reduced his confusion to zero"—Mathis's tone waxed evangelic—"and let him shine forevermore!"

Quinn had a mental image of Mathis, bearded and haggard, like the guy he'd shot, but taller, rawboned: a gaunt rack of a man with rotting teeth and blown-away pupils. Being able to fit even an imaginary face to his target tuned his rage higher, and he fired again.

"Aw right, man!" Mathis's voice was burred with anger; the cadences of his speech built into a rant. "You want bang-bang, you got it. But you stay out there, the queen'll do the job for me. She don't like nobody creepin' 'round her in the dark. Makes her crazy. You go on, man! Stay there! She peel you down to meat and sauce, motherfucker!"

His laughter went high into a register that Quinn's speakers distorted, translating it as a hiccuping squeal, and he continued to rave.

However, Quinn was no longer listening. His attention was fixed on the dead man's legs, spinning past on the current. A lace of blood eeled from the severed waist. The separate strands seemed to be spelling out characters in some Oriental script; but before Quinn could try to decipher them, they lost coherence and were whirled away by the jade-green medium into which—staring with fierce concentration, giddy with drugs and fatigue—he, too, felt he was dissolving.

At twilight, when streamers of mist unfurled across the water, Quinn stood down from his watch and went to find a secure place in which to pass the night: considering Mathis's leeriness about his queen's nocturnal temper, he doubted there would be any trouble before morning. He beat his way through the brush and came to an enormous ceiba tree whose trunk split into two main branchings; the split formed a wide crotch that would support him comfortably. He popped an ampule to stave off pain, climbed up and settled himself.

Darkness fell; the mist closed in, blanketing moon and stars. Quinn stared out into pitch-black nothing, too exhausted to think, too buzzed to sleep. Finally, hoping to stimulate thought, he did another ampule. After it had taken effect, he could make out some of the surrounding foliage—vague scrolled shapes, each of which had its own special shine—and he could hear a thousand plops and rustles that blended into a scratchy percussion, its rhythms providing accents for a pulse that seemed to be coming up from the roots of the island. But there were no crunchings in the brush, no footsteps.

No sign of the queen.

What a strange fantasy, he thought, for Mathis to have created. He wondered how Mathis saw her. Blond, with a ragged Tarzan-movie skirt? A black woman with a necklace of bones? He remembered driving down to see his old girlfriend at college and being struck by a print hung on her dorm-room wall. It had shown a night jungle, a tiger prowling through fleshy vegetation, and—off to the side—a mysterious-looking woman standing naked in moon shadow. That would be his image of the queen. It seemed to him that the woman's eyes had been glowing. . . . But maybe he was remembering it wrong; maybe it had been the tiger's eyes. He had liked the print, had peered at the artist's signature and tried to pronounce the name. "Roo-see-aw," he had said, and his girl had given a haughty sniff and said, "Roo-so. It's Roo-so." Her attitude had made clear what he had suspected: that he had lost her. She had experienced a new world, one that had set its hooks in her; she had outgrown their little North Dakota farm-

ing town, and she had outgrown him as well. What the war had done
to him was similar, only the world he had outgrown was a much wider
place: he'd learned that he just wasn't cut out for peace and quiet
anymore.

Frogs chirred, crickets sizzled, and he was reminded of the hollow
near his father's house where he used to go after chores to be alone,
to plan a life of spectacular adventures. Like the island, it had been
a diminutive jungle—secure, yet not insulated from the wild—and recognizing the kinship between the two places caused him to relax. Soon
he nodded out into a dream, one in which he was twelve years old
again, fiddling with the busted tractor his father had given him to
repair. He had never been able to repair it, but in the dream, he
worked a gruesome miracle. Wherever he touched the metal, blood
beaded on the flaking rust; blood surged rich and dark through the
fuel line; and when he laid his hands on the corroded pistons, steam
seared forth and he saw that the rust had been transformed into red
meat, that his hands had left scorched prints. Then that meat engine
had shuddered to life and lumbered off across the fields on wheels
of black bone, plowing raw gashes in the earth, sowing seeds that overnight grew into stalks yielding fruit that exploded on contact with
the air.

It was such an odd dream, forged from the materials of his childhood yet embodying an alien sensibility, that he came awake, possessed
by the notion that it had been no dream but a sending. For an instant, he thought he saw a lithe shadow at the foot of the tree. The
harder he stared at it, though, the less substantial it became, and he
decided it must have been a hallucination. But after the shadow had
melted away, a wave of languor washed over him, sweeping him down
into unconsciousness, manifesting itself so suddenly, so irresistibly,
that it seemed no less a sending than the dream.

At first light Quinn popped an ampule and went to inspect the island,
stepping cautiously through the gray mist that still merged jungle and
water and sky, pushing through dripping thickets and spiderwebs dia-
monded with dew. He was certain Mathis would launch an attack
today. Since he had survived a night with the queen, it might be concluded that she favored him, that he now posed a threat to Mathis's
union with her—and Mathis wouldn't be able to tolerate that. The
best course, Quinn figured, would be to rile Mathis up, to make him
react out of anger and to take advantage of the situation.

The island proved to be about 120 feet long, perhaps a third of
that across at the widest, and—except for a rocky point at the north

end and a clearing some thirty feet south of the ceiba tree—was choked with vegetation. Vines hung in graceful loops like flourishes depended from illuminated letters; ferns clotted the narrow aisles between the bushes; epiphytes bloomed in the crooks of branches, punctuating the grayness with points of crimson and purple. The far side of the island was banked higher than a man could easily reach; but to be safe, Quinn mined the lowest sections with frags. In places where the brush was relatively sparse, he set flares head-high, connecting them to trip wires that he rigged with vines. Then he walked back and forth among the traps, memorizing their locations.

By the time he had done, the sun had started to burn off the mist, creating pockets of clarity in the gray; and as he headed back to his firing position, it was then he saw the tiger cat crouched in the weeds, lapping at the water. It wasn't much bigger than a house cat, with the delicate build and wedge-shaped head of an Abyssinian, and fine black stripes patterning its tawny fur. Quinn had seen such animals before while on patrol, but the way this one looked, so bright and articulated in contrast to the dull vegetable greens, framed by the eddying mist, it seemed a gateway had been opened onto a more vital world, and he was for the moment too entranced by the sight to consider what it meant. The cat finished its drink, turned to Quinn and studied him; then it snarled, wheeled about, and sprang off into the brush.

The instant it vanished, Quinn became troubled by a number of things. How he'd chosen the island as a fortress; how he'd gone straight to the best firing position; how he'd been anticipating Mathis. All this could be chalked up to common sense and good soldiering . . . yet he had been so assured, so definite. The assurance could be an effect of the ampules; but then Mathis had said that the queen could slip thoughts into your head without your knowing—until you became attuned to her, that is. Quinn tasted the flavors of his thoughts, searching for evidence of tampering. He knew he was being ridiculous, but panic flared in him nonetheless and he popped an ampule to pull himself together. Okay, he told himself. Let's see what the hell's going on.

For the next half hour, he combed the island, prying into thickets, peering at treetops. He found no trace of the queen, nor did he spot the cat again. But if she could control his mind, she might be guiding him away from her traces. She might be following him, manipulating him like a puppet. He spun around, hoping to catch her unawares. Nothing. Only bushes threaded with mist, trembling in the breeze. He let out a cracked laugh. Christ, he was an idiot! Just because the cat lived on the island didn't mean the queen was real; in fact, the cat might be the core of Mathis's fantasy. It might have inhabited the lake shore, and when Mathis and his men had arrived, it had fled out here to be shut of them . . . or maybe even this thought had been slipped into his head. Quinn was amazed by the subtlety of the delusion, at the elusiveness with which it defied both validation and debunking.

Something crunched in the brush.

Convinced that the noise signaled an actual presence, he swung his gun to cover the bushes. His trigger finger tensed, but after a moment he relaxed. It was the isolation, the general weirdness, that was doing him in, not some bullshit mystery woman. His job was to kill Mathis, and he'd better get to it. And if the queen *were* real, well, then she did favor him and he might have help. He popped an ampule and laughed as it kicked in. Oh, yeah! With modern chemistry and the invisible woman on his side, he'd go through Mathis like a rat through cheese. Like fire through a slum. The drugs—or perhaps it was the pour of a mind more supple than his own—added a lyric coloration to his thoughts, and he saw himself moving with splendid athleticism into an exotic future wherein he killed the king and wed the shadow and ruled in hell forever.

Quinn was low on frags, so he sat down behind the fallen tree trunk and cleaned the upper barrel of his gun: it fired caseless .22-caliber ammunition. Set on automatic, it could chew a man in half; but, wanting to conserve bullets, he set it to fire single shots. When the sun had cleared the tree line, he began calling to Mathis on his radio. There was no response at first, but finally a gassed, irascible voice answered, saying, "Where the fuck you at, Quinn Edward?"

"The island." Quinn injected a wealth of good cheer into his next words. "Hey, you were right about the queen!"

"What you talkin' 'bout?"

"She's beautiful! Most beautiful woman I've ever seen."

"You seen her?" Mathis sounded anxious. "Bullshit!"

Quinn thought about the Rousseau print. "She got dark, satiny skin and black hair down to her ass. And the whites of her eyes, it looks like they're glowin', they're so bright. And her tits, man. They ain't too big, but the way they wobble around"—he let out a lewd cackle—"it makes you wanna get down and frolic with them puppies."

"Bullshit!" Mathis repeated, his voice tight.

"Uh-uh," said Quinn. "It's true. See, the queen's lonely, man. She thought she was gonna have to settle for one of you lovelies, but now she's found somebody who's not so fucked up."

Bullets tore through the bushes on his right.

"Not even close," said Quinn. More fire; splinters flew from the tree trunk. "Tell me, Mathis." He suppressed a giggle. "How long's it been since you had any pussy?" Several guns began to chatter, and he caught sight of a muzzle flash; he pinpointed it with his own fire.

"You son of a bitch!" Mathis screamed.

"Did I get one?" Quinn asked blithely. "What's the matter, man? Wasn't he ripe for the light?"

A hail of fire swept the island. The cap-pistol sounds, the volley of hits on the trunk, the bullets zipping through the leaves, all this enraged Quinn, touched a spark to the violent potential induced by the drugs. But he restrained himself from returning fire, wanting to keep his position hidden. And then, partly because it was another way of ragging Mathis but also because he felt a twinge of alarm, he shouted, "Watch out! You'll hit the queen!"

The firing broke off. "Quinn Edward!" Mathis called.

Quinn kept silent, examining that twinge of alarm, trying to determine if there had been something un-Quinnlike about it.

"Quinn Edward!"

"Yeah, what?"

"It's time," said Mathis, hoarse with anger. "Queen's tellin' me it's time for me to prove myself. I'm comin' at you, man!"

Studying the patterns of blue-green scale flecking the tree trunk, Quinn seemed to see the army of his victims—grim, desanguinated men—and he felt a powerful revulsion at what he had become. But when he answered, his mood swung to the opposite pole. "I'm waitin', asshole!"

"Y'know," said Mathis, suddenly breezy, "I got a feelin' it's gonna come down to you and me, man. 'Cause that's how she wants it. And can't nobody beat me one on one in my own backyard." His breath came as a guttural hiss, and Quinn realized that this sort of breathing was typical of someone who had been overdoing ampules. "I'm gonna overwhelm you, Quinn Edward," Mathis went on. "Gonna be like them ol' Jap movies. Little men with guns actin' all brave and shit till they see somethin' big and hairy comin' at 'em, munchin' treetops and spittin' fire. Then off they run, yellin', 'Tokyo is doomed!' "

For thirty or forty minutes Mathis kept up a line of chatter, holding forth on subjects as varied as the Cuban space station and Miami's chances in the A.L. East. He launched into a polemic condemning the new statutes protecting the rights of prostitutes ("Part of the kick's bein' able to bounce 'em 'round a little, y'know"), then made a case for Antarctica's being the site of the original Garden of Eden, and then proposed the theory that every President of the United States had been a member of a secret homosexual society ("Half them First Ladies wasn't nothin' but guys in dresses"). Quinn didn't let himself be drawn into conversation, knowing that Mathis was trying to distract him; but he listened because he was beginning to have a sense of Mathis's character, to understand how he might attack.

Back in Lardcan, Tennessee, or wherever, Mathis had likely been a charismatic figure, glib and expansive, smarter than his friends and willing to lead them from the rear into fights and petty crimes. In some ways, he was a lot like the kid Quinn had been, only Quinn's escapades had been pranks, whereas he believed Mathis had been capable of consequential misdeeds. He could picture him lounging around a gas station, sucking down brews and plotting meanness. The hillbilly con artist out to sucker the Yankee: that would be how he saw himself in relation to Quinn. Sooner or later, he would resort to tricks. That was cool with Quinn; he could handle tricks. But he wasn't going to underestimate Mathis. No way. Mathis had to have a lot on the ball to survive the jungle for two years, to rule a troop of crazed Green Berets. Quinn just hoped Mathis would underestimate him.

The sun swelled into an explosive glare that whitened the sky and made the green of the jungle seem a livid overripe color. Quinn popped ampules and waited. The inside of his head came to feel heavy with violent urges, as if his thoughts were congealing into a lump of mental *plastique*. Around noon, somebody began to lay down covering fire, spraying bullets back and forth along the bank. Quinn found he could time these sweeps, and after one such had passed him by, he looked out from behind the tree trunk. Four bearded, long-haired men were crossing the lake from different directions, plunging through the water, lifting their knees high. Before ducking back, Quinn shot the two on the left, saw them spun around, their rifles flung away. He timed a second sweep, then picked off the two on the right; he was certain he had killed one, but the other might only have been wounded. The gunfire homed in on him, trimming the bushes overhead. Twigs pinwheeled; cut leaves sailed like paper planes. A centipede had ridden one of the leaves down and was still crawling along its fluted edge. Quinn didn't like its hairy mandibles, its devil face. Didn't like the fact that it had survived while men had not. He let it crawl in front of his gun and blew it up in a fountain of dirt and grass.

The firing stopped.

Branches ticking the trunk; water slopping against the bank; drips. Quinn lay motionless, listening. No unnatural noises. But where were those drips coming from? The bullets hadn't splashed up much water. Apprehensions spidered his backbone. He peeked up over the top of the tree trunk . . . and cried out in shock. A man was standing in the water about four feet away, blocking the line of fire from the shore. With the mud freckling his cheeks, strands of bottom weed ribboning his dripping hair, he might have been the wild mad king of the lake—skull face, staring eyes, survival knife dangling loosely in his hand. He blinked at Quinn. Swayed, righted himself, blinked again. His fatigues were plastered to his ribs, and a big bloodstain mapped the hollow of his stomach. The man's cheeks bulged: it looked as if he wanted to speak but was afraid more would come out than just words.

"Jesus . . . shit," he said sluggishly. His eyes half-rolled back; his knees buckled. Then he straightened, glancing around as if waking somewhere unfamiliar. He appeared to notice Quinn, frowned, and staggered forward, swinging the knife in a lazy arc.

Quinn got off a round before the man reached him. The bullet seemed to paste a red star under the man's eye, stamping his features with a rapt expression. He fell atop Quinn, atop the gun, which—jammed to automatic—kept firing. Lengths of wet hair hung across Quinn's faceplate, striping his view of branches and sky; the body jolted with the bullets tunneling through.

Two explosions nearby.

Quinn pushed the body away, belly-crawled into the brush, and popped an ampule. He heard a *thock* followed by a bubbling scream: somebody had tripped a flare. He did a count and came up with nine dead—plus the guy laying down covering fire. Mathis, no doubt. It would be nice if that were all of them, but Quinn knew better. Somebody else was out there. He felt him the way a flower feels the sun—autonomic reactions waking, primitive senses coming alert.

He inched deeper into the brush. The drugs burned bright inside him; he had the idea they were forming a manlike shape of glittering particles, an inner man of furious principle. Mats of blight-dappled leaves pressed against his faceplate, then slid away with underwater slowness. It seemed he was burrowing through a mosaic of muted colors and coarse textures into which even the concept of separateness had been subsumed, and so it was that he almost failed to notice the boot: a rotting brown boot with vines for laces, visible behind a spray of leaves about six feet off. The boot shifted, and Quinn saw an olive-drab trouser leg tucked into it.

His gun was wedged beneath him, and he was certain the man would move before he could ease it out. But apparently the man was playing bird dog, his senses straining for a clue to Quinn's where-abouts. Quinn lined the barrel up with the man's calf just above the boot top and checked to make sure it was set on automatic. Then he fired, swinging the barrel back and forth an inch to both sides of his center mark. Blood erupted from the calf, and a hoarse yell was drawn out of Quinn by the terrible hammering of the gun. The man fell, screaming. Quinn tracked the fire across the ground, and the screams were cut short.

The boot was still standing behind the spray of leaves, now sprout-ing a tattered stump and a shard of bone.

Quinn lowered his head, resting his faceplate in the dirt. It was as if all his rectitude had been spat out through the gun. He lay thoughtless, drained of emotion. Time seemed to collapse around him, burying him beneath a ton of decaying seconds. After a while, a beetle crawled onto the faceplate, walking upside down; it stopped at eye level, tapped its mandibles on the plastic, and froze. Staring at its grotesque underparts, Quinn had a glimpse into the nature of his own monstrosity: a tiny armored creature chemically programmed to a life of stalking and biting and, between violences, lapsing into a stunned torpor.

"Quinn Edward?" Mathis whispered.

Quinn lifted his head; the beetle dropped off the faceplate and scur-ried for cover.

"You got 'em all, didn'tcha?"

Quinn wormed out from under the bush, got to his feet, and headed back to the fallen tree trunk.

"Tonight, Quinn Edward. You gonna see my knife flash . . . and then fare thee well." Mathis laughed softly. "It's me she wants, man. She just told me so. Told me I can't lose tonight."

Late afternoon, and Quinn went about disposing of the dead. It wasn't something he would ordinarily have done, yet he felt compelled to be rid of them. He was too weary to puzzle over the compulsion and merely did as it directed, pushing the corpses into the lake. The man

who had tripped the flare was lying in some ferns, his face seared down
to sinew and laceworks of cartilage; ants were stitching patterns across
the blood-sticky bone of the skull. Having to touch the body made
Quinn's flesh nettle cold, and bile flooded his throat.

That finished, he sat in the clearing south of the ceiba and popped
an ampule. The rays of sunlight slanting through the canopy were
as sharply defined as lasers, showing greenish-gold against the backdrop
of leaves. Sitting beneath them, he felt guided by no visionary purpose; he was, however, gaining a clearer impression of the queen. He
couldn't point to a single thought out of the hundreds that cropped
up and say, "That one; that's hers." But as if she were filtering his
perceptions, he was coming to know her from everything he experienced. It seemed the island had been steeped in her, its mists and mid-
nights modified by her presence, refined to express her moods; even
its overgrown terrain seemed to reflect her nature: shy, secretive, yet
full of gentle stirrings. Seductive. He understood now that the process of becoming attuned to her was a process of seduction, one you
couldn't resist, because you, too, were being steeped in her. You were
forced into a lover's involvement with her, and she was a woman worth
loving. Beautiful . . . strong. She'd needed that strength in order to
survive, and that was why she couldn't help him against Mathis. The
life she offered was free from the terrors of war but demanded vigilance
and fortitude. Although she favored him—he was sure of that—his
strength would have to be proved. Of course, Mathis had twisted all
this into a bizarre religion.

Christ!

Quinn sat up straight. Jesus fucking Christ! He was really losing
it—mooning around like some kid fantasizing about a movie star. He'd
better get his ass in gear, because Mathis would be coming soon.
Tonight. It was interesting how Mathis—knowing his best hope of
taking Quinn would be at night—had used his delusion to overcome
his fear of the dark, convincing himself that the queen had told him
he would win . . . or maybe she *had* told him.

Fuck that, Quinn told himself. He wasn't that far gone.

A gust of wind roused a chorus of whispery vowels from the leaves.
Quinn flipped up his visor. It was hot, cloudless, but he could smell
rain and the promise of a chill on the wind. He did an ampule. The
drugs withdrew the baffles that had been damping the core of his anger.
Confidence was a voltage surging through him, keying new increments
of strength. He smiled, thinking about the fight to come, and even
that smile was an expression of furious strength, a thing of bulked

muscle fibers and trembling nerves. He was at the center of strength, in touch with every rustle, his sensitivity fueled by the light-stained brilliance of the leaves. Gazing at the leaves, at their infinite shades of green, he remembered a line of a poem he'd read once: "Green flesh, green hair, and eyes of coldest silver. . . ." Was that how the queen would be if she were real—transformed into a creature of pure poetry by the unearthly radiance of Fire Zone Emerald? Were they all acting out a mythic drama distilled from the mundane interactions of love and war, performing it in the flawed heart of an immense green jewel whose reality could be glimpsed only by those blind enough to see beyond the chaos of the leaves into its precise facets and fractures? Quinn chuckled at the wasted profundity of his thought and pictured Mathis dead, himself the king of that dead man's illusion, robed in ferns and wearing a leafy crown.

High above, two parrots were flying complicated loops and arcs, avoiding the hanging columns of light as if they were solid.

Just before dusk a rain squall swept in, lasting only a few minutes but soaking the island. Quinn used it for cover, moving about and rigging more flares. He considered taking a stand on the rocky point at the north end: it commanded a view of both shores, and he might get lucky and spot Mathis as he crossed. But it was risky—Mathis might spot *him*—and he decided his best bet would be to hide, to outwait Mathis. Waiting wasn't Mathis's style. Quinn went back to the ceiba tree and climbed past the crotch to a limb directly beneath an opening in the canopy, shielded by fans of leaves. He switched his gun to its high-explosive setting. Popped an ampule. And waited.

The clouds passed away south, and in the half-light, the bushes below seemed to assume topiary shapes. After fifteen minutes, Quinn did another ampule. Violet auras faded in around ferns, pools of shadow quivered, and creepers seemed to be slithering like snakes along the branches. A mystic star rose in the west, shining alone above the last pink band of sunset. Quinn stared at it until he thought he understood its sparkling message.

The night that descended was similar to the one in the Rousseau print, with a yellow-globe moon carving geometries of shadow and light from the foliage. A night for tigers, mysterious ladies, and dark designs. Barnacled to his branch, Quinn felt that the moonlight was lacquering his combat gear, giving it the semblance of ebony armor with gilt filigree, enforcing upon him the image of a knight about to do battle for his lady. He supposed it was possible that such might actually be the case. It was true that his perception of the queen was growing stronger and more particularized; he even thought he could tell where she was hiding: the rocky point. But he doubted that he could trust the perception—and besides, the battle itself, not its motive, was the significant thing. To reach that peak moment when perfection drew blood, when you muscled confusion aside and—as large as a constellation with the act, as full of stars and blackness and primitive meaning—you were able to look down onto the world and know you had outperformed the ordinary. Nothing, neither an illusory motive nor the illusion of a real motive, could add importance to that.

Shortly after dark, Mathis began to chatter again, regaling Quinn with anecdote and opinion; and by the satisfaction in his voice, Quinn knew he had reached the island. Twenty minutes passed, each of them ebbing away, leaking out of Quinn's store of time like blood dripping from an old wound. Then a burst of white incandescence to the south, throwing vines and bushes into skeletal silhouette . . . and with it a scream. Quinn smiled. The scream had been a dandy imitation of pain, but he wasn't buying it. He eased a flare from his hip pouch. It wouldn't take long for Mathis to give this up.

The white fire died, muffled by the rain-soaked foliage, and finally Mathis said, "You a cautious fella, Quinn Edward."

Quinn popped two ampules.

"I doubt you can keep it up, though," Mathis went on. "I mean, sooner or later you gotta throw caution to the winds."

Quinn barely heard him. He felt he was soaring, that the island was soaring, arrowing through a void whose sole feature it was and approaching the moment for which he had been waiting: a moment of brilliant violence to illuminate the flaws at the heart of the stone, to reveal the shadow play. The first burn of the drugs subsided, and he fixed his eyes on the shadows south of the ceiba tree.

Tension began to creep into Mathis's voice, and Quinn was not surprised when—perhaps five minutes later—he heard the stutter of an M-18: Mathis firing at some movement in the brush. He caught sight of a muzzle flash, lifted his gun. But the next instant, he was struck by an overpowering sense of the queen, one that shocked him with its suddenness.

She was in pain. Wounded by Mathis's fire.

In his mind's eye Quinn saw a female figure slumped against a boulder, holding her lower leg. The wound wasn't serious, but he could tell she wanted the battle to end before worse could happen.

He was mesmerized by her pervasiveness—it seemed that if he were to flip up his visor, he would breathe her in—and by what appeared to be a new specificity of knowledge about her. Bits of memory were surfacing in his thoughts; though he didn't quite believe it, he could have sworn they were hers: a shanty with a tin roof amid fields of tilled red dirt; someone walking on a beach; a shady place overhung by a branch dripping with orchids, with insects scuttling in and out of the blooms, mining some vein of sweetness. That last memory was associated with the idea that it was a place where she went to daydream, and Quinn felt an intimate resonance with her, with the fact that she—like him—relied on that kind of retreat.

Confused, afraid for her yet half convinced that he had slipped over the edge of sanity, he detonated his flare, aiming it at the opening in the canopy. An umbrella of white light bloomed overhead. He tracked his gun across eerily lit bushes and. . . . There! Standing in the clearing to the south, a man wearing combat gear. Before the man could move, Quinn blew him up into marbled smoke and flame. Then, his mind ablaze with victory, he began to shinny down the branch. But as he descended, he realized something was wrong. The man had just stood there, made no attempt to duck or hide. And his gun. It had been like Quinn's own, not an M-18.

He had shot a dummy or a man already dead!

Bullets pounded his back, not penetrating but knocking him out of the tree. Arms flailing, he fell into the bush. Branches tore the gun from his grasp. The armor deadened the impact, but he was dazed, his head throbbing. He clawed free of the bush just as Mathis's helmeted shadow—looking huge in the dying light of the flare—crashed through the brush and drove a rifle stock into his faceplate. The plastic didn't shatter, webbing over with cracks; but by the time Quinn had recovered, Mathis was straddling him, knees pinning his shoulders.

"How 'bout that, motherfucker?" said Mathis, breathing hard.

A knife glinted in his hand, arced downward, and thudded into Quinn's neck, deflected by the armor. Quinn heaved, but Mathis forced him back and this time punched at the faceplate with the hilt of the knife. Punched again, and again. Bits of plastic sprayed Quinn's face, and the faceplate was now so thoroughly cracked, it was like looking up through a crust of glittering rime. It wouldn't take many more blows. Desperate, Quinn managed to roll Mathis onto his side, and they grappled silently. His teeth bit down on a sharp plastic chip, and he tasted blood. Still grappling, they struggled to their knees, then to their feet. Their helmets slammed together. The impact came as a hollow click over Quinn's radio, and that click seemed to switch on a part of his mind that was as distant as a flare, calm and observing; he pictured the two of them as black giants with whirling galaxies for hearts and stars articulating their joints, doing battle over the female half of everything. Seeing it that way gave him renewed strength. He shoved Mathis off balance, and they reeled clumsily through the brush. They fetched up against the trunk of the ceiba tree, and for a few seconds they were frozen like wrestlers muscling for an advantage. Sweat poured down Quinn's face; his arms quivered. Then Mathis tried to butt his faceplate, to finish the job he had begun with the hilt of his knife. Quinn ducked, slipped his hold, planted a shoulder in Mathis's stomach, and drove him backward. Mathis twisted as he fell, and Quinn turned him onto his stomach. He wrenched Mathis's knife arm behind his back, pried the knife loose. Probed with the blade, searching for a seam between the plates of neck armor. Then he pressed it just deep enough to prick the skin. Mathis went limp. Silent.

"Where's all the folksy chitchat, man?" said Quinn, excited.

Mathis maintained his silent immobility, and Quinn wondered if he had gone catatonic. Maybe he wouldn't have to kill him. The light from the flare had faded, and the moon-dappled darkness that had filled in reminded Quinn of the patterns of blight on the island leaves: an infection at whose heart they were clamped together like chitinous bugs.

"Bitch!" said Mathis, suddenly straining against Quinn's hold. "You lied, goddamn you!"

"Shut up," said Quinn, annoyed.

"Fuckin' bitch!" Mathis bellowed. "You tricked me!"

"I said to shut up!" Quinn gave him a little jab, but Mathis began to thrash wildly, nearly impaling himself, shouting, "Bitch!"

"Shut the fuck up!" said Quinn, growing angrier but also trying to avoid stabbing Mathis, beginning to feel helpless, to feel that he would have to stab him, that it was all beyond his control.

"I'll kill you, bitch!" screamed Mathis. "I'll. . . ."

"Stop it!" Quinn shouted, not sure to whom he was crying out. Inside his chest, a fuming cell of anger was ready to explode.

Mathis writhed and kicked. "I'll cut out your fuckin'. . . ."

Poisonous burst of rage. Mandibles snapping shut, Quinn shoved the knife home. Blood guttered in Mathis's throat. One gauntleted hand scrabbled in the dirt, but that was all reflexes.

Quinn sat up, feeling sluggish. There was no glory. It had been a contest essentially decided by a gross stupidity: Mathis's momentary forgetfulness about the armor. But how could he have forgotten? He'd seen what little effect the bullets had. Quinn took off his helmet and sucked in hits of the humid air, watched a slice of moonlight jiggle on Mathis's faceplate. Then a blast of static from his helmet radio, a voice saying, "You copy?"

"Ain't no friendlies in Emerald," said another radio voice. "Musta been beaners sent up that flare. It's a trap."

"Yeah, but I got a reading like infantry gear back there. We should do a sweep over that lake."

Chopper pilots, Quinn realized. But he stared at the helmet with the mute awe of a savage, as if they had been alien voices speaking from a stone. He picked up the helmet, unsure what to say.

Please, no . . .

The words had been audible, and he realized that she had made him hear them in the sighing of the breeze.

Static fizzling. "Get the hell outta here."

The first pilot again. "Do you copy? I repeat, do you copy?"

What, Quinn thought, if this had all been the queen's way of getting rid of Mathis, even down to that last flash of anger; and now, now that he had done the job, wouldn't she get rid of him?

Please stay . . .

Quinn imagined himself back in Dakota, years spent watching cattle die, reading mail-order catalogs, drinking and drinking, comparing the queen to the dowdy farm girl he'd have married, and one night getting a little too morbidly weary of that nothing life and driving out onto the flats and riding the .45-caliber express to nowhere. But at least that was proved, whereas this. . . .

Please . . .

A wave of her emotion swept over him, seeding him with her loneliness and longing. He was truly beginning to know her now, to sense the precise configurations of her moods, the stoicism underlying her strength, the. . . .

"Fuck it!" said one of the pilots.

The static from Quinn's radio smoothed to a hiss, and the night closed down around him. His feeling of isolation nailed him to the spot. Wind seethed in the massy crown of the ceiba, and he thought he heard again the whispered word *Please.* An icy fluid mounted in his spine. To shore up his confidence, he popped an ampule; and soon the isolation no longer troubled him but, rather, seemed to fit about him like a cloak. This was the path he had been meant to take, the way of courage and character. He got to his feet, unsteady on his injured legs, and eased past Mathis, slipping between two bushes. Ahead of him, the night looked like a floating puzzle of shadow and golden light: no matter how careful he was, he'd never be able to locate all his mines and flares.

But she would guide him.

Or would she? Hadn't she tricked Mathis? Lied to him?

More wind poured through the leaves of the ceiba tree, gusting its word of entreaty; and intimations of pleasure, of sweet green mornings and soft nights, eddied up in the torrent of her thoughts. She surrounded him, undeniable, as real as perfume, as certain as the ground beneath his feet.

For a moment he was assailed by a new doubt. "God," he said. "Please don't let me be crazy. Not just ordinary crazy."

Please . . .

Then, suffering mutinies of the heart at every step, repelling them with a warrior's conviction, he moved through the darkness at the center of the island toward the rocky point, where—her tiger crouched by her feet, a ripe jungle moon hanging above like the emblem of her mystique—either love or fate might be waiting.

ON THE BORDER

hapo, handsome twenty-three-year-old, with Aztec features, black hair, adobe-colored skin. Sitting on the cantina steps, gazing up at the unreal fire of the border: a curtain of shimmering blood-red energy that appeared to rise halfway to the stars before merging with the night sky. So bright you could see it for miles out on the desert, a glowing seam stretching from Texas to California, and in that seam were the old towns of Tijuana, Nuevo Laredo, Mexicali, and a dozen more, all welded into a single town of stucco bars and slums, of muzzle gleam and knife-flash, of paunchy whores and sleazy pimps and gringos on the slide from the fatlands of America: the Crust, they called it, the fucking Crust. Something useless and left over. But Chapo liked thinking of himself as part of that glow, that red meanness. At least that had been the case until three days before, when he had crossed over and come back with the gringa.

Now he wasn't sure what he liked.

Somebody heaved a bottle toward the border, and Chapo tracked the arc. Violet lightnings forked away from the impact point. Throw a man into it, and you got brighter colors but the same result.

Zap! Not even ashes.

He fingered an upper from his pocket and swallowed it dry. Then he picked up his mesh shopping bag and headed for home. Music poured from the bars, swaying his hips, setting his fists jumping in little karate strikes. Battered old 1990s rides rumbled past, dark heads behind the wheels. Tang of marijuana, stink of fried grease. The red light shone everywhere, and shadows were sharp like they would be in hell.

A crowd was gathered by the door of Echeverría's bar, which meant a country girl was riding the wire. The child some farmer didn't have enough money to feed, and so he'd sold her to Echeverría. A brown-skinned girl stripped naked, silver electrodes plugged to her temples. Her brains frying in a smoke of pleasure as she danced a herky-jerky path across the floor, and men touching her, laughing as she looked blindly around, trying to find them. Later when she slowed down, they'd take her upstairs and charge heavy for a short time. If he'd been smart, Chapo thought, he'd have sold the gringa to Echeverría. But the wire . . . that was where he stopped being part of the red glow. He didn't understand why, but he just couldn't hand her over to that fate.

A poster with the gringa's photograph was plastered to Echeverría's wall. Blond hair and angel face. It didn't do her justice, didn't show how her eyes were. At first glance they were blue, then green, and then you saw they were all colors like fire opals, with flecks of emerald and gold and hazel. Special eyes. Beneath the photograph, big black letters spelled out her name: Anise. Just like a gringa to be named for something you drink. Even bigger letters offered a twenty-five-thousand-dollar reward. Everybody was looking for her now, and no way Chapo would be able to move her until things calmed down.

"Hey, Chapo!" Rafael pushed out of the crowd and came up beside him. Big chubby guy with jowls and brown frizzy hair. He was always hassling Chapo, not for any real reason, just for something to do. "You oughta see inside, man!" he said. "They gotta sweet little lady ridin' tonight!"

"Fuck it!" Chapo popped another upper. "I don't go for that shit."

"Least she gonna have fun," said Rafael, and grinned. "Least she goin' fast . . . not slow like you." He pointed to Chapo's shirt pocket, his pills.

A flash of chemical fury, and Chapo knocked him back with a slap. Rafael rubbed his mouth, and a knife materialized in his hand. "Okay," he said. "You like it fast? You got it, man."

Everybody was staring, wanting it to happen, and the pressure of all those black eyes made Chapo feel a little loose, a little casual about his life. He started to go for his own knife, but thought about the gringa and held back.

"C'mon with it, man!" said Rafael, dancing back and forth. "C'mon!"

"Maybe later," Chapo said.

Jeering whistles sounded behind him.

"What's the matter, Chapo?" Rafael grinned and made passes with the knife, lunging close.

Chapo half-turned, then swung his shopping bag, heavy with cans of fruit juice; the bag struck Rafael in the jaw, and he came all unhinged, falling facedown in the dirt.

The whistles broke off, and as the crowd dispersed, laughing, a couple of them stopped to spit on Rafael.

Out on the edge of the desert, the edge of the Crust, that's where Chapo lived. A white stucco ruin with no windows, no doors. Inside, he waited a minute to make sure nobody had followed. Each of the window frames held a rectangle of golden stars and blue darkness.

When he was certain he was alone, he went into the back room. It was piled with rubble. He kneeled and knocked three times on the floor. Waited another minute. Then he lifted a heap of rubble that was glued to a round metal plate almost the size of a manhole cover. Lowered a rope ladder that had been concealed beneath the rubble. He climbed partway down, eased the metal plate back into place. "Okay," he said, climbing down the rest of the way.

A match scraped, a candle flared. Two candles. He made her out against the rear wall, sitting on a stained mattress, her legs tucked under her. Grime streaked her face, and her golden hair was getting stringy. She wore jeans and a torn white blouse.

"Got you some fruit," he said, holding up the shopping bag. "Some juice."

She didn't appear to register what he'd said. The hollows in her cheeks had deepened, making her look older . . . with that wide mouth, like a model in some fashion magazine. But he figured she wasn't much over eighteen. Nineteen, maybe.

He set the shopping bag beside her and sat a couple of feet away. The candles cast tiny dancing shadows on the dirt. Dark wings fluttered behind his eyes, making the room dimmer: the uppers playing tricks.

"Please," she said wearily. "Won't you help me?"

"That's what I'm doin'," he said.

"No, I mean won't you help me get back." Her voice broke, and he hoped she wasn't going to cry again.

"I keep tellin' you," he said. "Your papa's offerin' too much money. There's guys lookin' for you all over. They see some fat ol' lady, and they go peekin' under her dress to see if the fat's for real. We'd never make it to Immigration. And you know what happens if somebody catch you? They gonna tease you, touch you . . . touch you here." He tapped his chest. "And then they say, 'Hey, why don't we taste some of that 'fore we score the money.' And once they start, they'll give everybody a taste, and pretty soon there won't be enough left to be worth no reward. That's how it goes in the Crust. People don't think ahead."

"We could call the police," she said. "We . . ."

"The police! Shit! They even worse. They hold you awhile to jack up the reward. Maybe they send your papa a finger or somethin'. And when they get the money, they do you the same way. You be patient, and I'll get you out."

She stared at him a moment, hopelessness in her face. Then she reached for the shopping bag.

Sitting hunkered on the dirt floor of the cellar, gazing into nowhere, Chapo thought about the crossing. He'd been wanting to cross a long time, wanting some of that Stateside money. And Moro had given him a chance. Moro had owned one of the tubes that spat threads of light and punched holes in the red glow. Holes that spread to doorsize, lasted a few seconds, and then closed tight. In a single night they had stolen more money than Chapo had ever seen, and as they'd headed back to the crossing point, they'd seen the girl through a storeroom window, bound and gagged, lying on the floor. She'd been kidnapped by one of the Stateside gangs, and they were working out ransom with her rich papa. Moro had said to take her. At the crossing point, Chapo and the girl had gone through first. They'd squatted beside a dumpster, waiting for the others. But the others hadn't come through. Chapo had thought he heard a scream, but it had been hard to tell what with the hum and sizzle of the border so loud. Realizing the others were never going to show, he'd dragged the gringa to her feet and they'd made a run to Chapo's house. It had been almost dawn, the streets empty, and they'd been lucky to make it even then.

"Chapo?"

And maybe he *should* sell her. What the hell was he doing helping her? If things were reversed, she wouldn't help him. He was just a beaner to her. Just trash.

"Chapo!"

He looked up. She was smiling: it was a fake smile, but he was glad to see it. "Yeah?"

"I'm sorry," she said. "I know you're trying to help. It's just
. . . I'm scared, y'know."

Chapo made a noncommittal noise.

"You can sit over here if you want." She patted the mattress.
"I'm okay."

"You can't be comfortable," she said. "Come on, please. It'll
make me feel better."

"All right." He crawled over to the mattress and sat on the very
end. She gave a teasing laugh, told him he could sit closer, and kept
talking.

Three days without a shower, and she still smelled sweet. Out of
the corner of his eye he peeked at the tented-up sliver of her blouse.
Her breasts weren't very big, but he could tell they had a nice shape.
He could stand a taste himself. They said it was all the same, but she'd
feel different. Her body full of lazy afternoons and expensive sugars.
Plush and springy, a Cadillac ride. He'd sink forever into blond flesh.

She edged a little nearer, saying she was cold, and he knew what
she was doing, what was going to happen. Then her face was close
to his, lips parted, dazed-looking, and she said, "Oh, Chapo . . .
Chapo!" And her tongue was darting into his mouth, and his hand
cupped the underside of one of those breasts . . . soft. The kind of
softness that makes you dizzy, tipped with its little hard candy.

Like a fool, he pushed her away.

"We can do this," he said, his breath coming hard. "We can do
this, but I ain't gonna take you out 'fore I think it's safe."

Disappointment and humiliation flooded her face.

What was the matter with him? Why didn't he just grab her and
peel off the shell and pluck out the meat. That's what he wanted.
But maybe not, maybe with her he wanted it real. Something he could
never have. "You gotta be patient," he said.

"Patient!" She spat out the word. "For how long? Until you find
some way to use me?"

He got angry, then. "What you think? You think I couldn't make
money off you now? Dumbass bitch! I take you down to Avenida
Juárez tonight, if that's what you think. Sell your skinny butt till it's
wore down to gristle."

She aimed a slap at him, but he caught her wrist and shoved her
away. She scooted to the end of the mattress, waiting for him to attack. For a second, he thought he might. But all he did was to repeat,
"You gotta be patient."

"How long?" she asked, looking hopeless again.

"I dunno. A few weeks . . . that is, if your papa don't raise the reward."

"A few weeks." In her mouth it sounded like forever.

He couldn't figure why he wanted to save her. It might be he just wanted to save *something*, to see if anything *could* be saved. But that wasn't all of it. Trouble with words, they shrank your ideas to fit, and made you think they were what you'd meant.

She turned her face to the wall, curled up tight.

Chapo doubted she could last a few more weeks. One day she'd do something crazy, try for the border on her own. He could tie her up, drug her. But she'd get loose. Even though she cried, he could see she was strong. But her strength wasn't the kind that counted here in the Crust.

"Maybe there's a way," he said.

She didn't react. Probably didn't believe him.

"I'll check it out tomorrow," he said.

She mumbled something that he didn't catch.

What a goddamn fool he was!

He didn't want to sleep, so he did another upper. Something scrabbled in the shadows, then was still. The candles guttered low, and light seemed to be collecting around the gringa, burying her under a heap of yellow glow like an enchantment. Her breath deepened. Now and again she moaned. He studied the way the denim clung to her ass. Sleek, perfect curves. An ass Made in America. Chapo wondered what it had cost, what secrets had gone into the manufacture. And he wondered, too, what dreams were crowding that golden head. Even her nightmares would be beautiful.

The upper kicked in, and Chapo leaned back against the wall, feeling the crazy bounces of his heart, a mean wash of thoughts seeping up from the red glow of his blood.

Anise, he said to himself. What a stupid fuckin' name!

Like Chapo, Herreira lived on the backside of the Crust. An old, old man with sheet iron over his windows and big locks on his doors. He owed Chapo, owed him big. Two years before, a merchant named Ibáñez had taken Herreira's granddaughter in exchange for paper he held on him, and Herreira had asked Chapo to steal the paper, so his granddaughter could get free. They hadn't talked price, but Chapo had trusted Herreira to work something out. He'd broken into Ibáñez's house, and Ibáñez had caught him. Chapo had opened the merchant's belly with a knife. Afterward he hadn't been able to put a price on the man's life, and he'd told Herreira that sooner or later he'd need something. Now the time had come, and he needed the old man's jeep, his maps of the desert. He'd drive the gringa across the desert to the Pacific resort of Huayacuatla. There she'd be safe.

Herreira's face was as wrinkled as tree bark, and his hair was wispy and white. But his back was unbowed, his black eyes clear. He didn't much care to risk his jeep, but a bargain was a bargain, and besides, he didn't use it anymore. It was painted white to blend in with the hardpan of the desert, and was kept in an adobe building barnacled onto the rear of the old man's house. Herreira spread his maps on the hood and showed Chapo the hiding places, how he would have to drive during the night, and by day hide the jeep and sleep in the big rocks that stuck up from the desert floor. Herreira had once been a smuggler, bringing guns from the coast into the Crust, and he told Chapo it was very dangerous to make the crossing.

"They spot you, man, and that's it." He drew a finger across his throat. "You got no place to run. It's luck if you make it, and the odds ain't good."

"What are they?" Chapo asked.

"Sixty-forty, your favor. If there's no moon, a little better. But there'll be a moon for you."

Chapo studied the map. The border was a crooked red line, and he imagined himself living there like a roach in a crack. Sixty-forty odds. It seemed no worse than what he usually faced.

"How 'bout gas?"

"You gotta extra tank," said Herreira. "Enough to cross the desert. Three nights drivin'. But you'll need more when you head up into the hills. There's a village"—he pointed—"here. San Juan de la Fiebra. Know 'bout it?"

Chapo nodded.

"Well, you can deal with 'em . . . sometimes. You get past 'em, and it's only a few hours to Huayacuatla."

Again Chapo wondered why the hell he was doing this. It didn't feel smart or even the good kind of reckless. But he pushed the question aside. Why didn't matter. He was committed, and maybe it was just in him to do.

"Bring the jeep back," said Herreira, dead-serious. "Don't sell it if you get across."

"How you know I'm plannin' to come back?"

Herreira's laugh was sneering. "Shit, Chapo! Where you gonna go? You just like me, you border meat."

"Maybe," said Chapo.

"Maybe, my ass!" Herreira scowled at Chapo. "You bring that bitch back."

The first night.

They drove south from the border. The hardpan glowed white. Every once in a while they passed huge desert rocks, indigo under the moonlight, smooth depressions in their sides like dimples made by the pressure of enormous thumbs. The shadows of smaller things—stubby cacti and little rocks—were so deep and black, they hid the objects that cast them. Chapo was tense. He could feel the blazing pinpricks of the stars on his back. The engine noise and rattles were too loud for talk, and whenever the gringa wanted to stop and pee, she had to shout. Sometimes he'd catch her looking at him, and she would smile. Not a fake smile, but one that seemed to be trying to engage him, to give him encouragement, to say something friendly, and he would nod in response and think about the smile, and then his thoughts would be worn down by the engine noise, and he would just drive.

Hours like that.

An hour before dawn he came to the first hiding place, a mountainous rock that showed chalky pink under the brightening sky. There was a niche in the southern face large enough to hold the jeep, and after parking it there, he covered it with brush. They crawled up to a depression, almost a cave, from which they had a good view south and east. The gringa was excited and wanted to talk, but Chapo told her to sleep. Later, he said, it might be too hot to sleep. She drank a little water, chewed half a tortilla, and wrapped herself in a blanket. He had bought her a clean blouse—blue, with a pattern of white hibiscus—and when she turned in her sleep and the blanket slipped down from her shoulders, he could see her nipples pushing up the clingy material. He watched them rise and fall, not thinking, just watching, feeling mild arousal, until he began to get drowsy.

When he waked he couldn't remember having fallen asleep. Sweat was crawling down his sides, and the desert was rippling with heat haze; he thought he could hear the heat humming, but the sound was in his head, and after a second it switched off. At the base of the rock stood a green barrel cactus. He could have sworn it hadn't been there when he'd parked the jeep. There were supposed to be *brujos* in the desert: could be the cactus was one of them in disguise. He glanced around and found the gringa watching him.

"Good morning," she said cheerfully.

Her good spirits annoyed him. "Yeah, mornin'."

His mouth tasted like shit. He did an upper and washed it down with a sip of water from the canteen. Shook his head to clear away the cobwebs. He reached into his hip pocket and pulled out his wristwatch. It was nearly one o'clock. Six, maybe seven more hours of daylight. He wished he'd slept longer. That same old question of what he was doing here cropped up in his mind: the desert seemed a bad answer.

"Want something to eat?" she asked.

"Un-uh."

His automatic jabbed into his back; he reached behind him and eased it from his waistband, laid it beside his leg.

The gringa's eyes widened, but she made no comment. After a minute she said, "Do you wanna talk or something?"

"What for?"

"Just to pass the time."

He had another sip of water. "Yeah, sure . . . all right."

She waited for him to start, and when he didn't, she said, "Why didn't you think of this before? The jeep, I mean. It doesn't look like it's going to be too hard."

He didn't want to tell her what Herreira had said about the odds. "I dunno."

"Well," she said impatiently. "I'm glad you *did* think of it."

They were silent for a while, and then she said, "What do you want to be?"

"Huh?"

"What do you want to do with your life? I'm studying to be a dancer."

"You don't gotta study to do that. Dancin's just somethin' you learn natural. In the bars and shit."

"I mean formal dance."

"What's that?"

"You know . . . jazz, ballet."

He didn't know, and she tried to explain.

"Why you wanna do that?" he asked. "What's the point?"

"To make something beautiful."

For no reason he could figure, he laughed.

Irritated, she said, "I don't suppose you'd understand."

"I understand all right!" he snapped, and let his gaze range the length of her body. "I understand beauty just fine."

She flushed and lowered her eyes. "So what do *you* wanna be?"

He had an answer, but the truth of it was all tangled up in words, hidden in snarls of black thready sentences that he would never get to come out straight. The answer wasn't a thing or a job or anything like that, but a way to be. He was angry at being unable to express himself, and out of anger, he said, "I ain't rich like you, I ain't got no choice."

"Of course you do," she said.

"Don't gimme that shit! What you know 'bout it?"

"I know you don't have to stay in the Crust. I know if you left, you might find you had other options."

He was about to snap at her again, but a thin droning sound caught his attention. He scanned the horizon.

"What is it?" she asked, alarmed.

"Airplane comin' low. Smugglers, maybe."

He spotted it, then. Silver speck glinting to the south, resolving into a twin-engine job. No more than a couple of hundred feet high. The rear door was open, showing blackly against the silver finish, and as the plane drew near, something fell from the door. Something with arms and legs that pinwheeled crazily down to land spread-eagled on the hardpan about fifty yards away, looking like an **X** marking buried treasure.

"Oh, Jesus!" the gringa said. "It was a man, wasn't it?"

"Could be a woman."

The plane banked toward the east and soon was lost to sight.

"Maybe he's still alive," she said. "Maybe we should go look."

"You go," he said. "You wanna see blood and bone, you go look."

She peered at the unmoving figure, her face grim, registering shock. "He *might* be alive."

"What if he is?" Chapo said. "You wanna pick him up, take him to the hospital? Nearest one's back in the Crust."

The figure seemed to be blackening and dissolving in the heat haze. The gringa continued to peer a few moments longer, then settled back into the shade, her lips thinned.

They didn't talk much after that.

The last of sunset left a red seam of fire along the western horizon, as if north had become west, and the Crust was now ahead of them. The second night was like the first, except the moon was brighter and the gringa didn't bother to smile. She rode with her head down, picking at frays in her jeans, and Chapo knew she was thinking about the dead man. He thought she might start a conversation about him, and he was glad when she kept quiet. What was there to say? That they should have checked him out? Shit! She should thank her stars it hadn't been her. The man's death had given Chapo a lucky feeling. Two nights without being spotted, and the desert had taken someone else instead of them. The signs were favorable. He realized he hadn't been concerned thus far with whether or not they would reach Huayacuatla. The concept of survival had not been part of his plan; he had simply been acting upon some mysterious inner directive. But now he wanted to make it. Now he had hope.

They didn't arrive at the second hiding place until dawn: another rock, an immense red mushroom cap a hundred feet high. The hardpan had been eroded under its eastern edge, leaving a deep overhang. Chapo drove the jeep beneath the overhang, and worked feverishly at camouflage, finishing just as the fireball cleared the horizon. He poked around in the flaky detritus and stirred up a scorpion. Crushed it with his heel. They made a meal of beans and tortillas behind the jeep, and washed the food down with canteen water. The gringa dabbed water onto her face. In the pink glow she looked tired but more beautiful than she had the previous day, her features finer, as if a layer of drab insulation had been worn away. She pulled the blanket over her shoulders and sat looking out into the new morning.

Chapo couldn't decide whether to sleep or do an upper. He was tired, but if he waited until afternoon to sleep, he'd be fresh for the night drive. He took a pill from his shirt pocket, rolled it back and forth between his thumb and forefinger.

"Hello!" somebody shouted.

Chapo jumped up, knocking his head on the overhang with such force that he went back down to one knee. He grabbed his automatic and peeked from behind the jeep. Standing about thirty feet away was a wrinkled old Indian man wearing a straw hat and a grimy shirt and trousers of white cotton. When he spotted Chapo, he spread his arms and called out, "Welcome to my house!"

"Who is it?" the gringa asked, leaning over Chapo's shoulder.

"Stay back!" He pushed her to the side and moved out into the sun.

"Welcome!" the old man repeated. "My name is Don Augustín. And you?"

"Chapo."

"And the gringa . . . How is she called?"

"Anise," answered the gringa from Chapo's rear.

He spun around. "I told you to stay back!"

"Don't be afraid," said Don Augustín with a chuckle. "I won't hurt you."

He was standing slightly forward and dead-center of a pair of large branching cacti; they looked like two weird, pale green soldiers flanking him. Beyond him, emptiness spread to the horizon. Chapo thought again about *brujos*.

"Won't you come into my house?" Don Augustín asked. "It's been years since I've had visitors."

"Where is it?" asked the gringa.

"My house? Behind you." Don Augustín gestured at the rock. "It's cool inside, and there's water. You can wash and rest for your journey."

Chapo leveled the gun at him. "How you know we're on a journey?"

"Oh!" Don Augustín arched an eyebrow, and his wrinkles shifted into lines of good humor. "You've come to see me, then? I'm honored."

"We'll stay here," said Chapo.

"I want to wash," said the gringa defiantly. Before Chapo could stop her, she went a few steps toward the old man. "I don't understand about your house."

"The rock's hollow," said Don Augustín. "Oh, you'll like it, Señorita Anise. It's beautiful . . . Not so beautiful as you, of course." He delivered a gallant bow and gestured toward the far side of the rock. "If you will follow me. . . ."

"No," said Chapo.

Don Augustín came a couple of paces closer. "If I wanted to harm you would I have made so open an approach? No, I would have waited until you were asleep and"—he made a series of wild hacking motions—"chopped you into bits. I am a man of peace, Señor. When you enter my house, you also enter my place of worship, and I permit no violence there. And if it is magic you fear, the only magic here is the magic of this rock."

"Are you a *brujo?*" Chapo asked.

"That's not an easy question to answer." Don Augustín tipped back his hat and scratched his head; despite his apparent age, his hair was jet black. "Perhaps I am, and perhaps I'm not. But if I am, I have never sought the wisdom—it has simply been visited upon me, and I have no real use for it."

Chapo was inclined to believe him, but he distrusted this inclination and gave no reply.

"Please, Chapo." The gringa put her hand on his arm. "He's not going to hurt us."

"Listen to her, Chapo," said Don Augustín. "She has the wisdom of innocence, and because this place is innocent, here she must be your guide."

From these words Chapo had the idea that the old man knew everything about them, and if that were the case, if he had that much power, there was no point in being cautious. "All right," he said. "But careful, man. No tricks."

"Don't worry," said Don Augustín, and grinned. "Such a big gun! I'd never risk myself against it." And beckoning them to follow, he hustled off around the rock.

Sheltered beneath an overhang on the western side of the rock was a narrow entrance that led downward into blackness. Chapo held the gun on Don Augustín and let the gringa explore the opening. After a second she called back, "Come on! It *is* beautiful!"

"I told you," said Don Augustín with a wink.

Chapo forced him to take the lead, keeping a tight grasp on his shirt, and they entered together. Cool air washed over him, and in the moment before his eyes adjusted to the dimness he was overcome with fear; he had a sense of having intruded upon some inhuman presence, and he flung his arm around Don Augustín's neck in a choke hold. But an instant later, though that sense of alienness did not diminish, he felt secure and at peace. Gradually the interior of the rock melted up from the dark. Four kerosene lanterns were set high on the walls at what Chapo took to be the cardinal points, and in their glow he saw that the center of the hollow—which was quite large, maybe seventy across and forty feet high—was occupied by a sunken pool. The water captured a sheen of the lantern light and seemed to be radiating a golden energy. Kneeling beside it, her head turned toward them, the gringa resembled a magical creature surprised in the act of drinking.

"Isn't it wonderful?" she said, and Chapo could only nod.

Ranged along the walls were stacks of books, bulging grain sacks, bundles of kindling, a pallet, and what appeared to be an altar on which rested a glowing cube. Chapo crossed the hollow to the altar and saw that the cube contained a silver rose. From moment to moment, the rose would become opaque and then solidify; it floated in brilliant eddies of its own light and was revolving slowly.

"A hologram," said the gringa, coming up beside Chapo.

"Ah," said Don Augustín. "So that's what it was."

"Was?" said the gringa.

"Everything changes into its ideal here," replied Don Augustín. "That's why I stay." He laughed. "You should have seen me before I came. I was a truly despicable sort."

The gringa pointed at the rose. "And what is it becoming?"

Don Augustín shook his head. "Who can say? I will watch and learn. But it is already a very important something." He took the gringa by the shoulders and guided her a few steps toward the pool. "You must wash, Señorita Anise."

"But . . ." The gringa seemed flustered.

"You are concerned by lack of privacy?"

"I . . . yes . . ."

"We will marvel at your beauty . . . nothing more." Don Augustín gave her a gentle push forward, then took Chapo by the arm, led him to a pair of wicker chairs set at one end of the pallet, and urged him to sit. "Would you like some whiskey?" he asked. From behind his chair he withdrew a dusty bottle and two glasses, and poured them each half full.

Chapo could not keep his eyes from straying to the gringa. Poised on the brink of the pool, naked to the waist, her nipples showing lavender against the milky skin of her breasts.

"The feminine form," said Don Augustín, raising his glass. "Even in its most unlovely incarnation, a miracle to behold."

Chapo drank, shut his eyes against the fire burning his throat, and heard a splash. He was disappointed not to have seen the rest of the gringa.

Don Augustín smiled. "Why don't you call her by name?"

Certain now that he was in the company of a *brujo,* Chapo didn't bother to ask how the old man had known this. "I don't like it."

"It strikes you as artificial?"

"Yeah, I guess."

"And yet it suits her, does it not? Contemplate the meaning of the word, Chapo. A clear intoxicating liquid with a complex and tart flavor. You really should use her name. I have faith you soon will."

Before Chapo could speak, the old man produced a vial from his pocket and held it up to catch the light. Within was a quantity of brown powder. "Perhaps you'd care to try some?" Don Augustín asked.

Chapo grew suspicious. "I ain't takin' your drugs, man. You think I'm stupid?"

"Try it, Chapo, and you will receive strengthening insights." Don Augustín opened the vial and spilled a little into Chapo's glass. "Once this was a powerful drug that wrenched the soul and left the body aching for days on end. But here it has become perfected, and before Anise returns, you will also have returned. And you will understand much that now you do not . . . though you may not realize it."

Chapo felt no compulsion to drink, and yet he did: what the old man had said seemed not coercive but reasonable. He experienced a brief anxiety and a sensation of vertigo. Then he was back to normal. Standing on the verge of an underground lake in a vast cavern, its ceiling thronged with stars. Awaiting the arrival of a golden boat that would bear him to the other side. The boat drew up to shore, rowed by men with muscular torsos and the heads of eagles. Chapo boarded and sat among them as they propelled him along in long gliding strokes. Their speech was like music, and though he didn't recognize the separate words, he understood their meaning. They were counseling him to steadfastness, to resist wrong turnings, to moral wisdom. At last the boat reached the far side, and Chapo walked out into a world of such brilliance that every shape appeared to be shifting, alternately becoming larger and smaller. It was as if he were walking through a forest of living crystals that grew and changed in a rain of light. It was so bright that he could not see the companion who had met him at the landing, nor the king whose judgment he must endure.

"That wasn't so bad, was it?" said Don Augustín.

Chapo blinked to see the rough rock walls, the wicker chairs, the dimly lit pool beside which Anise was standing, doing the buttons of her blouse. "What was that place, man?" he asked.

"Making decisions is difficult even for the informed." Don Augustín removed his straw hat and ran a hand through his young man's hair. "And of course you won't think of this during the crucial moment. Just remember, Chapo. There's no such thing as happiness. Only fools like the Americans pursue it. To use strength wisely—that's the only happiness you can know."

Anise came walking up. She inclined her head and squeezed a few last drops of water from a cable of her long blond hair. Her skin shone. She looked brand new. "I had the oddest dream just now," she said. "I mean I was awake, but I could have sworn it was a dream."

The three of them sat beneath the altar of the silver rose and ate a meal of stew and tortillas that Don Augustín had prepared over a small fire; the smoke from the fire was drawn toward the roof of the cave as if by a draft, but Chapo could see no smoke hole. Don Augustín told them stories of his days selling blankets at a roadside stall north of Oaxaca. How he had cheated the gringos. How he had met a magician who had been transformed into a donkey. How once he had become so drunk on pulque that he had crossed over into the world of drunkards, where sidewalks sometimes ran along the sides of walls and the metal of lampposts was often pliant, where reflections were doubled and shadows were prone to turn into an inky liquid and drain off downhill. Finally he made them a bed of empty grain sacks and advised them to rest. They lay close together, almost touching, gazing up at the hypnotic revolutions of the silver rose, bathed in its eerie light, and soon were fast asleep.

The glow of sunset was shining through the cave mouth when they waked. Don Augustín was nowhere to be seen, but as they headed outside they discovered two objects lying just inside the entrance and knew without having to be told that these were his gifts. For Chapo there was a knife with a blood-red handle, and for Anise there was a blouse embroidered with a silver rose. Without the least sign of self-consciousness, she shrugged out of the one Chapo had bought and put the new one on. Only after she had done buttoning it did she display embarrassment. To make her feel at ease, Chapo pretended not to have noticed. They walked around to the white jeep, climbed in, and drove west toward a horizon brushed with streaks of slate and mauve, where the evening star was now ascending.

They reached the final hiding place several hours before dawn. It was the largest of the three rocks, resembling a miniature mountain chain with separate peaks and slopes, and it faced onto the first of a range of brown hills dotted with organ-pipe cactus. Centuries of wind had carved a deep bay into the rock, and they drove the jeep all the way in and covered it with mesquite. Then they climbed to the top of the lowest peak and lay down in a shallow depression from which they could see for miles in every direction. To the east, south, and north all was still. Under the full moon, the desert was a milky white plain flecked by a thousand shadows. But to the west among the hills there showed an intermittent green glow. Watching it flicker and vanish made the back of Chapo's neck prickle.

Anise edged closer to him. "What could it be?"

"That's where we gonna get gas."

"The village?" She looked horrified.

"San Juan de la Fiebra. They a buncha crazy fuckers. Some gringo come a few years back and give 'em Stateside drugs. All kinda extreme shit. And he preached this weird religion . . . like it's got Jesus, but other gods, too. You gotta watch your ass 'round there."

She stared out at the hills, her eyes narrowing as if focusing in on something he couldn't see. "We'll be all right," she said flatly. "Ever since we met Don Augustín, I've known that."

Chapo grunted. "You can't trust how *brujos* make you feel."

"It's hard to believe that's what he was."

"What else?"

She thought about it. "I don't know."

Pale clouds were drifting across the stars in the west, and Chapo wondered if the clouds were above the sea. He lay flat on his stomach, watching them cruise.

"What are you gonna do after we get to Huayacuatla, Chapo?"

"Head on back, probably."

She didn't say anything, but after a couple of seconds she ran her hand along the back of his neck. The touch made him shiver. He didn't look up.

"Chapo?" She whispered it, her voice burred.

He had to look at her, then. She was smiling just enough to show a sliver of teeth as white as the desert, and the centers of her all-colored eyes were pricked with moonlight, and her golden hair was outlined in stars. He felt he was falling up toward her.

"Yeah, I . . ."

"I want you," she said.

Nobody had ever said it that way to him. Let's fuck, maybe. Let's go upstairs, or Let's see what you got, Chapo. Never "I want you." He almost didn't know what it meant, and maybe it didn't mean what he thought. He wasn't sure how to answer. "Why?" he said, and felt foolish. Acting like it was his first time. But he *couldn't* understand why. Just because he'd been helping her? That was a good reason, he guessed. But he hadn't thought it would be her reason.

She took his hand and laid it on the silver rose, on the soft weights beneath. The nipple hardened against his palm. He closed his fingers around her breast, squeezing it, and she arched her back, pressing against his hand. She let out a hissing breath. He moved his other hand beneath the blouse, then moved both hands over her breasts, cupping them, rubbing the aureoles with the balls of his thumbs, knowing their shapes. She unbuttoned the blouse, tossed it aside. It floated away like a silver wing. Veiled in her hair, he kissed the milky flesh. So much warmth, so much sweetness. He lost track of where his hands were, what his lips were doing. It was all warmth, all sweetness, and she was whispering his name, saying she wanted him, wanted him now.

Going into her was like falling into a good dream, and it *was* different with her. . . . So different he couldn't say exactly how. He worried about her back on the stone, about hurting her. But soon he stopped worrying, and what he felt at the end was maybe a little stronger, a little more heat, but really was pretty much like all the other times, except for how happy he was at what *she* felt, at the way her body stiffened, her nails pricking him deep, holding him tight and still, as if were he to move, she'd break into pieces.

Afterward, becoming aware again of the cold desert wind, they got under the blanket, and Anise began talking excitedly, saying she loved him, saying he couldn't go back to the Crust, he should return to LA with her and go to school, and she loved him, and her father would help them get started, and Oh, Chapo, how much I love you, and he didn't know what to say. He had thought he'd known her before they made love, but though now he felt intimate with her, she also seemed a stranger, someone new. He realized he hadn't known her, that she had been in his eyes an emblem of foreign territory, of wealth and mysterious cities, a border he had finally crossed. Now she was no longer an emblem but real, and he was confused. Who was she? He turned on his side, pushed her gently onto her back and looked down at her, trying to find her inside her eyes, trying to understand what he felt.

"Chapo," she said, reaching up to him.

He laid a finger to her lips and studied her face.

"What are you doing?" she asked.

"Shh!"

"I know," she said after a while, "I know there's things you want to tell me, but you can't find the words."

He nodded.

"You'll find them," she said. "You will! But you have to come back with me . . . to LA."

She started talking again, but slower, her words as gentle as an easy rain, and everything she said clarified something behind her eyes, something he felt. He could see her strength, her goodness, and his recognition of those qualities seemed to make what he felt equally good and strong . . . though he couldn't put a name to his feelings. She told him about her city, the towers, the displays of light in the sky, the exotic pleasures and the roar of fifteen million souls. What she said began to make sense. He would go to LA, he would understand everything. And in that country of light, wealth would be a power, a power he could use in ways that the wealthy Americans had forgotten. He saw this was to be his destiny.

The sky paled to lavender, the stars thinned and shone gold, and they made love once again. They made love into the morning, into the blazing heat, and though he was bone-weary, Chapo could not stop making love to her. It was too beautiful to stop, too important a connection to break. And when at last they did fall asleep, they were still joined, still tangled like a knot of brown-and-white thread. In Chapo's dream he thought they were melting, becoming stone, and in the days to come they would be mistaken by other lovers who had climbed this high for a vaguely human shape produced from the rock by a miracle of wind and weather.

At dusk they drove into the hills and stopped on a rise above the village of San Juan de la Fiebra. At that distance it looked to be a peaceful place of white houses with red tile roofs and lights dancing in the windows. Chapo gave his pistol to Anise and told her to hide among the cactus until he returned. She begged him to take care, kissing him with such passion that when he drove away, he felt he was off on a noble mission and not simply going to find gas.

Though the rise was only a few hundred feet above San Juan de la Fiebra, the road wound through the hills, and it took Chapo half an hour to reach the village. Entering it, he passed the remains of an enormous bonfire, itself the size of a small hill, from which projected weird charred shapes that reminded him of giant insect legs, and he assumed this had been the source of the green glow. On the walls of the houses were painted horned goats and bearded corpses and creatures half fly and half man, all done in drips and spatters of red paint, making it seem they'd been rendered in a murder victim's blood. People dressed like campesinos in white cotton and straw hats came into the streets on hearing his engine. They stood in the street ahead of him, and he was forced to weave in and out among them, obscuring them in the wake of his dust. They were mostly wiry people of Indian stock, but he spotted a few with dark skin and blue eyes and a gringo cast to their features; they said nothing, only tracked him with their stares. A cold patch formed between his shoulder blades, and he had trouble swallowing.

At the far end of the village stood a Mexalina station, also adorned with grisly murals, its green pumps decorated like evil Christmas trees with garlands of cactus buds and wreaths of whitish leaves. As he approached, an amplified voice began speaking from somewhere. "GUARDIANS, AWAKE! FOR IN THE TIME OF THE FURY,THOU MUST BE EVER VIGILANT. BEWARE THE STRANGER WHO BEARS THE SEEDS OF

JOY IN HIS HEART, FOR FROM HIS JOY MAY SPROUT THE FRUITS OF COR-
RUPTION."

Chapo pulled up to the pumps and cut the engine. A gaunt man
wearing a grease-stained coverall, with coppery skin and gray streaks
in his hair, ambled toward him from the door. Chapo ordered ten
gallons, having to shout to make himself heard over the voice, which
continued its biblical admonitions; it was so loud, he could scarcely
think. Pretending to be at ease, unconcerned, he got out of the jeep
and went over to the Coke machine. Fed in coins. He uncapped the
frosty bottle and took a deep drink. Looked back along the street.
None of the people had moved. They were all gazing toward the station. The lights from the windows were unbelievably bright, spraying golden rays into the streets, as if each house contained a sun, and
above the crown of the hill where Anise was hiding, the stars were
showing this same golden color against the black sky.

". . . SHOW HIM THE MERCY OF MAD JESUS GONE SCREAMING FROM
THE TOMB, HIS NAILS TIPPED WITH BLOOD, HIS THOUGHTS LIKE
KNIVES . . ."

Chapo glanced into the window of the station. And froze. Sitting
on the counter beside the cash register was a hologram identical to
the one belonging to Don Augustín: a silver rose revolving in its own
glow. He didn't know what to make of it, whether it was a bad sign
or good.

". . . HARROW HIM, TEST HIM, FOR ONLY THUS WILL YOU KNOW
HIM . . ."

The voice was switched off. Turning, Chapo saw that six men on
motorcycles were ranged along the street facing the station. Their rides
were sleek and finished in black enamel that gleamed like chitin; they
wore red helmets, and their headlights were green and faceted like
insect eyes. Pistols at their sides. The attendant holstered the pump
in its socket and came over. Chapo fumbled for his wallet. But the
attendant held up his hand to ward off payment. "No charge, Señor,"
he said, and smiled. His incisors were rimmed with gold, and a red
stone like a drop of blood was set into one of the front teeth.

"It's all right," said Chapo. "I want to pay."

The attendant just kept smiling.

One of the motorcyclists revved his engine and glided to within
a few feet of Chapo. "Where are you going?" he asked.

Chapo couldn't see his face behind the black plastic of the helmet.
"To Huayacuatla," he said.

"And from where do you come?"

"The Crust."

The man shouted this information to the other motorcyclists, and they absorbed it without reaction. He turned back to Chapo. Lifted his visor and peered at Chapo. His face was bronzed and hawkish, and his eyes were balled and white like a statue's eyes, with no irises or pupils. Beneath his left ear, tracing the jawline, was a thin scar. Chapo's legs felt weak and boneless, and gooseflesh fanned across his shoulders.

"Are you a true believer?" the man asked.

Despite those eyes, Chapo knew the man could somehow perceive him, and he did not think he could successfully lie. "In what should I believe?"

"In the mysteries and the drugs." The man held up a vial of brown powder that dangled from a chain around his neck, and Chapo recognized it to be the drug he'd taken in the cave. "In the power of uncreated things, in the light bred from the final darkness."

"I know the drug," said Chapo. "But I don't understand these other things."

The man leaned toward him over his handlebars. "You are no seeker," he said, making it sound like an accusation.

Chapo shrugged. "I gotta be goin', man."

The man settled back on his seat. "Go, then."

As he walked back to the jeep, Chapo could sense the man's white eyes driving nails into his back. He climbed in, switched on the ignition. The needle on the gas gauge stabilized at almost three-quarters full. At least that much was all right. He gunned the engine. Then he pulled away from the pumps, swung the jeep into a U-turn, and passed behind the five motorcyclists. They didn't bother to turn and watch him.

Once again he had to weave in and out among the bystanders. But this time they paid him no mind. They gazed intently toward the station as if awaiting instructions. At the site of the bonfire, people were piling cactus limbs onto the charred heap, and Chapo wondered if that was how they got it to burn a funny color, if the cactus limbs yielded a green essence. He listened for the sound of motorcycle engines as he drove into the hills, and heard nothing. Yet he didn't feel right. How could you feel right in a place where blind men could see?

He stopped on the crest of the rise, and Anise came scrambling up from a gully. "Did you get it?" she asked breathlessly, climbing in.

"Yeah," he said, and was about to add that there might be trouble, when a shot rang out. Pinged off the hood. More shots. He pushed Anise out of the jeep and hauled her back down into the gully, behind a boulder. Grabbed the pistol from her and trained it on the slopes. The moon was just up, and in its light the ranks of cacti looked unreal: an alien army with shadowy upraised arms. Then he heard the motorcycles. They were buzzing, swarming nearby. He glanced right. Left. That way the gully gave out into a pitch of huge boulders. Gray shapes. Like frozen waves, melted statues. Motorcycles would never be able to penetrate them, at least not with any speed. Taking Anise's hand, he moved in a crouch along the gully.

Raspy whine of an engine winding out, and one of the motorcycles jumped the gully. Fire lanced down from a shadow hand, and Chapo returned the fire. Knew he'd missed.

"Who are they?" Anise clutched at his arm.

"I don't know."

He could still hear the engines buzzing as they entered the field of broken boulders, but he couldn't see any of them. Like spirits, invisible when you turned your eye on them, reappearing when you looked away. He crawled through the boulders until he found one with a cleft that offered a clear field of fire up and down slope. He drew a deep breath. Fear was stamped on Anise's face, and he couldn't think of anything to ease her. The silver rose on her chest heaved. Fuckin' *brujo!*

Chapo checked his clip. Seven left. Seven bullets for six riders. He dug the red knife from his pocket, handed it to Anise. For a split second, he thought she was going to fling it down. But then she flicked open the blade and set herself. Ready to fight. Chapo felt proud of her.

"Listen!" she said.

The engines had stopped.

He peeked out over the boulder. Spotted a couple of shadows edging toward them down slope. Maybe this wasn't such a great place to make a stand. He looked behind them. Adrenaline was pumping his heart, and his eyes were strained so wide, it seemed he could see every weed and pebble. The boulder field declined into the deep shadow of the next hill. Darkness like black gas. What the hell! There might be a cave. A trail. Something. He led the way through the rocks, keeping in a crouch. The amplified voice began to echo up from the village, the words unintelligible, booming out its nonsense. Loud enough that he couldn't hear the scrape of a boot, the rattle of a kicked pebble. The bastards might have planned it!

Halfway across the field, he began to feel a presence nearby. It was a trustworthy feeling, a Crust feeling. Tuning his senses higher.

But it didn't help.

As they passed between two of the larger boulders, a rider jumped him. Knocked him flat. Chapo lost his grip on the automatic. The rider pinned him with his knees, smashed a gloved fist into his chin, dazing him. Chapo could see his vague reflection in the visor above him. Then the rider leaped up, a red knife sprouting from his shoulder, and backhanded Anise to the ground. Chapo scrabbled for the automatic, found it. Squeezed off a round just as the rider dived at him. The bullet twisted the rider in midair, and he landed facedown beside Chapo. Muffled wet sounds came from inside the helmet.

Chapo came to his knees. A serpent of blood trickled from the corner of Anise's mouth, black-looking. He started to stand, but something cold touched the back of his head, and a hollow voice told him to put down the gun. Three more riders stepped from behind stones and stood over Anise. Chapo dropped his eyes. Studied the weeds springing up by his knees, the pattern of pebbles. He had been waiting for this moment all his life, and now it was here, he almost welcomed it.

Anise was speaking, but Chapo was too gone into his preparation for death to hear the words. He tried to think about something good. That's what Moro had told him before they had crossed to Stateside. "If you feel it comin', man," Moro had said, "think 'bout somethin' good. 'Cause then if you live forever, maybe you go with that good thing. And if you don't"—Moro had grinned—"what the fuck's the difference?" Chapo called up memories of the red glow, the border. Wild nights. None of it seemed good. His only good thought was that one time with Anise, and that was too much the reason for his dying to give him the peace he needed.

The last rider emerged from behind a boulder and looked down at Chapo. No way to tell because they were all dressed alike, all hidden behind their visors, but Chapo figured him for the one he'd talked to back at the Mexalina station. The rider nodded, as if seeing exactly what he'd expected. He turned and went a step toward Anise. Two of the men had hauled her to her feet and were gripping her arms. Their leader stopped dead and flipped up his visor. Lifted his chained vial, tapped a little powder onto his tongue. Gazed at her chest. From where Chapo was kneeling, he could see the rider's warrior profile. One white eye bright as new marble, set in a stern bronze mask. The rider removed his helmet. His black hair feathered in the breeze. He laid his hand flat against the silver rose on Anise's breast. She squirmed, and the two men holding her applied pressure, making her cry out. The rider tipped his head to the sky and stood absolutely still. After a second, his hand began to tremble. He jerked it away, said something in Indian to the two men. They let go of Anise.

She hesitated a moment. Then she scuttled to Chapo's side and kneeled beside him, throwing an arm around his shoulder. The cold thing at the back of Chapo's head went away. Blond hair curtained his eyes, and he brushed it aside. The rider walked over, holding his helmet under his arm like a knight after a tournament; the rest gathered behind him. He gestured to the body, and two of the others picked the dead man up, propping him erect between them. His knees were buckled, his chest a mire of blood and charred fabric. Yet Chapo had a funny notion that he wasn't dead. Not dead forever, anyhow. If blind men could see in San Juan de la Fiebra, maybe the dead could be reclaimed. The careful way they were treating the body supported that notion.

"Who are you?" asked the rider.

Chapo was still halfway to death. He didn't have an answer.

"I'm an American," said Anise tremulously, as if citizenship were at the core of her being.

One of the men laughed. "They don't know who they are."

"Who are you?" the rider repeated.

Chapo got slowly to his feet, feeling drained. He looked into the rider's white eyes. Depthless glowing surfaces like the desert. "Tell me why it's important," he said.

"It's not important," said the rider. "I merely wish to know."

"I'm Chapo, and she's Anise."

Once again there was laughter, and the rider said, "These are only your names. Perhaps you *don't* know who you are."

"Well, who are you?" Anise shrilled. "Just who the hell do you think you are to go. . . ." She broke off, cowed by the rider's stare.

"I am a Guardian of San Juan de la Fiebra," he said. "I am the madness of Christ, and the innocence of Moloch. I follow the northern teachings, and I have borne witness to the man in the desert . . . as have you, apparently." He indicated Anise's blouse.

"Don Augustín?" Anise looked at Chapo, then back at the rider. "Is that who you mean?"

"By his sign you may pass," said the rider. "But be warned. Do not return to San Juan de la Fiebra until you have learned who you are.''

He signaled the others, and carrying their dead companion, they headed up the slope, becoming lost among the shadows of the boulder field.

Anise slumped down, leaning against Chapo. "You see?" she said. "He did help us. I *knew* he did."

Chapo watched the slope, wanting to make sure the riders had gone. "The *brujo?*"

"Uh-huh."

"Maybe, maybe not."

The *brujo's* red knife lay on the ground. Chapo wiped the blade clean on his trousers, folded it, and slipped it into his pocket.

"How can you say that?" asked Anise.

"I told you . . . you can't trust *brujos*. The drug he gave me, the dream you had. All this might still be part of that. Could be none of it happened, or just a little of it happened, and this"—he tapped his forehead—"this did the rest."

"Why would you think that?" She stroked his hair, concern on her face.

"You believe a blind man can see? Shit! That coulda been what'cha call a hallucination."

"No it wasn't!"

"You believe in magic?"

"I don't know if I do or not. But that wasn't magic."

"What was it, then?"

"Little cameras in his eyes, wired to the optic nerves. Didn't you see his scar?" She touched Chapo's cheek beneath his left ear. "That's where they put the power source. I've seen the same thing a hundred times."

"You sure?"

"Of course." She took him by the shoulders. "Don't you start thinking none of this is real, Chapo." She kissed him, and like a slow magic, the kiss gradually brought him all the way back to life. Gold flecks seemed to have surfaced in her eyes, and everything about her seemed to have been refined. "There," she said, smiling. "Is that what you call a hallucination?"

"No," said Chapo, dazzled.

"It's all been real," she said. "That's how I know we're supposed to be together . . . because it's been so strong."

Chapo went along with her, but in his heart he wasn't so sure. Blind men with cameras in their eyes . . . That didn't sound real to him.

From a hilltop above the Pacific, Huayacuatla looked like Paradise. White sand fringed by a tame jungle of orchids and sapodilla, aguacate and sabal palms. The trunks of the palms were bowed toward the sea, and a westerly breeze blew their fronds back from it. Half-hidden among the vegetation were villas and hotels of all colors. Pastel blues and yellows and pinks. Late afternoon sun kindled diamond fires out on the sea. As they drove into the town, music came to their ears. Soft, sweet music that seemed to be part of the wind and not issuing from a mechanical source. Laughter came from behind the high walls of the hotels, and even the policemen smiled.

They drove onto the grounds of the biggest hotel beneath a blue stucco arch with ironwork letters that spelled CASA DE MILAGROS. The young man who parked their jeep wore a white jacket and creased blue trousers and shiny shoes, and looked a lot like Chapo. He gave Chapo a suspicious glance, smiled at Anise, and told them they could find the manager's office beyond the swimming pool. They walked leisurely along a flagstone path past bungalows with macaws tethered to perches beside the door. Bright things darted high in the branches of fig and mango trees. Chapo thought they were birds, but then one swooped close, circling him, and he saw it was a bright blue ball with stylized yellow wings and no head. Alarmed, he swatted at it. The thing let out a warbling squeal and broke into dozens of cartoon music notes that played a melody as they faded. Not wanting to appear unsophisticated, Chapo didn't ask what it was. The things kept swooping at him, giving him starts. He smiled and pretended he'd seen them many times before.

The pool was an Olympic-sized emerald lozenge filled with swimmers, and people were sitting beneath striped umbrellas around it. One woman whose face looked about sixty years old had the body of a teenager; her hair changed color as she talked, shifting from vivid green to crimson to a striped design of black and yellow. Something silver and saucer-shaped sailed through the air and landed at Chapo's feet; tiny silver animals swarmed off it, leaped into the pool, and vanished. Two kids ran over. One snatched the saucer up and sailed it across the pool toward another kid. A withered white-haired man was talking rapidly to three women, his words materializing in pale smoke above his head; when he stopped for breath, the smoke strung out into little dots, giving visible expression to his pause. Chapo felt lost. There were a hundred things going on that he didn't understand. He remembered Don Augustín's world of drunkards, and had the idea that he had stumbled into a sillier version of it.

In the manager's office, Anise placed a call to her father in the States. But he was on the border, and would be out of touch until late that night. No problem, said the manager. He'd arrange a couple of rooms and. . . .

"One room will do," said Anise. "And if you could pick up some clean clothes . . . for both of us."

The manager had difficulty repressing a look of disapproval, but said it would be his pleasure.

Two hours later, dressed in fine clothes, they ate dinner in the hotel restaurant: a dimly lit room with heavy silver and candelabras and linen tablecloths. White birds of pure light winged silently above their heads. Music seemed to be everywhere, even in the conversations of the people dining nearby. In the center of the room was a pit from which a sculpture made of fire leaped and crackled, shaping itself into image after image. Jaguar, swan, serpent, and a hundred more. The waiters went about their work as silently as the birds of light, depositing new dishes and bottles of wine. Chapo was astonished, delighted. He had never seen such beauty, never tasted such food. Though he had been nervous upon entering the restaurant, he soon felt at home. They drank and laughed, laughed and drank, talking of the things they would do in LA. With their dessert, the waiter brought a note for Anise; it said her father would arrive the next morning.

"You'll like him," she told Chapo. "He's different from these people. Strong like you."

Dizzy with the wine, Chapo believed her. Disbelief was not in him. Through the silver branches of the candelabra, she seemed to sparkle. Even the things she said seemed to leave a sparkle in the air, and he was coming to think that this sparkle was emblematic of the real world.

They finished eating, and as he stood Chapo knocked over a bottle of wine. A rich red stain spread over the tablecloth. Their waiter mopped at the stain, assuring him that it was no trouble, his tone apologetic. But the other diners stared and laughed behind their hands. Chapo was frozen by those stares, feeling as if he had been caught at something.

"Don't pay any attention to them," Anise said, pulling him away.

In the central pit a fiery eagle appeared to be looking straight at Chapo, regarding him with disfavor.

Making love that night was not as good for Chapo as it had been on the desert. The room was so large, so incomprehensible in its luxury. Everything vanished into the walls at the push of a button. Punch room service, and the image of a beautiful woman sprang out of nowhere to take your order. If you touched an ordinary surface, music would play or walls would turn into windows or video screens. And as he made love to Anise, he couldn't escape the feeling that any moment the wrong surface would be touched and the room would fold in upon them and he, too, would vanish or be transformed.

He waked around three o'clock, needing to go to the bathroom. But he couldn't find the button that made the toilet appear. Finally, not wanting to wake Anise and show what an idiot he was, he went out into the hall and urinated in a potted plant. A couple walked past the instant he had done zipping up, and he pretended to be examining the leaves. He returned to the room and lay down beside Anise. She was beautiful in the half-light, with the silken coverlet slipped down to her waist. Her breasts had the same glistening smoothness as the material, and her face had the serenity of a goddess. She would help him, he thought. She would teach him how to move in her brilliant world. But the thought did not comfort him, and he was unable to get back to sleep.

The next morning, waiting for her father, Chapo sat on the edge of a chair, his hands clasped in his lap. He sat very still as if posing for a photograph. No thoughts occurred to him. The inside of his head might have been poured full of cement. Anise was busy telephoning friends in the States, and didn't notice his silence.

Suddenly the door burst open, and a lean sunburned man with blond hair strode in. He didn't seem old enough to be Anise's father, but she ran to him and hugged him, talking a mile a minute. Chapo sat without moving. Anise pulled back from her father, and said, "Daddy, I want you to meet someone."

The man looked at Chapo and smiled thinly. "Oh, yeah." Keeping an arm around Anise, he reached into his jacket pocket and extracted a banded stack of bills. Held them out. "Here y'are, boy. Twenty-five thousand . . . just like advertised." His stare locked onto Chapo's, and in that exchange, in his pose, was a world of information. *This is mine,* said the arm around Anise. *This is yours,* said the hand holding the bills. *And that's all you're getting,* said the stare. Chapo wasn't afraid of him. But he understood something else from the man's attitude. He couldn't have put that sense of ultimate distance and difference into words, and maybe the man couldn't have done so, either. Yet they both were aware of it.

"No, Daddy," said Anise. "That's not how it is. He and I . . ."

Chapo could barely hear her. She was already receding from him, crossing the border into her own land. He got up and walked over to them and took the money. It had a good weight.

"Chapo!" Amazement, shock.

He eased past them into the hall. She cried out again, but then the door slammed shut, shearing off her voice.

The young man who brought the jeep from the parking lot extended his hand for a tip. Chapo cursed him and sped out beneath the blue arch. He sat for a moment beyond the arch, letting the engine idle, letting the warm sun soak into him. He felt empty, but the feeling was clean. A freedom from wanting, from dreams too sweet to digest. He had a final look around at Paradise. It wasn't so goddamn much! It was frail. One lapse in security, and the monkeys would come swinging back to retake the jungle, and the Devil would bask by the emerald pool, his laughter echoing through the ruins. One shot of heavy weather, and you wouldn't be able to tell it from the Crust. That was the Crust's strength: it was already down to the bone. Chapo blew out a long sighing breath, wishing he could get rid of memories as easily as bad air. Then he threw the jeep into gear and headed north along the coast, taking the legal roads home.

Back in the Crust, back in the cellar among the candles and shadows. Chapo hid the money a dozen places, two thousand dollars in each. He held back the last thousand. He'd take it and have himself a night. Spend it at La Manzanita. They had the best girls there. Young girls fresh from in the villages, still full of life, still believing the Crust was everything you could hope for. Maybe he'd have twenty-five such nights. What else could he do with the money? A bar, a business? He couldn't picture himself growing old and fat behind a counter. No, he'd have twenty-five nights to remind him of Anise. To light a thought like a blond candle, set it burning in the blackness of his skull. He wondered what had been between them. Love? Yeah, a little. But he thought it had more to do with innocence. Hers *and* his. Paring hers down, shoring his up. There was even more to it, though. You could never figure anything out, never say anything. The second you did, it became a lie, the truth shrunk to fit your words. He ran his thumb across the bills. They felt cool and slick, like strange skins. Twenty-four thousand. What if some opportunity came up, some big score?

Well, he'd have the one night, anyway.

Find a slim brown girl who'd fuck him mean and burn out the last sugars of Huayacuatla.

He swallowed one upper, then did another.

Out in the blood-red light, the wild laughter and crazy music, he walked briskly down Avenida Juárez toward the border. Every rut brimmed with shadow. In a house with black curtains a baby was screaming. Even with those curtains, crimson light penetrated and made it hard to sleep, and even when you slept, the light brought dreams that scared you awake. But the dreams made you strong, and it would be a strong baby, strong enough to dream about crossing that light.

The side wall of La Manzanita was six feet from the border. Before going in, Chapo stood an arm's length away, facing the shimmering redness. He'd seen guys jump into it, others just stroll on through. Drunks, suicides, men who believed the border was the door to a kind of afterlife. He'd had the urge himself to take that stroll. But no more. He felt satisfaction in being able to face it and not know that urge. Its hum and sizzle no longer an allure, no longer a humiliation, a weakness. Borders were everywhere, and once you recognized that, you could be strong in spite of them . . . or because of them. This unreal fire might be the least of borders. That much he'd learned on the trip to Huayacuatla, that much was true enough to say and not diminish. And having this one powerful truth was more important than having the money or Anise. It gave him a new purchase, a new perspective. He thought if he kept staring into the red glow, he would see the evolution of that truth.

He took out the *brujo*'s knife, its enamel the same color as the border. Considered tossing it through. Magic, huh? Would it penetrate, would its flight curve around buildings and find a secret target? After a moment, he decided to hang on to it.

Save it for some special bad heart.

"Chapo!"

Rafael was coming toward him, knife in hand. His jaw still bruised from where Chapo had nailed him with the shopping bag. He dropped into a crouch, cut lazy crescents in the air.

No easy way out this time.

Chapo tried to flick the red knife open, but the blade stuck.

*Brujo*s! Chapo silently cursed Don Augustín.

They circled each other, shoes hissing in the dirt, breath ragged. All the other sounds went away.

In the first thirty seconds Chapo took a slice on his left arm. It wasn't serious, it focused him. He sucked up the pain and studied Rafael's moves. Rafael grinned to see the blood.

Keep grinnin', asshole, Chapo said to himself.

He shook his guard arm, pretending it was bothering him.

Rafael went for the opening.

Chapo sidestepped the lunge, tripped Rafael, and sent him slamming into the wall of La Manzanita. As he slumped down, the knife slipping from his fingers, Chapo grabbed him in a choke hold. Lugged him toward the border. Held him up inches away. He hadn't been angry during the fight, but now he was almost sick with anger.

Rafael was too close to the red glow to want to struggle. He twisted his head, trying to see Chapo. Even the sweat beading his forehead shone red. Dull chubby face clenched in fear. But he wasn't going to beg. Code of the Crust. He'd die stupid and macho.

That was what drained off Chapo's anger, the recognition of his own stupidity, of a poverty that left you only with a fool's pride and a talent for dying. He dragged Rafael away from the border and let him fall. Rafael couldn't believe it. He stared at Chapo, uncomprehending.

To use strength wisely—that's the only happiness you can know.

Chapo could have sworn that he heard Don Augustín's voice speaking those words, and realized that if the knife had opened, he would never have come to this moment. The *brujo* might have done him a favor. He studied Rafael. "Wanna go to La Manzanita?" he asked.

"La Manzanita?" Rafael blinked, confused.

"Yeah, I did some business last week. Gonna celebrate."

"You want me to go with you?" Rafael was incredulous.

"Yeah, sure."

"Why?" Rafael said after a pause, suspicious. "Why you doin' this?"

" 'Cause this"—Chapo flourished his knife—"it's stupid. Why we gotta do it? What's the point?"

"You slugged me, man!"

Chapo displayed his bleeding arm. "We're even, okay?"

Rafael wasn't satisfied. "What kinda business give you the coin for La Manzanita?"

"Maybe I'll tell you sometime, maybe we'll do some business."

That appeared to stun Rafael. Nobody did business with him. He was too slow-witted to be slick. But, Chapo thought, maybe he could be loyal. Maybe he was born to be loyal, and no one had ever offered him a chance. It rang true. And loyalty could make up for a lot. He kicked Rafael's knife over to him. "Let's do it," he said.

Rafael picked up the knife. There was a moment. It showed in his eyes, glowing red like a little border. But the moment passed. "Okay," he said, pocketing the knife. He came to his feet, smiling. The smile was genuine, a signal as open and honest as a dog wagging its tail. Chapo wasn't ready to buy it . . . not all the way. But he did buy the concept that had produced it, and he was beginning to enjoy the feeling of control.

"La Manzanita!" said Rafael, looking at the building. "Man, I hear they got women in there can tie a knot in it, y'know. Man!"

"Let's find out," said Chapo.

"You go there a lot?" Rafael asked.

"Naw, man. Too much make you crazy . . . be bad for doin' business."

Rafael nodded sagely, like, Oh, yeah, he knew all about that.

Chapo clapped him on the back, tried to steer him toward the door; but Rafael balked, suspicion visible in his face.

"What's wrong?" Chapo asked.

"This don't make no sense, man," said Rafael.

"What you think . . . I'm gonna pay somebody to screw you to death?"

Rafael didn't respond to the joke, engaging Chapo's eyes soberly.

"Look," said Chapo. "Just 'cause we ain't killin' each other don't mean it don't make sense. You got anything better goin'? I mean, don't tell me you ain't taken chances for a lot less reward."

Rafael's hand snaked into the pocket where he kept his knife.

All Chapo's instincts cried out for him to open Rafael up for the flies; but he realized he had come to the end of those tactics. They brought you temporary survival, and that had always been enough for him. But now he wanted . . . he wasn't sure exactly what. Power for a start, and then something more. This hassle with Rafael was a test he had to pass.

"Hey," he said, throwing an arm around Rafael's shoulder. "You wanna cut me, or you wanna lie down on silk? You wanna watch me bleed, or you wanna hear a sugar voice sayin', 'Oh, Rafael! You so fine!' C'mon, man! We'll have a good time tonight, and then tomor-

row we can get back to killin' each other. Or maybe not. Maybe we'll
catch fire inside, maybe we'll find out we can burn together.''

Rafael's muscles relaxed, and he giggled, getting behind Chapo's
rap. "Yeah," he said. "Maybe we cross the border, cut some gringos.''

"Shit!" said Chapo. "We gonna do more'n that, man.'' He spat
at the border, and for a second he believed his spit would dissolve
the fire instead of merely sizzling and vanishing, revealing a fabulous
unknown America, a place of golden women with jeweled eyes and
occult powers. "We gonna raid the secret tower, bring back the magic
dagger. Know what I'm talkin' 'bout?''

"Yeah!" said Rafael gleefully, jittering with excitement. "Yeah!''

"We gonna dance on the moon, we gonna break the silver chains
and loose the final beast.''

From behind them came a shriek, curses. An old man dressed in
the cotton trousers and shirt of a campesino was lunging toward the
border, trying to hurl himself into it, while an old woman clung to
him, dragging him back. A crowd was gathering, hemming them in
against the shimmering curtain of energy. They laughed, talked,
pointed. The old woman called on God and the Virgin for help, her
cries as shrill as those of a frightened bird.

"Shit!" said Rafael, and spat. "I hate that weak shit, man! People
ain't got the strength to deal, they might as well be dead, y'know.''

Chapo started to say he had come to realize that what was usually
considered strength sometimes was a weakness and vice versa; but on
second thought, he decided it would be better for Rafael to remain
ignorant of subtleties such as this. They were not friends, after all,
only partners in crime. "Yeah," he said, pushing Rafael toward the
entrance of the club. "Fuck 'em! We ain't got to worry 'bout bein'
weak, right?''

Laughter and soft music issued from the door of La Manzanita.
White light veiled the threshold. Together, Chapo and Rafael crossed
over.

THE SCALEHUNTER'S BEAUTIFUL DAUGHTER

I

Not long after the Christlight of the world's first morning faded, when birds still flew to heaven and back, and even the wickedest things shone like saints, so pure was their portion of evil, there was a village by the name of Hangtown that clung to the back of the dragon Griaule, a vast mile-long beast who had been struck immobile yet not lifeless by a wizard's spell, and who ruled over the Carbonales Valley, controlling in every detail the lives of the inhabitants, making known his will by the ineffable radiations emanating from the cold tonnage of his brain. From shoulder to tail, the greater part of Griaule was covered with earth and trees and grass, from some perspectives appearing to be an element of the landscape, another hill among those that ringed the valley; except for sections cleared by the scalehunters, only a portion of his right side to the haunch, and his neck and head, remained visible, and the head had sunk to the ground, its massive jaws halfway open, itself nearly as high as the crests of the surrounding hills. Situated almost eight hundred feet above the valley floor and directly behind the frontoparietal plate, which overhung the place like a mossy cliff, the village consisted of several dozen shacks with shingled roofs and walls of weathered planking, and bordered a lake fed by a stream that ran down onto Griaule's back from an adjoining hill; it was hemmed in against the shore by thickets of chokecherry, stands of stunted oak and hawthorns, and but for the haunted feeling that pervaded the air, a vibrant stillness similar to the atmosphere of an old ruin, to someone standing beside the lake it would seem he was looking out upon an ordinary country settlement, one a touch less neatly ordered than most, littered as it was with the bones and entrails of skizzers and flakes and other parasites that infested the dragon, but nonetheless ordinary in the lassitude that governed it, and the shabby dress and hostile attitudes of its citizenry.

Many of the inhabitants of the village were scalehunters, men and women who scavenged under Griaule's earth-encrusted wings and elsewhere on his body, searching for scales that were cracked and broken, chipping off fragments and selling these in Port Chantay, where they were valued for their medicinal properties. They were well paid for their efforts, but were treated as pariahs by the people of the valley, who rarely ventured onto the dragon, and their lives were short and fraught with unhappy incident, a circumstance they attributed to the effects of Griaule's displeasure at their presence. Indeed, his displeasure was a constant preoccupation, and they spent much of their earnings on charms that they believed would ward off its evil influence. Some wore bits of scale around their necks, hoping that this homage would communicate to Griaule the high regard in which they held him, and perhaps the most extreme incidence of this way of thinking was embodied by the nurture given by the widower Riall to his daughter Catherine. On the day of her birth, also the day of his wife's death, he dug down beneath the floor of his shack until he reached Griaule's back, laying bare a patch of golden scale some six feet long and five feet wide, and from that day forth for the next eighteen years he forced her to sleep upon the scale, hoping that the dragon's essence would seep into her and so she would be protected against his wrath. Catherine complained at first about this isolation, but she came to enjoy the dreams that visited her, dreams of flying, of otherworldly climes (according to legend, dragons were native to another universe to which they traveled by flying into the sun); lying there sometimes, looking up through the plank-shored tunnel her father had dug, she would feel that she was not resting on a solid surface but was receding from the earth, falling into a golden distance.

Riall may or may not have achieved his desired end; but it was evident to the people of Hangtown that propinquity to the scale had left its mark on Catherine, for while Riall was short and swarthy (as his wife had also been), physically unprepossessing in every respect, his daughter had grown into a beautiful young woman, long-limbed and slim, with fine golden hair and lovely skin and a face of unsurpassed delicacy, seeming a lapidary creation with its voluptuous mouth and sharp cheekbones and large, eloquent eyes, whose irises were so dark that they could be distinguished from the pupils only under the strongest of lights.

Not alone in her beauty did she appear cut from different cloth from her parents; neither did she share their gloomy spirit and cautious approach to life. From earliest childhood she went without fear to every quarter of the dragon's surface, even into the darkness under the wing joints where few scalehunters dared go; she believed she had been immunized against ordinary dangers by her father's tactics, and she felt there was a bond between herself and the dragon, that her dreams and good looks were emblems of both a magical relationship and consequential destiny, and this feeling of invulnerability—along with the confidence instilled by her beauty—gave rise to a certain egocentricity and shallowness of character. She was often disdainful, careless in the handling of lovers' hearts, and though she did not stoop to duplicity—she had no need of that—she took pleasure in stealing the men whom other women loved. And yet she considered herself a good woman. Not a saint, mind you. But she honored her father and kept the house clean and did her share of work, and though she had her faults, she had taken steps—half-steps, rather—to correct them. Like most people, she had no clear moral determinant, depending upon taboos and specific circumstances to modify her behavior, and the "good," the principled, was to her a kind of intellectual afterlife to which she planned someday to aspire, but only after she had exhausted the potentials of pleasure and thus gained the experience necessary for the achievement of such an aspiration. She was prone to bouts of moodiness, as were all within the sphere of Griaule's influence, but generally displayed a sunny disposition and optimistic cast of thought. This is not to say, however, that she was a Pollyanna, an innocent. Through her life in Hangtown she was familiar with treachery, grief, and murder, and at eighteen she had already been with a wide variety of lovers. Her easy sexuality was typical of Hangtown's populace, yet because of her beauty and the jealousy it had engendered, she had acquired the reputation of being exceptionally wanton. She was amused, even somewhat pleased, by her reputation, but the rumors surrounding her grew more scurrilous, more deviant from the truth, and eventually there came a day when they were brought home to her with a savagery that she could never have presupposed.

Beyond Griaule's frontal spike, which rose from a point between his eyes, a great whorled horn curving back toward Hangtown, the slope of the skull flattened out into the top of his snout, and it was here that Catherine came one foggy morning, dressed in loose trousers and a tunic, equipped with scaling hooks and ropes and chisels, intending to chip off a sizable piece of cracked scale she had noticed near the dragon's lip, a spot directly above one of the fangs. She worked at the piece for several hours, suspended by linkages of rope over Griaule's lower jaw. His half-open mouth was filled with a garden of evil-looking plants, the callused surface of his forked tongue showing here and there between the leaves like nodes of red coral; his fangs were inscribed with intricate patterns of lichen, wreathed by streamers of fog and circled by raptors who now and then would plummet into the bushes to skewer some unfortunate lizard or vole. Epiphytes bloomed from splits in the ivory, depending long strings of interwoven red-and-purple blossoms. It was a compelling sight, and from time to time Catherine would stop working and lower herself in her harness until she was no more than fifty feet above the tops of the bushes and look off into the caliginous depths of Griaule's throat, wondering at the nature of the shadowy creatures that flitted there.

The sun burned off the fog, and Catherine, sweaty, weary of chipping, hauled herself up to the top of the snout and stretched out on the scales, resting on an elbow, nibbling at a honey pear and gazing out over the valley with its spiny green hills and hammocks of thistle palms and the faraway white buildings of Teocinte, where that very night she planned to dance and make love. The air became so warm that she stripped off her tunic and lay back, bare to the waist, eyes closed, daydreaming in the clean springtime heat. She had been drifting between sleep and waking for the better part of an hour, when a scraping noise brought her alert. She reached for her tunic and started to sit up; but before she could turn to see who or what had made the sound, something fell heavily across her ribs, taking her wind, leaving her gasping and disoriented. A hand groped her breast, and she smelled winey breath.

"Go easy, now," said a man's voice, thickened with urgency. "I don't want nothing half of Hangtown ain't had already."

Catherine twisted her head, and caught a glimpse of Key Willen's lean, sallow face looming above her, his sardonic mouth hitched at one corner in a half-smile.

"I told you we'd have our time," he said, fumbling with the tie of her trousers.

She began to fight desperately, clawing at his eyes, catching a handful of his long black hair and yanking. She threw herself onto her stomach, clutching at the edge of a scale, trying to worm out from beneath him; but he butted her in the temple, sending white lights shooting through her skull. Once her head had cleared, she found that he had flipped her onto her back, had pulled her trousers down past her hips, and penetrated her with his fingers; he was working them in and out, his breath coming hoarse and rapid. She felt raw inside, and she let out a sharp throat-tearing scream. She thrashed about, tearing at his shirt, his hair, screaming again and again, and when he clamped his free hand to her mouth, she bit it.

"You bitch! You . . . goddamn . . ." He slammed the back of her head against the scale, climbed atop her, straddling her chest and pinning her shoulders with his knees. He slapped her, wrapped his hand in her hair, and leaned close, spittle flying to her face as he spoke. "You listen up, pig! I don't much care if you're awake. . . . One way or the other, I'm gonna have my fun." He rammed her head into the scale again. "You hear me? Hear me?" He straightened, slapped her harder. "Hell, I'm having fun right now."

"Please!" she said, dazed.

" 'Please?' " He laughed. "That mean you want some more?" Another slap. "You like it?"

Yet another slap.

"How 'bout that?"

Frantic, she wrenched an arm free, in reflex reaching up behind her head, searching for a weapon, anything, and as he prepared to slap her again, grinning, she caught hold of a stick—or so she thought—and swung it at him in a vicious arc. The point of the scaling hook, for such it was, sank into Key's flesh just back of his left eye, and as he fell, toppling sideways with only the briefest of outcries, the eye filled with blood, becoming a featureless crimson sphere like a rubber ball embedded in the socket. Catherine shrieked, pushed his legs off her waist, and scrambled away, encumbered by her trousers, which had slipped down about her knees. Key's body convulsed, his heels drumming the scale. She sat staring at him for a long seamless time, unable to catch her breath, to think. But swarms of black flies, their translucent wings shattering the sunlight into prism, began landing on the puddle of blood that spread wide as a table from beneath Key's face, and she became queasy. She crawled to the edge of the snout and looked away across the checkerboard of fields below toward Port Chantay, toward an alp of bubbling cumulus building from the horizon. Her chest hollowed with cold, and she started to shake. The tremors passing through her echoed the tremor she had felt in Key's body when the hook had bit into his skull. All the sickness inside her, her shock and disgust at the violation, at confronting the substance of death, welled up in her throat, and her stomach emptied. When she had finished she cinched her trousers tight, her fingers clumsy with the knot. She thought she should do something. Coil the ropes, maybe. Store the harness in her pack. But these actions, while easy to contemplate, seemed impossibly complex to carry out. She shivered and hugged herself, feeling the altitude, the distances. Her cheeks were feverish and puffy; flickers of sensation—she pictured them to be iridescent worms—tingled nerves in her chest and legs. She had the idea that everything was slowing, that time had flurried and was settling the way river mud settles after the passage of some turbulence. She stared off toward the dragon's horn. Someone was standing there. Coming toward her, now. At first she watched the figure approach with a defiant disinterest, wanting to guard her privacy, feeling that if she had to speak she would lose control of her emotions. But as the figure resolved into one of her neighbors back in Hangtown—Brianne, a tall young woman with brittle good looks, dark brown hair, and an olive complexion—she relaxed from this attitude. She and Brianne were not friends; in fact, they had once been rivals for the same man. However, that had been a year and more in the past, and Catherine was relieved to see her. More than relieved. The presence of another woman allowed her to surrender to weakness, believing that in Brianne she would find a fund of natural sympathy because of their common sex.

"My God, what happened?" Brianne kneeled and brushed Catherine's hair back from her eyes. The tenderness of the gesture burst the dam of Catherine's emotions, and punctuating the story with sobs, she told of the rape.

"I didn't mean to kill him," she said. "I . . . I'd forgotten about the hook."

"Key was looking to get killed," Brianne said. "But it's a damn shame you had to be the one to help him along." She sighed, her forehead creased by a worry line. "I suppose I should fetch someone to take care of the body. I know that's not. . . ."

"No, I understand . . . it has to be done." Catherine felt stronger, more capable. She made as if to stand, but Brianne restrained her.

"Maybe you should wait here. You know how people will be. They'll see your face"—she touched Catherine's swollen cheeks—"and they'll be prying, whispering. It might be better to let the mayor come out and make his investigation. That way he can take the edge off the gossip before it gets started."

Catherine didn't want to be alone with the body any longer, but she saw the wisdom in waiting and agreed.

"Will you be all right?" Brianne asked.

"I'll be fine . . . but hurry."

"I will." Brianne stood; the wind feathered her hair, lifted it to veil the lower half of her face. "You're sure you'll be all right?" There was an odd undertone in her voice, as if it were really another question she was asking, or—and this, Catherine thought, was more likely—as if she were thinking ahead to dealing with the mayor.

Catherine nodded, then caught at Brianne as she started to walk away. "Don't tell my father. Let me tell him. If he hears it from you, he might go after the Willens."

"I won't say a thing, I promise."

With a smile, a sympathetic pat on the arm, Brianne headed back toward Hangtown, vanishing into the thickets that sprang up beyond the frontal spike. For a while after she had gone, Catherine felt wrapped in her consolation; but the seething of the wind, the chill that infused the air as clouds moved in to cover the sun, these things caused the solitude of the place and the grimness of the circumstance to close down around her, and she began to wish she had returned to Hangtown. She squeezed her eyes shut, trying to steady herself, but even then she kept seeing Key's face, his bloody eye, and remembering his hands on her. Finally, thinking that Brianne had had more than enough time to accomplish her task, she walked up past the frontal spike and stood looking out along the narrow trail that wound through the thickets on Griaule's back. Several minutes elapsed, and then she spotted three figures—two men and a woman—coming at a brisk pace. She shaded her eyes against a ray of sun that had broken through the overcast, and peered at them. Neither man had the gray hair and portly shape of Hangtown's mayor. They were lanky, pale, with black hair falling to their shoulders, and were carrying unsheathed knives. Catherine couldn't make out their faces, but she realized that Brianne must not have set aside their old rivalry, that in the spirit of vengeance she had informed Key's brothers of his death.

Fear cut through the fog of shock, and she tried to think what to do. There was only the one trail and no hope that she could hide in the thickets. She retreated toward the edge of the snout, stepping around the patch of drying blood. Her only chance for escape would be to lower herself on the ropes and take refuge in Griaule's mouth; however, the thought of entering so ominous a place, a place shunned by all but the mad, gave her pause. She tried to think of alternatives, but there were none. Brianne would no doubt have lied to the Willens, cast her as the guilty party, and the brothers would never listen to her. She hurried to the edge, buckled on the harness, and slipped over the side, working with frenzied speed, lowering in ten- and fifteen-foot drops. Her view of the mouth lurched and veered—a panorama of bristling leaves and head-high ferns, enormous fangs hooking up from the jaw, and pitch-dark emptiness at the entrance to the throat. She was fifty feet from the surface when she felt the rope jerking, quivering; glancing up, she saw that one of the Willens was sawing at it with his knife. Her heart felt hot and throbbing in her chest, her palms were slick. She dropped half the distance to the jaw, stopping with a jolt that sent pain shooting through her spine and left her swinging back and forth, muddle-headed. She began another drop, a shorter one, but the rope parted high above and she fell the last twenty feet, landing with such stunning force that she lost consciousness.

She came to in a bed of ferns, staring up through the fronds at the dull brick-colored roof of Griaule's mouth, a surface festooned with spiky dark green epiphytes, like the vault of a cathedral that had been invaded by the jungle. She lay still for a moment, gathering herself, testing the aches that mapped her body to determine if anything was broken. A lump sprouted from the back of the head, but the brunt of the impact had been absorbed by her rear end, and though she felt pain there, she didn't think the damage was severe. Moving cautiously, wincing, she came to her knees and was about to stand when she heard shouts from above.

"See her?"

"Naw . . . you?"

"She musta gone deeper in!"

Catherine peeked between the fronds and saw two dark figures centering networks of ropes, suspended a hundred feet or so overhead like spiders with simple webs. They dropped lower; and panicked, she crawled on her belly away from the mouth, hauling herself along by gripping twists of dead vine that formed a matte underlying the foliage. After she had gone about fifty yards, she looked back. The Willens were hanging barely a dozen feet above the tops of the bushes, and as she watched they lowered out of sight. Her instincts told her to move deeper into the mouth, but the air was considerably darker where she now kneeled than where she had landed—a grayish green gloom—and the idea of penetrating the greater darkness of Griaule's throat stalled her heart. She listened for the Willens and heard slitherings, skitterings, and rustles. Eerie whistles that, although soft, were complex and articulated. She imagined that these were not the cries of tiny creatures but the gutterings of breath in a huge throat, and she had a terrifying sense of the size of the place, of her own relative insignificance. She couldn't bring herself to continue in deeper, and she made her way toward the side of the mouth, where thick growths of ferns flourished in the shadow. When she reached a spot at which the mouth sloped upward, she buried herself among the ferns and kept very still.

Next to her head was an irregular patch of pale red flesh, where a clump of soil had been pulled away by an uprooted plant. Curious, she extended a forefinger and found it cool and dry. It was like touching stone or wood, and that disappointed her; she had, she realized, been hoping the touch would affect her in some extreme way. She pressed her palm to the flesh, trying to detect the tic of a pulse, but the flesh was inert, and the rustlings and the occasional beating of wings overhead were the only signs of life. She began to grow drowsy, to nod, and she fought to keep awake. But after a few minutes she let herself relax. The more she examined the situation, the more convinced she became that the Willens would not track her this far; the extent of their nerve would be to wait at the verge of the mouth, to lay siege to her, knowing that eventually she would have to seek food and water. Thinking about water made her thirsty, but she denied the craving. She needed rest far more. And removing one of the scaling hooks from her belt, holding it in her right hand in case some animal less cautious than the Willens happened by, she pillowed her head against the pale red patch of Griaule's flesh and was soon fast asleep.

II

Many of Catherine's dreams over the years had seemed sendings rather than distillations of experience, but never had she had one so clearly of that character as the dream she had that afternoon in Griaule's mouth. It was a simple dream, formless, merely a voice whose words less came to her ear than enveloped her, steeping her in their meanings, and of them she retained only a message of reassurance, of security, one so profound that it instilled in her a confidence that lasted even after she waked into a world gone black, the sole illumination being the gleams of reflected firelight that flowed along the curve of one of the fangs. It was an uncanny sight, that huge tooth glazed with fierce red shine, and under other circumstances she would have been frightened by it; but in this instance she did not react to the barbarity of the image and saw it instead as evidence that her suppositions concerning the Willens had been correct. They had built a fire near the lip and were watching for her, expecting her to bolt into their arms. But she had no intention of fulfilling their expectations. Although her confidence flickered on and off, although to go deeper into the dragon seemed irrational, she knew that any other course offered the certainty of a knife stroke across the neck. And, too, despite the apparent rationality of her decision, she had an unshakable feeling that Griaule was watching over her, that his will was being effected. She had a flash vision of Key Willen's face, his gaping mouth and blood-red eye, and recalled her terror at his assault. However, these memories no longer harrowed her. They steadied her, resolving certain questions that—while she had never asked them—had always been there to ask. She hadn't been to blame in any way for the rape, she had not tempted Key. But she saw that she had left herself open to tragedy by her aimlessness, by her reliance on a vague sense of destiny to give life meaning. Now it appeared that her destiny was at hand, and she understood that its violent coloration might have been different had *she* been different, had she engaged the world with energy and not with a passive attitude. She hoped that knowing all this would prove important, but she doubted that it would, believing that she had gone too far on the wrong path for any degree of knowledge to matter.

It took all her self-control to begin her journey inward, feeling her way along the side of the throat, pushing through ferns and cobwebs, her hands encountering unfamiliar textures that made her skin crawl, alert to the burbling of insects and other night creatures. On one occasion she was close to turning back, but she heard shouts behind her, and fearful that the Willens were on her trail, she kept going. As she started down an incline, she saw a faint gleam riding the curve of the throat wall. The glow brightened, casting the foliage into silhouette, and eager to reach the source, she picked up her pace, tripping over roots, vines snagging her ankles. At length the incline flattened out, and she emerged into a large chamber, roughly circular in shape, its upper regions lost in darkness; upon the floor lay pools of black liquid; mist trailed across the surface of the pools, and whenever the mist lowered to touch the liquid, a fringe of yellowish red flame would flare up, cutting the shadows on the pebbled skin of the floor and bringing to light a number of warty knee-high protuberances that sprouted among the pools—these were deep red in color, perforated around the sides, leaking pale threads of mist. At the rear of the chamber was an opening that Catherine assumed led farther into the dragon. The air was warm, dank, and a sweat broke out all over her body. She balked at entering the chamber; in spite of the illumination, it was a less human place than the mouth. But once again she forced herself onward, stepping carefully between the fires and, after discovering that the mist made her giddy, giving the protuberances a wide berth. Piercing whistles came from above. The notion that this might signal the presence of bats caused her to hurry, and she had covered half the distance across when a man's voice called to her, electrifying her with fear.

"Catherine!" he said. "Not so fast!"

She spun about, her scaling hook at the ready. Hobbling toward her was an elderly white-haired man dressed in the ruin of a silk frock coat embroidered with gold thread, a tattered ruffled shirt, and holed satin leggings. In his left hand he carried a gold-knobbed cane, and at least a dozen glittering rings encircled his bony fingers. He stopped an arm's length away, leaning on his cane, and although Catherine did not lower her hook, her fear diminished. Despite the eccentricity of his appearance, considering the wide spectrum of men and creatures who inhabited Griaule, he seemed comparatively ordinary, a reason for caution but not alarm.

"Ordinary?" The old man cackled. "Oh yes, indeed! Ordinary as angels, as unexceptional as the idea of God!" Before she had a chance to wonder at his knowledge of her thoughts, he let out another cackle. "How could I not know them? We are every one of us creatures of his thought, expressions of his whim. And here what is only marginally evident on the surface becomes vivid reality, inescapable truth. For here"—he poked the chamber floor with his cane—"here we live in the medium of his will." He hobbled a step closer, fixing her with a rheumy stare. "I have dreamed this moment a thousand times. I know what you will say, what you will think, what you will do. He has instructed me in all your particulars so that I may become your guide, your confidant."

"What are you talking about?" Catherine hefted her hook, her anxiety increasing.

"Not 'what,' " said the old man. "Who." A grin split the pale wrinkled leather of his face. "His Scaliness, of course."

"Griaule?"

"None other." The old man held out his hand. "Come along now, girl. They're waiting for us."

Catherine drew back.

The old man pursed his lips. "Well, I suppose you could return the way you came. The Willens will be happy to see you."

Flustered, Catherine said, "I don't understand. How can you know. . . ."

"Know your name, your peril? Weren't you listening? You are of Griaule, daughter. And more so than most, for you have slept at the center of his dreams. Your entire life has been prelude to this time, and your destiny will not be known until you come to the place from which his dreams arise . . . the dragon's heart." He took her hand. "My name is Amos Mauldry. Captain Amos Mauldry, at your service. I have waited years for you . . . years! I am to prepare you for the consummate moment of your life. I urge you to follow me, to join the company of the feelies and begin your preparation. But"— he shrugged—"the choice is yours. I will not coerce you more than I have done . . . except to say this. Go with me now, and when you return you will discover that you have nothing to fear of the Willen brothers."

He let loose of her hand and stood gazing at her with calm regard. She would have liked to dismiss his words, but they were in such accord with all she had ever felt about her association with the dragon, she found that she could not. "Who," she asked, "are the feelies?"

He made a disparaging noise. "Harmless creatures. They pass their time copulating and arguing among themselves over the most trivial of matters. Were they not of service to Griaule, keeping him free of certain pests, they would have no use whatsoever. Still, there are worse folk in the world, and they do have moments in which they shine." He shifted impatiently, tapped his cane on the chamber floor. "You'll meet them soon enough. Are you with me or not?"

Grudgingly, her hook at the ready, Catherine followed Mauldry toward the opening at the rear of the chamber and into a narrow, twisting channel illuminated by a pulsing golden light that issued from within Griaule's flesh. This radiance, Mauldry said, derived from the dragon's blood, which, while it did not flow, was subject to fluctuations in brilliance due to changes in its chemistry. Or so he believed. He had regained his lighthearted manner, and as they walked he told Catherine he had once captained a cargo ship that plied between Port Chantay and the Pearl Islands.

"We carried livestock, breadfruit, whale oil," he said. "I can't think of much we didn't carry. It was a good life, but hard as hard gets, and after I retired . . . well, I'd never married, and with time on my hands, I figured I owed myself some high times. I decided I'd see the sights, and the sight I most wanted to see was Griaule. I'd heard he was the First Wonder of the World . . . and he was! I was amazed, flabbergasted. I couldn't get enough of seeing him. He was more than a wonder. A miracle, an absolute majesty of a creature. People warned me to keep clear of the mouth, and they were right. But I couldn't stay away. One evening—I was walking along the edge of the mouth—two scalehunters set upon me, beat and robbed me. Left me for dead. And I would have died if it hadn't been for the feelies." He clucked his tongue. "I suppose I might as well give you some of their background. It can't help but prepare you for them . . . and I admit they need preparing for. They're not in the least agreeable to the eye." He cocked an eye toward Catherine, and after a dozen steps more he said, "Aren't you going to ask me to proceed?"

"You didn't seem to need encouragement," she said.

He chuckled, nodding his approval. "Quite right, quite right." He walked on in silence, his shoulders hunched and head inclined, like an old turtle who'd learned to get about on two legs.

"Well?" said Catherine, growing annoyed.

"I knew you'd ask," he said, and winked at her. "I didn't know who they were myself at first. If I had known I'd have been terrified. There are about five or six hundred in the colony. Their numbers are kept down by childbirth mortality and various other forms of attrition. They're most of them the descendants of a retarded man named Feely who wandered into the mouth almost a thousand years ago. Apparently he was walking near the mouth when flights of birds and swarms of insects began issuing from it. Not just a few, mind you. Entire populations. Wellsir, Feely was badly frightened. He was sure that some terrible beast had chased all these lesser creatures out, and he tried to hide from it. But he was so confused that instead of running away from the mouth, he ran into it and hid in the bushes. He waited for almost a day . . . no beast. The only sign of danger was a muffled thud from deep within the dragon. Finally his curiosity overcame his fear, and he went into the throat." Mauldry hawked and spat. "He felt secure there. More secure than on the outside, at any rate. Doubtless Griaule's doing, that feeling. He needed the feelies to be happy so they'd settle down and be his exterminators. Anyway, the first thing Feely did was to bring in a madwoman he'd known in Teocinte, and over the years they recruited other madmen who happened along. I was the first sane person they'd brought into the fold. They're extremely chauvinistic regarding the sane. But of course they were directed by Griaule to take me in. He knew you'd need someone to talk to." He prodded the wall with his cane. "And now this is my home. More than a home. It's my truth, my love. To live here is to be transfigured."

"That's a bit hard to swallow," said Catherine.

"Is it, now? You of all those who dwell on the surface should understand the scope of Griaule's virtues. There's no greater security than that he offers, no greater comprehension than that he bestows."

"You make him sound like a god."

Looking at her askance, Mauldry stopped walking. The golden light waxed bright, filling in his wrinkles with shadows, making him appear to be centuries old. "Well, what do you think he is?" he asked with an air of mild indignation. "What else could he be?"

Another ten minutes brought them to a chamber even more fabulous than the last. In shape it was oval, like an egg with a flattened bottom stood on end, an egg some one hundred and fifty feet high and a bit more than half that in diameter. It was lit by the same pulsing golden glow that had illuminated the channel, but here the fluctuations were more gradual and more extreme, ranging from a murky dimness to a glare approaching that of full daylight. The upper two-thirds of the chamber wall was obscured by stacked ranks of small cubicles, leaning together at rickety angles, a geometry lacking the precision of the cells of a honeycomb, yet reminiscent of such, as if the bees that constructed it had been drunk. The entrances of the cubicles were draped with curtains, and lashed to their sides were ropes, rope ladders, and baskets that functioned as elevators, several of which were in use, lowering and lifting men and women dressed in a style similar to Mauldry: Catherine was reminded of a painting she had seen depicting the roof warrens of Port Chantay; but those habitations, while redolent of poverty and despair, had not as did these evoked an impression of squalid degeneracy, of order lapsed into the perverse. The lower portion of the chamber (and it was in this area that the channel emerged) was covered with a motley carpet composed of bolts of silk and satin and other rich fabrics, and seventy or eighty people were strolling and reclining on the gentle slopes. Only the center had been left clear, and there a gaping hole led away into yet another section of the dragon; a system of pipes ran into the hole, and Mauldry later explained that these carried the wastes of the colony into a pit of acids that had once fueled Griaule's fires. The dome of the chamber was choked with mist, the same pale stuff that had been vented from the protuberances in the previous chamber; birds with black wings and red markings on their heads made wheeling flights in and out of it, and frail scarves of mist drifted throughout. There was a sickly sweet odor to the place, and Catherine heard a murmurous rustling that issued from every quarter.

"Well," said Mauldry, making a sweeping gesture with his cane that included the entire chamber. "What do you think of our little colony?"

Some of the feelies had noticed them and were edging forward in small groups, stopping, whispering agitatedly among themselves, then edging forward again, all with the hesitant curiosity of savages; and although no signal had been given, the curtains over the cubicle entrances were being thrown back, heads were poking forth, and tiny figures were shinnying down the ropes, crowding into baskets, scuttling downward on the rope ladders, hundreds of people beginning to hurry toward her at a pace that brought to mind the panicked swarming of an anthill. And on first glance they seemed alike as ants. Thin and pale and stooped, with sloping, nearly hairless skulls, and weepy eyes and thick-lipped slack mouths, like ugly children in their rotted silks and satins. Closer and closer they came, those in front pushed by the swelling ranks at their rear, and Catherine, unnerved by their stares, ignoring Mauldry's attempts to soothe her, retreated into the channel. Mauldry turned to the feelies, brandishing his cane as if it were a victor's sword, and cried, "She is here! He has brought her to us at last! She is here!"

His words caused several of those at the front of the press to throw back their heads and loose a whinnying laughter that went higher and higher in pitch as the golden light brightened. Others in the crowd lifted their hands, palms outward, holding them tight to their chests, and made little hops of excitement, and others yet twitched their heads from side to side, cutting their eyes this way and that, their expressions flowing between belligerence and confusion, apparently unsure of what was happening. This exhibition, clearly displaying the feelies' retardation, the tenuousness of their self-control, dismayed Catherine still more. But Mauldry seemed delighted and continued to exhort them, shouting, "She is here," over and over. His outcry came to rule the feelies, to orchestrate their movements. They began to sway, to repeat his words, slurring them so that their response was in effect a single word, "Shees'eer, Shees'eer," that reverberated through the chamber, acquiring a rolling echo, a hissing sonority, like the rapid breathing of a giant. The sound washed over Catherine, enfeebling her with its intensity, and she shrank back against the wall of the channel, expecting the feelies to break ranks and surround her; but they were so absorbed in their chanting, they appeared to have forgotten her. They milled about, bumping into one another, some striking out in anger at those who had impeded their way, others embracing and giggling, engaging in sexual play, but all of them keeping up the chorus of shouts.

Mauldry turned to her, his eyes giving back gleams of the golden light, his face looking in its vacuous glee akin to those of the feelies, and holding out his hands to her, his tone manifesting the bland sincerity of a priest, he said, "Welcome home."

III

Catherine was housed in two rooms halfway up the chamber wall, an apartment that adjoined Mauldry's quarters and was furnished with a rich carpeting of silks and furs and embroidered pillows; on the walls, also draped in these materials, hung a mirror with a gem-studded frame and two oil paintings—this bounty, said Mauldry, all part of Griaule's horde, the bulk of which lay in a cave west of the valley, its location known only to the feelies. One of the rooms contained a large basin for bathing, but since water was at a premium—being collected from points at which it seeped in through the scales—she was permitted one bath a week and no more. Still, the apartment and the general living conditions were on a par with those in Hangtown, and had it not been for the feelies, Catherine might have felt at home. But except in the case of the woman Leitha, who served her meals and cleaned, she could not overcome her revulsion at their inbred appearance and demented manner. They seemed to be responding to stimuli that she could not perceive, stopping now and then to cock an ear to an inaudible call or to stare at some invisible disturbance in the air. They scurried up and down the ropes to no apparent purpose, laughing and chattering, and they engaged in mass copulations at the bottom of the chamber. They spoke a mongrel dialect that she could barely understand, and they would hang on ropes outside her apartment, arguing, offering criticism of one another's dress and behavior, picking at the most insignificant flaws and judging them according to an intricate code whose niceties Catherine was unable to master.

They would follow her wherever she went, never sharing the same basket, but descending or ascending alongside her, staring, shrinking away if she turned her gaze upon them. With their foppish rags, their jewels, their childish pettiness and jealousies, they both irritated and frightened her; there was a tremendous tension in the way they looked at her, and she had the idea that at any moment they might lose their awe of her and attack.

She kept to her rooms those first weeks, brooding, trying to invent some means of escape, her solitude broken only by Leitha's ministrations and Mauldry's visits. He came twice daily and would sit among the pillows, declaiming upon Griaule's majesty, his truth. She did not enjoy the visits. The righteous quaver in his voice aroused her loathing, reminding her of the mendicant priests who passed now and then through Hangtown, leaving bastards and empty purses in their wake. She found his conversation for the most part boring, and when it did not bore, she found it disturbing in its constant references to her time of trial at the dragon's heart. She had no doubt that Griaule was at work in her life. The longer she remained in the colony, the more vivid her dreams became and the more certain she grew that his purpose was somehow aligned with her presence there. But the pathetic condition of the feelies shed a wan light on her old fantasies of a destiny entwined with the dragon's, and she began to see herself in that wan light, to experience a revulsion at her fecklessness equal to that she felt toward those around her.

"You are our salvation," Mauldry told her one day as she sat sewing herself a new pair of trousers—she refused to dress in the gilt and satin rags preferred by the feelies. "Only you can know the mystery of the dragon's heart, only you can inform us of his deepest wish for us. We've known this for years."

Seated amid the barbaric disorder of silks and furs, Catherine looked out through a gap in the curtains, watching the waning of the golden light. "You hold me prisoner," she said. "Why should I help you?"

"Would you leave us, then?" Mauldry asked. "What of the Willens?"

"I doubt they're still waiting for me. Even if they are, it's only a matter of which death I prefer, a lingering one here or a swift one at their hands."

Mauldry fingered the gold knob of his cane. "You're right," he said. "The Willens are no longer a menace."

She glanced up at him.

"They died the moment you went down out of Griaule's mouth," he said. "He sent his creatures to deal with them, knowing you were his at long last."

Catherine remembered the shouts she'd heard while walking down the incline of the throat. "What creatures?"

"That's of no importance," said Mauldry. "What is important is that you apprehend the subtlety of his power, his absolute mastery and control over your thoughts, your being."

"Why?" she asked. "Why is that important?" He seemed to be struggling to explain himself, and she laughed. "Lost touch with your god, Mauldry? Won't he supply the appropriate cant?"

Mauldry composed himself. "It is for you, not I, to understand why you are here. You must explore Griaule, study the miraculous workings of his flesh, involve yourself in the intricate order of his being."

In frustration, Catherine punched at a pillow. "If you don't let me go, I'll die! This place will kill me. I won't be around long enough to do any exploring."

"Oh, but you will." Mauldry favored her with an unctuous smile. "That, too, is known to us."

Ropes creaked, and a moment later the curtains parted, and Leitha, a young woman in a gown of watered blue taffeta, whose bodice pushed up the pale nubs of her breasts, entered bearing Catherine's dinner tray. She set down the tray. "Be mo', ma'am?" she said. "Or mus' I later c'meah." She gazed fixedly at Catherine, her close-set brown eyes blinking, fingers plucking at the folds of her gown.

"Whatever you want," Catherine said.

Leitha continued to stare at her, and only when Mauldry spoke sharply to her, did she turn and leave.

Catherine looked down disconsolately at the tray and noticed that in addition to the usual fare of greens and fruit (gathered from the dragon's mouth) there were several slices of underdone meat, whose reddish hue appeared identical to the color of Griaule's flesh. "What's this?" she asked, poking at one of the slices.

"The hunters were successful today," said Mauldry. "Every so often hunting parties are sent into the digestive tract. It's quite dangerous, but there are beasts there that can injure Griaule. It serves him that we hunt them, and their flesh nourishes us." He leaned forward, studying her face. "Another party is going out tomorrow. Perhaps you'd care to join them. I can arrange it if you wish. You'll be well protected."

Catherine's initial impulse was to reject the invitation, but then she thought that this might offer an opportunity for escape; in fact, she realized that to play upon Mauldry's tendencies, to evince interest in a study of the dragon, would be a wise move. The more she learned about Griaule's geography, the greater chance there would be that she would find a way out.

"You said it was dangerous. . . . How dangerous?"

"For you? Not in the least. Griaule would not harm you. But for the hunting party, well . . . lives will be lost."

"And they're going out tomorrow?"

"Perhaps the next day as well. We're not sure how extensive an infestation is involved."

"What kind of beast are you talking about?"

"Serpents of a sort."

Catherine's enthusiasm was dimmed, but she saw no other means of taking action. "Very well. I'll go with them tomorrow."

"Wonderful, wonderful!" It took Mauldry three tries to heave himself up from the cushion, and when at last he managed to stand, he leaned on his cane, breathing heavily. "I'll come for you early in the morning."

"You're going, too? You don't seem up to the exertion."

Mauldry chuckled. "It's true, I'm an old man. But where you're concerned, daughter, my energies are inexhaustible." He performed a gallant bow and hobbled from the room.

Not long after he had left, Leitha returned. She drew a second curtain across the entrance, cutting the light, even at its most brilliant, to a dim effusion. Then she stood by the entrance, eyes fixed on Catherine. "Wan' mo' fum Leitha?" she asked.

The question was not a formality. Leitha had made it plain by touches and other signs that Catherine had but to ask and she would come to her as a lover. Her deformities masked by the shadowy air, she had the look of a pretty young girl dressed for a dance, and for a moment, in the grip of loneliness and despair, watching Leitha alternately brightening and merging with gloom, listening to the unceasing murmur of the feelies from without, aware in full of the tribal strangeness of the colony and her utter lack of connection, Catherine felt a bizarre arousal. But the moment passed, and she was disgusted with herself, with her weakness, and angry at Leitha and this degenerate place that was eroding her humanity. "Get out," she said coldly, and when Leitha hesitated, she shouted the command, sending the girl stumbling backward from the room. Then she turned onto her stomach, her face pressed into a pillow, expecting to cry, feeling the pressure of a sob building in her chest; but the sob never manifested, and she lay there, knowing her emptiness, feeling that she was no longer worthy of even her own tears.

Behind one of the cubicles in the lower half of the chamber was hidden the entrance to a wide circular passage ringed by ribs of cartilage, and it was along this passage the next morning that Catherine and Mauldry, accompanied by thirty male feelies, set out upon the hunt. They were armed with swords and bore torches to light the way, for here Griaule's veins were too deeply embedded to provide illumination; they walked in a silence broken only by coughs and the soft scraping of their footsteps. The silence, such a contrast from the feelies' usual chatter, unsettled Catherine, and the flaring and guttering of the torches, the apparition of a backlit pale face turned toward her, the tingling acidic scent that grew stronger and stronger, all this assisted her impression that they were lost souls treading some byway in hell.

Their angle of descent increased, and shortly thereafter they reached a spot from which Catherine had a view of a black distance shot through with intricate networks of fine golden skeins, like spiderwebs of gold in a night sky. Mauldry told her to wait, and the torches of the hunting party moved off, making it clear that they had come to a large chamber; but she did not understand just how large until a fire suddenly bloomed, bursting into towering flames: an enormous bonfire composed of sapling trunks and entire bushes. The size of the fire was impressive in itself, but the immense cavity of the stomach that it partially revealed was more impressive yet. It could not have been less than two hundred yards long, and was walled with folds of thin whitish skin figured by lacings and branchings of veins, attached to curving ribs covered with even thinner skin that showed their every articulation. A quarter of the way across the cavity, the floor declined into a sink brimming with a dark liquid, and it was along a section of the wall close to the sink that the bonfire had been lit, its smoke billowing up toward a bruised patch of skin some fifty feet in circumference with a tattered rip at the center.

As Catherine watched, the entire patch began to undulate. The hunting party gathered beneath it, ranged around the bonfire, their swords raised. Then, with ponderous slowness a length of thick white tubing was extruded from the rip, a gigantic worm that lifted its blind head above the hunting party, opened a mouth fringed with palps to expose a dark red maw, and emitted a piercing squeal that touched off echoes and made Catherine put her hands to her ears. More and more of the worm's body emerged from the stomach wall, and she marveled at the courage of the hunting party, who maintained their ground. The worm's squealing became unbearably loud as smoke enveloped it; it lashed about, twisting and probing at the air with its head, and then, with an even louder cry, it fell across the bonfire, writhing, sending up showers of sparks. It rolled out of the fire, crushing several of the party; the others set to with their swords, hacking in a frenzy at the head, painting streaks of dark blood over the corpse-pale skin. Catherine realized that she had pressed her fists to her cheeks and was screaming, so involved was she in the battle. The worm's blood spattered the floor of the cavity, its skin was charred and blistered from the flames, and its head was horribly slashed, the flesh hanging in ragged strips. But it continued to squeal, humping up great sections of its body, forming an arch over groups of attackers and dropping down upon them. A third of the hunting party lay motionless, their limbs sprawled in graceless attitudes, the remnants of the bonfire—heaps of burning branches—scattered among them; the rest stabbed and sliced at the increasingly torpid worm, dancing away from its lunges. At last the worm lifted half its body off the floor, its head held high, silent for a moment, swaying with the languor of a mesmerized serpent. It let out a cry like the whistle of a monstrous teakettle, a cry that seemed to fill the cavity with its fierce vibrations, and fell, twisting once and growing still, its maw half-open, palps twitching in the register of some final internal function.

The hunting party collapsed around it, winded, drained, some leaning on their swords. Shocked by the suddenness of the silence, Catherine went a few steps out into the cavity, Mauldry at her shoulder. She hesitated, then moved forward again, thinking that some of the party might need tending. But those who had fallen were dead, their limbs broken, blood showing on their mouths. She walked alongside the worm. The thickness of its body was three times her height, the skin glistening and warped by countless tiny puckers and tinged with a faint bluish cast that made it all the more ghastly.

"What are you thinking?" Mauldry asked.

Catherine shook her head. No thoughts would come to her. It was as if the process of thought itself had been canceled by the enormity of what she had witnessed. She had always supposed that she had a fair idea of Griaule's scope, his complexity, but now she understood that whatever she had once believed had been inadequate, and she struggled to acclimate to this new perspective. There was a commotion behind her. Members of the hunting party were hacking slabs of meat from the worm. Mauldry draped an arm about her, and by that contact she became aware that she was trembling.

"Come along," he said. "I'll take you home."

"To my room, you mean?" Her bitterness resurfaced, and she threw off his arm.

"Perhaps you'll never think of it as home," he said. "Yet nowhere is there a place more suited to you." He signaled to one of the hunting party, who came toward them, stopping to light a dead torch from a pile of burning branches.

With a dismal laugh, Catherine said, "I'm beginning to find it irksome how you claim to know so much about me."

"It's not you I claim to know," he said, "though it has been given me to understand something of your purpose. But"—he rapped the tip of his cane against the floor of the cavity—"he by whom you are most known, him I know well."

IV

Catherine made three escape attempts during the next two months, and thereafter gave up on the enterprise; with hundreds of eyes watching her, there was no point in wasting energy. For almost six months following the final attempt she became dispirited and refused to leave her rooms. Her health suffered, her thoughts paled, and she lay abed for hours, reliving her life in Hangtown, which she came to view as a model of joy and contentment. Her inactivity caused loneliness to bear in upon her. Mauldry tried his best to entertain her, but his mystical obsession with Griaule made him incapable of offering the consolation of a true friend. And so, without friends or lovers, without even an enemy, she sank into a welter of self-pity and began to toy with the idea of suicide. The prospect of never seeing the sun again, of attending no more carnivals at Teocinte . . . it seemed too much to endure. But she was either not brave enough or not sufficiently foolish to take her own life, and deciding that no matter how vile or delimiting the circumstance, it promised more than eternal darkness, she gave herself to the one occupation the feelies would permit her: the exploration and study of Griaule.

Like one of those enormous Tibetan sculptures of the Buddha constructed within a tower only a trifle larger than the sculpture itself, Griaule's unbeating heart was a dimpled golden shape as vast as a cathedral and was enclosed within a chamber whose walls left a gap six feet wide around the organ. The chamber could be reached by passing through a vein that had ruptured long ago and was now a wrinkled brown tube just big enough for Catherine to crawl along it; to make this transit and then emerge into that narrow space beside the heart was an intensely claustrophobic experience, and it took her a long, long while to get used to the process. Even after she had grown accustomed to this, it was still difficult for her to adjust to the peculiar climate at the heart. The air was thick with a heated stinging scent that reminded her of the brimstone stink left by a lightning stroke, and there was an atmosphere of imminence, a stillness and tension redolent of some chthonic disturbance that might strike at any moment. The blood at the heart did not merely fluctuate (and here the fluctuations were erratic, varying both in range of brilliance and rapidity of change); it circulated—the movement due to variations in heat and pressure—through a series of convulsed inner chambers, and this eddying in conjunction with the flickering brilliance threw patterns of light and shadow on the heart wall, patterns as complex and fanciful as arabesques that drew her eye in. Staring at them, Catherine began to be able to predict what configurations would next appear and to apprehend a logic to their progression; it was nothing that she could put into words, but watching the play of light and shadow produced in her emotional responses that seemed keyed to the shifting patterns and allowed her to make crude guesses as to the heart's workings. She learned that if she stared too long at the patterns, dreams would take her, dreams notable for their vividness, and one particularly notable in that it recurred again and again.

The dream began with a sunrise, the solar disc edging up from the southern horizon, its rays spearing toward a coast strewn with great black rocks that protruded from the shallows, and perched upon them were sleeping dragons; as the sun warmed them, light flaring on their scales, they grumbled and lifted their heads and with the snapping sound of huge sails filling with wind, they unfolded their leathery wings and went soaring up into an indigo sky flecked with stars arranged into strange constellations, wheeling and roaring their exultation . . . all but one dragon, who flew only a brief arc before coming disjointed in midflight and dropping like a stone into the water, vanishing beneath the waves. It was an awesome thing to see, this tumbling flight, the wings billowing, tearing, the fanged mouth open, claws grasping for purchase in the air. But despite its beauty, the dream seemed to have little relevance to Griaule's situation. He was in no danger of falling, that much was certain. Nevertheless, the frequency of the dream's recurrence persuaded Catherine that something must be amiss, that perhaps Griaule feared an attack of the sort that had stricken the flying dragon. With this in mind she began to inspect the heart, using her hooks to clamber up the steep slopes of the chamber walls, sometimes hanging upside down like a blond spider above the glowing, flickering organ. But she could find nothing out of order, no imperfections—at least as far as she could determine—and the sole result of the inspection was that the dream stopped occurring and was replaced by a simpler dream in which she watched the chest of a sleeping dragon contract and expand. She could make no sense of it, and although the dream continued to recur, she paid less and less attention to it.

Mauldry, who had been expecting miraculous insights from her, was depressed when none were forthcoming. "Perhaps I've been wrong all these years," he said. "Or senile. Perhaps I'm growing senile."

A few months earlier, Catherine, locked into bitterness and resentment, might have seconded his opinion out of spite; but her studies at the heart had soothed her, infused her both with calm resignation and some compassion for her jailers—they could not, after all, be blamed for their pitiful condition—and she said to Mauldry, "I've only begun to learn. It's likely to take a long time before I understand what he wants. And that's in keeping with his nature, isn't it? That nothing happens quickly?"

"I suppose you're right," he said glumly.

"Of course I am," she said. "Sooner or later there'll be a revelation. But a creature like Griaule doesn't yield his secrets to a casual glance. Just give me time."

And oddly enough, though she had spoken these words to cheer Mauldry, they seemed to ring true.

She had started her explorations with minimal enthusiasm, but Griaule's scope was so extensive, his populations of parasites and symbiotes so exotic and intriguing, her passion for knowledge was fired and over the next six years she grew zealous in her studies, using them to compensate for the emptiness of her life. With Mauldry ever at her side, accompanied by small groups of the feelies, she mapped the interior of the dragon, stopping short of penetrating the skull, warned off from that region by a premonition of danger. She sent several of the more intelligent feelies into Teocinte, where they acquired beakers and flasks and books and writing materials that enabled her to build a primitive laboratory for chemical analysis. She discovered that the egg-shaped chamber occupied by the colony would—had the dragon been fully alive—be pumped full of acids and gasses by the contraction of the heart muscle, flooding the channel, mingling in the adjoining chamber with yet another liquid, forming a volatile mixture that Griaule's breath would—if he so desired—kindle into flame; if he did not so desire, the expansion of the heart would empty the chamber. From these liquids she derived a potent narcotic that she named brianine after her nemesis, and from a lichen growing on the outer surface of the lungs, she derived a powerful stimulant.

She catalogued the dragon's myriad flora and fauna, covering the walls of her rooms with lists and charts and notations on their behaviors. Many of the animals were either familiar to her or variants of familiar forms. Spiders, bats, swallows, and the like. But as was the case on the dragon's surface, a few of them testified to his otherworldly origins, and perhaps the most curious of them was Catherine's metahex (her designation for it), a creature with six identical bodies that thrived in the stomach acids. Each body was approximately the size and color of a worn penny, fractionally more dense than a jellyfish, ringed with cilia, and all were in a constant state of agitation. She had at first assumed the metahex to be six creatures, a species that traveled in sixes, but had begun to suspect otherwise when—upon killing one for the purposes of dissection—the other five bodies had also died. She had initiated a series of experiments that involved menacing and killing hundreds of the things, and had ascertained that the bodies were connected by some sort of field—one whose presence she deduced by process of observation—that permitted the essence of the creature to switch back and forth between the bodies, utilizing the ones it did not occupy as a unique form of camouflage. But even the metahex seemed ordinary when compared to the ghostvine, a plant that she discovered grew in one place alone, a small cavity near the base of the skull.

None of the colony would approach that region, warned away by the same sense of danger that had afflicted Catherine, and it was presumed that should one venture too close to the brain, Griaule would mobilize some of his more deadly inhabitants to deal with the interloper. But Catherine felt secure in approaching the cavity, and leaving Mauldry and her escort of feelies behind, she climbed the steep channel that led up to it, lighting her way with a torch, and entered through an aperture not much wider than her hips. Once inside, seeing that the place was lit by veins of golden blood that branched across the ceiling, flickering like the blown flame of a candle, she extinguished the torch; she noticed with surprise that except for the ceiling, the entire cavity—a boxy space some twenty feet long, about eight feet in height—was fettered with vines whose leaves were dark green, glossy, with complex venation and tips that ended in miniscule hollow tubes. She was winded from the climb, more winded—she thought—than she should have been, and she sat down against the wall to catch her breath; then, feeling drowsy, she closed her eyes for a moment's rest. She came alert to the sound of Mauldry's voice shouting her name. Still drowsy, annoyed by his impatience, she called out, "I just want to rest a few minutes!"

"A few minutes?" he cried. "You've been there three days! What's going on? Are you all right?"

"That's ridiculous!" She started to come to her feet, then sat back, stunned by the sight of a naked woman with long blond hair curled up in a corner not ten feet away, nestled so close to the cavity wall that the tips of leaves half-covered her body and obscured her face.

"Catherine!" Mauldry shouted. "Answer me!"

"I . . . I'm all right! Just a minute!"

The woman stirred and made a complaining noise.

"Catherine!"

"I said I'm all right!"

The woman stretched out her legs; on her right hip was a fine pink scar, hook-shaped, identical to the scar on Catherine's hip, evidence of a childhood fall. And on the back of the right knee, a patch of raw, puckered skin, the product of an acid burn she'd suffered the year before. She was astonished by the sight of these markings, but when the woman sat up and Catherine understood that she was staring at her twin—identical not only in feature, but also in expression, wearing a resigned look that she had glimpsed many times in her mirror—her astonishment turned to fright. She could have sworn she felt the muscles of the woman's face shifting as the expression changed into one of pleased recognition, and in spite of her fear, she had a vague sense of the woman's emotions, of her burgeoning hope and elation.

"Sister," said the woman; she glanced down at her body, and Catherine had a momentary flash of doubled vision, watching the woman's head decline and seeing as well naked breasts and belly from the perspective of the woman's eyes. Her vision returned to normal, and she looked at the woman's face . . . *her* face. Though she had studied herself in the mirror each morning for years, she had never had such a clear perception of the changes that life inside the dragon had wrought upon her. Fine lines bracketed her lips, and the beginnings of crow's-feet radiated from the corners of her eyes. Her cheeks had hollowed, and this made her cheekbones appear sharper; the set of her mouth seemed harder, more determined. The high gloss and perfection of her youthful beauty had been marred far more than she had thought, and this dismayed her. However, the most remarkable change—the one that most struck her—was not embodied by any one detail but in the overall character of the face, in that it exhibited character, for—she realized—prior to entering the dragon it had displayed very little, and what little it *had* displayed had been evidence of indulgence. It troubled her to have this knowledge of the fool she had been thrust upon her with such poignancy.

As if the woman had been listening to her thoughts, she held out her hand and said, "Don't punish yourself, sister. We are all victims of our past."

"What are you?" Catherine asked, pulling back. She felt the woman was a danger to her, though she was not sure why.

"I am you." Again the woman reached out to touch her, and again Catherine shifted away. The woman's face was smiling, but Catherine felt the wash of her frustration and noticed that the woman had leaned forward only a few degrees, remaining in contact with the leaves of the vines as if there were some attachment between them that she could not break.

"I doubt that." Catherine was fascinated, but she was beginning to be swayed by the intuition that the woman's touch would harm her.

"But I am!" the woman insisted. "And something more, besides."

"What more?"

"The plant extracts essences," said the woman. "Infinitely small constructs of the flesh from which it creates a likeness free of the imperfections of your body. And since the seeds of your future are embodied by these essences, though they are unknown to you, I know them . . . for now."

"For now?"

The woman's tone had become desperate. "There's a connection between us . . . surely you feel it?"

"Yes."

"To live, to complete that connection, I must touch you. And once I do, this knowledge of the future will be lost to me. I will be as you . . . though separate. But don't worry. I won't interfere with you, I'll live my own life." She leaned forward again, and Catherine saw that some of the leaves were affixed to her back, the hollow tubes at their tips adhering to the skin. Once again she had an awareness of danger, a growing apprehension that the woman's touch would drain her of some vital substance.

"If you know my future," she said, "then tell me . . . will I ever escape Griaule?"

Mauldry chose this moment to call out to her, and she soothed him by saying that she was taking some cuttings, that she would be down soon. She repeated her question, and the woman said, "Yes, yes, you will leave the dragon," and tried to grasp her hand. "Don't be afraid. I won't harm you."

The woman's flesh was sagging, and Catherine felt the eddying of her fear.

"Please!" she said, holding out both hands. "Only your touch will sustain me. Without it, I'll die!"

But Catherine refused to trust her.

"You must believe me!" cried the woman. "I am your sister! My blood is yours, my memories!" The flesh upon her arms had sagged into billows like the flesh of an old woman, and her face was becoming jowly, grossly distorted. "Oh, please! Remember the time with Stel below the wing . . . you were a maiden. The wind was blowing thistles down from Griaule's back like a rain of silver. And remember the gala in Teocinte? Your sixteenth birthday. You wore a mask of orange blossoms and gold wire, and three men asked for your hand. For God's sake, Catherine! Listen to me! The major . . . don't you remember him? The young major? You were in love with him, but you didn't follow your heart. You were afraid of love, you didn't trust what you felt because you never trusted yourself in those days."

The connection between them was fading, and Catherine steeled herself against the woman's entreaties, which had begun to move her more than a little bit. The woman slumped down, her features blurring, a horrid sight, like the melting of a wax figure, and then, an even more horrid sight, she smiled, her lips appearing to dissolve away from teeth that were themselves dissolving.

"I understand," said the woman in a frail voice, and gave a husky glutinous laugh. "Now I see."

"What is it?" Catherine asked. But the woman collapsed, rolling onto her side, and the process of deterioration grew more rapid; within the span of a few minutes she had dissipated into a gelatinous grayish white puddle that retained the rough outline of her form. Catherine was both appalled and relieved; however, she couldn't help feeling some remorse, uncertain whether she had acted in self-defense or through cowardice had damned a creature who was by nature no more reprehensible than herself. While the woman had been alive—if that was the proper word—Catherine had been mostly afraid, but now she marveled at the apparition, at the complexity of a plant that could produce even the semblance of a human. And the woman had been, she thought, something more vital than mere likeness. How else could she have known her memories? Or could memory, she wondered, have a physiological basis? She forced herself to take samples of the woman's remains, of the vines, with an eye toward exploring the mystery. But she doubted that the heart of such an intricate mystery would be accessible to her primitive instruments. This was to prove a self-fulfilling prophecy, because she really did not want to know the secrets of the ghostvine, leery as to what might be brought to light concerning her own nature, and with the passage of time, although she thought of it often and sometimes discussed the phenomena with Mauldry, she eventually let the matter drop.

V

Though the temperature never changed, though neither rain nor snow fell, though the fluctuations of the golden light remained consistent in their rhythms, the seasons were registered inside the dragon by migrations of birds, the weaving of cocoons, the birth of millions of insects at once; and it was by these signs that Catherine—nine years after entering Griaule's mouth—knew it to be autumn when she fell in love. The three years prior to this had been characterized by a slackening of her zeal, a gradual wearing down of her enthusiasm for scientific knowledge, and this tendency became marked after the death of Captain Mauldry from natural causes; without him to serve as a buffer between her and the feelies, she was overwhelmed by their inanity, their woeful aspect. In truth, there was not much left to learn. Her maps were complete, her specimens and notes filled several rooms, and while she continued her visits to the dragon's heart, she no longer sought to interpret the dreams, using them instead to pass the boring hours. Again she grew restless and began to consider escape. Her life was being wasted, she believed, and she wanted to return to the world, to engage more vital opportunities than those available to her in Griaule's many-chambered prison. It was not that she was ungrateful for the experience. Had she managed to escape shortly after her arrival, she would have returned to a life of meaningless frivolity; but now, armed with knowledge, aware of her strengths and weaknesses, possessed of ambition and a heightened sense of morality, she thought she would be able to accomplish something of importance. But before she could determine whether or not escape was possible, there was a new arrival at the colony, a man whom a group of feelies—while gathering berries near the mouth—had found lying unconscious and had borne to safety.

The man's name was John Colmacos, and he was in his early thirties, a botanist from the university at Port Chantay who had been abandoned by his guides when he insisted on entering the mouth and had subsequently been mauled by apes that had taken up residence in the mouth. He was lean, rawboned, with powerful thick-fingered hands and fine brown hair that would never stay combed. His long-jawed horsey face struck a bargain between homely and distinctive, and was stamped with a perpetually inquiring expression as if he were a bit perplexed by everything he saw; and his blue eyes were large and intricate, the irises flecked with green and hazel, appearing surprisingly delicate in contrast to the rest of him.

Catherine, happy to have rational company, especially that of a professional in her vocation, took charge of nursing him back to health—he had suffered fractures of the arm and ankle, and was badly cut about the face; and in the course of this she began to have fantasies about him as a lover. She had never met a man with his gentleness of manner, his lack of pretense, and she found it most surprising that he wasn't concerned with trying to impress her. Her conception of men had been limited to the soldiers of Teocinte, the thugs of Hangtown, and everything about John fascinated her. For a while she tried to deny her feelings, telling herself that she would have fallen in love with almost anyone under the circumstances, afraid that by loving she would only increase her dissatisfaction with her prison; and, too, there was the realization that this was doubtless another of Griaule's manipulations, his attempt to make her content with her lot, to replace Mauldry with a lover. But she couldn't deny that under any circumstance she would have been attracted to John Colmacos for many reasons, not the least of which was his respect for her work with Griaule, for how she had handled adversity. Nor could she deny that the attraction was mutual. That was clear. Although there were awkward moments, there was no mooniness between them; they were both watching what was happening.

"This is amazing," he said one day, while going through one of her notebooks, lying on a pile of furs in her apartment. "It's hard to believe you haven't had training."

A flush spread over her cheeks. "Anyone in my shoes, with all that time, nothing else to do, they would have done no less."

He set down the notebook and measured her with a stare that caused her to lower her eyes. "You're wrong," he said. "Most people would have fallen apart. I can't think of anybody else who could have managed all this. You're remarkable."

She felt oddly incompetent in the light of this judgment, as if she had accorded him ultimate authority and were receiving the sort of praise that a wise adult might bestow upon an inept child who had done well for once. She wanted to explain to him that everything she had done had been a kind of therapy, a hobby to stave off despair; but she didn't know how to put this into words without sounding awkward and falsely modest, and so she merely said, "Oh," and busied herself with preparing a dose of brianine to take away the pain in his ankle.

"You're embarrassed," he said. "I'm sorry. . . . I didn't mean to make you uncomfortable."

"I'm not . . . I mean, I. . . ." She laughed. "I'm still not accustomed to talking."

He said nothing, smiling.

"What is it?" she said, defensive, feeling that he was making fun of her.

"What do you mean?"

"Why are you smiling?"

"I could frown," he said, "if that would make you comfortable."

Irritated, she bent to her task, mixing paste in a brass goblet studded with uncut emeralds, then molding it into a pellet.

"That was a joke," he said.

"I know."

"What's the matter?"

She shook her head. "Nothing."

"Look," he said. "I don't want to make you uncomfortable . . . I really don't. What am I doing wrong?"

She sighed, exasperated with herself. "It's not you," she said. "I just can't get used to you being here, that's all."

From without came the babble of some feelies lowering on ropes toward the chamber floor.

"I can understand that," he said. "I . . ." He broke off, looked down, and fingered the edge of the notebook.

"What were you going to say?"

He threw back his head, laughed. "Do you see how we're acting? Explaining ourselves constantly . . . as if we could hurt each other by saying the wrong word."

She glanced over at him, met his eyes, then looked away.

"What I meant was, we're not that fragile," he said, and then, as if by way of clarification, he hastened to add: "We're not that . . . vulnerable to one another."

He held her stare for a moment, and this time it was he who looked away and Catherine who smiled.

If she hadn't known she was in love, she would have suspected as much from the change in her attitude toward the dragon. She seemed to be seeing everything anew. Her wonder at Griaule's size and strangeness had been restored, and she delighted in displaying his marvelous features to John—the orioles and swallows that never once had flown under the sun, the glowing heart, the cavity where the ghostvine grew (though she would not linger there), and a tiny chamber close to the heart lit not by Griaule's blood but by thousands of luminous white spiders that shifted and crept across the blackness of the ceiling, like a night sky whose constellations had come to life. It was in this chamber that they engaged in their first intimacy, a kiss from which Catherine—after initially letting herself be swept away—pulled back, disoriented by the powerful sensations flooding her body, sensations both familiar and unnatural in that she hadn't experienced them for so long, and startled by the suddenness with which her fantasies had become real. Flustered, she ran from the chamber, leaving John, who was still hobbled by his injuries, to limp back to the colony alone.

She hid from him most of that day, sitting with her knees drawn up on a patch of peach-colored silk near the hole at the center of the colony's floor, immersed in the bustle and gabble of the feelies as they promenaded in their decaying finery. Though for the most part they were absorbed in their own pursuits, some sensed her mood and gathered around her, touching her, making the whimpering noises that among them passed for expressions of tenderness. Their pasty doglike faces ringed her, uniformly sad, and as if sadness were contagious, she started to cry. At first her tears seemed the product of her inability to cope with love, and then it seemed she was crying over the poor thing of her life, the haplessness of her days inside the body of the dragon; but she came to feel that her sadness was one with Griaule's, that this feeling of gloom and entrapment reflected his essential mood, and that thought stopped her tears. She'd never considered the dragon an object deserving of sympathy, and she did not now consider him such; but perceiving him imprisoned in a web of ancient magic, and the Chinese puzzle of lesser magics and imprisonments that derived from that original event, she felt foolish for having cried. Everything, she realized, even the happiest of occurrences, might be a cause for tears if you failed to see it in terms of the world that you inhabited; however, if you managed to achieve a balanced perspective, you saw that although sadness could result from every human action, that you had to seize the opportunities for effective action that came your way and not question them, no matter how unrealistic or futile they might appear. Just as Griaule had done by finding a way to utilize his power while immobilized. She laughed to think of herself emulating Griaule even in this abstract fashion, and several of the feelies standing beside her echoed her laughter. One of the males, an old man with tufts of gray hair poking up from his pallid skull, shuffled near, picking at a loose button on his stiff, begrimed coat of silver-embroidered satin.

"Cat'rine mus' be easy sweetly, now?" he said. "No mo' bad t'ing?"

"No," she said. "No more bad thing."

On the other side of the hole a pile of naked feelies was writhing together in the clumsiness of foreplay, men trying to penetrate men, getting angry, slapping one another, then lapsing into giggles when they found a woman and figured out the proper procedure. Once this would have disgusted her, but no more. Judged by the attitudes of a place not their own, perhaps the feelies were disgusting; but this *was* their place, and Catherine's place as well, and accepting that at last, she stood and walked toward the nearest basket. The old man hustled after her, fingering his lapels in a parody of self-importance, and, as if he were the functionary of her mood, he announced to everyone they encountered, "No mo' bad t'ing, no mo' bad t'ing."

Riding up in the basket was like passing in front of a hundred tiny stages upon which scenes from the same play were being performed— pale figures slumped on silks, playing with gold and bejeweled baubles—and gazing around her, ignoring the stink, the dilapidation, she felt she was looking out upon an exotic kingdom. Always before she had been impressed by its size and grotesqueness; but now she was struck by its richness, and she wondered whether the feelies' style of dress was inadvertent or if Griaule's subtlety extended to the point of clothing this human refuse in the rags of dead courtiers and kings. She felt exhilarated, joyful; but as the basket lurched near the level on which her rooms were located, she became nervous. It had been so long since she had been with a man, and she was worried that she might not be suited to him . . . then she recalled that she'd been prone to these worries even in the days when she had been with a new man every week.

She lashed the basket to a peg, stepped out onto the walkway outside her rooms, took a deep breath and pushed through the curtains, pulled them shut behind her. John was asleep, the furs pulled up to his chest. In the fading half-light, his face—dirtied by a few days' growth of beard—looked sweetly mysterious and rapt, like the face of a saint at meditation, and she thought it might be best to let him sleep; but that, she realized, was a signal of her nervousness, not of compassion. The only thing to do was to get it over with, to pass through nervousness as quickly as possible and learn what there was to learn. She stripped off her trousers, her shirt, and stood for a second above him, feeling giddy, frail, as if she'd stripped off much more than a few ounces of fabric. Then she eased in beneath the furs, pressing the length of her body to his. He stirred but didn't wake, and this delighted her; she liked the idea of having him in her clutches, of coming to him in the middle of a dream, and she shivered with the apprehension of gleeful childish power. He tossed, turned onto his side to face her, still asleep, and she pressed closer, marveling at how ready she was, how open to him. He muttered something, and as she nestled against him, he grew hard, his erection pinned between their bellies. Cautiously, she lifted her right knee atop his hip, guided him between her legs, and moved her hips back and forth, rubbing against him, slowly, slowly, teasing herself with little bursts of pleasure. His eyelids twitched, blinked open, and he stared at her, his eyes looking black and wet, his skin stained a murky gold in the dimness. "Catherine," he said, and she gave a soft laugh, because her name seemed a power the way he had spoken it. His fingers hooked into the plump meat of her hips as he pushed and prodded at her, trying to find the right angle. Her head fell back, her eyes closed, concentrating on the feeling that centered her dizziness and heat, and then he was inside her, going deep with a single thrust, beginning to make love to her, and she said, "Wait, wait," holding him immobile, afraid for an instant, feeling too much, a black wave of sensation building, threatening to wash her away.

"What's wrong?" he whispered. "Do you want. . . ."

"Just wait . . . just for a bit." She rested her forehead against his, trembling, amazed by the difference that he made in her body; one moment she felt buoyant, as if their connection had freed her from the restraints of gravity, and the next moment—whenever he shifted or eased fractionally deeper—she would feel as if all his weight were pouring inside her and she was sinking into the cool silks.

"Are you all right?"

"Mmm." She opened her eyes, saw his face inches away, and was surprised that he didn't appear unfamiliar.

"What is it?" he asked.

"I was just thinking."

"About what?"

"I was wondering who you were, and when I looked at you, it was as if I already knew." She traced the line of his upper lip with her forefinger. "Who are you?"

"I thought you knew already."

"Maybe . . . but I don't know anything specific. Just that you were a professor."

"You want to know specifics?"

"Yes."

"I was an unruly child," he said. "I refused to eat onion soup, I never washed behind my ears."

His grasp tightened on her hips, and he thrust inside her, a few slow, delicious movements, kissing her mouth, her eyes.

"When I was a boy," he said, quickening his rhythm, breathing hard between the words, "I'd go swimming every morning. Off the rocks at Ayler's Point . . . it was beautiful. Cerulean water, palms. Chickens and pigs foraging. On the beach."

"Oh, God!" she said, locking her leg behind his thigh, her eyelids fluttering down.

"My first girlfriend was named Penny . . . she was twelve. Red-headed. I was a year younger. I loved her because she had freckles. I used to believe . . . freckles were . . . a sign of something. I wasn't sure what. But I love you more than her."

"I love you!" She found his rhythm, adapted to it, trying to take him all inside her. She wanted to see where they joined, and she imagined there was no longer any distinction between them, that their bodies had merged and were sealed together.

"I cheated in mathematics class, I could never do trigonometry. God . . . Catherine."

His voice receded, stopped, and the air seemed to grow solid around her, holding her in a rosy suspension. Light was gathering about them, light from a strange heatless burning, and she heard herself crying out, calling his name, saying sweet things, childish things, telling him how wonderful he was, words like the words in a dream, important for their music, their sonority, rather than for any sense they made. She felt again the building of a dark wave in her belly. This time she flowed with it and let it carry her far.

VI

"Love's stupid," John said to her one day months later as they were sitting in the chamber of the heart, watching the complex eddying of golden light and whorls of shadow on the surface of the organ. "I feel like a damn sophomore. I keep finding myself thinking that I should do something noble. Feed the hungry, cure a disease." He made a noise of disgust. "It's as if I just woke up to the fact that the world has problems, and because I'm so happily in love, I want everyone else to be happy. But stuck . . ."

"Sometimes I feel like that myself," she said, startled by this outburst. "Maybe it's stupid, but it's not wrong. And neither is being happy."

"Stuck in here," he went on, "there's no chance of doing anything for ourselves, let alone saving the world. As for being happy, that's not going to last . . . not in here, anyway."

"It's lasted six months," she said. "And if it won't last here, why should it last anywhere?"

He drew up his knees, rubbed the spot on his ankle where it had been fractured. "What's the matter with you? When I got here, all you could talk about was how much you wanted to escape. You said you'd do anything to get out. It sounds now that you don't care one way or the other."

She watched him rubbing the ankle, knowing what was coming. "I'd like very much to escape. Now that you're here, it's more acceptable to me. I can't deny that. That doesn't mean I wouldn't leave if I had the chance. But at least I can think about staying here without despairing."

"Well, *I* can't! I . . ." He lowered his head, suddenly drained of animation, still rubbing his ankle. "I'm sorry, Catherine. My leg's hurting again, and I'm in a foul mood." He cut his eyes toward her. "Have you got that stuff with you?"

"Yes."

She made no move to get it for him.

"I realize I'm taking too much," he said. "It helps pass the time."

She bristled at that and wanted to ask if she was the reason for his boredom; but she repressed her anger, knowing that she was partly to blame for his dependence on the brianine, that during his convalescence she had responded to his demands for the drug as a lover and not as a nurse.

An impatient look crossed his face. "Can I have it?"

Reluctantly she opened her pack, removed a flask of water and some pellets of brianine wrapped in cloth, and handed them over. He fumbled at the cloth, hurrying to unscrew the cap of the flask, and then—as he was about to swallow two of the pellets—he noticed her watching him. His face tightened with anger, and he appeared ready to snap at her. But his expression softened, and he downed the pellets, held out two more. "Take some with me," he said. "I know I have to stop. And I will. But let's just relax today, let's pretend we don't have any troubles . . . all right?"

That was a ploy he had adopted recently, making her his accomplice in addiction and thus avoiding guilt; she knew she should refuse to join him, but at the moment she didn't have the strength for an argument. She took the pellets, washed them down with a swallow of water, and lay back against the chamber wall. He settled beside her, leaning on one elbow, smiling, his eyes muddled-looking from the drug.

"You do have to stop, you know," she said.

His smile flickered, then steadied, as if his batteries were running low. "I suppose."

"If we're going to escape," she said, "you'll need a clear head."

He perked up at this. "That's a change."

"I haven't been thinking about escape for a long time. It didn't seem possible . . . it didn't even seem very important, anymore. I guess I'd given up on the idea. I mean just before you arrived, I'd been thinking about it again, but it wasn't serious . . . only frustration."

"And now?"

"It's become important again."

"Because of me, because I keep nagging about it?"

"Because of both of us. I'm not sure escape's possible, but I was wrong to stop trying."

He rolled onto his back, shielding his eyes with his forearm as if the heart's glow were too bright.

"John?" The name sounded thick and sluggish, and she could feel the drug taking her, making her drifty and slow.

"This place," he said. "This goddamn place."

"I thought"—she was beginning to have difficulty in ordering her words—"I thought you were excited by it. You used to talk. . . ."

"Oh, I am excited!" He laughed dully. "It's a storehouse of marvels. Fantastic! Overwhelming! It's too overwhelming. The feeling here . . ." He turned to her. "Don't you feel it?"

"I'm not sure what you mean."

"How could you stand living here for all these years? Are you that much stronger than me, or are you just insensitive?"

"I'm. . . ."

"God!"

He turned away, stared at the heart wall, his face tattooed with a convoluted flow of light and shadow, then flaring gold.

"You're so at ease here. Look at that." He pointed to the heart. "It's not a heart, it's a bloody act of magic. Every time I come here I get the feeling it's going to display a pattern that'll make me disappear. Or crush me. Or something. And you just sit there looking at it with a thoughtful expression as if you're planning to put in curtains or repaint the damned thing."

"We don't have to come here anymore."

"I can't stay away," he said, and held up a pellet of brianine. "It's like this stuff."

They didn't speak for several minutes . . . perhaps a bit less, perhaps a little more. Time had become meaningless, and Catherine felt that she was floating away, her flesh suffused with a rosy warmth like the warmth of lovemaking. Flashes of dream imagery passed through her mind: a clown's monstrous face; an unfamiliar room with tilted walls and three-legged blue chairs; a painting whose paint was melting, dripping. The flashes lapsed into thoughts of John. He was becoming weaker every day, she realized. Losing his resilience, growing nervous and moody. She had tried to convince herself that sooner or later he would become adjusted to life inside Griaule, but she was beginning to accept the fact that he was not going to be able to survive here. She didn't understand why, whether it was due—as he had said—to the dragon's oppressiveness or to some inherent weakness. Or a combination of both. But she could no longer deny it, and the only option left was for them to effect an escape. It was easy to consider escape with the drug in her veins, feeling aloof and calm, possessed of a dreamlike overview; but she knew that once it wore off she would be at a loss as to how to proceed.

To avoid thinking, she let the heart's patterns dominate her attention. They seemed abnormally complex, and as she watched she began to have the impression of something new at work, some interior mechanism that she had never noticed before, and to become aware that the sense of imminence that pervaded the chamber was stronger than ever before; but she was so muzzy-headed that she could not concentrate upon these things. Her eyelids drooped, and she fell into her recurring dream of the sleeping dragon, focusing on the smooth scaleless skin of its chest, a patch of whiteness that came to surround her, to draw her into a world of whiteness with the serene constancy of its rhythmic rise and fall, as unvarying and predictable as the ticking of a perfect clock.

Over the next six months Catherine devised numerous plans for escape, but discarded them all as unworkable until at last she thought of one that—although far from foolproof—seemed in its simplicity to offer the least risk of failure. Though without brianine the plan would have failed, the process of settling upon this particular plan would have gone faster had drugs not been available; unable to resist the combined pull of the drug and John's need for companionship in his addiction, she herself had become an addict, and much of her time was spent lying at the heart with John, stupefied, too enervated even to make love. Her feelings toward John had changed; it could not have been otherwise, for he was not the man he had been. He had lost weight and muscle tone, grown vague and brooding, and she was concerned for the health of his body and soul. In some ways she felt closer than ever to him, her maternal instincts having been engaged by his dissolution; yet she couldn't help resenting the fact that he had failed her, that instead of offering relief, he had turned out to be a burden and a weakening influence; and as a result whenever some distance arose between them, she exerted herself to close it only if it was practical to do so. This was not often the case, because John had deteriorated to the point that closeness of any sort was a chore. However, Catherine clung to the hope that if they could escape, they would be able to make a new beginning.

The drug owned her. She carried a supply of pellets wherever she went, gradually increasing her dosages, and not only did it affect her health, her energy; it had a profound effect upon her mind. Her powers of concentration had diminished, her sleep became fitful, and she began to experience hallucinations. She heard voices, strange noises, and on one occasion she was certain that she had spotted old Amos Mauldry among a group of feelies milling about at the bottom of the colony chamber. Her mental erosion caused her to mistrust the information of her senses and to dismiss as delusion the intimations of some climactic event that came to her in dreams and from the patterns of light and shadow on the heart; and recognizing that certain of her symptoms—hearkening to inaudible signals and the like—were similar to the behavior of the feelies, she feared that she was becoming one of them. Yet this fear was not so pronounced as once it might have been. She sought now to be tolerant of them, to overlook their role in her imprisonment, perceiving them as unwitting agents of Griaule, and she could not be satisfied in hating either them or the dragon; Griaule and the subtle manifestations of his will were something too vast and incomprehensible to be a target for hatred, and she transferred all her wrath to Brianne, the woman who had betrayed her. The feelies seemed to notice this evolution in her attitude, and they became more familiar, attaching themselves to her wherever she went, asking questions, touching her, and while this made it difficult to achieve privacy, in the end it was their increased affection that inspired her plan.

One day, accompanied by a group of giggling, chattering feelies, she walked up toward the skull, to the channel that led to the cavity containing the ghostvine. She ducked into the channel, half-tempted to explore the cavity again; but she decided against this course, and on crawling out of the channel, she discovered that the feelies had vanished. Suddenly weak, as if their presence had been an actual physical support, she sank to her knees and stared along the narrow passage of pale red flesh that wound away into a golden murk like a burrow leading to a shining treasure. She felt a welling up of petulant anger at the feelies for having deserted her. Of course she should have expected it. They shunned this area like. . . . She sat up, struck by a realization attendant to that thought. How far, she wondered, had the feelies retreated? Could they have gone beyond the side passage that opened into the throat? She came to her feet and crept along the passage until she reached the curve. She peeked out around it and, seeing no one, continued on, holding her breath until her chest began to ache. She heard voices, peered around the next curve, and caught sight of eight feelies gathered by the entrance to the side passage, their silken rags agleam, their swords reflecting glints of the inconstant light. She went back around the curve, rested against the wall; she had trouble thinking, in shaping thought into a coherent stream, and out of reflex she fumbled in her pack for some brianine. Just touching one of the pellets acted to calm her, and once she had swallowed it she breathed easier. She fixed her eyes on the blurred shape of a vein buried beneath the glistening ceiling of the passage, letting the fluctuations of light mesmerize her. She felt she was blurring, becoming golden and liquid and slow, and in that feeling she found a core of confidence and hope.

There's a way, she told herself. *My God, maybe there really is a way.*

By the time she had fleshed out her plan three days later, her chief fear was that John wouldn't be able to function well enough to take part in it. He looked awful, his cheeks sunken, his color poor, and the first time she tried to tell him about the plan, he fell asleep. To counteract the brianine she began cutting his dosage, mixing it with the stimulant she had derived from the lichen growing on the dragon's lung, and after a few days, though his color and general appearance did not improve, he became more alert and energized. She knew the improvement was purely chemical, that the stimulant was a danger in his weakened state; but there was no alternative, and this at least offered him a chance at life. If he were to remain there, given the physical erosion caused by the drug, she did not believe he would last another six months.

It wasn't much of a plan, nothing subtle, nothing complex, and if she'd had her wits about her, she thought, she would have come up with it long before; but she doubted she would have had the courage to try it alone, and if there was trouble, then two people would stand a much better chance than one. John was elated by the prospect. After she had told him the particulars he paced up and down in their bedroom, his eyes bright, hectic spots of red dappling his cheeks, stopping now and again to question her or to make distracted comments.

"The feelies," he said. "We . . . uh . . . we won't hurt them?"

"I told you . . . not unless it's necessary."

"That's good, that's good." He crossed the room to the curtains drawn across the entrance. "Of course, it's not my field, but. . . ."

"John?"

He peered out at the colony through the gap in the curtains, the skin on his forehead washing from gold to dark. "Uh-huh."

"What's not your field?"

After a long pause he said, "It's not . . . nothing."

"You were talking about the feelies."

"They're very interesting," he said distractedly. He swayed, then moved sluggishly toward her, collapsed on the pile of furs where she was sitting. He turned his face to her, looked at her with a morose expression. "It'll be better," he said. "Once we're out of here, I'll . . . I know I haven't been . . . strong. I haven't been. . . ."

"It's all right," she said, stroking his hair.

"No, it's not, it's not." Agitated, he struggled to sit up, but she restrained him, telling him not to be upset, and soon he lay still. "How can you love me?" he asked after a long silence.

"I don't have any choice in the matter." She bent to him, pushing back her hair so it wouldn't hang in his face, kissed his cheek, his eyes.

He started to say something, then laughed weakly, and she asked him what he found amusing.

"I was thinking about free will," he said. "How improbable a concept that's become. Here. Where it's so obviously not an option."

She settled down beside him, weary of trying to boost his spirits. She remembered how he'd been after his arrival: eager, alive, and full of curiosity despite his injuries. Now his moments of greatest vitality— like this one—were spent in sardonic rejection of happy possibility. She was tired of arguing with him, of making the point that everything in life could be reduced by negative logic to a sort of pitiful reflex, if that was the way you wanted to see it. His voice grew stronger, this prompted—she knew—by a rush of the stimulant within his system.

"It's Griaule," he said. "Everything here belongs to him, even to the most fleeting of hopes and wishes. What we feel, what we think. When I was a student and first heard about Griaule, about his method of dominion, the omnipotent functioning of his will, I thought it was foolishness pure and simple. But I was an optimist, then. And optimists are only fools without experience. Of course I didn't think of myself as an optimist. I saw myself as a realist. I had a romantic notion that I was alone, responsible for my actions, and I perceived that as being a noble beauty, a refinement of the tragic . . . that state of utter and forlorn independence. I thought how cozy and unrealistic it was for people to depend on gods and demons to define their roles in life. I didn't know how terrible it would be to realize that nothing you thought or did had any individual importance, that everything— love, hate, your petty likes and dislikes—was part of some unfathomable scheme. I couldn't comprehend how worthless that knowledge would make you feel."

He went on in this vein for some time, his words weighing on her, filling her with despair, pushing hope aside. Then, as if this monologue had aroused some bitter sexuality, he began to make love to her. She felt removed from the act, imprisoned within walls erected by his dour sentences· but she responded with desperate enthusiasm, her own arousal funded by a desolate prurience. She watched his spread-fingered hands knead and cup her breasts, actions that seemed to her as devoid of emotional value as those of a starfish gripping a rock; and yet because of this desolation, because she wanted to deny it and also because of the voyeuristic thrill she derived from watching herself being taken, used, her body reacted with unusual fervor. The sweaty film between them was like a silken cloth, and their movements seemed more accomplished and supple than ever before; each jolt of pleasure brought her to new and dizzying heights. But afterward she felt devastated and defeated, not loved, and lying there with him, listening to the muted gabble of the feelies from without, bathed in their rich stench, she knew she had come to the nadir of her life, that she had finally united with the feelies in their enactment of a perturbed and animalistic rhythm.

Over the next ten days she set the plan into motion. She took to dispensing little sweet cakes to the feelies who guarded her on her daily walks with John, ending up each time at the channel that led to the ghostvine. And she also began to spread the rumor that at long last her study of the dragon was about to yield its promised revelation. On the day of the escape, prior to going forth, she stood at the bottom of the chamber, surrounded by hundreds of feelies, more hanging on ropes just above her, and called out to them in ringing tones, "Today I will have word for you! Griaule's word! Bring together the hunters and those who gather food, and have them wait here for me! I will return soon, very soon, and speak to you of what is to come!"

The feelies jostled and pawed one another, chattering, tittering, hopping up and down, and some of those hanging from the ropes were so overcome with excitement that they lost their grip and fell, landing atop their fellows, creating squirming heaps of feelies who squalled and yelped and then started fumbling with the buttons of each other's clothing. Catherine waved at them, and with John at her side, set out toward the cavity, six feelies with swords at their rear.

John was terribly nervous, and all during the walk he kept casting backward glances at the feelies, asking questions that only served to unnerve Catherine. "Are you sure they'll eat them?" he said. "Maybe they won't be hungry."

"They always eat them while we're in the channel," she said. "You know that."

"I know," he said. "But I'm just . . . I don't want anything to go wrong." He walked another half a dozen paces. "Are you sure you put enough in the cakes?"

"I'm sure." She watched him out of the corner of her eye. The muscles in his jaw bunched, nerves twitched in his cheek. A light sweat had broken on his forehead, and his pallor was extreme. She took his arm. "How do you feel?"

"Fine," he said. "I'm fine."

"It's going to work, so don't worry . . . please."

"I'm fine," he repeated, his voice dead, eyes fixed straight ahead.

The feelies came to a halt just around the curve from the channel, and Catherine, smiling at them, handed them each a cake; then she and John went forward and crawled into the channel. There they sat in the darkness without speaking, their hips touching. At last John whispered, "How much longer?"

"Let's give it a few more minutes . . . just to be safe."

He shuddered, and she asked again how he felt.

"A little shaky," he said. "But I'm all right."

She put her hand on his arm; his muscles jumped at the touch. "Calm down," she said, and he nodded. But there was no slackening of his tension.

The seconds passed with the slowness of sap welling from cut bark, and despite her certainty that all would go as planned, Catherine's anxiety increased. Little shiny squiggles, velvety darknesses blacker than the air, wormed in front of her eyes. She imagined that she heard whispers out in the passage. She tried to think of something else, but the concerns she erected to occupy her mind materialized and vanished with a superficial and formal precision that did nothing to ease her, seeming mere transparencies shunted across the vision of a fearful prospect ahead. Finally she gave John a nudge and they crept from the channel, made their way cautiously along the passage. When they reached the curve beyond which the feelies were waiting, she paused, listened. Not a sound. She looked out. Six bodies lay by the entrance to the side passage; even at that distance she could spot the half-eaten cakes that had fallen from their hands. Still wary, they approached the feelies, and as they came near, Catherine thought that there was something unnatural about their stillness. She knelt beside a young male, caught a whiff of loosened bowel, saw the rapt character of death stamped on his features, and realized that in measuring out the dosages of brianine in each cake, she had not taken the feelies' slightness of build into account. She had killed them.

"Come on!" said John. He had picked up two swords; they were so short, they looked toylike in his hands. He handed over one of the swords and helped her to stand. "Let's go . . . there might be more of them!"

He wetted his lips, glanced from side to side. With his sunken cheeks and hollowed eyes, his face had the appearance of a skull, and for a moment, dumbstruck by the realization that she had killed, by the understanding that for all her disparagement of them, the feelies were human, Catherine failed to recognize him. She stared at them—like ugly dolls in the ruins of their gaud—and felt again that same chill emptiness that had possessed her when she had killed Key Willen. John caught her arm, pushed her toward the side passage; it was covered by a loose flap, and though she had become used to seeing the dragon's flesh everywhere, she now shrank from touching it. John pulled back the flap, urged her into the passage, and then they were crawling through a golden gloom, following a twisting downward course.

In places the passage was only a few inches wider than her hips, and they were forced to worm their way along. She imagined that she could feel the immense weight of the dragon pressing in upon her, pictured some muscle twitching in reflex, the passage constricting and crushing them. The closed space made her breathing sound loud, and for a while John's breathing sounded even louder, hoarse and labored. But then she could no longer hear it, and she discovered that he had fallen behind. She called out to him, and he said, "Keep going!"

She rolled onto her back in order to see him. He was gasping, his face twisted as if in pain. "What's wrong?" she cried, trying to turn completely, constrained from doing so by the narrowness of the passage.

He gave her a shove. "I'll be all right. Don't stop!"

"John!" She stretched out a hand to him, and he wedged his shoulder against her legs, pushing her along.

"Damn it . . . just keep going!" He continued to push and exhort her, and realizing that she could do nothing, she turned and crawled at an even faster pace, seeing his harrowed face in her mind's eye.

She couldn't tell how many minutes it took to reach the end of the passage; it was a timeless time, one long unfractionated moment of straining, squirming, pulling at the slick walls, her effort fueled by her concern; but when she scrambled out into the dragon's throat, her heart racing, for an instant she forgot about John, about everything except the sight before her. From where she stood, the throat sloped upward and widened into the mouth, and through that great opening came a golden light, not the heavy mineral brilliance of Griaule's blood, but a fresh clear light, penetrating the tangled shapes of the thickets in beams made crystalline by dust and moisture—the light of day. The tip of a huge fang hooking upward, stained gold with the morning sun, and the vault of the dragon's mouth above, with its vines and epiphytes. Stunned, gaping, she dropped her sword and went a couple of paces toward the light. It was so clean, so pure, its allure like a call. Remembering John, she turned back to the passage. He was pushing himself erect with his sword, his face flushed, panting.

"Look!" she said, hurrying to him, pointing at the light. "God, just look at that!" She steadied him, began steering him toward the mouth.

"We made it," he said. "I didn't believe we would."

His hand tightened on her arm in what she assumed was a sign of affection; but then his grip tightened cruelly, and he lurched backward.

"John!" She fought to hold on to him, saw that his eyes had rolled up into his head.

He sprawled onto his back, and she went down on her knees beside him, hands fluttering above his chest, saying, "John? John?" What felt like a shiver passed through his body, a faint guttering noise issued from his throat, and she knew, oh, she knew very well the meaning of that tremor, that signal passage of breath. She drew back, confused, staring at his face, certain that she had gotten things wrong, that in a second or two his eyelids would open. But they did not. "John?" she said, astonished by how calm she felt, by the measured tone of her voice, as if she were making a simple inquiry. She wanted to break through the shell of calmness, to let out what she was really feeling, but it was as if some strangely lucid twin had gained control over her muscles and will. Her face was cold, and she got to her feet, thinking that the coldness must be radiating from John's body and that distance would be a cure. The sight of him lying there frightened her, and she turned her back on him, folded her arms across her chest. She blinked against the daylight. It hurt her eyes, and the loops and interlacings of foliage standing out in silhouette also hurt her with their messy complexity, their disorder. She couldn't decide what to do. Get away, she told herself. Get out. She took a hesitant step toward the mouth, but that direction didn't make sense. No direction made sense, anymore.

Something moved in the bushes, but she paid it no mind. Her calm was beginning to crack, and a powerful gravity seemed to be pulling her back toward the body. She tried to resist it. More movement. Leaves were rustling, branches being pushed aside. Lots of little movements. She wiped at her eyes. There were no tears in them, but something was hampering her vision, something opaque and thin, a tattered film. The shreds of her calm, she thought, and laughed . . . more a hiccup than a laugh. She managed to focus on the bushes and saw ten, twenty, no, more, maybe two or three dozen diminutive figures, pale mongrel children in glittering rags standing at the verge of the thicket. She hiccuped again, and this time it felt nothing like a laugh. A sob, or maybe nausea. The feelies shifted nearer, edging toward her. The bastards had been waiting for them. She and John had never had a chance of escaping.

Catherine retreated to the body, reached down, groping for John's sword. She picked it up, pointed it at them. "Stay away from me," she said. "Just stay away, and I won't hurt you."

They came closer, shuffling, their shoulders hunched, their attitudes fearful, but advancing steadily all the same.

"Stay away!" she shouted. "I swear I'll kill you!" She swung the sword, making a windy arc through the air. "I swear!"

The feelies gave no sign of having heard, continuing their advance, and Catherine, sobbing now, shrieked for them to keep back, swinging the sword again and again. They encircled her, standing just beyond range. "You don't believe me?" she said. "You don't believe I'll kill you? I don't have any reason not to." All her grief and fury broke through, and with a scream she lunged at the feelies, stabbing one in the stomach, slicing a line of blood across the satin-and-gilt chest of another. The two she had wounded fell, shrilling their agony, and the rest swarmed toward her. She split the skull of another, split it as easily as she might have a melon, saw gore and splintered bone fly from the terrible wound, the dead male's face nearly halved, more blood leaking from around his eyes as he toppled, and then the rest of them were on her, pulling her down, pummeling her, giving little fey cries. She had no chance against them, but she kept on fighting, knowing that when she stopped, when she surrendered, she would have to start feeling, and that she wanted badly to avoid. Their vapid faces hovered above her, seeming uniformly puzzled, as if unable to understand her behavior, and the mildness of their reactions infuriated her. Death should have brightened them, made them—like her—hot with rage. Screaming again, her thoughts reddening, pumped with adrenaline, she struggled to her knees, trying to shake off the feelies who clung to her arms. Snapping her teeth at fingers, faces, arms. Then something struck the back of her head, and she sagged, her vision whirling, darkness closing in until all she could see was a tunnel of shadow with someone's watery eyes at the far end. The eyes grew wider, merged into a single eye that was itself a shadow with leathery wings and a forked tongue and a belly full of fire that swooped down, openmouthed, to swallow her up and fly her home.

VII

The drug moderated Catherine's grief . . . or perhaps it was more than the drug. John's decline had begun so soon after they had met, it seemed she had become accustomed to sadness in relation to him, and thus his death had not overwhelmed her, but rather had manifested as an ache in her chest and a heaviness in her limbs, like small stones she was forced to carry about. To rid herself of that ache, that heaviness, she increased her use of the drug, eating the pellets as if they were candy, gradually withdrawing from life. She had no use for life any longer. She knew she was going to die within the dragon, knew it with the same clarity and certainty that accompanied all Griaule's sendings—death was to be her punishment for seeking to avoid his will, for denying his right to define and delimit her.

After the escape attempt, the feelies had treated her with suspicion and hostility; recently they had been absorbed by some internal matter, agitated in the extreme, and they had taken to ignoring her. Without their minimal companionship, without John, the patterns flowing across the surface of the heart were the only thing that took Catherine out of herself, and she spent hours at a time watching them, lying there half-conscious, registering their changes through slitted eyes. As her addiction worsened, as she lost weight and muscle tone, she became even more expert in interpreting the patterns, and staring up at the vast curve of the heart, like the curve of a golden bell, she came to realize that Mauldry had been right, that the dragon was a god, a universe unto itself with its own laws and physical constants. A god that she hated. She would try to beam her hatred at the heart, hoping to cause a rupture, a seizure of some sort; but she knew that Griaule was impervious to this, impervious to all human weapons, and that her hatred would have as little effect upon him as an arrow loosed into an empty sky.

One day almost a year after John's death she waked abruptly from a dreamless sleep beside the heart, sitting bolt upright, feeling that a cold spike had been driven down the hollow of her spine. She rubbed sleep from her eyes, trying to shake off the lethargy of the drug, sensing danger at hand. Then she glanced up at the heart and was struck motionless. The patterns of shadow and golden radiance were changing more rapidly than ever before, and their complexity, too, was far greater than she had ever seen; yet they were as clear to her as her own script: pulsings of darkness and golden eddies flowing, unscrolling across the dimpled surface of the organ. It was a simple message, and for a few seconds she refused to accept the knowledge it conveyed, not wanting to believe that this was the culmination of her destiny, that her youth had been wasted in so trivial a matter; but recalling all the clues, the dreams of the sleeping dragon, the repetitious vision of the rise and fall of its chest, Mauldry's story of the first Feely, the exodus of animals and insects and birds, the muffled thud from deep within the dragon after which everything had remained calm for a thousand years . . . she knew it must be true.

As it had done a thousand years before, and as it would do again a thousand years in the future, the heart was going to beat.

She was infuriated, and she wanted to reject the fact that all her trials and griefs had been sacrifices made for the sole purpose of saving the feelies. Her task, she realized, would be to clear them out of the chamber where they lived before it was flooded with the liquids that fueled the dragon's fires; and after the chamber had been emptied, she was to lead them back so they could go on with the work of keeping Griaule pest-free. The cause of their recent agitation, she thought, must have been due to their apprehension of the event, the result of one of Griaule's sendings; but because of their temerity they would tend to dismiss his warning, being more frightened of the outside world than of any peril within the dragon. They would need guidance to survive, and as once he had chose Mauldry to assist her, now Griaule had chosen her to guide the feelies.

She staggered up, as befuddled as a bird trapped between glass walls, making little rushes this way and that; then anger overcame confusion, and she beat with her fists on the heart wall, bawling her hatred of the dragon, her anguish at the ruin he had made of her life. Finally, breathless, she collapsed, her own heart pounding erratically, trying to think what to do. She wouldn't tell them, she decided; she would just let them die when the chamber flooded, and this way have her revenge. But an instant later she reversed her decision, knowing that the feelies' deaths would merely be an inconvenience to Griaule, that he would simply gather a new group of idiots to serve him. And besides, she thought, she had already killed too many feelies. There was no choice, she realized; over the span of almost eleven years she had been maneuvered by the dragon's will to this place and moment where, by virtue of her shaped history and conscience, she had only one course of action.

Full of muddle-headed good intentions, she made her way back to the colony, her guards trailing behind, and when she had reached the chamber, she stood with her back to the channel that led toward the throat, uncertain of how to proceed. Several hundred feelies were milling about the bottom of the chamber, and others were clinging to ropes, hanging together in front of one or another of the cubicles, looking in that immense space like clusters of glittering, many-colored fruit; the constant motion and complexity of the colony added to Catherine's hesitancy and bewilderment, and when she tried to call out to the feelies, to gain their attention, she managed only a feeble, scratchy noise. But she gathered her strength and called out again and again, until at last they were all assembled before her, silent and staring, hemming her in against the entrance to the channel, next to some chests that contained the torches and swords and other items used by the hunters. The feelies gaped at her, plucking at their gaudy rags; their silence seemed to have a slow vibration. Catherine started to speak, but faltered; she took a deep breath, let it out explosively, and made a second try.

"We have to leave," she said, hearing the shakiness of her voice. "We have to go outside. Not for long. Just for a little while . . . a few hours. The chamber, it's going. . . ." She broke off, realizing that they weren't following her. "The thing Griaule has meant me to learn," she went on in a louder voice, "at last I know it. I know why I was brought to you. I know the purpose for which I have studied all these years. Griaule's heart is going to beat, and when it does the chamber will fill with liquid. If you remain here, you'll all drown."

The front ranks shifted, and some of the feelies exchanged glances, but otherwise they displayed no reaction.

Catherine shook her fists in frustration. "You'll die if you don't listen to me! You have to leave! When the heart contracts, the chamber will be flooded . . . don't you understand?" She pointed up to the mist-hung ceiling of the chamber. "Look! The birds . . . the birds have gone! They know what's coming! And so do you! Don't you feel the danger? I know you do!"

They edged back, some of them turning away, entering into whispered exchanges with their fellows.

Catherine grabbed the nearest of them, a young female dressed in ruby silks. "Listen to me!" she shouted.

"Liar, Cat'rine, liar," said one of the males, jerking the female away from her. "We not goin' be mo' fools."

"I'm not lying! I'm not!" She went from one to another, putting her hands on their shoulders, meeting their eyes in an attempt to impress them with her sincerity. "The heart is going to beat! Once . . . just once. You won't have to stay outside long. Not long at all."

They were all walking away, all beginning to involve themselves in their own affairs, and Catherine, desperate, hurried after them, pulling them back, saying, "Listen to me! Please!" Explaining what was to happen, and receiving cold stares in return. One of the males shoved her aside, baring his teeth in a hiss, his eyes blank and bright, and she retreated to the entrance of the channel, feeling rattled and disoriented, in need of another pellet. She couldn't collect her thoughts, and she looked around in every direction as if hoping to find some sight that would steady her; but nothing she saw was of any help. Then her gaze settled on the chests where the swords and torches were stored. She felt as if her head were being held in a vise and forced toward the chests, and the knowledge of what she must do was a coldness inside her head—the unmistakable touch of Griaule's thought. It was the only way. She saw that clearly. But the idea of doing something so extreme frightened her, and she hesitated, looking behind her to make sure that none of the feelies were keeping track of her movements. She inched toward the chests, keeping her eyes lowered, trying to make it appear that she was moving aimlessly. In one of the chests were a number of tinderboxes resting beside some torches; she stooped, grabbed a torch and one of the tinderboxes, and went walking briskly up the slope. She paused by the lowest rank of cubicles, noticed that some of the feelies had turned to watch her; when she lit the torch, alarm surfaced in their faces and they surged up the slope toward her. She held the torch up to the curtains that covered the entrance to the cubicle, and the feelies fell back, muttering, some letting out piercing wails.

"Please!" Catherine cried, her knees rubbery from the tension, a chill knot in her breast. "I don't want to do this! But you have to leave!"

A few of the feelies edged toward the channel, and encouraged by this, Catherine shouted, "Yes! That's it! If you'll just go outside, just for a little while, I won't have to do it!"

Several feelies entered the channel, and the crowd around Catherine began to erode, whimpering, breaking into tears, trickles of five and six at a time breaking away and moving out of sight within the channel, until there were no more than thirty of them left within the chamber, forming a ragged semicircle around her. She would have liked to believe that they would do as she had suggested without further coercion on her part, but she knew that they were all packed into the channel or the chamber beyond, waiting for her to put down the torch. She gestured at the feelies surrounding her, and they, too, began easing toward the channel; when only a handful of them remained visible, she touched the torch to the curtains.

She was amazed by how quickly the fire spread, rushing like waves up the silk drapes, following the rickety outlines of the cubicles, appearing to dress them in a fancywork of reddish yellow flame, making crispy, chuckling noises. The fire seemed to have a will of its own, to be playfully seeking out all the intricate shapes of the colony and illuminating them, the separate flames chasing one another with merry abandon, sending little trains of fire along poles and stanchions, geysering up from corners, flinging out fiery fingers to touch tips across a gap.

She was so caught up in this display, her drugged mind finding in it an aesthetic, that she forgot all about the feelies, and when a cold sharp pain penetrated her left side, she associated this not with them but thought it a side-effect of the drug, a sudden attack brought on by her abuse of it. Then, horribly weak, sinking to her knees, she saw one of them standing next to her, a male with a pale thatch of thinning hair wisping across his scalp, holding a sword tipped with red, and she knew that he had stabbed her. She had the giddy urge to speak to him, not out of anger, just to ask a question that she wasn't able to speak, for instead of being afraid of the weakness invading her limbs, she had a terrific curiosity about what would happen next, and she had the irrational thought that her executioner might have the answer, that in his role as the instrument of Griaule's will he might have some knowledge of absolutes. He spat something at her, an accusation or an insult made inaudible by the crackling of the flames, and fled down the slope and out of the chamber, leaving her alone. She rolled onto her back, gazing at the fire, and the pain seemed to roll inside her as if it were a separate thing. Some of the cubicles were collapsing, spraying sparks, twists of black smoke boiling up, smoldering pieces of blackened wood tumbling down to the chamber floor, the entire structure appearing to ripple through the heat haze, looking unreal, an absurd construction of flaming skeletal framework and billowing, burning silks, and growing dizzy, feeling that she was falling upward into that huge fiery space, Catherine passed out.

She must have been unconscious for only a matter of seconds, because nothing had changed when she opened her eyes, except that a section of the fabric covering the chamber floor had caught fire. The flames were roaring, the snaps of cracking timber as sharp as explosions, and her nostrils were choked with an acrid stink. With a tremendous effort that brought her once again to the edge of unconsciousness, she came to her feet, clutching the wound in her side, and stumbled toward the channel; at the entrance she fell and crawled into it, choking on the smoke that poured along the passageway. Her eyes teared from the smoke, and she wriggled on her stomach, pulling herself along with her hands. She nearly passed out a half dozen times before reaching the adjoining chamber, and then she staggered, crawled, stopping frequently to catch her breath, to let the pain of her wound subside, somehow negotiating a circuitous path among the pools of burning liquid and the pale red warty bumps that sprouted everywhere. Then into the throat. She wanted to surrender to the darkness there, to let go, but she kept going, not motivated by fear, but by some reflex of survival, simply obeying the impulse to continue for as long as it was possible. Her eyes blurred, and darkness frittered at the edges of her vision. But even so, she was able to make out the light of day, the menagerie of shapes erected by the interlocking branches of the thickets, and she thought that now she could stop, that this had been what she wanted—to see the light again, not to die bathed in the uncanny radiance of Griaule's blood.

She lay down, lowering herself cautiously among a bed of ferns, her back against the side of the throat, the same position—she remembered—in which she had fallen asleep that first night inside the dragon so many years before. She started to slip, to dwindle inside herself, but was alerted by a whispery rustling that grew louder and louder, and a moment later swarms of insects began to pour from the dragon's throat, passing overhead with a whirring rush and in such density that they cut off most of the light issuing from the mouth. Far above, like the shadows of spiders, apes were swinging on the vines that depended from the roof of the mouth, heading for the outer world, and Catherine could hear smaller animals scuttling through the brush. The sight of these flights made her feel accomplished, secure in what she had done, and she settled back, resting her head against Griaule's flesh, as peaceful as she could ever recall, almost eager to be done with life, with drugs and solitude and violence. She had a moment's worry about the feelies, wondering where they were; but then she realized that they would probably do no differently than had their remote ancestor, that they would hide in the thickets until all was calm.

She let her eyes close. The pain of the wound had diminished to a distant throb that scarcely troubled her, and the throbbing made a rhythm that seemed to be bearing her up. Somebody was talking to her, saying her name, and she resisted the urge to open her eyes, not wanting to be called back. She must be hearing things, she thought. But the voice persisted, and at last she did open her eyes. She gave a weak laugh on seeing Amos Mauldry kneeling before her, wavering and vague as a ghost, and realized that she was seeing things, too.

"Catherine," he said. "Can you hear me?"

"No," she said, and laughed again, a laugh that sent her into a bout of gasping; she felt her weakness in a new and poignant way, and it frightened her.

"Catherine?"

She blinked, trying to make him disappear; but he appeared to solidify as if she were becoming more part of his world than that of life. "What is it, Mauldry?" she said, and coughed. "Have you come to guide me to heaven . . . is that it?"

His lips moved, and she had the idea that he was trying to reassure her of something; but she couldn't hear his words, no matter how hard she strained her ears. He was beginning to fade, becoming opaque, proving himself to be no more than a phantom; yet as she blacked out, experiencing a final moment of panic, Catherine could have sworn that she felt him take her hand.

She awoke in a golden glow that dimmed and brightened, and found herself staring into a face; after a moment, a long moment, because the face was much different than she had imagined it during these past few years, she recognized that it was hers. She lay still, trying to accommodate to this state of affairs, wondering why she wasn't dead, puzzling over the face and uncertain why she wasn't afraid; she felt strong and alert and at peace. She sat up and discovered that she was naked, that she was sitting in a small chamber lit by veins of golden blood branching across the ceiling, its walls obscured by vines with glossy dark green leaves. The body—her body—was lying on its back, and one side of the shirt it wore was soaked with blood. Folded beside the body was a fresh shirt, trousers, and resting atop these was a pair of sandals.

She checked her side—there was no sign of a wound. Her emotions were a mix of relief and self-loathing. She understood that somehow she had been conveyed to this cavity, to the ghostvine, and her essences had been transferred to a likeness, and yet she had trouble accepting the fact, because she felt no different than she had before . . . except for the feelings of peace and strength, and the fact that she had no craving for the drug. She tried to deny what had happened, to deny that she was now a thing, the bizarre contrivance of a plant, and it seemed that her thoughts, familiar in their ordinary process, were proofs that she must be wrong in her assumption. However, the body was an even more powerful evidence to the contrary. She would have liked to take refuge in panic, but her overall feeling of well-being prevented this. She began to grow cold, her skin pebbling, and reluctantly she dressed in the clothing folded beside the body. Something hard in the breast pocket of the shirt. She opened the pocket, took out a small leather sack; she loosed the tie of the sack and from it poured a fortune of cut gems into her hand: diamonds, emeralds, and sunstones. She put the sack back into the pocket, not knowing what to make of the stones, and sat looking at the body. It was much changed from its youth, leaner, less voluptuous, and in the repose of death, the face had lost its gloss and perfection, and was merely the face of an attractive woman . . . a disheartened woman. She thought she should feel something, that she should be oppressed by the sight, but she had no reaction to it; it might have been a skin she had shed, something of no more consequence than that.

She had no idea where to go, but realizing that she couldn't stay there forever, she stood and, with a last glance at the body, made her way down the narrow channel leading away from the cavity. When she emerged into the passage, she hesitated, unsure of which direction to choose, unsure, too, of which direction was open to her. At length, deciding not to tempt Griaule's judgment, she headed back toward the colony, thinking that she would take part in helping them rebuild; but before she had gone ten feet she heard Mauldry's voice calling her name.

He was standing by the entrance to the cavity, dressed as he had been that first night—in a satin frock coat, carrying his gold-knobbed cane—and as she approached him, a smile broke across his wrinkled face, and he nodded as if in approval of her resurrection. "Surprised to see me?" he asked.

"I . . . I don't know," she said, a little afraid of him. "Was that you . . . in the mouth?"

He favored her with a polite bow. "None other. After things settled down, I had some of the feelies bear you to the cavity. Or rather I was the one who effected Griaule's will in the matter. Did you look in the pocket of your shirt?"

"Yes."

"Then you found the gems. Good, good."

She was at a loss for words at first. "I thought I saw you once before," she said finally. "A few years back."

"I'm sure you did. After my rebirth"—he gestured toward the cavity—"I was no longer of any use to you. You were forging your own path, and my presence would have hampered your process. So I hid among the feelies, waiting for the time when you would need me." He squinted at her. "You look troubled."

"I don't understand any of this," she said. "How can I feel like my old self, when I'm obviously so different?"

"Are you?" he asked. "Isn't sameness or difference mostly a matter of feeling?" He took her arm, steered her along the passage away from the colony. "You'll adjust to it, Catherine. I have, and I had the same reaction as you when I first awoke." He spread his arms, inviting her to examine him. "Do I look different to you? Aren't I the same old fool as ever?"

"So it seems," she said drily. She walked a few paces in silence, then something occurred to her. "The feelies . . . do they. . . ."

"Rebirth is only for the chosen, the select. The feelies receive another sort of reward, one not given me to understand."

"You call this a reward? To be subject to more of Griaule's whims? And what's next for me? Am I to discover when his bowels are due to move?"

He stopped walking, frowning at her. "Next? Why, whatever pleases you, Catherine. I've been assuming that you'd want to leave, but you're free to do as you wish. Those gems I gave you will buy you any kind of life you desire."

"I can leave?"

"Most assuredly. You've accomplished your purpose here, and you're your own agent now. *Do* you want to leave?"

Catherine looked at him, unable to speak, and nodded.

"Well, then." He took her arm again. "Let's be off."

As they walked down to the chamber behind the throat and then into the throat itself, Catherine felt as one is supposed to feel at the moment of death, all the memories of her life within the dragon passing before her eyes with their attendant emotions—her flight, her labors and studies, John, the long hours spent beside the heart—and she thought that this was most appropriate, because she was not reentering life but rather passing through into a kind of afterlife, a place beyond death that would be as unfamiliar and new a place as Griaule himself had once seemed. And she was astounded to realize that she was frightened of these new possibilities, that the thing she had wanted for so long could pose a menace and that it was the dragon who now offered the prospect of security. On several occasions she considered turning back, but each time she did, she rebuked herself for her timidity and continued on. However, on reaching the mouth and wending her way through the thickets, her fear grew more pronounced. The sunlight, that same light that not so many months before had been alluring, now hurt her eyes and made her want to draw back into the dim golden murk of Griaule's blood; and as they neared the lip, as she stepped into the shadow of a fang, she began to tremble with cold and stopped, hugging herself to keep warm.

Mauldry took up a position facing her, jogged her arm. "What is it?" he asked. "You seem frightened."

"I am," she said; she glanced up at him. "Maybe . . ."

"Don't be silly," he said. "You'll be fine once you're away from here. And"—he cocked his eye toward the declining sun—"you should be pushing along. You don't want to be hanging about the mouth when it's dark. I doubt anything would harm you, but since you're no longer part of Griaule's plan . . . well, better safe than sorry." He gave her a push. "Get along with you, now."

"You're not coming with me?"

"Me?" Mauldry chuckled. "What would I do out there? I'm an old man, set in my ways. No, I'm far better off staying with the feelies. I've become half a feelie myself after all these years. But you're young, you've got a whole world of life ahead of you." He nudged her forward. "Do what I say, girl. There's no use in your hanging about any longer."

She went a couple of steps toward the lip, paused, feeling sentimental about leaving the old man; though they had never been close, he had been like a father to her . . . and thinking this, remembering her real father, whom she had scarcely thought of these last years, with whom she'd had the same lack of closeness, that made her aware of all the things she had to look forward to, all the lost things she might now regain. She moved into the thickets with a firmer step, and behind her, old Mauldry called to her for a last time.

"That's my girl!" he sang out. "You just keep going, and you'll start to feel at rights soon enough! There's nothing to be afraid of . . . nothing you can avoid, in any case! Goodbye, goodbye!"

She glanced back, waved, saw him shaking his cane in a gesture of farewell, and laughed at his eccentric appearance: a funny little man in satin rags hopping up and down in that great shadow between the fangs. Out from beneath that shadow herself, the rich light warmed her, seeming to penetrate and dissolve all the coldness that had been lodged in her bones and thoughts.

"Goodbye!" cried Mauldry. "Goodbye! Don't be sad! You're not leaving anything important behind, and you're taking the best parts with you. Just walk fast and think about what you're going to tell everyone. They'll be amazed by all you've done! Flabbergasted! Tell them about Griaule! Tell them what he's like, tell them all you've seen and all you've learned. Tell them what a grand adventure you've had!"

VIII

Returning to Hangtown was in some ways a more unsettling experience than had been Catherine's flight into the dragon. She had expected the place to have changed, and while there *had* been minor changes, she had assumed that it would be as different from its old self as was she. But standing at the edge of the village, looking out at the gray weathered shacks ringing the fouled shallows of the lake, thin smokes issuing from tin chimneys, the cliff of the frontoparietal plate casting its gloomy shadow, the chokecherry thickets, the hawthorns, the dark brown dirt of the streets, three elderly men sitting on cane chairs in front of one of the shacks, smoking their pipes and staring back at her with unabashed curiosity . . . Catherine felt that superficially it was no different than it had been ten years before, and this seemed to imply that her years of imprisonment, her death and rebirth, had been of small importance. She did not demand that they be important to anyone else, yet it galled her that the world had passed through those years of ordeal without significant scars, and it also imbued her with the irrational fear that if she were to enter the village, she might suffer some magical slippage back through time and reinhabit her old life. At last, with a hesitant step, she walked over to the men and wished them a good morning.

"Mornin'," said a paunchy fellow with a mottled bald scalp and a fringe of gray beard, whom she recognized as Tim Weedlon. "What can I do for you, ma'am? Got some nice bits of scale inside."

"That place over there"—she pointed to an abandoned shack down the street, its roof holed and missing the door—"where can I find the owner?"

The other man, Mardo Koren, thin as a mantis, his face seamed and blotched, said, "Can't nobody say for sure. Ol' Riall died . . . must be goin' on nine, ten years back."

"He's dead?" She felt weak inside, dazed.

"Yep," said Tim Weedlon, studying her face, his brow furrowed, his expression bewildered. "His daughter run away, killed a village man name of Willen and vanished into nowhere . . . or so ever'body figured. Then when Willen's brothers turned up missin', people thought ol' Riall musta done 'em. He didn't deny it. Acted like he didn't care whether he lived or died."

"What happened?"

"They had a trial, found Riall guilty." He leaned forward, squinting at her. "Catherine . . . is that you?"

She nodded, struggling for control. "What did they do with him?"

"How can it be you?" he said. "Where you been?"

"What happened to my father?"

"God, Catherine. You know what happens to them that's found guilty of murder. If it's any comfort, the truth come out finally."

"They took him in under the wing . . . they left him under the wing?" Her fists clenched, nails pricking hard into her palm. "Is that what they did?"

He lowered his eyes, picked at a fray on his trouser leg.

Her eyes filled, and she turned away, facing the mossy overhang of the frontoparietal plate. "You said the truth came out."

"That's right. A girl confessed to having seen the whole thing. Said the Willens chased you into Griaule's mouth. She woulda come forward sooner, but ol' man Willen had her feared for her life. Said he'd kill her if she told. You probably remember her. Friend of yours, if I recall. Brianne."

She whirled around, repeated the name with venom.

"Wasn't she your friend?" Weedlon asked.

"What happened to her?"

"Why . . . nothing," said Weedlon. "She's married, got hitched to Zev Mallison. Got herself a batch of children. I 'spect she's home now if you wanna see her. You know the Mallison place, don'tcha?"

"Yes."

"You want to know more about it, you oughta drop by there and talk to Brianne."

"I guess . . . I will, I'll do that."

"Now tell us where you been, Catherine. Ten years! Musta been something important to keep you from home for so long."

Coldness was spreading through her, turning her to ice. "I was thinking, Tim . . . I was thinking I might like to do some scaling while I'm here. Just for old time's sake, you know." She could hear the shakiness in her voice and tried to smooth it out; she forced a smile. "I wonder if I could borrow some hooks."

"Hooks?" He scratched his head, still regarding her with confusion. "Sure, I suppose you can. But aren't you going to tell us where you've been? We thought you were dead."

"I will, I promise. Before I leave . . . I'll come back and tell you all about it. All right?"

"Well, all right." He heaved up from his chair. "But it's a cruel thing you're doing, Catherine."

"No crueller than what's been done to me," she said distractedly. "Not half so cruel."

"Pardon," said Tim. "How's that?"

"What?"

He gave her a searching look and said, "I was telling you it was a cruel thing, keeping an old man in suspense about where you've been. Why, you're going to make the choicest bit of gossip we've had in years. And you came back with. . . ."

"Oh! I'm sorry," she said. "I was thinking about something else."

The Mallison place was among the larger shanties in Hangtown, half a dozen rooms, most of which had been added on over the years since Catherine had left; but its size was no evidence of wealth or status, only of a more expansive poverty. Next to the steps leading to a badly hung door was a litter of bones and mango skins and other garbage. Fruit flies hovered above a watermelon rind; a gray dog with its ribs showing slunk off around the corner, and there was a stink of fried onions and boiled greens. From inside came the squalling of a child. The shanty looked false to Catherine, an unassuming facade behind which lay a monstrous reality—the woman who had betrayed her, killed her father—and yet its drabness was sufficient to disarm her anger somewhat. But as she mounted the steps there was a thud as of something heavy falling, and a woman shouted. The voice was harsh, deeper than Catherine remembered, but she knew it must belong to Brianne, and that restored her vengeful mood. She knocked on the door with one of Tim Weedlon's scaling hooks, and a second later it was flung open and she was confronted by an olive-skinned woman in torn gray skirts—almost the same color as the weathered boards, as if she were the quintessential product of the environment—and gray streaks in her dark brown hair. She looked Catherine up and down, her face hard with displeasure, and said, "What do you want?"

It was Brianne, but Brianne warped, melted, disfigured as a wax-work might be disfigured by heat. Her waist gone, features thickened, cheeks sagging into jowls. Shock washed away Catherine's anger, and shock, too, materialized in Brianne's face. "No," she said, giving the word an abstracted value, as if denying an inconsequential accusation; then she shouted it: "No!" She slammed the door, and Catherine pounded on it, crying, "Damn you! Brianne!"

The child screamed, but Brianne made no reply.

Enraged, Catherine swung the hook at the door; the point sank deep into the wood, and when she tried to pull it out, one of the boards came partially loose; she pried at it, managed to rip it away, the nails coming free with a shriek of tortured metal. Through the gap she saw Brianne cowering against the rear wall of a dilapidated room, her arms around a little boy in shorts. Using the hook as a lever, she pulled loose another board, reached in and undid the latch. Brianne pushed the child behind her and grabbed a broom as Catherine stepped inside.

"Get out of here!" she said, holding the broom like a spear.

The gray poverty of the shanty made Catherine feel huge in her anger, too bright for the place, like a sun shining in a cave, and although her attention was fixed on Brianne, the peripheral details of the room imprinted themselves on her: the wood stove upon which a covered pot was steaming; an overturned wooden chair with a hole in the seat; cobwebs spanning the corners, rat turds along the wall; a rickety table set with cracked dishes and dust thick as fur beneath it. These things didn't arouse her pity or mute her anger; instead, they seemed extensions of Brianne, new targets for hatred. She moved closer, and Brianne jabbed the broom at her. "Go away," she said weakly. "Please . . . leave us alone!"

Catherine swung the hook, snagging the twine that bound the broom straws and knocking it from Brianne's hands. Brianne retreated to the corner where the wood stove stood, hauling the child along. She held up her hand to ward off another blow and said, "Don't hurt us."

"Why not? Because you've got children, because you've had an unhappy life?" Catherine spat at Brianne. "You killed my father!"

"I was afraid! Key's father . . ."

"I don't care," said Catherine coldly. "I don't care why you did it. I don't care how good your reasons were for betraying me in the first place."

"That's right! You never cared about anything!" Brianne clawed at her breast. "You killed my heart! You didn't care about Glynn, you just wanted him because he wasn't yours!"

It took Catherine a few seconds to dredge that name up from memory, to connect it with Brianne's old lover and recall that it was her callousness and self-absorption that had set the events of the past years in motion. But although this roused her guilt, it did not abolish her anger. She couldn't equate Brianne's crimes with her excesses. Still, she was confused about what to do, uncomfortable now with the very concept of justice, and she wondered if she should leave, just throw down the hook and leave vengeance to whatever ordering principle governed the fates in Hangtown. Then Brianne shifted her feet, made a noise in her throat, and Catherine felt rage boiling up inside her.

"Don't throw that up to me," she said with flat menace. "Nothing I've done to you merited what you did to me. You don't even know what you did!"

She raised the hook, and Brianne shrank back into the corner. The child twisted its head to look at Catherine, fixing her with brimming eyes, and she held back.

"Send the child away," she told Brianne.

Brianne leaned down to the child. "Go to your father," she said.

"No, wait," said Catherine, fearing that the child might bring Zev Mallison.

"Must you kill us both?" said Brianne, her voice hoarse with emotion. Hearing this, the child once more began to cry.

"Stop it," Catherine said to him, and when he continued to cry, she shouted it.

Brianne muffled the child's wails in her skirts. "Go ahead!" she said, her face twisted with fear. "Just do it!" She broke down into sobs, ducked her head, and waited for the blow. Catherine stepped close to Brianne, yanked her head back by the hair, exposing her throat, and set the point of the hook against the big vein there. Brianne's eyes rolled down, trying to see the hook; her breath came in gaspy shrieks, and the child, caught between the two women, squirmed and wailed. Catherine's hand was trembling, and that slight motion pricked Brianne's skin, drawing a bead of blood. She stiffened, her eyelids fluttered down, her mouth fell open—an expression, at least so it seemed to Catherine, of ecstatic expectation. Catherine studied the face, feeling as if her emotions were being purified, drawn into a fine wire; she had an almost aesthetic appreciation of the stillness gathering around her, the hard poise of Brianne's musculature, the sensitive pulse in the throat that transmitted its frail rhythm along the hook, and she restrained herself from pressing the point deeper, wanting to prolong Brianne's suffering.

But then the hook grew heavy in Catherine's hands, and she understood that the moment had passed, that her need for vengeance had lost the immediacy and thrust of passion. She imagined herself skewering Brianne, and then imagined dragging her out to confront a village tribunal, forcing her to confess her lies, having her sentenced to be tied up and left for whatever creatures foraged beneath Griaule's wing. But while it provided her a measure of satisfaction to picture Brianne dead or dying, she saw now that anticipation was the peak of vengeance, that carrying out the necessary actions would only harm her. It frustrated her that all these years and the deaths would have no resolution, and she thought that she must have changed more than she had assumed to put aside vengeance so easily; this caused her to wonder again about the nature of the change, to question whether she was truly herself or merely an arcane likeness. But then she realized that the change had been her resolution, and that vengeance was an artifact of her old life, nothing more, and that her new life, whatever its secret character, must find other concerns to fuel it apart from old griefs and unworthy passions. This struck her with the force of a revelation, and she let out a long sighing breath that seemed to carry away with it all the sad vibrations of the past, all the residues of hates and loves, and she could finally believe that she was no longer the dragon's prisoner. She felt new in her whole being, subject to new compulsions, as alive as tears, as strong as wheat, far too strong and alive for this pallid environment, and she could hardly recall now why she had come.

She looked at Brianne and her son, feeling only the ghost of hatred, seeing them not as objects of pity or wrath, but as unfamiliar, irrelevant lives trapped in the prison of their own self-regard, and without a word she turned and walked to the steps, slamming the hook deep into the boards of the wall, a gesture of fierce resignation, the closing of a door opening onto anger and the opening of one that led to uncharted climes, and went down out of the village, leaving old Tim Weedlon's thirst for gossip unquenched, passing along Griaule's back, pushing through thickets and fording streams, and not noticing for quite some time that she had crossed onto another hill and left the dragon far behind.

Three weeks later she came to Cabrecavela, a small town at the opposite end of the Carbonales Valley, and there, using the gems provided her by Mauldry, she bought a house and settled in and began to write about Griaule, creating not a personal memoir but a reference work containing an afterword dealing with certain metaphysical speculations, for she did not wish her adventures published, considering them banal by comparison to her primary subjects, the dragon's physiology and ecology. After the publication of her book, which she entitled *The Heart's Millennium,* she experienced a brief celebrity; but she shunned most of the opportunities for travel and lecture and lionization that came her way, and satisfied her desire to impart the knowledge she had gained by teaching in the local school and speaking privately with those scientists from Port Chantay who came to interview her. Some of these visitors had been colleagues of John Colmacos, yet she never mentioned their relationship, believing that her memories of the man needed no modification; but perhaps this was a less than honest self-appraisal, perhaps she had not come to terms with that portion of her past, for in the spring five years after she had returned to the world she married one of these scientists, a man named Brian Ocoi, who in his calm demeanor and modest easiness of speech appeared cast from the same mold as Colmacos. From that point on little is known of her other than the fact that she bore two sons and confined her writing to a journal that has gone unpublished. However, it is said of her—as is said of all those who perform similar acts of faith in the shadows of other dragons yet unearthed from beneath their hills of ordinary-seeming earth and grass, believing that their bond serves through gentle constancy to enhance and not further delimit the boundaries of this prison world—from that day forward she lived happily ever after. Except for the dying at the end. And the heartbreak in between.

SURRENDER

JK

've been down these rivers before, I've smelled this tropical stink in a dozen different wars, this mixture of heat and fever and diarrhea, I've come across the same bloated bodies floating in the green water, I've seen the tiny dark men and their delicate women hacked apart a hundred times if I've seen it once. I'm a fucking war tourist.

My bags have stickers on them from Cambodia, Nicaragua, Vietnam, Laos, El Salvador, and all the other pertinent points of no return. I keep telling myself, enough of this bullshit, your turn to cover the home front, where nobody gives a damn and you can write happy stories about girls with cute tits and no acting ability, in-depth features on spirit channeling and the latest in three-piece Republicans who do it to the public doggie-style and never lose that winning smile, but I always end up here again, whichever Here is in this year, sitting around the pool at the Holiday Inn and soaking up Absolut and exchanging cynical repartee with other halfwits of my breed, guys from UPI or AP, stringers from Reuters, and the odd superstar who'll drop by from time to time, your Fill-In-The-Name-Of-Your-Favorite-Blow-Dried TV Creep, the kind of guy who'll buy a few rounds, belch platitudes, and say crap like, Now Katanga, there was a *real* war, before going upstairs drunk to dictate three columns of tearstained human interest. I used to believe that I kept doing all this because I was committed, not a pervert or deluded, but I'm not too sure about that anymore.

A few years back I was in Guatemala City: Mordor with more sunshine and colonial architecture, diesel buses farting black smoke, and a truly spectacular slum that goes by the nineties-style name of Zone

Five. I was just hanging out, doing yet another tragic piece on the disappeared, dodging carloads of sinister-looking hombres in unmarked Toyotas, and pretending to myself that what I was going to write would Make A Difference, when this colleague of mine, Paul DeVries, AP, a skinny, earnest little guy with whom all the Guatemalan girls are in love because he's blond and sensitive and in every way the opposite of the local talent, who tend early on to develop beer guts along with a mania for sidearms and a penchant for left-hooking the weaker sex . . . DeVries says to me, "Hey, Carl, let's haul our butts down to Sayaxché, I hear there's been some kinda fuckup down there."

"Sayaxché?" I say. "What could happen in Sayaxché?"

Sayaxché's a joke between me and DeVries, one of many; we've been covering back-fence wars together for four years, and we've achieved a rapport based on making light of every little thing that comes our way. We call Sayaxché "the one-whore town," because that's how many ladies of the evening it supports, and she's no bargain, with horrible acne scars and a foul mouth, screaming drunk all the time. The town itself is a dump on the edge of the Petén rain forest, with a hotel, a regional bank office, whitewashed hovels, an experimental agricultural farm, a ferry that carries oil trucks across the Río de la Pasión on their way to service the ranches farther east in the jungle, lots of dark green, lots of starving Indians, Joseph Conrad–land, what could happen?

"Forget it," I tell DeVries at first.

But I'm getting fatigued with the disappeared, you know; I mean what's the point, if they'd been disappeared by magic everyone would love to hear about it, but another tragedy, more endless nattering of miserable Third World gossip . . . ho hum, and so I end up hopping a DC-3 for Flores with DeVries, then it's a bus ride on a potholed dirt road for an hour, and we are there, drinking beer and smoking on the screened verandah of the Hotel Tropical, a turquoise cube on the riverbank with three-dollar rooms and enormous cockroaches and framed photographs everywhere of Don Julio, the owner, a roan-colored man with gold chains and a paunch, posing proudly with a rifle and a variety of dead animals. We're listening to ooh-ooh-ah-ah birds and howler monkeys from the surrounding jungle, staring at the murky green eddies of the River of Passion, trying to pry some information out of Don Julio, but he has heard of no fuckup. He's a real stand-up guy, Don Julio. Hates commies. One of those patriotic souls who will in drunken moments flourish his mighty pistola and declaim, "Nobody takes this from me! A communist comes on my land, and

he's a dead man." And so he's doubtless lying to us in order to protect his pals, the secret police. He shrugs, offers more beer, and goes
off to polish his bullets, leaving me and DeVries and a Canadian nurse
named Sherril—she's on her way south to do volunteer work in
Nicaragua—to indulge in the town's chief spectator sport, which is
watching the oil trucks rolling off the ferry getting stuck in this enormous pothole, which is artfully placed at the end of the dock and
the beginning of a steep incline so that it's the rare truck that avoids
getting stuck. In front of the bank across the street, a two-story
building of pink cement block, some Indian soldiers with camo gear
and SMGs are advising the driver of the current truck-in-distress on
possible methods of becoming unstuck; they favor a combination of
boards and sand beneath the tires, and rocking back and forth. The
driver, who's been frustrated now for more than an hour, is close to
tears.

"Well, this is fucking terrific," I say to DeVries; he's ten years
younger than me, and our relationship has been established so that
I have the right to express stern fraternal disapproval. "There's no
end of newsworthy material to be found here."

"Something might turn up," he says. "Let's hang for a while and
see what surfaces."

"What're you guys looking for?" Sherril asks. She's long, she's
tall, she's looking good, she's got light brown hair and no bra, and
she's waiting for this guy who promised to paddle her upriver to the
Mexican border to see the Mayan ruins at Yaxchilán but hasn't showed
up yet and, being two days late, probably won't show at all; she acts
very engaged-disengaged, very feminine-in-control, like I want to do
my thing with the rebels so I can live with myself, you know, and
then raise my children to love animals and never say bad words in
Calgary or somewhere, and me, I'm beginning to think that if she's
stupid enough to go paddling up the River of Doom with some sleaze
she met in an Antigua bar, she'll be idealistic enough to choose to
sleep with a war-torn journalist such as myself. I can tell she's impressed by my repertoire of cynicisms, and there is definitely a mutual
attraction.

"We heard there was some trouble here," I say. "Soldiers all over."

"Oh, you must mean out at the farm," she says.

DeVries and I exchange glances and say as one, "What happened?"

"I don't know," she says, "but a lot of soldiers were out there
the other day. I think they're still there. They'd have to come back
through here if they left."

The farm is, like Sayaxché, a kind of joke, though not so funny as the one-whore bit. Some years before in a canny exercise of graft, the Banco Americano Desarrollo, the leading development bank in the region and thus first among many in the economic villainy that maintains the status quo of death squads and inhuman poverty throughout Central America, all in the cause of keeping the USA safe from Communism and the killer bees or whatever, negotiated an agreement with the then chief of corruption in Guatemala, a president by the name of Ydigoras Fuentes; this agreement traded the rights in perpetuity to oil leases in the Petén in return for what the agreement called an aggressive US policy directed toward land reform and agricultural development, a policy that—behind a veil of wonderfully vague promises—actually promised only to establish one experimental farm, this being the one in Sayaxché. It employs thirty Guatemalans and is considered a model of sanitation and efficiency; land reform and agricultural development are, needless to say, still a good ways off.

Wellsir, DeVries and I are hot to trot on out to the farm and see what's cooking, but Sherril tells us we'll never make it . . . not in the daytime, anyway. Too many soldiers blocking the roads. She knows a way, however; if we wait until night, she'll take us. It seems that while waiting for her tardy tour guide, she ran into a right-wing nasty from Guat City who owned a ranch downriver and was dumb enough to go for a jungle walk with him. All he talked of were the discos, Cadillacs, his many girlfriends, and she thought him a fool, not recognizing that such fools are dangerous. When he tried to put a move on her, she was forced to run away and lose him in the jungle, and so discovered a nifty secret route to Ye Olde Experimental Farm, which appeared to be heavily guarded.

There are journalistic ethics involved here, we realize. Should two guys who're wise to the way of the world let this naïve Calgarette lead us into the mouth of hell at the risk of her all and everything? Probably not. But this is show biz, right, and so, rationalizing the shit out of the situation, we say, okay, honey, what an adventure we'll have! We drink beers, watching oil trucks buck and hump in the Pothole of Death, and we wait for nightfall. Toward dusk I take a little walk with Sherril, tell her sad stories about the death of grunts, and am rewarded for my valorous past by several deep wet kisses and proof positive of her no-bralessness. "God!" she says, flushed and dewy with delight, as we stroll arm in arm toward the hotel. "God, I never expected to meet somebody like you in this awful place." There is, I realize, vast potential here. Who says Canadians can't kiss?

At this point it all stopped being a joke. It really hadn't been much of a joke up until then, but this is show biz, right, and I just wanted to get you to here. I don't know what to tell you people. I'm probably coming off in all this as wearing the moral superiority hat, but it's only defensiveness. See, I'm just so used to waxing passionate and having you look down your noses at me as if to say, Interesting Specimen, or My Goodness, he's certainly opinionated, or Yawn, boring, so the West is in decline, so what, know where we can cop some Ecstasy, or Jeez, I mean it's too bad and all, but I don't wanna hear it, I work hard all the livelong while that lucky old sun just rolls 'round heaven all day, and when I get home at night, I wanna kick back, pop a cold one, and be entertained. So what do I tell you people? I can't argue with you. You either give a shit or you don't, and nothing I say is going to change your mind. But if it's entertainment you want, I suggest you take a walk around, say, the vicinity of Tolola in El Salvador, where you can see the intriguing results of a foreign policy that has Apache helicopters dropping forty thousand pounds of bombs on the countryside every month, repeating the tactic we used in Vietnam to destroy popular support for the VC (oh, yeah!), in this case, the FMLN, and in the process causing one-fifth of an entire nation to become refugees. It would be a most entertaining walk. See the empty towns littered with skeletons! See the curious collection of left hands rotting in a basket in front of the bombed church! See the village of legless men! If you liked *The Killing Fields,* you'll love Tolola!

Seriously, folks, it will live in your memory.

The smell alone will make it An Experience.

But I digress. Maybe the fact is that in the United States it's become easy to achieve moral superiority, even for fuckups like myself. In that case, I suppose I would do well to finish my story quickly and let you get back to your MTV.

Off we went, trudging through the jungle, following Sherril's perfect denim-clad butt through the slimy night air. It took us almost two hours of steady humping to reach the farm, vampire mosquitos, creepy scuttlings, and when we spotted lights shining through the foliage, we crept up to the margin of the jungle, went flat on our stomachs, and peered through a bed of ferns. Personnel carriers with M-60s mounted on the rear, about a dozen altogether, ringed a one-story building of white stucco: the farm office. The lights proved to be spotlights and were aimed at a field of what appeared to be agave . . . though God only knew why anyone would want to cultivate agave. About fifty or sixty soldiers were visible, and none of them looked to be having big fun; they were all on alert, fanned out in front of the office, their guns trained on the field. It was very weird.

I don't know what we would have done. Nothing, probably. No way I was planning to get any closer. The chances are we would have gone back to town and done a little investigative reporting. But free will did not turn out to be an option. A few minutes after we had reached the farm I heard at my back the distinctive snick of an automatic weapon being readied for fire, and then a voice telling us in Spanish to lie with our faces down and our arms spread. Moments later, we were hauled to our feet, blinded with flashlights, and, despite crying, *"Americanos, Americanos,"* we were herded roughly by a group of soldiers toward the farm and into the office building. Laid out in the dirt beside the door was one of your basic Central American vistas: a row of bullet-riddled naked bodies. The soldiers hustled us past the bodies before we could get a good look at them. Sherril started to object, but I pushed her along, whispering for her to keep quiet. Inside, we were met by another basic CA element, your sadist officer, this one a major named Pedroza who would have scored high in a General Noriega look-alike contest: the pitted skin, the vaguely Oriental cast to the features. He gazed dreamily at us, visions of cattle prods and Louisville Sluggers dancing in his head; his eyes lingered upon Sherril.

It may seem that I was leaping to conclusions concerning the major, but not really. He had attained high rank in one of the most conscienceless and brutal military forces in existence, and one does not do that without having caused a world of torment; his face had the cruel sleekness of someone who has indulged in torture and enjoyed it. There is a slowness, a heaviness, attaching to such men, a bulky slovenly grace like that of an overfed jungle predator, one whose kills have come too often and too easily. To anyone who has seen them in action, they are inimitable; their evil dispositions as manifest as are their beribboned and bemedaled chests.

Pedroza asked us a number of questions and was, I believe, about to begin getting physical, when a distinguished silver-haired man in his early fifties entered the room. On seeing him, I felt greatly relieved. He was Duncan Shellgrave, a vice president with the development bank. His nephew was a friend of mine, and I'd stayed at his house in Guat City on a couple of occasions.

"What the hell's going on here, Duncan?" I said, hoping aggressiveness would establish some tenuous spiritual credential.

"Just take it easy, Carl," he said, and told the major in Spanish that he'd take care of this.

The major, with a despondent sigh, said, "As you will," and Shellgrave led us into the adjoining office, a white room with a window of frosted glass and an air-conditioned chill.

"We're having a little problem," Shellgrave said, favoring us with his best loan-denied smile, indicating that we should take chairs. "I'm afraid you'll have to sit it out in here. Otherwise Major Pedroza will be quite annoyed."

There were two folding chairs; I left them to Sherril and DeVries, and perched on the edge of the desk. "What kind of problem?" I asked.

Another smile, hands spread in a show of helplessness.

I should tell you a story about Shellgrave to illustrate his character. A week after the Nicaraguan revolution, which I'd covered for a number of leftist rags, I was passing through Guat City when I ran into Shellgrave's nephew and he suggested we take dinner at his uncle's; he thought it would do his uncle a world of good to hear the straight shit concerning the state of affairs in Managua. Well, we got to the house, typical American paranoid chic with guard dogs, high walls topped with broken glass, and lots of electronic security, and when Shellgrave heard I'd just come from Managua, he said, "My God! You're lucky to be alive. They're slaughtering people in the streets down there."

I knew that this was absolutely not the case, but when I attempted to persuade Shellgrave of this, he put on that bland smile and said, "You must not have seen it. They were probably steering you away from the action."

I assured him that I'd been all over the streets; I'm no chump for the Sandinistas, but as revolutions go, Nicaragua had started out as a pretty clean one, and nothing like Shellgrave had suggested was going on. Still, I wasn't able to convince him. The fact that I'd just come from Managua seemed completely irrelevant to him; he gave his CIA informants ultimate credibility and me none. It didn't suit his basic thesis to believe anything I said, and so he didn't. He wasn't stonewalling me, he wasn't playing games. He simply didn't believe me. Men like Shellgrave, and you'll find them all over Latin America, they have a talent for belief; they *know* they're right about the important things, the big picture, and thus they understand that any information they receive to the contrary must be tainted. They thrive on the myth of *realpolitik,* they dance with who brung 'em, and their consciences are clear. They are very scary people. Perhaps not so scary as Major Pedroza and his ilk, but in my opinion it's a close call either way.

I knew there was no use in badgering him for details; I stared at the white walls, tried to cheer up Sherril with a wink and a smile.

DeVries started questioning Shellgrave, and I told him, "Don't waste your time."

He got angry at me for that; he pushed back that blond forelock that drove all the girls at the University of San Carlos to delirium, and said, "Hey, you may have burned out, man, but not me. This is more than a little hinkey here, y'know. This is some bad shit. Don't you smell it?"

"The man"—I pointed at Shellgrave—"is not responsible. For him, heaven's a room with a view of Wall Street. He doesn't know from hinkey. He's eaten so many people he thinks it's normal."

Shellgrave's smile never wavered; he may actually have been pleased by my characterization.

"See there," I said to DeVries. "He's fucking beatific. He knows the empire's crumbling, and that it's his sacred duty to hold on to the last crumb for as long as he can."

But DeVries, God bless him, was a believer; he kept after Shellgrave, though without intelligent result.

The shooting began about ten minutes after we'd entered the white room. Caps popping, that's what it sounded like above the shuddery hum of the air conditioner, and then the heavier beat of the M-60s. Sherril jumped to her feet, and Shellgrave, smiling, told her not to worry, everything was all right. He believed it. He wanted us to believe it. For our own good.

"So what's that?" I asked him. "The sound of Democracy in Action?"

He shook his head in bemusement: I was an incorrigible, and he just didn't know what to do with me.

The screaming began about three minutes after the shooting, and Shellgrave's reaction to this was not so calm. He stood, tried peering through the frosted glass, and that failing, started for the door, stopped, then went for it and locked it tight.

"Don't worry," I told him. "Everything's all right."

Sherril said, "What is it? What's happening?"

Her face was the color of cheesecloth, and her hands were twisting together; DeVries, too, looked shaky, and I wasn't feeling so hot myself.

"Yeah, what is happening?" DeVries asked Shellgrave.

Shellgrave was standing at the center of the room, his head tilted up and to the side, like a man who hears a distant call.

The screams were horrid, throat-tearing screams of pure agony and fear; they were either drowning out most of the gunfire, or else there weren't as many people firing as there had been. Then somebody screamed right outside the window, and at that Shellgrave bolted for a filing cabinet, threw it open, and began stacking papers on the desk. I picked one up, saw the word *mutagenic* before he snatched it from my hand.

I still believed we were going to survive, but my faith was dwindling, and maybe that was why I decided to live in ignorance no longer. I shoved Shellgrave hard, knocking him to the floor, and began leafing through the papers. He tried to come at me again, and I kicked him in the stomach.

DeVries and Sherril came to stand beside me. I couldn't make much sense out of the papers, but they appeared to outline a project that had been going on for twenty years, something to do with a new kind of food and its effects on a local settlement of Indians, who—being severely malnourished—had probably leaped at the chance to eat the shit.

"Jesus Christ!" said Sherril, staring at one of the documents.

"What is it?" I asked.

"Wait!" She began going through more of the papers.

Shellgrave groaned, said, "Those are classified," and this time it was DeVries who kicked him.

There was a sudden intensification of gunfire, as if the tide of battle had turned.

"God," said Sherril weakly, and dropped into Shellgrave's chair.

"Tell us, damn it!" DeVries said.

"I think," she said, and faltered; she drew a steadying breath. "I don't believe this." She looked at us hollow-eyed. "Mutants. The food's worked terrible changes on the second generation. The brain tissue's degenerated. The children of the ones who first ate the food, they're idiots. There's some stuff here I can't understand. But there've been changes in the skin and the blood, too. And I think . . . I think they've become nocturnal. Their eyes . . ." She swallowed hard. "They're killing them. They've stopped feeding them, and they can't eat anything else but the plant they grow here."

I kneeled beside Shellgrave. "And now they're trying to kill your ass. That's them outside, right?"

He was having trouble breathing, but he managed a nod; he pointed to the papers. "Burn 'em," he wheezed.

"Uh-huh," I said. "Sure thing."

It suddenly struck me as being metaphorical, us being in that cool white room, insulated from the screams and the gunfire and the monstrous dying that was happening out in the humid heat of the jungle. It was very American Contemplative, it was the classic American circumstance. All my years of filing horror stories, stories that had nothing of the bizarre technological horror of this one, yet were funded by equally demonic evil, stories that ended up in some city editor's wastebasket . . . I guess it was all this that allowed me then to editorialize my own existence. This was, you see, a particularly poignant moment for me. I realized the horror that was transpiring outside was in character with all the other horrors I'd witnessed. I'm sure that reading this as fiction, which is the only way I can present it, some will say that by injecting a science-fictional element, I'm trivializing the true Central American condition. But that's not the case. What was going on was no different from a thousand other events that had happened over the previous hundred and fifty years or so. This was not the exception, this was the *rule*. And it displayed by its lack of contrast to other horrors the hideous nature of that rule. The excesses of United Fruit, the hellish sadism of men such as Torrijos, Somoza, D'Aubuisson, and thousands of less renowned minions, the slaughters, the invasions, the mass graves, the dumps piled high with smoldering corpses, cannibalism, rape, and torture on a national scale, all thoroughly documented and all thoroughly ignored, all orchestrated by a music of screams like that now playing . . . this was merely part of that, a minor adagio in a symphony of pain, the carrying-forward of a diseased tradition.

I understood that whoever won this battle would have little sympathy for journalists, and in this DeVries was way ahead of me. He'd dug out a pistol from the paperstorm of Shellgrave's desk, and after sticking it in his belt, he picked up a folding chair, told us to head for the trees, and then swung the chair at the window, clearing away shards of frosted glass. I clambered through, helped Sherril out, then DeVries—he had a folder of pertinent papers in one hand. After the coolness of the room, the fetid heat nearly caused me to gag. Glancing at the field beyond the office building, I spotted dozens, no, hundreds of dark and curiously twisted naked figures scampering through the agave; some were kneeling and tearing at the leaves, and there were bodies scattered everywhere, many showing bloody in the spotlights—the sort of flash Polaroid that takes about a second to develop fully in your mind and stays with you forever after, clear in all its medieval witchiness and savage detail. It was about fifty yards to the trees, and I thought we were going to make it without incident; all the screams and shooting were coming from the front of the office building. But then there was an agonized shout behind me, and I saw Shellgrave, who had struggled out the window, being dragged down by a group of the twisted figures. Blood on his face. The next moment more of those figures were all around me.

Since the spotlights were aimed toward the field, it was fairly dark where we were, and I never did get a good look at our attackers. I had the impression of something resembling a hard bumpy rind covering their faces, of slit eyes and mouths, and punctures for nostrils. Even for Indians, they were tiny, dwarfish, and they couldn't have been very strong, because I'm not very strong and I knocked them aside easily. There were, however, a lot of them, and if it hadn't been for DeVries I'm sure we would have died. He started firing with Shellgrave's pistol, and, as if death posed for them a great allure, they left off clutching at me and Sherril, and they went for DeVries. I grabbed Sherril's arm and bolted for the jungle. We were about sixty or seventy feet in under the canopy when I heard DeVries scream.

I'd been friends with DeVries for—as I've said—four years, but our friendship went by the boards, replaced by panic, and with Sherril in tow, I kept running, busting down rocky defiles, scrambling up rises, stumbling, falling, yelling in fright at every hint of movement. We must have been in flight for about five or six minutes when after a spectacular fall, rolling halfway down a hill through decayed vegetation and ferns, I discovered the mouth of a cave.

The limestone foundation of the Petén is riddled with caves, and so this was no miraculous occurrence; but being out of breath and bone-tired, I viewed it as such at the time. The opening, into which my legs had wound up dangling at the end of my fall, was narrow, choked with vines, no more than a couple of feet wide, but I could sense a large empty space beyond. I cleared away the vines, caught Sherril's hand, and led her inside. Cool musty smell, water dripping somewhere near. I held up my cigarette lighter for a torch, illuminating a portion of a large domed gallery, the walls white and smooth, except for the occasional volute of limestone; against one wall was a tarpaulin with the edge of a crate showing beneath it. I clicked off the lighter, felt my way toward the tarp; when I reached it, using the lighter again, I examined the crates—there were four of them, all stamped with code designations and marked US AIR FORCE. There was the distinct odor of machine oil.

"What are they?" Sherril asked.

"Smells like weapons," I said. "Automatic rifles, I hope."

I began working at one of the crates, prying at the boards, but I wasn't making much headway. Then I heard a noise from outside the cave, something heavy moving in the brush. There was a large boulder beside the mouth, and in hopes that we could block the entrance with it, Sherril and I hurried back across the cave; but by the time we reached the entrance, the source of the noise was already halfway in, blocking out the faint gleam of moonlight from above. We flattened against the wall next to the opening. A shadow stepped into the cave, too big to be one of the Indians; a beam of light sprang from its hand. I made out camouflage gear, a holstered pistol, and knowing that we had no choice but to attack, I jumped the man, driving him onto his back. Sherril was right behind me, clawing at his face. The man cursed in Spanish, tried to throw me off, and he might have if Sherril hadn't been bothering him. I managed to grab his hair; I smashed his head against the stone; after the third blow he went limp. I rolled away from him, catching my breath. Sherril picked up the flashlight and shined it on the man's slack pitted face. It was Major Pedroza. That made sense to me—the major was likely stockpiling weapons for his own little coup, or else was making a neat profit selling to the *contras* or some other group of courageous freedom fighters.

While I hadn't had time to absorb DeVries's death, the whole affair of the experimental farm, it seemed those things were moving me now, that and everything else I'd seen over the years, all the bad history I'd reported to no avail, and it also seems that Sherril was directed by similar motives, by anger born of disillusionment. Although she hadn't seen as much as I, although I hadn't given her the respect she deserved, I realized she had the instincts I'd once had for compassion, for truth, for hope. Now, in a single night, all those instincts had been fouled.

We went about tying up Pedroza with lengths of vine that I cut from around the cave mouth, using the knife I'd taken from him. I felt stony and emotionless, as if I were wrapping a package of meat. I turned him onto his belly and tied his arms behind him; then I tied his legs and connected them to a noose that fitted tightly around his neck. If he struggled, he would only succeed in strangling himself. I was sure of one thing—no matter what happened to me and Sherril,

Pedroza was going to die. This may strike some as unfair. What certain knowledge, they may ask, did I have about him? He certainly had done nothing to me. But as I have detailed earlier, he was no innocent. In truth, it should have been Shellgrave whom I was preparing to kill; he was the true villain of the piece, or at least the emblem of true villainy. Pedrozas would be impossible without Shellgraves. But the major would do, he would satisfy. I tore my shirt to make a gag and stuffed it into his mouth, lashing it in place with my belt. This accomplished, Sherril and I pushed the boulder to seal off the entrance; then we sat down to wait.

Neither of us said much. I was busy dealing with my desertion of DeVries; I knew I could have done nothing for him, but knowing that was little help. I saw him in my mind's eye firing Shellgrave's gun, a glimpse of blond hair, a pale strained face, then I saw him swarmed by the Indians, and then I heard him scream. I should have been used to that sort of quick exit; I'd had it happen many times before, but this one wasn't going down easily. Maybe I'd been closer to DeVries than I had realized, or maybe it was the nightmare surrounding his death that made it seem insurmountable.

I'm not sure what was running through Sherril's mind, but I felt that the currents of our thoughts were somehow parallel. She began to shiver—it was dank in that cave—and I put an arm around her, let her lean against me. I asked her if she was okay, and she said, "Yeah," and snuggled up close. Her clean girl smell made me wistful and weak. Soon after that I kissed her. She pulled away at first, and said, "No, don't . . . not now."

"All right," I said evenly; in my mind I was ready to go along with her, but I kept my hand on her breast.

"What are you doing?" she said.

"I don't know, I just needed to touch you."

I took my hand away, but after a moment she put it back, held it against her breast. She made a despairing noise.

"I guess I need it, too," she said. "Isn't that something?"

"What do you mean?"

"To want this now. Isn't that"—she gave a dismayed laugh—"wrong or something." Another laugh. "Wrong." She said the word as if it had gained a whole new meaning, one she was only now capable of understanding.

I had no answers for her. I kissed her again, and this time she kissed back; not long after that we spread our clothing on the stone for a mattress and made love. It was the only hope we had, the only thing we could do to save ourselves from the blind shadows and bloody shouts thronging our heads, and as a result our lovemaking was rough, more an act of anger than one of compassion. Involved in it, too, was the mutuality we'd had to begin with, the thing that might have grown to health, but now—I thought—fed by the food of that grotesque night, would bloom twisted, dark, and futureless. And yet by engaging that mutuality, I had the sense that I was committing to it in a way from which it would be impossible to pull back.

It must have been while we were making love that the Indians found us, because when I surfaced from the heat and confusion that we had generated, I heard their voices: odd fluted whispers issuing not from the cave mouth but from somewhere overhead, leading me to realize there must be a second entrance. We struggled into our clothes, and I broke into the crates with Pedroza's knife; I had his pistol, but I doubted that would be sufficient firepower. The first crate contained antipersonnel rockets; I had no idea of how to use them. The second, however, contained M-16s and full clips. I inserted a clip into one and made ready to defend. I was surprised that they hadn't already attacked us, and when after several minutes they still hadn't made a move, I shined Pedroza's flashlight toward the ceiling.

In the instant before they ducked away from the second entrance, which was halfway up the side of the dome, I saw the glowing yellow cores of their eyes; the sight was so alarming, I nearly dropped the flashlight. I handed it to Sherril and fired a short burst at the opening; it wasn't very big, a mere crack, but it might, I thought, be large enough to admit those twisted bodies. The drop was about forty feet.

"The papers," I asked Sherril, "did they say anything about whether they'd be able to take a long fall?"

She thought it over. "There was some stuff about low calcium content. Their bones are probably pretty brittle."

"They might think of lowering vines."

"Maybe, but according to the papers they're . . . they're animals. Their IQs aren't measurable."

I heard a strangled noise and had Sherril shine the flashlight toward Pedroza; his eyes were bugged, his face suffused with blood.

"Be careful," I advised him in Spanish. "You'll hurt yourself."

His eyes looked more baleful than those of the Indians.

"I think we'll be all right," Sherril said. "If we can hold them off till morning, we'll be all right."

"Because they're nocturnals?"

"Uh-huh. They can't take much light. They might be able to wait until midmorning, what with the canopy, but by noon they'd be in terrible pain." The flashlight wavered in her hand. "They burrow."

"What?" I said.

"They move around at night, and when daylight comes, wherever they are, they dig burrows in the dirt, they cover themselves with dirt and sleep . . . like vampires. They scarcely breathe at all when they're asleep."

"Christ," I said, unable to absorb this, to feel any more revulsion than was already within me.

I glanced at Pedroza; he had a lot to answer for.

Sherril was looking at him, too, and from the loathing that registered in her expression, I knew that Pedroza would be in for a bad time even if I weren't there.

We sat down by the boulder, keeping our weight against it in case the Indians tried to move it; we kept the light shining on the entrance overhead, and we talked to drown out the incessant and unsettling fluting of their voices, not speech in all likelihood, mere noises, the music of a pitiless folly reverberating through the cave. I told Sherril stories, but they weren't the stories I would have told her under other circumstances. They were stories about the brave good things I'd seen, stories that still hoped, stories that gave storytelling a good name, and not my usual rotten-with-disgust tales of Businessmen From Hell and their global sleights-of-hand. Those stories were the best parts of my life passing before my eyes, and it wasn't that I was afraid of dying, because I thought we were going to make it; it was that the last of my foolish ideals were giving up the ghost, having their final say before wisping up into ectoplasmic *nada*. Although I'd convinced myself that I'd given up on my ideals a long time before, I believe it was then that I utterly surrendered to the evil of the world.

It was the same for Sherril. She talked about nursing, about the good feeling it gave her, she talked about her home, her old friends, but she kept lapsing. I would have to tune her in with questions as if her station were fading from the dial. I watched her face. She was more than pretty, so damn pretty I couldn't believe that I'd had the fortune to make love to her—a stupid thing to consider, but stupid thoughts like that were occurring constantly. Her eyes were green with hazel flecks in the irises, her hair was silky, but her most attractive feature was that she knew what I knew. She was changing before my eyes, toughening, learning things that she shouldn't have had to learn all at once; she was a nice girl, and it was a shame for her to have to understand so young what a shuck niceness was. All the while as

I listened, I could hear the sick music of the doomed tribe wanting to kill us, Pedroza grunting as he tried to enlist our attention. None of that mattered. In a way, I was almost happy to be up against it, to know how bad it could get, and yet there I was, still able to look at a pretty woman and hope for something. I was aware that even this could be taken from me, but I was beyond being afraid. And I was learning, too. Although I didn't recognize it at the time, I was learning that you can fall in love through hate, by being with someone in a crucible of a moment when everything else is dying and the only thing left is to try to live. Or maybe it wasn't love, maybe it was just the thing that takes the place of love for those who have surrendered.

Just before dawn, some of the Indians began dropping through the crack. About twenty of them in all made the jump, but no more than a third of that number survived the landing, and they were incapable of swift movement, their bones shattered. The first one down startled me and drew a shriek from Sherril; but after that it wasn't even dramatic, merely pitiful. The wounded ones crawled toward us, their razor-slit mouths agape to reveal blood-red tongues within, their strangely unfinished faces displaying what struck me as a parody of desperation. I finished them off with bursts from the M-16. I didn't know what had caused them to try, nor did I know why they had stopped, why they didn't just keep coming like lemmings; perhaps both the jumping and the stopping had been stages along the path to their own surrender. When I was sure that no more would be coming, I dragged their bodies deeper into the cave, out of sight around a bend; I tried to avoid looking at them, but I couldn't help noticing a few details. Shriveled genitalia; a faint bluish cast to the skin as if they suffered from cyanosis; the S-curved spines, the knotted shoulder blades. They were light, those bodies, like the bodies of hollow children.

The sun rose about a quarter of six that morning, making a dim red glow in the crack overhead, a slit evil eye, but the voices kept fluting for a while after that. Pedroza's eyes pleaded with us; he had wet his pants, the poor soul. We watched him wriggle and grunt; we made it a game to see which of us could get him to produce the most interesting noise by doing things such as picking up the knife and walking behind him.

Eventually we let him alone and sat talking, planning what we'd do once we left the cave: avoid Sayaxché, strike out for Flores, maybe hitch a ride with an oil truck returning from the jungle.

Sherril looked at me and said, "What are you going to do afterward?"

"I'm not staying around here. The States . . . maybe I'll go back to the States. How 'bout you? Nicaragua?"

She shook her head. "I can't think of anywhere that sounds right. Maybe home."

"Calgary."

"Uh-huh."

"What's Calgary like?"

She opened her mouth, closed it, then laughed. "I don't know." Then after a pause. "The Rockies, they're close by."

I thought about the Rockies, about their clean, cold rectitude, their piney stillness, so different from the malarial tumult I had traveled in for all those years. I said their name out loud; Sherril glanced at me inquiringly.

"Just seeing if it sounded right," I said.

It was almost noon before we decided it was absolutely safe to leave the cave. I went over to Pedroza and unplugged his mouth. He had to lick his lips and work his jaw for a few moments in order to speak; then he said, "Please . . . I . . . please."

"Please what?" I asked him.

His eyes darted to Sherril, back to me.

"Don't shoot me," he said. "I have money, I can help you."

"I'm not going to shoot you," I said. "I'm going to leave you tied up here."

That was a test to see his reaction, to determine whether he had any allies left alive; if he flunked I intended to shoot him. His fear was no act, he was terrified. He babbled, promising everything, he swore to help us. I hated him so much, I cannot tell you how much I hated him. He was all the objects of my hate.

"I could shoot you," I said. "But I think I'll just leave you here. Of course you've got an option. I bet if you jerk real hard with your legs, you can probably kill yourself."

"Listen," he began.

I clubbed him in the jaw with the rifle butt; the blow twisted his head, and he had to fight to keep from overreacting and strangling himself. I kept talking to him, I told him if he confessed his sins I might give him a chance to live. I was very convincing in this. He was reluctant at first, but then his sins came pouring out: rape, massacre, torture, everything I'd expected. He seemed emptied afterward, drained of strength, as if the secret knowledge of his crimes had been all that sustained him.

"Say a hundred Hail Marys," I told him, and made the sign of the cross in the air. "Jesus forgives you."

He started to say something, but I stuffed the gag back in.

Sherril was staring at him, her face cold, unrelenting.

I kissed her, intending to cheer her, boost her spirits, but when I looked at Pedroza, I had the idea that the kiss had wounded him. I kissed her again, touched her breasts. He squeezed his eyes shut, then opened them very wide; he wriggled a bit. Sherril knew what I was up to, and she was all for it; her antipathy for the major was as strong as mine. We spread our clothes on the stones and we made love a second time, showing Pedroza the sweetness that life can be, letting him understand the entire pain of his fate—once again it seemed the only thing we could do. He was nothing to us, he was simply everything, an abstract, a target as worthlessly neutral as a president.

By chance, we were making love beneath the crack in the limestone, and a slant of dusty sun like those you might see falling through a high cathedral window fell across Sherril, painting a strange golden mask over her eyes and nose, the sort of half-mask worn by women at carnivals and fancy balls, creating of her face a luminous mystery. And what we were doing did seem mysterious, directed, inspired. It was no performance; it was ritual, it was a kind of hateful worship. We were very quiet, even at the end we stifled our cries, and the silence intensified our pleasure. Afterward, though I could hear the glutinous noise of Pedroza's breath, it was as if we were alone with our god in that holy dome of stillness, the white cold walls like the inside of a skull, and we were its perfect thoughts. I felt incredibly tender. I caressed and kissed her, I accepted her caresses and kisses, bathed in that streak of gold, illuminated, blessed in our purpose. I suppose we were mad at that moment, but we were mad like saints.

We dressed, smiling at each other, unmindful of Pedroza, and it wasn't until we began shifting the stone back in front of the cave mouth that we looked at him. He was still pleading with his eyes, wriggling toward us and whining, making choked gargling noises. I felt no sympathy for him. He deserved whatever was in store for him. He was trying to nod, aiming his eyes at the gun, begging me to shoot him.

"*Adiós,*" I said—a word that means "to God," an ironic conceit of the language in these godless times.

We shifted the stone into place.

Before we set out for Flores we were brought up short by what
we saw just beyond the mouth of the cave. The side of the adjoining
hill was dotted with mounds of black dirt, each one about five feet
long. There were hundreds of them, tucked in among ferns, under
rotten logs, beneath bushes. Like infestations of ants I'd seen in South
America. It was horrible to see, and thinking about those tiny de-
formed bodies lying moribund beneath the dirt, I became sick and
dizzy. The ultimate attitude of surrender. I suppose I could have been
merciful and shot them as they lay; the crates in the cave contained
a sufficiency of death. But someone might have heard, and, too, I
had gone beyond the concepts of mercy and humanitarian aid. I wasn't
in the game anymore. I felt bad about that, but at least I'd tried, I
had spent years trying, whereas most people surrender without even
making an effort. There was nothing I could do except to leave. So
we walked away from the cave, from Sayaxché, from Guatemala, from
those pathetic little things with slit eyes and malfunctioning brains
in their sleep of dirt and nightmares, from Major Pedroza in the final
white church of his terror, from the whole damn world. And because
we had nowhere we wanted to go any longer, we went there together.

Sometimes I look at Sherril, and she looks at me, and we both wonder
why we stay together. We're still in love, but it doesn't seem reasonable that love should survive an act of surrender as complete as the
one we made, and we keep expecting some vile mutation to occur,
the product of that night in the jungle beyond Sayaxché. I suppose
that's why we don't have any children. We don't think about all this
very much, however. Life is sweet. We've got money, food, a future,
a cabin in the Rockies not far from Calgary, work we care about—
though perhaps not with the same passion we once evinced. It's good
to make love, to walk, to smell the wind and watch the sun on the
evergreens. We're not really happy, too much has happened for us
to buy that chump; but we neither one of us ever required happiness. It's too great a chore to be happy when the world is going down
the tubes, when the shitstorm is about ready to come sweeping in
from the backside of creation and surprise us with a truly disastrous
plague or cosmic rays from hell, and there are signs in the sky that
it's time to get right with God or maybe make a few moves to change
things, and all you hear is the same placid generic bullshit about shoring
up the economy and possibly kicking a few bucks over to the extremists
who would kind of like to have breathable air and keep the ice caps
from melting and would prefer not to alienate the rest of humanity

by supporting every sadistic tumor in a uniform who decides he's going to be God of Mangoland and run the cocaine franchise for the South Bronx in return for saying No to the Red Menace. Central America isn't just Central America. It's what's happening, it's coming soon to your local theater, and if you think I'm overstating the case, if you don't see the signs, if you haven't been taking notes on the inexorable transformation of the Land of the Free into just another human slum . . . well, that's cool. Just kick back, and pop yourself a cold one, maybe catch that ABC special on the Starving Man and get a little misty-eyed, it'll make you feel cozier when it's time for "Monday Night Football," or "Miami Vice," like you've paid your dues by almost feeling something.

And don't worry, everything's all right.

I promise I won't mention any of this again.

Adiós.